The Academy

Tales of the Marketplace

A Novelogy

by Laura Antoniou

Edited by Karen Taylor

With Guest Authors

M. Christian
Michael Hernandez
david stein
Cecilia Tan
Karen Taylor

Novelogy by Laura Antoniou,
Contributing authors: M. Christian, Michael Hernandez, david stein, Cecilia Tan, and Karen Taylor
Editing by Karen Taylor

Karen would like to thank the following for their assistance, advice, and support in the creation of The Academy:
Seattle's "No Safewords" Writers Group
Shmarr Mustapha
Audrey Hart Sparks
Glenda Rider and Sara Humble
Rie Brosco and Naomi Segal

Published by

Mystic Rose Books
P.O. Box 1036/SMS
Fairfield, CT 06432.

ISBN 0-9645960-3-2

First Edition, first printing 2000

Dedication

This one is in honor of the readers who never stopped
asking me for more, and the 1999 International Master/
slave Conference that was held in Atlanta. And for my
wife, Karen Taylor, who is muse, editor, critic, co-writer
and my number one fan as well. Tough job on a good
day. Amazingly, she's there on bad days, too.

Contents

The Academy, Tales of the Marketplace is a novelogy, a complete novel containing short stories within the text. The short stories have been written by guest authors, and are indicated in the table of contents and chapter headings with a byline. The exceptions to this are two stories also written by Laura Antoniou, Mandarin Style and Clocking. This book is intended to be read as a novel, but the reader may enjoy the short stories by themselves as well.

ethics are the rules of the game
morals are why you play

Isn't it a pleasure when you can make practical use
of the things you have studied?
Isn't it a pleasure to have an old friend visit from afar?
Isn't it a sure sign of a gentleman, that he does not take offense
when others fail to recognize his ability?
Kung Fu-tzi, known as Koshi-sama, or Confucius

1 Welcome to Okinawa

The murmur of voices had that peculiar polyglot cadence of a mixture of languages. English dominated, as it always did, a combination of sheer numbers and the decibel level of its native speakers. But Japanese was a close second, and the lilting tones of French wove in and out like snatches of melodic static. The excitement level was high, matched by the energy of people in motion, going from one to another, hands and arms outstretched.

"Parker-san." It was a strong voice, cutting through the din as neatly as though it had been pitched perfectly for one listener without seeming like a shout.

Chris Parker glanced up as the automatic shading in his glasses finally began to fade. He smiled and waited until the man who had called to him came closer, and then bowed low in greeting. His bow was met by one noticeably less deep, and they both smiled when they rose to look at each other.

Sakai Tetsuo hadn't changed much in the three years since they had last met in person. His hair was a dense mixture of gray and white, trimmed just a little longer than current Tokyo fashion, his blue suit impeccably tailored and pressed, his shoes hand-made and Italian. His tie was knotted tight to his throat, perfectly neat, matched by the shining peaks of his pocket square. He was only slightly taller than Chris Parker, and as they shook hands, they looked like a strange pair of brothers, small and compact and precise in every movement.

"You are looking excellent, my friend," Tetsuo said warmly. "It has been too long! You must stay after the conference and come back to Tokyo and visit with me."

"Oh, no, Sakai-san, I must look like something the cat dragged in.

1

Spending a day on airplanes doesn't do much to improve one's disposition or appearance. Thank you very much, but you are too kind." Chris ruefully ran a hand through his hair and shook his head. "I would love nothing more than to visit with you, and it might be possible." He avoided the direct and rude negative that they both understood would have been improper, and Tetsuo nodded slightly in pride.

"You are always a welcome guest," he said simply. "Perhaps we could speak later, upon some insignificant items concerning mutual business?"

Chris hid his shock at Tetsuo's directness. To bring up business first was unknown of in this rigid instructor in all things Japanese. "I am at your service," Chris answered, this time in Japanese.

Tetsuo smiled again. "Excellent! In this too, you have improved," he said. "But perhaps we shall speak English, so that I may practice my own poor efforts?" They could continue this dance back and forth all night — as in fact, they had, on several occasions. The rhythm of Japanese conversation, especially concerning business, was soft, rolling, and required patience which few untutored Westerners could finesse. However, Tetsuo's English was excellent, a language he had begun to learn as a child and had honed with years in America. His business acumen was also honed in America, with a Harvard MBA. Chris' Japanese was of much more recent vintage and rudimentary at best. The areas of knowledge which he had studied both at college and during his first extended contact with Tetsuo would simply not be adequate to the subtle nuances of negotiation.

"I will be honored to see you at your convenience," Chris said, inclining his shoulders slightly. Tetsuo immediately reciprocated, and the two of them straightened at the sound of a delighted low pitched laugh.

"I could watch you all day, bobbing up and down like those strange toys in the backs of American cars," Ken Mandarin said, sliding up to them. Today, she was not in her usual Western cross-dressing drag, but in a stunning Japanese outfit. She whirled for their approval, indigo hakama trousers flaring out, the heavy jacket wrapped more tightly around her body than perhaps necessary or customary.

The two men bowed to her and she laughed again, dipping elegantly into an enormously exaggerated one. "All this up and down, up and down!" she exclaimed, tossing her head back. "One might get dizzy!"

"I see you've already been shopping," Chris said.

"What, this old thing?" Ken looked pleased, though, and she leaned forward to give him a peck on the cheek. "And look at you!!" she exclaimed, backing up to arms length. "I like your new haircut! Very modern, oui?" She glanced lightly to her right. "Good to see you, Sakai."

"A delight to see you again," Tetsuo said, his voice equally light. But they both had acquired a slight edge. "I did not realize that your name also revealed an interest in a martial art."

"It's Ken-da, not ken-do," Ken said. "And I wouldn't know which end of that bamboo sword to hold, let alone how to beat my opponent to bits. But this - this is a fine outfit, no?" Her eyes became sharply drawn; no matter why she choose an outfit more suited for a dojo, she was clearly ready for some kind of battle. There was a reason why Ken did not often work in Asia, but preferred the West. Her battles with the various Marketplace establishments in the Far East were legendary, as were her father's before he died; they had both shared a marked dislike of the Japanese block for their own reasons. Memories were long in the East, she would sometimes say with a shrug. No matter how carefully the Marketplace cultivated an air of neutrality, there were always political and historical differences between some people. Chris was grateful for the sight of a convenient excuse to move on.

"Michael!" Chris snapped. "Find out what room I'm in and don't dawdle."

"Yes, sir," Michael said, struggling with the luggage and too obviously dismayed that he couldn't join in the mingling. As slaves approached, he had to shake his head over and over again, until the message spread not to help him. He turned toward the registration room to the left of the main stairs and both Ken and Tetsuo relaxed somewhat at the distraction. Tetsuo was the first to excuse himself, omitting the usual reminder to schedule a meeting, and Ken kissed Chris again and gave him a hug.

"Is that the boy you told me about?" she said appraising Michael's body from behind, cocking her head as if she could see his hips and flanks through the hanging garment bag. Apparently the edge she had acquired was gone again as she switched her attention to something new. "Pretty! Lend him to me. I've brought the Two - they haven't had a toy in months!"

Chris chuckled at the thought of Ken's rapacious matched set of personal servants and what twisted and exhausting use they could make of Michael. He nodded. "Done," he said. "But there is a price."

"Anything!" she replied extravagantly. Then, her eyes narrowed again and she adopted an arms akimbo stance that looked rather appropriate in her new outfit. "Oh, you mean a real price!" she said accusingly. She wagged her finger at him, making tsking sounds between her teeth. "You should know better, white boy. The proposal you've placed before the Academy is more complicated than it seems to be — I am still not quite comfortable with all the potential. . .ramifications."

Chris shrugged. "I am sure we can find some grounds to agree upon," he said. "But I was really thinking of asking you for a proper introduction to your friend from Seattle and the junior she's brought with her."

3

Ken had the decency to look abashed, and Ken Mandarin looking ashamed was quite a sight. "I am so sorry," she said, with just the slightest evidence of a blush underneath her wheat colored skin. "Of course, I shall introduce you to Marcy, she wishes to make your acquaintance as well. Naturally! But now, you must excuse me, so that I can go and commit suicide over my stupidity." She reeled away in a false swoon, and threw herself through the open panels of the exterior wall into the garden beyond. Her gutter Cantonese trailed behind her as she cursed herself. Chris smiled as he saw two Chinese gentlemen gaze after her in shock and horror.

But her gaffe had communicated more than she had perhaps thought. Chris' smile faded as he turned to look for Michael, thinking of the comfort of a long, hot bath. It wasn't even the first day of The Academy, and the battle flags were out. And for the first time ever, he wasn't the squire on this crusade — he was a goddamn knight.

Trainers from all over the world were converging on the Shimada Resort and Ryokan, located deep in the green hills about forty miles outside of Naha, the capital of Okinawa. Autumn in this tropical area was lush and warm, and the gleaming wood beams of the Japanese country-style inn glowed in the sunlight. It had been specially emptied for the week, entirely staffed by Marketplace employees and servitors of varying levels. Stone lanterns marked the long drive into the property, and a beautiful red and gold gate framed one of the splendid views of the valley to the east. There was a bubbling stream on the northern edge, where outdoor baths were also available, framed by raised dark oak platforms. Ornamental gardens could be seen from almost every window. Small ponds were dense with almost garishly colored lilies, hidden between the trees. It was a breathtakingly beautiful site which invited exploration and an experience of sensuality. The army of service staff moved with the practiced ease of slave veterans — no one would embarrass themselves by sending a marginally acceptable piece of property to serve at the Academy. In fact, it was common for trainers to bring a special slave with them, a way for those lucky individuals to see perfection in action.

The resort was cunningly split between Western and Japanese style accommodations. Much of the actual conference area was Western, with high tables and straight backed office chairs and rooms that were exact copies of every other hotel room in the world, clean, small and efficient. But in his annoying way, Chris had insisted upon a room in the ryokan section of the resort, a traditional Japanese room, and Michael had prepared to deal with one. The pictures he had studied and the descriptions in the tourist guidebooks had been enough to let him know that there were in fact, beds in the room — or at least they were behind panels somewhere. He gazed at the perfectly proportioned room, counting the tatami mats that made every room in such a traditional arrangement uniform sizes. There was an ikebana arrangement of a floating lily set in shallow water over dull gray water-smoothed stones, set in a niche across from the door; a perfect position for the late afternoon sun to hit it. He found that he couldn't remember what the little niche was called, and tried to hide his panic by unpacking.

Belatedly, he remembered his shoes, and took them off immediately, carrying them to the door. He had been gratified to see that many of the guests were shod in the shoes they wore outside. But in this traditional wing, where the flooring in the rooms was the ubiquitous tatami matting, you had to leave your street shoes outside, wear slippers on the wooden floors and socks or bare feet inside.

Oh, jeeze, and I walked through the whole place! Why didn't someone stop me?

Did I pass the slippers on my way in without noticing? Wasn't there supposed to be a special kind of porch, a genkan, something like that? Were staff people right now snickering over his error and whispering about him? He was about to slide the door open and dash down the hall to the main entrance, but naturally, that was when Chris got there.

"That'll be ten," Chris said, brushing by him. Chris had already removed his boots, and his small feet were neatly encased in Japanese slippers. He kicked them off and stooped to place them neatly by the door, toes facing out. "Excellent," he said with a sigh, after turning again to scan the room. "I'll be bathing. Have everything unpacked and my strap out by the time I'm finished."

"Yes, sir," Michael said glumly.

"And don't worry, Michael," Chris said cheerfully as he took one of the ryookan yukatas hanging on one wall. The light cotton robes all bore a stylized gate pattern in soft, pale gray on a much darker background. "You have an infinite number of potential fuck-ups ahead of you over the next couple of days. You had to start somewhere." He chuckled as he padded out the door, leaving Michael to slide the lightweight panel shut after him.

Michael bit back even the thought of a retort, one of the hardest things in his new regimen of exercises. Back in the spring, when he had impulsively volunteered to be trained as "a classic" — a rigorous, seven year process involving everything from this current apprenticeship assignment to actually being sold and living for a term as a slave — he thought he had considered every possible drawback to the situation. As usual, however, he was dead wrong.

He hadn't counted on being immediately assigned to Chris Parker, the

5

man he had somehow developed a massive crush on, despite years of knowing that 1) he was just not very attracted to men, and 2) he was certainly not a bottom. He hadn't counted on suddenly becoming the real low man on the totem pole at an entry-level training house, subject to the whims of everyone except the damn slaves in training, and occasionally to them as well. And finally, he hadn't counted on liking it so damn much.

It was perverse beyond belief. No matter how difficult things got, from Chris' degrading taunts about his skill level or thought processes, to the various hazards of working with no less than three demanding trainers, to the sheer pain of his continual punishments, erotic and not so, his heart beat out a passionate plea for more and he slept like a baby. Even his constant stream of self castigation seemed to be part of this whole process to make him stunningly aware of his place in the world — and more firmly convinced that it was right for him.

And this was only the beginning! If Anderson and Chris weren't bullshitting him, they intended to actually sell him to someone within the year. At first, he had been eager for the chance to prove himself, but lately, he had been wondering if, in fact, it was all some sort of head-game. After all, they both admitted that almost no one was trained like that any more, and Chris hadn't mentioned this potential sale since they were both at Anderson's place. Plus, there was the fact that despite his occasionally insufferable arrogance about these "Old Guard" methods, Chris admitted that he had not fulfilled them himself. Not adequately, at any rate.

Of course, Chris had been in some sort of service, somewhere. It showed in the way he perfectly deferred to Grendel and Alex back at the House, and in the way he acted toward Anderson. But there were no sale records for him in the Marketplace. His experience had to have been some sort of private arrangement that somehow still counted. Michael was convinced that his own "sale" was really just going to be some kind of reassignment to another trainer, possibly Grendel and Alex, since they seemed friendly with Anderson and busy enough to use him. But if that happened, he feared that Chris would no longer be part of the picture. There was no way they really needed two under-trainers, and the house seemed over-staffed as it was, what with Rachel pretty much running things and the trainee slaves doing the scut work.

The thought of continuing his training without Chris — no matter how much he hated him — was very disturbing.

It was, in fact, mortifying.

Even now, as he found the closets and hung up Chris' suits and smoothed out his ties, (and found a western style shoe rack), Michael could feel his cock straining against the narrow cotton rope that Chris had wrapped around it before their connection in Tokyo. It had been almost three hours to Okinawa, and another hour and a half on the road to get here. But that was nothing, Michael thought ruefully. At least the rope didn't have little spikes on the inside of it, like the parachute/cock-ring assembly that he had been directed to pack along with the other items that Chris used to keep him aware of his status. It didn't matter, really. Anything that Chris used on him, touched him with, said to him, seemed important beyond all logic now. Imbued with erotic and emotional significance.

The only regularly used toy not in the bag, as a matter of fact, was Michael's now well-used gag. Because, for once, he was free to speak for the entire trip — free to ask questions, engage in conversations, even — chat about the weather. After months of isolation, he was almost feverishly eager to have those experiences. And cautious as hell, too. Just because you are allowed to do something doesn't mean you can do it badly. That was one of his most underlined notes in his precious book of hints and rules, compiled since Anderson, the Trainer of Trainers, reminded him that obedience to her was more important than what he felt was correct. If he took the opportunity to speak up, his voice had to be controlled, his questions intelligent, his conversation appropriate. If not…

He pulled Chris' strap out of the garment bag pocket and laid it out on the low, polished pine table. The handle was dark with palm sweat, the smooth leather worn by years of use. Michael couldn't remember three days that had gone by in the past five months without feeling it. Even now, there were fading bruises on the backs of his thighs.

As he moved and felt them, he sighed in pleasure. Oh man, he thought, fighting to keep his motions sure, his attention on the task before him. This is as far from where I was a year ago as I could get!

And it felt so damn good!

He had no illusions about his presence here. He was not here to serve anyone but Chris, and he was not here as an example of anything except for what he was — a raw, untrained man marked by Anderson as having a chance at becoming a trainer. And while some people would envy his position, Michael still felt the tug of ambivalence from time to time. Was he crazy, thinking that he stood a chance at being anything but a dilettante, Chris' favorite accusation? Was he clinging to this trainer-in-training facade in order to avoid considering becoming a full time slave?

As if to relieve his worries, his cock gently settled underneath its bondage, no longer strangling itself in frustrating tumescence. There was never a true erotic attraction to being a full time slave, never that jolt of feeling right that he had read about in so many slave interviews and reports. So clearly, he was made to be a trainer, and this newfound passion for use, abuse and humiliation was directed toward one man and one man only. And since Chris made it clear that his loyalties lay in only one direction — that of Imala Anderson and her methods and traditions — and that he was certainly not interested in owning a slave, then that settled things. Period. Nothing more to say.

Yet when Chris came back and Michael got on all fours and presented his ass up for a beating, his traitorous cock was hard as a rock, red and straining painfully between the white strands of rope, and every stroke drove the breath from him in gasps that were ecstatically pure. And his thanks were as genuine as his obedience and his gasps. As usual, he forgot all about how cut and dry everything was, needing only to feel the slight brush of Chris' hand on his head to make him wriggle with pleasure and ache to be better — so much better — in the future.

"Ladies and Gentlemen, thank you for attending this year's Academy. On behalf of the International Coalition of Trainers and Handlers and the Asian and South Pacific offices of The Marketplace, I welcome you to Okinawa and this beautiful resort, provided for our use by the Shimada family." The speaker was Noguchi Shigeo, the undisputed Trainer of Trainers in his part of the world. At least eighty years old, (some said ninety) he seemed to be made of seasoned timber, as ancient and creaky as the central beam of an old country house. His English was precise and British, his manners impeccable, his training methods unspeakably brutal. It was said that his school rejected at least a dozen applicants for each position, and then weeded out half of those who were accepted. In the small world of the Marketplace, that was quite considerable, especially because although he was always cordial and respectful, no gai-jin — no foreigner — had ever been accepted for training in his house. Plus, his rejections were still considered among the most desired of private trainers, especially if they had survived the first year.

Tetsuo Sakai had been trained by Noguchi. Like all of those who had received the touch of this venerable master, he was standing to Noguchi's left side, mingled with the crowd, yet easily within sight of the old man and proudly attentive. It didn't matter that Tetsuo had been an independent trainer for decades or that his house was the acknowledged second, right behind Noguchi's, in slave training. What mattered was knowing where you came from.

The rest of the room was still settling as Noguchi went into the extensive list of welcomes and introductions of the various Marketplace representatives who were going to be present for the Academy's session. Slaves circulated, bearing bound copies of the schedule and various position papers which were to be shared, discussed and debated. There was also one formal proposal this year, requiring a vote of the membership. Interpreters buzzed constantly; there was a tight edge of excitement in the air.

Ken Mandarin had made the attempt to look interested and be quiet, but as soon as she got hold of the Academy schedule, she flipped it open, scanned the contents, and immediately began turning pages to the section she wanted to read first. Several of Noguchi's men gave her short, stern glances, but she ignored them, preferring the circle of spotters who had congregated around her, just as eager to see what was going to be the real business of the week. We are the real outlaws here, Ken thought smugly, as she and her peers began to scan the items which might affect them. Perhaps it is not at all where you came from, she reflected, but where you are going. And neither this old man nor my pompous little American friend is going to tell me where I am going.

Yes, there it was. They had scheduled an obscene amount of time for debating, as usual. Talk, talk, talk, they always had to talk everything to death! She sighed theatrically and shut the binder sharply, noting who ignored the sound, who jumped and tried to pretend they didn't hear it, and who actually turned to see. It was gratifying to have her powers of observation. It was all part of what made her so good at what she did. Damn to hell anyone who thought they could tell her what her job was. She felt that the critical mass of her fellows had digested the material, and deliberately scanned each of them in turn, letting them see that she was prepared to fight. Even the oldest one there deferred to her — as was only correct. A pity that she and Parker would come to heads over this, but c'est la guerre. She turned her attention back to Noguchi, who was finally getting to some of the information she had come to hear.

"As our schedule is heavy and our time limited, we shall limit discussion on the major proposal to our formal debates. I respectfully request that the usual 'hallway discourse' be as limited as possible, so that all of our attendees will have the most complete information possible." There was a slight wave of laughter at this valiant attempt to control the second oldest human instinct in the world, that to gather and gossip. Noguchi gave the slightest of shrugs, acknowledging the futility of his position, but his face was stern, his voice slightly harder. "When matters of such import come before us, they deserve our best efforts for resolution," he added. "It is not an exaggeration to say that the very character of our institution might change after this meeting of the Academy. I encourage all of our members to be cooperative both in the process, and in the final results, whatever they may be."

"Even if we are disenfranchised by this process?" Ken called out, stirring those around her to muted agreements.

Shigeo Noguchi lowered his gaze to her, slowly and with the great majesty that was his to bear. The anger of his students and the surprise of those who would never presume to interrupt such a grandfather in their midst was perfectly palpable. Ken tossed it all off with a casual sniff and stared back at the man with a perfectly insolent smile on her lips.

"I look forward to the debates with great pleasure," the old man said simply. "But I know no amount of talk will ever disenfranchise you, Ms. Mandarin."

The light laughter broke the momentary tension until Ken laughed herself. She gave another of her dramatic bows toward Noguchi and turned to leave. He seemed not to take any offense, and continued his introductory words as she and several others quietly left the room.

Michael itched to follow her. Now, there was a hot babe, he thought, fully aware of the massive disrespect such a thought entailed. He had never been formally introduced to her, had only heard of her, seen her from afar. He knew that she and Chris were old acquaintances, if not friends, and that she had spotted several excellent clients, both for Chris and for Chris' employers, Alex and Grendel. In fact, Chris had told him that Ken's patience when scoping out potential clients by far exceeded his own. Not a bad compliment from a man who thought that patience came before obedience in the proper attributes of someone in service. Or those who trained them.

Even still, Michael liked the way she looked, exotic and playful, strong and passionate. He liked the way she moved quickly and gracefully, assuming that people would move out of her way. She looked like the kind of women who had had people surrounding her to see to her every whim for a long, long time. It was frankly sexy, enticing, yet slightly dangerous. In his older days in California, he would have played with her in a minute. Gone hunting with her, if she wanted to, and enjoyed her wickedness when it was aimed at someone who was helpless before it. He smiled slightly, imagining her in a latex catsuit and spiked heels.

"I'm loaning you to her later," Chris said casually. The level of sound rose in the room as people applauded Noguchi and broke up into their little social groups. Michael paled, unsteady for a moment. Damn him! Damn all of them! Was he so transparent that they could all read his mind, or was he so simple that they could all stay two steps ahead of him?

"Speak," Chris snapped.

"Yes, sir. Thank you, sir," Michael replied smartly. He had learned that gratitude fit almost every occasion and used it liberally. This time, it seemed appropriate, because Chris nodded and let the matter drop. In any event, there was someone approaching, from behind Michael's shoulder, according to how Chris' eyes were tracking. Carefully, Michael edged out of

10

the way, and sighed when he managed to move to the side just as the new-comer came close enough for a personal greeting.

"Mr. Parker, what a pleasure to see you again." The voice behind him was low, smooth, and gently accented; he turned his body to stand behind Chris and to his left, and saw one of the most beautiful women he could possibly imagine.

There he had been, just seconds into a full-fledged erotic fantasy about this slender, angular Asian woman with spiky hair and high cheekbones. But now, Ken Mandarin faded before something ever so much more — ethereal. And Michael struggled to understand why.

She was in her fifties, maybe even her sixties, it was hard to guess. Her smooth, olive toned skin was faintly glowing in health, that kind of color you got when you lived in a warm place. Her hair was a rich, lush black, touched lightly with silvery white, making you guess at her age, mocking you with the possibilities. She had large, bold dark eyes, and a body that Americans would describe as heavy. But when she stood and offered an elegantly manicured hand toward Chris Parker, she seemed as tempting as Aphrodite freshly come from the waves, as stunning as an Italian movie actress, as inviting as a warm embrace.

Chris took her hand and kissed the back, European style. Michael couldn't think of any other way to greet this woman. He realized that his mouth and lips had dried out, and nervously swallowed, hoping that Chris would not introduce him. I'll just fade into the background, he thought, praying that his palms weren't sweating.

"Ninon," Chris said, pronouncing it like it was French. "I was so pleased to get your note."

"And I was pleased to see that you have at last truly joined us," the woman said. "Your writings have been so useful to me, it seemed a shame you were not more active among us. I hope that I am among the first to give you my full support and encouragement."

"I'm honored by your interest," Chris replied. "I just hope that the upcoming discussions won't be — unpleasant to you."

"Oh, my young friend," she laughed, and her laugh was like something warm and soft thrown over bare shoulders. "I have been here much longer than you, and have faced terrible battles in the past. Surely, you know that it is those moments of unpleasantness which accentuate the moments of joy."

"Of course." Chris smiled, and was that just the slightest touch of color in his cheeks? Well, there was certainly a lot of heat pumping through Michael's face, and it intensified when Chris turned toward him and indicated him. "Ninon, please allow me to present Michael, who was chosen by

11

Anderson to train under me."

Michael felt buffeted when the women turned her gaze toward him. He bowed deeply, appropriately for a person of such little status, and, he hoped, low enough for Chris' judgment. She smiled at him, though, and it made everything instantly better. She did not extend her hand to be kissed, for which he was terribly grateful. He didn't think that it would be appropriate to take one of those pretty hands into his suddenly huge and sweaty paw.

"Ninon is one of the greatest gifts the modern Marketplace has," Chris said. "And her specialty will interest you, Michael."

"Yes, sir?" Michael managed to say.

"Ninon exclusively trains pleasure slaves." Chris smiled again, and Michael gulped as Ninon turned to look into his eyes again.

"Is that truly a field of interest to you, Michael?" she asked, her eyebrows raising delicately. "As a client, or a trainer?"

"I — I hope to be a trainer," Michael stammered.

"How charming. And fortunate for you, as well. You are at an awkward age for pleasure training," she said gently. "Too young for the proper experience, too old to be fully trained in the most proper way. But a few months with me, and I would teach you things about pleasure which you could have never imagined."

I bet, Michael thought, bitterly hating the way the spikes were digging into his balls and around the base of his cock. "It would be an honor for me to study under you ma'am," he said. He hated the way it sounded the minute the words left his mouth, but again her smile made everything better. When she turned her attention back to Chris, he tried to breathe in deeply and gently and regain his composure.

"Surely, you have many allies in this," she was saying.

"All I need," Chris said confidently. "And I suspect that many of those who have indicated opposition will come around before our meeting is over. I've found that there are a lot of irrational fears surrounding what this might mean for independents, especially spotters." He gave her a meaningful look, and she nodded wisely.

"Still," she said gently, "it is needed. The quality of merchandise has been declining for years now. I have seen common threads; a lack of dedication, a lack of the proper spark, the passion." She shook her head sadly. "However, we cannot place the blame entirely upon the clientele. We must bear this responsibility, as we are the foundation upon which the Marketplace exists. We are more than the conduit, Mr. Parker — we are the shapers of service. Surely, we must admit that there are universal standards of acceptability."

"Of course we do," came a deep voice from behind her. "We accept the standards and teach them. But we can't allow any governing board authority over us and our methods. That would go against the very essence of our origins and place in the world."

Michael cringed at the sound of that confident, cheerful voice. Chris and Ninon turned to welcome Geoff Negel into their little conversation, and Michael wished even harder that he could sink into the floor, unnoticed.

"Mr. Negel," Ninon said, extending her hand. He shook it, American style, and offered his hand to Chris as well. Michael half expected his trainer to refuse it, but without the slightest hesitation, Chris returned the greeting.

"A pleasure to see you again, Ninon, Parker," Geoff said. His eyes sparkling, he turned deliberately to Michael and held his hand out. "And great to see you, Mike! You're looking well."

"Thank you, Mr. Negel," Michael said softly, surrendering to the moment. He shook his old trainer's hand nervously, and stepped even further back away from the little group.

"Oh, please, we've never stood on that kind of formality," Geoff said cheerfully. "Call me Geoff, the way you always did."

Michael glanced at Chris, but the man didn't come to his rescue. "Uh, thank you, Mr. Negel, I'm honored. But, I'm — it would be improper for me to address you so informally. Please excuse me."

"Of course, of course," Geoff murmured. "You're quite the stickler for formality, Parker, aren't you?"

"Quite." Chris said with a slight smile. "Which is why I see we shall be the principle opponents over this issue."

Geoff opened the binder and read, "'Proposed: That the International Coalition of Trainers and Handlers create a standing committee of Standards of Training, including a certification process for accrediting new Trainers.' It sounds so innocuous, Parker. But what you're suggesting could destroy one of the primary freedoms we enjoy in the Marketplace — the ability to create new and innovative methods, to challenge the past and create for the future. I mean no disrespect, I hope you realize this. Your own methods are documented successes, and I have learned much from your input in Anderson's reports. Anderson herself is truly the greatest American trainer of our generation, I will admit that freely. But there are other styles — perhaps better, perhaps equal, certainly worse. But styles which deserve to succeed or fail on their own merits, not on your personal judgment."

"What makes you think that my standards would be the sole basis for accreditation, Negel?" Chris asked. "My proposal clearly outlines a method for establishing the criteria by committee."

"And who selects the committee?" Geoff asked, waving one hand dismissively. "We all know that's where the real issue is. Who is selected to rule over us, and what training methods will be approved of, hm?"

"Gentlemen, gentlemen. Surely, this is one of those discussions best left for the debating floor?" Ninon said lightly, touching each man and smiling at both in turn.

Geoff immediately assumed a contrite expression. "Of course, Ninon! I apologize. I really just meant to come over and say hello. I'm sorry I interrupted your conversation. You'll both hear enough from me later! See you in session, Parker. Bye, Mike." He turned and entered the crowd, immediately greeting someone else and getting drawn into another conversation.

"The battle is joined," Ninon said softly.

"I wish that he was the worst of my opponents," Chris said lightly. "You know where the real battle will be — with the spotters." He coughed, and then added, "And the British."

The older woman nodded, and laid her hand lightly on Chris' arm again. She looked sympathetic. "Yes, I have heard. Still, I believe we should gather our friends close, and be sure to listen very carefully to what Mr. Negel and his supporters are saying. It would be a shame to lose because we have underestimated the feelings of those like him. I think I shall see who else is here and in agreement. Let us share our resources at breakfast, yes?"

For a second, Chris Parker looked almost shocked, but he recovered and nodded gravely. "An excellent idea, thank you, Ninon."

"No, no, thank you. And may I say, Chris, you are looking more handsome than ever! Good-bye, young Michael, and do try to calm down." She smiled kindly, and as she turned to leave, Mike colored into a blush.

God, this was going to be difficult! It was one thing to just be there, acting as Chris' valet and all around flunky, being nice and polite to everyone. But he had been dreading this eventual meeting with Geoff Negel. To have it coincide with the erotic flush he had felt upon meeting Ninon was just typical of the exquisite timing which made his life so hard.

Geoff Negel had been the first Marketplace professional that Michael had ever met, back when his first exposure to this underground world was through his Uncle Niall, a Hollywood writer. Somewhat undecided as to what his own professional life was going to look like, Michael had leapt at the chance to become a trainer of real-life slaves, and for many months, lived the idyllic life of a man for whom no pleasure was denied. But then, he screwed up royally and put his own training in jeopardy. By sheer luck, the East Coast trainer known as Anderson responded to his request for further training. Little had he known where that trip would take him, exactly how far from the warm, sheltering hedonism of Geoff Negel's California based house of slave training. *

He felt ashamed; as though he had been stripped and exposed before Geoff, and made to grovel like a penitent slave. Geoff hadn't gone for all this "in order to be a good trainer, you have to know how to be a good slave" stuff. In fact, he had spoken derisively of it, confident in his own methods, his own style. To stand there in front of him behaving like a slave in training, to refuse his invitation to call him by his first name — it was humiliating. How could something that was so right, day to day, be so damn hard minute to minute?

"Was it really so difficult?" Chris asked, in his casually maddening way.

"Yes, sir," Michael said. "I'm sorry I let it show."

"Well, it takes practice to know exactly how much emotion to display," Chris said. Apparently, he was in a generous mood. "If your intention was to show Geoff that he could effectively humiliate you, you did well. If your intention was to make Ninon treat you like a clumsy, shy adolescent, I'd say you were marvelously successful."

Or, maybe he was just saving the cutting remarks for last, Michael thought.

"Never mind that, though — Ninon has that affect on many people, regardless of orientation or taste." The corner of Chris' mouth twitched slightly, and Michael knew he was flashing on some pleasant memory. "If she had not produced that affect on you at first, she would have no doubt tried for something even more devastating."

"I've never been attracted to a woman who — " Michael hesitated, trying to find the right words.

"Was so much older than you? Who was not two slender legs supporting breasts of a more than moderate size?"

"It's not that, it's just she's — I mean, she isn't — she's hardly unattractive!" Michael sputtered.

"Certainly not. But it is her profession to make people who can attract attention, divert it, keep it. Naturally, in order to pass that knowledge on, she is the master of the art."

Oh, so it was a lesson. Michael tried to compose himself. "If I heard her physical description, I wouldn't have thought she could have that effect on me," he admitted. "Is she Italian? I couldn't place the accent."

"Greek," Chris said, with a slight nod. "Her house is on Mykanos, surely one of the most beautiful spots on earth. I guarantee that you would find it absolutely intoxicating. Most trainees do. But such training isn't for you. Think about that, and write me a few words on it tonight."

"Yes, sir," Michael said. He was doing a lot of writing these days. And unlike Anderson, Chris not only checked up on him, but read and commented on everything. In fact, Michael mused, this seemed an awful lot like Junior High School. He spent far too much time reading and writing, and kept getting interrupted by inconvenient boners. He hid a grin as he wondered whether that would make a good entry in his journal. Probably not.

As trainers would continue to arrive the next day, dinner was an informal affair, with ad hoc groups meeting in separate rooms or enjoying an array of fresh sushi being prepared on one of the open porches. Michael finally was freed from his duty at Chris' side, as Chris went off for some private meeting with one of the Japanese trainers. Michael had practically jumped for joy; instead, he smiled and thanked Chris as politely and warmly as he could imagine and dashed off to enjoy a tour of the premises uninhibited by anything save his fear of being unintentionally rude to someone. I can manage to stay out of trouble, he swore to himself, after trying a few clearly identifiable pieces of raw fish from a table hosting two stern sushi chefs. He found that the food was not quite what he knew as Japanese food per se, and tried to act as nonchalantly as possible when confronted by dishes of what looked like little nuggets of something pale and soft. Noticing several people digging into them and popping them like peanuts, he tried them and found himself chewing something that tasted remarkably like incredibly dense Velveeta.

Weird. Also weird was the fact that a lot of the foods seemed spicy hot, especially when dabbed with a red pepper sauce that seemed very popular with the locals. He smeared a healthy portion on top of a piece of sashimi and took a bite, and felt like his mouth was being seared. As he gasped and tried not to choke, someone pressed a small cup into his hand and he swallowed its contents compulsively. Not the best idea, as it turned out. Expecting the light taste of fine sake, he was met with a much denser, harsher feel, like a brandy, which did precious little to soothe his tongue and quite a bit to make him dizzy.

"Uchinaa guchi wakai miseemi?" A tall, broad and bearded Japanese man demanded of him. It was one of the local trainers, of course, and his face was so composed that the loud voice seemed terrifying. He helpfully repeated himself in a slower, and much louder tone and Michael made a helpless gesture, still spitting around the array of tastes in his mouth.

"Sir, please excuse my rudeness, but Master Sato wishes to know if you speak Okinawan Japanese," said a young woman suddenly next to him. By the collar around her throat and the careful phrasing, he knew she was one of the many interpreter slaves who were wandering around, and he was very grateful for her sudden appearance. She had a ribbon pinned to her blouse that listed English, Deutsch, Espanol, Italiano, and two names in kanji, one of which he assumed was Okinawan Japanese. Michael wasn't even sure whether there was a big difference between Okinawan and mainland Japanese, or whether it was like the difference between Mexican and Puerto Rican Spanish. But he was glad to see her anyway.

"Yes — er, no," he said carefully, finally feeling a slight easing in the burning sensation. "Thank you, please tell Mr. Sato that I am sorry that I don't speak Okinawan, but thank him for his kind concern for me." Michael handed the little cup back with a sheepish grin, and as Sato heard his response, he nodded and smiled. The smile barely broke through the stone of that face. He said "Ma'asan, eh?" and elbowed Michael and winked, and then bowed slightly and left.

"Ma'asan?" Michael asked the interpreter.

"It means, 'tasty', Sir." she replied with a brilliant smile. She was not even five feet tall, Michael realized. Tiny, like all the women in adventure books about big burly men finding themselves in Japan. Her ink black hair was short, though, appalling short. He wondered if it was custom, or her owner's taste, or even a punishment. Without thinking about it, he brushed one hand across the soft layers of shorn hair, so much like an animal's coat. She didn't even blink, only took his caress with the same calm confidence she had radiated when interpreting. But her smile seemed to waver and then get suddenly wider.

"Thank you for your help," he said, suddenly embarrassed by his action. It had been so long since he felt free to touch a slave, he thought. Yet how natural it felt, how comforting to know that she would stand there and allow him to run his hand across her head. But did he do something wrong by touching her? No one had said anything to him about such things.

"It is my honor to serve, Sir," she said. "Do you require anything more from me?

"Yes — yes," Michael said. He didn't want her to leave. He wanted to touch her again. Most of all, he wanted to take her into one of those secluded groves and fuck her brains out. Instead, he asked her what he had been drinking, and how to get another one.

"It is called Awamori, Sir," she said, elegantly indicating in which direction he should walk. "It is considered one of Okinawa's most famous exports. It is like brandy, and the Awamori here is of the finest quality." She remained calm and polite, but that initial smile was now barely a memory. Her face was frozen in a kind of cheerful grin that made him shiver, and he recalled that one of the ways that Japanese people showed embarrassment was by smiling. So he had done something wrong by touching her, dammit. Also, he knew a factoid when he heard one; she was slipping into a tour guide mode, and she was much more important as an interpreter. He sighed and shooed her away to help someone else while he waited for one of the servers to pour him a new cup.

"You must watch yourself when you drink this fine beverage," came Ken Mandarin's voice from over his shoulder. "It is a drink that seduces, you know. You think you have not had enough, and then suddenly, you find yourself in — how do you say it? A compromising position."

"Ms. Mandarin, I'm honored to meet you," he said, surprised at how cleanly it came out. The he remembered that Chris had arranged to "loan" him to her, and he blushed. She smiled in her predatory way, and tossed back a cup of the strong drink and sighed with satisfaction. How dangerous she seemed, especially in contrast to the slight, composed translator who had come to his rescue a moment before.

"Yes, I am sure you are!" she replied, putting her cup down. "So, what are you doing off of your leash, hm?" She started to walk away, and he felt compelled to follow — a question was hardly a dismissal, and she was one of the big shots here.

"I've been freed to wander," he said, keeping up with her. "I am even allowed out to play from time to time," he added daringly.

"Oh, ho, you are? How terrible for you. Do you not find it easier to be controlled, knowing that your world is ever safer than the traffic you are playing in now?" She waved merrily to someone who had nodded her way and turned suddenly back into the hotel. The cool shade of the evening was so pleasant inside, warm wood everywhere, muted light in the corners. Michael scrambled to keep up with her, because she seemed purposeful now.

"I'm not a good porch dog," he said.

"That's not what I heard," she said, suddenly stopping and flashing a very nasty grin. "In any event, you shall certainly meet a rather fascinating doggie trainer later on, and we shall see what he makes of you."

What the hell am I supposed to say to that? Michael wondered. "Well — I'll be honored to meet anyone you wish to introduce me to, Ms. Mandarin."

"Ha!", she laughed, smacking him smartly on the arm. "You're a good boy. Come in and meet some of my friends — I make no promises that they will not bite!"

He looked around, and saw the half open sliding door that she was pointing to. Instantly, he slid it open wide enough for them to enter, and found himself in a small western-style meeting room, with a regular sized table and real chairs. Seated around the table were five individuals he had seen earlier with Ken. Her fellow spotters, most likely. Suddenly, he realized that this might not be the smartest place for him to be. If Chris was stirring up trouble with the spotters, and he was Chris' — Chris' — trainee. Student. Junior trainer. Boy? Whatever.

"Heya, this is Mike here," Ken said, sprawling across one of the chairs, one leg dangling over the arm. "Meet the real people who make the Marketplace work, Mikey."

Michael sighed and bowed as the people in the room introduced themselves. There was no awkwardness with these people, and no one extended a hand to shake his. Only one of them was known to him, a man named Paul Sheridan from New York City, a friend of Chris' older brother, Ron. Paul had literally decades of experience in the field, and this was the first time Michael had seen him out of some form of leather. In fact, Paul was wearing a rather loud Hawaiian shirt over a pair of cut off jeans, certainly one of the most informal people there. But he had never met the darkly tanned woman who introduced herself as Shoshana, or the vaguely sinister Italian man who barely scanned him for an instant before nodding and shrugging as though the meeting was of no consequence at all. The last man was a slender, brown skinned man who was more engaged in the Academy schedule and barely nodded to him when he was introduced. It was one of those moments when Michael realized he had been examined and quickly regarded as a person of little consequence, and as always, it hurt.

Michael felt an increasing need to leave, but couldn't figure out how to elegantly get out of the situation without insulting Ken Mandarin or showing how scared he was.

"Do you know why we are here?" Ken asked him, as he bowed to his final introduction. She looked pointedly at him, and he felt that sinking sensation that meant he was about to Learn a Lesson.

For a second, he thought of answering her with a quip, but decided against it. "I know the purpose of the Academy is to encourage communication and learning among the trainers," he said carefully. "You meet every year, but not everyone attends. I know that for years, it has been the custom of the Academy to bestow an honorary accreditation to senior trainers who are sponsored by previous members, and that this was always a voluntary process, something like getting a certificate from a civic organization. And I know that this year, there's a proposal to make accreditation into a formal status instead of an optional one, and you have to vote on that."

There was a derisive snort from the only other Californian in the room, a man Michael had never worked with when he was out there.

"Oh, don't be so harsh, Daniel, everything he says is true," Ken said waving a hand at him. "So what do you think happens to us, Mike, hm?

What will happen to the freelance people, the spotters who train, the trainers who spot? What will happen to those who might not get this, this accreditation, eh?"

"Well — we can't know that until it's tried," Michael said, knowing how awful it sounded. "Besides, it's not even clear what the qualifications of accreditation will be, you don't know who might be accepted and who not. And I know there's nothing in the works to deny people access to the Marketplace — "

"Yet!" snapped Shoshana. "Nothing yet! First they want to register us, make sure we are all in agreement, and then those who are not will be cast out."

Michael instantly put his head down and his hands behind his back. It was a posture meant to receive a rebuke, and it calmed the entire room as though they were all alpha dogs and he had turned his throat to them. Ken laughed, delighted.

"Oh, poor thing, poor thing," she crooned. "Come here and sit by me, and learn something, mmm?"

"Ma'am—" Michael began to speak, but she shushed him. "No, no, we shall not frighten you any longer. I only want you to leave here knowing what we do for the Marketplace. Actually. . ." she paused meaningfully and looked into his eyes, "actually, I think you understand quite well what a spotter should and should not be, is that not true?"

Michael wished he could just hang himself there and then. But instead he sat gingerly where she pointed, even more subdued than before. She knows! he thought with a moment of anguish. Of course, Geoff must have told her, they were on the same side now.

Daniel pointed a finger at Michael and said, "People always say that spotters are the gateway to the Marketplace, and leave it at that. Well, sometimes I don't think that anyone really understands how must time and effort —and money! — goes into being a successful spotter. Come on, folks, who here spotted ten clients last year?"

Ken waggled a finger, but the rest of them scowled. Daniel waved at Ken with one hand and said, "Well, we have to expect that from you, Ken, you have no other life! Besides, you pick 'em and send them off for training faster than anyone I ever heard of. I doubt you remember the names of the people you spotted last year!" That was met with friendly laughter and Ken grinned with satisfaction.

"But look at me — 5 damn clients last year, and I was grateful for every damn one. And you know how many people I spotted and let go?" He looked around the table.

Shoshana shrugged. "One hundred? Two? It is the same all over."

"I built the playroom, I go to all the soft events, every damn one of them. Plus, I do the swinger circuit, and the post military rounds. Know what that means? I'm on the road three weeks out of four sometimes. And when I find a good one and get 'em into training, there's no guarantee I can see 'em to the selling floor, because we're getting a higher return rate now than ever!" He was obviously worked up about this, prepared to say all these things, and in the saying, some of his anger seemed to deflate. He sank back into his seat. "What I don't need from the Academy, thank you very much, is more rules to learn, so I have to make it even harder for a new client to get into shape. And the last fucking thing I need is someone else telling me what trainers I can use if I don't have the time or talent to train."

"Trainers tend to think they have the hardest job," Shoshana said. "They are always whining about how much time they spend getting a client ready for market. But what about the time we spend making sure they are market material? What about the number of times we throw back bad merchandise, the ill-bred, the ill-motivated, the. . . the fakers. How many times we find out only at the last minute that they truly do not have the wish to serve and must be gotten rid of so that we can move on? How many times are our hearts broken because we cannot get a client to the right level to send them on?"

"Don't ever let them break your heart," Ken scolded. "You must be more positive! But it is true, we toss so many back into the sea! We are more than the gateway, Mike, we are the funnel, the, what is it? The strainer. Without us, these exalted trainers would be wasting all of their time going to meetings on. . ." she thought for a moment. "On Twenty-Four-Seven! Yes, that was the phrase, 24/7!"

"What is that supposed to mean?" the Italian asked.

"All the time. Twenty-four hours in a day and so forth. How to, 'live the lifestyle', nes't ce pas?" Ken laughed and the others joined in. Even Michael spared a slight giggle. He had been to several seminars on just that topic, and couldn't begin to imagine what Chris would look like at one, let alone how he would participate.

"I went to one last year, as a matter of fact," Ken said, sitting up in her chair. "I go to several of these conventions, these weekend meetings, although I prefer the ones most concerned with fashion for my own uses! I have found some very good clients there, very good ones. But, oh, what I go through to find them! The agony! The hours of looking, and waiting! The teasings, the bindings, and oh, oh, all the sex I must have! But you know — when the bird is in the bush, you must beat the bush to get it to fly out."

"I'm sure you hate all that bush beating," laughed Daniel.

"Oh, sometimes," Ken agreed. "But sometimes, also, one finds a moment of truth."

2 Mandarin Style

by Laura Antoniou

She was like a knifeblade in twilight, attractive and dangerous and oh, so obvious in her presence. I felt for her like I sometimes feel when I stand on the edge of a balcony, like I should really bend my knees and launch myself out and down, to my certain destruction.

I dampened my jockeys right through to the seam of my 501s, and turned away before I leapt.

I was late for the seminar, the booklet folded back in my hands, slipping and sliding among the dozen handouts and schedule updates, glancing down from time to time to make sure I was in the right place. The hotel hallways were crowded, and I could barely make it from one room to another without running into ex-girlfriends, former bottoms, current fuck buddies, and assorted community acquaintances, who all had to be acknowledged. Hugs and back pounding, kisses and casual gropings, promises to meet later, later, after the next one, before the contest, at the dungeon.

How many people have I slept with, based on a relationship that lasts ten minutes at a time, while we're both on our way to something else? I amused myself by trying to count while I scanned the room looking for a seat behind someone not too tall.

As usual, the presenters weren't ready, just milling around at the front of the room, playing with the microphones and pouring glasses of ice water. I stuffed the papers into my vest pockets and settled my dick comfortably against my right thigh. It was itching today, probably too dry. The straps of the harness settled up tight, and I sat up straighter to relieve the pressure.

Finally, with nods all around, the leader of the seminar coughed and tapped the mike, and people began to settle down. I waved at a pal across the room, and they turned the tape recorder on, and the man introduced the

22

topic.

"Twenty-four-slash-seven, or, Do People Really Live This Way?" There was scattered laughter; I smiled a little. The amusement didn't make me feel comfortable. I pulled the program booklet out of my pocket again to check the description of the seminar. It said: "An examination of the possibilities in a full-time D/S relationship. Presenters will discuss the realities of this most difficult lifestyle."

I tried to sit tall while they introduced themselves. Yes, yes, the middle guy has been in the scene for twenty years, he has two lifestyle subs under him. Yes, the woman at the end has been in the scene for 30 years, and she is up to her third slave. The two leathermen have been together for five years, and they are master and slave. I read it all in the program. Let's get to the point. How did they meet? How did they know? What did they do — and how can I find someone to do that with me?

Well, isn't that the point of all these things? I mean, I had fun watching the fire demonstrations earlier, but really, I'm here to hook up. If not for tonight, then maybe — maybe much longer.

As they took turns explaining how real their relationships were to them, I was dismayed to find my mind wandering. Yes, it's sweet that you love each other so much, I said mentally, but what does it say in your contracts? Do you really do anything you want with your lover? What does it feel like? And why weren't there more bottoms on the damn panel?

Instead, I began to hear how compromise made things work for them all. The same stuff I'd heard before, last year as a matter of fact. This one had a trick for making sure that his slave knew that certain things were his right to do — but that he didn't have to exercise that right. Another one sat down with his slave once every quarter, to discuss things like equals, just to make sure things were going great. Not that she couldn't ask to do that at any time, he added quickly. It was just to make sure that they both had a safety net. That started a discussion on the burdens of being the top in a full time relationship. Nods of agreement all around.

I stifled a yawn, and wondered when the dungeons were going to open that night, and whether there was a women's party.

As my mind wandered, so did my eyes. And that's when I saw her slip into the room, followed by this tall blonde haired man who looked like he would be more at home posing for an advertisement for milk.

But she was the one who grabbed me. Five foot four or five was my guess, with spiky ink-black hair that looked like it ran down between her shoulder blades. Her high cheekbones and narrow, dark eyes spoke of an Asian background, but she wasn't obviously Chinese or Japanese — maybe Filipina? She was wearing faded jeans and tight chaps with a silky leather uniform shirt, aviator glasses hanging from a correct loop in the front. There wasn't a ring of keys dangling left, but what looked like a silver snake of a collar, with a lock hanging tantalizingly low on her thigh.

I instantly saw myself crawling to her and rubbing my face against that thigh, pushing that loop of silver, begging for it to embrace my throat.

I turned back to the seminar and pressed my lips closed. Swallowing hard, I then had to take a deep breath, because a wave of dizziness had washed over me.

You got it bad, baby, I thought to myself. Calm down! Jeeze, you'd think you weren't getting laid often enough!

But I didn't dare look back at her. I stared at the presenters, waiting for wisdom, or at least a clue.

"You have to recognize that your sub is a human being, with feelings and needs just like you have," one of the guys was saying. "Sometimes, she's going to need some time off, maybe to just chill out and take inventory. It's your responsibility to provide her with that time."

"And what if you should require that person's services during that time?" came a voice from the back of the room. I knew who it was. This time, I was not the only person who turned to look at her.

She was still standing, and the blonde guy was behind her and to one side, looking kind of casual, but attentive. And very cheerful. She, on the other hand was dead serious.

"Well, what do you mean? Like to talk or something?"

"No. I meant, what if, when you have dismissed your slave for this free time, you realize that there is a task which needs completion, or that you wish to have sex with them. What if you have an unexpected guest whose comfort requires the services of your slave? What if you are merely bored and wish them to come and act as a footstool while you take tea?"

Her voice was low pitched, but clear, and there was some kind of accent there I couldn't recognize, like an English person speaking French, or a Frenchwoman who learned English in London. She made short gestures when she spoke, little, sharp movements which emphasized words, added ironic accents to her phrases. The room swayed as attention went back to the panel.

"I'll take that," the woman on the end offered. "It's simple — the agreement I have with my slaves is just that — an agreement. In it, I have made promises, too. I have to uphold them, on my honor as a mistress. If I have to deal with a minor inconvenience from time to time, it's my responsibility to deal with it."

There were noises of agreement, affirmation.

"Then why do you call them slaves? Would a slave not be pleased to be

24

used by their owner? Would a slave not be utterly available, at all times, even if this is inconvenient to them — because that is their purpose? Does not an owner have the right to use their slave, so long as such use does not cause them to be incapable of serving?" I was beginning to flush. Every line from her made my cunt throb and pulse, and by now, I was so wet I wondered if the seat was going to be spotted. But I was also shaking. When I turned back to the panel, I grabbed hold of the laces on the side of my vest and wrapped them around my fingers to keep my hands from trembling.

"Well, I guess it depends on your definition of slavery," one of the men countered. "The way I see it, I have just as much responsibility as my sub, more, in fact. As a dom, I have to make sure that she is safe, and — "

"Happy?" The woman asked.

"Well, yes, of course," he admitted, with heads bobbing up all around.

"What's the point of doing all this unless both partners are happy?" asked another one. There was some applause, and then the room swished as heads turned back to the woman in the rear. A few hands danced and waved, trying to get in on this, but it was obvious that they were going to have to wait.

"It seems strange to me," the woman said, this time allowing a thin smile to show through, "that you will spend all this time and effort to create happiness when a man or woman who truly wishes to be a slave will be happy once they become one." She made an abrupt gesture to one side, and blondie stepped away, opened the door, and she slid through.

"Hey — don't leave — you can't do that —" came an outraged cry from the podium.

"Oh, that was nice," the woman on the end snapped. "Come in, say your piece, and then leave before anyone can argue with you. That was useful."

"Well, let's just say that that sort of judgmentalizing doesn't help anyone," the leader said, regaining focus. "Slaves and masters are whoever they decide themselves to be. Now, let's get back to the real topic, OK?"

I heard one person down the row from me whisper, "Do you know who she was?" I saw the head shake, no, and then I gathered up my papers and made my way out.

By the time I got to the hall, she was long gone.

I saw her again, skirting the edges of the room where the fundraising auction was held, but lost her in the crowd. In vain, I looked for her at the dungeon space, even loitering in mixed space for two hours, asking people if they'd seen her. Almost everyone had — but not there.

I didn't know what I would say to her. I didn't even know how I'd say it. But that night, after a few half-hearted friendly scenes with some other girls, I fell asleep alone, twisting under the covers, hot but unable to jerk off. It was like being love sick, except that I didn't even know her name, or whether she liked girls, or shit, even if she'd take one look at me. It hurt, real bad. And no, not in a good way.

On Sunday, after the last of my marked off seminars, I packed and stowed my luggage at the front desk. I would have three hours until I had to take the shuttle to the airport and then home. Because of that woman, this had been one of the strangest conferences I'd ever been to — I hadn't taken anyone new to bed, and I hadn't bottomed to anyone new, and I didn't even come, not once. I was wondering how long this was going to last.

"Excuse me," came a voice from the door. No, it wasn't her — it was him. Blondie. I turned and jumped a little — but she wasn't next to him. He flashed a smile. "I'm sorry, I don't know how to address you," he said easily. "Is it Miss, Ma'am, or Sir?"

God, you could hear the capitals when he talked. "Jessie," I said, clearing my throat. "Jessie is just fine."

"Thank you, Jessie. My Mistress has asked for the pleasure of your company if you are currently free."

My heart beat out the rhythm of a tango. I stood without thinking and nodded, and he held the door open for me. How did he find me? Why did she want to see me? How did she pick me to see? I walked with him to the elevator, where he punched up the penthouse suite floor, naturally, and I began to feel a little giddy.

"This is like being in a book," I said out loud.

"Yep," he agreed.

"I mean, wealthy, mysterious woman who I don't know asks to see me the last day of a conference. This doesn't happen on a regular basis."

"Nope!"

I wiped my hands against my jeans legs and looked at my traveling clothes in horror. I was as vanilla as you can be, not even packing. I didn't even look like a dyke, let alone a tough, butch bottom leatherdyke.

The elevator door slid open and Blondie waited for me to exit, and then kind of sailed across the hall to tap on a door. He opened it slowly, and ushered me in like he was going to announce me.

She was sitting in one of the big wing backed chairs by the wall of windows that gave a great view of the city. She was also not in her leathers — she was wearing a man's tailored white shirt, French cuffs and gold at her wrists, and one of those fancy silk ties that cost more than what I make and will never, ever be used for makeshift bondage.

"So," she said right away, before I had a chance to even step into the room. "What do you want?"

My mouth went dry, and my mind went blank. I stared at her for an incredibly long moment and then mentally shook my head to get the cobwebs out. "Er — you sent for me," I managed to say.

"You sent for me, what?"

"You sent for me — Ma'am." This time, I put in the capital. It was real easy.

"Sir," she corrected genially.

"Yes, Sir," I whispered.

"You were looking for me, and now, you've found me. Tell me, little girl with a big cock, what it is you were going to say when you followed me out of the workshop yesterday."

"Well," I started.

"No, wait! First, straighten your back. Place your hands in the small of your back, and push them forward. Do not, do not fidget, yes, do not fidget. Look at me. Tell me."

I did as she said, and my hands burrowed into place before I figured out how to do it. "I wanted to tell you," I said, shaking, "that I liked what you were saying. Sir."

"Yes, you did. And you wanted what else?"

"To — to see if you knew — to find out if you might —" I lost the nerve. Sweat was covering my body, and I was trembling too hard to concentrate. It all seemed so stupid, that I was standing there like that, so scared yet so fucking turned on that I couldn't even move. I hung my head, and took deep breaths.

"You must say it, or I will have Andy open that door and send you on your way."

I looked back up at her, and felt my knees shaking. There was only one response to that — I hit the floor, hard, and she made a hissing sound that was almost like a whistle. "Then come closer and tell me," she said.

Flashback to that moment in the seminar — but now, I was there, literally crawling to her on my knees, crossing that hotel room in an agonizingly embarrassing halting shuffle, until I was as close as I dared to be, her curious, hard eyes following my every move.

"I want to be a slave like that," I choked out, bowing my head again. "Sir. I would be happy if I were a real slave."

The scissoring whisper of steel caught my attention, and like magic, there was a knife in her left hand and her right hand was gripping the collar of my t-shirt. "Everyone says that," she said, catching my eyes with hers. "Whose slave would you be?"

"Yours," I gasped. Anything else was cut off as swiftly as she swept that knife along the front of my shirt, stabbing it down below where her fist was, and then cutting straight through the straps of my bra, and not stopping at my waistband. Instead, she switched grips and pulled my shirt from the jeans and finished severing it. I felt a tug from behind and gasped again, but it had to be Andy, pulling the newly made rag from my shoulders, along with the remains of my bra.

She reached down and pinched one of my nipples, gently. "You would be my slave? I have enough slaves. Be my toy, right now, and show me how much you meant what you claimed."

This is crazy, I thought. I have a plane to catch, and I don't have anything to wear down to the lobby, and that was a good bra!

"As you wish, Sir," I said, shaking.

To describe what we did would be fairly pointless. If I told you she spanked me, how would you know that every blow of her hand made me want to cry? Not because of the pain, but because she was telling me with every heavy swat, that spanking was for children, and only with my tears would this end. Every time I felt that, I fought the battle with never wanting it to end and wanting so much to give her what would please her.

How could you know that?

And if I told you that I crawled and whimpered on the floor, following her boots with my tongue as she parted my legs with a slender and wicked cane, leaving so many slashes on the inside of my thighs that the very thought of pulling my jeans back on was terrifying, would you realize that I didn't care about the pain or the discomfort? would you believe me when I said that my thoughts were only on the boots which I had been commanded to shine, and that until they were gleaming with my spit, nothing, nothing would distract me? Could you possibly understand how pleased I was when she braced her heels, one at a time, against my back, and pronounced the job done to her satisfaction? That I came, grinding my cunt against her foot, only to repeat the exercise, knowing that this was a trap set for me yet also understanding that I was to fall into it, eagerly?

It's impossible to describe.

And when I say she possessed my body, you may think that her fingers in my mouth, in my cunt, in my asshole, were all just that — fingers, penetrating and opening me, spreading me wide to examine and tease, to empty and fill again, until I squirmed with ecstasy and groaned in pain. But to me, she was taking possession of me — marking her territory. I begged for more, not with words, but with every time I arched my back, every time I relaxed to take more, every time I cried, or moaned or licked hungrily at her offered fingers in gratitude.

The knife was in her hand again, but her other hand was indicating her fly. "Take me," she said, "take me well, and all that I wish to do with you, and I will mark you. And if I mark you, I will see you again."

I forced my hands into stillness as I worked the fly open. Underneath the expensive trousers, dampened with my tears, were silk boxer shorts, never so sexy on a woman before. I reached in, and felt the bulge I would have to take to earn her favor, and licked my lips desperately. It was large. No, it was huge. One of those black silicone things that doesn't look anything like a real cock, and as it came free of her clothing, I despaired of ever really taking it with any expertise. I could only hope to survive on sincerity. She passed me an unlubricated condom, and slowly, I worked it over the tip, using my lips to push it on.

"Eeeee— yes," she sighed, watching me. "That is good, ma petite. I know you cannot swallow all of me. But make love to it nonetheless. Do not allow what is happening to you to distract you."

What was happening to me? I wondered about that for scarcely a moment before I felt my thighs being spread wider. It had to be Andy again, and his fingers lightly touched my cunt, and I shivered.

I had not had a man touch me there in years.

The cold shock of that made me stop what I was doing — exactly what I shouldn't have done. What she said she didn't want me to do. Instantly, her hand was in my hair, jerking my mouth off of her cock, and turning my eyes to hers.

"You are not a virgin," she stated with the assurance of one who has already had access to my open holes. "You may be a lesbian, but you are my toy right now, are you not?"

"Yes, Sir," I said, feeling a wash of betraying tears. The fingers had left me, and I shook, half in fear and half in anger at myself.

"And if I choose to have my toy penetrated by my hand, or my fist, or my cock, that is my right, is it not?"

"Yes, Sir!"

"Or any hand or fist or cock. It is of no import who or what they are attached to. I wish it done — you will accept it."

I felt a word dancing around in my mind, and captured it before it could escape. Safeword, I was thinking. Dammit, safeword! I want you, not your boytoy, I don't want any man's dick in my cunt.

But I want to be a slave, your slave, like you said, serving you —

But I don't want anyone else —

But other women, that would be all right —

But I could be happy —

She pushed my head back down, and speared my mouth, expertly. I

choked at the intrusion, and almost fell backward, but caught myself with a
fist wrapped around each of my ankles. There was no intruding hand between my thighs this time, only the hard, slick cock of a woman, the pounding and sliding penetration that no flesh and blood phallus could duplicate.
I set my lips around it, and pushed back, taking as much as I could, coughing and gagging as she took me. I didn't know what to think, and soon
enough couldn't. At one point, she held me suspended on this gag, filling
me until I couldn't breathe, and laughing as I swayed back.

And then, I was on all fours, and that big, awful cock took me, first
driving into my cunt, slick with the dampness of cum and sweat and every
drop of lube my body could possibly manufacture. By the time she spread
my asscheeks, I was near blind with confused pleasure, drunk on endor-
phins, exhausted with the strain of holding my own body up. I felt the
tearing pressure as though it came from outside my body, and when she
sank her teeth into my neck, pinning me to the floor, I screamed and thrashed
around in something so shattering it couldn't be contained in the word orgasm. Think of one mind-blowing electrical shock that zaps you from head
to toes. Now, sustain it until you can't breathe.

I lay there, panting and oozing, clutching at the carpet fibers, trembling. I felt a weight on my back, and a sharp cut on my shoulder, and cried,
sobbed, really, when I realized that she was marking me.

Then, I felt Andy lifting me up, and allowed him to lead me to the
glorious bathroom. He bathed me like an invalid, wiping me down, and left
the room with me sitting on the john, utterly wasted.

I stood, and turned to see my back in the mirror. On my left shoulder
was an odd mark — two vertical lines, one with a shorter line flying up on
the right side, the other with a line extending from the top at perhaps a 30
degree angle. They were trickling blood. When Andy came back, he put a
bandage over both. He brought my clothes with him — at least my jeans,
socks and boots. A conference t-shirt was with them, probably his, since the
woman's would be too small for me.

I realized that I didn't even know her name.

I walked out into the room, unsure of what to say, or what to do.
Should I kneel again? What would happen now?

"You may go," the woman said. She was placing a business card on the
table by the door.

I stood still. Confusion must have been quite apparent on my face.

"You are not ready," she said, with a shrug. "C'est la vie. But you were
fun to play with, and so I have given you a souvenir. Perhaps you will be
ready one day, and then you will call this number, and I will see you, and if
you prove suitable, I shall finish the cuts. But do not dare call if you are not

prepared to give me everything."

Tears came quickly — how could I still have them to cry? And she shook her head at me.

"There is no failure with me, little girl-boy, only partial success. You have been entertaining, and so we part as so many do, mm? Without rancor, without tears. Surely, you will find other happiness, even if you never call me."

I hated her, with every fiber of my being. I hated her for teasing me, for playing with me, for cutting my shirt and making me miss my fucking flight, but I hated her for making me leave, oh yes, that was the worst part. Stiffly, determined not to make a scene, I strode to the door. My back and thighs and ass and cunt and tits ached, and I thought, well, at least I have that. I picked up the card in shaking fingers and put it in my pocket. Andy was holding the door open and I was almost through it before I turned and hit my knees again, this time bowing my head all the way to the floor.

"Yes," I heard her say. "You are welcome."

Andy took me to the airport in a big shiny rent a car. We didn't say much to each other. And I didn't look at the card until I got home. It was very plain. It had a New York telephone number on it, and the initials KM. She had written on it, "When you are ready."

I slid it into the frame of my mirror, where I see it every morning, and every time I check myself out before hitting the bars. I don't exactly know how I feel about this readiness, what it really means, and whether I'll ever call that number.

But I do know this: the price of freedom has never been so low.

3 Fortunate Bastard

As I knelt, trembling on the polished wooden floor, my back a tight bow, the growling words of my new master came too fast for me to even hope to follow, punctuated by sharp, staccato sounds that dripped with contempt and anger. From time to time, I felt a slight kick — against my shoulder, against my thigh, but I did not raise my head, not an inch, holding myself as still as possible, as Anderson had cautioned me to do.

Finally, the command to look up came, and I carefully brought my body up, not moving my knees, sliding my arms alongside my body as carefully as possible, even though I felt the tingles of worn and sleeping muscles all over myself. Sakai Tetsuo was a handsome but severe man, his eyes dark and narrow, his cheekbones drawn tight over an aristocratic face. He was holding a rod, and too fast to follow, it descended and smacked hard, making a loud crack that cut through the room. I couldn't help it; I flinched as it struck, and that began the first of many, many beatings. I didn't know what I had done, or what I had neglected to do. I wasn't to know for days. It would be three weeks before I found out that my new master even spoke English. All I knew that day was that I was held as beneath contempt — not only because I was an American, but because I was a freak.

And yet, she had sent me there. After all the time it took for her to see me as what I was, she had sent me there.

Chris snapped himself out of his reverie as he stood by the door to the room Tetsuo had invited him to. It was a lifetime ago, his first visit to Japan. Yet still, it seemed unnatural for him to approach this door on his feet; strange to merely tap against the pine door frame and wait to be invited in. Surely, if he dared to walk in, eyes level, Tetsuo would erupt in rage and

32

nearly take his head off with one blow.

But he heard the invitation come, slid the door open, and entered without a trace of the tremors which threatened to rise in him like waves. Tetsuo was already seated by his table, soft lamps illuminating the one corner of the room.

There was never a need to say the empty things that were taught to slaves in the States. No "I am here, Master", or "What may I do for you, My Lord?". Here, one is summoned, and one comes.

I need a drink, Chris thought, settling opposite Tetsuo and forcing the memories into a corner of his mind.

"Sake?" Tetsuo offered.

"Thank you, no," Chris said. "Just water please."

Tetsuo nodded, and the door to the adjoining room slid open like a whisper. A tray appeared, followed by a woman in a kimono, and Chris stopped watching as she went through the ritual of closing the screen, picking up the tray, and all of the movements which you had to learn in order to bring someone something as simple as a drink. He didn't comment on how quickly whoever was in the other room had found a cup of water for him, or arranged the tray. To notice a serving slave, as opposed to an ornamental one, was a breach of etiquette.

There was the usual exchange of courtesies; Tetsuo asked polite questions about the state of affairs in New York, and Chris inquired about Tetsuo's school in Tokyo. They agreed that the Shimada resort was quite an excellent blending of Eastern and Western styles, and the weather was fine, and that they both regretted being so busy that they could not spare any time to cheer for their favorite baseball teams in person, although they hoped that they might find an afternoon this year to do just that. Finally, Tetsuo changed his posture in that minute way that showed he was ready to talk business.

"As to the matter at hand," he said, "I have been most interested in this proposal of yours. I must tell you that I and my house support it wholeheartedly."

Chris bowed his head down slightly in acknowledgment and gratitude, but did not comment. It was only natural that Tetsuo would support it. He waited for better news.

"Noguchi-sama is also in favor," Tetsuo continued, as though this were of no singular importance. But that was the real blessing, Chris thought. As Noguchi goes, so do the great Japanese houses, trainers and spotters alike.

"That is encouraging news," Chris said.

"But that is not why I asked to see you." Tetsuo emptied his sake cup and put it gently down. He made a slight motion with his right hand and no slave returned to the room to refill it. It was so very subtle; so designed to make it seem that slaves just knew when to do things and when not to.

"I have some proposals of my own to present this week," Tetsuo continued. "This first one is for you. I have been following your progress for these few years. Your record has been exemplary; you have been of great value to the house of Elliot and Selador. Your writing style varies enough from Sensei Anderson's that I can see where your influence has been growing in her own reports. In addition, I have found your independent style of training to be most instructive, particularly considering the nature of the North American clients you have trained."

Chris picked up his cup and drank slowly. Tetsuo had never been so — effusive — in his compliments. It was almost too much to process cleanly. Without thinking, his left hand made a gesture, and the slave returned to refill his cup. Tetsuo didn't hide a smile, and Chris almost blushed.

"You are too kind to this poor, ignorant student," he finally murmured in Japanese.

Tetsuo didn't argue, as an American teacher might have, only grunted in response to the use of his language. He continued in English. "There has been one mark against your record, and that is a disappointment However, considering your youth and the pressures of the market, I believe I understand the complete situation. Our failures often point directly at our weaknesses."

Chris nodded.

"And if your greatest weakness is your loyalty, then you are to be commended upon choosing a remarkable fault for this age," Tetsuo said with a slight smile. "A fault which I wish to exploit. It is time you — moved on, Parker—san. I realize that in your country, it is common for one in your position to begin a house of your own. I propose something different. An alliance, and a business proposition. Between my house, and the house of Sensei Anderson. Between myself, and you. Come to Japan, Parker-san. As a trainer in my house." He signaled for more sake, and held up one finger toward Chris, who had taken a breath to speak. "I am not finished."

Chris composed himself smoothly and waited as the sake was poured, allowing the girl to serve him some. When she was gone again, Tetsuo reached next to him on the floor and picked up a carved wooden box, which he placed on the table. As Chris stiffened in surprise, he pried the top of the box off and pushed it across the table so that Chris could see the contents. Even though there was no real reason to look, Chris did. The coil of dark metal was threaded with the stylized magnetic lock and identity cylinder that Tetsuo used on his personal slaves, and not the large orange tag that was used on trainees.

"Not only as a trainer," Tetsuo added, settling back comfortably. "But as my personal slave. I wish to purchase you from Sensei Anderson."

Chris reached for the sake, and drank it down like water.

* * *

"And then what happened?" Michael asked, when he finished giggling. The other people around him were wiping tears from their eyes and calming their own snickers. "What could I do?" The speaker shrugged. She was a broad faced, bright-eyed young Korean who called herself "just Kim!". "I bowed low, backed out of the room and went back later with a can of paint. . ." More laughter followed and she grinned.

Earlier that evening, Michael had pried himself free of the brooding spotters as soon as he could. After wandering aimlessly for almost an hour and considering turning in, he found a group of folks who were all his age and younger hanging out by the hot tubs furthest away from the ryokan. To his delight, they were almost all trainees themselves. He tossed off his clothes, cleansed himself quickly and thoroughly in the glorious outdoor area set up for it, and joined Kim and a quiet Canadian man named Benjamin, while others sat at the edge or lounged on the platform. Kim had turned out to be quite a storyteller — and very funny. Two translators knelt nearby — the Brazilian man's bad English wasn't quite as good as Michael's bad Spanish sprinkled with bad Portuguese, and Kim's French wasn't as good as she had hoped it would be, although her English was fine, so Catherine, the Swiss woman who spoke only German, French and a little English had felt left out. Now, they all traded stories and jokes with the gentle murmuring of translation going on throughout it all.

"So what about your teacher, Michael?" Kim turned to him and he felt her toes nudge against him in the tub. "Does he make you do stupid things?"

"Don't they all?" Michael said a bit too loudly. But beer, sake, and that incredible local rice brandy had made them all a little bold, and everyone laughed. He wanted to nudge her back — firmly — but stopped himself ruefully. He couldn't explain that he often thought that Chris read his mind, and that speaking ill about him would almost certainly cost Michael whatever freedoms he had this week. "I want to be Ninon's trainee," he quickly said with a leer. Everyone laughed some more.

"So do I!" several of them said at once, and cups banged against each other in toasts to the Mistress of Pleasure. "I would train for two more years to spend one year with her!" swore Catherine, the Swiss lady.

"Three!" swore the Brazilian. "By God, three years, with beatings every week!"

35

"I would give myself to her as a slave," Kim said, " and I do not like women!"

"But neither do I!" said the Brazilian, and they exploded in laughter.

Oh, this is better, Michael thought. This is fun! Nice people, no politics, just a little vacation, that's all. Talking about sex instead of business was a bonus, too.

"But the market for pleasure slaves is down," Benjamin said soberly, killing Michael's last thought. "At least it is in the Americas. How is it out here, Kim?"

Kim shrugged. "Better than you have, I think. Many more people here want pleasure slaves than in your country. You are so strange in America — and Canada!" she amended. "Here in Asia, people always think of slaves as property to be fucked. In America, you wanted slaves to work in fields, and were ashamed that you want to fuck them. For Marketplace slaves, it is the same! Here, we use them for pleasure, and in America, you make them do housework."

"Aw, that's not true!" Michael immediately protested. "We produce hundreds of pleasure slaves in the US! And they're still popular!"

"Sure, yes," Kim agreed. "But see how the international sales go, eh? The most pleasure slaves are trained in the East, and the most specialty slaves are now coming from the West."

"Huh?"

"It's true," Benjamin agreed. "I've been studying sales records for the past ten years, and comparing them to the previous fifty. America and Canada are producing more slaves with cross-training than anyone else right now, and the Asian markets are supplying more pleasure slaves than ever. The Mediterranean and Middle East markets are full of pleasure slaves, too. But we North Americans are putting out specialists. Cooks and butlers and doctors and drivers and teachers, eh? "

"I wonder what that means," Michael mused out loud.

"It means you Yankees don't know how to have fun!" Kim teased.

"I know how to have fun!" he protested, finally giving her that nudge with his toe. She nudged him back, and they ended up splashing each other like kids, until Benjamin protested and they all settled down again.

Specialists, huh? Michael thought as he settled into the warm water up to his chin. Well, it was true — so many of the slaves whose files he'd seen in his studies were supposed to be doing specific jobs. The kind of basic training that the Elliot/Selador house did — designed to make a person easy to place in a simple job — was pretty rare. It was one of the reasons they were so successful; not only did they specialize in newcomers, but in slaves whose only talent was their desire to serve. Some owners liked that, certainly enough to keep the house in the black. But the real demand — and the high prices — were reserved for the slaves who had valuable training in specialized skills. And it had been a surprise for Michael to find out that there were plenty of slaves who did not expect to be used sexually; and even slaves whose contracts said so! Very strange, at least to him.

It was all so confusing sometimes. Chris had made him painfully aware of the essential humanity of the slaves that they handled, yet the little bastard was a cold, distant, absolutely scary topman when he deigned to play. One of the harshest things he had ever called Michael had been "user"; yet he was the first to tell a would-be slave that their entire purpose was to be used and useful.

It was enough to make you nuts, Michael reflected. "I don't want to talk business," he drawled, stretching luxuriously. "This is the first time I haven't been under supervision, underfoot, or just plain under the weather in ages. I need to have some fun out here before I go back to all-work-and-no-play! Did you see some of the pleasure slaves they were showing off at the party? I want a few pieces of every one. Who's with me on that?"

There was a moment as the interpreters managed the idioms, and some light laughter in response. Kim sighed dramatically and shook her head. "I am still celibate this trip," she said easily, with no trace of embarrassment or annoyance. "Next year, when I finish my apprenticeship, I will be a goddess of sex! My slaves will never sleep until I have been satisfied a thousand times. But this year, you will all have to lust for me in vain."

"Man, that sucks," Michael said honestly. "For real, you can't get laid?"

"You can?" translated the two interpreters simultaneously.

"Well, yeah!" Michael said, and then suddenly paused, thinking. When was the last time he got off? Was it that time when Rachel did a toy inventory with him? He had ended up with what seemed like a sex shop's worth of things clamped, strapped and chained to and in him while she and one of the slaves-in-training went at it like a couple of hungry weasels in front of him. Unable to touch himself, every time one of them even brushed his cock, he almost came, and when Rachel finally started taking all the toys off and out of him, the little slave girl stroked his cock until he exploded. He had almost fainted, it was so intense. But that was — ages ago.

His face told the story, and they all laughed at him, and he blushed, deeply. Yeah, he was horny all the time, and no, no one had really had sex with him since he left Anderson's house, but he hadn't thought that he was necessarily celibate.

"I don't understand!" he said in a burst of annoyance. "Why the hell do we have to suffer so much, when we're the fucking trainers?"

"Oh, you might be a trainer," the Brazilian man said with a snort.

"But I am a maggot!"

"And I am slut," added Catherine with a brilliant smile.

"I'm just 'the kid'," said Benjamin cheerfully.

"'You want to be a trainer that fast, you go train with Negel in California," Kim said wagging a finger at him. "He will call you whatever you like! I hear he says you are a trainer after only six months, very easy!"

Michael slid quietly back into the water as they laughed, and felt his ears burning. He had no way of knowing which of his new friends — if any — knew how he had gotten here and wished he had not raised the issue of training at all. But their laughter seemed general and not cruel, so he counted his blessings and allowed part of his mind to follow their outrageous conversation. But even as he managed a few soft laughs and a nod or two, the practical side of his brain was occupied with figuring out how to keep his secrets safe during the conference. Suddenly, he was keenly aware that it wasn't just his face that was on the line here, but Chris Parker's as well.

Lucky bastard, he thought, flashing a grin at Kim. Chris never has to worry about anything.

4 Tightening Coils

Pickled papaya? Rice porridge with bitter melon? And were those misshapen things really considered donuts? Michael gulped in some air and tried to concentrate past the throbbing in his skull. The unfamiliar food wasn't making his hang-over any more friendly. He passed the entire table by and snagged a cup of American coffee and went outside to drink it.

It was steamy in the early morning, and the local birds seemed in on the conspiracy to tear his eyeballs out through his ears. He tossed back three aspirin with his coffee and groaned. Why on earth did he drink so much last night?

He had made his way back to the room sometime between two and three. Chris liked his privacy, and Michael had thought to just tip-toe in and find his futon in the dark. But to his surprise, the room was empty, a single lamp lit and no sign of his trainer. There was a shoji screen set up, blocking half of Chris' futon, but it was amply clear that he wasn't in the room.

He had somehow managed to get out of his clothing and shove it all in his luggage to minimize any mess he might make, before collapsing face down onto the shockingly thin sleeping mat. The next thing he knew, a strange slave was gently opening the shutters and once again, he was the only one in the room. Chris' futon, out and pristine last night, was already put away, and on the table was a note that simply read "Review the track 1 seminars and choose two". The Academy schedule was open to the event listings and there were several tabs inserted on various pages, with Chris' neat script indicating papers for Michael to read.

When does he sleep? Michael wondered, clutching the coffee mug protectively. Back in the states, coffee was a treat for him, despite the fact that

Chris was rather a caffeine freak himself, drinking it at all hours, even late at night. But this is no treat, he thought, grimacing. This is life-saving medication. He gulped at it desperately and groaned again. The schedule and its attached papers seemed so huge and complex, with lists of meetings, seminars, presentations and special discussion groups. He hadn't been ready to examine it, only shoved it under his arm for later perusal. He thought that maybe another coffee, then another shower, and he might be ready to read fine print.

"You're looking a little worn this morning, kiddo," came Geoff Negel's nauseatingly cheerful deep voice.

Great, Michael thought. I'm never going to get rid of him, ever.

""Morning, Mr. Negel," he mumbled. As he started to rise, he felt Geoff's hand gently on his shoulder.

"No need to get up for me, Mike. There was a time when we were equals, remember?" He walked around Michael's spot on the stairs and took a deep, theatrical breath. He was dressed in white shorts and a soft looking summer sweater, his tan clean and glowing, his silvered hair brilliant in the sun. Michael felt like he was a troll looking at a knight. "Beautiful day, isn't it?"

"Yes, sir," Michael grunted.

Geoff looked down at him, his mouth compressed suddenly in what looked like genuine hurt. "I'm sorry you're mad at me, Michael, and somewhat in the dark as to why you are. I'm very happy for you; accepted to study with Anderson, and now the single student of her protégé — that's very impressive. You've come far since I first met you. You deserve to go much, much further. If you're holding some sort of grudge against me, I wish you'd tell me what I did, so I can apologize for it."

Michael lowered his own head to avoid those piercing, ever so earnest eyes. What am I supposed to say now? I hate you because I spent all that time with you learning things that my new teachers think are the cause of every thing bad in the universe? I want to avoid you because you were there for one of the biggest fuck-ups of my life, and I have no idea how many people you've told about me?

"I — I'm just not feeling well today, sir," he mumbled. "I'm sorry that I've made you feel uncomfortable. I — I'll try to be in a better mood." Not an acceptable apology at all, in addition to being a piece of misdirection that Chris would slap him into next week for, but what did he care? Geoff wasn't like these people he was learning with now, he wouldn't be able to tell. Besides, Geoff Negel was nothing to him. Nothing.

"I see," Geoff sighed. "Well, if you're going to hide behind what passes for manners, there's not much I can do. Sorry to bother you, Mike. Try to drink some grapefruit juice, that'll help rehydrate you. Feel better." He started to move away, and Michael made no move to stop him.

Other people came and went, exploring, or on their way to one of the out-buildings. Michael sat as still as possible, waiting for the pounding to stop echoing. He was also waiting for the feelings of self pity and anger to wash away. Damn Geoff Negel anyway! Damn him for being so strong and healthy and positive he was right; damn him for being handsome and fit and sexy and confident, and so, so damn wrong.

Most of the time, Michael knew that the methods and philosophies that he was being taught by Imala Anderson and her golden boy Parker were tested by time. He saw the results, met them, studied them in files and folders, and in the flesh. And although he also saw other training methods that were excellent, he knew the value of being trained according to one tradition and then teaching it to others. He also knew, in retrospect, that the time he had spent with Geoff's house in California was wasted. That in time, Geoff and his methods will vanish like a fad.

But it was one thing to know something because logic and wiser people than you tell you so, and another thing to feel it in your heart. And seeing Geoff glide effortlessly through his detractors, white teeth gleaming and hand always out, was humbling. Maybe he's right for now, Michael thought in a torrent of confusion. Maybe it really is his time. And what's wrong with being right for the moment?

At least no one answered him. He was getting tired of Chris sneaking up behind him and answering his thoughts. With a sigh, he got up and went back inside for his second cup of coffee. And maybe some grapefruit juice.

Chris took a seat on the floor, crossing his legs comfortably. Several of the people at this invitation—only breakfast demonstration and discussion had pillows and bolsters brought for their comfort, but there were no chairs in the room. It was all for the best — the view from the floor was quite stimulating enough.

The sinuous dark skinned man with intricate scarification traces on his back and legs had been holding wrapped coils of colored rope, waiting until the last guest had been made comfortable. Then, with patience and grace, he unwound the rope from the perfect coils, re-winding it around the bodies of the man and woman who had started out by standing and holding onto a ribbon-like strand of heavy-weight silk that had been thrown over one of the exposed beams overhead. It had looked disarmingly unsafe and unstable.

That had added immeasurably to the charm of the scene.

41

As the coils became more intricate, wrapping around limbs and body parts, the dark man began to link one part to another, and the two slaves used for his demonstration were slowly drawn down, one to her knees, the other onto his back. The three of them were nude — but as the rope was used, coils of red, dark blue, pale green, the bodies of the couple in bondage became clothed. Uncomfortably so — the male was bent backwards with his legs tucked up underneath him, and the female had no way to balance except on her knees and toes — but they bore it with only slight moans and a light sheen of sweat to mark their trial.

They both screamed sex. So did the binder, whose circumcised cock was fully erect. But he paid no attention to it, other than to make sure his ropes never touched it.

Nice touch, that.

When he had used up the last inch of rope, the binder then moved his human packages from side to side — handling their immobilized bodies with ease as he showed them to the guests. It was cleverly done. If you wanted to, there was access to genital openings and nipples. It might require rolling them over — and in the man's case, pushing apart his lower limbs to such an extent that he groaned — but they had neatly been both tied up and arranged for use. The binder demonstrated this with a gentle thrust of his hips in the direction of each available orifice — a cute movement that showed his arousal and control and teased the viewers. Both bondage arrangements left "handles" that could be used to lift the slaves, which the binder also demonstrated, his muscles bunching and gleaming.

He ended his demonstration by bringing the silk ribbon down from the rafter and elegantly draping it around the two bound slaves, making them into an attractive package. Then, in silence, he bowed his way behind the screen, leaving the guests to politely applaud and murmur praise. The bound slaves, of course, had no place to go. They both closed their eyes; Chris could see them straining to breathe quietly, their bodies hot and slick, the ropes tight and just so slightly yielding.

"All this to make slaves ready to be used?" Walther Kurgan laughed, and stretched his shoulders. "The master must have great patience, I think."

"Well, not everyone thinks that foreplay consists of 'bend over', my friend," Ninon replied, fanning herself lightly.

"What more do you need?" The ex-military man grinned and eyed the bondage arrangement again. "It is attractive, though. I can see this on the auction block. After the examinations, before the bidding."

There was some general agreement with him on that score. Chris was one of the only dissenters. "I don't think Americans have that kind of patience, Mr. Kurgan. As a special demonstration, yes. But they want to be able to go right from exams to bidding."

"Americans don't have any patience," Kurgan said strongly. "Present company excepted, of course!"

Of course, thought Chris, as he nodded.

"Mr. Parker," Ninon said gently, after giving Kurgan one of her pointed "I am ignoring you" head tosses, "When can we expect Anderson to arrive?"

"I don't know if she is at all," Chris said, feeling the ripple of shock that followed his words. "The last time I spoke to her, she was still considering." Across the room from him, Tetsuo sat comfortably, no sign that he was paying any particular attention to this announcement.

"That is not like her," Corinne said petulantly. The French trainer whose translator clients were making the week easier for everyone was a woman in her late fifties, with a narrow, elegant nose and long, sandy hair. She was easily fluent in over a dozen languages and functional in half a dozen more, and her slaves were in high demand as tutors and translators, but she cherished opportunities to dabble in less—specialized property. She moved forward on her knees to examine the slaves up close, running her fingers across the ropes. "I know she does not like to attend, but this is too important for her to miss. She supports the proposal, of course."

"Yes," Chris nodded. "I do know that her vote is assured, and her - cadre - will support her as they always do."

"But we will not have her presence. That might be a problem." The female slave groaned — Corinne had apparently found a sensitive spot. She smiled briefly and then turned her attention back to the little group. "I hope you understand that I am not disparaging your presence, Chris."

"I understand perfectly."

But it was a problem, and they all knew it. Kurgan yawned and stretched again and then prodded the nearest slave with his toe. "I will tell you what I think," he said bluntly. "We must make alliances with the South American factions; they will appreciate the need for order among our members, even if they chafe at the thought of . . .hmm. . . regimentation? You find a better word, Corinne."

"No, I don't think that military terms will serve us best here," Corinne agreed, her eyes mischievous. "Present company excepted, hm?"

Alone, away from their students and apprentices, away from their lesser rivals and the need to keep up that all important appearance of absolute control and formality, the trainers in the room delighted in teasing each other. Among themselves, they were not rivals; each had their areas of expertise and their countries of origin (or residence) to separate them. They were an un-elected elite, formed by habit and tradition, and maintained, some said, throughout the history of the Marketplace. Although Chris had met

43

with all of them separately on different occasions, this was the first time he had taken a place among them. Of the fifteen people in the room, he was the youngest; he had paid his deference early, and was rewarded with a position next to Ninon and frequent nods when he spoke. They seemed gratified that he took their teasing in stride without being baited into replying sharply. If any of them had expected him to be as blunt as Anderson, they hid their surprise. In fact, it was almost as though they were ready to accept him as an individual.

It was beginning to look like this Academy was going to be nothing but a series of shocks.

Ninon passed him a sheet of paper, and he scanned the list of trainers on it. She had placed her initial next to several whom she agreed to speak to. As they chatted and joked, he initialed three he already knew, sighing as he saw the familiar names. He then passed it onto Walther who scowled at it. But he would agree; he would do his best as they all would. Whatever Anderson meant by leaving her attendance a mystery, whether it was to pass on her mantle to her favored protégé or to protest this very battle among her kind, they could not afford to waste time in group speculation.

And in fact, Walther seemed to snap out of his displeasure as easily as he had slid into it. He scrawled his initials across several names and tossed the sheet of paper onto the male slave's stomach. "I am due at a discussion now," he announced. "If any of you can do this favor for me, see if this female is available for later tonight."

"After the demonstrations?" Corinne asked. "I will share with you, if you like."

"Good God, no, during them. Thank you for your offer, but I don't know if I can stand another two hours of this sort of thing," Walther laughed, waving his broad hand dismissively over the bound bodies. "I want some diversion while any new styles of bondage or singing and dancing are going on. Perhaps we can share someone tomorrow." A few of the trainers laughed or smiled politely.

"I will ask Honore," Tetsuo promised. As the German left, the remaining trainers all took a moment to study the bondage sculpture again, and then moved in closer to each other to talk about business, ignoring them. It was one of the many small differences between the trainers; some of them brought sex to their business, others brought business to their sexuality. It was no dishonor to Walther that he would rather fuck a slave than watch something new and distinct; it was just his style. Everyone had their own priorities, and as long as they did their jobs well, a certain amount of individual taste was always allowed for. It was only the eternal presence of the slaves themselves, clients or property, that remained the same.

44

After his first seminar, a kind of basic over-view of the current market conditions, Michael's head was reeling with something other than the hangover. It was one thing to understand that the Marketplace was international and old and established; it was another thing to hear people discussing things ranging from rescuing Marketplace property from places that were splitting apart in political anarchy to how to recreate the huge Russian market that was broken up after the Revolution. The Chinese representatives were eager to discuss what might happen when Hong Kong was returned to the mainland — would that hurt them, or would it open greater mainland China, the largest potential customer base in the world? That the hand-over wasn't scheduled for years didn't matter — apparently, some of the Marketplace plans were decades in the making.

American software millionaires, Russian businessmen and Asian import/export pioneers were dominating a rise in new ownership. Fewer slaves were renewing contracts with the same owners after their first years. Contracts themselves were getting more complicated all the time. So many little facts were jotted down in his notebook, so many questions alongside them. How on earth had he ever thought this was all easy to understand?

"Ah tell you, it's getting harder and harder to figure out where the new clients kin come from," came a distinctly southern-American voice from over his shoulder. "An' yet, Ah see the numbers go up every quarter! We gotta put the brakes on, Ray!" Michael half turned to see a middle-aged man in a light, tropical suit waving his hands for emphasis, his Asian companion nodding.

"Far too many failures," the younger man agreed. "Yet the demand is extraordinary. Too much money, far too easy to get certified as an owner right now. I think we must eventually consider cutting the market back, sharply."

"Restrict the number of available slaves?' Michael asked out loud. "Sorry to intrude — but is that what you meant? And can we do that?"

The American looked at him for a moment and smiled indulgently. "We sure can, son. When you control the manufacturing process, you can sure as hell slow down the shipments! Ah'm Sebastian Pettibone Tucker, Tucker to my friends. This here is Mr. Ray Wong."

Michael shook their hands and introduced himself. "Oh — you're the kid Anderson picked out last year, right?" Tucker said genially. "Well, she ain't exactly the one to start her trainees on market share principles, tha's the truth!"

"But — I don't understand. Why should we slow down training new clients if the demand is so high?"

"'Cause when the demand gets high and the money flies, people get sloppy," Tucker said, heading to one of the inner western-styled rooms and signaling for a slave. When she came, he said sternly, "Coca Cola, with plenty of ice, and keep it coming!" As he collapsed into a tall, bamboo chair, he fanned himself with the schedule. His face was slightly flushed, and his sandy hair curling around his ears. The three of them watched the slave for a moment of silence, and then looked at each other and laughed out loud.

"Well, you can't help it," Tucker said, sighing. "You come to the Academy, and you see everything that was wrong with your last three clients."

Mr. Wong motioned to Michael and they sat side by side on a comfortable bench. "Did you notice that the return figures for slaves are up? And the contract renewals are not?"

"Yeah."

"This indicates to me — and to my esteemed colleague —" Tucker nodded, as he accepted a frosted glass of cola from the elegant servant — "that the quality of clients may be suffering. We are noticing a general shortening of training periods. Perhaps you have as well?"

"Um — actually — Anderson said the same thing to me last time I saw her," Michael began. He paused as he saw the two men smile in what looked like triumph, and for the first time, got a glimpse of what it must feel like to be representing the Trainer here among her peers. He warmed to the feeling, and continued, "And I think I agree. If it takes years to train a trainer, how can we expect to put a slave on the market in a few weeks?"

Tucker lifted one hand in an elegant "so there" gesture. "My friend, you are wise beyond your years."

"But — then the problem is with the training, not with the clients, right?"

Mr. Wong shook his head. "It is interrelated, I think. If a trainer thinks he can make a slave in a month, he wants to make 12 a year. And where is he going to find 12 clients worth the training time? That is my question."

"Ditto," sighed Tucker. "I swear, I just don't know what the damn spotters are thinkin' of anymore. I had to outright refuse seven 'pre-selected' clients last year — and let me tell you, I only work with the best spotters! But there they were — lazy, dumb as a caseload of hammers, and a few that had no idea what they might be gettin' themselves into! And lemme tell you, son, when I have to do my own spotting, what happens to my training schedule, huh?"

"I only trained three new clients last year," Mr. Wong admitted. "Plus, I spent time in New Zealand at a new training facility. I am considering joining a partnership this year."

"Do you think — that maybe people don't really need what the Marketplace offers anymore?' Michael suggested cautiously.

46

Tucker laughed. "Hell no, Mike, I think we'll always have a demand for high quality flesh!"

"Oh — well, I meant the slaves. The clients. Maybe they don't need to come to the Marketplace, because they have so many modern outlets for kinky sex now. I mean, why give up all your freedom if all you want is some top to slap you around and fuck you every once in a while?"

Mr. Wong and Tucker looked at him as if he had uttered blasphemy.

"Sir, that is the very core of our problem!" Tucker exclaimed, sitting upright. "Spotters who think that people with the latest fetish are somehow acceptable for our Way Of Life. Clients who believe that they can learn to be a proper slave by taking classes in it; that's just a — a fad, that's what it is. Ten years ago, they thought they could be slaves because they saw a coupla movies about masters n' slaves. Forty years ago, because they read all the smutty books about it. People like that are just a fact o'life, son. The problem is when they are convinced that they can — and should! — seek something beyond their ken, as it were."

"Although it is true that a significant number of new clients are reaching us through the fetish arenas," noted Mr. Wong with a pointed look. "And many of them are as true to their new life as any client who was not a part of that world. We cannot simply recommend that spotters not cast their nets over a portion of the sea just because many of the fish need to be thrown back!"

"But how can we make sure that those fish don't end up in my tank, that's what I want to know!" Tucker laughed and heaved himself to his feet. "Well, hello there, stranger!"

Michael half-turned in his seat and then rose himself, with Mr. Wong at his side. Alexandra Selador joined them, hugging Tucker warmly.

"Hello, Tucker, good to see you!"

"It's always a pleasure to see you, Ms. Selador," he said genially. "Do y'all know Alex here, boys?"

She turned and shook Mr. Wong's hand and then smiled at Michael, who had automatically put his hands behind his back and taken half a step back. "Well, hello there, Mike! I see you're meeting all the important people here."

He grinned; he really liked Alex. Of the two partners in the Long Island House he was working in, she was more likely to offer a kind word or a hint when things got bad. "Yes, ma'am," he said cheerfully. "I didn't realize that you had arrived! If I had, I would have seen to you this morning."

"I got onto an earlier flight and slept in," she said, sitting down. "You don't have to worry about me, Mike. I know Chris will keep you busy enough, and it looks like they almost brought a slave for everyone this year. My it's hot, isn't it?" The men took seats around her and a slave brought her a glass of iced tea with that same fluid grace that they all did.

"I couldn't help but overhear what you gentlemen were talking about," she said after taking a sip. "I wish I hadn't missed the report, Michael. You'll have to give me your notes later. But you know, Tucker, there is only one way to make sure you don't spend six weeks training someone who will run off and marry the first self-appointed master or mistress who gives them an orgasm - and that's to listen to them. We seem to have to learn that lesson every year."

"But they all say the same damn things, Alex," Tucker said. He cocked his head to one side and said in an innocent sing-song voice, "Why Masta' Tucker, I was just born to be a slave, I was! It's in my dreams, it's in my blood, I'd do anything for my masta!" They all laughed.

"Yes," Alex agreed. "They often do. But you know what? We have to stop believing them. Oh, we toss back the obvious loose cannons and flakes, at least I hope so. But sometimes, you find someone who is as honest and hungry as they claim to be — but the Marketplace still isn't right for them."

"The ones who wish a more conventional life?" asked Mr. Wong. "Marriage and children?"

"No, I wasn't thinking of them, although I think we have to consider expanding our resources to cover that sort of matchmaking. I'm thinking more of the ones who know exactly what they want to be and limit themselves right into a niche that is best served off the block."

"Now, see, I like that kind of thinking," Tucker said. "More private sales, that's a good direction to go in. The old fashioned way, really, owner to owner, trainer to owner."

Alex shrugged elegantly. "That too! But what I was really thinking of is all the arrangements we can make without involving the contract people at all. Not everyone needs the kind of protection and system we offer; especially if they only want one owner, or only one role. I think we need to consider our secondary market; slaves who co-exist in our world without belonging to it. With the proper relationships in place with responsible owners, there's no reason why we can't admit that there are some people who belong to our world without ever being formally registered as a client."

"But what do people like that need from us?" Michael asked.

"They need the assurance that we are there for them when — or if — their time comes," Alex said. "They need to know that we will act on their behalf if they need us to. And most of all, they need to know that we exist."

"Why?" Tucker asked, a look of amused disbelief on his face.

"Because," Alex smiled, "It will make their lives ever so much more . . . delicious."

5 Thank You, Miss Claudia,   by Karen Taylor

"I can't believe this is actually happening to me." I stared out the window as the driver turned left onto a tiny lane that I hadn't even seen from the road we had been on. The hedges were high and thick on the right, the left opening into an enormous, meticulously kept lawn with formal flower beds rolling in great curves and swirls across the grass. I couldn't even see the house yet! I clenched my fists, relieved that the white cotton gloves were actually absorbing some of the sweat from my palms. Did this all belong to Mistress Madeline? Of course it does, I told myself, digging my covered nails deeper into my cotton-covered palms. Why, someone like Mistress Madeline was probably fabulously wealthy, to keep such an estate. And to have people — people like me — under her care.

I still couldn't believe my luck. After spending months as Miss Cruz's personal maid-in-training, she had recommended me for a long-term position with Mistress Madeline, and I was accepted to the position of second chambermaid, with possibilities of advancement in her house. Miss Cruz told me that if Mistress Madeline was pleased with my work, there was the possibility I might be trained for the Marketplace, even sold on the auction block. The idea of being owned, a slave maid for the rest of my life, was frightening — and intoxicating.

I smoothed my skirt down, trying unsuccessfully to cover my knees. Opening my purse, I pulled out a compact to check my make-up one last time. Breathing a sigh of relief that my mascara wasn't running, I refreshed my lipstick and snapped my purse shut just as the car came to a stop. The driver opened my door, helped me out, and was turning the car around before I even remembered to thank him.

I stared up at the house. It reminded me of something out of an E.M.

Forster novel. Brideshead displaced to New Jersey. A great, Georgian door centered in the building, with small wings spreading off to each side. Windows everywhere, so I made sure I was standing straight and moving as gracefully as possible across the driveway, just in case anyone was watching. Drawing a deep breath, I rang the bell.

The door opened, and a man who could have played a butler in any movie for the last 50 years glared at me. "What are you doing here?" he asked, the chill in his voice so noticeable I wished I had a sweater on.

"I'm, I'm the new chambermaid, sir," I said, curtseying as Mistress Cruz had taught me. If possible, his glare was even more chilling.

"Don't you think I know that?" he hissed at me. "I'm asking you what you are doing here, at the front door, as if you were a guest of Mistress Madeline instead of the kitchen door where it is proper for someone in your position."

Gulping, I felt my cheeks burning hot, and tears filling my eyes. I can't believe I made such a horrific mistake! I turned even as the butler was closing the door and ran to the side of the house, hoping to find the kitchen door before he alerted anyone to my amazingly stupid act.

The wing I was sprinting for was obscured by hedges, and as I skidded around the corner, hair disheveled under my hat, I knew it was the wrong side of the house. Full length windows, which offered a view of the garden (and me) covered the entire south side. Through a set of open French doors I could hear someone singing German lieder accompanied by a piano. When the music stopped abruptly, I knew they had seen me. I wished myself invisible and sped on around the back of the house, finally stumbling to a halt in front of the a door that stood wide open, once again facing the baleful glare of the butler.

Gathering the last of my emotional strength, I curtseyed again, panting. "Sir, I'm the new chambermaid, sir, reporting in."

As I gasped for breath, I felt his eyes move over me. My skirt was hanging wrong now, there was a run in my left stocking, and my felt hat was wilted. I had scuffed my shoes and the heels had bits of earth on them. His nose twitched as if he could smell me sweating profusely through my blouse. The palms of my gloves were stained and damp. "I will inform the housekeeper of your arrival," he said, gesturing for me to wait under the covered roof of the breezeway, next to the recycling and compost bins.

Just before the tears spilled out of my eyes, a flash of memory. "You are not a quitter, you got chutzpah." Miss Cruz. She said it to me so many times, sometimes after watching me drag myself off the floor after a beating, other times when I was perfecting my tea serving skills in her Chelsea apartment. "Remember that, my dear. It's your greatest strength."

Allison Cruz had been the best thing that ever happened to me. While meeting her had been through an odd set of accidents and misunderstandings; she had taken a liking to me, and she introduced me to the world I was now entering. First, she took me to some of the s/m clubs in New York, and later, to some of the private parties held by the professional doms. I found a partial answer to my desires there, but I wanted more. I begged her to let me serve her, to become her personal maid. Reluctantly, she agreed to a trial arrangement. I moved in with her, and for three months I served her. In return, she taught me how to speak properly, and to perfect my make-up so as to enhance my features without calling undue attention to them. When I took her to lunch after being accepted into my current position, she expressed her confidence again. "You are a natural, Francie, I knew that when I first saw you," she said. "You will go to the Marketplace. I'm betting on it."

So instead of running, instead of breaking down into tears, instead of doing all the things I wanted to do, I snapped open my purse, fetched my brush and pulled it through my hair, refastened my hat, and fixed my make-up. I thought about removing the sweat-stained gloves, but I heard footsteps approaching and settled for straightening my skirt. The door opened and the housekeeper stepped out to the breezeway.

"Welcome, Miss Francie," she said formally. "I am Miss Claudia, the housekeeper and Mistress Madeline's personal maid. You will be working under me."

Miss Claudia was a petite woman who wore a dark green dress with a neckline decorated with lace in a manner that appeared modest while inviting attention to her cleavage. There was lace at wrists, and decorating her apron. Her brown hair was drawn back in a French twist, held in place by a complicated arrangement of long hairpins decorated with tiny pearls. There were curly wisps that had freed themselves, softening the overall effect to such success I knew it was deliberate. She looked like a perfect little china doll, absolutely delicious.

I curtseyed in acknowledgment of her introduction. "Thank you, ma'am," I whispered, keeping my voice soft.

"My Mistress says you have very high recommendations from Miss Cruz," she said. "She expects good work from you, and I intend to ensure she receives it." The housekeeper stepped closer to me, looking up into my eyes. I could smell a light floral scent from her hair. She reached forward, as if to smooth a wrinkle in my blouse, her fingers brushing my left nipple, which immediately hardened. With a small smile, her hand traced its way down my buttons to my skirt, and patted the bulge I had tried so hard to hide under a tight jockstrap. "I expect you to work hard to please me in

51

every way, Miss Francie," she said, a twinkle in her eye. "It is not until I am satisfied that you will be allowed to personally serve Mistress Madeline."

I gulped. It wasn't that I was ashamed of my cock. I wasn't like the men who thought dressing in women's clothes and licking the shoes of a dominatrix was the height of sexual satisfaction. Dressing in women's clothes wasn't degrading or humiliating for me, in fact, it exhilarated me. But I didn't want to change my sex. I just wanted to be a maid.

A maid with a dick.

Being a maid had been a lifelong dream. When I was a little boy I devised elaborate tea parties for my stuffed animals, and served them all. I devoured old etiquette books, memorizing the details of setting tables and changing bed linens. My favorite television show was "Upstairs/Downstairs." As I grew older, I became devoted to Merchant/Ivory films, like "Howard's End" and books like Remains of the Day. I never wanted to be the butler or the chauffeur in my fantasies. I wanted to be a maid.

I fantasized that I lived in Edwardian England, working in one of the great country halls, starting as a scullery maid and working my way up the servant hierarchy until I was moved Upstairs, eventually serving as Lady's maid. I dreamed of lacing her corsets, brushing her hair (100 strokes). Sometimes in my fantasies I was caught doing something wrong, and was disciplined severely. The punishment would depend on my position in the household: if I was a scullery maid, for instance, the cook would beat me with a wooden spoon. If I was a Lady's maid, it would be a spanking with her silver-backed brush. Or I might lean forward and place my hands on the fireplace mantel in the parlor, my crisp black dress yanked up above my buttocks and caned by the butler or housekeeper. Never in my dreams, however, had I imagined a housekeeper so delicate and beautiful.

Pulse pounding, I followed Miss Claudia through the kitchen. She took me up the back staircase to the third floor, showed me the room I would share with the other maids, and instructed me to freshen up and prepare to meet the rest of the staff. "Your uniform is on the bed. We will be waiting in the parlor at 4:00 p.m. precisely, Miss Francie," she said, and closed the door behind her.

I kicked off my pumps let myself slump against the wall momentarily. I was awash in a mix of emotions: awe, fear, joy, and an unrelenting horniness ever since the pretty housekeeper had touched me. I undressed, washed my upper body and shaved my face at the basin in the corner of the room. Foundation, blush, mascara, a hint of eye shadow and lipstick in a soft coral were next. Then I padded over to the bed, and looked at the uniform. It was exactly as I had dreamed about all those years: simple, black rayon dress, starched white apron, crisp white cap. Black leather pumps and sheer black stockings. Each garment was an erotic delight to handle and put on. I could have spent hours just running my fingers across the silk slip, and pulling the tight, high-waisted girdle over my throbbing privates nearly made me come. But I only had a few minutes before my introduction to the staff, so I contented myself with snapping the garters against my thighs as I secured the stockings.

Standing in front of the room's full-length mirror, I studied myself. My short dark brown hair was once again brushed firmly into an old-fashioned pageboy, bangs marching straight across my brow, cap fastened firmly on top. The dress had been made from my measurements, and showed off my slender waist, the hem line precisely at my knees. I would still tower over most of the women in the house, but I kept my shoulders down and my back straight. I knew other men who slumped to hide their height when they were in women's clothes; Miss Cruz had cured me of that habit long ago. Besides, my shoes had low heels, keeping my height at a manageable 5'8". Taking a deep breath, I headed down the stairs.

The parlor was just off the main hall. I knocked quietly at the door, and once again came face to face with the frosty eyed butler. I curtseyed again, mostly to avoid his eyes, and he stepped to one side, allowing me to enter. The staff was lined up in front of the fireplace, Miss Claudia standing in front of them.

"Welcome, Miss Francie," she said warmly, indicating that I should join her, then turned to the staff. "Miss Francie is to be the new second chambermaid. Her responsibilities will cover the guest rooms, and to assist the first chambermaid and myself in any other duties." She then introduced me one by one to the rest of the staff: the parlor maid, Miss Charlene; the first chambermaid, Miss Susan; the Cook ("Cook," of course); and finally, the butler, Mr. Fletcher. As I was introduced to each, I curtseyed and they would respond with a curtsey (or in the case of Fletcher, a bow).

"Jefferson, the chauffeur, is out with Mistress Madeline," Miss Claudia explained, "and the garden is managed by a company, and is not part of the house. But in any event, you would have little contact with Jefferson or the gardeners, as your duties should not take you even downstairs, except for meals and to assist Charlene for special events. We don't need chambermaids running through the gardens, interrupting music lessons in the Conservatory, despite evidence to the contrary." I blushed a deep crimson, and heard someone snigger. The housekeeper's head snapped in the direction of the sound, and her pretty eyes narrowed.

"Susan," she said quietly. The plump red-head stepped forward quickly, her face filled with dread. "Fetch me a cane from the stand, please." I watched the maid's eyes fill with tears, but she didn't protest. She trotted to what I had mistakenly thought was an umbrella stand, and pulled a cane from the half dozen that were kept there. She returned to hand the cane to Miss Claudia, and curtseyed. The housekeeper pointed to the fireplace mantle, and with a nervous whimper, the red-head turned to the mantle and pulled her skirt up, revealing creamy white buttocks barely covered with black lace panties, and a black garter belt. With trembling fingers, she lowered those wispy panties to just below the curve of her bottom.

"Susan, you are to receive four strokes for inappropriate verbal behavior," the housekeeper stated.

"Yes, Miss Claudia," the girl answered, her voice quavering. The first stroke came almost immediately after she finished speaking, and I winced involuntarily at the sharp sound of cane hitting flesh. The impact had hit the softest, fleshiest part of the maid's buttocks, just above her thighs, and two red, parallel lines were already appearing in sharp relief against her skin. She had gasped, but made the formal reply. "Thank you, Miss Claudia." The swish of the cane and its impact cracked through the air again, and again two parallel marks appeared, directly below the first set. "Thank you, Miss Claudia," the maid whimpered. The third stroke bit into her thighs, and I flinched again, in sympathy. The housekeeper flicked the cane through the air one last time, and now there were eight angry red lines paralleling each other perfectly across the chambermaid's buttocks and thighs. "Thank you, Miss Claudia," she responded, a sob catching in her voice. I watched the housekeeper step forward and touch the girl reassuringly on the shoulder.

"Don't cry now, Susan, it's not seemly," she said, "Mistress Madeline will be home for dinner, and we can't have your eyes all puffy and red, can we?" I watched her hand dropping to caress the chambermaid's buttocks, cupping them briefly, and running a finger across the marks. "What if she wants a juicy red-head to turn her bed down tonight, hmmm?" The maid nodded, a smile lighting up her face now, and Miss Claudia patted her once more before pulling her panties up and smoothing her skirt back over her buttocks. She then returned her attention to the rest of us. Other than a slight rise of color in her pretty cheeks, the housekeeper was as calm as she was before she had so viciously caned the young maid. I shivered. What composure!

"Mistress Madeline will be returning at 6:00," she informed us. "Mr. Linden will be joining her for dinner, and is expected to stay through the weekend next. Dinner will be served at 7:30. Charlene, please assist Cook in preparations. Mr. Fletcher, I must ask you to attend to the table, as I will be instructing Francie in her upstairs duties. I expect to be finished before 7:00, and will assist you at that time. That will be all, thank you." With her dismissal, the servants left quickly, to attend to their various tasks.

I followed Miss Claudia to the back stairs, still in shock. I knew I would have trouble sleeping tonight, thinking of her sweet smooth hands wielding a cane that would come sizzling down on my backside, but I kept that thought in the back of my head and made a determined effort to concentrate. On the second floor, Miss Claudia began opening doors.

"This is the guest wing," she explained. "There are four rooms, each with their own bathroom. Linens are kept here." She continued the tour, pointing out where supplies were to be found, the closet for storing dirty linens until they were to be taken to the laundry room in the basement, and the dumbwaiter located between the second and third rooms.

"Mr. Linden will be using the blue room," Miss Claudia said as she showed me the room, which was decorated in the more masculine Federal style, with a sturdy four-poster bed dominating the room. "He takes a snifter of brandy at night, and prefers his windows open." She hesitated, looking at me. "Previously, Mr. Linden has requested that Mr. Fletcher attend to him because we don't have a valet on staff, but Mistress Madeline has decided that you shall be called upon for those duties." She hesitated, and I wondered if Mr. Linden was expecting someone like me to appear at his door. Then the housekeeper seemed to come to a decision. "Follow me, Miss Francie," she said, and we headed to the other wing, passing through a hidden door into a small bedroom that I knew instantly was hers.

The room was petite and very feminine. The walls were bisected with a chair rail, and floral wallpaper reached up to the ceiling. Pink curtains moved slightly in the afternoon breeze. A double bed with a fluffy comforter was pushed against one wall, a vanity set, a straight-backed chair and a chest of drawers the other furniture. I stood in the center of the room on a round rug decorated with a rose pattern, while the housekeeper went to her vanity and opened one of the drawers, retrieving something that I couldn't see. "Francie, please take off your undergarment," she requested. I pulled the skirt up to grasp the top of the restrictive girdle, and peeling it off my body. As I started to pull my skirt back down, she interrupted. "No, keep your skirt up." She walked slowly toward me, her eyes fixed on my cock. I blushed, and I felt my cock get harder under her gaze.

"That's such a pretty package, it's a shame to hide it under something so binding," she said. "I think an alteration in your uniform is required." She gently gathered my balls into her hand. I breathed hard at her touch, my insides melting in embarrassment and desire.

"Francie, from now on, this will be worn beneath your uniform instead of underwear." In her hand was a leather strap with snaps that I immediately recognized as a cock ring. She smiled at me as she wrapped the leather around my cock and balls. "This was a special gift from a friend, a fellow maid when I first met him," she remarked as she snapped it tightly around my privates. "Oh, I'm so pleased it fits," she said.

She started to pat my balls, the palm of her hand coming up between my legs, first gently, then harder, until she was lightly and rapidly slapping my scrotum. A moan escaped my lips, and she smiled wider. She stopped slapping and grasped my cock in her hand, moving up and down on the shaft, encouraging it to grow. I was panting from the intensity until she slapped it as well, and the pain stabbed through my groin. Even as I gasped she returned to fondle my balls again, tormenting me to the edge of pleasure, then slapping, never so hard as to cause real agony, but enough to make me gasp.

Finally, she stopped, but the leather ring kept my balls engorged and my cock was protruding nearly straight out from my body. Miss Claudia stepped back to admire her handiwork. "Yes, that will do splendidly," she decided. "I'll have your uniforms shortened to enhance the effect, but this will do nicely for this evening." She smoothed my skirt down, her eyes twinkling as my throbbing package showed in sharp relief through the fabric. "Yes, this will do quite splendidly," she repeated, and gestured for me to follow her out of the room. Glancing at the grandfather clock in the corridor, she ordered me to my duties, and started downstairs to assist Mr. Fletcher.

I was dusting the windowsills in the blue room when Susan knocked timidly on the door and entered.

"Francie, I wanted to apologize to you personally for my behavior earlier today," she said, after curtseying to me. "I hope you won't be mad at me — I'd like us to be friends."

"Oh, I hope we can, too," I responded eagerly. "But I must admit I was rather taken aback by your punishment. After all, you barely made a peep. Is Miss Claudia always so stern with the maids?"

"Oh, yes," said Susan, with a bit of relish in her voice. "It's one of the reasons I love being here. You know," she added, lowering her voice conspiratorially, "she wasn't always that way. When I was first working here, Miss Claudia was a timid little thing. She would cry at the slightest thing. I thought she was rather brainless, really, the way she would flutter about. She wasn't much good for anything other than serving tea and polishing the silver."

"No!" I cried, astonished. By this time we were huddled together like schoolgirls. "What happened?"

"Miss Madeline sent her to a special training house, a place where they train slaves for the Marketplace," Susan informed me. I could hear the capital letters in her voice when she mentioned the Marketplace, and shivered in fear. "When she came back she was a different person. You've seen!"

"What kind of training would make someone change like that?" I wondered out loud, but before we could continue, we heard footsteps in the hall. We turned quickly and curtseyed as the housekeeper appeared in the doorway.

Looking at both of us shrewdly, she said "Mistress Madeline and her guest, Mr. Linden, are on their way here. Please come downstairs to welcome them." We quickly trotted behind her, and stood in the hall, where this time I lined up with the rest of the staff.

Mistress Madeline was taller than I, and dark, the color of milk chocolate. She wore her hair long, and in a complicated arrangement that must take nearly an hour to prepare. I ached at the vision of brushing her hair out (100 strokes). She was dressed in a simple, but elegant dress, and had clearly been shopping, as witnessed by the packages being carried by the two gentlemen following her in. Since one was in uniform, I guessed he was Jefferson, making the other Mr. Linden.

"Carl, give those to Fletcher," she said in a light, musical voice. The butler was already stepping forward to relieve the man of the packages, and he and the chauffeur took their burdens into the parlor. Mistress Madeline turned her attention to Miss Claudia, and at her signal we all curtseyed. That was when I heard Mr. Linden gasp — well, snort, really.

"Good heavens, Madeline, what's this?" Mr. Linden exploded. I knew he meant me, but I stayed in position, eyes fixed downward, hands clasped together — and my bound cock now pushing slightly against the fabric of my skirt.

"Well, Carl, you kept complaining that I didn't have enough available men around the place," Mistress Madeline answered. "I decided this would be a good compromise: another man for you without taking away from the feminine ambiance that I've taken such pains to create here."

"But, a sissy maid!" he protested. I kept my eyes down, staying in position. I can't stand the term, but I was certainly in no position to contradict the Mistress' companion. She made a shushing sound to him.

"Claudia, I will want a bath before dinner. And a brief consultation with you as well — we're going to have a party this weekend." She turned to walk briskly up the grand staircase, indicating that the housekeeper accompany her. With a long sigh, Mr. Linden followed. I followed the other servants to the kitchen.

"Well, you shore wuz a surprise for Mista Linden," said Miss Charlene flicking a lock of caramel colored hair out of her eyes. "You even made Mista Fletcher's eyes jump, even though he knowed aboutcha ahead to time. But I gotta admit, you look cute as a bug's ear in that yooniform, 'specially with that little package y'all got under theah." Susan giggled, and nodded in agreement. The attention of the two maids made me blush even more.

"Thank you," I said awkwardly, and she flashed a smile that lit her whole face. "Aw shucks, Francie, I really jest meant to say welcome. But I gotta go," she said, standing up as a little bell rang on the servant's board. "That's Mista Linden ringing for you, and I gotta give Cook a hand finishin' the salads."

I headed up the back stairs to the second floor, hesitated, then knocked at Mr. Linden's door.

"Come in," he called, and I entered, with a curtsey. He was sitting on the edge of the bed, waiting. He pointed to his boots. "Give me a hand with these," he said, and I immediately dropped to my knees and gently removed the boots, setting them carefully by the fireplace. "So, what's your name?" he asked me.

"Francie, Sir."

"Francie, huh? Well, if that's the way it is." He was unbuttoning his shirt. "I'll want a bath, hot, and I'll want you to shave me." I went into the bathroom and started the hot water pouring into the iron claw foot tub. As steam began to fill the room, he joined me, stark naked. He was a big man, darker than Mistress Madeline, with an upper body that he clearly kept up with weights and thick, stocky legs. His head was beautifully shaped, and he kept it shaved. An enormous gold earring weighed down his left earlobe, and a amappalang piercing framed the head of his thick, heavy cock. He looked at me, and sighed again, and stepped into the bath.

"My shaving items are in the cabinet there," he directed. "Give my head a once over. I usually have it shaved every other day." I found the razor, shaving brush and the cup containing the hard bar of soap. Working the soap into a lather, I covered his head with the bay-scented foam, and began to shave him carefully. It was a strangely erotic sensation, rubbing my hand over the smoothness of his head, checking for stubble.

"Wonderful, Francie, just wonderful," he said as I handed him a mirror to inspect the results, and I glowed at his compliment. He must have noticed, because as he dried himself he gave me another once-over.

"Francie, take off that uniform." I obediently stepped out of my shoes, untied the apron and unbuttoned the dress, letting it fall to the floor. I then unhooked my garter belt and slipped the stockings, still attached, off my legs. As I reached up to unpin my cap, he interrupted me.

"Is that part of your standard uniform?" he said, pointing to the cock ring.

"Yes, Sir," I answered, embarrassed.

"I don't think I've ever seen a maid wearing one of those before," he said, cocking an eye at me. I blushed.

"Miss Claudia has decided I am to wear it under my garments," I explained. He threw back his head in a roar of laughter. "Claudia!" he laughed. "Oh, that sweet, wicked thing! I'll have to thank the wench personally." I stood silently, wondering what was going on, and feeling very naked. But he didn't seem to be laughing at me, but at some joke I didn't yet understand.

"Francie, get over here and suck my dick," Mr. Linden said, still chuckling. I dropped to my knees and opened my mouth, stretching wide to include the ends of the ampallang, as he continued to laugh quietly. The laughter changed into grunts, as I worked my tongue around the shaft of his thickening dick. I found that I could grasp one side of the barbell piercing with my teeth. He moaned with enjoyment as I tugged on it gently, then worked my mouth to the other side and did the same. I felt one meaty paw on the back of my head, keeping me in place as he thrust harder and harder down my throat, finally pulling out to shoot his orgasm onto my bare chest with the roar of a tiger.

"You know, I think I like the cap," he said, as I gently cleaned the cum from his shaft and then from myself. "From now on, whenever I call you to this room, I want you in just the cock ring and the cap."

"Yes, Sir," I answered. He laughed again, and dismissed me for the evening.

After that, life began to settle into a routine. Every morning I would present myself to Mr. Linden, dressed as requested. I would help him dress for the day, and then straighten his room. Then I would change into my uniform and help Miss Susan or Miss Charlene with other tasks in the house. In the afternoons, I would undress again, draw a bath for Mr. Linden, and suck his cock before dinner. In the evenings, after we finished our chores, I would join Susan and Charlene in our attic room while we prepared for bed. I would brush Susan's curls (100 strokes) until they shone like copper, and Charlene would beg one or the other of us to offer her our feet for a massage or pedicure. We would giggle like young schoolmaids as we shared snippets of gossip. Nearly every night, however, our talk would eventually turn to the housekeeper.

All of us were in awe of Miss Claudia. She was so pretty, so efficient, and so, so sexy. The maids gave me tidbits about her punishments that made me wriggle on the bed. I became obsessed with perfecting my appearance and my work, in the hopes that she would notice. At night I would fantasize that I had invited her wrath, and dreamed of that dreadful cane whipping through the air to bury itself in my flesh.

As the weekend approached, we all grew busier. Miss Claudia had informed us that Mistress Madeline was hosting a small party on Saturday night, for about 20 slave owners and friends, and that a dozen additional slaves were expected. Some would be there to help us in our duties, others for the enjoyment of the Owners. "Not that any of us are exempt from that duty, as well," the housekeeper reminded us. "Should an Owner request your personal services, you are expected to comply immediately." We nodded, excited, and I listened eagerly to the stories my roommates had to tell of previous parties in the house.

Early Saturday morning, the first of the slaves began to arrive. These were mostly additional kitchen staff, which made Cook both happy and testy, so we did our best to stay out of her way unless we were absolutely needed. Two additional maids were brought in to help in the downstairs with rearranging the furniture and arranging flowers, and another joined me upstairs in the afternoon, airing out the other guest rooms and scrubbing the floors. By four o'clock the house felt crowded with slaves, and Miss Claudia was in the midst of it all, with a clipboard, checking off items and sending slaves to the garden, the kitchen, the garage, anywhere they were needed. I was in awe of her control, and couldn't reconcile the woman before me with the vision Susan and Charlene both insisted had been what the housekeeper was like before she was trained in the Marketplace.

As we came closer to the hour of the party, I took advantage of a lull in the house to change into my evening uniform. The bell rang as I was pulling my stockings on, and I glanced quickly at the bell board. It was Mr. Linden's room. Mr. Linden! His bath! I immediately stripped off the clothes I had so recently put on and raced downstairs, skidding to a stop before the open door. There he was, waiting. And next to him was Miss Claudia, cane in her hand.

"Francie, Mr. Linden had expected his bath drawn nearly 30 minutes ago," she said quietly. I nodded, and apologized without making any excuse for myself. I had learned from Mistress Cruz that slaves never had an excuse for forgetting their duties. She ordered me to the bathroom, and I hurried in, starting the water splashing into the tub, then returned to the bedroom.

"Thank you for bringing this to my attention, Mr. Linden," said the housekeeper. "I'll send her in to you as soon as I'm finished."

"Thank you, Claudia," he answered formally, and strode into the bathroom, shutting the door behind him. The housekeeper stood before me, and took a deep breath.

"Francie, until this moment your first week here has been quite without complaint," she began, her words piercing my heart. "I understand that you are getting along very well with the other maids and Mr. Linden speaks highly of your services. However, Francie, there is no excuse for forgetting your primary routine, even in the midst of preparing for a party. Especially in the midst of preparing for a party where Mr. Linden is expected to appear." I nodded, miserable that I had failed her, failed the one person I wanted to impress.

"Francie, you are to receive six strokes for forgetting your first duty to Mr. Linden," Miss Claudia announced formally. "You will also scrub the grand staircase tomorrow morning. The usual punishment is 12 strokes and a week's extra chores, but Mr. Linden requested that in light of your new employment and the extra activity in the house, that I should be lenient with you." I nodded to indicate I understood, and at her gesture, bent over, resting my hands on the bed. "Let's make this quick, Francie, you have Mr. Linden to attend to and I am needed downstairs. I want quick responses from you."

"Yes, Miss Claudia," I answered. I heard the whistle of the cane only a moment before the stinging rod struck my buttocks. The pain shot through me like lightening, but I fought my urge to cry and quickly answered "Thank you, Miss Claudia."

The second came while I was still feeling the white hot of the first stroke, and a burst of flame went through me again. I gasped, and as I released my breath I remembered to thank her again. The third stroke caught me on the soft spot where the flesh of my buttocks melted into my thighs, and I nearly cried out. "Th — thank you, Miss Claudia," I stammered, trying to gain my breath before the next stroke. It came too soon, and I was gasping again. There were spots in front of my eyes, and I felt my knees begin to tremble.

"Thankyoumissclaudia," I rushed out, taking a gulp of air just before the cane whistled through the air again. I cried out, tears spilling out of my eyes. "Thank you, Miss Claudia," I moaned. I was sobbing as the last stroke struck my upper thighs. "Oh, Miss Claudia, thank you," I wailed.

I felt, rather than saw that she had put the cane down. Her touch was cool, soothing against the white hot of my buttocks. "There, there, my dear," she murmured, handing me a crisp white handkerchief. "You don't have time for this, and neither do I. Go into Mr. Linden, and as soon as you're finished, I'll need you downstairs." I nodded, dried my eyes, handed her back her handkerchief, and scurried quickly into the bathroom to shave Mr. Linden.

The party was a blur. I was too busy carrying trays and picking up champagne glasses to notice much. There were handsome men and women, scantily dressed pleasure slaves, with Mistress Madeline holding several attentive people in thrall in the parlor. Every once in a while I heard the familiar roar of Mr. Linden's laughter coming from a smoke filled corner of the den. I was certain that I had seen a very famous movie star coming down the stairs with a man who had been linked to him for years in the press.

On one of my trips through the servant's corridor, carrying a load of empty champagne glasses to the kitchen, I caught something out of the corner of my eye. I glanced again into the canning pantry, and saw one of the slaves who had arrived earlier that day to help park cars. The uniform he was wearing was very old-fashioned, and emphasized his height and the span of his shoulders. He was also kissing the top of Miss Claudia's head, and her arms were wrapped tightly around his waist.

"Oh, Robert it's so good to see you," she was saying to him. I had never seen her look so happy, and I must have made some sort of noise, because she looked up and saw me. I cringed, sure that I was going to be punished, but she instead broke into a delighted laugh.

"Francie, this is Mr. Grafton, who belongs to Ms. Pauline of Pound Ridge. I met him when we were both undergoing Marketplace training." I curtseyed as best as I could with the heavy tray in my hands. Robert nodded his head formally, and turned to the housekeeper with a mischievous grin.

"I hope he's more coordinated than I was when you first met me," he said, and she laughed in response. "Francie is very good," she responded, and I blushed at her compliment. "But as you can see, there were some things about her that reminded me of you." The housekeeper stepped forward and pulled my dress up. Helpless because of the serving tray, I could only stand there as she displayed my semi-hard cock. "Notice the decoration?" she asked him, and Robert clapped his hands in glee. "You romantic thing, you," he cried, and once again gathered the petite woman into his arms for a quick hug. "I have to return to my duties, Claudia. It's been a pleasure to see you again." He stepped carefully around me, and strode quickly down the corridor.

"Return to your duties, Francie," the housekeeper ordered, and I quickly retreated to the kitchen, thoughts rushing around in my head. Mr. Grafton trained with Miss Claudia? Was he the maid she had referred to when she first strapped on this cock ring? That huge, muscular, masculine entity? Could Marketplace training really change a person so much? It was a dreadful thought. Dreadful, I firmly told my erect cock.

By midnight I was exhausted. My buttocks ached from the caning, my feet were sore from all the running around, and my arms ached from carrying the heavy trays of food to the buffet. When Miss Claudia dismissed me for the night, I barely had the energy to climb the stairs to the third floor, and was asleep before my roommates were even undressed.

The next day, I pulled myself out of bed at the usual time and took a tray with coffee and croissants to Mr. Linden's room. He thanked me, and told me not to return until he called for me. When I left his room, Miss Claudia was waiting for me in the hall.

"Don't bother to change into uniform before starting on the stairs." She walked with me to the grand staircase, where a bucket of hot water and a stiff brush were set on the top stair. "You know what I expect from you," she said, and left me there. I immediately went to the task.

I had learned how hard physical labor can numb the mind from my training with Miss Cruz. It was also a dangerous trap, inviting a slave to become lazy. I struggled against that natural tendency, watching carefully that I had reached every spot, using a smaller brush to work the dirt from the corners of the risers, crawling across each stair to check for smoothness against my knees. I was careful to rinse each stair with clean water that I replenished from the kitchen, and to rub a soft cloth over each completed stair. By the eighth stair, halfway down, I was seeing double, my mind begging me to skip the spots that didn't look dirty, but I forced myself to be thorough. When I grew tired, I slowed down, but forced myself to be even more vigilant, bending down until the risers were nearly in front of my nose. It was almost noon when I had finally reached the last stair. As I wearily crawled across the floor with my brush, I found myself staring at a shoe. I looked up, and it was Miss Claudia before me. Beside her was Mistress Madeline.

I struggled to stand, but after the hours I had spent on my hands and knees, it took a few moments. My curtsey was awkward, but Mistress Madeline didn't seem to notice, she seemed more interested in my uniform — or rather, the lack of it.

"Mr. Linden has requested that Francie appear to him only in this costume," Miss Claudia explained. "I assigned him this chore to commence immediately after his morning duties with Mr. Linden."

"Ahh," was Mistress Madeline's only comment. She stepped forward, and walked slowly around me. I felt as I would on the slave block that I had once imagined, completely exposed and vulnerable. I felt her pinch me, deliberately twisting one of the bruises left by the caning. I squeezed my eyes shut, willing my body to stay still.

"Trouble?" she asked her housekeeper.

"A minor incident," Miss Claudia replied. "Easily remedied."
Her hand then slid between my legs and fingernails scratched the underside of my balls.

"And this?" I felt her fingers tug at the cock ring, and saw a remarkable sight — Miss Claudia blushing.

"I, I thought it might make Francie more acceptable to Mr. Linden, Mistress," she replied. The color in her cheeks made Miss Claudia look younger, and for a moment I could imagine what she might have been like before her Marketplace training.

"That was good thinking, Claudia," she said, releasing my balls and gliding back to the housekeeper, lifting the girl's chin with a long, delicate finger.

"Did you put it on yourself?" Mistress Madeline asked her. I watched Miss Claudia blush even more prettily and lower her eyes demurely.

"Yes, Mistress. When I first gave it to him to wear with his uniform."

"With your own pretty little hands, my dear? Did you tug on this lovely cock gently, play with him? I bet you did, you naughty little thing." Her voice was teasing, and the effect on Miss Claudia was astonishing. She shifted on her feet and fluttered her lashes as if she were ashamed of herself. But at the same time, her nipples were pressing quite noticeably through the white blouse she was wearing. Her lips were parted, and I heard her breathing quite rapidly.

"Did you, Claudia?" her voice was sharper.

"Yes, Mistress, I touched him. I played with him, Mistress."

"Did you enjoy it? I bet you did, you hungry little pet." Mistress Madeline tapped a fingertip on the housekeeper's lips, and she opened her mouth to kiss it, her tongue flicking out like a kitten's.

"Well, my dear, I think I'd like to see that. Perhaps later this afternoon, after my bath. Francie can brush my hair while I watch you finger yourself into readiness for his equipment." At that, I felt my cock tug hard against its restraint, and I knew I was blushing as deeply as Miss Claudia. I didn't know which thought made me more excited — brushing Mistress Madeline's hair, or knowing my maid's cock was to be put to use for her entertainment.

"Yes, Mistress." We answered in unison, and both of us curtseyed as the tall, dark woman glided past us up the stairs.

I glanced at Miss Claudia, who was gazing after our Mistress. Her color was still high, and she was panting. She was more beautiful than ever. With a catch in her voice, she turned to me with a light of joy in her eyes. "Oh my, Francie, let's finish here quickly, shall we? We mustn't keep Mistress waiting!"

6 Willows

At the lunch break, Michael was gratified to discover that he had an appetite and that the lunch was sponsored by the Italian trainers and consisted of fresh salads, pasta and wonderful, lightly grilled fish sizzling with garlic and basil. Traditional Japanese meals were also available, and he saw many of the local people pick up what looked like a beautifully arranged box of food. But there was no question for himself; after a large, tangy helping of green salad, he dove into linguini with wild mushrooms. Alex had her own agenda to turn to, and didn't require his services, so he picked through Chris' suggestions in the program. Suitably fortified and feeling much better, he was able to attend a discussion on managing re-training negotiations with a clear head and a lot of curiosity. His hot-tub buddy of the night before, Benjamin, was there, also taking notes like mad, and with him what looked like a tribe of his relations. Mike wasn't surprised to find that they were in fact a large family and after the discussion was formally ended, he drifted over to join them, and got introduced all around.

"Da, this is Mike LaGuardia, he's apprenticed to Chris Parker, eh?"

"Parker? Good kid, that one. Good old Anderson, eh?" the older man said, warmly shaking Mike's hand. Ezekiel ("call me Zeke") Urquhart was a tall, rangy man, with a craggy face and kind, slightly squinty eyes. His large hands were rough surfaced but gentle to grip.

"Yes, sir," Michael said, smiling. It was hard not to instantly like this old man, so like his disarmingly charming son. "What part of Canada are you from?"

"Saskatchewan, son, near the south. Afternoon drive from Medicine Hat. You know the area, eh?"

"No, sir, I don't. The only part of Canada I've visited is Vancouver."

Father, brother, and two children all laughed gently. "Now, that ain't

Canada, son. You ever want to see the most beautiful land God put on earth, you come up and spend a visit with us. Take your breath away, eh?"

"I'm sure it would. But — isn't that kind of — isolated? Doesn't it make it hard for the clients to — well — find you?"

"You'd think it would," Benjamin said with a grin. "But we have to beat 'em off with a stick, don't we Da?"

"That would just encourage 'em," Ben's hard eyed sister said, with the slightest of smiles.

"Yeah, we're a piece aways from the big cities," Zeke admitted. "Used to be a real workin' ranch, back before the depression. Came the money troubles, herds had to be cut back to pay off the debts. To live. That was when my own Da started on the new family business. Seems Grand-da put together a pretty interesting group of ranch hands, and most of them had stayed on, because, well. Like attracts like, eh? Some of them done some rodeo stuff, trick riders and calf ropers and such. Turns out they was practicing on each other, least that's the way Da explained it to me! Pretty friendly bunch — I remember old Jeremiah, he's the one that taught me how to use a bullwhip. Used to take a fly off a bull's ear without touching the flesh; he was that good."

"Wow," Michael said, in spite of himself. "So your father and grandfather actually started training slaves for the Marketplace?"

"Yup. Da was the one got involved with official training, Grand-da was more of a recreational man. But Da, he brought it all together. Specialty stuff, animal training. Started with a few of the hands, just for kicks. Then this woman came by with a few friends and two eager-looking fellas. She asked Da if he could teach them to pull a cart that she could ride. She offered him good money. Six weeks later those boys were pulling as good as any matched set of thoroughbreds. I've seen the pictures — she's riding in a surrey, carriage whip in hand, and those boys are dressed in nothing but harnesses. We've been busy ever since, eh?"

One of the other listeners, a youngish woman with a British accent nodded. "I've seen your work with some of the owners at Saratoga," she said. "In New York."

"Oh, yeah," Zeke nodded. "Those pony folks really like to mix it up with the real horse crowd. Me and the kids here, we're figuring on setting up meets an' the like, throughout the Triple Crown. Do our own derby, eh?" He cackled.

"And then there's the steeplechase folks and the hunting folks, too," added Benjamin. "And we make our own harnesses, custom fitted to the critters we train. Can't say we don't have enough work."

"There's a rather large pony community in Britain," the woman said thoughtfully. "We should see if we can arrange some business. Who does your harness work?"

"Oh, that would be ol' Roger Carrigan, one of Da's best finds," Zeke replied. A collective sigh of recognition came from the group listening in. "Guess you know him, too, eh? Came up from Australia dozen, maybe more years ago, looking for ranch work. Didn't think we'd recognize his name, but I did — ol' Jeremiah used to swear by Carrigan Aussie whips. It's a fine arrangement. My daughter is apprenticed to him, learning how to make harnesses and them pretty single-tails. Good work, too," he added with fatherly pride.

"Da will be speaking tomorrow, at the morning specialty seminar," Ben said excitedly. "You should come, Mike, if you can, eh?"

"Well — I have to check with Mr. Parker," Mike said. "But I'd love to be there. Do you train ponies too, Ben?"

"Oh, I help Da with 'em, sure. Ma's pretty much got the kennel wrapped up by herself. Lately, I've been doing dogs and cats."

"Cats?" Michael laughed at the image of a grown human being sleeping all day and taking breaks to stretch and eat. "Is there much of a demand for kitty cats?"

"Big cats," Ben said with a grin. "Y'know, lions and tigers and such. Pretty much a new fetish, as far as we know, but we get calls every month now, eh? An' I'm the chief lion tamer!" They laughed, and Michael could easily see the tall, spare young man with a coiled whip in one hand, coaxing a feline featured, acrobatic, strong and sensuous woman to move carefully, curling her body into intriguing poses. He wondered briefly what a leonine man would be like — and what you would use one for.

"We've brought a few of our critters for the show tonight," Zeke said casually. "If you're not too busy, you might take a peek, eh?"

"I'd like that," Michael said happily.

"An' here's your Mr. Parker, then," Zeke said, raising a hand in greeting.

"Mr. Urquhart, a pleasure to see you again." Chris shook hands and then turned to greet the younger members of the clan. "I look forward to tonight's demonstration, I've never seen your work in action for longer than a few minutes."

"Well, we'll have a bit more than that," Zeke said. "I'd love to stay an' chat, but you know, there's details to be tending. You kids just carry on for now, eh?"

"Sure, Da." "See you later, Da."

Michael would have liked to stay with the Urquharts and get to know Abigail, the quiet, harness-making sister a little better, but he could almost feel Chris' attention pulling at him. So, he quietly made his farewells after Chris excused himself, and followed the smaller man away from the crowds.

"Sir, before you say anything, I admit I didn't finish my assignment last night, but I did it today, before lunch," Michael said all in a rush, as soon as they were in a slightly less crowded area.

"Assignment?" Chris looked up for a moment, and Michael felt a strange tingle of dissociation. Had Chris — the infallible Chris Parker, actually forgotten something?

"The — the writing assignment. About pleasure slave training. . ."

"Oh, yes." Chris nodded, looking thoughtful. "Very well, you can just leave it out for me in the room."

"You — you're not going to punish me?"

Chris sighed and brushed one hand over the top of his head. "No, Michael, I'm not. It's minor enough. Sorry to disappoint you."

Michael flushed and felt it down to his toes. "I didn't mean it that way," he began.

"Of course not."

Michael groaned out loud. "You always do this to me!' he said sharply. "Sometimes, I don't know whether you're treating me like a trainer in training, or just some slave you like humiliating."

"And why is that a problem?" Chris asked.

"Oh, come on, sir, you know why! I never know where I stand." Michael took a deep breath and then dived in. "For instance — am I allowed to get laid?"

Chris laughed for a moment. "Why, has someone made an offer?"

"Well — sort of. Maybe. Hell, I'm not sure! It's plain that there are plenty of available slaves, anyway. If I wanted to, could I — use one?"

Chris actually looked like he was thinking about it. "No, I don't think so," he said carefully. "You don't have the seniority to just pick one out, and you don't have the experience to really evaluate the ones brought as samples. No, I think your chances of — getting some — are not very good here. At least, not from the slaves present, and not on your own terms."

Michael felt a note of danger there, but set it aside for the moment. "But am I allowed to?"

"Certainly," Chris said. "If it doesn't interfere with your training or your duties."

"But — but —" Michael drew his thoughts in. Should he mention anything else, or just take his victory and run with it?

Was it really a victory?

"Some of the other junior trainers and I were talking last night," he finally said.

"Ah! And you found out that many of them are not allowed to dally with the clients."

"Or with anyone! They said that they're not supposed to have sex until they, I don't know, reach some higher level in training, I guess. And since you treat me like a slave most of the time anyway, I was just wondering if — well — if this was supposed to be spelled out to me or something."

"It could have been part of your training period with me," Chris said evenly. "But the Trainer and I decided that it might be too worrisome for you, that the restriction might distract you too much. As it turns out, your training schedule doesn't allow you a lot of free time, so I suppose you haven't had much opportunity to enjoy this particular freedom, but neither have you fretted over it."

"You mean — you decided not to put the restriction on me because you thought — I couldn't take it?"

"Mm—hm," Chris nodded. "Now, quickly — tell me what you are thinking."

"I — I don't know what to think. Part of me says, great, I can get laid, and now part of me is saying the only reason I can get laid because you think I'm so ruled by my dick that if I knew I couldn't use it, I'd think of nothing else." Michael's voice was bitter, and he could hear a slight whine in it. He tried to control himself better.

"And which part of you do you believe?"

Michael's shoulders slumped. "The part that wishes you had more faith in me. And the part that wishes I was worth it."

"Well, we're working on both of those, aren't we? When you get back to the states, I suggest you discuss it with Anderson, and see if she wishes to place that formal restriction on you. In the meantime, you're going to be too busy and the potential partners you would find here are mostly unavailable, so there is nothing to worry about."

"You know, sometimes I wish things were just a little more clear for me," Michael said, keeping his voice even.

"Oh, don't be so passive, Michael. Think of every difficulty you encounter as a matter of training and see if that helps. And for God's sake, be grateful that your training is so lenient, because I promise you, a more regimented and controlling environment would only upset you more." Chris' voice edged up just a little, and Michael was startled to see both a flash of anger and deep seated annoyance — something Chris hadn't let show in weeks. "If you were in a different style of training, you'd be having all the sex you could imagine, boy. At my whim, exactly as you will tomorrow night, except that I'd be using you regularly myself."

"Tomorrow night?" Michael repeated in shock.

"Yes, I told you I was loaning you to Ken. I don't imagine that what she has in mind is tea serving and boot polishing. What's more, I expect you to be clean, groomed and eager, to cooperate with whatever she has planned, and in other words, behave exactly as what you think a slave in your position should. And, to be suitably grateful for the experience afterward. You wanted to get laid, Michael? You've got it. Or at least something approximating it."

A thousand protests, questions and complaints crowded on the edge of Michael's lips, and he struggled to keep them back. It had been a long time since he had seen Chris angry, really angry and not just putting on a show for the slave trainees. But that nasty sneer of condescension, that tone that just raised his hackles, was so provoking, so infuriating!

"So you're really going to hand me off to a stranger, and I have to go, no questions asked? Just like that, no preparation, no build up, no warning? How the hell is that supposed to make me feel? Like I'm ready to perform for you?"

"You're supposed to feel like a slave, Michael, remember? Remember how you requested this? 'I want to be trained as a classic', you said, and I warned you that you didn't even know what that meant. Now, you know. Imagine what it will feel like when you're actually sold."

"Oh, that's bullshit," Michael snapped, feeling a deep warning pain in the pit of his stomach. But he was committed; he kept going. "No one trains like that any more, not even Anderson. You guys even told me that! It's a whole new world out here, and you are absolutely fixated on the past. You're working some kind of big scam on me, that's what you're doing. These other trainers might be horny for a while, but no one's passing them around like slaves!"

"Your manners, Michael."

Fury welled up in Michael's throat like bile. "Dammit, you always do this! Just when I'm being totally honest with you, you cut me off!"

His voice was raised — and suddenly he could hear shushed voices in corridors not far away. The feelings of panic and anger and confusion tore at him in heavy pounding waves as he realized how much of this conversation might have been overheard.

"Oddly enough, Michael," Chris said. "It is possible to be both honest and respectful."

"Yes, sir," Michael whispered, ashamed of his outburst. "I apologize."

"Properly," Chris said sharply.

Michael sank to his knees, feeling the shame grow throughout his body. His anger was still hot, and the corridor seemed stifling. "I apologize for raising my voice," he began, shaking. "For using profanity, and being . . . difficult, sir. I — I ask you to forgive me. I beg you to forgive me. I will try to be better controlled and more respectful." The formula for the apology assembled itself in his mind and he tried not to rush it. "Please tell me what I can do to make amends for my . . . outbursts."

"Two things, Michael. You can submit your body for chastisement as I see fit, tomorrow evening, in front of Ken Mandarin and before she makes use of you. But right now, I want you to ask that question that's burning out of you, this time properly."

Michael's head snapped up, and with all his strength, he asked, "Sir — were you really trained this way? Like a classic?"

"Yes, I was. In every aspect of the training, except that there was one major difference between your training and mine. Unlike you, I didn't choose to be trained that way. I didn't get it explained to me every step of the journey." Chris said the words calmly, but there was something in him that made Michael feel like he was on the edge of violence.

"But — did she — she never really — just handed you off to someone, did she? Anderson? And were you really — sold? I mean — there are no records — you aren't listed. . .you were never really sold, right?"

Chris looked down at Michael and caressed his right hand with his left, his face tightly drawn. For a second, Michael was sure he was going to be hit, and hard. But Chris' eyes shifted away from him for a second, and when they turned back, Michael felt even more ashamed then he was embarrassed. Because the look of pain in Chris Parker's face was worse than the anger had been.

Chris sighed and waved one hand. "You are dismissed, Michael. I was going to invite you to the debates, but I don't think you've earned that right. Meet me at room 5, Western wing, before dinner tonight. Wear a suit. Try not to get into any trouble between now and then." He turned and walked away.

Michael waited until Chris turned a corner and then sat back onto the polished floor heavily, clenching his hands into fists. His cock was hard, his face unbearably hot. He crossed his legs and buried his face in his hands, wishing he could scream, or punch one of these beautiful walls, or just jump off a damn cliff, anything to free himself from these tightening bands of pressure. Every time he thought he was coming close to understanding, he had one of these episodes. It was like they came on a schedule, exactly in time to make things worse for him.

I wish I knew what I was doing here, he thought wildly. And dammit, I wish Anderson was here. There's something going on here that's beyond him and me and I can't figure out what.

There were meditation rooms in a small outbuilding a short walk down one of the marked paths. As Chris stopped to cleanse his hands and face and mouth in the basin set by a small bubbling fountain, he tried to compose himself as he was taught; it came slowly. He removed his shoes and left them outside, and felt the silence of the space coax him toward sleep. But he shook off that wonderful temptation and sank into a kneeling posture on the smooth polished floor, his only company a simply framed print which he thought exhorted him to be like a willow. He had not gotten far in actually reading Japanese, only a few hundred kanji in addition to a more simple 47 character syllabary. He was, as Tetsuo's undertrainer once called him, a dull child in spoken Japanese. But he was a complete idiot in the written forms.

Yet the print spoke to him all the same.

He was unused to sitting like this; out of practice. Not surprising, really. Neither Grendel nor Alexandra had required it of him for longer than a token of his position, and that only rarely. When he had returned from Japan, he had practiced meditation regularly. But like his Japanese, it had faded from his life. He had not even bothered to practice the language when Anderson had a client who was learning it last year; he had judged his own memory too faulty to give her the proper examples in speech.

Odd how some of it had returned last night.

He had finished the sake, feeling the faint warmth of it flowing down his throat, and then looked at Tetsuo, who was staring at him in that familiar, penetrating way that made him so damn sexy. Chris almost replied automatically, saying the words he had said on those few occasions before when people had come close to figuring out how he fit into the scheme of things, but then simply bowed his head with a sigh. "How long have you known, Sensei?"

"I am glad you didn't feel the need to deny it," Tetsuo said, showing his pleasure.

"Oh, I feel the need," Chris said, with a slight smile. "But I would never insult you like that."

"Thank you. In answer to your question, I have not really known, not in fact. I have deduced this, from the years of our association." Tetsuo poured more for his guest and then set the bottle down carefully. "I know you, Chris Parker. And I know Anderson-sensei. There are many mysteries of your life which I have been given the favor of knowing; this was the one remaining. How was it that one who was so suited to a life of service was not secure in someone's collar? At first, I considered that you had decided against it for — pragmatic reasons. Later on, as you completed your training and remained a trainer yourself, I considered that you had forgone the auction out of gratitude to your Sensei, to serve her as so many of us do, forgoing the simpler temptation of the collar."

"That is often assumed," Chris nodded. He refilled Tetsuo's cup, since it was clear that they were not to be interrupted by the slave any more. It would be impolite for either of them to refill their own cups.

"To go through the formal training and then to give it up for a collar would be a grave waste of her time and efforts, but you would hardly be the first nor the last," Tetsuo said. "But the truth of the matter is that she owns you, and that is how she compels your continued service as a trainer. You have belonged to her since before we met, I assume."

Chris nodded again. "Yes, Sensei."

"You are to be noted for your fortune, Chris Parker. The Trainer who owns no slaves has placed her mark upon you in more ways than one." Tetsuo lifted his cup gently, and Chris took up his own. He sipped the warm liquid in honor of his trainer/owner.

"I have been — touched by fortune — in many ways, Sensei," he said, as he placed the cup back on the table. "But I must ask you, Sensei, with all respect; since you do know, why are you discussing this with me?"

"Because you can ask that question and expect an answer," Tetsuo said, with a look of satisfaction. He leaned back slightly, stretching. "Changes are coming, far greater ones than even the one you propose this week." His eyes smiled, slight crinkles that reminded Chris of the deep sense of humor this man had, and how rarely he allowed it to show. "I honor my House and my Sensei with my life and deeds, but I am not blind. In order to maintain my position in this world, my own House must grow and expand. Having you as a trainer in my House will aid my program of expansion."

Chris said nothing; it would be hard to come up with anything that didn't sound like completely false modesty or smug pride. Besides, Tetsuo had not answered the question yet.

Tetsuo snorted appreciatively. "I discuss it with you, Chris Parker," he said, leaning forward again, "for the joy of surprising you. For a youngster, you are often world-weary, cynical, too assured of your place under heaven. I am sure I was not the only one in your life who enjoyed shaking you from your calm acceptance of your circumstances."

Astonishingly, Chris felt the pleasurable warmth of embarrassment spread through him. He couldn't bring himself to blame the sake.

"I have never forgotten training you," Tetsuo said thoughtfully. "At the start, your very presence was only suffered because of my long friendship and respect for Sensei Anderson. I expected you to leave, to fail, to break. And after Noriko. . ." He sighed, and Chris lowered his head again, this time closing his eyes for a moment. They let the name waver in the air between them, acknowledging their shared past, and Tetsuo's great loss.

"After Noriko, I realized that having you at my service had given me greater ease than I could have assumed possible. I do enjoy shocking you, Chris Parker. I enjoy it now as much as I did years ago. I also enjoyed your small rebellions and your great disobediences. I enjoyed making your will bend to mine. It is a rare slave that catches my attention in these ways, and I find I miss having such a diversion for longer than it takes to place a new client into the Marketplace. I am not like my respected colleague, Sensei Anderson, I own with pleasure. It would please me to own you.

"So I discuss it with you because I know that valuable property such as you cannot be held lightly. I would not have you unaware; that is a test for novices. I already know that you would mount the auction tables and go willingly and serve with honor. That would be the greatest surprise for you, would it not? And from that moment, your experiences would diminish."

"I don't know that," Chris said quietly. "Since I have not experienced the auction block."

"You are experiencing it now," Tetsuo said casually. "Your new .. form, your modern haircut, your tailored suit, none of these things hide your essence from me. Your throat is bound with silk instead of chain, but we both know where the true mark of your ownership lies. We sit here as proper men, sharing sake as friends, but you have not forgotten my rule, at least I do not think so."

"No, Sensei, I have not," Chris admitted.

"Then do not be fooled, Chris Parker. You are here as an independent trainer, honored by your peers, leader in an honorable struggle for order, yes. But you are also here displaying your worth. If I can see how it is you come to be here, you must realize that there are trainers much wiser than I. Who can say which of them are assessing your value as we speak? Who among them might also be wondering how to acquire you in one way or another? As these hours and days pass, I will begin my negotiations with Sensei Anderson, whether she comes here or not. You are Merchandise, young trainer. Merchandise I have decided to acquire." Tetsuo stretched again and smiled, his eyes sharp with a sudden pleasure. "Aside from that, I have taken the liberty of reserving a bath-house, and I am all consumed with curiosity about this campaign of physical fitness and art of the body upon which you have embarked. I cannot compel you by rights, but I can invite you as a friend, and a former student, to bathe with me. Can you do this, or must you retire?"

"More surprises?" Chris asked, raising one eyebrow.

Tetsuo laughed, a warm sound in the warm room. "Oh, yes," he said. "I don't think I can still surprise you with a bamboo rod, so I must find other ways." He turned and barked an order. Two slaves entered instantly, both of them male this time, wearing only fundoshis. They carried light robes and as Tetsuo stood, one of them instantly went to him to take his jacket. Tetsuo loosened his dark, narrow tie, never taking his gaze from Chris. It was still an invitation — but the sheer force of his request was almost like a command. As he unbuttoned his shirt, his eyes seemed to be almost teasing; I am ready for you, they said. I dare you.

After a moment, Chris also stood, and held his arms slightly back, feeling the weight of the jacket slide into waiting hands. As he reached for his own tie, he felt a familiar ache. He wanted it to be natural and comfortable, he wanted to be as free as this older man and strip with ease, but it was still hard to shed the armor, even when he saw Tetsuo's eyes slightly widen in pleasure. He stood with the robe open for an extra moment, the slave stopped in mid-motion by Tetsuo's hand, and then found that he needed a longer breath when the belt was finally wrapped around him and tied. But Tetsuo said nothing, only grunted when they were both ready to go.

They walked to the bath-house with the two slaves following behind, leaving the empty sake bottle and the elegant wooden box on the table.

By the time Chris returned to his room, Michael was gently snoring on his futon. It was almost dawn. His body longed for sleep, but instead he wrote a brief note to his student, changed into fresh clothing, and found an empty meeting room to review his notes and plan his day. It was so tempting to try to call the States and confess, or to simply slip away and leave the entire gathering to its own devices.

Of course he didn't do either. He went to his meetings and he started his lobbying and now he had to stand up and address his peers. Peers, hell. His superiors. His teachers, his models. And at least one old master.

Chris opened his eyes and looked at the print again. He didn't feel rested. But he did feel a little like a willow.

"Caught in a tai-fun," he said out loud. He stood up, feeling and hearing a slight crack in his knees, and slowly left the room to go to the debates.

7 In Exile

Michael tried not to look like he was moping. But it was hard. Everyone — or at least all the trainers and spotters — were closed off in the large meeting room to begin the most important discussions of the week, a proposal presented by his own damn Trainer, and he wasn't allowed to go.

Not only that, but apparently his old trainer, Geoff Negel, was the chief opponent to this accreditation program that Chris wanted to create. What an opportunity, to see those two butt heads in this formal atmosphere! Chris had never forgiven Geoff for granting trainer status to a fellow Californian who had placed a dishonest slave in the same household that Chris had a former client in. There had been some stupid mix up, the ill-trained slave either stole or just hid some jewelry and Chris' client got blamed for it and brutally punished. Chris had actually flown out to California to intervene and set things right, and when he got back, told Michael that it was trainers like Geoff who were responsible for everything short of global warming.

After Chris had cooled off over the incident and Michael felt safe about bringing the topic up again, he had asked Chris why, if Geoff Negel's methods were so sloppy, was the trainer so successful?

"How do you measure success?" Chris had asked.

"Number of sales versus number of returns," Michael answered.

"That's the fallacy then," Chris said. "It's not the number of sales that makes you successful — I can find someone every other week and manage to sell them to someone else. It's the success rate of the actual contracts that we have to measure."

"What's the difference?"

They had been out riding. Michael had only ridden in Western saddles before, mostly beach trail rides, and Chris wanted him to have some experience with the English style. So, he was sitting somewhat gingerly on the tiny saddle with his knees bent, his elbows tight and his heels back, feeling self conscious and trying not to show it by carrying on a casual conversation.

"What's a better deal, Michael — a car that you have to trade in every two years, or a car that will run for ten?"

"The one that lasts longer, of course."

"The same thing applies to slaves." Chris looked comfortable in his saddle, moving naturally with the horse, using his hands to gesture freely. "If the slave is motivated enough, a two year contract is not much to ask. In fact, many of them barely realize that two years have gone by when you call them to ask if they are interested in renewing. If slave and owner have been well matched, they will both want to renew, and there is a good chance that the renewal will be for a longer period as well. That was how we measured success; not by the first sale, but by the first renewal. And the ones thereafter, of course. The ultimate success is a lifetime contract, but that's also considered pretty rare."

Michael digested that; it seemed reasonable. "But," he said cautiously, tugging on his reins to keep his mount from breakfasting on some clover, "some people lease cars because they want a new one every three years. So some owners might not want a slave for ten years or more."

"Good!" Chris nodded encouragingly, and turned his horse to one side so he could comfortably face Michael. His horse stepped sideways with a snort of annoyance, but obeyed. "Yes, there are owners — and slaves — who prefer short term contracts. And that is where Mr. Negel has established the majority of his trade."

"But he's successful at that, then," Michael said. "It's just like having a specialty."

"Not exactly. Here, we train novices for general use. So by Marketplace guidelines, we generally don't write contracts for more than two years. But we assume that the customers will want more and the slaves themselves are looking forward to a long time in service. If the same client can't seem to renew a contract with several owners in a row, we have to examine why. There are a lot of reasons why an owner will keep an otherwise unsuitable slave for the duration of their contract, not the least of which is sentimentality. But if more than, say, two owners don't express an interest in renewing a contract with the same client, then we ask for in depth interviews with them to discover the root of their dissatisfaction. And then, we will examine the client in question to make sure they should go back to the block."

"But what if things just didn't work out?" Michael asked. "It happens all the time in the soft world, and that's where you have the advantage of dating and engagements and living together and all the ways people get to know each other first. Buying someone off the block can't possibly end up in long lasting relationships all the time."

"Owning a slave and marrying someone is not the same thing," Chris said with a slight smile. "At least, not in this day and age. With the exception of companion slaves, owners want a particular service performed, and will generally be satisfied if it is. Slaves likewise crave a system in which to serve and not necessarily become a best friend and lover to share the covers with. You can never account for personal taste, or course, and some of the best slaves may end up with several owners before finding a situation that is mutually suitable.

"But what Geoff Negel is creating — and selling — are slaves who are not prepared for service of more than two years. They fulfill their initial contracts and move on, either to another two year contract with a new owner — or an even shorter one! — or they leave altogether. And since leaving the Marketplace is not counted as a failure, he seems to be a success."

Michael thought about that for a minute, continuing his battle with the dumb horse, who was determined to sample every bush they passed, and trying not to get distracted by Chris' handsome riding boots.

"I — I don't think that's fair," he said finally. "Other people's clients must leave the Marketplace after one contract, too. Maybe it wasn't right for them. But if they fulfill their contracts and then leave and there are no complaints, that isn't a failure."

"You are right, from the strictly technical perspective. But we can't survive on two year slaves who pop into the Marketplace to 'see if they like it' and then leave, taking with them the knowledge of our existence and our methods and leaving nothing behind. Neither should we allow people to be called 'trainers' when their experience is constrained to preparing someone for such a limited relationship. Yet Mr. Negel registers more new trainers than any other trainer of his level in the United States. What's more to the point, he registers more owners."

"What does that have to do with anything?" The horse bent her head sharply to one side, and Michael lost the struggle with her. She gleefully grabbed a clump of weeds and started to graze, and Michael grunted with the effort to pull her head up. Chris came to the rescue by miming a pull on one rein, and Michael followed his instruction until the mare gave in with annoyed snort.

"The difference is the same as the difference in our riding styles," Chris said with a short laugh. "We have horses that seem similar on the outside, and the same equipment and we proceed from the assumption that the horses will perform according to our wishes. But your mount is getting the message from you that she can bend the rules; you are not consistent in reminding her of her duty, so she cheats. But you can't blame her alone for her behavior because she doesn't know any better. So the ride won't be exactly what you want at the end — but it won't be worth giving her away, either. You know you don't have the experience to take her in hand, so you forgive the cheating until it gets tiresome or embarrassing. At a certain point, you might get frustrated enough not to want to ride her any more.

"But a more experienced rider takes the mount in hand and will know whether it's the horse or themselves that is lacking in schooling. You may harbor some doubts — is it your riding, or her training? If you take no more lessons with me, you may leave here and never expect more from a horse or know what to do to keep them behaving. You are like a new owner right now — aware that you should have the potential for great power and pleasure, but not exactly sure how to manage it." Chris turned his mount again, showing off, walking the horse backward for a few steps.

"Geoff Negel creates the market for his unschooled mounts," Chris said with a sharp gleam in his eye. "He proposes ownership status for people he cultivates to require less from property than a more traditional owner does. You told me yourself that he trains owners — invites them to his house and makes matches between them and his clients. If he sets up a system of lower expectations and doesn't give his owners exposure to the potential world they might have access to, then he controls the market for his own product! And frankly, I think he encourages short term contracts, although you would be more knowledgeable about that than I am. It's hard for me to imagine a trainer who would so work against the standards of Marketplace tradition."

"But — but — a lot of his owners want short term slaves — some people really like variety!"

"In a bed partner, a pleasure slave? Yes, many owners do. But in a housekeeper? A childcare expert? A personal assistant? These are positions that benefit from a long term relationship. As does a good sexual partner, but that's more a matter of taste. If you will always and only like 23 year old blondes, that's your fetish. And if all Geoff did was train those 23 year old blondes and make them available for the two years that they will fulfill that fetish, that might be acceptable. But he trains them and sells them as general clients, supposedly available for any use. When they grow dissatisfied and leave, he finds a new one to replace them. When the owners go from slave to slave, distracted by the variety at their hands, they never learn that something more stable and rewarding is available to them. He is only in one corner of the world, Michael. But his influence has the potential to be vast. Every slave he trains, every trainer he vouches for and every owner he nominates will pass on what they learned to someone else. And because there are few obvious failures on his record, he continues to look successful. Don't confuse the image with the reality, Michael. You are better schooled, now.

"In fact, you can show me how much better; let's get back at a trot, shall we? Post, Michael. It'll hurt less if you post."

And posting did make a difference, of course. Michael tried to remember all the ways that Geoff taught clients, and what kinds of values he tried to instill in them, and contrasted with the things he was learning now, what he had learned in his time at Anderson's house. And he compared the slaves he worked with under Anderson and Parker and now under Grendel and Alex. He couldn't help but notice that there were differences between them and the slaves he was used to in California, and hated the way he felt guilty when he wrote as much in his notebooks.

It was very uncomfortable, he reflected as he wandered, feeling like you're trapped between two philosophies. Geoff wasn't a bad man, in fact, he was a very good man, patient and kind and generous. A sexy man who celebrated a sexy lifestyle. And living with him was always a joy, comfortable and happy and easy going. The slaves were mostly cheerful and grateful and eager to please.

But none of them, Michael thought, looking around the resort as he walked, could serve here this week. None of them. Even as pure pleasure slaves — there wasn't a single pleasure slave here who didn't know at least two languages and was skilled in some non-sexual entertaining skill.

It seemed like most of the junior trainers had gone to the debates as well, and although the resort was bustling with all these perfect slaves preparing the banquet hall for the evening, the hallways and smaller meeting rooms felt strangely empty. He had never actually felt the difference between the presence of free people and slaves before.

And although he got reverences and respectful murmurs and offers of service, he missed the fun of the place when there was a mixture of trainer and slave in the halls. The play of power and control. Not to mention the noise of people who were free to raise or lower their voices at will. The place was just too damn quiet when the slaves took over. When he finished looking through the meeting rooms and had turned down two offers of refreshments, he saw a third slave, this one American, approach him. He was ready to just wave him off, but the man leaned into a respectful bow and asked, "Are you looking for company, sir? There are others who are not attending the debates."

"Oh — sure, thanks. I was — wondering where the others were," Michael said.

"This way, sir." The slave led him out of the business section back toward the traditional Japanese side, and through a courtyard. There was a beautiful outdoor pavilion set up, softly swaying banners shading stone benches and a few more conventional canvas backed outdoor chairs. And to his pleasure, he could see Kim laying on her back in the grass, two other junior trainers with her, and one of Corinne's ubiquitous translator slaves kneeling to one side.

"Hey," Michael called out, as he approached them. Kim sat up and grinned easily.

"Hey," Kim answered. "Come and join the exiles!"

Michael snorted; so much for trying to pretend that it was his choice to be there. He collapsed into a comfortable cross-legged position on the ground and leaned over to give Kim a peck on the cheek. "The exiles?" he asked.

"I am unworthy of the presence of my betters," Kim shrugged. She pointed to another young woman sitting to her left and said, "This is Luciana, she is training with the great Arturo Massimiliano."

Michael knew just enough Italian to get into trouble, but he knew when to be polite. "Buon pomeriggio," he said, reaching out to shake her hand. Her smile was immediate and he was glad of it. He turned to the other person sitting nearby and almost laughed.

Because this — this boy — surely couldn't be old enough to be here! There was no doubt about one thing, though; he was a beautiful young man. There had been a movie he had seen recently; some weird film about a kid named Gilbert Grape. There had been a young man in that movie, with haunting, ethereal eyes, and a lock of hair that fell over them in a wonderfully bashful way. An Italian name, he thought, not exactly remembering. But this young man before him was just like that; a little slender, almost delicately boned, with a chin almost too smooth to boast that tiny goatee. He was dressed in a suit small enough to have been bought in a boy's section, but the chin fuzz and a certain look in his light blue eyes actually did suggest that he was older. It was his body that gave him away — slight, with small hands and a pointed chin.

"I'm Michael," he said, sticking his hand out.

"Stuart," said the young man, shaking Michael's hand warmly. His accent was pure American, so the translator was for Luciana's benefit.

"The exiles," sighed Kim dramatically. "Left behind as our masters discuss important things."

"My trainer thought the topic wasn't important for me," Stuart said with a slight, toothy smile. "Plus, I think she just wanted me out of her hair for a while. But man, I really wanted to go!"

Luciana shrugged as she listened to the translation. "I wanted to go too," she said, her translator working almost simultaneously. "But I think I'm also glad to not be working for just a little while." She looked up, over Michael's shoulder and smiled again, and started to strip. Michael swallowed hard and then half-turned to see three slaves approaching with towels and pillows and bottles.

Kim grinned. "We might not be having sex," she said gleefully, "but we can certainly have massage!"

"You devil you," Michael said with a grin of his own. "So order one for me, too! How about you, Stu, are you getting rubbed?"

Stuart coughed nervously, looking away briefly from the two women busily disrobing. "I — I'd rather not, thanks. But I'll hang out with you, if that's OK."

The three slaves laid out large, soft towels and sheets and the three junior trainers arranged themselves face down, comfortably. In no time, three slaves were industriously working on tense muscles and bruised egos, and the sounds of sighs filled the garden. Michael's slave was a Eurasian woman with long hair and dense muscles, and he practically purred under her ministrations.

"Who needs all the politics anyway?" he asked rhetorically, rolling over so the woman could work on his legs. "This is exactly what I needed!"

"Mmmmmmm," Kim sighed, stretching and relaxing while her masseur worked her buttocks. "Politics? What is that? I am in heaven. Politics are hell."

"Well, I still wish I was there," said Stuart, his knees drawn up against his body. "Or if not there, I wish there was something else to do — another seminar, or maybe even a discussion group. I wanted to learn everything I could this weekend. It feels kinda silly to just be hanging out. Not that you guys aren't great, but I could be, you know — learning something."

"He's a good student," Luciana mumbled, so thickly that her translator had to bend next to her to hear. "Not like me, eh? Not like we three exiles." She laughed and the others joined her.

"Oh, I'm happy if one minute goes by and I don't have a lesson," Michael said. "Sometimes, it seems like the only things I hear are criticisms and lessons..."

"It is our place in life," said Kim without a trace of bitterness.

"Wow — you guys must have really tough trainers," Stuart said admiringly. "Marcy is hard on me, yeah, but I love it. I love learning everything she can tell me."

What a fucking boy scout, Michael thought, hiding a snicker. "So, what did you learn today, Stu?"

"Oh God, I don't even know where to start — this morning, I went to a demonstration of posture training, it was really hot. Then I caught the end of this discussion of computer technology, they're thinking of making identity disks with imbedded chips in them, you wouldn't believe how useful that could be! Marcy told me I could be in charge of her computer, I'm learning all the software and stuff, keeping up on what the Marketplace is planning to do in the future. It's awesome. Have you guys heard about the World Wide Web? It'll be an awesome way to preview sales! Live chat, too. I tell you, with some more speed, our new internet connections will blow the old BBS system away. And then, at lunch time, I met some really big names, it was like, I don't know, like meeting people you only read about. Because, you know — I um, read about them before I came here. Jeeze, listen to me, I sound like an idiot!" He laughed at himself, and Michael revised his earlier judgment.

Not a boy scout, he thought. A fucking space cadet. How the hell does he rate being here?

"So teach us something," Kim said cheerfully. "I am a worthless, stupid cow without brains enough to seek cover in the rain, but I try to learn. Teach me something about how this computer thing will make a better slave."

"Oh, don't be unkind," Luciana said, poking Kim in one arm. "He is excited, and that is only correct. I don't know whether computer chips or internets can make our lives any easier or more fun, but I do know that if you say you were not once like Stuart, you are lying."

Stuart blushed and coughed again, nervously. "Jeeze", he complained. "You guys are so, like, blasé about it all. But look at yourselves! You're laying on a tropical island with these hot slaves massaging your body and there's another one headed this way right now, and I bet he's got cold drinks. Your job is to make people like them, and you get to play with them and train them and get served by them — it's the most awesome job in the whole universe!"

"And how long have you been at it, Stu?' Michael teased.

"Well — I started my training about two years ago."

Michael squinted in the afternoon sun and looked at Stuart again. Two years ago? Hell, the kid must have been — practically a teenager! Shit!

"I know I haven't been at it long, I admit that. But age is a self-correcting flaw, right?" He grinned, and the women smiled back at him. "And I love it all," he continued. "I love waking up and realizing that I'm living a fantasy life. Everything I always dreamed of is coming true for me. I've got the best trainer in my area to teach me, and I've seen some of the most amazing slaves. I mean slaves that make you cry they're so awesome, so dedicated."

"There you go!" cried Kim, brushing away her masseur with one impatient hand and taking the cold drink that Stuart had seen coming from the slave who was kneeling patiently next to her. "That's what we need, an inspirational lesson. Tell us about some extraordinary slave of your acquaintance. Remind me why I am enduring all this." She helped herself to a damp towel as well, and wiped at the sweat on her throat and breasts.

"Help us pass the time, you mean," Luciana said, rolling over into a sunny patch of grass and dragging her fingers through her burnished hair. "I am willing, though."

Michael really wasn't — but the company of two naked woman and the warm afternoon were two things that kept him laying comfortably on the soft sheets, his arm folded under his cheek. He wiggled his toes, and felt the slave move to massage his feet and sighed loudly.

"Yeah, teach us about how amazing this life can be," he said. "I am all ears!"

"You guys," Stuart sighed. But he took a tall glass of iced tea and sipped it thoughtfully. "OK, you want something inspirational? Lemme tell you about this one slavegirl; this'll knock your socks off."

"Knock away," Michael said, prepared to fall asleep. But his stomach churned with the heavy knowledge of Chris' displeasure, and the shame of being denied the right to even stand in the back of the room while Chris stood up and delivered the most important topic to be discussed this week. I'm no inspiration, he thought sadly. I'm practically a liability.

8 The Tiger In the Dining Room   by M. Christian

"I'm very disappointed in you —"

Fancy had undergone many experiences since ... well, since she'd really started to live. Her body vibrated with the echoes of some of them, slight tremors keyed to special memories; ripples of sensation set into motion by the right sound, just the right smell.

The touch, the feel, even the smell of old, warm leather, immediately brought up intense memories of penetration and orgasm. All of her senses except that of sight — she'd been blindfolded and bound by thick strips of soft tanned hide. A scent of violet recalled a special kind of pain, a special kind of penetration: memories of the time Mistress Caroline had inserted a needle through her left nipple. Mistress Caroline, to whom she'd been loaned for a weekend, always wore a soft violet perfume.

Many feelings, sensations, and many of them carrying along what others — and what she might have called before she'd been brought into her real life — would consider pain. The simple fact was that word rarely had any meaning anymore. Pain was just another form of experience, part of her travels as a submissive.

But then, staring down at the tightly-woven Chinese rug at her feet, Fancy did feel pain — not needles, not a cane, not a whip, not a scalding form of humiliation — the sharp sting of shame.

In some small place inside, she felt it had not been her fault. Still, a far greater part of her knew that it was, indeed, her fault — she should have looked where she was going, should have seen the imperfection in the woven surface. She should never have allowed herself to trip on it and fall, fragmenting her Master's priceless porcelain tea set with a crash in front of his friends, fellow Masters and Mistresses.

If she had been a perfect slave, an ideal slave, she never would have tripped.

"I try to be a forgiving sort," her Master said, standing firmly at attention to one side. "I endeavor to give everyone in my immediate circle the benefit of the doubt: to place myself in their position, in their shoes — so to speak — and not let my rather, well, high standards rule my judgment."

He began to slowly pace, a short march from one side of the small room to the other. His heavy boots, all gleaming, finely-tooled leather, softly thumped with each step on the Chinese rug. "But this ... severe display of what I could only call profound clumsiness — especially as it was, conducted in full view of my esteemed colleagues — has truly stretched the limits of my patience."

Fancy didn't say anything. Not only was she forbidden to speak unless spoken to, but she was too deeply shamed. She couldn't stop her lip from quivering enough to even frame a response, even if she were allowed to.

Mute by order and her own humiliation, she knelt in the center of the room, arms behind her back, eyes heavily downcast.

"I have invested a good portion of my very valuable time and resources in your acquisition, and personal time to train in the methods I prefer."

Tears, as hot as molten lead, started to slowly inch their way down her cheeks and Fancy desperately wanted to blow her nose. She didn't — and instead just let the snot slowly drip.

"By your behavior this afternoon I am beginning to think that all this time, all my time with you has been for nothing."

When Fancy had first met her Master she had been entranced, shocked by
his perfection into a kind of adoring stupor: tall, strong, with finely chiseled features, raven-dark hair, a finely manicured beard and mustache, intelligent, and with a profound knowledge of what was wonderful pleasure and, well, wonderful pain. His accent, more than anything though, was what made Fancy stand and simply drool — from both her mouth and her cunt: James Mason, Jeremy Irons, Alec Guiness, Pierce Brosnan ... he was dignity, refinement, strength, and civility.

But now he was disappointed, and she discovered — for the first time —
that his perfect Oxford tones could also project icy menace, cold distance, and dismissive indifference.

"But, as I have stated, I do try and understand, to forgive transgressions and failures — after all, I can't hold you, an American, to my own British standards of excellence. Because of this, I am not prepared, at this time, to simply return you to the Marketplace. Do you understand how

86

fortunate you are that I am endeavoring to expand this portion of my otherwise rigid and demanding personality?"

Fancy nodded, saying, "Yes, Sir; thank you, Sir," and tried not to sniffle.

Suddenly an elegant hand appeared in her field of vision, coming between her bare thighs and the Chinese rug. In this hand was a silk handkerchief, a brilliant square of red. "Blow your nose, Fancy — have some pride. Until this incident you have done nothing to give me any form of displeasure. You have been a most satisfactory slave."

Despite the compliment, Fancy felt herself smile. Before she had been ... well, before she had been that young woman kneeling on that Chinese rug, she would have snorted a quick gust of disgust at his patronizing and been "outa here."

But she was Fancy now — no, that's not it. She was finally the woman she had always wanted to be, she was finally Fancy — and Fancy glowed at this kind gesture from her Master, this touch of approval.

"'Have been', Fancy — until now, you had been an adequate slave. But your behavior this evening has shown that you may not be able to achieve the level of excellence I demand from those in my service. I may be trying to develop a sense of ... patience with people's flaws, but I am also firm in my requirements for my slaves. Tonight, Fancy, you must prove to me your worth as a slave, you must show me — your Master — that you have within yourself the ability to grow from your disappointing state into a truly memorable possession."

He hadn't given her permission, but Fancy knew her Master well enough to know when she was — unspoken — being allowed to speak. "Thank you so much, Sir. I won't disappoint you again, Sir."

"Perhaps you won't," he said — and was that a touch of humor in his precise voice? "You shall stay here tonight, while I go out to amuse myself, and you shall think about your error. In the morning, when I return to fetch you, I expect to hear the exact words that will show me that you are indeed worthy of my time as your Master."

With that, her Master turned and walked out — but not before turning out the lights, drenching the room in cool darkness.

For the first hour Fancy berated herself, pummeling her self-esteem with her Master's disappointment. *Why do I even try? I can't even do this right. Why do I always fail at everything I try? This was going to be it; this was going to be the life I always wanted — and now I fucked it up.* Her Master flashed through her mind. His wicked smile as he selected the toy of the evening, the taste of his lips, the biting smell of his excitement, the time he'd bathed her and made her sneeze from the bubbles. That afternoon when he taught her how to properly make tea, that night he'd presented her to what he called his 'Circle' and the rest of that night as she was delightfully passed from one to another — and I fucked it up, just as I always do.

For the next hour she tried to calm herself, back away from the hideous pit yawning before her. Stop — it's not over yet! You have to try, you have to pull yourself together and keep going. He hadn't thrown her away, he hadn't ended his wonderful time with her. He was still here, and she was still here. He had taught her so much — how to make real English tea and how to burn the crumpets, but — more importantly, lessons in pleasuring others, in understanding sensation, in the glory of service and, more than anything, the skill to love what you have been, are, and could be. I want this too damned much!

From ten to eleven she wandered through her own mind, a little trip through her personal history. It wasn't a voyage she wanted to go on, but for some reason thinking of her Master and their good times brought to mind the long, hard years she'd spent trying to get where she was.

Unlike some of her friends, her special desires hadn't always been there. There had been no tying the next-door kids up, no getting wet watching pirate or gladiator movies, no self-bondage, not even dog-eared copies of famous naughty books. Before she was Fancy, she was happy enough — a good home, good folks, complete education, and even some traveling.

She'd had lovers, women as well as men, but something had always seemed ... missing, as if every time she orgasmed a part of her would stay hungry for something spicy. It took her a while, several years in fact, before she found it. It hadn't been the expected route either — no sudden stumbling over an S/M emporium, no lover who liked to spank — or be spanked. No, she had been masturbating one lazy Sunday morning, just like of drifting along in her own mind, fantasizing about that time at the lake three years before when she'd had that little informal three way with the Philip and Nick. In the middle of her memories of that hot morning on the dock when Nick playfully had taken off her bikini top and Philip had gently flicked a cool finger over one of her exposed nipples, she found herself imaging Philip — instead — grabbing her head and forcing it down towards his gentle pulsing cock while Nick mumbled in her ear, "You want it, slut — you want it bad."

It had shocked her — the reality of the fantasy and the power of her orgasm. Sitting in the little dark room of her beloved Master, she remembered thinking through the rolling after-quakes of her coming, I want this.

After that, it was easy — the information was right at hand, as if it had always been hovering just out of reach. She just hadn't seen it.

She was lucky, though, that when she had seen it, had realized she wanted it, that she'd been able to find it.

The trip, at first, had been rocky — a couple of 'Masters' that were all bluster and thunder without passion, or a few with passion but no power. Some were silly ("Call me 'My Liege'"), some hurt her spirit as well as her body, and others ... well, others had been just too boring to even remember. She was especially lucky that the road didn't wander off into self-destruction or shame — every step had seemed in the right direction ... even if it meant an occasional detour ("Call me 'Fire Lady'").

Then, just when it seemed she was ready, a rumor changed into a possibility, and then into a name and a phone number.

Sitting in that small room, the darkness a warm blanket around her, she remembered that first call — the quavering in her voice, the man's firm tones on the other end; when she hung up the phone she knew, then and there, that she was not what she had been. The next step was just to find a name for her new self.

She became Fancy: a well-trained, elegant, skilled, and — mostly — valued slave. First to her Trainer, Jason, and then — after a frightening turn on the auction block — to Master Graham. Her Master was all that she could hope for — powerful, dynamic, passionate, and — until her foot caught on the edge of the rug — surprisingly sensitive dominant.

In the dark, she felt the shame boil in her and the tears start to fog her already dimmed vision. It had all been for nothing, she'd finally discovered what she wanted to become, where she wanted to be, and then she'd thrown it all to the wind. Because of a knot in a carpet. A foot too close to the floor.

It wasn't just the sex — though, okay, that was a wonderful part — or the servitude — which was terrific. More than anything was was the thought that she was prized, she hadn't just been a slave, she'd been a damned fine one. For the first time in her life she'd felt true, deep pride, in what she did, what she'd become. She understood that this one mistake wouldn't send her back to Jason in disgrace. Master Graham wouldn't sell her or return her because she tripped. But if she didn't maintain high standards of behavior, it was a distant possibility. And without a doubt, she would miss her Master's hands caressing her body, the way his strong chest felt, tasted; and she'd certainly miss being the object of his powerful will but... most of all, she'd miss being Fancy, and the pride that made her the best.

The darkness outside was close to mirroring the sadness inside her when she heard the noise.

It took a while, the sadness smothering her, making anything except for her pain insignificant, but it was very persistent — too much to ignore.

In a hammering heartbeat her attention was on the closed and shaded window. The sound was there, sharp and clear — too irregular to be wind, way too precise to be anything natural.

She was frozen, deer-in-the-headlights paralyzed. Oh, shit — she thought in a tone she thought she'd left behind when she'd become Fancy — what the fuck is that?

She knew what she had to do, too many years of living in the city had instilled her with a kind of territorial feral instinct: get up, turn on the light, yell "Get away from my window, youcocksuckingmotherfucker!!" and, if her blood was sufficiently boiling, throw something cheap and heavy at the window.

The sound continued — but Fancy just stood at attention, frozen. Part of it was fear, even from that ballsy woman who would have grabbed the nearest ceramic ashtray, heaved, and called the landlord to fix the window afterward. But a bigger portion was ... something that sent a shiver of fear up her back. She was wet.

Fuck, she was wet — with the revelation that the sound was someone outside, forcing their way inside. She'd felt it: a feeling she'd only felt before during the wonderful depths of servitude. Graham's hands on her ass, Graham's cock in her mouth, Graham's cock in her cunt, Graham's whip on her back — and, now, the little scratching that meant someone was trying to break in.

Standing there in the dark, she felt herself drip. When the window finally cracked and then softly squeaked open, she knew she must have been painting her thighs with a sheen of molten desire.

He was big. As he stepped through the window his shoulders brushed the sides of the frame, and when he stood his head was only a foot or two from the top. Dressed in black, he looked like the darkness made human-form: the dead of night out for a prowl.

Gloves, dark jeans, a black sweater and ski mask — Fancy couldn't tell if he was young, old, black, white, Asian, or anything else. He was — her nipples felt like knotted cords, and each heavy thump of her pounding heart-beat seemed to send a exciting tremor through them. Her cunt was heavy, and hungry for any touch, any penetration; her clit was as hard as she ever felt it. It was only her terror that kept her from dropping a hand down to part her plump lips and stroke it. Suddenly her throat hungered for a cock — any cock — to plunge down, fill her with salty come. There, in the dark, she was the perfect slave, the perfect object of lust ... just waiting to be used by a pure man; an animal walking upright. He was a hunter, a lion, a beast. Graham was powerful, certainly, but this intruder was a crack of lightning.

It was all Fancy could to keep from whimpering, from dropping to her knees and begging him — pleading with him — to take her, use her, fuck her.

Then he saw her.

"Whatthefuck —!" he said in a thick voice, too full of thunder and alarm for her to recognize the accent. In a burst of dark movement he was facing her, crouched down and perfectly focused. One hand was cocked back in a leather-covered fist, the other ... gleamed.

Fancy was on her knees, hands outstretched in perfect submission — terror collapsing under the weight of her trained desire. Legs slightly spread, heavy breasts resting on the scratchy rug, nipples shimmering as if shocked by the contact, she was his: perfectly, absolutely, totally.

Knives did that to her.

"Jesus, bitch —" he said, stepping back and breathing heavy.

She couldn't speak. One half too much panting desire at the sign of the sharp steel, one half sizing him up: letting him do the talking.

"Get up, bitch," he said, voice deep, hoarse — as if scratched by too many fierce screams. "What the fuck you doing?"

Slowly, the fear making her hands shake, she climbed back up onto her feet. The room seemed to sway.

For the first time he seemed to notice she was naked. "Fuck ..." he said, that rough voice dropping register as he looked.

He raped her with his eyes. Even though the room was dark, there was more than enough ambient light from the busy city outside. In the intermittent flashes, his hard stare was as cold as the knife he still held: her shoulders, her large breasts, knotted nipples, the gentle swell of her tummy, her bare mons (Graham not having a fondness for pubic hair) — and he couldn't very well miss her swollen majora or the shine of juice on the inside of her thighs.

Fancy stood stock still, feet planted firmly, eyes downcast — focused on the brilliant shine of the knife in his hand. She wanted that knife, as much or more so than his cock. She wanted that knife to hover, a hair's breath, from her throat. She wanted to feel his fire, his ferocity — she wanted to be trapped with this beast, this urban tiger. Fancy wanted to be his toy, and his victim.

The darkness was thick like syrup — as if from the bottom of a well, she looked up at his knife, trying to anchor herself in cold logic: burglar in the house, knife positioned at her naked belly, Graham nowhere to be found, maybe not even at home. But even cold logic betrayed her, and the so-hungry slave named Fancy, instead looked at a powerful animal, glittering knife in his hand, hard cock in his pants, sopping moisture between her legs.

"You want it, bitch, don't you?" he said, tone still gravel, but now tempered with what must have been mean-ass come-on.

She almost nodded, almost said, "Yes, Master", almost dropped down to her knees again to hunt for his hard cock through those black jeans. Almost — but she didn't. She stood, frozen — a deer in his feral headlights — and trembled from equal parts fear and want.

The knife blade flashed in front of her downcast eyes, so close it made her start, made her eyes flicker up from the blade to his arm, his broad shoulders, his dark eyes. "Yeah, bitch — you want it ...."

She did — Lord, she did. It was like the absolute slave that Fancy wanted to be, was standing there. She was pure. She was want. She was an object. She was a victim....

Fancy heard his hands fumbling with his belt, heard his jeans tumble around his ankles. Heard, because she suddenly wasn't looking down, but rather had brought her head up to stare into a pair of hard brown eyes. She saw him for the first time: not power, just violence; not domination, but destruction.

"Yeah, bitch, you fuckin' want it. You want it fuckin' bad —" he said, equal parts desire and rage. A kid, a little boy, who finally got his wish: a toy to use, break, then throw away. "You ready to take it, bitch?"

"No," Fancy said, "and I'm not a bitch. I'm Fancy — and I'm the best fucking slave there is."

Then she took a step back, carefully aimed — that brown belt in Tai Kwon Do never far from her mind — and power kicked him right in the balls.

In the end, she really wished she could have stolen away for a quick shower. But the instant the thought filled her mind she pushed it aside. Her Master had told her to remain in this room, and that's what she would do — even if she reeked of cunt juice and sweat.

Her arms still ached, and she smiled. She'd stayed where she'd been put — but that hadn't prevented her from getting a work—out.

He certainly hadn't looked heavy — big, maybe, but not like the monster sack of cement he'd felt like as she'd dragged him, groaning and cursing, over to the window. Even with his balls kicked up his ass, he'd tried to grab her — but she'd just fallen back into a perfectly balanced stance (Thank you, Master Ko) and given him three quick shots to the face, throat, and solar plexus — which had left him in a pliant, if heavily fetal curl.

Once she knew he wasn't going to do anything remotely threatening, her breathing settled back into its regular, slow rhythm. She picked the knife up — noticing for the first time it was a cheap Chinese piece of shit —

and flipped into a far corner. Call the police? She should, it was, after all, her civic duty ... but then she hesitated. First, explaining to the cops why she was naked, why one room of Graham's lavish apartment was decked out with a sling, stocks, GYN table; why ... well, there was just too many whys. Too many things had to be hidden, changed, covered, and Master would have to be summoned and disturbed as well. His much valued privacy would be invaded. Besides, the burglar — between sobs and almost-shrieking groans — was quite adamant about coming back to "fucking kill you, bitch."

She debated, quite coolly, taking the knife and ... well, not really seriously.

In the end, she settled for simply dragging him over to the window and heaving him out. He made a very satisfying thud and then some almost childish screams after he landed in the alley two floors below. She made a mental note to have the ornamental railings outside the windows checked for damage, and returned to her place in the center of the room. To her shock, it was morning already — somehow, the night had passed, taking with it her shame and terror, her deeper fears and her unholy arrousal. She was once again Fancy.

"I am not pleased," her Master said, standing in front of her. "Yes, you have performed the simple physical task I set out for you to remain in this room till my return ... but, this is not all I ordered you to accomplish — is that not right, slave?"

"Yes, Master. I apologize, Master."

"With all this time to think, to ponder what it means to be a slave, to be the ideal submissive, I have found your answer to be simple — no, that implies elegance. More childish. 'Because I'm proud of who I am.' Does that speak of the complexities of servitude? Does that even touch on the physical sensations of your position, on the philosophical attributes of true service? No, Fancy — this is just not an acceptable answer."

"Yes, Master. I am so sorry, Master."

"And answer me this, pray—tell, what was that God-awful noise a few minutes ago? God, girl, did I give you permission to bang around like a bloody marching band? And look here — first that din and now this. I did not give you permission to open a window. Were my orders unclear? Were my instructions too complex? You were just to remain here — quietly — in this room, and to come up with an answer that would show me that you have what it takes to remain in this house, to stay my property."

"Your orders were quite clear, Master. Please forgive me."

"I have even begun to wonder about your sanity: it's chilly outside and this room is close to being cold. Don't you have enough sense to even close a window?"

"I'm sorry, Sir; it won't happen again."

At the window now, he rested his hands on the frame, preparing to close it — but then something caught his eye. Leaning out, he looked down for a few moments.

Distantly, Fancy could hear a few pitiful moans — as if, for instance, from someone who'd been severely beaten and then dumped out a second floor window.

After peering down into the alley for what seemed like a very long minute — at what, Fancy had a pretty good idea (if he'd been too banged up to hobble off) — Graham calmly stood back up and slid the window slowly shut. He glanced around the room, and found the silver glitter of the cheap knife laying where Fancy had tossed it aside. Then, he swept his eyes over to his property.

Her eyes were downcast, focused on the Chinese rug. Suddenly, he was beside her, his hand gently cupped her chin and lifted her face to his. His eyes were sparkling. "I do believe," he said, "I am in possession of a very, very fine slave. Perhaps pride shall suffice."

Fancy didn't say anything. She just smiled.

9 The Dog and Pony Show

The afternoon session ended and the explosion of trainers and spotters leaving the debates was as bustling as the check-in period, with the added pressure of evening activities looming ahead. By the time Michael pardoned himself from his sweet afternoon on the grass and dressed for dinner, he was feeling a lot calmer. Jet lag, he decided. I'm over tired and just plain cranky-mean. I know I shouldn't even talk to anyone when I'm like this, and I definitely shouldn't be asking impertinent questions of Mr. Touchy. I'll write about it in my journal, later.

He had dashed back to the room after young Stuart finished his story, to lay out Chris' clothing and make sure his shoes were polished. Since the dinner was hosted by the Canadians, it was North American style formal wear. Chris had brought two different tuxedos, Michael his best suits.

He was actually looking forward to it. Formal dinners were never difficult for him; his family had a few when he was growing up. His Uncle Niall had more than his share. He had thought about renting a tuxedo, but at the very idea, he had gotten a withering look of contempt from Chris. And no wonder; when he started to pack, he discovered that Chris had a separate closet for his formal wear.

"How many tuxedos do you own?" he had asked, in amusement.

"The better question is, 'how many suits in there are tuxedos?'" Chris had responded. And sure enough, there were vast differences between the carefully hung sets of formal wear to what Chris casually called his working clothes.

Until that time, Michael hadn't even known that Chris had ever been a butler.

Naturally, he thought that was amusing too. "I mean," he had said trying not to giggle, "think of what butlers are in American culture, OK? Alfred at stately Wayne Manor. Or that guy in the movie, the one who was a butler for Dudley Moore, remember? 'I'll alert the media', that was funny!"

Well, the beating he got later on was no laughing matter, although he could swear that Grendel and Alex thought the whole thing was pretty amusing. And it wasn't that Chris ever got into the whole formal costume at their house, either; least not when Michael was there. He tended toward the same clothing he wore at Anderson's — suits and ties, collared shirts and ties with jeans for days when he worked outside.

Michael secretly thought that maybe Chris had some sort of tux fetish. It was occasionally a funny thing to consider, although he was very careful not to ever say anything out loud. But it also started him wondering what other huge secrets Chris Parker had. Man of mystery, indeed. Just when you think you had him pegged, he went out to a leather bar and hustled tourists at pool, or watched some cheesy monster movie with Rachel, the two of them leaning into each other and laughing around buttered popcorn. Or, well, he turned out to have been a butler.

As he brushed the jacket off and opened the box of studs and cufflinks, Michael thought about the entire formal service wardrobe. Where had Chris actually been a butler? And when? Was that something he had been sent away to do? Was that the context in which Anderson — loaned him out? Because there was now no doubt that Chris had been handed off to someone unspeakable. The memory of it was apparently so terrible, he couldn't even hide it from Michael, the traditional 'last-to know' guy.

And the fact that Chris had actually experienced it meant that Michael was himself more likely to suffer, too. It was frightening now, too frightening to really spend a lot of time considering. He decided that he would ask for a meeting with Anderson when he got back to the states to clarify things. But while he was here, he had to concentrate on doing better. He had to focus on serving and pleasing Chris, making up for his lost temper and showing what all these months of learning were worth.

So, knowing that Chris wouldn't let him play valet because of his little temper tantrum, he left the room and sought out a little time with other people his age as they congregated in the halls and on the outskirts of the banquet hall. It was nice being part of a crowd that might be discussing genital piercings as easily as sports scores. He kept an eye on the time, and strolled over to the Western wing as promptly as possible. Serving slaves dashed about in western-style uniforms, some of them more provocatively dressed than others. As he turned into Room 5, he thought he had walked into the wrong room, because the first person he saw was Stuart.

He was dressed in a tux now, a modern one without a lapel. He looked for all the world looked like the junior groomsman who was getting up the nerve to ask the junior bridesmaid to dance.

But instead of a too-tall girl in a pastel party dress, Chris, looking relaxed and elegant himself, was chatting with him. Michael stationed himself a discreet distance away, but could hear them very well. He lowered his head and focused away from them.

"What do you think of the Jorgenson Center?" Chris was asking, showing no sign that he had noticed Michael at all.

"It's OK, Sir," the kid replied. "Not equipped for someone like me, I can tell you that! If I had told them everything at first, I don't think they might have been as helpful. You gave me the best advice though, and I can't tell you how much it meant to me."

"I'm glad I could help," Chris said gently. "And from what I've heard — and what I see — they're better equipped than anyone was when I was your age. You make me feel ancient."

"Wow, I'm sorry!" The kid blushed. "It's just that — when Marcy told me about you, and said that I could write to you — it was like a lifeline."

Michael shuffled a little, wanting to move even further away. This seemed embarrassingly personal. At the same time, his sense of jealousy came right up. What the hell was Chris doing with that — that — child? How did this angelic looking space cadet end up being pen-pals with my trainer? Stuart was still speaking.

"And Sir — with all respect — I have to say again that you should consider publishing it. If you only saw what was happening on the west coast — it's like an explosion. And we need the kind of stuff you wrote to me." He was so sweetly earnest.

"Publish it? I don't know, Stuart." Chris paused and shook his head. "It was a different world for me, I'm afraid. There are things I'm not comfortable with as common knowledge. I — I would need to think about that."

"Thanks, Sir, that's all I can ask."

Michael cleared his throat slightly, and was gratified to see Chris check his watch.

"Time we should be going," he said. "Michael, come here a moment. This is Stuart. He is Marcy Teodor's trainee, from Seattle. Stuart, this is my student, Michael."

"Hello, Stuart," Michael said, feeling foolish as he nodded. "Good to see you again, I didn't know you knew Mr. Parker."

"You never said who your trainer was," Stuart said with a touch of excitement and respect. "It's an pleasure to formally meet you, sir."

Michael almost rolled his eyes. No one had called him 'sir' in ages.

"I am sorry to interrupt you, sir," Michael said quickly, turning to Chris. "But —"

"Yes, it's time for dinner. We will be sitting with Marcy and Stuart and a few of the other Americans. Let's get going." He led the way, with Michael and Stuart falling in behind him.

"It is like, such an honor to actually meet him," Stuart whispered. "I can't believe you're actually training with him! You are the luckiest guy, like, anywhere!"

This time, Michael did roll his eyes.

Marcy Teodor turned out to be a tall, solidly built woman with a crooked nose but beautiful, expressive eyes. She was elegantly dressed in a long black skirt and a cunningly tailored tuxedo jacket which gathered around her breasts, a perfect frame for the smoky jade of her necklace. She shook hands like a man, though, and ruffled Stuart's hair in greeting exactly as though he were an Irish Setter. Michael felt suddenly grateful for the dignity Chris allowed him most of the time, and tried to keep from grinning.

Seating took time, as elegantly dressed slaves escorted people to the glittering tables. There was a subtle 'cowboy' motif in the formal service; and when people discovered touches like the wire-wrapped lasso which encased their napkins, there was muted laughter. If there was any sign of how the debates went, it was only that a few people seemed even more formal than usual. Men and women acknowledged each other with nods, and bows, by standing, and by extending their hands. Michael couldn't even keep up with the messages they were sending to each other, as some men rose for all women and everyone rose for some senior Trainers. He saw Geoff across the room, accompanied by what looked like a knot of young people, some trainers and some spotters.

When Ken Mandarin swept in, eyes turned, as she intended. She was wearing tails, with a formal white tie, and a top hat that would have done Dietrich proud. Behind her were her pair, wearing matching shirt cuffs, black loin cloths and starched collars with satin bow ties. They were remarkably pretty — and funny, too. Just exactly the kind of silly costume that people expected to see at a formal banquet of slave trainers. And Ken knew it, too — she laughed her way through the room, pausing only to blow kisses to various friends. When she was seated, she waved her slaves away, and they took her hat, collapsing it in a flourish that actually got applause.

"What would we do for laughs without Ken?" Marcy said. But her eyes were slightly hooded; Michael could hear a certain tension in her voice as well. But before he could ask anything, he was pleased to see his new friend

Tucker approaching to take a seat, with Alexandra on his arm. It was very strange, feeling so much in the center of things yet being in the minority, only part of the American group.

After the men at the table seated themselves again, Chris leaned slightly over toward Marcy and said, "You know, there's no need to be angry with Ken. You've known her longer than I have, she's a good friend. And she doesn't mean harm."

Marcy harumphed and watched her wine poured with a critical eye. "No, she doesn't mean it, but come on, some of what she said was uncalled for. She almost accused you and everyone who supports you of being fascists. That's a bit over the top, don't you think?"

Chris shrugged as he laid the napkin in his lap. "I've been called much worse. She feels threatened. Frightened people often say things they regret later. I'm supposed to meet with her to discuss this tomorrow, and then I have a play date scheduled sometime in the evening. Join us. Bring your puppy and don't let a disagreement spoil an otherwise good relationship."

"My, you're busy," Alexandra joked.

Chris looked up at her with a mix of warmth and respect that Michael could almost feel across the table. His eyes looked tired, but he was clearly keeping himself focused. "I'm following your recommendation to socialize," he said.

Marcy laughed. "Oh, you're one of those all-work-and-no-play people, aren't you? Somehow, I've gotten that impression from your reports. Tell you what, if Ken says it's OK, I'd love to come play for a while. And Stuart here hasn't been out in company yet, it'll be good for him."

Finally, Michael saw someone who could be as easily embarrassed as he was. Stuart almost turned purple, he blushed so deeply. It deepened the difference between his fair skin and fair hair. He cleared his throat and took a drink of water amid the slight, knowing smiles.

"So, I see the whole goatee thing made it to New York," Marcy said, leaning back a little to get a better look at Chris.

"I have — a thing?" Chris' pause was priceless, and if Michael wasn't already feeling a little heat run up his collar, he would be giggling hysterically. As it was, Alex was laughing.

"Oh, God, yes — sometimes I think there isn't a male in the Seattle area over the age of 12 who doesn't have a little chin fuzz on him. Look at Stuart here!" She grinned and winked at the young man, who was now stubbornly paying attention to unfolding his napkin. "Yeah, there's a thing all right. Somehow tied into that depressingly exciting music they're churning out in basements while they drink their $2 cups of coffee."

Chris sighed. "I must admit I haven't been paying attention to modern trends as much as I should." He eyed Michael with mild amusement. "Coffee is $2 a cup and I have a . . .thing."

"Oh, it's not as bad as I make it out to be," Marcy said. "At least it looks good on you."

And that was something in which Michael could take some satisfaction, at least. It was just over a month ago when Rachel and Alex had both complained to Chris about his full beard, and Michael had caught him upstairs getting ready to shave it off.

"Don't take all of it off," Michael had suggested. "Let me do something, it'll look hot."

Chris put down the old fashioned straight razor he had been honing and looked at Michael in that rare way that meant he was carefully considering it, and Michael rushed ahead, eager to be of interest.

"I can barber, really!"

"You can use one of these?"

"My dad taught me when I was 14, and Uncle Niall uses one, too. I can shave your nuts, if you wanted me to, without a single nick." The minute the words were out of his mouth, he almost choked. "Oh my God, I don't believe I said that." But apparently Chris thought that was funny.

"All right," Chris decided. "I'll sit by the window. And I'll let the women of the house decide if what you do is acceptable, and what to do to you if it's not."

For once, Michael was confident in his abilities. With a flourish, he heated a towel, worked up a thick lather in the enameled mug, and went to work in a way that would have made his Italian uncle, the family barber, proud. He carefully trimmed Chris' hair, thinking of the photos in the latest men's magazine that he had been admiring. Chris had a surprisingly simple haircut, but it wasn't the best for his face. As hairs fell around the chair, Chris seemed uninterested, the perfect customer, quiet and allowing his head to be moved easily.

When the haircut was done, Michael worked at removing most of the beard. He trimmed and shaped Chris' mustache, and when he was finished, looked critically at the results. Now, instead of a simple parted hairstyle with loose curls, Chris had a short-top with a little flair — the front cowlicks curled up and then down again over his eyebrows. His slightly straight cut and deliberately longer sideburns gave his face more length. And the close cropped goatee looked pleasingly masculine yet a little dandyish, too. It was all even, very precise. Michael found some gel in the bathroom and ran a little of it through Chris' hair with satisfaction.

And when the trainer looked at himself in the mirror, he fingered the goatee with suspicion, but then leaned back and nodded. "You'd best add this skill to your file," he said simply.

Michael lived for praise like that. It was even better when Rachel pronounced it beautiful and Grendel and Alex approved. Admit it, Michael thought, looking at Chris as the conversation continued. It looks good on you, and you like the attention. Never mind that the little space-cadet brat sitting across from you has the exact same cut.

Michael hid his laughter with a fit of coughing and was rescued from explaining it when the first course began to arrive.

The meal was sponsored by the Canadian branch of the Marketplace. Not, as Michael had first thought, by the trainers alone. "Hell, we couldn't afford McDonalds for this crowd," Benjamin had joked. "There's only seven of us here out of maybe 25 trainers in all!" But each geographic segment of the Marketplace took turns sponsoring special meals and events in honor of their trainers, to showcase both their best properties and various cultural items of interest.

For example, the meal itself was arranged of dishes prepared by slave chefs from different cities in Canada. Sweet fresh salmon with an herbal dressing, wild greens arranged with a rich foie gras, a variation of cock-a-leekie soup with a spicy taste from the wild garlic that was shaved over the top — each course had its home region and chef identified, leading to the beautifully arranged crispy ducks with Saskatoon berry compote. It was a delightfully decadent menu, but that was expected.

As if to compete with the food, the service staff was perfection itself. How could they not be? Every eye in the room rested on one team of servers or another at all times, watching movements, listening for sounds of discontent, pointing out a handsome body or a sensuous mouth.

Multi-lingual wine stewards discussed vintages while their juniors poured; servers of all genders laid plates down without a sound, smiled pleasantly but not engagingly, encouraging the diners to ignore them. Michael watched his table mates as closely as he could without being obvious. Alex, Tucker and Marcy were comfortable with and amused by the service and the servers. Chris was rating them, when he bothered to look at them at all. And poor Stuart spent half of his time being delighted how things appeared and disappeared while he looked away, and the other half making the servers have to sway gently out of his way as he gestured broadly or leaned in the wrong direction. Marcy whispered corrections to him from time; Michael knew what they were because of the remarkably familiar way that Stuart realized how he had misbehaved, immediately corrected himself and then fell silent in quiet self-annoyance. But it never took long for his natural exuberance to have him acting up again.

Chris ate sparingly, and as the meal progressed, Michael became aware that his trainer looked exhausted. He didn't stumble over words or let his attention wander too much, but when he sat back in his chair he looked almost ready to let his shoulders sink into the back. As Michael watched, he realized that Chris' reactions were slightly off, too. It was strange, to be sitting there and studying Chris so closely, but Michael actually shivered when he realized that no one else at the table seemed to notice. Even Alex, often engaged in a cheerful conversation with Tucker, didn't give Chris more than the attention she usually did — friendly and slightly commanding, with just a touch of teasing. Michael wondered if Chris had in fact gotten any sleep the night before, and then wondered what to do about it. It seemed pretty clear — but it would be ballsy, especially for him.

In the slight lull after the main course had been cleaned away but before the dessert, Michael leaned over and said softly, "Sir, you asked me to remind you about your appointment this evening."

The corner of Chris' mouth tugged up, and he nodded. "Quite right," he said. "I've been preoccupied. Ladies, Mr. Tucker, I'm afraid I must excuse myself from your company for this evening."

"Busy, busy," said Alex with a smile. "I'll see you in the morning, Chris."

When Chris leaned forward to rise, Michael intercepted the eager-to-please slave who stood by and got up to take Chris' chair himself. Chris nodded and said "Thank you, Michael," and Michael felt a pleasant warmth in the words. "You may stay for the festivities if you wish. Please extend my sincere regrets to the Urquharts for missing their demonstration."

"Thank you, sir, and I will," Michael said, and watched as Chris slowly made his way out of the room. *Nicely done,* he congratulated himself, as he took his seat again.

Stuart looked at him, wide eyed. He leaned over and whispered, "You're being trained in the old Anderson style, aren't you?"

Michael nodded casually.

"Oh, wow!" Stuart slumped a little and then corrected his posture with a look of chagrin.

Michael decided that a little touch of worship felt just fine. He smiled in what he felt was an indulgent way, and then turned to Alexandra. "What do you know about the entertainment tonight, Ms. Selador?"

"A display from the Urquharts was all I heard," she said, looking toward Tucker. "The animal trainers?"

"That's them," Tucker agreed. "Saw them settin' up kennels in the back, so I'm bettin' it'll be your typical dog 'n' pony show!" He laughed heartily. "But tomorrow it's the Japanese trainers' turn up at bat, and I must admit I am dreadin' the very thought."

"Why?" Michael asked.

"What with the sittin' on the floor, drinkin' hot wine and eatin' raw fish, that would be more than enough for me," Tucker replied. "But you know what their entertainments usually are? Skinny gals in pancake makeup plunkin' on long guitars and wailing like stuck cats."

Marcy laughed so hard she almost choked, and Alex shook her head sadly. "Oh, Tucker, really. It's not that bad. Besides, it could be much worse. They could have — kareoke."

Michael snickered, but Tucker's eyes widened and he leaned forward with glee. "Now, I wouldn't be sayin' such a thing, my dear Ms. Selador, since you ain't heard my rendition of 'Born in the USA'."

"This is my — seventh Academy in ten years," Marcy said, rescuing Alex from trying to make some sort of comment in response to Tucker's revelation. "And there hasn't been a single entertainment yet that didn't make me feel like my slaves were the most boring creatures on the planet!" She laughed. "But damned if I've met more than a dozen owners who really want the fancies."

"Not our niche," Alex shrugged. "But fun to watch, in that 'we've dined, now divert us' sort of way."

"Remember that year on Santorini?" Tucker asked with a broad smile. "Now, that banquet made you feel like a goddamn Roman." He turned to Michael and Stuart to explain. "Sixteen different rooms, because we reclined, boys. On damn couches! They had to put up tents for all the slaves they sent in. We're talking cup-bearers, footmen, washin' up slaves, and then they had jugglers and tumblers and contortionists and who-knows what else."

"It was damn uncomfortable if you ask me," Alex said with a smile of her own. "But I did think it gave you a great sense of being really overcome with service. Something like this," she swept the room with her hand, "this is a little old fashioned and exactly like any formal dinner. But a Roman banquet with twelve courses and one server per guest? It's a taste of what you can do with unlimited power over a vast amount of people. It was too sweet — like those honey dipped fruits at dessert, remember? One bite, and you felt like it was the most delicious thing you ever tasted. Two bites later, you needed that strong coffee just to wash the taste out of your mouth."

Tucker nodded. "Moonshine madness. Well, that's why I'm a trainer and not an owner. That, plus what my accountant tells me!"

Michael shook his head, wishing he had been there. "So the Academy is one way for you to all feel like owners?"

"Extravagant owners," Marcy said. "Very few of the owners I know actually live like this, even when they have the wealth to justify it."

"And speaking of extravagance," Alex said. She nodded her head toward the double doors that opened up to the back of the building.

Conversations, while not stopping altogether, shifted in tone as the ponies were herded in, prancing around the edges of the room in pairs. Michael was delighted to find that instead of the more typical English carriage style of harness and costume, these were obviously western ponies, with heavily inlaid leather harnesses and brightly colored rodeo head-dresses. Trick ponies! Benjamin's father, in brown leather batwing chaps and a matching vest, drove one group while the steel-eyed Abigail whistled and drove the other. Michael hardly recognized her in her fringed white leather skirt and vest and beautifully decorated silver-toed boots. Images of Dale Evans tickled at the back of his mind as she expertly cracked her driving whip over the tossing heads of her team.

"'Bout time they found out that everyone who likes ponies ain't English," Tucker said with a chuckle.

The ponies were arranged by height, the smallest ones in the front ranks. When Abigail's team passed by the table, Michael especially admired a young Asian woman, her black eyes sparkling over the silver bit in her mouth. As she tossed her silky hair, making the purple ostrich plumes in her head harness dance like flags, he noticed that the hair descending from her butt plug looked exactly the same color and texture as the hair on her head. He scanned all the ponies as they passed, and laughed out loud; they all wore their head hair long, and their tails matched. Several of them were fairly expert in flicking those tails too, to the audience's delight.

The two teams rounded the room, crossed each other at the main dais and continued to trot, knees high, through intricate figure eight and double circle patterns. They split, the pairs passing each other in perfect movements, advancing and turning under Zeke's firm gaze and Abigail's expert whip cracks. It was not as much a rodeo show as a weird kind of horsy square dancing.

In their final formation, to the applause of the diners, the ponies gathered in a row across the dais, advancing forward and then sideways, their heads moving in unison now. They turned and moved expertly, all the while keeping their eager eyes on their handlers, showing a combination of spirit, strength and obedience to command. It was stunning to look at, down to the final movements, where they wheeled so energetically that it gave the impression of rearing, and then all bowed low, their trainers bowing with them, to thunderous applause.

"Just like the Rockettes," Michael joked.

"Actually, it looks like a routine pioneered with the Royal Lippizanner Stallions," said Alex. "I think that would predate Radio City by about 150 years."

"Fancy stuff for rich owners," said Tucker. "Just imagine what that herd must be worth, huh?"

"And the owners just loan their slaves to us for shows and service?" Michael asked. "No remuneration?"

"Listen, owners like to know that their slaves are good enough to be here," Marcy said. "I wish I could have supplied a half a dozen myself, but I only felt good about one recommendation last year. How about you, Alex?"

"We've got three alumni here," Alex replied. "At least I think it's three — after a while, I lose track of some of our older graduates, especially if we don't represent them any more."

Michael frowned. "Damn — then how many. . .?"

"Anderson slaves?" Alex filled in. "Here this week? We might not be able to get a good accounting, so many of her clients get credited to their first trainers, even though she's the one who perfected them. Hm. Maybe twenty?"

"Twenty?"

The trainers looked around, estimating how many slaves made up the service arm, while the ponies trotted prettily out the back doors again and people started to rise.

"At least," said Tucker, squinting. "Yeah, at least. Anyhow, let's shove off and see part two."

"You mean that wasn't it for the entertainment?"

"Oh no, my wild dog, that was not the extent of the entertainment!" Michael twisted in his chair and then stood up as Ken Mandarin approached. "Betting will close in ten minutes; does Parker allow you such pursuits?"

"Betting on what?"

"The races, boy," Tucker said genially, taking Alex's arm again. Their chairs were slid away by silent, smiling slaves and everyone started to head for the rear doors. The evening was slightly cooling, but still lush and wonderfully fragrant, and the breezes whispered through the room. "Ponies dancin' ain't much of an entertainment, no matter how pretty they are. And that wasn't nearly long enough. It ain't a real entertainment until you start to feel drowsy!"

"Oh, Tucker, you love every minute," Alex said. "And I know you've been waiting for this part, because I saw you placing your bets earlier."

"Indeed," Ken agreed. "I too, have wagered heavily. Upon the team from Calgary, Canada. They are not as pretty as the Swedes, but they seem strong, and virile."

Once outside, in one of the few large open spaces on the land owned by the ryokan, a makeshift track had been laid, marked with brightly colored silk flags. Michael was surprised to find the race was not between the hardy western ponies who had just performed, but by teams of dogs. Three thick wheeled, chariot-like vehicles had been placed at spaced intervals, obviously weighted down with packs of something bound in more silk ribbon, and hitched to each one was a team of five naked human dogs. Slaves in loincloths were lighting high torches along the side of the track, and blankets, pillows and low seats were arranged for the spectators.

The dogs were panting, sometimes barking at each other and at the crowd. They whined and whimpered and nosed their handlers with the same wiggly ecstasy that any dog owner would recognize, and occasionally growled and snapped when they jostled each other too roughly. As Michael maneuvered his way through the crowd, he found Benjamin, bare chested but wearing a light leather vest, checking the harnesses on one team. He waved happily when he saw Michael, and Michael slipped under the guide rope to join him.

"They look great, eh?" Benjamin asked proudly, ruffling the long hair of his lead dog affectionately.

"I have never seen anything like it!" Michael cried, laughing with delight. "Dog sled racing?"

"Well, you know, not all dogs can be lap dogs," Benjamin said. In fact, one of the dogs, a muscular female with blue eyes and tattoos and scars all over her body, had started to assertively nose Michael with a certain gleam that was a savage cross between a grin and the baring of teeth before a fight. Michael almost drew back, but instead decided to reach down and pet her. She sniffed at his hand, and along his leg, and then decided he must be all right, because she accepted his stroking and made happy growling noises deep in her throat. Michael had never seen someone so devoted to an animal role before, and much to his surprise, it excited him. He just knew that if she was properly fucked from behind that she would growl and snarl and then howl when she came. His cock sprang at the image.

"This is the first team Da had me train by myself," Benjamin said. "Now, be good, Livia, don't do that," he added, when the female had started to nose toward Michael's crotch. "Bad dog! Stay in place!"

She whined, but grinned, wuffed and moved back beside her harness partner. Michael laughed again in sheer delight.

"All of 'em are from Calgary, three different owners. Da is running the Alaskan team, and Georg Lundgram has the European team. Not that it's much of Europe, eh?" Ben was obviously excited — he sounded more like his father and spoke faster. "They're the only dog trainers who are our competition, I guess, puttin' out workin' dogs as well as sportin' ones."

"So you're competing against your own father?" Michael asked, incredulous. It sounded so strange, in this ever-so hierarchical world, where one never challenged one's superior. "What happens if you win?"

"Better to ask what happens if I lose," Benjamin laughed. "Losers get extra chores, I reckon."

Seven trainers who had been given garish ribbons to declare them the Honorable Racing Officials began to signal for silence for the starting line-up, and Michael quickly shook Ben's hand and ducked back under the rope.

And what if you do win, my friend, he thought, as the handlers walked the track once together and the betting was closed. Does that mean you're not a junior trainer any more? Is it like one of those 'beat the master and become a master' things? Will it embarrass your father, or will it make people respect the two of you more?

Lately, Michael had thought a lot about status, and it was so much more complicated than he ever imagined. But before he could get too lost in his thoughts, there was a sharp gunshot, and the three teams rose, barking and howling. Their shoulders and hips pulled tightly against the harnesses as they rose on their feet, hands reaching in front of them as though they were walking limbs and not tool holders, and then the heavy sleds lurched into motion over the shorn grass. The handlers stood, braced in the chariot portion of the sled/cart, one hand wrapped firmly on a padded handle set into the frame, the other hand free to use a remarkably fluid long whip. Each vehicle had a traditional, short dog whip that was hung from the side, but it was clear that unlike those, which were primarily meant to make noise and break up fights, these handlers actually used their whips to hit their dogs. It was hard to know which to be more impressed by — the beautiful reactions and struggles of the teams as they both pulled and jerked against the harness in pain when the lashes struck them, or the skill of the handlers who had to use a single tail while perched on the back of a narrow, precariously balanced cart.

At the beginning, the teams pulled together into a tight, equal formation, trading off first place only when they rounded the tighter corners and were forced to make room. Michael was amazed at the ferocity with which Benjamin laid onto the shoulders and flanks of his team. It wasn't that Zeke or the slender Swede were any more gentle — it was just that it was strange to see Benjamin, so friendly and lighthearted and openly cheerful, was also clearly a sadist who enjoyed his work.

But clearly, no matter whether he enjoyed it, he got results. Gradually, into the second circuit of the race, he began to pull ahead of the other two teams, to the roar of the crowd. Ben's team strained and howled, dropping onto all fours and rising up against the harnesses in an impressive show of spirit and strength, finally pulling ahead of the other teams by the entire length of the sled, and from then on, they never relinquished first place. They surged across the hastily erected tape at the finish line, with Benjamin howling as loudly and lustily as his team, leaping off the sled to run up alongside them and collapse to his knees to shower them with pats and hugs. They howled and licked and kissed his body, their shoulders and arms shaking with tension, their hips wriggling and thrusting in excitement. Someone could easily be buried under five human dogs like that, overwhelmed. But Benjamin was laughing and slapping playfully at them all, crying their names with affection and pride.

Michael had to really push his way through, but he made it to his friend, cheering at the top of his lungs. Ben grinned wildly, his face dripping with sweat, as he rose and accepted a big ribbon and a large brassy medal from the laughing Honorable Officials and hardy backslaps from his peers. But he shook them all off when his Da came through the crowd, and got pulled into a big bear hug that elicited even more cheers. Zeke looked proud enough to pop the buttons off his shirt, and was as equally covered in sweat as his son. "Get your team cleaned up, boy," he said with a smile. "You done real good."

"Thanks, Da," Benjamin said with a grin. He turned to Mike and asked, "Want to help?"

"Sure," Michael said, coming forward to learn how to undo the harnesses and what exactly one does with five sweaty, over excited slaves who wouldn't be able to tell you what they needed and probably wouldn't like it if allowed to. As he listened to Benjamin tell him what to do and stop frequently to praise his team, Michael wondered even more about the roles of parent and child, trainer and trainee, master and man.

10 Snack Run

The entertainments carried on through more exhibition horsy demonstrations and some nice obedience trials, and Michael smiled a little when he saw people politely hiding yawns, as Tucker predicted. Jet lag and a long primary day caused the crowd to thin gradually and elegantly as the Canadians wrapped up their presentations.

Michael himself felt fine; the little rest he had in the afternoon had left him refreshed and feeling strong at dinner time. He wandered aimlessly for a while, and thought of just going back to the room to force some sleep. But the thought of tossing and turning while Chris slept — and possibly disturbing him — was not attractive. He decided to only go to bed when he was sure he could actually sleep.

It was a great time, though, to set down his observations of the day. He had stashed his travel journal into his breast pocket, and finding a peaceful spot to write was easy. An observant slave even found a lap desk for him, so he could sit on a verandah and feel the slight breezes that suggested rain in the distance. Twin lamps provided more than enough light. He removed his tie and rolled it up neatly into his pocket, and then draped his jacket over the railing. He was still too hot; he desperately wanted to be in shorts and a t-shirt, or just shorts, period. But if Chris could stand to be in long sleeves and a jacket every day, dammit, he could, too.

He filled several pages before he took a break and flexed his fingers. How could someone be expected to absorb so much in a few days, he wondered. Training techniques, sales records, world-wide political and social changes, it was all so — big. And the slaves themselves — Michael had never seen such an array of service minded adults. Ranging from their early twenties to way past their sixties at least, they spanned every description of human being he could possibly imagine. It was daunting to know that these were just the slaves whose owners made them available, nominated by the trainers as the best in their fields. There seemed to be so many of them that you would be tripping over them every other minute. But instead, they kept neatly in the background, coming at a glance, a gesture or a word, and sometimes they seemed to become available at a thought.

Like Anderson trains them, he thought. He wiped some sweat off his forehead and decided that this was enough time spent without air conditioning. As he got up, he debated putting the tie and jacket back on, but carried them instead. He was shocked to see that he had somehow killed two hours on the porch and shook his head ruefully.

It had been months since he had that much uninterrupted time alone. And what had he chosen to do with it? His homework. That should count for something, he thought.

He wandered through the western wing and found that there were a few tables occupied in the main entrance area, trainers engaged in what looked like some killer games of backgammon and poker. There was even a mah-jong game going hot and heavy in one corner. This was the only indoor area where cigarettes and cigars were allowed, and the air was both chilly and bitter with smoke. As he watched a few games — and decided that most of the players would eat him for lunch and serve left-overs — he was reminded of Anderson's evening card games and the way she genially lost to her staff until the stakes were high enough for her to care. That was when she took you for everything you had, no apologies.

The spotter Paul was dealing 5-card-stud, and when he saw Michael, he waved him over. "Come on and grab a seat, Mike!"

"Sorry, but my allowance isn't big enough," Michael joked. The trainers and spotters laughed but didn't press him, and he made his way into the hallways toward the passageway to the Eastern wing. He still wasn't sleepy. Maybe he should go check out the hot tubs again? That was sure relaxing.

It's so damn weird, he thought. Here I am at a slave trainers convention with more slaves then you can shake a stick at, and is there a single orgy going on? Was there some sort of organized play space, a dungeon with stocks and crosses and whips and chains? No. Instead, there's a room full of people playing cards and board games, and a lot of people who went to bed early. There had been two road trips he had been invited on after the demonstrations were over; one group of golf fanatics were off to a driving range, and another group of mostly younger people had headed off to Naha to find a pachinko parlour. He had thought that either one would wear him out, yet here he was, wide awake with nothing to do.

A slave passed him, carrying what looked like a banana split on a tray.

He stopped her — a middle aged red-head with sharp, classically green eyes — and gazed at the ice cream longingly. "Where did that come from?" he asked.

"Fresh from Wu the nighttime chef, Sir" she answered quickly. Her voice had a rolling lilt to it which was as charming as her face. "The kitchen is straight back from me, and the honorable Chef Wu has opened two informal dining rooms in the Eastern wing as well. Shall I send a server to you, Sir?"

Ordinarily, Michael was not one for midnight snacking. And the dinner had been lavish earlier — but the silky texture and the haze of frost from the dish of ice cream tempted him. "I'll find it," he said, nodding to her. "Thank you."

"Thank you, Sir, for allowing me to be of service! Enjoy your evening, Sir." She continued on her way after a slight, elegant dip, and Michael shook his head, watching her. Just the right combination of saucy and respectful, colorfully different, yet somehow homogenous here.

He went through the passageway, pausing to slip out of his shoes and into sandals again. Thank goodness he had been warned to bring loafers, he thought with amusement. This was definitely not the place to be hopping around untying running shoes or tugging off your heavy boots. Not that a slave wouldn't be happy to assist you, though. Cubbyholes for shoes and trays of indoor slippers had been available at every entrance of this wing, but cleverly shaded and set back, easy to miss, if you forgot about it. He was already used to it, and grateful that he had noticed others making the same mistake he had.

The first informal dining room he discovered had about a dozen people in it, and he was pleased to see the Englishwoman he had met earlier with Benjamin and his dad, along with a few others he recognized. Ken Mandarin was there, too, looking for all the world like a dissolute aristocrat, her bow tie draped around the open throat of her silk shirt, the tails replaced by a light half robe. Her handsome slave Andy was kneeling to her left, his hands behind his back and a slight smile on his face. Everyone was seated on the floor, in various postures that they found comfortable, and the snacks ranged from fresh sushi and bowls of noodles to more of the luscious looking ice-cream and an assortment of what looked like French or Belgian chocolates. In one corner sat a brunette that Michael had seen earlier, although he was never introduced. She had Asian eyes, but an American accent, and seemed comfortable in the background. But she was not clearly with one particular senior trainer or another, which was strange, seeing as people dropped their pedigrees quicker than their names around here. She was quietly engaged with a bowl of soba, listening to the gossip and jokes, and when

Michael nodded a greeting to her, she looked surprised for a moment and then nodded gravely back.

Bronwyn, the Brit, was holding forth on what was obviously a favorite topic, and Michael folded himself comfortably down to listen in.

"Really, so much of our so-called fetish scene is based entirely upon shame, and there is no good basis for service in that, is there?"

"Shame works very well here," laughed a young Japanese man examining a platter of raw tuna. His accent was thick, but he seemed at ease participating in the conversation. He was part of the group that came with Chris' old friend, Tetsuo Sakai, Michael remembered.

"Oh, yes," Bronwyn nodded, "but that is shame directed toward not failing the group, yes? I am referring to the erotic shame, the type that makes one's client pleasantly aroused. That does not inspire hard work, I must say!"

Ken waved her hand to join in the fun. "But you British have gifted us all with the history of the rod, have you not? Indeed, our disciplinary fashions were once called the British vice!"

Bronwyn shook her curls firmly, apparently not afraid to contradict so strongly. "You can get some obedience with the cane, but not loyalty," she said firmly.

Michael laughed out loud. He had just whispered his desires to a short haired, deeply tanned man who crept out of the room with a remarkable agility. "You know what my trainer would say to that," he said. "You can't get loyalty out of Americans, either. We're all just a bunch of hedonists who don't care anything about service, honor or loyalty as long as we're getting our rocks off. So you can't find a good basis for service there, either."

Ken laughed, too. "Oh yes, the wild dog speaks the truth! We are nothing but decadent fools over in your old colonies!"

Bronwyn shot them both defiant glances. "Most amusing," she said. "Especially since more decent slaves come out of your little sadomasochistic societies now than anywhere else in the western world. Look at how many clients Matson spotted, hm?"

No one answered that for a moment, although a few of them lowered their eyes, suddenly fascinated with what was left on their trays and in their bowls.

Ken leaned forward. "Yes, Matson. A man who has been absent from these conclaves for some time, if I am not mistaken. Michael, has your trainer told you of him?"

"No, ma'am," Michael said, taking his chocolate sundae from his server gratefully. "At least not that I remember."

She sat back, looking annoyed. "Well, he should have," she said. "I cannot say much, myself."

"What a mystery," Michael exclaimed, his spoon poised.

"Do you really want to know?"

All eyes turned to the quiet, dark haired woman putting down her noodle bowl. "I can tell you. It's kind of a long story, but if you want to hear it. . ."

"I would not miss it," said Ken Mandarin. She gestured, and Andy fetched another bolster for her, and she draped herself over it in a dramatic flinging of her body. "Please tell us all."

11 Bullseye   By Cecilia Tan

You don't hear Matson's name much anymore, but for a while his streak of hot prospects created a little buzz and earned him the nickname Bullseye. The Marketplace has many talented and scrupulous spotters, with sound instincts and sharp eyes, but he managed to build himself a little bit of a legend. His specialty was slaves culled from s/m societies and soft-world contract relationships—glorified sexual-service-cum-marriage arrangements.

Matson claimed that "picking the winners" was simple. He had an eye for the true spirit of service, he said, people for whom s/m sex was the key that could unlock their potential. Before referring a prospect for training he would test their responses for three specific things: one, whether pain would distance them from their own bodies, break down the concept of their bodies as their own or if it would heighten it, two, whether humiliation would distance them from their own ego or incite rebellion, and three, whether he could then access the deep-seated, non-rational emotional centers necessary for contentment in a slave role, either by sexual love, reward, or other means.

Here is how it began: with a slave we shall call Lily. They were introduced by her then boyfriend-cum-master at a public dungeon party and became intrigued by one another. Through a long series of flirtations, correspondence, and negotiations, it so happened that he arranged to see her shortly after she and her "significant other" had parted ways. He invited her to stay the weekend with him and she immediately accepted.

The scene began the moment she arrived at his doorstep. She stepped inside with her valise of personal articles and closed the door. He took the valise from her, and without a word, began stripping her clothing from her. She neither helped him nor hindered him in that activity and when she was naked in the foyer he asked her "Why did you not help me to remove your
114

clothing?"

"Because you seemed to take such pleasure in tearing it from me," she replied. "I could not tell which was your intent, to tear it from me, or to merely denude me."

"Why did you not ask?"

"Because I had not been given permission to speak."

Matson was apparently impressed, for he bent the girl over his knee there and spanked her twenty times on each buttock. Then he said "While you are with me, you always have permission to ask questions, and you always have permission to answer questions directed at you. Is that clear?"

"Yes, sir. Is 'sir' the correct title to use, sir?"

"Yes, it is. Now come with me."

He led her directly to a play room replete with spanking bench, raised futon, suspension rack, and various other dungeon standards. He led her to a gynecologist's examining table and bound her feet into the stirrups. He instructed her to spread her labia wide. Lily expected to see a speculum next, but no, he probed her gently with his fingers.

"You are lubricating. Is this from the spanking?"

"From the spanking, yes, and also the stripping and the general excitement of your presence, sir."

"Ah, well. We'll see about excitement. Keep your lips spread. When I ask you, you must tell me what you are feeling." And he began to stroke her clit.

At first, he began with a short downward stroke, about one per second. After about a minute of that he asked, "On the arousal scale, where would you say you are?"

"On a scale from one to a hundred," she answered, "About twenty-five."

He continued with that motion without variation, for several more minutes, asking her and continuing it until she said the number had dropped between ten and fifteen. He dipped his finger into her lubrication then, and switched to moving his finger in a lazy circle around her clit. Her breathing and heart rate accelerated.

He instructed her to call out numbers as they changed. As his finger circled the numbers again climbed, until she reached fifty. At that point he stopped and left the room.

He returned some fifteen minutes later, now dressed only in a thin silk robe. She did not appear to have moved a muscle while he was gone and he was enormously pleased by this. Other women would have looked bored, or defiant, or curious, and he would have punished them, fought them into submission, or ordered them to satisfy him, respectively, and later sent them back to their husbands or boyfriends with an amusing story to tell. But this one lay still and placid, her fingers still stretching her labia wide as if they never tired, awaiting his next move with measured calm.

He was determined to shatter that calm. He ordered her to close her eyes, silently slicked his manhood to hardness, rolled on a condom and positioned himself between her legs. He grasped her hips and with one difficult thrust, buried himself in her.

Her eyes clenched tighter, and she drew her breath, but there was no scream, no litany of begging, no curse, as he felt her insides spasm as they tried to accommodate his size. Yes, he was large, I'll leave it at that. Large enough that any pussy would not have it easy, especially not one left open to the air for a quarter of an hour. Now his feelings teetered between disappointment that his rape of her had not elicited more of a response, and pleasure at how well she obeyed him and accommodated him. He bit her breasts, slapped her face, and fucked her mercilessly. And eventually she did cry, she did gasp and wail. But she never begged for him to stop, never pushed him away or did anything to lessen her own suffering even though her two hands were unbound. After he came, he jerked out of her and watched her closely to see if she would assume the scene was over. Her eyes did not open, she did not move. He stood there for long minutes, expecting her to beg for her own release or request some reward. But she said nothing.

"Is there something you would like to say?" he asked.

She cleared her throat of tears before speaking. "Yes, sir. I would like to apologize for crying out if the sound of it did not please you."

An answer like that from his last visitor, a cheeky Californian he'd sent back whence she came, would have been dripping with sarcasm, and yet Lily was able to say it with just enough hesitation and choking that it rang sincere. Quite unexpectedly he found himself close by her side, his hands stroking her as he answered into her ear "Oh no, my Lily, your cries pleased me very much." Perhaps that was the moment from which there was no return.

A few phone calls, a few delivered messages—he made sure his calendar was clear of obligations for a while, and mentioned her name for the first time to a trainer of his acquaintance in the Marketplace.

The next day Matson changed his tactic with her. Certainly she could obey his orders when they were not to do something. But how well could she perform when ordered to do something? Her "master" had bragged about her abilities to please man or woman, special talents of her tongue, and other parts of her as well. But he let her first task be to clean his kitchen.

At first he watched while she scrubbed the inside of the sink with baking soda and cleaned each black metal stove spider with steel wool. Flecks of soap speckled her bare breasts and sweat shone on her back as she worked.

He instructed her to continue for an hour, unsupervised, while he took care of some things.

* * *

"Come dear, don't dwell on the drudgery," Ken said. "We all know all there is to know about housework."

The young woman smiled. "Very well. But you'll want to hear about what happened when he came back."

"By all means."

* * *

Suffice to say that when he returned to the kitchen fully dressed he found her picking the dead leaves out of his house plants... there was nothing left to do, she explained, unless she was going to begin repainting... To his eye she had been so thorough his stovetop looked like new and even the grout between the kitchen tiles had been bleached.

He pushed her into the shower stall in the bathroom. While he sprayed her skin with stinging water from the hand-held massager-head, he asked her "Why did you do all of those things?"

"To please you, sir."

"To earn my favor or reward?"

"Not specifically, sir. To do any less than my best would be wrong."

"So, my pretty pet, do you pride yourself on your thoroughness?"

"Pride...? If you approve, then I am happy." She seemed to struggle for a moment with the explanation, as if the concept were so basic she had never before put it into words. "I... can not do what I think would not please you, and I can't not do what I think might."

He cut off the spray and handed her a towel. "Well then, make me happy."

"Sir?" She stopped patting herself dry with the towel.

"Exactly that. Please me."

She sank to her knees in front of him, clutching the towel close. "Yes, sir." Her eyes showed her hesitation, as she tried to guess what he meant. She let the towel fall and ran her hands down her front. Her nipples tightened and her stomach flattened as she drew in her breath. Then her delicate fingers reached out for him, caressing the fine silk of his shirt, creeping upward into his hair as she pressed her naked body against him. One hand loosened the top buttons of his shirt.

He would have faulted her for being presumptuous, except that yes, it did please him. She inflamed his senses and excited him in a way that made him want to make her cry out in pain and shelter her from harm all at once.

He scooped her up then and carried her to the bedroom, where he put her on her feet and told her to continue.

Her cool fingers reached inside his shirt to untuck it from his pants and she scratched his back until every itch was gone. She undressed him with kisses and lay him back upon the bed where she knelt and worshipped his rising hard cock. She lavished attention on it, with her fingers, her breath, her lips and her tongue. He liked being worshipped; he liked being her god.

After he came, and after he had inspected her pussy and found it again wet and ready, after he ordered her to lie still beside him, he told her this: "You have succeeded in pleasing me, and yet you have failed."

"How, sir?" She trembled slightly in his arms.

"I was so hoping that you would NOT please me, so that I could punish you. And so by pleasing me, you have disappointed me, and robbed me of that satisfaction."

She pressed closer to him. "Well, then, do I not deserve the punishment for disappointing you so? I am yours to do with as you will." With that she slipped out of the bed to the floor, where she knelt with her head touching the soft carpet. "If it would please you to punish me," she said, "I would be pleased to suffer."

"Later," he said. "Get dressed. I have some errands for you to do."

The next twenty-four hours were a whirlwind of pain and passion for both of them, as he turned from one tactic to another, one toy to another, playing with her skin and her mind and her sex—and he felt a stab of thrilling electricity every time he looked into her eyes and saw himself reflected there.

That night he invited his acquaintance the trainer, Alayne, to dinner, eager to exhibit his prize. Alayne had protested vehemently; it was much, much too soon! But Matson insisted, so she agreed with a laugh.

Lily, who did not know Alayne was anything but a friend to be impressed, prepared and served them a gourmet meal, beginning with stuffed mushrooms that he chose to eat off her soft skin, her flat belly like an hors d'oeuvre tray, followed by a cunning consommé served in shallow china bowls she set on the table without a sound. The roast lamb was succulent and savory and he tucked a sprig of meat-soaked rosemary into her pubic hair where she knelt beside him. And although they talked of everything else, Lily could feel Alayne's eyes on her, and his eyes on Alayne's eyes. The meal finished with cognac and liqueur-soaked bananas brulee on tangerine almond salsa.

Alayne's spoon clinked into her dessert dish as she sat back. And finally she asked "Where did you get this one, again? Are you sure she's not one of ours, run away from someone less deserving?"

Matson didn't answer. He stroked her hair with one hand.

"Have you told her...?"

"Why don't we retire to the other room," he suggested, and stood. "Heel," he said, though he hadn't taught her how to heel and didn't dare turn his head to see if she was following him. But when he sat down in the living room, she had crawled alongside him. He set down his half-finished cognac. He tugged on her hair until she was on all fours in front of him and he ran his hands over her smooth buttocks and thighs.

Alayne settled into the couch opposite him with her snifter.

His hands stroked her up and down until one fingers slid down her spine and through the wet folds of her cunt. He stuck a finger inside of her, almost reflexively, just as he might stroke her hair or scratch his own chin. With his free hand he picked up his snifter and luxuriated in the fine, woody scent.

They talked more, those two, now about slaves and scenes and service. And he would occasionally add a finger, or subtract one, as he caught Alayne up on the latest leather community spat, and they discussed people they knew in common, how someone named Mildred was now in a household in France, Rick under the boot of an ex-Marine...

Lily's cunt tightened as she realized they were speaking of slaves like her, speaking seriously of people who lived this sort of lifestyle, not just on weekends or in professional dominant's dungeons.

The sudden tug on his fingers brought Matson back to life. He shoved her roughly down onto the thick carpet. "I do believe," he said to Alayne, "that tonight's entertainment is about to begin."

"Oh, good," Alayne declared, spreading her legs. "I could use a good cunt-licking. Come over here, honey."

Lily looked up at him, questions in her eyes, and Matson's pride swelled as he realized she awaited his word before beginning. So many slave sluts he'd played with would do anything anybody said, but not her. He nodded his approval to her and stood up.

Between the two of them they flogged her, blindfolded her and tickled her, made her pleasure Alayne with her tongue while Matson impaled her with his, all manner of decadence until in the early hours of morning Alayne declared that she had to get going.

"You could stay the night," Matson said as Lily helped her put her boots back on.

"No, no, I want some time to think this over. We'd better have that conversation soon, though. I'll call you tomorrow and we can discuss this when I'm not so... distracted." Alayne blew a kiss at Lily and slipped out the door.

Discuss this? Lily thought. This? Me?

That night, as she lay at the foot of Matson's bed, she lay awake despite the exhaustion of use and effort. They had been careful, so careful, as they talked around the subject, but she knew, somehow, that there was more there than they had told her. They had tantalized her with hints, but she knew to be patient was the only way.

Or, perhaps not. Did he not say she could always ask questions of him? What could she say, how could she ask about what she did not know? She feared offending him, though, and put her questions out of her head, and kept silent.

Matson did not keep her waiting long. That afternoon in his study he explained to her the basic workings of the Marketplace, and Alayne's role as a trainer, and then spoke to Alayne on speaker phone so that Lily could hear.

"You know," Alayne told him, "I don't usually like to rush things, but there's an auction in Vienna I could certainly put her into. That's three months, and I've already got quite a full plate. But considering her skills and her potential value... did you mention she speaks French?"

"Spanish," Lily corrected, at his prompting.

Matson and Alayne went back and forth over financial dealings, until finally Alayne said "Matt, this is really quite a generous deal. Why are you being so standoffish about this? Are you listening to me?"

"Mm," he agreed, looking at Lily. Maybe he had the idea then, or maybe he'd had it in mind all along and was waiting for this moment. "I'd like to make a proposal," he said, never taking his eyes off the curve of Lily's neck, he luminous naked skin, "regarding Lily's training."

Lily listened in amazement as Matson proposed that he "continue" her training, with Alayne's periodic supervision, and that rather than be given spotters credit and fee, he'd share the training credit with her.

"I didn't know you wanted to be a trainer, Matt." Alayne's voice was alive with sing-song.

He stroked Lily's hair. "She's responding so well to me."

Alayne was silent for a few moments. "Could you pick up the receiver?"

He picked up the receiver and Lily waited with her head bowed. Matson did not know if she heard Alayne's next comment or not but he liked to think not. His Lily was surely trying to block out the sound of her private comments.

What Alayne said was "That's — a sudden proposition, Matson. It may be as much work for me to supervise you than to train her myself."

"Don't be ridiculous. You've known me for a long time Alayne."

120

"That's true. I'd like to talk it over with a colleague though."

"Fine. But you know I will not disappoint you."

He hung up the phone and slid down beside her on the floor, burying his lips in the dark smoothness of her hair.

He had been training her since the first day, he decided. He took her to public parties and was pleased at the way her eyes rarely strayed from him, her attention always on his needs. She learned he hated cilantro and cooked with basil instead. When he left her free to her own devices, she did things for him that he did not even know he needed, like replacing the batteries in his smoke detectors and retacking the playroom carpet where old nails had begun to come up.

Alayne visited from time to time, but never stayed longer than a meal or a brief evening, and as time passed, Matson spoke on the phone with other people in the Marketplace as well, or so Lily overheard. He was unconcerned that she should hear what might be her own fate, and made sure that she knew that one evening their guests would be special, that several trainers would be coming to evaluate her performance. "I'm sure you will make me proud," he said.

The night arrived only a few days later, giving him plenty of opportunities to push her. If anything he was harder on her then than he had been at any other time, priming her with severe canings and merciless sex. He marveled at how even after beating her across the back with the dog whip and then fucking her long and hard for over an hour, when he told her immediately afterward that she had free time, that she spent that free hour doing the things she knew he loved after a scene, pouring his cognac, rubbing his feet. God, she was everything he had ever wanted, he realized. He wanted her more than he wanted to become a trainer, more than he wanted the respect and approval of the others.

And, if all went right according to his plan, he would have both.

The trainers arrived in ones and twos on an evening pouring rain. Lily, clad in nothing, shook wet raincoats and hung them to dry, fetched clean socks, and stowed umbrellas. Once everyone was gathered, all total four men and two women: two of the men and one of the women trainers, the other three possibly some kind of slaves themselves, Matson seated them all in the living room and began to run Lily through her paces. They observed while the female slave and she were made to spank each other, while the two male slaves were made to put her through various acrobatic sexual positions. But the physical portion of this was easy. Then came the interviews. They sat in a circle around her, sunk into plush couches or leaning forward with elbows on knees, while Matson stood behind her in shadow.

"Lily, do you understand fully what we say when we mean entering into service in the Marketplace?" Alayne began.

"Yes, ma'am."

"And do you feel you're ready to enter service?" This from a man off to her left, his face unclear to her.

"I feel I am already in service," she answered. "And yes, I feel I am ready to enter the Marketplace."

"Nice answer," said another man, she could make out his longish hair and knew he was the one called Gerard, who had been the last to arrive.

"Or nicely coached," continued the man on her left. "Why do you think you crave this lifestyle? What drew you to it?"

Lily spoke clearly, but not so quickly that she seemed to have canned answers. "There's very little honor in the world, very little to believe in. I was unhappy when I had no direction, no focus. Through service, I have something to believe in, a reason to be." She did not fidget where she knelt but looked down at the carpet instead of into the darkened faces. "As to your second question, I..."

"Tell the truth, Lily," Matson commanded.

"I came into the scene looking for someone special. But I'm not looking anymore."

Matson's heart pounded to hear her say it. When the questioning was done, he locked her in the playroom and said good-bye to everyone else himself.

When he entered the playroom, she was kneeling in the center of the carpet, as he'd taught her to do. There were indentations in the carpet that fit her knees.

He knelt in front of her, his hands clasped together. Candles burned at the periphery of the room. He inhaled as if to settle his stomach in that moment that felt so holy, so right.

"Did I please them, sir?" she said. Asking a question was always allowed.

"Oh, yes, you pleased them. They would take you into the Marketplace in a flat second." He lifted her chin and held her gaze. "But, consider this, my sweet Lily..." He interrupted himself to kiss her, to bury his tongue deep in her and smother himself in her scent. "Consider this." He held in his hands a length of chain, a collar. "Consider that you are mine. I know you want to make me proud. But, Lily, you do not have to go into the Marketplace to do that. You have proved you can pass muster, that you can stand with the finest slaves on Earth. That has made me more proud than you know. But you can stay here with me. You need never leave my service."

He held up the chain with two hands, a near beatific smile on his face.

We can only suppose what he must have been thinking. Perhaps he was expecting a moment of triumph, when she would at last set aside her calm to declare how much she loved him, how deeply she knew she had found the right master and need look no further. As he held the collar out to her, though, her eyes did not light with joy and his smile faded a bit as she asked a question, "Are you offering me a choice, sir?"

He stammered, as if he had not expected there to be choice involved. "I.. I want to hear it from you. You know what would please me most."

Her head stayed where it was but her eyes seemed to focus past him. "I thought... I thought you wanted to train me for sale. Sir?"

"Yes, Lily, I acted as your trainer, but did you come to me looking for a trainer, or a master?" He fairly growled with growing frustration and confusion. "I am not a trainer." He proffered the collar again.

"But," she said, trying to make her words slow and cautious, "I thought that until I enter the Marketplace, no one owns me."

"I own you!" He bellowed then, and leapt upon her.

Lily was a strong woman, but small and caught unawares. The struggle was brief as he wrestled her into bonds that locked her hands behind her back. The struggle only seemed to excite him. The resistance he had expected from her in the beginning was finally showing itself and it was time to remind her of his tenets.

He forced her to stand and clipped her bonds to a chain hanging from the ceiling, so that she stood on her feet, her back bent over horizontal and her ass displayed for him. First, pain, to reinforce the conviction that her body was his and not her own. Her flesh was still sore from that week's beatings, and he went directly for the cane, not waiting for her to count or ask, merely laying it on while she cried and cried.

Then humiliation, to distance her from her ego and her sense of self. He lowered the chain and cuffed her ankles apart, and set about trying to find what would humiliate her most. An hour ago, he would have said nothing would humiliate her other than to catch her making a mistake—she would submit willingly to any activity or attention. But she was no longer playing willing. She needed to be overcome, he decided, this was not so far off from his original plan, and through this they would be cemented and bonded forever. He squatted down in front of her.

"Yes, Lily, you are mine, just as Marketplace slaves belong to their owners, to use, or abuse, as we see fit." And he...

* * *

The young woman stopped and looked at the people around her. Many had stopped eating, others had taken their quiet conversations into other rooms. Michael had left half of his ice-cream to melt, and the bowl had vanished without his noticing.

"Go on," Ken urged, her face a mask of scandal.

"Can we just say that it does not matter what he did next? Pick the most horrible thing you can think of one human being doing to another short of murder. Whatever it is you are each thinking, hold that thought."

* * *

Lily had not been quiet through all this. After she was put in bondage she tried from time to time to talk to him, to explain what was going on in her mind, but it was clear that they had vastly divergent opinions of what was transpiring, and anything she said only served to egg him on. Eventually she saved her breath, waiting for him to tire and knowing that he could not keep her a prisoner forever. In the morning perhaps, she could leave.

Beyond a certain point, once she gave up talking to him, she had not even thought to hope for anything to happen other than to wait for him to simply stop. So can you imagine how her heart leapt when she heard the sound of the doorbell ringing. The playroom, remember, was directly off the main foyer, that long-ago space where he had stripped her. Matson ignored the bell. But after it rang several more times, and knocks and thumps came on the door, he threw on a robe and went to answer it.

So complete was his delusion that he was mastering Lily he did not even think to close the dungeon door nor expect that she would cry out for help. At the door it was one of the male slaves who had apparently left something very important at the house and had come back to see about getting it before his own ass was in the proverbial or literal sling. As the front door opened, Lily screamed for help. And maybe it was her scream, or maybe it was the look on the slave's face, or maybe it was whatever incriminating evidence of his unspeakable act that showed on his hands or his body or wherever, but Matson's charade ended then and there.

As he put the shaking, injured, and angry Lily into the hands of that slave he said "I thought you loved me."

"Maybe I did," she answered.

"I thought... I thought you were doing it all for me, because of me. I loved you..."

Lily tried to pull away but he held onto the elbow of the slave who

124

waited a moment more. "Matson," she said, "You lied to me. We started out as play partners. I started to feel things for you, of course. But the moment you told me about the Marketplace, that was the moment it became real for me. Don't you see? You showed me there's a world of reality beyond the play. But you didn't own me in the Marketplace. You told me you wanted to be a trainer." She began to sob but held her ground. "I thought I was doing what you wanted. You wanted a slave to train and sell, isn't that what you said? You wanted to raise your status..."

"No, no..." Matson was saying, mostly to himself.

"If what you wanted was for me never to forget you, then you can be sure I am serving you still," she said, her voice low and bitter and almost lost in the sound of the rain. "If what you wanted was someone who loved you more than the service itself then... then..." Her voice caught on her tears and the slave who held a raincoat over her shoulders finished the sentence for her:

"Then you don't belong in the Marketplace. Sir."

* * *

"And he has not been numbered among us since then," came a voice from the doorway. Michael snapped his head and scrambled up to his feet as he heard that voice.

"It is a cautionary tale," Ken agreed, glancing up at Chris Parker. "Most valuable to hear. Thank you for telling it, cherie."

The young woman nodded in acknowledgment and rose elegantly to pass her bowl to the slave who had been approaching her to retrieve it.

"I didn't see you come in, sir," Michael said. Chris was wearing the long cotton robe and Japanese sandals, and looked a little better rested, but hardly tousled from sleep.

"That's all right, Michael, I didn't want to interrupt the story."

"Indeed, you are the one who most often tells it," Ken said, stretching and sitting up again. "The evil nature of impudent, undisciplined spotters, no?"

"In fact," Chris said softly, "I often tell it to illustrate how trainers can allow hubris and lust to destroy their own work. And how important it is to have standards upon which to base our behavior."

Michael watched as the tale telling young woman quietly exited the room with a brief half-bow toward Chris, who nodded as she slid by.

"You — you were there, weren't you?" Michael asked, as he moved up next to Chris in the doorway.

"But of course he was," Ken laughed. "He is the rescuer, oui?"

125

"You read too many trashy novels," was all Chris said. "I barely knew the man. Sorry to interrupt your evening, I was just getting some tea." He raised the little pot and cup to the room and got a few salutes back, and then turned back into the hallway, with Michael trailing behind him.

"Sir — sir," he said, letting his longer legs catch him up. "I — I really wanted to apologize. For earlier. Better then I did then. I don't know what gets into me, sometimes, it's like I can't control myself."

"That is exactly it," Chris agreed. "When you are in control of yourself, you will not have such problems. But you didn't need to apologize again, Michael. At least not verbally. You behaved very well at dinner, you didn't pout, and frankly, I am grateful for being freed from the dog and pony show."

Michael laughed as they turned into their corridor. He lowered his voice appropriately. "It was fun, actually. I liked watching it. I liked meeting the dogs, too."

"Hm." Chris paused and Michael darted forward to slide open the door to their room. "I should teach you how to do that formally," the trainer mused as he moved in. "I have no doubt you enjoyed the show. But I was much too tired to properly appreciate it. I almost never work with clients like that, and it would do me no good to see them when I can't be appropriately attentive." He turned around to face Michael and sat carefully on his futon. "Michael — you were attentive tonight. The way I suspect you can be much more often than you are. But I think the reason why you were so attentive was because you were purposefully on your best behavior. You were trying to make amends for your earlier lapse. Please correct me if I am wrong."

Michael slumped into a cross-legged position and shook his head ruefully. "I guess that's true."

"And that's where all your problems really originate," Chris said, gently. "Michael, you must learn to be on your best behavior all the time. Because nothing but your best will do for this life. I can't explain it better than that."

"Thank you," Michael said with a sigh. "I'll try to do better, sir."

"Very well. Give me your journal and get ready to sleep. We will be running in the morning, so you need to rest. This absurd energy of yours is making me feel old." Chris took the little book and his tea and settled comfortably to read while Michael stripped and crawled onto his futon. "You know, sir," he said, suddenly feeling drowsy, "you could have sent a slave to get the tea."

"Perhaps I did," Chris said.

Michael frowned, thought he actually heard Chris chuckle, and tried to figure out what that meant. And why Chris was suddenly mentioning his age so much — the man couldn't be that old himself. Michael thought back to everything he knew about Chris and tried to figure out his age. Mid thirties was what he came up with, and hell, that wasn't old, especially in this crowd, where everyone bowed and scraped to everyone over fifty. He gave up wondering and allowed sleep to overtake his thoughts, long before Chris turned out the light.

12 The Specialists

What a difference a full night's sleep and no alcohol made on the day! Michael didn't even mind the morning run with Chris. It wound up with the two of them joining the early tai-chi workout that a wide faced, smiling Hawaiian woman named Pua was leading. Michael was not surprised to find that Chris was at least a little familiar with the discipline, but he knew that Chris was surprised to find that Michael was as well.

"Learned it at school," Michael admitted, as they went back to their room to clean up for the morning seminars and meetings. "Great way to meet chicks."

He felt damn lucky not to get his butt kicked over that one. They split up after that, this time with Chris telling Michael that he could — if he continued to behave — attend that day's debates.

Chris shook his head as he watched Michael enter the room where the specialty trainers were gathering. What a damn shame it always seemed to take a crisis to bring out the young man's best instincts. What does Anderson see in him that I don't, he wondered for the tenth or hundredth or thousandth time. He had set himself to discover this while he worked with Michael, and it was a constant mystery. Yes, the boy showed spirit, and he was devilishly handsome and charming in his artless way, at least when he wanted to be. But he was constantly in motion, from his hands to his mind, always flitting from one position to another, always glancing around to see what was happening around him. That one will never drink tea from an empty cup, Chris thought with mild amusement. And speaking of tea —

He turned into a private meeting room to find a beautiful, Colonial tea service waiting on a sideboard. There was a man seated at the table, his back to the door, an English language newspaper open in front of him.

"May I serve you tea, Sir?"

"Hrmph." The paper rustled.

Chris draped a tea towel over his forearm and served quietly, adding a lump of sugar and a dash of cream. When he replaced the teapot, the man behind the paper chuckled.

"And who shall serve you, then, you puppy?"

"I suppose I shall have to do that myself, Mr. Dalton." Without turning back, Chris prepared his own tea, black, and took the cup to the table. "With your permission, Sir?"

"Damn it, Parker, will you never learn not to call me that?" The paper folded neatly down. Mr. Dalton was almost completely bald now, with a carefully trimmed fringe of pure white hair and an angular face, creased with wrinkles and filled with great dignity. Only his eyes showed that he wasn't truly upset, as he set the paper aside carefully. "Sir, indeed. I have a name, puppy!"

"Blame your sister trainer, Mr. Dalton, who instructed me to never embarrass her by showing insufficient courtesy to my betters." Chris took Dalton's complaint as an invitation to sit and pulled up to the table.

"Kindly inform my damnable sister that she is an arse, Mr. Parker." He laughed, a scratchy, low sound, and sipped the tea.

"I most certainly will not, Mr. Dalton, but I will give her your warm greetings and affection, as usual."

"Hmph. Impertinent, as usual. And what, might I inquire, has taken to nest upon your chin? You look like a junior footman, Mr. Parker. Or the gardener's lad."

Chris had to smile; of course Dalton would be the only one to not like his new look. He leaned forward, his eyes sharp and said, "Perhaps I deserve a good caning, Mr. Dalton," he said.

"Perhaps you do, puppy! And don't think I'm not the man to do it, either. But we'll lay aside such pleasantries, shall we? And shall we also agree that the weather is dreadfully hot, the Labour Party has gone too far, your Republicans are quite a shower, and football hooligans are a sorry lot?" He folded his hands serenely as Chris laughed.

"It's beginning to look like one 'tokoro ga' conversation after another this week," he said with a slight smile.

"Yes, yes, 'as to the matter at hand' indeed," Dalton agreed. "Our Japanese hosts have a useful phrase for everything. And it is regrettable, since we have not had time to socialize as gentlemen for several years now. But I will engage in more banter with you, however, if that is why you requested this meeting."

"*Tokoro ga,*" Chris replied, "I would like to hear now, in private, the reason why the United Kingdom block will not support my proposal."

Dalton sighed and took another drink of tea. "Because we have lost enough already, Mr. Parker."

Chris frowned. "I'm afraid I don't understand, Mr. Dalton."

"Don't you? I suppose not. Bless you, boy, you still see our ways as elegant reminders of civilization. As do we, of course." His eyes looked weary as he gazed into the past. "We *were* the Marketplace, Mr. Parker. We laid the groundwork, we created the international scope of it all. We brought the British soul to bear in its ways — discipline, honor, tradition, loyalty, reserve — all exported like great ships laden with iron and timber. And now, we are nothing but a small special interest group; a minority, as you would say, deserving of special consideration for our age, but not for our ways."

"Forgive me, Mr. Dalton, but isn't that exactly why you *should* be supporting the proposal?"

Dalton eyed the younger man with regret. "Your confidence in your fellow trainers is impressive, Mr. Parker. You see your proposal as a way to establish the ways you have been taught. And perhaps for the immediate future, that would be the case. But what will happen, Mr. Parker, ten years from now — or twenty — or fifty — if you and those who believe as you do are no longer strong enough to hold this august gathering to such high principles?"

Chris sat back with a slightly frustrated sigh. "If the commission is established firmly and supported well, that shouldn't be an issue," he said.

"You are correct. It is the continuing support we question. As matters stand, we of the old houses and ways — the old guard, as you would have it — may continue to train in our methods and create clients of a certain caliber. But should your proposal succeed, there may be a time in which these methods are discredited, or even banned outright. That would create a schism from which we could not recover easily, don't you agree?"

"I — don't agree, Mr. Dalton. But now I understand your concerns. I just wish I could convince you otherwise. Your influence is hardly insignificant. Other trainers still look to the United Kingdom for guidance, and I would be much more confident if I had your support."

"Is that so, Mr. Parker? Pray tell me then, what was served for breakfast yesterday?"

Chris lowered his eyes, and felt even worse when Dalton reached across the table to touch his shoulder. There had been no British trainers at the private early meeting.

"Thank you, Mr. Parker, you are kind to an old man. But our time has passed, I'm afraid. We must hold on to what we still posses — our traditional houses and the trainers and clients we make there. For our own safety, we cannot support a resolution which one day may make us outcasts entirely from our own creation. As we sit here in this lovely room, a new generation of British trainers is rising, based upon American and Far Eastern methods and a bit of the Continent thrown in for good measure. They would certainly welcome our quiet exit from the scene. I am truly sorry."

Chris raised his head and forced a thin smile. "Thank you for speaking to me so candidly, Mr. Dalton. And for letting me play mother one more time. I will consider what you've said. Perhaps some sort of compromise might be in order."

"Nothing would please us more than to find some sort of agreement with you, Mr. Parker. Although," Dalton said, looking pointedly at Chris' goatee, "if you persist in looking like some sort of starving artist, you may win a certain sympathy vote."

Michael's mind was reeling again when he left the meeting room. After an initial introduction to about a dozen different trainers, the room had broken up into special interest groups. As a trainee, he wandered from group to group, taking notes furiously.

If you had asked me what a specialty slave was, I think I could have named about a dozen, he thought, flipping through the imprinted booklet of trainers and their areas of expertise. Pleasure slaves. Novice work—all slaves. House management slaves, like maids and butlers and cooks and drivers. Bodyguards. Fancy slaves for entertainment purposes only, like the dogs and ponies.

But architects? Marketing professionals? Pilots? Personal trainers, yes, but coaches too? Tutors in everything from childhood education to different languages — why hadn't he thought that people might buy one of Corinne's multi-lingual slaves not as a translator, but as a language tutor? "For," the Frenchwoman said with a twinkle in her eye, "it is well known that we learn much of our conversational skills in the bedchamber — we might as well have a tutor to entertain us as well as engage our minds."

Mechanics and engineers. Computer language and programming experts, and repair people. Professionals in competitive sports, like wrestling, body-building, and horse racing. Even soccer and baseball players! Writers, photographers and film makers to create for one owner alone, or for the enjoyment of their family and friends.

Slaves as investment counselors and money managers — men of business who would never complain about spending too much time on the road, or enduring the inconveniences of accompanying a powerful person without ever gaining a rise in rank. Secretaries and personal assistants, yeah, that was easy. But a slave chief financial officer?

"Just what today's modern executive needs — a loyal employee who can be counted on not to stab him in the back," assured the gray haired, square-jawed man who handed out business cards to everyone who paused by him.

Even the pleasure slaves were divided into categories. Certain slaves were trained to be suitable for general use — accepting and eager for both men and woman, for conventional as well as fairly kinky sex. But there were pleasure slaves trained for specific uses and specific people — the kind of slave an owner would keep to themselves and never offer to friends. Professional companions who could be counted on to exactly judge mood and intent at all times, molding themselves to one person — or perhaps a couple — so perfectly that it might seem that they were born for such a position. Slaves trained to top, either for their owner's private pleasure, or for owners who enjoyed watching SM acts performed for them. Slaves who were better at enduring pain — slaves who were sexually insatiable — slaves who were trained to struggle and resist — experienced role players who became their owners fantasies' — it just went on and on!

"It's too much," Michael laughed. To his pleasure, his new pal Kim had come to the same room, her own pad ready for pages of notes.

"Yes — why can't they just be all general purpose, huh?" she agreed, pushing her hair out of her eyes. "I will never remember all of this, I am dog meat."

Michael saw Chris approaching and backed away slightly. "Kim, this is my trainer, Mr. Chris Parker. Sir, this is Kim."

"Hello, Kim," Chris said with a slight bow. Kim blushed and threw herself down in a deeper one. "You're Choi Jin Yong's student, aren't you?"

"Yes, Sir," she said. Michael held back a grin; this was the first time he had actually seen Kim with someone considered her superior, and it was kind of funny. But he didn't want to embarrass her. "Peace be upon you, Sir."

"And upon you. Did you both learn much at the seminar?" He turned to join the flow of people toward the outdoor pavilions where cool drinks were being served and two slaves knelt back to back playing a gentle, intricate melody on long, somber sounding flutes.

"It was amazing," Michael said, consulting his notes. "I never even imagined some of the areas of specialty they had there. And there was this guy who had charts of how the specialty sales have been going for a hundred years!"

"That would be Japic van Beem. His research has been invaluable. You could do worse than study those charts of his — they're very revealing. What did you find so surprising?"

"Where do I start? Medical professionals?"

"That's a big specialty," Chris nodded.

"But — who would have thought that people needed private doctors these days?"

"Imagine that you are a wealthy businessman, relocated to some new territory. Through honest appraisal or xenophobia, you have decided that local medical care is unacceptable for the safety and comfort of your family, or your staff. You can either add a company budget line for such an individual, or simply purchase a slave who will be at your service and perhaps of other use to you as well. Of course, there is Greta as well, you've met her."

Michael nodded and turned to Kim to explain. "Greta is this general practice doctor who belongs to a psychiatrist. They pretty much examine half the slaves that come out of the New York area."

"Most convenient," Kim said.

"Slave doctors will also not balk at finding bruises, piercings and examples of ill use on their customers," said Chris. "But you are correct; a doctor is a very expensive piece of property, and fairly rare. Do you remember what Mr. van Beem said about the field right now?"

Michael nodded. "He said that the demand for nurses and physical therapists remains high. But he didn't go into any detail."

"So what does that one line tell you?" Chris addressed the question to the two junior trainers, and they glanced at each other in a moment of panic. Michael cleared his throat.

"That — it's a steady market for them?" he hazarded.

"You can do better than that!"

Kim chewed her lip thoughtfully. "Remains," she said softly. "Remains means — that this is a new trend? One that he thought might pass?"

"That's better," Chris nodded. "The market for nurses and other health care professionals has grown dramatically. I'm sure you can figure out why. You two have grown to adulthood taking safer sex for granted. But six, eight years ago, we were devastated by what was happening in our ranks. There isn't one of us here who hasn't lost friends, clients, customers — no one was unaffected." He folded his arms and sighed heavily. "Like the sex radicals in the soft world, we were hit early and hard. It took years for the information to spread and more years for it to be adhered to. Now, every slave and trainer gets the usual battery of tests with every medical check-up, and owners register their own results and we have entire booklets of guidelines for what is permitted under which circumstances . . .and still, the most frequent contract violation is lack of safer sex considerations." Chris shook his head.

"That's terrible!" Michael said. "Who would want to put someone's life in danger like that?"

"It's a terrible truth, Michael. It's often hard for us to face our terrible truths. Now, consider — why would a slave nurse be useful other than in health care?"

"On duty all day and night," Kim answered quickly, counting on her fingers. "Devoted to serving their master. What is the word — motivation — motivated — to serve."

Chris turned to Michael with an eyebrow raised, and Michael wished he could kick Kim neatly in the shins. He thought quickly. "A slave nurse. . . would be confidential. If you wanted to keep things quiet."

"Good!" Chris said encouragingly. "What else?"

"Well — if their contract had general duties in it as well, then you could — use them. For sex, or something."

"Yes indeed," Chris said, taking a seat under a tree. "Or something."

13 The Nurse   by Karen Taylor

"Life doesn't get better than this," Lamont sighed as he pulled his cock out of the slave's mouth. Pulling the condom off, he smiled down at the boy. "Akichan, you're getting better and better. Now hop up, hand me that towel, and freshen my drink."

"Hai, Lamont-san," Akira answered, unbending his body smoothly, handing a towel to his master. Picking up the glass next to Lamont, the young Japanese man walked to the house, leaving his master staring at the pool. He returned silently with a vodka tonic, and retired again to the house, to assist Pedro in preparing dinner.

Lamont remained at the pool, his ebony skin glistening from the sweat brought on from the harsh Southwest summer afternoon. Dropping the towel on his lounge, he dived back into the pool to cool off, before dressing for dinner. Two friends of Roberto's from the LA area were expected within the hour. Lamont remembered Eric from a shoot a few years back when they were both working the same clothing line, about the time he met Roberto. The other guy's name escaped him, but Lamont remembered how boring the talk of investments were when he and Roberto visited the couple the last time they were in LA. Their house staff, though, had not been boring.

"Are they — Marketplace people?" he had whispered to Roberto that night.

"Yes, but not everyone else at this party is," Roberto murmured back, and Lamont took the hint. Roberto warned him never to reveal the existence of the Marketplace to the uninitiated. So instead, he tried to spot who else at the party might be in the Marketplace, periodically checking with Roberto for confirmation. It had amused him for a few hours, and later that evening

Eric sent one of the young men from his house staff to their room for some personal attention.

I wonder if that boy is still there, Lamont thought idly as he pulled himself out of the pool and walked to the house. What was his name? Kevin? Carlos? Not that it mattered, Lamont smiled to himself. The slave would answer to anything if ordered to.

Lamont was dressing when Roberto returned home. Despite his wealth, which included the family's rich mining lands in Mexico, Roberto taught sociology at the local University, his specialty being Southwest indigenous peoples. Lamont was proud of his lover, proud to find Roberto's name in the various scholarly journals that came to the house, even if Lamont didn't bother to read them. He just loved smart men, and Roberto was definitely that. He even spoke several languages, employing a line of slaves over the years to keep him brushed up. Lamont remembered the icy blue eyes of the Russian slave whose body was the closest he had ever seen to a real "Tom's man." He had been in the house when Lamont first moved in with Roberto, and Lamont delighted in the man's careful English, even as he was being flogged or fucked. Akira, the latest of Roberto's language tutors, was delightful in other, quieter ways. Pedro, the elderly, pudgy cook with broad Indian features, on the other hand, apparently spoke almost no English. Lamont didn't find the mestizo attractive in the least, and left him alone except to plan dinner menus for the various parties he and Roberto would throw.

"Why don't you find a cook who's also fuckable?" Lamont asked his lover once. Roberto merely smiled.

"Pedro has been with me for a long time. His value as a cook and chauffeur are more than enough for me. Besides," Roberto added with a twinkle in his eye. "I don't want you to use up all your energy on the slaves. There *is* someone else living here too, remember."

Yes, Lamont remembered every time Roberto returned home. Graying hair bleached white by the Arizona sun, tan skin and twinkling green eyes that betrayed his Spanish ancestry and set off his white teeth, Roberto was handsome in a slightly rugged way that tugged at Lamont's urban-bred heart. Lamont met him at the bedroom door and kissed him.

"How was your day?" Lamont asked as Akira held out two shirts for his deliberation. Roberto grunted as Lamont decided upon the cantaloupe-colored button down to offset his dark skin. Akira immediately turned to Roberto to assist him with dressing, but the older man shrugged him off irritably. "Aki, leave us. Go see if Pedro needs help with anything, otherwise wait for our guests."

"Hai, Roberto-sama." With a small bow, Aki left the room. Lamont turned to Roberto in surprise.

136

"Roberto, what's the matter? I've never heard you speak like that to —
"

"I went to the doctor today," said Roberto. Lamont froze as buttoned his shirt, but kept his voice casual.

"And? What did Martha have to say?" He was met with silence. Roberto sat on the bed, putting his head in his hands.

"Roberto?" Lamont sat on the bed next to his lover. He placed a hand on Roberto's thigh, and Roberto covered it with one of his own.

"I've got it, Lamont," he answered, looking solemnly into his lover's eyes. "I'm Positive."

Suddenly, life wasn't so good anymore.

In the early 1980's, AIDS was a slowly emerging fact of life for Lamont. In the first wave of the virus, after the test had been made available, he had tested positive, but remained asymptomatic. It was almost miraculous — so many of his friends seemed to die within weeks of their diagnosis. Not that anyone other than Roberto knew, of course. In his business, if word got out, jobs disappeared. He just took care of himself, ate right and worked out regularly, and avoided fund-raisers unless the real celebrities were going to be there. Lamont barely remembered having sex without barriers — certainly every slave contract had safe sex guidelines written in, so latex was a big part of his life now, whether he was fucking Roberto or getting sucked by Akichan. Somehow, though, it had never occurred to Lamont that his lover might get ill. Roberto always seemed oblivious to all of those human things that Lamont felt daily — irritation, depression, anger, pain. Lamont wasn't prepared to think of his lover as being just another human.

It took several weeks for the shock to fade. Lamont would panic any time Roberto coughed or sneezed, he ran Pedro ragged in the kitchen coming up with hot beverages or strange concoctions involving grasses or root vegetables, and snapped at Akira if the slave was slow to respond to Lamont's constant demands for blankets (in September? Roberto would say incredulously, but Lamont nodded grimly.) Finally, Roberto stopped Lamont just as he was about to berate Aki for not anticipating the need to purchase an additional hot water bottle.

"Lamont, you're going way out of proportion on this," Roberto said firmly. "I am not sick, I don't intend to be sick, and all you're doing is making me irritated, and making the slaves too jumpy to perform properly. I demand you stop it." He wrapped his strong arms around his lover. "Lamont, you're driving all of us nuts — I'll end up in the hospital because of my nerves if you keep this up." But the attempt at a joke failed miserably as Roberto's words caused Lamont to burst into tears.

"Roberto, Roberto," he said helplessly. "I don't want you to die. Please don't die." Roberto caressed his lover tenderly. "I'll do my best," he promised, kissing Lamont's tear-streaked face.

And so for a while, the house returned to normal, Roberto teaching three classes a week, Lamont taking a short job in Albuquerque. And then, in November, Roberto got sick. Really sick. It began as a cough that refused to go away. Then the nausea. When, after the third day of vomiting up food, Roberto's fever soared above 102, Lamont refused to listen to Roberto's denials and called the doctor.

"He's burning up, and he hasn't kept anything down for ages," Lamont cried hysterically into the phone. "Martha, he's going to die!"

"He's not going to die, Lamont, now stop it" said the voice on the other side of the phone line. "Meet me at the hospital."

Pedro drove the car around as Lamont and Akira supported Roberto's weight down the stairs. "Lamont-san, you will call?" Akira pleaded in his limited English. Lamont promised he would as soon as he had any news. Were those tears he saw on the young slave's face? But there was no time to wonder. Pedro sped the car into town as Lamont held his feverish lover in the back seat. "What will I do?" he whispered to himself.

The diagnosis was pneumocystis pneumonia, treatable with a regimen of pentamadine and a combination of other drugs. As Martha had predicted, Roberto did recover, although it took several weeks and he now tired more easily. Lamont demanded that his lover cut his class schedule down to one a week, and was forced to compromise with one class and a senior independent study. Lamont taught Roberto yoga exercises, and the older man would stretch and watch his lover's dark body pump weights or climb the stair exerciser. Sometimes Lamont would drop next to Roberto on the floor, breathing heavily, and tease his lover's body into arousal, caressing Roberto's heavy uncut cock, sucking on Roberto's coffee colored nipples. Sometimes Roberto would find that Lamont's strong masculine scent aroused him enough that he would be the one to initiate an hour of gentle sex, and they would retire to the bedroom. When that happened, Pedro would prepare a quiet but celebratory meal, and Akira would prepare the master bath with special soaps and heat the towels, his timing impeccable, exiting through the hall just as the door handle from the inner door began to turn. For a few days after, the slaves would glow in the reflected light of their masters' joy.

That spring, Akira's contract was up for renewal, and Roberto scheduled a telephone call with the young man's trainer of record. Lamont was in Houston for the week on a shoot, but had already talked extensively to Roberto about his delight in the slave. "Oh, and see if you can get to know that guy

Parker better," Lamont said on the phone. "He was pretty weird. I'm not sure what it was."

It had been two years since Roberto had last seen Chris Parker, but the memory remained strong of the short, stocky trainer. They met at the Tokyo auction, where three slaves Chris had trained were on the block: a petite blond woman with elaborate tattoos, an exotically attractive Eurasian gentleman, and Akira. Their conversation that evening was strictly business, and very limited; Chris' boss was there hovering over everything, and he was one tough customer. Chris practically kow-towed every time the guy passed by, moving stiffly at times. It was unnerving.

But the next night Roberto and Lamont ran into Chris at a gay bar near the auction house, and bought him a drink. When Lamont found that his beautiful looks and easy smile did not penetrate Chris' shield of polite distance, he wandered off for easier prey. It had seemed kind of kinky and powerful, the idea that he could seduce a trainer of slaves, but there was no need to waste his time. There were plenty of lithe Japanese men who were delighted to find a handsome black American in their midst, and the short, stumpy little Marketplace professional seemed to have a chip on his shoulder along with a rather recent scar on his cheek. Roberto, however, stayed to talk. Chris was more than he seemed, and Roberto appreciated that, and gave the trainer the respect he would give another owner — or a good slave. They talked extensively about training; it seemed that Parker was on some sort of exchange program, not in Japan for long, and he expected to be going home to New York fairly soon. When Roberto gently asked about the scar, Chris told him that he was recovering from a minor accident and politely brushed off further interest. But he did show a genuine interest of his own in Roberto's family, which had employed three families of slaves in Central Mexico in a line which extended back through the Revolution to the first Spanish settlers in the New World. Roberto was only too pleased to be able to share this heritage with someone who obviously appreciated it for its romantic value. He remembered the gleam in Chris' eyes when he told him about the love and respect his family had for the fewer members of each generation of servitors who returned to their tradition proudly.

When the trainer called, Roberto picked up the phone himself. "I hope you have a single malt scotch at hand, Mr. Parker," he said. Akira was bringing him a drink as he sat in his comfortable chair by the window, feeling the warmth of the afternoon sun on his shoulders.

"You have a good memory, Señor Vasquez," answered Chris. "I do indeed, and all the relevant papers as well."

"You are not an easy man to forget," answered Roberto, who dismissed Akira with a wave of his hand, then lifted his drink slightly in a toast to the absent trainer. "I wish you could have taken me up on my invitation to visit us here; you would have enjoyed the weekend, I assure you."

"I thank you, sir, for your kind invitation. But business presses me these days," Chris said. "Perhaps some other time."

They spoke lightly about insignificant topics — the weather, the economy. And when they had both sipped from their drinks more than twice, Chris got down to business. "I have already spoken with Akira of course. He is quite happy with you, and is willing to renew his contract. He did, however, mention that your health has been in question."

Roberto nodded absently. "Yes," he said. "I have AIDS. My doctor has been very positive, but I am sick, and I expect to die soon. I'm not being dramatic, merely accepting. I have lived a good life, and I hope to die with dignity. You understand?"

"I understand," Chris responded, compassion in his voice.

"My biggest concerns, frankly, are for Pedro and Lamont," Roberto continued. "Akira is young and will be of use to Lamont over the next two years. But Pedro has been with me for, well, for all of my life, and most of his. I'm not certain how to address his contract in my will, I was hoping you could advise me. And Lamont, well . . ." his voice trailed off. Chris allowed the silence to remain until Roberto collected himself. "I don't know how to help Lamont. He is very courageous, but he does not know it. And he's very angry about my getting sick. Not that I blame him, but you can't beat this virus out of my body." He chuckled.

"I understand your dilemma, Señor Vasquez," Chris said gently. "You are not the first owner who has faced this regrettable situation. However, I do have some suggestions that might be of use to you at this point." As he began to talk, Roberto looked amused, and then intrigued. It was much later when he finally hung up and retired to his bed, thoughtful.

When Lamont returned from the Houston shoot, he was disappointed to learn that Roberto had decided not to renew Akira's contract. "Why?" he pouted. "Akira was great fun, and very useful. I liked him."

"I liked him, too, and he is getting a good recommendation from us," Roberto said. "But I've decided it's time for a change. Let's go to Amsterdam next month."

"Amsterdam!" Lamont threw his arms around Roberto. "How fabulous! "Let's find us a big old blond Scandinavian to round out the household." Roberto merely smiled.

The Amsterdam auction had little in common to the one in Tokyo, Lamont's only other experience at major Marketplace events. The Japanese auction was very businesslike, held in a towering office building, the slaves posed carefully under bright lights, over-sized television screens showing each slave up close in the adjoining room where elaborately tattooed women and men served sushi to the buyers. Here in Amsterdam, the hors d'oeuvres were excellent cheeses and a sharp white wine, more in keeping with the centuries old house that served as the auction house's headquarters. No garish, exposing TV here, but the rooms were large and interesting, filled with antiques and art.

Lamont left Roberto reading the catalogue and wandered to the viewing room. He saw a lovely pair of twins — two men, beautifully displayed and clearly the highlight of the season's offerings. There were several well presented women and men who probably served as general house staff, and Lamont spent a few minutes looking at the men. An older woman, photographs of her dressed in a business suit adorning her table, bent cheerfully as a gentleman used a paddle to spank her. Lamont wondered idly what her skills were — cooking? Bookkeeping? Law? He didn't bother to read the catalog. But just beyond her he saw a profile he wanted to investigate.

The man was gorgeous. His blond hair reached to his shoulders. Happily, he wasn't shaved, and a soft gold dusted his chest and then grew deeper as the hair developed in a line starting just below his navel and continuing down to his groin. Lamont's eyes traced the strongly developed muscles, lingering at the meaty cock and balls. He reached out a hand to caress the slave's chest, to discover if the hair was as soft as it appeared to be. Lamont's hand brushed slowly down the muscled wall of stomach, stopping just above the hairline. Touching the genitals was permitted, but was considered an assertion of serious intent to purchase. With a sigh, Lamont moved around the slave, his hand enfolding the hard buttocks, sliding between them to run down the inside of his thighs. He imagined the slave bending over for him, spreading his ass cheeks wide to take his dark cock. It was maddening, looking at this blond angel, knowing that if he was at home, the slave would do anything he wished. Where was Roberto?

Returning to the front hall, Lamont found Roberto examining a printout of statistics. "Oh, Roberto," he cried, "there is an angel in there, a fabulous, blond angel — you must come and see." Roberto smiled and shook his head.

"I'm looking at them from the other side," he smiled, indicating the table where the Marketplace records were kept. "This is what's important to me, you know that." True, Lamont thought to himself. Pedro was an excellent example of Roberto's interest in skills over looks. Roberto never seemed to notice what was important, Lamont thought crossly. But the vision of the blond man kept him pulling at his lover's arm.

"Roberto, this man, this — you've just <u>got</u> to see him," Lamont pleaded.

141

"Quick, before the viewing ends." But even as he pried his lover away from the auction books, the doors to the viewing room were closing, signaling that the bidding would begin in minutes.

Because Lamont was not technically an owner, it was considered bad taste for him to pay too much attention to the bidding. Casually, he wandered away from Roberto and back to the bar, smiling at one or two of the Marketplace owners on his way. Lamont knew the Marketplace rated his performance in Roberto's household as part of his owner potential. Roberto had explained to him the importance of keeping up his contacts and being on his best behavior at Marketplace events. Lamont was well familiar with networking in his own line of work, and the smiles came easily to his face when he met the eyes of Marketplace owners. But the other people there were more interested in the bidding than he was, and shortly he lost their attention.

At last, after his third vodka tonic, Lamont heard the change in the crowd noise and knew the business was over. He strolled over to Roberto, who was shaking hands with several other men. "Good luck, Roberto," said one, clasping his hand before turning away.

"Lamont, we have a new purchase," Roberto informed his lover happily. Lamont's eyes opened wide. "Really? Who? Which one?" he jabbered, as his lover laughed and shook his head as the doors to the slaves' display area were reopened.

"His name is Joshua, and he is an Anderson slave." Roberto was consulting the numbers as they moved through the room. Lamont looked vaguely around, frustrated that he hadn't bothered to read the slaves' books when he was looking at them earlier. "He's 30, Bachelor of Science in Nursing," Roberto continued, but Lamont was barely listening, reading the information quickly at each station to find a Joshua, stopping before a tall French maid to check whether the name was female or male. He vaguely heard Roberto's voice talking about credit hours in immunosuppression, certification in something called oncology, before the realization broke through. He turned and stared at Roberto.

"You bought a nurse!" He cried. "A nurse!" Roberto shushed him as other owners turned briefly toward them, then away politely. "You aren't that sick, Roberto, you don't need a nurse!.."

Robert shushed him, answering in a quieter tone. "Lamont, my darling, I don't need one now. But I will need one soon. Probably sooner than either of us wants to think about. Ah, here he is!" And Lamont once again found himself staring up at the blond god he had been so taken with earlier. But now the muscles lost their appeal, the blond tuft brushing across the slave's brows was no longer entrancing. As Lamont stared numbly, Roberto snapped a collar onto the slave. Immediately, the slave knelt, and presented himself to his new owners.

You may look like an angel, Lamont murmured silently, but you are really the Angel of Death.

"He is a beautiful man," Roberto said as they returned to the hotel. But Lamont was not to be placated.

"Roberto," he said tersely, "I cannot — I cannot accept that you will ever be so sick as to need a nurse in the house, no matter how handsome he is." As Roberto started to object, Lamont raised his hand. "I know I overreacted when you were sick last time, but I wasn't sure what to do then. I can do it now, Roberto. You don't need a nurse, you have me! I can take care of you." He glared at his lover, and they stayed that way for what seemed an eternity.

"Lamont," said Roberto after a moment. "You are my lover. You are my companion. Asking you to be my nurse on top of that is simply too much for anyone. Especially you."

"What?!" Lamont exploded. "What do you mean, *especially* me?"

"Lamont, face it. You're a wonderful friend, fabulous lover, great at parties, but you hate dirty work," Roberto replied firmly. "There may be a time when I need help feeding myself, or, God forbid, when I am unable to leave the bed to relieve myself. Lamont, you can't even stand the smell of cerviche, how will you handle my vomit and shit?" As he watched his lover shudder at the thought, Roberto continued more gently. "Lamont, I've just purchased someone whose job it will be to take care of all of those problems. Someone who will change my sweat-soaked bed sheets and smile when I fart." Roberto paused for a moment, his eyes far away. "Joshua will be there for the worst of it. When you need a break from it, I'll still have someone to take care of me."

"But Roberto —" Lamont protested, interrupted by a knocking at the door.

"That would be Joshua," Roberto said. "Let him in." With a groan, Lamont walked to the door. "Lamont," Roberto added. "I think you will thank me for this decision. Maybe not now. But someday."

For the next several weeks, Lamont avoided Joshua, unless he was called upon by Roberto when the two of them were together. Joshua was aware of Lamont's discomfort, and kept out of his way. It was a relief, because every time the slave would walk past him, Lamont could feel his cock twitch. He longed to touch the slave, but his desire would deteriorate to hatred, and he would dream of beating the blond man into a bloody pulp. Sometimes Lamont dreamed of fucking him first, and sometimes he would imagine driving his dark cock between bruised and marked buttocks. But mostly Lamont dreamed of Roberto gaining strength and health as Joshua slowly grew sicker and sicker, giving up his life for Roberto. It was a dream that Lamont held onto.

But that summer, Roberto began to drop weight. While there was nothing immediately pressing, both he and Lamont knew that it was a symptom of worse times to come. Lamont often found Roberto sitting in the kitchen talking quietly with Pedro in Spanish. On Sundays, Roberto would have Pedro drive him to early Mass, preferring the small dilapidated church founded nearly three centuries earlier by Spanish missionaries over the modernized cathedral in the better part of the city. Martha came to the house, and was introduced to Joshua, and they spent many hours in private, going over Roberto's medical records. Joshua was now more present in Lamont's life, as he watched the slave prepare medications and serve Roberto when the man was too tired to leave their bed.

In early autumn, Roberto decided to visit the family estates in Ocotlan, outside Guadalajara. "I want to see it again while I can still walk on my own," Roberto told Lamont.

"Do you want me to come with you?" Lamont had visited Roberto's home about seven years ago, and his memory was of unbearable humidity and an inability to communicate with anyone other than the simple phrases of Spanish he pulled from his Frommers Guide. Some of his discomfort must have shown on his face, because Roberto chuckled and kissed him.

"No, but I will take Pedro. After all, it is his home, too." Roberto smiled. "I'm sure Joshua can take care of you while I'm gone. I've told him that he is to obey you in all things during my absence."

It was after lunch on their first day alone that Lamont called Joshua to join him in the workout room.

"Present," Lamont ordered as soon as the slave appeared. Immediately, Joshua sank to his knees, keeping his legs spread and his fingers clasped behind his neck. Lamont silently moved behind the slave. He was so beautiful, Lamont admitted. He reached out to caress the slave's head, then trailed his hand down the back, admiring the light golden fuzz across the man's shoulders. Lamont returned to stand in front of the slave, and unbuttoned his pants. Reaching into his pocket, he pulled out a condom, and carefully rolled it onto his long, hard dick. "Suck this," he said, and immediately Joshua leaned forward, keeping his hands locked behind his neck, to pull Lamont into his mouth.

Lamont felt the slave's mouth close on the head of his cock, and a tongue began to rub itself across his piss slit. His eyes closed as he reached down to curl his fingers in the slave's hair, pushing his face slowly deeper, feeling his cock finally press against the back of the slave's mouth. Joshua's throat relaxed, and Lamont pressed himself even father in, until the slave's nose was brushing his jeans. Lamont pulled Joshua's face away only a little, then pulled it back toward his body. Never letting his dick leave the back of the slave's throat for more than a second, he started a fast a cruel stroke, punishing Joshua's mouth with his cock.

Joshua was good, Lamont thought in a small corner of his mind, the slave had not yet gagged nor was he gasping for breath. It irritated him. He shoved the slave's head up and down the length of his cock, smashing the man's nose against his torso. He was rewarded with the sound of gasping, and smiled a cruel smile. "Take it, slave," he growled as he began pumping hard into the slave's mouth. He pulled his cock away slightly, and made Joshua just work the head, worrying it with his lips and tongue until Lamont felt the pressure building in his balls. With a groan he pushed Joshua's face farther down on his dick, grabbing the slave's hair and using his head like a giant, warm fist, the slave unable to resist as Lamont's cock thrust deeply into the back of his throat. With a groan that started deep in his belly, Lamont shot into Joshua's mouth. He held the slave's head tight against his body, knowing that his cock would be gagging the man, and wishing that his cum was jetting down the slave's throat to fill his stomach.

That thought reminded him as to why the slave had been purchased in the first place. His warm relaxation began to heat up to anger. "You," he whispered as he pulled his cock out of Joshua's mouth. "How dare you try to placate me?" Even as he was speaking, he struck the slave across the face.

"Sir?" Joshua asked confusedly. "I was trying to please you, sir."

"Please me," Lamont sneered as he buttoned his fly. "Please me with your mouth, your body, is that what you were trying to do?" He grabbed the man by the hair and hauled him up to his feet. "You haven't, you know," he said, glaring at Joshua. "You have to try harder."

"Please, sir, tell me what you wish me to do," Joshua pleaded.

"Then follow me." Lamont moved to a corner of the room where a large chest was sitting against the wall, and opened it. Pulling out a heavy flogger, he turned back to Josh. "Face the wall," he hissed.

The first lashes hit Joshua's back before the slave had even completed the order. Lamont smiled as the slave gasped, and placed his hands firmly against the wall to prepare himself for the next blow. Lamont let his arm throw the whip forward and watched in delight as the lashes landed across Joshua's shoulders, leaving a bright pink mark that wasn't given a chance to fade before the whip landed again. Joshua gasped, and then let his breath out hard as a blow came across his ass. Lamont heard the slave emit small noises as the flogger pounded against his flesh, and smiled. The muscles in his arms sang as they did when he was pumping weights.

Methodically, he worked the slave's back and ass over with the flogger, his arm rising and falling, his biceps flexing as he prepared to land another barrage of blows across Joshua's shoulders. Almost without breaking his rhythm, he reached to the box and picked up a cat-o-nine tails. The knots left hard raspberry-looking marks on Joshua's fair flesh, and made the slave groan. Lamont sighed as he alternately flicked the whip to catch the tails against Joshua's ass, and then used his entire arm's force to drag the ugly knots harder into Joshua's back. Detachedly, Lamont felt his anger drive the rhythm and pattern of the blows as he beat the slave. Joshua was beginning to tremble from the onslaught. After a particularly vicious blow from Lamont's whip, his knees buckled, and he fell to the floor.

"Over the box, you worthless bag of shit," Lamont growled, watching in grim delight as the slave scrabbled feebly to pull his body over the chest. Pulling off his belt, Lamont smiled cruelly. "I'm not done with you yet, boy," he sneered as he wrapped the buckle around his hand.

"Please sir, please," the slave cried. "Have I done something to anger you?"

"Done?" Lamont laughed, the sound empty of any merriment. "You exist." He brought the belt down across the slave's ass. "You came into my house," the belt crashed down again. "You wait to use your real skills," Lamont's voice became hoarse with the effort of talking and beating. "You are a daily reminder of death," he panted, as his belt landed again and again. He let his anger work its way out through the belt, watching the welts grow across Joshua's ass and thighs. The noises from the slave moved from groans to howls, then to whimpers. But Joshua asked no more questions.

Finally, Lamont felt his mind calm again. He stood, and threw the belt down on the floor next to the quivering slave. "Pick this room up when you're able to move again," he spat out, and left to take a long, hot shower in the master bathroom. Later that evening, he was amused to watch the slave moving less gracefully than usual as he served Lamont dinner.

The next day, Lamont called Joshua to him again. "You are afraid of me now?" Lamont murmured, making the slave move through various positions that left his body so open and vulnerable to attack. Lamont inspected the red traces of welts on the insides of the slave's thighs, pinching one cruelly. Straightening, he struck Joshua brutally across the face. The slave flinched, but retained his position. "You belong to Roberto, but he isn't here. Your fancy-schmancy nursing degree isn't needed." Lamont sneered. "I guess that just leaves your pretty face and body, doesn't it? Not that it looks so good today," he smirked, looking at the dark bruises that had spread over Joshua's ass. "And it's only going to get worse." A shudder moved through Joshua's body. "Good, good, you realize the implications," said Lamont, and he struck Joshua's face again. "Get up against the wall again."

This time, Lamont took his time with the slave, deliberately causing as much pain as possible. First, he fastened a huge ball gag into Joshua's mouth, forcing the slave's jaws wide apart and causing his saliva to slowly drip from the corners of his mouth. Returning to the box, Lamont pulled out ugly alligator clips and pressed them on Joshua's nipples, then tugging to ensure that they bit hard into the tender flesh. He pulled a handful of smaller clips out of the box, and began to attach them to the slave's balls and cock, until they glittered with metal. He then drew a long metal chain through the clamps on the slave's balls and pulled it up to attach to the nipple clamps. Lamont watched Joshua's eyes fill with pain, and he felt his cock grow hard. He reached back to the chest to bring out one of his favorite handmade toys, a series of clothespins attached with thin cord. He methodically attached the clothespins to the tender flesh on the underside of Joshua's arms. The slave groaned through the ball gag as each clip bit into his flesh, but his discomfort only spurred Lamont on. He pulled more of the objects from the chest, and began to fasten them to the inside of Joshua's thighs. The slave was whimpering now, his eyes filling with tears.

"On your hands and knees now, slave," Lamont ordered, pulling off his shorts as he watched Joshua painfully lower himself to the floor, knowing that the clips were pulling his skin cruelly against the movement. It was delightful. He knelt behind the slave, and pulled a condom over his rock hard dick. "Ass up, slave," he barked, and Joshua struggled to comply. But Lamont didn't wait, and pulled the slave's ass closer to him admiring the lines of bruises that appeared from yesterday's treatment, and ignoring the soft cries of pain. He pressed his cock slowly into Joshua's pink ass, listening to the slave's cries become groans as he was slowly filled by Lamont's dark flesh.

"Arch your back, slave," Lamont demanded as he began to slowly pump his cock in and out. As Joshua obeyed, he cried out involuntarily — the chain attaching his nipple clamps to the clamps around his cock and balls was tight, punishing the front of his body as Lamont began to work his ass harder.

"That's right, it's supposed to hurt," Lamont said as he fucked the slave. "I want you crying by the time I'm done with you today. Arch!" Lamont felt his cock twitch in Joshua's ass canal as the slave obeyed the painful command. This was going to be good, he decided, thrusting his cock in and out of the tight hole. He felt his balls brush against the clothespins on Joshua's thighs, and the sensation drove him closer to the edge. Joshua was gasping, his words unintelligible behind the huge gag, but the pleading in his voice apparent. It was nearly enough for Lamont. When he felt his body burst over the top, speeding toward an orgasm, he gripped the cords on each side of Joshua's thighs and jerked hard, ripping the clothespins off the slave's flesh in an instant. Joshua screamed as Lamont came, his battered body shaking under Lamont's thrusts. As if in a dream, Lamont found himself slowly reaching forward and grabbing the cords dangling from each arm of the body below him, and pulled once again. The clothespins snapped off like gunshots, and Joshua howled. Lamont pumped his ass a few more times as the slave cried from the pain.

The treatment continued for two more days. Lamont would wake, and watch the trembling, bruised slave serve him a late breakfast. Then he would call the slave to the workout room, devising other tortures to release his anger and frustration. He beat Joshua's cock and balls until the slave sobbed uncontrollably. He tied Joshua to a chair and covered his face with a swim cap, watching the slave's features appear in sharp relief against the latex in a struggle to breathe. He beat new welts over the bruises left on the first day, and poured hot wax across the marks. And with each session, Lamont felt his anger wash through him, its intensity slowly abating with each stroke of the belt, with each cry of pain from Joshua.

On the fifth day, there was a phone call from Pedro.

"Joshua!" Lamont shouted after he hung up the phone. The slave appeared immediately, despite his limping from the caning he had received on the soles of his feet only hours before. "Joshua, it's Roberto. He's . . . he's coming home today." Lamont touched the slave tentatively, then burst into tears. "He's sick. Pedro says he collapsed, he has a fever," he choked. "He's unconscious," Lamont wailed. He looked at a slave helplessly. "What do we do?"

The next week was a whirlwind of activity at the house. A hospital style bed appeared with a load of equipment that Lamont couldn't identify, and Roberto's life signs became monitored by a series of machines, aided by plastic bottles attached to IV tubes dripping clear liquid in a steady rhythm into his veins. Joshua spent entire days at Roberto's side, relieved for a few hours each morning by Pedro, who sat next to his master with a rosary laced through his fingers as he murmured quietly in Spanish. Lamont hovered like a maddened hornet, demanding to know everything that was happening, his presence so disruptive that Joshua physically removed him from the room during a visit from Martha. When she came into the living room after an hour, she found Lamont fuming.

148

"Who the hell does he think he is?" He burst out. "I'm Roberto's lover, for god's sake. How dare he remove me?"

"Lamont, Lamont," Martha said. "We needed to examine Roberto. You know how he values his privacy in medical matters."

"How is he, Martha?" Lamont asked. "No one tells me anything, and he — he doesn't really ever seem to wake up anymore. Martha, I —" his voice broke. The doctor sighed, and put Lamont's hand in hers.

"He's not in pain," she said. "I promise we'll keep him comfortable. You're lucky you have Joshua here — he can do anything I can, I promise."

Later that evening, Joshua knocked quietly on Lamont's door. "Yeah, come in," Lamont snarled from his bed. The slave entered and knelt next to the bed, remaining silent. He was naked, as Lamont had mostly kept him when they were alone in the house. Lamont looked down at the slave. "Well?" he asked impatiently.

"Sir, I apologize for my abrupt behavior this afternoon," Joshua began. His beautiful blue eyes stared pleadingly into Lamont's. "I felt it was necessary at the time, however it is inappropriate to treat you in such a way, and I will accept any punishment you wish."

Lamont felt another wave of anger wash over him. Abruptly, he reached down and grabbed Joshua by the hair, hauling the slave up on the bed. He briefly glanced at the still noticeable bruises on the slave's shoulders and ass as the man landed next to him.

"Answer me truthfully, Joshua," Lamont demanded, his hands tightening in the slave's hair. The slave didn't flinch. "Was it absolutely necessary to make me leave the room this afternoon?"

"Sir, in my best medical opinion, it was." After a moment, Lamont released Joshua.

"Does Roberto know that I — what I've been doing to you these past few days?"

"Sir, Master Roberto has not made any mention of my physical condition," Joshua answered. "To be honest, sir, I don't believe Master Roberto has noticed anything since he returned."

"Joshua, I haven't finished with you."

"I understand, sir."

"But I want you to make Roberto your first priority."

"Of course, sir."

"How — how is he?"

"Sir, Master Roberto is resting as comfortably as possible."

"No, don't give me that shit. How _is_ he? Don't pretty it up for me." Lamont backhanded the slave with a blow that thrust him off the bed. He watched Joshua gather himself into a kneeling position on the floor. "Well?"

149

"Sir, I'm terribly sorry. He may not live through the weekend."

With a moan, Lamont turned away from the slave and pulled a pillow across his chest, clutching it to him. He rocked silently, tears streaming down his face. "I knew it," he choked. "I knew he'd leave me, even after he promised. Oh god, what will I do?" He buried his face in the pillow.

"Sir, I must return to Master Roberto," Joshua whispered. Lamont nodded, letting Joshua leave the room without further comment.

It was Saturday when Roberto passed away. Martha worked silently to remove the tubes and needles from Roberto's body, tears streaming down her cheeks. Pedro was also weeping, pulling a rosary through his fingers until Joshua led him gently from the room, leaving Lamont alone with his lover. It was nearly two hours later when Lamont emerged from the room, his eyes red but no longer crying.

Still, it was Joshua who took charge. For the next several days, he assisted Lamont with funeral arrangements, gave Pedro assignments regarding guest accommodations and menus. Lamont was thankful for the slave's competence, and decided to give himself the time he needed to recover.

Several weeks later, seated at Roberto's desk, Lamont called Pedro to the library. Lamont looked at the slave as if for the first time. Pedro was still slightly overweight, but his hair seemed grayer, his body bowed more than Lamont remembered. But then, Lamont reminded himself, he rarely ever truly paid attention to Pedro, ignoring him except to order special meals or to get some special arrangements for the table. But today Pedro seemed very calm, his chiseled features at peace, his movements not betraying the age Lamont suspected him to be. It was strange to realize that he had never before thought of this man as attractive.

"Sit down, Pedro," he said, waving the slave to a chair. "I wanted to let you know of Roberto's personal wishes regarding your contract here, and allow you to make some choices." The slave remained inscrutably silent. Lamont noticed that he still had the rosary wrapped through his fingers.

"Pedro, Roberto told me you were his slave since you were both very young," Lamont began. "His will gives you the option to be freed, with appropriate financial compensation for your lifetime of service, or to return to the Ocotlan estates.

"You also have the option to remain with me, but I would like to encourage you to take one of the other options," Lamont continued. "To be honest, Pedro, you were always Roberto's, not mine. It doesn't feel right to me to have you stay."

150

"Gracias, señor," Pedro replied. "Si me lo das, solamente quiero un favor en esta vida. Si usted y Dios lo vendigan, en mi corazon quisiera ir a Ocotlan."

"Ocotlan it is," said Lamont. "I'll make arrangements with Roberto's family to get you home." Pedro rose from his chair when Lamont stood. For the first and last time, the two men embraced each other. As Pedro left, Lamont asked him to send Joshua to the room. Within moments, the blond slave was in the doorway.

"Joshua, come in and sit down." The slave did as he was told, sitting across from Lamont as the black man pulled a piece of paper from the pile next to him.

"Joshua, this is your contract," Lamont said. "According to this, in the event of Roberto's death, you belong entirely to me for the remainder of your contract."

"Yes, sir."

"Because you're my first Marketplace slave, I'm required to meet with a Marketplace representative within six weeks following Roberto's death to ascertain that I am treating you properly. Anderson is not available, she is sending Parker as her representative. He's arriving tomorrow."

"Yes, sir."

Lamont began to pace the room. "Joshua, I don't dare put this contract at risk. I'm too new to the Marketplace to have this go wrong — I may never own another slave if I fuck up on you. And frankly, well, I don't want you here. You're good at your duties, don't get me wrong. I just — I can't bear to have you here. Not with Roberto gone.

"I'm not stupid," Lamont continued, looking everywhere but at Joshua. "I know you weren't responsible for this horrible, despicable disease. But having you in the house with Roberto sick — Joshua, your health was a constant reminder of my lover's illness. I, I couldn't bear seeing you so healthy when he was dying."

Joshua leaned forward, speaking carefully. "Sir, your anger was an expected reaction to your lover's illness, and I welcomed the opportunity to serve you."

Lamont ignored the slave. "If I try to get rid of you so fast, that damn Parker is going to wonder why," Lamont muttered. "But if you stay, I'll probably end up killing you unless I get too sick. Hah," Lamont laughed despairingly. "What irony to have the angel of death at my bedside as well. What possible choices does this leave me with?" He stared accusingly at Joshua.

"Sir, perhaps Mr. Parker will have some suggestions," the slave offered hesitantly.

"Parker?" Lamont exclaimed. "What the hell would he know about it? What I need to do is, is —" he stopped suddenly, and fell into his chair again, and put his head into his hands. "I need to talk to Roberto," he whispered. "Roberto always knows what to do." His body began to shake. "Oh, Roberto, Roberto," Lamont moaned, "I need you. I can't do this myself." His voice began to choke. "Please, please help me." Silently, in response, the slave moved to the side of his new master.

14 Honorable Opponents

"The next speaker is Mr. Geoffrey Negel, from California, America," said William Longet, the Swiss parliamentarian who ran all the formal meetings. "Please consider time limits. Rebutting statements may be made after the speaker is finished. Mr. Negel, you have the floor."

"Thank you, Mr. Longet." Geoff rose to address his peers. He was dressed in a lightweight ivory colored suit, with a shirt the color of a clear afternoon sky open at his throat. The folds of the clothing fell handsomely on him, and when he gestured, his heavy gold watch glittered under the harsh florescent lighting.

"Fellow trainers and spotters, thank you for your attention today. And thank you for your participation in Academy politics. It may be beneath some of our membership to actually engage in what creates this world we live in, but everyone here knows how important it is to have a participatory system of organization. You are all to be congratulated on your attention to what our hosts would call *giri*, or duty." He directed a neat bow to Noguchi Shigeo, who gently nodded back.

"Participation is what I want to address today," Geoff continued. "I am against this proposal. I don't think anyone here could deny that the scope of what we do could not be managed without the cooperation of a massive number of people. We're no longer a British-European organization with offices in four countries. In fact, with the first international sale scheduled in St. Petersburg since 1904," — this was slightly interrupted by cheers from the small knot of trainers from various cities in the former Soviet Union — "we are now in more nations, trading our treasured clients across more borders than ever before. We are a truly cosmopolitan organization, withstanding wars, national divisions, political uprisings and downfalls, even the winds of cultural change. There is a need for us, my friends, a deep, abiding human need, and it is truly miraculous that we have persevered to come together here in this beautiful corner of the world to teach and learn together."

"Is he ever going to come to some sort of point?" growled Walther, fiddling with a silver pen.

Chris Parker nodded. "This is called 'softening them up." he murmured.

"Ah. Perhaps he hopes to lull us to sleep, and call for the vote?" The big German leaned back in his seat, folded his arms comfortably and let his head dip down, insultingly plain to anyone in his line of sight. That included Michael, who was standing along a side wall with an assortment of other junior trainers and a few slaves. He was amazed at how much his stomach fluttered when Geoff rose to speak. How handsome the Californian looked, how self assured and pleased with himself! It hurt to look at him.

"It almost seems impossible for us to have lasted as long as we have," Geoff was saying. "After all, look at how much could divide us — religion, skin color, gender, political beliefs, national and regional alliances, philosophies — all the things which have sent us to war against each other over the years. Yet ultimately, we have refused to let this happen — through years when the entire globe was torn apart in strife, still the network of independent trainers met and spoke and taught and learned from each other."

"That is a lie," Walther said, without opening his eyes. "There are eighteen nations right now that we do not do business with, and there are many trainers not with us today because they are — constrained within their own homelands!"

"Then correct him when he is through," Ninon suggested, her voice a light whisper.

"I will," he muttered.

"So when you look at our history, I think you will join me in being a little surprised at the dissension that has arisen over something as ultimately petty as training styles." Geoff gazed across the room, sweeping his body to cover everyone. If he noticed Walther noticeably dozing, he didn't react to it.

"Yes — that is what this resolution boils down to. Different training styles. And frankly, my fellow trainers, different training styles is what I come to the Academy to learn!"

There was some scattered laughter, and a few multi-lingual words of encouragement. Geoff smiled briefly.

"At one time, there was a need for a certain unity in style. After all, we had to invent a structure for voluntary slavery in a world that still traded human beings like animals. We redefined it, helped people to achieve an identity that was safe and controlled. We needed uniform standards so that we could be assured that no one entered our clientele unwillingly — that

154

there were ways to remove clients from abusive situations — that our owners could be monitored and judged suitable. And fellow trainers, we have those systems in place! Look at how well we manage our insular little world here; and we do it without subscribing to any code but the same basic, ethical guidelines laid down for us by our forebears.

"In the old days of the Marketplace, we needed rigid codes of behavior and styles of training because we were a small group united by a belief in a way of life we knew would not be acceptable to the larger world. Of course there were initiations, ranks, status struggles, old houses versus new houses, there might have been secret handshakes as far as I know." He grinned and demonstrated, waving one hand around and wiggling his fingers. More trainers smiled, a few laughed, but several began to sit up with wariness evident in their eyes.

"But let's face the facts, my friends — our older ways were tribal ways. Honorable ways, with success in their wake, but no longer suitable for a large, international venture such as ours. I am not saying that they are wrong; I want to be really clear about that! If that's what works for you, that's great. There are many of you here whose words I've studied for years, whose work I respect with all my heart. You find your students and clients and you teach them your way, and we can see the results on the auction blocks, as it should be. But there is no one way that will serve us all, just as there isn't one slave who can serve any owner.

"This is a wondrous world we now live in. Clients find their ways to us by methods we never imagined. Underground clubs gave way to newspapers and magazines — people found ways to connect over the phone, for crying out loud, and now, who knows where this Internet revolution might take us? There are now hundreds of established organizations that teach people safe ways to experience a form of slavery —"

"Soft world clubs, you mean?" came a sharp voice, one of the three Australian trainers.

Geoff swiveled quickly and stabbed a finger out, "Yes! And let me say that I don't like that term much. Soft world, indeed. We marginalize people that way, we hold them up for ridicule. And yet where do we go to hunt?"

"The army for one," snapped Walther, sitting up.

"Mr. Kurgen, I'm glad you brought that up — because in fact, we are getting fewer clients from the armed services these days — and do you know why? Because they are reading these books and magazines and going to these clubs and finding that they don't have to be taught to kill and submit blindly to governmental authority in order to serve!"

"Now, see here," Walther started to say. But Longet stopped him with a rap on the table. "Mr. Kurgen, please wait to be recognized during the rebuttal."

"I'll kick his rebuttal all over Japan," Walther muttered. When he saw Chris choking back a laugh, he grinned. "It is good to pun in English," the German said with satisfaction.

"With more clients coming to us with some experience — not the best experience, to be sure, but some knowledge of the language to describe their desires, we need to be adaptive, to grow and change, so that we can welcome them. A strict, restrictive style of training might not be able to be so open to cultural changes —"

"Fads, you mean!"

Geoff smiled sadly. "Fads go away in time. What I'm talking about is a sea change, a gradual shift in paradigms from which there is no turning back. We can't afford to limit our scope any more than it already is, and I'm afraid, my friends, that this proposal, so innocent at first glance, so noble and high-reaching, is in reality a way to try to keep us focused upon our tribal past instead of charging forward into our shared future.

"I have other points to make, but I see that my initial statement time is up. I welcome your comments." He sat down after a slight bow to the audience and to Mr. Longet, who immediately pointed at Walther.

"I don't know about *tribal* things," the German man said, rising. He scanned the room, a look of contempt on his chiseled features. "I am not from the wild west of America! And even if I were, I would be riding my great black stallion, Rih, being a cowboy, instead of wearing feathers and hunting the buffalo, eh?" He laughed, joined with most of the room.

"But I do know this; the future is only worth advancing to when one knows and teaches the traditions of the past. Honors them, yes, and not just as — as — icons, as stories to tell to inspire us." He wheeled around and gestured to himself, "I was trained by Karl Wein! And he trained with Jurgen and Marta Perlman, and they were trained — well, you all know who they were trained by! Or," he said, with a meaningful pause, "you should know."

"The reason I name them is because I would not be here without their mastery. The methods they used and the way they instructed are in me like bone and blood. And they are effective! We have generations of proof as to their effectiveness, their efficiency. I think my respected American friend says he does not mean to insult when he suggests that we are out-dated, but in fact he wishes we would all go away and leave him and his wild Indians to take over!"

"Now, wait a minute," Geoff said, rising.

"No, no, you must wait now, it is my turn to speak!" yelled Walther.

"Gentlemen, please," called out Mr. Longet. "Mr. Negel, you are not recognized. Herr Kurgen, you may continue."

156

The German smiled in satisfaction as Geoff sat again. "In addition, I wish to say that we do have a tradition of barring trade when we must. Right now, we do not trade within the nations which will not honor visas and allow for the immigration of clients — and we must not forget that the Perlmans left their homeland not only because of personal danger, but so that they could aid in removing their clients and students from the…the nightmare. Every few years, we must examine ourselves and the world to determine where and when we are safe, and how we may continue to operate; this proposal, which I support, is but one way to assure us of continuity." He looked at William Longet and nodded firmly. "I have finished speaking now."

"We recognize the author of the proposal."

"Thank you, Mssr. Longet." Chris rose and bowed once to the parliamentarian and once to Noguchi. "Honored trainers and spotters, please allow me to remind you all, once again, that this proposal does not contain any language suggesting that there should be one approved training method. I would be the last one to suggest that; I have benefited from learning several radically different styles and have in fact developed my own, which many of you have examined.

"'Proposed: That the International Coalition of Trainers and Handlers create a standing committee of Standards of Training, including a certification process for accrediting new Trainers.' A committee, my fellow trainers, not a single entity with one vision. A process; not a rule by fiat. And new trainers; not previously established ones. No one here would or should fear that their own styles, as long as they continued to be effective, would be disenfranchised."

"And what does that mean, continue to be effective, eh?" Ken Mandarin asked.

"Exactly what it means to us now, Ms. Mandarin," Chris replied. "We are all in service to three things — our consciences, our clients, and our customers." There were agreeable nods to that summary, and he continued. "If we find that we are betraying ourselves in what we do, we will fail. If we don't produce effective, pleasing and content clients, we fail. And if there are no customers for those clients we train — then we have not only failed ourselves, but our clients as well. These things keep us honest, regardless of which styles we use."

"Then why bother with this controlling committee?" Ken asked with a dismissive wave of one hand.

"For the same reasons that Mr. Negel used as arguments why we do not need it," Chris said with a slight smile. "Yes, we are a large organization, and we can no longer all meet annually, trainers and spotters and slaves and owners. We have divided into our worlds, and even within the divisions, we cannot all know each other. But if all new trainers were presented for examination and certification — then at least we know that someone other than their direct line teacher or master has attested to their fitness.

"We already encourage that clients be examined by two or more trainers before being presented for sale. What greater care should we take, then, when we establish a new trainer, who could touch the lives of perhaps hundreds of clients?

"I am also encouraged by the growth of the Marketplace in the modern age. But I know you will agree that by our nature, we are exclusive. One of the ways we maintain our organization to the level of efficiency and confidentiality is by continually enforcing behavioral standards among ourselves. This commission, this process I propose will only serve to formalize what is already in place informally. We must keep our older values alive while we grow, or else all our growth will only lead to dissolution. To greater dissatisfaction among our clients and customers. To more exposure to the uninitiated outside world. To a greater emphasis paid to fads and fancies than to building the foundations for future generations of our people." He sighed and unwrapped his fist from the paper he had been crushing without noticing, taking in the eyes of friends and foes. "Thank you for your kind attention." He sat down, feeling suddenly nervous, even though Ninon leaned over to pat his thigh and Walther grunted in agreement.

No wonder the feeling of dread — the next recognized speaker was Howard Ward, the chief speaker for the group from Great Britain. Chris felt his mouth go dry as he forced himself into a polite and relaxed position of attendance, and found that Dalton was doing the same thing. As Mr. Ward began by announcing his opposition to the proposal, they both nodded and looked as though this was of no more interest than the luncheon menu.

But the session just got worse from there.

"I understand the reasons behind your proposal perfectly, Parker," said Fiona "Fi" Larabey, the only trainer currently working in Perth. She was a short and stocky woman with tanned and weathered skin and a shock of almost bleached hair that fell in staggering waves down her back. She reminded him of Jack, the stableman at Alex and Grendel's house on Long Island. Maybe it had to do with the way she tossed her hair back and looked you right in the eye. Like most of the Australians he had met, these were two people who enjoyed the trappings of authority without really showing respect for them. They'd work at something until it came out perfectly, but wouldn't call you "Sir" unless they bloody well felt like it. They had an enduring belief that if you could handle something well, you should be left alone to do it, without interference.

"And honestly, I think some of the boys in there got a little out of hand with the name callin' and such, and that's a damn bloody shame, an' I apologize for how nasty it got at the end. There's no need for that kind of talk! But even if I disagree with the shouting an' cursing, I still can't see votin' for your plan there. It's just that I chafe under harness, you know?" she said. "Don't like the idea of a governing committee sitting in judgment over me."

Chris sighed again; so many of the objectors turned the proposal into something personal, as though he had been thinking of them individually when he labored over the wording. At this point, he was almost ready to start asking them not to flatter themselves.

"All I can ask of you is that you examine it again," he said. "I think you will find that it is far more open to diversity than some of the more vehement opponents might believe."

"I'll give it another go, then," she said kindly.

"Thank you," he murmured. And realized that in their walk, they had come to the junction between the wings, and the crowd had thickened as people went to their choice of dining areas for a light lunch. Tonight's banquet would by tradition be sponsored by their hosts, but there was still a long afternoon to endure. One more debate session to go, and then another round of seminars, during which he had to present his paper.

Funny how unimportant that little thesis had become. He glanced at the options before him for food, and decided to stay in the western wing. There would be Japanese food in plenty later on. As he turned into the main dining hall though, he found that not only was Geoff Negel holding court in the center of the room with most of his supporters arrayed around him, but Michael was there as well, apparently listening.

A slave came up to him immediately and he felt the way her eyes scanned his body language followed by the unhesitating way she held one hand out to indicate an empty seat to Negel's back. Chris admired the way it was done, very neat, very discreet. But he shook his head, and without a second of hesitation, she guided him to an empty seat at the table to Geoff's right. He was barely seated when a cup of coffee appeared, and finally, Michael noticed him.

Poor Michael, how awkward for him.

"Sorry, sir, I lost track of you in the halls," the younger man said, as he hurried over to lean down next to Chris' chair. "Um — I just came in here for a bite—"

Chris turned to nod at the offered tray a slave was displaying, and allowed himself to be served a green salad but declined the curried prawns. "That will be all," he said, and then turned back to Michael.

"You are here to learn," he said softly. "Learn."

"Hello, Mr. Parker," Geoff called from the next table. Chris nodded to him. "It was a pleasure to debate with you again today; you're an excellent speaker, and you made some pretty compelling arguments." He smiled warmly, the kind of smile that made other people feel ungracious for not returning one just like it. Chris nodded again, a little more slowly.

"Thank you, Mr. Negel. Then I can count on your support during the voting?"

"Funny, too," Geoff said quickly. "You know, Parker, you should come out to California one day. Actually see what it's like in my corner of the world."

"I've been," Chris said, drinking his coffee.

"Well, you haven't been to my place," Geoff laughed. "You might consider coming; I would be honored to arrange a special training seminar and introduce you around. I think someone has given you a bad impression of who we are and what we do on the West Coast, and I'd give anything to correct it."

Michael almost laughed out loud at the thought of the oh-so-formal Chris Parker at Geoff Negel's free-and-easy training center, where dressing for dinner meant putting pants on over your bathing suit, where there were often more guests entertained than slaves trained, and everyone called each other by their first name.

"I try not to be a generalist," Chris said. "And although I am concerned about things like Marketplace personnel having too close ties to the — non-Marketplace kinky population — and I am puzzled by the rise in family style relationships which incorporate our clients with non-clients in the same setting and blur the hierarchical differences, I don't believe that the entire state of California is either responsible for these trends or filled entirely with people enacting them."

Paul Sheridan, the spotter, laughed out loud. "Damn if they aren't though," he said genially. "You should see what I saw last year at Folsom." He shuddered. "There's some scary shit coming from that side of the country, that's for sure."

Geoff's smile faded a little, to one that was more tolerant than warm, and he shook his head sadly. "Gentlemen, gentlemen. Really now. We're still *people* in California, you know. With all the glorious variety that I'm sure you can find in every region in the world. But the fact remains that we, on the west coast of the United States, lead the way in the spread and acknowledgment of alternative sexualities." One of the Asian men at Geoff's table huddled with a translator, and Geoff paused until the man nodded in understanding.

"We are the center of the radical sex movements — from the leather lesbians in Seattle to the large fetish parties in San Diego. And do I even have to mention San Francisco, the gay mecca of the United States? Of course we're experimental — we're pioneers. Forward thinkers. We find new ways to relate every day, and others come and learn them from us. Sure, there's always some resistance, there always is to new ideas. But you'll find that sooner or later, our ways seep into the lives and fantasies of the SMers across the country and around the world. Even to people in the Marketplace."

15 The California Way   by M. Christian

Turbulence over the Rockies had made her stomach into a gastrointesti-
nal cauldron of potentially explosive embarrassment. The sudden drops, fists
clenched tight enough to give her palms the commas of her fingernails, and
equally spontaneous climbs had also pitched the fat, greasy salesman for Hunter
Farm Equipment's ("Finest Backhoes in Oskwa County, girlie") whiskey sour
onto the arm of her best — and only — blue suit. The harsh smell was a nail
rammed into her sinuses, turning up the heat under her stomach.

She didn't sleep and the movie was one she'd already seen. She ended up
faking it, trying to relax in the torturous seat for the rest of the trip — shutting her eyes to short-circuit the predatory small-talk and puffery from "the
best damned salesman in Southeastern Louisiana —"

Slaves aren't supposed to be grouchy. Nonetheless, Doris was red-eyed,
bone-tired, sharp and testy when she finally retrieved her one small bag from
the chaos of the carousel and went out into a crisp September morning.

All that and she was back in San Francisco. Home was the last place she
wanted to be.

When Max Bloom, her Trainer, had told her to sever her ties with the
outside, to sit and methodically dial one number after another, cutting away
job, friends, apartment, job . . . and family . . . it had been easy to imagine that
she was casting them off forever, call after call: closing doors so she could
walk into the life she'd always wanted.

One call had been to Richmond. Luckily she'd gotten her father's answering machine. The message had been short, a quick flick of a verbal knife:
"Good-bye. I'm leaving and I won't be back."

But there she was, waiting as patiently as she could, struggling to fit
herself into the carefully created persona of a Slave ... but all the time feeling
the ghosts of San Francisco waiting around every corner. Doris waited: Slave

Doris for her new Master, Little Doris — who'd run away from home — for pain to start again.

Even the mystery of her new life wasn't enough to exorcise the ghosts. She still felt like she was waiting for Betsy to show up, to take her by the hand and drag her off into another adventure: The Chinese New Year Parade, the Cherry Blossom Festival, the Bay to Breakers, lunch in the Japanese Tea Garden, spaghetti in North Beach, closing clubs in SOMA — anything to distract, to keep from thinking of having to eventually go back to Richmond.

Waiting in the cool concrete shadow of the airport, she took a nervous deep breath, trying to find the Slave that, just a few days before, had been bought — sold into a blissful life as sensual property. She tried to capture her life before the auction, to hang onto her erotic dream of a life — the smell of Max's aftershave; the cool feel of his brass foot board she'd slept against; the curve of his long, hard cock entering her mouth, her cunt. The memories helped, putting her back into the Doris who'd been on the auction block, was *property*, a desired Slave, and not the Doris who'd run away to San Francisco every chance she'd got.

Slowly, the weight of the city and her sour memories lifted from her — that and breathing crisp, natural, air. Her stomach settled a bit and her sour attitude changed to that of simple annoyance mixed with a sharp spike of anxiety: I wonder what he'll be like —

Max Bloom, watching her pack, had given her a few hints about her life to come — but, by far, few too many. She knew that her life as a Slave rarely had to do with her direct wishes — the whole reason, in fact, why she'd become one — but, still, to fly clear across the country to walk, basically blindfolded about everything that her life would be was a little ... well, she was irritated enough with the flight and coming back to San Francisco.

"Yes," Bloom admitted as he'd supervised her packing (or at least the amount of objects he'd allow her to take with her), "it is rather unusual. But then you *are* going to California.

"Let me put it this way," he'd continued, "I've heard there's some very unusual arrangements that get made for Slaves on the West Coast. It wouldn't surprise me in the least if you are going to find yourself in one of them."

The memory of the auction haunted her through her packing, her trip to the airport, the flight. Her nervousness had been almost physiological — no matter how hard she tried she couldn't calm her body: her memories of the auction vibrated with excitement and fear. The hall had been a flurry of Masters and Mistresses claiming their purchases — some trying them out with an echoing chorus of trial punishments — but not for Doris. She had stood and waited for what seemed like an eternity till a round little Japanese man in an immaculate black silk suit, all bottle-bottom glasses and little bowler hat, presented her with a small card and a thick envelope and left, without giving her a chance to even blink.

In the envelope is a plane ticket to San Francisco, the note had said in hard courier type (an affectation she'd realized as the card was computer-printed). *Leave immediately. You will be met.*

So there she was, better — not so miserable — but, still, not completely comfortable at being whisked back to the city of her childhood, her painful adolescence.

At least, she mused, waiting, she was coming back as the Slave she always wanted to be.

"You the new slut?"

At first Doris didn't hear him — the cold echoes of the terminal drowned out his deep voice. That, and the source being so unexpected: If she had to pick anyone out of the tourists, businessmen, the casual travelers it would not have been him.

Tall, almost disturbingly so. He was thin, almost touching on emaciated — he stared at her from behind mirrored sunglasses, a wickedly lascivious grin breaking across the lower half of his face. A brilliant rooster-crest of a Mohawk leapt from the top of his otherwise brilliantly smoothed and polished head. A spill of silver earrings caught even the crappy fluorescent lights of the terminal and brilliantly flashed.

He wore threadbare denim cut-offs and a stained white T-shirt that might have said something, one time or another, but was now just a pale pink blob of illegibility.

"Hey," then he whistled, painfully shrill in the closed concrete overhangs, "*you.* I said, 'Are you the new slut?'"

Doris passionately resisted pointing to her chest with a stupid *Who, me?* gesture. Instead she dipped her eyes and folded her hands over her blue-suited stomach. "I'm from the Marketplace," she said, not wanting to use "sir" in case he was just the punk he seemed, and hoping that dropping it wouldn't get her in bad graces — if he was, indeed, her new Master.

"Cool. I'm Spunk," he said, tossing her a small black helmet. "Get on."

She caught it, clumsily, almost dropping it onto the hard concrete. "I don't know what you —" she started to say as 'Spunk' (her new Master?) stepped aside, showing her a gleaming chrome motorcycle. Doris didn't know that much about cycles but she knew enough to hold her breath in reverent awe of its elegant power, its erotic, throbbing, majesty.

"Excuse me," she said, trying assertive timidity, as she walked towards him, "but I really don't know what's going on."

"Sure you do, slut — sure you do!" Spunk walked up to her, meeting her halfway, and towering over her. "Marketplace, right? You're what's commonly called a 'slave', right? Well, see my Pa is the one that just bought you, which means that you belong to Pa and if you belong to Pa you also belong to me."

That was enough for Doris. Bloom would have been proud of her: "Yes, Sir," she said, standing straight and dipping her head down to look at his scuffed, battered combat boots. "I'm sorry, Sir; I misunderstood."

Spunk laughed, deep and short, like a shotgun blast in the echoing corridors. "At ease, slut. Yeah, you're property and all that, and, yeah, you're gonna be used like you've never been used before, but, fuck, you're still ... what the fuck's your name, anyway, slut?"

"Doris, Sir."

"Doris? Fuck, that's a slut's name if ever I heard one," he said, smiling. "Well, <u>Doris</u>, stick that thing on your head, stash your junk in the saddlebag, and let's go meet the folks."

Not in a million years —

Well, maybe in five hundred thousand —

Doris hung onto the back of Spunk's bike, all conversation, and most of her thoughts, lost to the thrumming power of the machine between her legs — all, save, for her bubbling incredulity of her situation: Spunk? Pa? Folks?

Spunk wasn't what she'd call a Masterful type. But, still, she had to admit that she had a certain powerful ... attraction to the slim punk. Agreed, a big helping of that was the fact that she had spent the better part of a half hour with her arms wrapped firmly around him, her breasts pressed against his strong back, his throbbing ... engine between her legs, thumping stronger than any vibrator ever could.

And his hand. Mustn't forget his hand.

The trip had started out with a bang — with her heart in her throat: Once she was on and seated as securely as she could, Spunk fired the bike up and tore out of the terminal — a pair of screams echoing behind his tearing sprint: One from the bike's tires on the abrasive concrete and the other from Doris.

Soon though, sooner than she would have expected, the ride floated down over Doris and her fear dropped down to a dull vibration that closely matched the rumble of the bike — that and most likely because she couldn't see forward because of Spunk's back. She could, however, look to the right or the left — but after seeing a few blurring streaks that she realized were cars being passed at their maniac speed she decided it was much better to stare at either Spunk's back or the inside of her own eyelids by closing her eyes.

The ride, thankfully, wasn't long — but it was ... interesting. About the time she'd decided that watching traffic pass by them (or, better yet, them passing traffic by) was risky to either her stomach — again — or her sanity she felt his hand push its way insistently between her left thigh and Spunk's back.

At first she thought that Spunk might be trying to tell her something, maybe to get her to stop trying to squeeze his stomach out his back, but then she realized that his hand was reaching for.

A flash of shivering fear blasted through her. Well, actually two, distinct, spasms. One was that Spunk would lose control of the bike and they'd spill —horribly — down onto the freeway. The second was almost as primordial — that she didn't know what her Master wanted, and how to please him.

Shortly, though, what he wanted became clear — and that the bike never dipped or wove even in the slightest diminished her first fear as well — as his hand reached precariously back and under her, cupping her ass.

The drumming hum of the bike, the powerful strength of Spunk; the delightful mystery of what her life was going to be like; the warm return of the sense of being property, of being a slave; all of it — of course Spunk's thumb curled up and roughly dipped into her cunt and found wetness. Of course — was there ever a question? She was a Slave, he was her Master (at least she thought so).

He stayed inside her for what seemed like ages — because you don't measure time when you're riding on a bike (especially not with a thumb in your cunt), you measure distance: Spunk's hand stayed inside her cunt for miles and miles.

She didn't expect to come —not at all. Coming, what with the fear of falling off, the oppressive doubts that ricocheted around in her dazed mind, didn't feel like a possibility.

But, still, she shivered and shook, a quaking spasm that raced up from his thumb, tapping with the echoing rumble of the bike against her G-spot — if not a true come then a damned good near one.

Just as she was about to reach down — so pleasurable was the thrill that she was about to delusionally risk her balance on the speeding bike — and position his hand and thumb better to push her completely over the edge, he pulled his hand firmly out to replace it on the clutch of the bike.

Dizzy with fear and the near-shattering come, Doris relaxed against his strong back, losing herself in the bike's throbbing vibration and the sudden tilts and swings as Spunk easily glided them off the freeway and down into the city proper.

Even though Doris had spent a big chunk of her adolescence — too big a chunk — in the city, she couldn't really tell where they were headed, and where they ended up. Her brain was addled and fried by the clenching fear of the ride and the thumping of her heart from the near orgasm for anything as delicate or right-brain as navigation.

Still, she was able to pick out certain landmarks: A cafe all glass and golden lettering, a shuttered and dark church, the grumble of LRV tracks under the bike's tires, the sudden — stomach grabbing — lurch of a severe hill ... placed her somewhere near Dolores park, maybe touching the Castro, maybe kissing Noe valley.

Then they stopped. Doris had shifted her vision, turned her head, to the right so she missed their approach — in fact, she was so rattled both from the ride and Spunk's thumb in her cunt, that she didn't realize they'd completely stopped till he heeled the kickstand down and leaned the bike onto it.

"Come on, slut — we're here," he said, smiling, as he pulled off his own helmet, then helped her extract her befuddled head from her own. Freed from its almost too-tight headlock, she shook her head — both to clear it and to free the many tangles of her long brown hair — and had the delightful sight of Spunk, smiling, as he sucked her juice off his leather-gloved hand.

Then she saw the house.

Still, seeing it, she didn't know exactly where she was. The street was like so many, too many, in San Francisco; Tall elegant homes like the sides of a filigreed canyon, a gingerbread gulch. Even simplicity seemed baroque in the ornamental chaos of the street — a window in San Francisco could never escape being just a window. Stickers, age-old political posters, and a citywide delightful kaleidoscope of gay pride rainbow flags decorated or despoiled in colorful confusion.

The house that Spunk nodded her towards was hardly simple. Yet it wasn't the fractal busyness of some of San Francisco's more outré homes. It walked a neat line without falling one way of the other. Not plain with windows colored with signs, posters and flags, and not achingly busy. It's basic form was Victorian, three floors; Three bay windows; three smaller, square ones; and one delightful oval peering out of a peaked attic. It was blue — a peaceful, just after dawn blue — trimmed with a lighter — a little later after dawn — blue. It looked well-kept and serene without the anal retentive fragility of never-touched china. People lived in this house, Doris knew, but didn't live *for* the house.

"Come on, slut," Spunk said, retrieving the helmet from Doris with a playful grab, "you gotta meet the folks."

"Yes, Sir," she said, reflexes kicking the words out of her numb mouth as her — maybe — Master walked up a short set of stairs to the little-after-dawn blue of the front door.

"Jeese, slut," he said, turning to smile and gently shake his head, as he fed a key into the lock, "knock it off, willya? Sound like a fucking Stepford slave or something —"

Then the door was open, and Spunk stepped aside, a Mohawked gentlemen bidding her to enter and — taking an unconscious breath — Doris did.

The room was surprising, enough to stop her one foot inside: If there's one thing that never seems to go with ridiculous baroque San Francisco architecture it was austere Japanese — yet that's what she was facing, in all its meditative simplicity: Shoji screens, tatami mats, elegant cabinetry, futons placed with a powerful Feng Shui precision, leafless branches polished to religious smoothness set in deep islands of oval black rocks, and even a tiny wood-framed alcove — a miniature zen garden filled with immaculately raked sand and focused with elegantly placed stones, brilliant with redirected sunlight.

"Ma! Pa! We're *HOME!*" bellowed Spunk from behind her as he closed the door and dumped their helmets discordantly on the polished hardwood floor.

"Hi, honey — we're in the kitchen. Did everything go okay?" a chiming, elegant voice said somewhere behind the Asian decorating.

"No problem, man. Found her turning tricks in the garage. Had to wait my turn —" Spunk said, smiling down at her, twinkles dancing in jewel-blue eyes after he took off his glasses. Doris was so shocked by their beauty that, for all of three seconds all she could do was stare — till he took her gently by the hand and pulled her, still shocked and more than a little frightened, through the serenity of the living room and past an open, immaculate, Shoji screen and into the kitchen.

Three heartbeats to take it all in:

Japanese outside, smooth, cool, crisp industrial inside: A set of absolutely clean windows overlooking a riotous green backyard of vines, painfully brilliant flowers, and a distant high wooden fence. Simple steel cabinets lining almost every other surface of the kitchen, surrounding a massive wooden cutting block.

Doris liked to cook, so, naturally, her eyes first danced over the equipment: Wolf, Krup, and all their expensive kin. She lingered over the brass pots and skillets, paused at the ornate and beautifully displayed jars of herbs, spices, and dried fruit and vegetables.

Doris was a slave, so next her eyes quickly saw the people there:

"Welcome," said a large man with that musical voice she'd heard. It would have been easy to call him fat, but not accurate: he was large, tall (though sitting down), broad, and his skin — what Doris could see of it — was smooth and supple, but he wasn't fat. Bald, eyebrowless, he had a playful elegance about him, a kind of divine contemplation of the universe. He wasn't as fat as the Buddha, but he was almost as serenely powerful. He was dressed in a deceptively simple black silk shirt and pants, and sat, contemplative and immobile, on a black barstool. On his feet were a pair of split-toed tabi slippers. "I'm Maurice. You can call me, 'Ma'," he said with a beautifully balanced nod of his finely sculpted head.

Then someone slapped her hard on the back, pitching her forward against the pull from her single bag she still carried. She didn't fall, but she did stumble a bit, reaching, but not needing to catch, the side of the butcher-block table.

"Ain't she a fine one, hon? Dig this ass — ain't that a divine ass? Man, can I pick 'em, or can I pick 'em?" said a thunderous voice from behind Doris. Dropping her bag, completing the motion of her near fall, she turned.

If Ma was regal elegance, then this woman was raw power, barely caged. She was tall and evenly distributed, almost as tall as Spunk who was standing behind her, with a face that was hard but not brutal: as if she'd sculpted herself, manipulated her demeanor to hang somewhere between male and female. Her breasts, for instance, were obviously large and well-shaped, but were trapped behind a firm sportsbra, under a spotless T-shirt, then behind a shiny leather vest decorated with perhaps a dozen brilliant insignia. On her head was an equally immaculate leather cap, and on her legs were polished leather chaps over a pair of artistically worn jeans. She didn't have any earrings or jewelry of any kind — but she did have a mustache: it was fine and delicate, a soft brown line that was only a shade or two away from her own butch-cropped color.

Roughly, she reached out and took Doris' hand and shook it firmly. "Put 'er there, babe. Welcome to the house of the rising ass —" She thought that was hysterical, and laughed like a longshoreman. "I'm Pauline — 'Pa' around here. Glad ta *have* ya!" Then bent down and picked Doris completely off her feet, touching her head on the ceiling, in a wild hug — laughing even more.

"I'm happy to be here ... Sir," Doris mumbled, shaken (literally). It had all been too much: The flight, her stomach, the ride, Spunk's thumb, the strange house, the even stranger ... masters? ... all of it was a jumble, a mad chaos in her mind. She wanted to scream for order, for someone to say Me: Master. You: Slave. She wanted to please, to be what she always wanted to be: Doris the prized property, Doris the cherished object.

She felt like she was on the motorcycle again, tearing through unfamiliar territory at breakneck speed — and she feared she was going to fall off at any second ....

Seeing the elaborate play of emotions across her face, the woman who wanted to be called 'Pa' smiled, and as she did her mask of roughness seemed to lift a bit, to be lifted to show a thin slice of firm reality beneath it: "You're among friends here, slut; friends and much more. We might not be the 'ideal' as far as the Marketplace is concerned, but we are all skilled Masters, good Slaves, and fine people. It might seem odd at first, but before you know it you'll know ... you're home."

Home was a bad word, it kicked her hard in the gut, making her already weak knees even weaker. It was a frightening word, the last word in a thought, a spoken phrase that meant humiliation (of the bad kind), pain (of the bad kind), and sex (of the very, very bad kind) as in "I have to go home now."

But she wasn't that Doris, the frightened Doris. She could feel her Trainer behind her, his warm, firm hand on her back, reminding her that she was Slave Doris — and that Slave Doris was very, very special.

Still ... *San Francisco ... family ....*

"Thank you ... Sir?" She put a warbling inflecting in the last word, a slight beg for clarity.

"Now, now, now — " the strong woman said, wagging a finger under Doris' nose and smiling broadly, "— it's Pa, remember? That's Ma, I'm Pa, and you know Sonny already —"

"*Spunk*," he said from the doorway with a teenager's practiced disgust and embarrassment. "It's Spunk, remember?" But it was done with a drag queen's performance, a routine of broad gestures and winks at the audience.

"Kids these days," Pa said, playfully putting Spunk in a headlock and wrinkling his Mohawk. "To me you'll always be that little snot-nose kid I picked up at the bus station."

Dazed, glazed, floating a few inches off the floor, Doris felt a firm hand on her shoulder. "Are you hungry, dear? I bet you are — what with nothing but airplane food all the way here. What would you like? I can cook just about anything," Ma said, his voice like a slowly running brook: Musical and shimmering. It was a voice, Doris realized, she could listen to for hours.

Was she hungry? It was a strange feeling, to be asked rather than told. She had expected to be asked to serve, and then serve herself. But to be asked was just as staggering as the strange environment. She thought, probably longer than she would have normally, before deciding that she actually wasn't. "I'm actually fine, Sir — I mean, 'Ma'. Thank you."

"What a precious child," Ma said, beaming with delight. "So polite ... and so sexy."

"She is at that," Pa said, hooking her thumbs into the top of her chaps. "Can I pick 'em or can I pick 'em!"

"I'll say," winked and leered Spunk, pushing past Pa and moving towards the sink. "She'll fit right in."

"You'll have lots of fun here, dear," Ma said, rising from her stool to step

170

towards Spunk. "We all get along famously." With the practice reactions of people who've lived together too long, Spunk opened a cabinet, pulled out a stainless steel container and wolfishly started eating the .. granola? ... he found there, till Ma walked over to him and calmly pulled the container out of his hands, put the lid back on, closed the cabinet, and said, "You'll spoil your dinner."

"I ... I'm sure I will, Ma," Doris said, watching them, wondering if she ever would, really.

"I know we will, kid: We're one hellava fun family. You could say that we get along ... real well." Pa might have looked like a leatherman but her — his? tone and gestures were a broad parody of a leering heterosexual male.

There was something there, something in the playful absurdity of the act that made Doris relax a bit, and smile. It was like a bit of proof that this was all a game, a kind of act that simply overlaid the game she knew too well.

As if reading her mind, Pa said: "It's real simple, kid. I'm the head of the household: The fucking breadwinner, the man of the house. Ma here is the lady of the house. She stays home and does the ironing or whatever she does all day."

"I cook, I clean, and I write mystery novels," Ma said, smiling as he hugged a widely-grinning Spunk.

"And that good-for-nothing is our sort-of son. We call him Sonny just to piss him off."

"Which they do — all the time," Spunk said, smiling.

"We might not look it but we *are* something you're used to — just all little different packaging: You'll get the hang of it."

Confused, but more at ease, Doris nodded.

"Fer instance — *get over here you worthless lay-about*," Pa said sharply to Spunk.

"So what the fuck do you want ... *dad*," Spunk said, sarcastically, disengaging himself from the tender embrace of Ma and walking over to the stern visage of Pa.

"Now didn't I tell you that you were supposed to pick up ... Doris?" The last of what he said died in a question. "Got to change that name. I'm sure we'll think of something. Weren't you supposed to just pick up *Doris* and bring her here."

"Yeah, Pa, that's what you said."

"Well, sport, if these superbly trained nostrils are right then I think you did more than just pick this poor young thing up —" Quicker than she'd seen anyone move before, Pa had Spunk's still-gloved left hand in his own and brought it sharply up in front of his nose.

Spunk, in response, hissed in delight at the sudden movement and the domination, sagging slightly to his knees.

Pa gave a long sniff of Spunk's glove. "Definitely did more than just pick her up, I'd say — isn't that right, Sport?"

In delighted submission, Spunk whined: "Yes, Pa."

"You've been a bad boy."

"Yes, Sir."

"What have you been?"

"A bad boy, Sir."

"I think we'll have to punish you, Sport. Something, I think, appropriate — right, Ma?" Pa said, dripping power and strength, pure masculine dominance.

"I think a little discipline would do wonders for his whole attitude on life," said Ma, in his musical tones.

"But not tonight. Oh, no, I want you to have to wait till later on — to really think about how you've misbehaved. Then, maybe, we'll teach you a nice, firm, lesson."

Spunk caved in even more, dropping his eyes and whimpering like a punk puppy. "I'm sorry, Pa. It won't happen again."

"What's the worst thing to do to a masochist?" Pa said, a stage-whisper in Doris' ear.

"Make them go to bed without any ... *supper*," chimed Ma in response, behind her.

"Now you, young lady —" Pa said, straightening and putting her male-echoing voice down at Doris.

"Yes, Sir? I—I, mean, 'Pa'?" Doris said, stumbling into the familiar dynamic, but with the unfamiliar terms.

"You're getting it," Ma said softly from behind her.

"I don't think Sonny was the only one completely guilty in this. Am I right?"

"Yes, Pa," Doris said, eyes downcast, focused on her polished black boots. A slave by any other name: She hoped, immediately, that one day in the future she'd be able to polish them. And she was terribly glad that Max Bloom had carefully instructed her in the ability to tell the difference between being punished because you did something wrong and being punished because Master wishes to play the game. It was delicious to play the game.

"I know you've been a very bad girl, a real slutty girl. I do believe, Ma, that we're going to have to punish this slut — to show her the error of her ways."

"It's for her own good," Ma said, laughter and smiles in his voice.

"Come on now, slut," Pa said, bending down to look up into Doris' downcast eyes, "time to face the music." Hooking a finger in the top of

Doris' blue suit, she gently tugged her towards the Japanese front room. "Come along, slut."

Stunned, Doris did. Emotions played around her mind, dazzling her vision: She was Slave Doris, tingling with anticipation of what her new Masters might have use of her, already feeling the familiar sensation of desire flooding her body. But she was also Just Plain Doris — shocked and scared, not knowing how to feel, how to act, and waiting for the bad things of "family" to start.

The whole gang of them, the whole ... (deep breath Doris) "family" walked into the oriental austerity of the front room. Spunk sat on a little black cushion, with his back to an immaculate screen. Ma went over to one of the low cabinets and, with the grace and perfect motions of a geisha or a samurai, bent down and began to remove and display an assortment of objects.

Pa, who still had her finger tucked into her suit, led her into the middle of the room. "I think you're gonna enjoy this, you nasty little girl. It's punishment, true, but something tells me that this is not going to be all that punishing —" she said, smiles in her words, play in her words, but, still, the firm hand of a Master.

"I want you to look over at what Ma is laying out there. Tell me what you see," Pa said, turning her head gently with one finger.

Beautifully polished ocher, fine strips of butter-fine black leather. Even from where she stood the workmanship and power was evident. "A whip."

Coils and coils of it, dyed midnight black so as to be not so much lengths as a great corded cloud. "Rope."

Hard and long, a curved scimitar that would have been ridiculous for its dimensions if not for its fine, sculpted workmanship. "A dildo."

"You have an assignment ... Doris (we have to do something about that name). As you are punished, as you are used and abused I want you to think of one thing —" Pa said, leaning close, running a steel-firm finger down the side of her cheek and down into the narrow valley of the suit Doris remarkably still wore. "— what we should do to Spunk for his punishment."

"Hey —" Spunk protested, humor dancing in his outrage.

"Do you understand me, slut?"

"Yes, Pa."

"Good — now get rid of this ridiculous outfit and show us all what we paid good, hard money for."

She was Doris the Slave and her Master — Pa? — had ordered her to strip. So she did. The jacket first: The scratchy, uncomfortable fabric slipping off her arms and shoulders. Free, she briefly wondered what she should do with it (on the floor? Folded or dropped?) when Ma appeared at her side and gently took it from her, saying, "I'll put it away so it won't get wrinkled."

Then her shoes (ugly, uncomfortable things), and her stockings (Bloom had sent her in garters, a little gift to her new Master) — rolling them down and again handing them to Ma.

Then her blouse, the finer material sliding over her arms, dusting them with gentle goose bumps. The skirt was next — since she was a narrow, slim woman it was a quick, short trip: past her supple thighs, past her firm ("Exercise is important to maintain property" Bloom had said) ass, and down to the floor. Ma elegantly descended and offered her a supportive hand as she stepped out of it, then took them away as well.

In bra and panties she stood. Her pause wasn't long, but Pa said: "All of them."

All of them — bra unhooked and gone the way of the rest of her clothes. Panties, dainty and fringed, over those same thighs, that same, tight, ass. Naked, she stood before Pa — who looked at her with cool appraisal, before Ma — who looked at her with an artist's refined vision, and Spunk — who smiled and licked his lips.

"Ma, Sonny, I do think we've got ourselves a winner," Pa said.

From somewhere behind one of the glowing white screens, Ma produced an elegantly formed bench. The top was smoothly polished leather and — again — Doris found herself wishing that she would be allowed to polish it.

"Can you guess which one these wonderful objects you get to experience first?" Pa said, running a firm finger across the polished leather.

Across the room, Spunk mouthed "Dil—do."

"The dildo, Pa?" Doris said, keeping her eyes lowered from Pa's burning gaze.

"Nope! Dead wrong — and just for that you get twenty extra strokes," Pa said, patting the top of the bench. "Lean over and get yourself ready."

"And you," Doris heard Pa say to Spunk as she leaned over the bench and gripped the lower ends to balance yourself, "you'd better fucking behave yourself — remember, she gets to name your punishment when this is over."

"Oh, fuck —" she heard Spunk say, a (mock) painful revelation in his words.

"This is a simple game — one, I think, you'll enjoy," Pa said, bending down to whisper in her ear. "It's very simple. I'm going to whip you. You're going to tell me, when I ask, how many times you've been whipped. Get it right and you get one of Ma's delicious flans. Get it wrong ... and you get twenty more strokes."

"Yes, Pa," Doris said, already feeling the delicious pre-warmth spread through her. Like a warm blanket, the knowledge that she was where she was, where she wanted to be, fell over her. Family .. San Francisco .. retreated till it was just her, Slave Doris, and her Masters. It was good. Very, very good.

A firm finger traced the shape of her ass. "Very lovely —" said Pa.

"Quite spectacular": The music of Ma.

"Fucking 'A'": The boyish tones of Spunk.

Then: The first impact. More of a kiss than a strike, the smooth leather of the whip glided over her thighs, up and off her ass, setting a gentle gust of warm room air tumbling over her back. Almost unconsciously, she thought *one*.

Then another, and she felt the familiar warmth spread up and through her ass, touching, but not burning, her cunt. After so much strangeness, it was welcome familiarity — something she was trained to receive, loved to receive. It wasn't a strange house anymore with strange people who might or might not be her new masters, in a city that conjured bad memories — rather, she was a Slave and she was being punished.

Ten, eleven, twelve, more — the strokes slowly becoming more intense, progressively heavier. The warmth, the gentle radiance from her ass boiled down into her cunt and she felt herself grow expectedly wet. The tease, the fluttering hint of excitement became even more real, a glow from a rising sun.

Doris felt each stroke as a fleshy surge up from her ass, along her back and into her shoulders — and down, naturally, into the smoldering cauldron of her cunt.

Twenty, twenty ... one, twenty-two, twenty ... three, twenty-four?

Stroke, stroke, stroke — impact, impact, impact. Maybe, somewhere in that dim and distant land that was her first leaning over the bench, the whip might have seemed like pain, could have been called something akin to discomfort, but as they progressed and drum-beat into her, the sensations had evolved and moved. Now it wasn't anything but a thunderous, rhythmic bliss that moved through her body: Waves, crests, surges, rolls ... they rocked from her ass to her cunt (wet, very wet) and through the rest of her body.

Doris, the Slave, felt good.

Somewhere very far away, maybe from New York (since she was in that mythical land called San Francisco) a woman with a very butch — gravel and thunder — voice said: "How many, slut?"

The voice was asking for something — something Doris knew was important but didn't know hot to respond. A body orgasm was hiding close by, too close to allow her mind to function as anything but as a receiver of firm pleasure. Numbers? The concept tasted familiar but the meaning was flushed away. She didn't know how many, hadn't a clue, but she did know one thing: She wanted more.

"I ..." she managed to say, breathing heavily, "... ten, Si — I mean, <u>Pa</u>."

Thunder and gravel: "Wrong-on, slut! Yeah, like we had any idea that you'd get it right — or want to get it right."

She heard someone she thought might be Spunk say, "Yeah, right."

She heard someone she thought might be Ma say, "Isn't that just so precious!"

Then she heard someone she thought might be Pa say, "I guess the little slut should get some more."

Then she did. The first might have been a leather rainfall on her ass, vibrations into her cunt, but the next series was different: Simple rain turning to powerful storm.

The body come that was coming, in sight but undefined, was suddenly clear and close — a quaking, epileptic orgasm that Doris reached out for, touched (shiver, shiver!) and tried to bring into herself.

Then it stopped — and it was all Doris could to not to complain, to open her mouth, to speak.

Pa spoke first: "Not yet, slut. Don't be greedy your first night at home."

That word. That bad word reached down into her like bucket of ice water. "Sorry, Pa. I'm sorry."

"Don't worry your sweet little head about it," Ma said, his musical voice close, his breath on her back. "You'll have your treat before the night is over. Now stand up, dear —"

Doris did, her head swimming with redirected blood. Ma looked at her, an artist gazing for the first time at a blank canvas. In his pale hands was the length of dyed rope.

Pa said. "Ma's *real* body is thin, long, black and very, very strong. She's going to make love to you now."

Then, magically, that's just what Ma did. At first it was a confusing dance, full of strange steps and odd movements: Loops mysteriously appearing and vanishing over and around her body. She kept waiting for knots .. and waiting and waiting .. but none seemed to appear. The rope was, literally, a thing alive: An extension of Ma's self, a kind of hand, arm, finger around her arms, waist, thighs, chest, tits, between her legs, and between her lips. Just as she expected knots, she also expected — and didn't get — the focused restriction of other forms of bondage. Yes, it was tight. Yes, it was firm. But the pressure was so elegantly distributed over her body that she couldn't really say where the points really were — the sensations blurred into just a general firmness: Arms, chest, tits, cunt, legs ... she was caught in an elaborate black web, a network of no-knots, tying her into artistic immobility.

Then Doris, Slave Doris, was flying. How else to describe it? One moment she was bound by coils and beautifully stylish contortions of nothing but simple rope and the next she was suspended. After the whipping, and because of the rope, her position was vague. She suspected she was standing, one leg forward, one leg back — with hands over her head and laced together with a ladder of simple coils. She had heard of the art of Japanese bondage and had even seen some examples in some magazines she'd masturbated over — long before she'd heard of the Marketplace, or become the Slave she loved to be — but she had no idea that it could be ... like that: like flying. Doris was a butterfly — a beautiful creation of black rope and meticulous talent.

She was somewhere else — not the same place Pa's flogger had brought her, but somewhere else entirely. Ma had brought her somewhere more ... supported. She flew, yes, but it wasn't a kind of dreamlike flight. There, caught in his supportive web, Doris was soaring on thin black wings.

Of course, she realized — in a coolly rational part of her mind that was, surprisingly, able to make this observation — having the rope be a throbbing pressure between her slick lips and a strategic knot placed just where it would tap (a quaking heartbeat in her cunt) with every movement she made, every breath she took, could have been a large part of her trip, her flight.

"Beautiful," said someone who could have been Ma.

"Fucking 'A'" said someone who could have been Pa.

"Pretty enough to fuck," said someone who could have been Spunk.

"None for you, young man — you've been grounded. Till, that is, you get your punishment," said someone who could have been Pa.

"Awww, man...," said someone who could have been Spunk.

"Part of which, you bad boy, is getting to watch but not touch," said someone who could have been Pa.

Then something slightly cool, and very hard, touched her hot, melting lips. The touch was electric — but not literally: She was flying, hot and height, and the touch there was only slightly less steaming that she was ... thus, cool. She was confused, floating on her ropy wings, buoyed by the near come from Pa's whip, so she wasn't capable of any kind of even lower mathematics: Doris couldn't add anything up — so she didn't really know what Pa meant when she said: "What is it, dear?"

"I—I don't know, Pa," she managed to mumble out.

"Come on, slut. You know. Take a guess. But if you guess Spunk you're wrong — he's being punished."

Then it clicked — a remarkable achievement considering how her consciousness was floating somewhere around Jupiter. An image: A fine sculpture of wood, burnished and glowing with natural warmth. Too big? Maybe, or maybe she was so excited, so on fire she'd try anyway — if just to push her over the end: "The dildo, Sir."

"Right, slut. Very right —" and the touch turned into a slowly increasing pressure. With a will focused to an extraordinarily tight tiny point, Doris could imagine the wooden cock slowly press against her wet, open lips, pushing aside with gentle insistence the rope, the knot, that she knew was there. She could see it in her mind — since here eyes were staring at the whiteness of a screen — glistening with reflections from her hot juice, as Pa slowly withdrew, inserted, withdrew, inserted the sculpture till, painstakingly, but painlessly, it moved into her one fraction of an inch at a time.

It was hard to say where Doris was right then — Jupiter, possibly — but wherever it was, it was good. Damned good. Screamingly good, which was what she did — an earthen, primordial scream of pure joy — as the cock made its way, the final inch, into her.

"Now, slut," someone who might have been Pa said, "you may come."

"Yes, dear," someone who might have been Ma said, "*now.*"

"Oh, man," someone who might have been Spunk said, "I'm so fucking *hard!*"

Then she did — and, lifted by the wondrous ropes of Ma, fucked by the magnificent cock of Pa — she passed out.

Words, during or since, could never do it justice.

Dreamily, because Doris could never be sure how much of the rest of that evening was reality or the soft, billowy, illusions of her sleeping, happy, mind, the cock was withdrawn from her clenching, spasmodic cunt. She then was slowly, carefully, uncoiled from the thin grasps of Ma, and gently lowered to the floor.

Then, before a shiver could even begin to race across her body, she was bundled up in a beautifully ornate quilt (that she knew Ma must have sewn) and was carried up a flight of stairs and into a simple, yet warmly beautiful room (all rosewood and oak, peaceful paintings and flowers), and was tucked into a comfortable bed.

"Tomorrow," Pa may or may not have said, kissing her on the forehead "you'll fix us all breakfast. Then we'll decide what to do with Spunk."

"Tomorrow," Ma may or may not have said, also kissing her on the forehead "you'll help me bake some cookies. Then we'll get Spunk."

"Tomorrow," Spunk may or may not have said, playfully ruffling her hair, "is going to be *a lot* of fun."

Then the light was put out, and darkness closed in. "Welcome home," they may or may not have said as definite dreams started to close in around Doris — and she smiled.

16 Honorable Opponents II

There was a lot of grumbling when the trainers reassembled in the large room. A lunch time spent re-hashing debates — or trying to avoid the subject — did not serve to make many of them eager to continue. Despite the strong showing that the anti-proposal speakers had made in the morning, there was a heavy expectation of formidable verbal combat in the air. Toward the end of the morning session, the debates had started to get — nasty.

"Academy members," said William Longet as he took his seat again, "please attempt to observe decorum! There is no need for the sort of name-calling or harsh language evident in our last session."

But apparently there was. Corinne was called a 'narrow-minded, stuck up Frenchie who didn't know what language to think in', and Sam Keesey from Nevada was called an anarchist; Tetsuo Sakai was accused of supporting the proposal in order to maintain an unethical control over the Asian market, and Ken Mandarin almost throttled an elderly Irish woman who called her a slut who spotted only to support her own promiscuity.

Longet appealed to order again and again, until he had to rise and bang his gavel repeatedly to get their attention. And each time, they sent quick apologies to him and sometimes to each other, sat down, and allowed at least one more person to speak for a minute uninterrupted.

Ninon was one of the few who was granted a moderate amount of time and attention.

"I support this proposal with all my heart," she said clearly, her voice achieving a bell-like quality as she pitched it to the room. "For I have seen what happens when unsuitable trainers allow unsuitable slaves to be traded. Twenty years ago, you heard of such things in whispers, as rare happenstance which caused shame to fall upon a house and all the trainers within. Now, it is too easy to say, oh, so-and-so trained with this man, but he has not been with him in two years. Or that woman, she was training with this one, but she left early and found someone who would present her clients. That is not only bad karma, as our kind hosts would say, but it is bad business."

That was more to the point, and the trainers listened, many of them nodding.

"If we had the power to approve all new trainers, we could establish a formal apprenticeship period — create a way for local coalitions of trainers to nominate new, younger trainers to us - and encourage the more established houses to create opportunities for these fresh, new faces to study and learn — "

"See? See how easy it is to go from a general approval committee to something even more insidious?" That was Keesey, standing to face her, his broad, burnished face red from a previous confrontation. "Already, they're thinking of establishing training guidelines, sending new juniors to the old schools! Why not just take my trainees from me and indoctrinate them right now?"

"Now, see here!" shouted Tucker, raising a fist, "Don't you go callin' Ninon insidious, you fat prick!"

The sound of the gavel falling and the sight of Ninon, drawn up with her arms carefully crossed in front of her steadily brought the general outrage down to quiet again.

"As I was saying before I was interrupted," she said easily, "yes, I do believe that the old style of apprenticing new trainers is perfect the way it is. I have had great success with it — and so have all the older houses which have been using it for generations. I am not ashamed to say that I think all trainers would be improved by it, and if I served upon this committee, I would ask whether such methods were used in one's training." She leveled her gaze at several of the more outspoken opponents. "I do not fear such a commission, because I know that if I had failed myself and a student, I would want to know before my student wasted the time, passion and love of creating a slave. I would wish to know whether I had not given my student enough time and experience before I sent them out to affect the lives of the living treasures we call clients. I would rather be called names here, by all of you, than to hear from one owner that one slave coming from my trainer line was unsuitable. A committee to approve new trainers in our midst? I regret only that the proposal did not also give us a way of dealing with some of the unsuitable ones among us now. I am finished; you may resume your shouting." She sat down elegantly, and no one shouted.

"Ninon, I hear what you are saying," said Geoff, rising. One of his supporters who actually had been pointed at by Longet waved the parliamentarian off and yielded his place. "But let's be serious here. You advocate a training period of five years. Tetsuo here says six. And Anderson, not to be outdone, asks for a commitment of *seven* years to make a trainer like her. Seven years, ladies and gentlemen! You could train a surgeon in less time!

"This isn't an effective way to continue our lines! This is lunacy!" The stress of the day was showing on him, too, although he seemed to handle his voice level very well. "And the methods of training trainers often make slave training look like a vacation week in the Bahamas!" This got a laugh from some of the trainees standing along the edges of the walls. "Really; how much longer do you think people will stand for the kind of strict, hierarchical — and downright brutal — methods that are advocated by some of our more — traditional — members? You would ask young and new trainers if they endured the years of humiliation and abuse required of these pathologically sadistic styles of training and judge them acceptable because of it? I would like to know myself, so that I can keep clients out of their hands!"

Chris Parker almost choked, and a wave of gasps spread through the room, accompanied by scattered laughter and one or two claps. Tetsuo was signaling to be recognized, though, so Chris kept his own hand down.

"Surely my esteemed colleague does not mean to suggest that trainers numbered among us today are actually *harmful* to their clients and novice trainers," he said reasonably. "I beg his pardon if I misunderstood, I am not attended by a translator at this moment, an unforgivable error at a meeting of this importance."

No one was fooled. Of the Japanese contingent, Tetsuo Sakai had the best mastery of idiom and cultural vocabulary in American English. Geoff drew a hesitating breath, but before he could respond, Tetsuo continued, "I agree that the training programs we use here are difficult; who would wish that a teacher or master is ill-informed, or ill-instructed? We do not teach a simple matter here. We have a sacred duty to our clients, to provide them with instructors who can be respected because of what they have achieved — and yes, what they have endured. It is a path of honor, to grow in this way. But it is not — inhuman as much as it is occasionally inhumane. It is heat which tempers the sword, after all." He bowed to Mr. Longet. "My apologies for my rude interruption."

"Please, please, it was no interruption," Geoff said quickly. "I am thankful for your wisdom, of course, Sakai-san." He gave a slight bow, but it was clear that he was not ready to surrender the floor, either. "But I respectfully disagree.

"Once, it was thought that the only way to achieve mastery was to start out life as a slave. But that philosophy never held true on any real cultural level, it was an invention."

"What?" came several affronted cries.

"Look at history, my friends! Every human culture had its elite classes, born to be served, and its poor and disenfranchised, born to be enslaved by one method or another. Only when society grew to appreciate democratic values did the concept of a man — or woman — working their way up the ranks to the top come to realistic fruition.

"So now we have the concept of a voluntary slave — an oxymoron if there ever was one — and we provide an arena in which we encourage people to act out the erotic fantasy of owner and owned. We are merely the intermediaries here, serving two real masters — our clients and our customers."

"I beg your pardon," Mr. Ward said strongly, "but to some of us present, this is no fantasy!"

Geoff waved a hand casually. "Use any word you like then. We control the paradigm. We create the alternate reality. But I'm afraid that when you believe too passionately in this lifestyle as a series of earned ranks, that only a former slave may make a future one, that only pain and humiliation and blatant trickery can mold someone into a good trainer, then you are encouraging a system of abuse!"

"My God man, you *are* callin' us abusers!" shouted Tucker.

"Mr. Negel, I think you might wish to reconsider what you've said," said Chris, rising two rows back from Tucker.

"Gentlemen and ladies, please attempt to—" started Mr. Longet, but Geoff directed himself back at Chris.

"I chose my words deliberately, Mr. Parker! Yes, if what you are doing is setting out to inflict the same patterns of shame and physical pain and a steady stream of humiliating duties and behaviors on someone just because that was what was done to you, then you are nothing more than another abusive parent figure, getting your own back for the pain you experienced in the past."

"Damn, that's one of the best parts," Bronwyn whispered to Dalton, who barely suppressed a tight smile.

"Gentlemen!" Longet managed to get himself heard. "The topic we are addressing is the proposal!"

"This pertains to the reasoning *behind* the proposal," Geoff insisted. "To create a slow and steady monopoly on new trainers, by denying non-traditional houses any new 'approved' trainers! You can count on discouraging the truly creative, the spirited individuals who have no intention of giving up their privacy, their free wills, their very sexual orientation — or their bodies — and retain only the ones who are best molded by your will-breaking, and with all due respect to Mr. Sakai, *inhuman* program of brainwashing. When will you people understand that we are trainers, not slaves?"

Rumbles grew into outbursts as Longet started thumping his gavel again.

"My fellow trainers, those among you who are still clinging to these outmoded ways are just hoping that by controlling the new trainers in the field, you'll keep your dominance throughout the Marketplace by default, instead of by merit."

Michael trembled, he was so tense; the room had exploded into knots of trainers and spotters yelling at each other. He watched Chris, who was still standing — and saw his teacher exchange a long look with an old, balding gentleman seated with the bunch of Brits — he could see Bronwyn sitting right next to him. And then Chris turned to eye Ken Mandarin, who was scowling. Gradually, the riot subsided again, leaving Chris and Geoff facing each other.

"Your comments, sir," said Chris, "were beneath contempt. And perfectly illustrative of the need for this proposal." He took his seat as casually as if he had been up to make a point of order, leaving Geoff Negel frowning for a moment in confusion. Then, with a heavy sigh, the Californian man sat as well, and hands and fingers waving gave William Longet something to do.

17 Smoke Rings

Chris smelled her before he actually heard her approach. "Cuban?" he asked, without turning his head.

"*Oui*, but of course! And I brought one for you."

Ken Mandarin stepped across the stone pathway and leaned over the edge of the decorative fencing, looking over the edge, down the sloping hill. It was thick with tropical vegetation, rich in heavy, misty scents. Her cigar cut through the air like a trumpet blast, and she grinned around it. She turned back to Chris, seated on a stone bench and offered him one from her leather case.

"I've given it up," he said lightly.

"Nonsense! Giving up American cigarettes is wise. They are tasteless tubes of nothing. Giving up expensive cigars rolled upon the thighs of virgins, however, is stupid. Take it." She waved it enticingly. "Take it! You can always smoke it later, when no one is looking."

Chris sighed and took the cigar from her, a *Romeo y Julietta*. He slid it into his breast pocket carefully and moved to make room for her. "Rolled on the thighs of virgins?" he asked.

"It is a pleasant image," Ken declared, sitting down. "Even if it was truly some ancient Cuban man who has more fingers than teeth."

Chris nodded, the scent of the rich, bitter tobacco working its seductive dance on his senses. "Ken, why are you still against me on this?' he asked suddenly.

"Because I don't like to be told what to do," she said simply. "I am an Owner from birth; I am a Spotter by trade, an Agent by whim, and sometimes I am a Trainer by choice. If you, Chris Parker, come to me and say, 'train your slaves in thus and such a way, I know it to be useful', I can listen to you, or tell you to go fuck yourself. Either way, it is my choice, and I continue to do my work and I succeed or fail according to what I deserve. Your way, this accredited way — it would take away my choice, no?"

"No," Chris said calmly, even though this would be the fifth or sixth time he had explained this. "I never suggested that there should be one accepted method, or even that the governing committee should have the power to force a single method onto unwilling trainers. You should know me better than that. But you have to admit that we are getting far too loose. It's all the buzz in the hallways, isn't it? Too much time spent weeding out unsuitable clients, dealing with owners who want refunds, slaves who want out. We need a little more centralization of the training process, and a way to — deal with trainers who consistently turn out poor clients."

"But who gets to be in the center? That is my question." Ken took a long, gentle drag on her cigar and leaned back to blow smoke rings. They drifted around her head lazily until she waved them into nothingness. "I understand you, I truly do. And there is nothing I wish more than for business to be a little easier on us all. But to give one group of trainers the right to rule over the others? Not acceptable."

Chris shook his head. "I wish I could find a way to assure you it won't be like that."

"Power is power is power, Mr. Parker. I will tell you now, here, alone, that I think you are a magnificent trainer. I think you are one of the best I have ever seen, and I like to work with you. I like to play with you! But you are a hard man. You don't like people to come in and. . .how would you say. . .make a mess in your clean life. But we spotters and part-timers, we are a messy people!" She waved her cigar around and some of her ash fell onto the smooth gray stones beneath their feet. She laughed delightedly at her perfect illustration.

"I don't understand you," Chris said with a slight, crooked smile. "I know for a fact that you are every bit as conservative as I am. You've said the same things I have about some of the alternative training methods, and much worse! All you third and fourth generation Marketplacers are like that, you always remember the good old days when trainers were owned by houses, and houses were run by pure owners whose bloodlines ran back for centuries, and slaves signed away lifetime contracts like this." He snapped his fingers arrogantly, jerking his arm to one side in a campy gesture.

For a moment, they were both still, and then they both laughed together.

"Well, it was like that!" Ken insisted, brushing her hair back with one hand. "Exactly so! But you know, Parker, even though I do think there are fools out there, I worry about the day I am called a fool. It is my low self-esteem, no?"

Chris snorted, and she laughed again, louder. "Oh, I do not like being cross with you. Come, let us come up with some way past this thing, so that we can be friends again."

"Then help me," Chris insisted firmly. "Help me find the way to make it - safe — for you. I swear I will listen to everything you say. But something has to be done, Ken, or we will surely pass away in this generation, and there will be no Marketplace for the next Mandarin or the next Parker."

"You truly believe that?"

"With all my heart. Anderson believes it too, if that's what you need to hear."

She looked at him dead on and stubbed her cigar out on the bench. "Do you know something, Parker? I do not need to hear that. These others might think you are no more than her lackey, but I know better. Very well. I will ask some of my friends, I will give it some thought. But I do not promise anything, mon ami. You must be prepared to listen to what we say."

"Of course I will. Thank you." His relief was visible.

Ken took a long look at him and nodded. "Yes, I will think upon it. But in the mean time, I have spoken to Marcy and her new trainee. You do not mind if they attend my little private entertainment tonight?."

"That would be fine," Chris said, not revealing that it had been his idea.

"*Bon*. It shall be a meeting of dogs, I think - your wild dog and Marcy's tame one." Chris looked at her in confusion and she laughed. "I am glad we can discuss things like friends, Parker."

"Me too," Chris said. "You have been a good friend to me, you know."

"Well, we traditionalists must stick together in the end," Ken laughed. "Otherwise, we shall be eaten by turkeys. Isn't that a strange thing to say? I saw it on a poster at the airport. 'Don't let the turkeys get you down'. You Americans always come up with the strangest idioms."

"At least we don't swear by the excrement of turtles."

"Ayeeeya! You keep your dirty thoughts to yourself, white boy."

When Chris finally got back to his room to dress, Michael was already in his best suit and his tuxedo was properly laid out. But also present was a large, flat box covered with an icy green paper with gold threads running through it, and another, smaller box on the floor. Kneeling on the tatami flooring on one side of the table next to these precisely placed boxes was a slave whose throat bore the house identity disk from Sakai-san's training facility.

"Sir," Michael said, with only the slightest hesitation, "this — and he — were delivered for you." He extended a folded message, on heavy, cream colored rice paper. Chris took it and sat down next to the table to open it.

Michael watched curiously as Chris carefully unfolded the paper and removed the contents with both hands. The slave had told him nothing, except that he had been told to wait for Mr. Parker as long as necessary. He had yielded the message easily enough, and Michael had known better than to ask him about it.

Chris laid the message down thoughtfully and then pried the top of the box off. Michael peered in and saw carefully folded dark garments, half-wrapped in layers of more gilt paper. Chris lifted the corners of the top garment and revealed it to be a long jacket in dark gray, almost black. Under it was a slate colored kimono, and under that still was something that had a lot of pleats.

"Wow — what's all this?" Michael asked.

"It — it's a men's formal kimono," Chris said. His voice shook, and Michael almost stepped back in shock. The color seemed to have drained from Chris' face as he sat there and examined the box contents.

"Rarely worn, actually," Chris continued, laying the pieces gently back in the box. He steadied himself a little, and took a deep breath. Then his voice took on a purely informational tone, as though he was reciting a lesson. "These days, when you see Japanese men at a formal event, they are more likely to wear a morning coat than one of these. Even at weddings where the bride may wear a unique bridal kimono, the groom is more likely to wear a western tuxedo."

"So — who sent you this? And why, if I can ask."

"Sakai-san sent this," Chris said, and the slave immediately bowed down in response to the name. "Apparently, several of the Japanese trainers are wearing kimono tonight, and he thought I might like to try a different kind of fancy dress."

Michael cocked his head to one side. "But — you're not Japanese. Is this some kind of special honor or something? Because they support your proposal?"

"It could be," said Chris. He adjusted the jacket slightly and stared down at the ensemble in thought. "In any event, I shall wear it." He stood up and nodded to the kneeling slave. "Please attend me," he said, starting to strip.

"May I help?" Michael asked, as the visiting slave rose and stepped over to Chris..

"No, but you may watch," Chris said. "I have never worn a kimono — at least not a formal one like this." He made the admission awkwardly, and Michael immediately retreated to his side of the room and sat down.

The slave knew his business, and was elegantly trained to move with a graceful economy. He smiled gently or broadly and rarely spoke, except to say a short phrase that Michael decided meant "like this, sir". And Chris was as cooperative and non-committal as he had been during his haircut, prepared to be wrapped or shown a particular knot as the peculiar costume required.

Michael had never seen hakama trousers outside of a dojo, and he admitted that the strange pinstriped pattern on these gave them a decidedly elongating effect. The pleats, though, made them look like some sort of wide over-skirt. There was a white cotton kimono that was worn under the darker one. The dark gray silk jacket fastened with a long, braided cord which the slave tied twice in illustration before Chris tried it himself. Tabi and zori, the traditional Japanese socks and sandals, were in the smaller box. When Chris was dressed, the slave slid open one of the storage closets and drew out the mirror.

Chris looked at himself and felt his stomach tighten.

"This would normally be the time to teach you Japanese dress," Sakai-sama said, glowering down at me. I began to feel the fear—nausea again. He spoke slowly now, in English, treating me like a very stupid child on his good days, and like a stubbornly ignorant fool on days like this.

"But how do we dress you?" he continued, his arms folded. "Eh? Eh? Answer me."

"As my honorable master wishes," I answered in Japanese, as well as I was able. It was the phrase I was most familiar with, right after 'please excuse the inexcusable behavior of this worthless person'.

"I wish you would go home," he snapped back. "But since you will not, I do not see why I should honor you with the proper clothing of a proper person. You will stay in American clothing. You will never be called upon to wear kimono anyway. Any kimono!"

"Looks great, sir," Michael was saying. "Just like the Seven Samurai!"

Chris pulled himself away from the mirror and his memories. "You realize, of course, that they were a pack of ronin," he said, surprised at the genuine humor in his voice. He moved gently, taking a moment to figure out how to walk confidently, and the slave nodded and bowed happily. "I will deliver my thanks to Sakai-san myself; thank you for your help," Chris said, nodding to him. The slave bowed very deeply and left the room in an elaborate series of moves that involved him kneeling to open the door, edging his way through to bow again, and then sliding it closed. Michael stared after him in amusement.

"Is that they way they have to do it all the time?"

"As with everything else, it depends on their owner," Chris said, turning and settling his shoulders comfortably. "I'm going to take a few more minutes to get used to this, Michael. You may go ahead of me; I've no doubt we'll be at separate tables tonight anyway."

Michael nodded and left immediately. As he walked out, Chris shook his head. Michael should have tried the formal exit — would it have killed him to just think ahead by that much?

He stretched, feeling the soft cotton of the layers brush against him in whispers. He bent down, flexing his knees, and caught himself in the mirror again.

And what kind of idiot am I, he thought, with another stab of pain in his gut. Castigating poor Michael for not thinking ahead? If this night doesn't kill me, facing the Trainer when she finds out about it certainly will.

But he consoled himself by imagining what Ken would say when she saw he had a *much* more authentic outfit than she did.

Ayeeyah, indeed.

18 Identities

A rumbling patter built up to thunderous, echoing explosions of sound. The three drummers, all wearing nothing but sandals and loin coverings with broad belts, moved their muscular arms and shoulders with perfect precision.

It was a different kind of dinner bell, to be sure. But when the doors to the main dining hall opened, there were gasps and murmurs from the trainers as they edged in. For instead of the anticipated low tables and cushions and backrests on the floor, the dining hall had been transformed into an ultra-modern vaguely futuristic looking eatery with shining black plates on silver-gray tablecloths, sterling accents glinting off of slender halogen lamps and perfectly posed and bound slaves mounted on silver stands, their skins dusted with powder that scintillated under colored spotlights.

The army of service slaves were all in black, unrelieved by color. The slender ones wore tight bodysuits; those who would not be improved by such a garment wore a non-descript yukata. All of them were covered, though, their duty to disappear.

Michael gave his name to a slave, who guided him to a table where he was seated next to Paul Sheridan. Paul was in a Naval officer's white dress uniform tonight, and it looked good on him. He introduced Michael to Joost de Graaf, the good looking, light skinned black man sitting next to him. "He's from Amsterdam," Paul said with a smile. Joost, who had ignored Michael the first time they met, back when he had been hanging out with Ken Mandarin, seemed far more friendly now. He was dressed in a white linen suit, which contrasted beautifully with his cafe au lait skin and looked wonderfully tropical next to Paul's severe uniform. "This is my country's for-mal wear," Joost laughed, brushing invisible dust from his jacket with his long, slender fingers.

Chucking at Michael's grin of confusion, Joost explained, "I am from

Suriname, ja?" They chatted for a few minutes, and Michael realized that he had never even heard of the country formerly known as Dutch Guyana, and certainly never imagined that Amsterdam had a population of dark skinned, Dutch speaking "natives".

"Suriname is a most beautiful country," Joost said, carefully, accentuating his words precisely. "Tropical and lush. But difficult for this trade. Amsterdam is much, much better."

The three men started to compare experiences with and rumors about the large Amsterdam auction houses. But as the Japanese trainers came in, conversation stilled, gradually spreading silence throughout the entire room. They were all wearing the kind of kimono that Michael had seen Chris dressed in, and in fact, it looked like most of the Asian members were wearing their national clothing over more western styles. He was fascinated by the sight of Kim in what looked like a long, colorful gown topped with an extremely short jacket. But Ken Mandarin took his breath away.

Tonight, she was not wearing masculine costume, but a long, impossibly tight cheongsam, the Chinese dress that had become the preferred style for millions of Asian women. It was slit up the side, almost to her hip. And it was a work of art! A rich pattern of bamboo shoots rose up from the bottom almost to her thighs, where the deep green and browns gave way to a gradual night sky, with blue and purple fading into black, and a moon hiding behind clouds on one shoulder. As she turned to greet someone, Michael grinned when he saw that crouched in the bamboo at the back of the dress was a tiger, mostly hidden, but his orange stripes and bright eyes showing in flashes of bright color.

Paul whistled through his teeth. "You know, if I went for girls," he said with a grin.

"I do," Michael laughed.

"Oh, ya," Joost almost purred.

"More's the pity for you two, then!" Paul laughed too, and as Ken got closer to them, Michael realized that she was being escorted to their table. He rose, biting his lip.

"Fantastic as usual," Paul said, saluting her. "You always know exactly what to wear!"

She smiled at him, pleased. "But you, you with this white uniform, how charming you are! Much more interesting than all the black leather. Joost, you pretty man, where have you been hiding? And look, here is the wild dog, the dingo."

Michael snorted. "Why, thank you for the nickname, ma'am," he said.

She laughed and sat casually in her held chair, the men following her. Joost leaned over to tell her about his meeting with the South American trainers earlier in the day. Their table quickly filled with two people from Australia, a rough looking fair eyed and gray haired woman named Fi and a dark skinned man who had straight black hair and Asian eyes. He introduced himself as Juan Matalino, and he turned out to be from the Philippines, relocated to Sydney.

"But where is your teacher?" Ken asked of Michael as the last seat was filled.

Michael repressed a grin and pointed. Ken followed his finger across the room to where the Japanese were being seated, and her eyes widened. Then she muttered something that made Mr. Matalino and Joost cough into their napkins.

"You know," Ken suddenly grinned, "when I say such things in America, or Egypt or England, no one understands me. I must remember that here I am among those who might."

"Really, Ken," Juan said, shaking his head. "His mother *and* his sister?"

"And brother too!" she said defiantly. And then she reconsidered. "Well — perhaps not his brother."

Paul laughed. "If it's kinky, then sure, throw him in. Because Ron Avidan is a major kinkster."

Michael blinked. "Avidan? But — I didn't know they had different last names."

"Listen, I don't think half of us here have the names we were born with," said Paul, sitting back and watching as large, shining carts were rolled into the room. "Nature of the business. You don't get here by staying the same person you were when you were a kid."

"That is true," said Ken, choosing a wine from the selection arrayed for her pleasure. Michael was grateful to see that there was also beer, and he had an ice cold one sitting in front of him before he even finished nodding. "Many of my slaves changed and lost many names before they found me."

"It's not just the slaves, though," said Fi, after softly making a special request of a server. "Lots of us just want to make sure that mum and da back home don't look us up at the wrong time! Can't have the nephews come over for a dip in the pool when you've got a different kind of party goin' on." She cackled and grinned when a can of Fosters was brought out for her on a mirrored tray. "Bless the little details," she said.

Paul nodded. "Between the real names, the married names, the scene names and the Marketplace names, sometimes I need two rolodex cards for one person," he said. "And what's worse is that I finally got my new computer and modem hooked up, and now I have e-mail names, too!"

"E-mail is a wonderful thing!" Ken declared. "I have many computer names, now. Andy keeps my records anyway, he tells me when who I am reading and who I am when I am answering." She laughed. "You must all give me your e-mail, so I can send you amusing stories and pictures of all the beautiful slaves I find."

"Bloody mess, all this Internet rot," Fi grumbled. "Spend more time sittin' in front of the damn screen than out lookin' at folks, sometimes!"

"Join the 20th Century," laughed Paul.

"Yes, join we forward-looking people," Ken echoed. "Michael, you have e-mail, correct?"

"I did when I lived on the West Coast," Michael said, "but right now, the only access I have is through the Marketplace BBS. Chris doesn't even have his own access code, he uses Anderson's. Eliot and Selador are pretty hooked in, though, both on the BBS and out there on one or two of the big commercial providers. I've tried to tell Chris about some of the stuff out there, discussions and live chat and everything, but he doesn't think it'll amount to much. I don't think he's looking forward to having auctions advertised on the 'net, let alone this idea of catalogs on web pages."

Ken looked scandalized. "No wonder he is wearing some old clothes tonight," she scoffed. "He is — what is the word — he hates the future?"

Luckily, before anyone could provide a word that Michael might consider an insult, Paul leaned his arm over the back his chair as slaves industriously unfolded and arranged great silver carts arrayed all over the room. "Now — what do you think they're doing with those things?"

The devices were scattered throughout the room, one for every three or four tables. Slaves took up positions next to them and bowed to incoming chefs, who bowed to the tables surrounding their positions and ceremoniously took up a pair of knives.

"It is *teppanyaki*," declared Ken. "Excellent, I was getting weary of sushi."

"Like at Benihana?" Michael raised an eyebrow as he accepted an exquisitely arranged tiny platter of fresh and pickled vegetables.

"Boy are you lucky Chris isn't here to smack you for that one," Paul said genially. "This is like some Americanized chain restaurant like Monaco is like Las Vegas."

Michael shut his mouth as the dinner was served. The chefs were in fact not much like the somewhat tired but showy men he had seen the last time he was dragged out for "Japanese steak". They were acrobatic with their knives, yes, but didn't rely on tricks like banging things loudly to startle the diners. And even though he had been very good about accepting the variety of raw seafood available to him on this trip, the sight of still living shrimp hitting the grills and actually wriggling for a moment was a little troubling.

And when a server gave him what looked like one slender cut of really rare meat, sliced into a three-section fan onto a special little plate and bowed with a flourish, he raised an eyebrow to his table, afraid to ask.

"Kobe beef," Ken purred. "Do not even chew. It is like heaven."

"Massaged and fed beer all day, that's the life for a cow, huh?" Fi said, shamelessly requesting another serving. "You have to hand it to the Japanese — they know how to live it up."

Ken shrugged. "They live in houses smaller than a cat's eyebrow. They work more hours than almost anyone, *oui*? If they find that massaging cows is what makes them happy—" she shrugged again. But ate the slices of beef slowly.

Michael ate in silence, mostly, afraid to open his mouth again. The tender, fat-laced beef did indeed melt on his tongue, and he almost groaned in pleasure. But when Fi brought up the afternoon debates, he cautiously raised his eyes.

"I tell you, it's a tough one for me," she said thoughtfully. "I understand what Parker's saying, and I agree — somewhat. But I figured I was gonna vote against it, because, well, I don't like being managed, you know?"

"I know," sighed Ken.

"But now — I dunno. I have to think some more."

Ken snorted in frustration and neatly decapitated some of the shrimp that were brought to her at her special request with their heads intact. (Michael had preferred his naked of all reminders that they had been in swimming shape before being grilled alive.) "It is an awkward thing, when one who is your ally arranges to embarrass one, that is true."

"Well, I warned you, Ken," said Paul. "But really, we're not allies as much as we're coincidentally on the same side. We don't have to take responsibility for what he said."

"We do not? I disagree. I choose my friends. I choose my politics." She ate one of the heads thoughtfully. "Right now, I am considering my choices."

"Excuse me," Michael dared. "But — I thought that maybe Geoff got a little strong in some language — but — what was the big deal? I mean there have been three debates over this, hasn't everything been said a dozen times now?"

Matalino looked surprised. "No one suggested that we are *better* than the clients, the slaves, before today," he said.

"Did Geoff?" Michael asked. "I don't remember him saying that."

"He said that we were *trainers*, not *slaves*," Paul prompted. "He implied that because we are trainers — and spotters, I suppose — that we didn't deserve to be treated like slaves. And Mike — that was fucking out of line. I understand what his point was — the old fashioned ways of training trainers aren't for everyone. But he insulted every former and current slave in that room. By saying that old fashioned training is abuse and some people don't deserve abuse — do you see where that goes? That somehow, the slaves deserve to be abused. Idiot." He shook his head angrily and stabbed at the last piece of beef on his plate. "And I guess Ken is right, if it looks like we're on his side, that we let him talk for us, then we're fucked, too."

"Current slaves? There — there are trainers here *now* who are — really slaves? Right now, in service?"

"Always," said Ken strongly. "There are always slaves among us. Once, more than half of all trainers were themselves owned. Now there are fewer, yes, but they are here."

Michael thought about his next question carefully. "But how can you tell?" he asked finally. "Everyone is so dressed up, no one seems to be wearing a collar. And although some of the junior trainers respond like slaves — when they're being good," he added with a grin, "I don't think I've met one who said that they are in service and owned."

"We are first trainers and spotters here, not masters and slaves," Ken said indignantly.

"But sometimes they forget," laughed Fi. "They're still talkin' about the year that Andorjan, that Hungarian fellow, told Nelka to fetch him a drink and then put her mouth to proper use between his legs. By God, she nearly ripped his lungs out."

"You mean it's like a secret?" Michael asked.

"No, it can't be a secret," Paul answered. "After all, we can all look up sales records. But think about it — lots of trainers are former slaves, whether they're old guard or not. Spotters, too. Nowadays, some large houses own their own trainers, and then there are owners who like to own and then lease a trainer to other owners. Not to mention trainers who are just so happy being slaves that the only way to keep 'em is to keep 'em collared." He laughed and shook his head with a shrug. "But it's — impolite — to mention someone's status as owned or not when we're together. You know."

"It is simply not done," said Joost firmly. "We already operate on formal manners to try and keep the peace together; imagine how complicated it would be if we had to consider the rankings of slaves as well? When the Academy gathers, we are all trainers and spotters, and we have status based on what we do, not who we might belong to and what we might do in private."

Paul nodded. "So when Negel said that the old training styles were abusive and cruel and that we — the trainers — didn't deserve to be treated that way — well — he dissed a lot of important people, Mike."

"More importantly, he — *dissed*? He *dissed* many *good* people," Ken said. She worked her mouth carefully around the slang word. "Dissed. He disses? They diss? I don't like that word, it sounds stupid."

Michael tried to control his urge to look around the room and try to figure out who might be a slave and who used to be one. But apparently something gave him away, and Paul clapped him on the back. "We are not telling you a thing, Mike. And neither will Chris."

"But — how does a trainer work when they're also a slave?" Michael asked. "Do they only train people that their owner provides? How can you maintain communication with spotters? What about training facilities, housing — who supervises them?" Two days of listening to people discuss slave management gave him dozens of questions all at once, and they spilled out of him. "How can they be sure that their owner won't interfere with training? Or that the people they've been told to train are even — suitable? What if they want to reject someone that the owner picked? It's all so — complicated!"

"Same way the owner of a master chef leaves the guy with the kitchen staff and doesn't go in to add parsley to the soup, kiddo. You got an investment like that, you better be prepared to let it do what it does, and don't get in its way."

"It's hard to even imagine," Michael said. "It's hard to imagine a lot of the people here as slaves, really. Even though I know all about the older training methods now, it just seems so unreal sometimes. I mean, everyone here is respectful and knowledgeable and they can *make* slaves — but they all seem so damn — I don't know. Confident. In control." He paused and added sheepishly, "Dominant."

"And you've never met a dominant slave?" laughed Fi. "Lucky you, I run into 'em more times than not!."

"Well, you know, there's a reason why we never mention one without the other," Paul said. "Sadomasochism, right? S/M. Slave and Master, dominant and submissive. For lots of us, it's just as right to do one or the other. For some of us, it's a matter of where we really want to be at any given time. I did my time in a collar, sure, and I don't care who knows it. But I couldn't do that now. I don't *want* to do that now. It's not in my blood any more. I changed, you know?

"Some people will never change. Lifelong slaves until they retire to Florida or something. But what happens if you can't leave this life? What if all your friends are here, what if this is the only world where you feel like a complete human being? Then you do what you have to do to stay in it. You train because your owner says to train, and then you're fulfilling your service. See?"

"I guess," Michael said. He picked at some wasabi, mashing it and moving it around his plate.

"Doesn't look like it. Maybe I'm not explaining it well, I'm no story teller," Paul said. "Well — lemme see — there was this guy . . . OK I can tell you about this one guy, because he's not here." Paul thought for a minute and accepted another cold glass of Sapporo from the server who whisked away his old one. "In fact, I don't know if any of you have met him. Let's see, what to call him. . .Mr. Benjamin." He snorted, choking back a laugh. "Yeah, he'd like that."

19 In Service   by david stein

At precisely 8 o'clock, I took a deep breath and rang Mr. Benjamin's door buzzer. I'd been waiting there in the foyer of his brownstone for ten minutes because I didn't want to risk being late — or a moment too soon, either.

The door buzzed in response. I pulled it open and walked inside, my heart pounding. A year ago, I had no idea who he was, had never heard the name. But a year ago I barely knew who I was, or what I needed. I'd come a long way since then, racked up a lot of experiences with some very talented topmen, and a few with other bottoms, too. I'd thrown myself into the s/m scene several years earlier, in my mid-20s, with the eagerness of the newly converted, and the more I tried, the more I wanted.

The feelings that flooded through me at the beginning of a scene, those first moments when I knelt in submission, or offered my wrists to be cuffed, were so exhilarating, so fulfilling, that they were almost enough to make up for the typical let-down at the end, after I'd been tormented, fucked, and allowed to come, then released from bondage. That's when the men I'd worshipped and served turned into buddies — anxious to be reassured that I'd had a good time, and was I going to the party so-and-so was throwing next week?

I forced myself to smile and chat like a regular guy, when inside I wanted to scream with frustration. Is this all there is? I wondered. Just a complicated way to get off? Didn't it mean anything that I'd crawled on the floor and licked their boots and drunk their piss? Was it all just an act we did for each other, this whole apparatus of dominance and submission?

From the first, I'd never felt like I was acting. I felt more real, more me when I was naked and chained, with my tongue on a man's boot and my ass burning from his belt, than I ever felt in the office where I worked or the apartment where I ate and slept. Which was the act and which was real?

Finally I started to ask people who seemed to know what they were doing, who'd been around the scene a lot longer than me: Is there anything beyond playacting? Is it possible to submit for real, not just a scene? Or is that only another fantasy?

"Well, if you're serious about this, you should see Mr. Benjamin," I was told again and again. "He can help you, if anyone can."

Was I serious? Of course I was, I insisted — to myself as much as anyone else. It wasn't a game to me anymore. Been there, done that. I was less and less interested in a weekend's sport. I wanted to put my life on the line in a way that would matter. I wanted to become a real slaveboy, not just a Stand&Model Chelsea boy.

Eventually I met a man who knew a man who could get in touch with a man who knew Mr. Benjamin well enough to pass on the message that I was interested in training with him. He responded eventually by e-mail, and we corresponded for a couple of weeks — mainly, I answered his questions, including filling out a very detailed questionnaire that covered everything from my financial status to how often I jerked off, and what I thought about while doing it! Whatever questions I asked him he deflected, saying only that there would be time enough to explain things after we met in person. He did make it clear that despite all the information I'd provided, he wouldn't decide whether to take me on until he saw how I responded in our first session.

It's almost laughable, I thought as I climbed the stairs to the fourth floor. A man so hard to reach, you'd expect him to live in Trump Tower or some mansion, not this slightly rundown apartment building in Manhattan's West 80s. When I arrived at his door I took a few moments to pull myself back into a more respectful, receptive mood. Before I could press the bell, however, the door was pulled open.

I'd been warned what to expect, but the man who looked coolly up at me, as if reconsidering whether I was worth his time after all, was unimpressive by the usual standards of the gay world. I towered over him, and if he had a physique sculpted by Nautilus, the three-piece suit he wore hid it well. Not even boots, for crissake, just well-polished black dress shoes.

His thinning hair was trimmed very short, and his clean-shaven features were of the pleasant but undistinctive kind you can't remember five minutes after the person leaves the room. So this was the elusive Mr. Benjamin? If he'd been a blind date, I'd have turned around and left immediately, muttering lame apologies. But this isn't about sex, I told myself firmly. If he can teach me what I need, it doesn't matter what he looks like.

"You must be Jeffrey," he said with the bare trace of a smile. His voice was firm, quietly commanding.

"Sir, yes, Sir," I answered crisply, louder than I'd intended.

"Come in, then." He waved me past him into the hallway, shutting the door behind us. "Take off all of your clothes here, and place them neatly in this closet." He opened its door to show me. "You'll always undress here when you visit me. You may not wear clothes anywhere else in my home. Understood?"

"Sir, yes, Sir!" I said with alacrity. Now this was more like it!

"Drop that military affectation, boy. A simple, 'Yes, Sir,' will do, if a response is necessary." I was about to answer when his raised eyebrow forestalled me. "And don't apologize, either," he said, "unless I demand one. Just listen, remember . . . and learn. When you're stripped, go down the hallway and through the first open door on the right. Wait for me there. Do not go anywhere else. And don't dawdle." With that last injunction, he walked away down the hallway — and at the end turned left.

How quickly he'd taken control of me! I shrugged out of my leather jacket and hung it up. I deliberately hadn't worn anything too flashy, just enough leather to make a good impression. All wasted on Mr. Benjamin, apparently. I took off my chaps, then sat on the floor to unlace my black lineman's boots, then pulled them off, followed by my jeans. Would he make me wear suits, too?

I hadn't worn briefs, of course, so the last thing I had to remove was my tight gray T-shirt, the one with the neat little "In training" logo on it. I wondered if Mr. Benjamin had even noticed it — probably better if he hadn't!

Taking a couple of deep breaths to calm myself, I padded down the parquet-floored hallway in my bare feet. The hallway was bare, too, with no pictures or bric-a-brac, and the large room through the open door on the right certainly wasn't a typical home "dungeon" or "playroom." Only a few items suggested that it was used for anything less innocent than a quiet evening of leisure reading.

Most of the parquet floor was covered by a beautiful oriental rug, in deep reds and golds, thickly padded — my feet sank into it as I walked toward the overstuffed armchair covered in dark-brown leather. A low table stood next to it and a reading lamp behind it. The only other furniture was a matching ottoman, a tall brass-bound Chinese apothecary's chest against the wall, and a torchière floor lamp that filled the room with light reflected off the ceiling. The one window was completely covered by dark curtains, the far wall by floor-to-ceiling mirrors. If there was a closet, it was behind them. The wall with the door, however, held a number of strategically placed rings, chains dangling from them, and a steel-barred "puppy" cage hulked brutally on the elegant carpet.

He hadn't told me where to wait, or how, so I stood there, naked, and pondered the matter. Was this a test? He knew I'd read all the usual stuff and had some experience. Wouldn't he expect me to know enough to kneel?

I was just arranging myself on my knees, facing his chair from a yard away, when he came into the room.

"On your feet, boy. You don't know how to kneel yet."

I leaped up, my cheeks reddening in embarrassment. I cast my eyes down as he came toward me. Nothing was said as he slowly circled my naked body. He was behind me when I felt something thin and hard tap my inner left thigh. It tapped again, on the other side.

"Take a wider stance," he ordered. "Feel where your shoulders are and where your knees are. Whenever you stand for inspection, or wait in readiness, there should be a straight line from each shoulder through the corresponding knee and down to the floor." I shifted my legs outward in compliance, and my cock started to get hard.

"Now put your hands behind you — no, don't clasp them, just cross them at the wrist. . . . Higher. Higher. Yes, hold them right there, above your waist. Always leave your ass clear and unobstructed. . . . Yes, good. Now bend forward at the waist."

I heard the unmistakable rustle behind me of a rubber glove being pulled on, and then my asscheeks were pulled apart and a finger was inserted in my hole, unlubricated. I relaxed as well as I could to permit the invasion. He fingered my prostate, and I sprang a boner.

"You're used to being fucked, I see. Good control, though it's always possible to do better. A well-trained slave has complete control over his anal sphincters and can relax them completely or tighten them like a vise as required. Straighten up."

He came around in front of me again, and I saw that he carried a pointing stick, rather like an elongated conductor's baton. It was slim and looked smooth, but I figured it could give quite a sting if he chose to hit me with it.

"The way you're standing now is my 'Ready' position for a slave," Mr. Benjamin explained, pulling the used rubber glove inside out and off his hand as if it were the most ordinary thing in the world. He stepped over to the table and dropped it, then turned back to me and continued in the same calm, even tone. "The same position but on your knees is called 'Presenting.' Normally you Present first when you enter a room, and you take the Ready position after you've been acknowledged, unless some immediate service is required. Please keep in mind that there are many styles of posture training; this is the first you must learn. If you prove to be satisfactory, I may instruct you in others."

My cock was still hard, and he couldn't help but notice it.

"Well, well," he said, lightly tapping it with his stick. "So the boy likes being inspected and probed. Is that true, Jeffrey?"

"Yes, Sir." It was true. I was pleased with my body and happy to show it off. And I liked being handled like a piece of property. That's why I was there!

"You realize, don't you, that not all Masters will appreciate this? Some will require you to suppress your erections, or They'll do it for you. If you always respond like this to being dominated, you'll need to look for a Master who likes that in a slave...But we're getting far ahead of ourselves, boy. You're no slave yet. You're just a boy who thinks he wants to be a slave. And you came to Mr. Benjamin to find out for sure, didn't you?"

"Yes, Sir...Please, Sir — train me, Sir?"

"We'll see. Now pay attention." He tapped my balls with his springy stick, not hard enough to hurt — much. "The reason to keep your legs apart is to expose your balls and asshole. When you're a slave, they won't belong to you anymore, and you'll have no right to protect them or withhold them. Remember that you're supposed to be vulnerable and exposed. In time, you'll feel strange and uncomfortable when you're not naked and spread, when you have to wear clothes, for instance, or sit normally in a chair instead of standing or kneeling with your legs apart.

"Take this as an example," he said, sharply tapping my chest, my nipples, my abs. "There's a reason for everything I'll teach you, and it all comes down to helping you stop thinking like a free man and start thinking like a piece of intelligent property. Some of the reasons will seem obvious, and some will be obscure. Don't worry about them. You don't need to understand all the reasons behind what I tell you. All you have to do is accept and obey. It's not about acting like a slave; it's about being a slave. The two are totally different. Understand?"

"Yes, Master."

"No!" he said, and underscored it with a slash of his pointer across my chest. It raised a welt immediately. I winced and glanced up at him but managed to suppress anything more than a small hiss between clenched teeth.

"I am not your Master," he said in a tight voice, as if I'd touched a sore point underneath the armor of his formality. "I'm not anybody's Master. I am simply a trainer of slaves. I take eager, clumsy, unformed boys like you and turn them into first-class pieces of property that any Master would be proud to own...Eyes down, boy. Focus on the floor between my feet. Whenever you have no need to look up, keep your eyes on the floor. If you're standing or kneeling in front of a superior, you may look at His feet but no higher — unless ordered otherwise, of course. Your place is at the bottom, the base of the hierarchy, and that's where your eyes should always return."

He came close to me then and reached up to my neck, kneading each side of it with his hand. Despite his self-deprecation, the confident, assured touch thrilled me, and my cock waved in the air.

"Relax these muscles, boy. A stiff neck is a sign of pride and self-regard. You don't need to do anything; just stop tightening them. Let your head fall forward a little — it won't break off. Just let it go, let yourself be relaxed and vulnerable. This is all about dropping your guard, learning how to be defenseless and unresistant."

His hand moved over my shoulder and down my left arm, then the right. "You're too tense here as well, boy. You won't be able to hold your arms in that position for long if you lock them up like that. Let the weight of your arms flow down to your wrists and then into your back. It really needs very little energy to keep them there, if you don't try too hard." I felt the tension in my arm muscles ease as his fingers traced lightly along them.

"Now it's time for you to kneel, Jeffrey," he said from behind me, putting his hands back on my shoulders. "I'll guide you. Keep your back straight and bend your knees. . . . Slowly, let yourself sink down. Don't move your arms or your head; nothing above your waist needs to move. . . . That's right, good. . . . Now extend your right leg back and lower that knee to the floor. Always begin each change of position from your right side, unless there's some reason to do otherwise."

Normally, I'd have bent my torso forward and my ass back as I went down, but Mr. Benjamin's hands prevented that. Feeling awkward as hell, I kept my back straight and concentrated on not toppling. It felt as if my center of gravity was a foot in front of me, but I reached the floor without major mishap.

"Good," he said. "You'll get better with practice. It only felt strange because you're used to doing it differently. Now feel where your shoulders and knees are and line them up." I edged my knees a little further apart, feeling my balls hanging loose between them.

"Unless you're given permission to sit back on your heels, or told to take some other position, always kneel up like this, with your back and thighs straight. Remember to bow your head about 30 degrees and keep your eyes down. That's right. Good boy. Now stand up again, starting on the right."

I almost fell over in the process of standing up — amazing how dependent I was on my arms for balance! — but Mr. Benjamin kept me centered with light touches on one side or the other. He stayed in contact with me as I moved, either correcting my position or just reinforcing a correct direction. I became accustomed to his constant touch; it was reassuring, even pleasant, to be manipulated by his warm, dry hands.

"Again," he said, after I achieved the standing position. I bent my knees and began the process of moving down.

"And up . . . And down . . . Again . . . Again . . . Again . . ."

My muscles began to burn a little after a dozen repetitions, but with each cycle my movements became smoother, more graceful. My cock was no longer hard; there was nothing erotic about these exercises, yet they were curiously satisfying in another way. I was glad to let go, stop questioning, and allow my responses to be reshaped by Mr. Benjamin.

"Go all the way down this time," he said when I was next on my knees. "Lower your torso and head, and move your ass back, till your forehead is on the floor. Yes, that's right, now move your arms and clasp your hands behind your head. That's right. Feel how your ass is now the highest point of your body." His hand caressed my asscheeks, firmly and possessively. My balls dangled, loose and vulnerable, between my legs, and my cock started to fill out again. I didn't know if he'd beat me or fuck me, but I was ready for either. It felt so right to be exposed like this, and not to have any say in how I'd be used.

"Focus on your ass, not your head or cock. Right now that's what you are, a male ass with a slave attached. You have a fine ass, boy, and I'm going to enjoy beating it. Be glad that you can give me that pleasure." Time stretched out as I waited for it to start. I thought I could hear him walk away from me, toward the other side of the room, and return, but with the thick carpet it was hard to be sure.

"I'm going to beat you now, Jeffrey," he said directly behind me. "Remain as motionless as you can, and don't say anything. Remember that you are here of your own free will. If you want me to stop, you may put your hands over your ass, then get up and leave. But you won't be allowed to come back. Understand, boy?"

"Yes, Sir."

Wham! The first blow slammed into my ass. Whap! Whack! There was no gentle, erotic warm-up, just pain. I gritted my teeth and ground my forehead into the carpet. Wham! Whack! It wasn't the pointer stick I felt — he must have retrieved a wide leather strap from the closet, or wherever he kept his equipment. Whap! He worked me over methodically, from my thighs up to my shoulders, as if he were out to paint my backside an even red. Wham! Whack! How I wished I'd been tied down! The beating would have been so much easier to take with restraints to pull against. But this was a test, of course, and I had to prove I could control myself. Whap! Whack! Wham! God, he was good! Every stroke landed solidly, laying down a broad stripe of pain that flared white-hot and slowly faded into the background, not quite disappearing before the next one arrived. It was like a forest fire leaping from one thicket to the next, flames engendering flames, until the whole forest was alight. Except the conflagration was in me, was me.

Wham! Whap! I'd endured heavier floggings, beatings so severe my throat was raw from screaming, but never one so thorough, so precisely controlled, so relentless. Whack! The force and rhythm of Mr. Benjamin's blows never varied. Wham! Whap! He wasn't playing with my sensations, ramping up and then down to pull me along, keep me turned on. It didn't matter if I was turned on or not. All that mattered was that he was beating me, and I was letting him. Whack! Whap! Wham!

"Don't forget to breathe," he softly reminded me in between strokes.

I didn't scream, just held still and whimpered. My nose filled with the smell of damp wool as my tears soaked the carpet under my face. Finally I was able to relax into the rhythm of the beating and let the pain carry me away. My ego shriveled — I had no consciousness to spare for self-awareness. I stopped separating myself from what I was feeling, stopped judging it as good or bad, stopped trying to anticipate an end to it. Wham! Whack! Eventually even the feeling of the individual blows was lost as the blaze engulfed me . . .

"That's enough for now, boy," Mr. Benjamin said finally, as if from a great distance, and the beating stopped, though it took me some moments to realize it. "Straighten up and sit back. You can rest your arms on your thighs."

I groaned as my welted ass settled back onto my heels.

"No complaining, boy," he said from in front of me. "Just take a deep, deep breath, fill your lungs down to the bottom. Now hold it for a count of five . . . Now release it, all the way, let it carry the pain out of you. . . . Repeat: deep breath . . . hold . . . release . . . Again." He made me repeat the breathing exercise four more times, and by the end I was feeling much better. A warm afterglow suffused my body, and Mr. Benjamin, standing there with his jacket off and his shirt sleeves rolled up, even looked a lot sexier to me than he had at first. I wiped my face as well as I could with my hands and sniffed to clear my nose. My cock, which had deflated during the beating, was hard again. I snuck a look at his face — he was smiling. I quickly dropped my eyes and stifled an answering smile of my own.

"You took that well, boy," he said in an amused tone. "Did you enjoy it?"

"Thank you, Sir," I said, still looking down at those damned shoes of his. "Not while it was happening, Sir, but now I'm glad that you beat me, Sir. Thank you, Sir."

"Slaves need to be beaten regularly. Not as punishment — it's better if there's no particular reason, except to remind the slave of who and what he is. It's hard to stay focused on the idea that you're property, and a good beating brings that home to a slave's mind in a very direct and unmistakable way. Most slaves come to enjoy their beatings and to miss them if the routine is interrupted. In fact, it's a form of abuse to deny them that discipline, because nothing else seems to reinforce the special bond between Master and slave, or slave and trainer, as well as a regular, expected beating. While you're being beaten, you have the full attention of the one beating you, and He has yours. Did it seem that the beating I gave you was mechanical or impersonal?"

"Umm," I hesitated, not wanting to voice what might seem like a complaint, "yes, Sir, perhaps a little less personal than I'm used to, Sir."

"Well, you're wrong. It wasn't impersonal at all. I was intensely aware of your reactions at every moment, almost as if I was reading your mind through the quivering of your flesh. But I deliberately put that aside. Instead of playing on your responses, adapting the beating to you, I wanted to see how you would adapt to a methodical, unmodulated beating. Taking a beating because it turns you on is one thing. Taking a beating just because someone else wants you to is quite another. . . . As I said, you did well."

He seated himself in the chair and picked up a manila folder from the side table. My file? I looked at his shoes while he shuffled papers. Why couldn't he wear boots at least?

"Look at me, Jeffrey." I raised my eyes to his. They were brown and large, surrounded by halos of tiny lines in his 50-something skin. Was he ever young? I wondered. Did he have any idea what it was like to be 28 and constantly horny and have your head filled with images of bondage and torture? Of being unable to look at a strong, handsome man without wanting to kneel at his feet? Of being so desperately ready to be taken over? I was afraid I'd turn rotten with cynicism and frustration if it didn't happen soon.

"Are you with me, boy?" he asked, shaking me out of my reverie.

"Yes, Sir," I said as firmly as I could. He chuckled.

"This session's not what you expected, is it?"

"Sir, I'm not sure what I expected. They warned me, Sir, that you wouldn't behave like any Master I'd ever met."

"And just how many real Masters do you suppose you've met, boy?"

"A few, Sir," I said cautiously.

"Damned few, I expect," he said dismissively. "Those leather-clad studs you see at the bars with their keys on the left aren't 'Masters,' you know. Most of them would be hard—pressed to know what to do with a real slave if they had one. They aren't ready to own another man; they barely own themselves. Some of them may be competent tops for a scene, but as soon as they come their scripts run out. Those aren't the kind of Masters I work for." He looked down at the papers in his lap again, and I returned my own gaze to the floor between his feet.

"Your replies to my questionnaire are quite complete and satisfactory, Jeffrey. And accurate, as far as I can see. They give me a reasonably full picture of your experience, your interests, and your qualifications. All the usual domestic skills — very good. Computer savvy, experienced with a wide variety of programs — that's very important now. Read French and German — excellent. You don't speak them?"

"Not well, Sir. Only a little. But I could learn, Sir, if needed."

"I'm sure you could. Fine, then." He studied the papers some more.

"I see you were unsure about one of the items on the sexual part of the questionnaire, 'Toilet training.' Are you unsure what it is, or unsure whether you can do it?"

"Both, Sir."

"Of course!" he laughed. "How can you know if you can do it when you don't know what it is? Toilet service, which you didn't question on the form, is when you take your Master's piss or, sometimes, shit. Few American Masters will require you to eat their shit, though it's more common in Europe. Piss-drinking is common here, though, and it's not dangerous as long as you're both healthy. Toilet training, however, means that you are not allowed to relieve yourself except with
permission, and when you do so you may not stand to piss or sit on the toilet seat to shit. You sit on the bowl, or crouch over it, not touching it — or your cock — for both functions. It also means that you cannot close the door when you use a bathroom in your Master's home. Or any other Master's home or playspace. Is that clear enough?"

"Yes, Sir."

"And you think you can do that with no trouble?"

"If necessary, Sir," I said, betraying some distaste for the prospect.

"Believe me, boy, it's entirely necessary, even more than toilet service, which not all Masters care for. Few things are so effective in teaching a slave that he's property as taking away his ability to control his own bodily functions. Some training regimens even require you to be catheterized and plugged at all times so that you can't go on your own even with permission. I don't take it that far — too much work for me! Like other disciplines, toilet training can be very hard at first, but after awhile you won't give it a second thought. It'll just be the way things are."

I felt his eyes on me before he told me to look up.

"You're a healthy, intelligent, educated, attractive young man," he said. "You have a good job and marketable skills, your own apartment, no heavy debts. You're out of the closet, apparently comfortable with being gay and kinky, no evidence of debilitating mental or emotional problems. So why do you want to be owned? . . . Oh, I know what you said on the form, and it was very well expressed, too. But I need to hear it from your own mouth, in words you haven't rehearsed and polished."

I took a deep breath and tried to explain, as much to myself as to him.

"Sir, there's something missing in my life. It's like I have a hole in me, Sir, that never gets filled. Even when I trick with a good Topman, Sir, he never seems to demand enough from me. After they get their rocks off, Sir, they always go soft and want to treat me like a buddy. It was even worse, Sir, when I had a lover. He was always asking me what I wanted, Sir, or expecting me to make decisions. It's not that I can't make decisions, Sir, when I have to. I do it all the time at work. But I don't want to have to make them at home, Sir . . . That sounds selfish, Sir, doesn't it?"

"Yes," he said. "Is that it, then? You want to be spared having to make decisions? You're not willing to be responsible for your own life?"

"No, Sir! I didn't mean it that way, Sir. It's true, Sir, that I don't like making decisions, but that's because I don't know what my life is for, Sir! It all seems pointless sometimes. I work, I eat, I sleep, I jerk off — why? What's the purpose, Sir? I need someone who'll give my life meaning, Sir, by taking all I have to give Him, by demanding the best from me, Sir. What I do for myself doesn't count, Sir. I only feel real when I'm serving someone else, Sir, making Him happy or more comfortable. If I have to take care of myself so I can serve Him better, Sir, that's okay. Then it's not for me but for Him. I'm not expecting a free ride, Sir, or to be taken care of like a baby."

"And how much of this feeling is sexual, Jeffrey? Do you feel the same pleasure in service after you've had an orgasm?"

I flushed with embarrassment, because of course a lot of it was sexual. And I remembered how lazy I could feel right after coming. But he spared me having to confess that, and he seemed to understand that it wasn't just sexual.

"Well, that proves you're normal, my boy! Nearly all slaves find their calling because sex drives them to it. But those who stay in this life discover rewards beyond the sexual — they have to, because most Masters allow orgasms very sparingly! A horny slave is an attentive slave, and the same goes for a trainee. If I accept you for training, Jeffrey, the very first rule is that you will never touch your cock except to clean it, and then with a washcloth, and you will never come except on my order — unless you have a wet dream! And you can be sure I won't order you to come for a long time, at least four weeks to start. These rules don't apply only when you're here. You'll follow them all the time, everywhere. Can you accept and abide by that?"

"Yes, Sir!" I vowed, my cock paradoxically rock-hard at the thought of being denied release. "It'll be hard, Sir, but I know I can do it." Four weeks!

"Good. There are devices that can help insure your chastity, and I'll look into getting something practical for you. But any device can be defeated if the slave is determined to disobey. Your obedience is much more important than your chastity. You will demonstrate that obedience by keeping a daily journal, and, among other things, you will note down in it every time you 'slip' and touch your cock. I will discuss your slips with you and encourage you to do better. If the violation was flagrant, I will punish you. A failure to be truthful with me is unforgivable. If I ever catch you in a lie, you will be instantly dismissed. Understood?"

"Yes, Sir."

"A word about punishment. I don't believe that you can train a slave to behave properly by physical punishment. I use pain as a reminder, or for emphasis, and to help a trainee focus. But the main force must always be your own desire to succeed and excel, to become what you say you want to be. I'm not going to beat that into you or any of that nonsense you've probably read about in porn stories.

"Oh, I'll beat you plenty — every session will include some kind of a beating. As I told you before, slaves need to be beaten regularly. But I won't beat you for punishment. I expect you to learn not only to accept regular beatings but to welcome them and enjoy them. The last thing I want is for you to associate them with misbehavior, or to encourage you to think you need to screw up in order to get beaten!

"Most of our sessions will be much like this first one, though longer and with more varied training in how to move, especially in chains, how to talk, and how to serve. If I think you need heavier torture or extended bondage, I'll give you that, too. You won't need to play games anymore the way you've been doing in the bars. You won't have to try to seduce me into giving you what you need. Giving you what you need is what I'm here for. Think of me as your coach. I will prepare you to endure anything that may be imposed on you in service, and to do anything you'll be asked for. Is that clear?"

"Yes, Sir." My head was spinning with questions! But I didn't know where to begin, or how to ask them without irritating him. Of course, he saw that, too.

"If you think of questions after you leave today, you may write me, and I will answer them, if I can, when I see you again."

"Thank you, Sir!"

"I don't hold much with written contracts during training. Either your word is your bond, or you're not worth anyone's time. So here's the deal: If you will agree to do whatever I tell you, to the best of your ability, until I release you, I will agree to train you to be the best slave you are capable of being. I promise that I will not dismiss you except for cause or when I judge you are ready to offer yourself to a Master. You, however, will have the option of quitting at any time for any reason — with the proviso that such a decision is final, and that if you quit I won't see you again. Is all that clear, Jeffrey?"

"Yes, Sir."

"And do we have an agreement?"

Sweat broke out all over me as I wrestled with the decision. He made it seem so . . . so sweeping and irrevocable, although there was that escape clause. . . . Wasn't this what I wanted? How could I back out now, without even trying? Just because he's not a sexy stud? You don't need to be a sexy stud to be a good teacher! But what if he expects to fuck me, or have me suck him off? . . . Well, so what? I can close my eyes and pretend it's someone else. When I'm a slave I won't have any choice about who uses my holes. Why worry about it now? I'm sure he'll keep it safe; he's no fool, that's for sure.

"Why are you hesitating, boy?" he demanded finally. "Either you know what you want, or you don't. Having sought me out with considerable effort, you know what I am. You know my reputation. You came here asking to be trained as a slave, and I have agreed to do so. Yes, I'm demanding a blank check from you, but you can stop payment on it at any time. We're both adults. We've been candid with each other — or at least I have. You've had a chance to see and feel what my teaching is like. Trust your heart. Decide."

"Yes, Sir, thank you, Sir," I forced out. This was so hard!

"Does that mean you agree? Don't hedge."

"Yes, Sir, I agree, Sir. I will do whatever you tell me, Sir, to the best of my ability, until you release me, Sir. Thank you, Sir." There! It was done. I was committed.

"Good boy. Put your hands behind your back again. Now bend forward and kiss my shoes. The left one first. Always begin on the Master's left when you are offering service. Begin on your right side when you change your own position." I could barely reach his gleaming black shoes, but he helped me by moving his feet out a few inches. After I kissed his left and then his right shoe, I knelt upright again, keeping my head bowed. Something cold and metallic slipped over my head and settled around my neck — a dog chain. He had slipped one end through the other, instead of locking it, and the loose end hung down my chest.

"Your collar, boy. It's unlocked, because you still have the freedom to take it off at any time. But you'll keep it on, won't you?" Tears welled up in my eyes. I couldn't imagine ever wanting to take it off!

"Oh, yes, Sir, thank you, Sir!"

"You'll have to earn a lock for it, boy, and that won't be easy. You need to understand exactly what you're giving up in becoming a slave, and this un-locked collar will be there to remind you. It's almost time for you to go, but I'll expect you back here tomorrow at 6 p.m. You get off work at 5:00, you said, so be punctual. You're going to serve my dinner, and I don't like to eat late. Tomorrow is Friday, so expect to stay here through the weekend. If you had other plans, cancel them. Bring a small bag with anything you think you absolutely need as well as clothes for work on Monday. Remember that your cock and balls are off limits to you now. Don't worry too much about all the other rules I've given you today. We'll go over them again and again until you're incapable of forgetting them. Tonight just concentrate on not touching your cock — that should be hard enough, I expect! You can even sleep in your bed instead of on the floor; time enough for that later. Any questions yet, boy?"

"Yes, Sir. Forgive me, Sir, if this is too personal . . . but were you ever a slave?"

"Yes, boy," he said with a laugh, "I've been where you are — that's really what you're asking, isn't it?" He didn't wait for me to reply but continued, more gravely. "I was trained just as I will train you — if anything, more harshly and forcibly. I wasn't allowed to live on my own at all once I entered training. I was brought into my Master's home, stripped, collared, and regimented 24 hours a day from Day 1. I won't ask anything of you that hasn't been demanded of me. Understand, boy?"

"Yes, Sir. But. . . but..." His eyes flashed, and I left the obvious question unstated, suddenly afraid I'd angered him. His expression softened, however, and he actually smiled down at me — kneeling before him put my head lower than his even though I was taller and he was sitting.

"Why am I not a slave now? Is that your question, boy?"

"Yes, Sir," I said in a small voice.

"Who said I'm not, boy? There's more than one way to live a life of service. We can't all stay naked and on our knees, much as we might like to. For instance, right now you need to get on your feet, get dressed, and go home."

"Yes, Sir!" I said, smoothly rising to my feet in the Ready position before turning to leave the room.

"Stop!" Mr. Benjamin said sharply. I froze in place. "Turn around!" I faced him, filled with distress at having fucked up already — and I didn't even know how! "Do not ever turn your back on me, boy, or on any other superior. When you're dismissed, you back away slowly until I turn my attention elsewhere, then turn and leave normally. Get down and give me fifty pushups! Now, boy!" I lowered my chest to the floor and then pushed back up onto my toes. "Count off each one, boy, and thank me for it. They'll help you remember this lesson."

"One, Sir, thank you, Sir! . . . Two, Sir, thank you, Sir! . . . Three, Sir, thank you, Sir! . . ." I was slick with sweat by the time I'd finished the punishment set, and my muscles burned, but I felt good! I'd learned a new lesson, and I'd been given a new boundary. I smiled to myself as I got onto my knees and faced him in the Present position, then rose to my feet again. Despite his words earlier, I could recall each of the rules Mr. Benjamin had already taught me. I recited them to myself as I backed away under his critical gaze. Every rule was a link in a chain of obedience, and the longer the chain, the safer and more secure I felt. As his eyes released me, I noted just the hint of a smile on his face. I smiled to myself, too, as I turned to leave the room — and enter into my new life.

20 Play Party

Ken Mandarin did not have a *ryokan* style room. Ken had a suite on the top floor of the hotel building, overlooking the thick foliage and a waterfall to the south. Ken had a small stereo and CD player that had amazing sound quality, and an array of low, soft furniture and trays of chilled fruits and chocolates and bottles of champagne everywhere, and she had an array of sex toys and pain toys that must have caused an army of raised eyebrows at customs.

None of this was visible to Michael, however, kneeling on the floor wearing nothing but a blindfold and feeling very much like he was about to be sacrificed to some rude god.

"You know, my English is not very good," Ken was saying to him. "Please explain again why you are here looking like this?"

Michael could hear Marcy snicker, and his ears burned. "Ma'am, I was disrespectful to my teacher, impatient and rude, I raised my voice and called attention to myself and to him. Ma'am, for those offenses, I am offering my body for chastisement, and I hope that the memory of this will keep me from making similar mistakes in the future. I beg my trainer's pardon for my offenses and beg yours for having to witness this." Oh yeah, he would never, never forget this night.

Earlier that evening, right after dinner, when the entertainment began and a woman walked out onto the stage with a koto, her face covered with a thick white mask and her body covered with a long, ornate golden kimono, Michael had sat back, expecting to hear some examples of Japanese classical music. From where he sat, he could see a long suffering look on the face of Tucker, who was busy signaling for another beer. Michael was going to do the same, when suddenly, from the wings, came two figures all dressed in

213

solid black, who ran up to the startled woman and reached for what looked like golden strings attached to her kimono. As she stood up, uttering one or two words of what seemed like genuine surprise, the black clad 'helpers' pulled on the strings, which unraveled through the sides of the kimono in whirls of motion. Another black clad figure dashed in front of them and grabbed the koto, and as he darted off to the left, the kimono broke apart and was pulled away, leaving the woman dressed — in a shiny, satin suit, with a black shirt and red tie. One flick of a wrist and the white mask, with its painted-on eyebrows came off, and it revealed a feminine Japanese face topped with a stylish pompadour. Two twists of the body and a standing microphone was planted in her hand. A familiar riff filled the air, from large speakers on either side of the stage, and a warm American southern voice started singing — "Uh—one for the money, two for the show. . ."

She was an Elvis impersonator. As the room exploded in laughter and applause, she gyrated and made love to the mike the way the King used to, her every move sexual and exciting and a wonderful cross between feminine and masculine.

Michael could just hear Tucker shouting, "Now, that's more *like* it!"

And they all laughed even harder when the two black-clad assistants came back at the end of her song to tear off her suit to reveal — a slender *man* underneath it all, his smile going from the sexy snarl of Elvis to the coquettish look of the actors who played female roles in Kabuki.

The rest of the entertainment was similar — gender twisting and dancing, with some slaves clearly of one sex or another but most of them either blurring the lines or outright leaving the trainers arguing. Some lip-synched, others sang legitimately, there was even a comedy routine, but it was all delightful — funny, exciting, curious and gradually mysterious. And damn if it didn't lift the mood of the room. The fluidity of gender and sexual messages was just exhilarating, and pleasantly teasing, the slaves energetic and skilled, and thrilled by applause and attention. It was a perfect show — silly and seamless, thought and discussion provoking and yet casual. When the "cast" was brought out for a final round of identification, all of them clad only in training collars, roars of delight and amusement rose as the trainers got to settle on who had clocked the correct genders, or at least had come close. The slaves all bowed deeply, in the Japanese style, before they exited.

By the time the black clad slaves scurried through the hall setting up a series of small black machines as they had set up the grills earlier, and smaller, hand held microphones were appearing, people seemed eager to scan lists of songs to sing. But before Michael even got his hands on the black and silver covered book of song titles, a figure in black and gray appeared at his side, and his heart leapt in surprise. It was Chris, and he touched him lightly on the shoulder. "Time to go, Michael."

And when Ken got up to leave as well, Michael wished that he could say that he really, *really* needed to hear Tucker's version of *Born in the USA*, but they were gone from the building before the Southern man even got to thank his hosts for such a fine, *fine* dinner.

The same slave that helped Chris dress got him all undressed, leaving Michael to wait in a clean jockstrap and a yukata until Chris put on jeans and a t-shirt. Chris picked up the strap and they walked to the other building in silence, and once they got into the room, it was "Strip, present and report to Ms. Mandarin why you are in such a sorry state of affairs", and boom, that was it.

How did they *do this* on a regular basis, Michael thought, as Ken discussed his explanation and apology with Marcy. How can any human being sleep at night knowing that at any moment, they can be stripped naked and made to do humiliating things in front of people — people they might have to deal with later on? He had always assumed that slaves — people who wanted to be slaves anyway — had some quirk in their nature that always made these things hot, or at least acceptable. But what if their erotic attachment was to only one person, or only one situation? What if all they needed or wanted *was* to be the upstairs maid? Or to be one master's fuck toy? And what if their owner could still compel them to do things like this? How did they cope?

"Well, I can hardly reward your dingo with the attentions of my two perfect angels if he has been naughty," Ken said, drawing one finger along Cindy's back and making her slave shiver. Ken had changed into a handsome pair of red silk boxer shorts and a loose robe knotted around her hips. Andy knelt at her feet, watching Michael intently, his lips parted and slightly wet. There were red marks around his pale pink nipples, bright and new, bites or crop strikes, it was difficult to tell. Michael's last sight was Andy's face, and his hard little nipples.

"You're going to have to explain the dingo comments to me later," Chris said. "But I agree. I was going to beat him myself. But my beatings are steadily losing their effectiveness, as he is increasingly enjoying them. Quite a nuisance, actually."

Michael wished a whole troupe of demons would descend on his trainer and rip him to shreds.

Marcy rolled her eyes. "What else is new? It's an old story, Parker, physical punishments have to be non-erotic, come on, that's stuff you figure out when you're a kid, for crissakes."

"Well, as you must have guessed by now, Marcy, I am fond of old ways;

I rely on a higher instinct to guide behavior, a desire to please and not be disappointing. I beat people because I enjoy it, and prefer that their reaction be appropriate to the situation. Since Michael will not be held to such an exacting nature of service, I am open to other methodology, and therefore — I call upon your experience to aid me. And to aid Michael, of course."

"Tsk, tsk, Marcy, one must be patient," interjected Ken. Michael could hear the whisper of her boxer shorts as she walked around him, could imagine her stroking her jaw, or laying a long finger against one lip. "Yes, we agree that one should not please a slave — oh, Michael, I do apologize, we all know you are not a slave — but still, one must not please a — a — target of punishment? If the target does not know the difference between pleasure and punishment. But I think it is clear that he does not *enjoy* enjoying it is that not true, dingo?"

Michael groaned. Why couldn't they just get it over with?

And then he realized that Chris was next to him, and he could feel, actually *feel* the menace, and he knew that he had to answer, and quickly.

"Ma'am," he said, thinking as fast as he could, "I am ashamed that my bad behavior has — caused me to be punished."

"Not — a — direct — answer." said Chris, and gave Michael a firm push in the center of his back. Michael allowed himself to fall onto his hands and braced himself. There was one blow of the strap for each word that Chris had said, and when he finished with the last one, he grabbed Michael by the hair and pulled him up, and jammed one foot under his cock and balls. Michael could feel the stiffness, and his heartbeat echoed in his brain and he wished he could scream and struggle and just run out of there, but he stayed still, allowing Chris to push him back down again.

"See?" was all Chris said.

"Let Cindy do it then," suggested Marcy. "Or Stu here, he can handle one of those canes if you want something different."

Not the boy, not the boy, not the boy, Michael thought furiously.

"No — let Andy do it," Ken said firmly. "He has a strong arm. I wish to see if the dingo reacts to all men, or just to one man."

There was silence then, and Michael knew that Chris had agreed, and he tensed his body. As he felt Andy take up a position beside him, he ground his teeth together, vowing to remain silent for as long as he could. It didn't take too long for him to break his vow, because whatever Andy was using, it wasn't Chris' strap and it wasn't a cane, but something hard and stingy, some kind of whip with knots on the ends, short enough to use kneeling, but wicked enough to make his breath come out in tight hisses. He tried to keep silent, at least keep to gasping, but the first time those knots crept up and hit the underside of his balls, even at half strength, he yowled.

"He doesn't know to tuck?" Ken asked idly.

No one answered her, but the whipping stopped, and Michael felt a strange hand part his legs further, and humiliatingly pull his cock and balls tighter under his body. Then the same hand tapped his spread thighs, and Michael pulled them in. He was now tucked. The whipping continued, and he could dimly hear conversation in the background. Thank goodness, they weren't all just staring at him.

But — shouldn't they be? His brain started to hurt from the contradictions. How could he so much want them all to disappear and yet feel bad that they weren't paying attention?

When it was over, he gasped for breath and almost whimpered. His ass and legs felt like they had been sand blasted. A hand fisted in his hair again, and he knew that it was Chris, and as he was jerked up, it was amply clear that there was a difference between when Chris disciplined him and when some other man did. Chris gave him a slight shake, and Michael gasped, "Thank you sir."

"Well, that ends that experiment," Marcy said. "What next?"

"Now he belongs to Ken, for whatever deviltry she's planned," Chris said, untangling his fingers. Cindy came up to him with her trademark combination of shyness and invitation and held a glass of champagne for him; he smiled at her when he took it, and stroked her hip gently as he retreated to one of the low, comfortable chairs.

Ken walked around Michael again with one finger tapping her lips. "I was going to let the twins have him, but on second thought — perhaps just Cindy."

With the slightest of pouts, Cindy left Chris' side to go to her owner. She was wearing a thong and her smile, and when Ken signaled, she dropped the thong. "Let him see," Ken said, and Cindy knelt gracefully to pull off the blindfold, so that the first thing that Michael saw since he had knelt in the middle of the room were her beautiful, tanned breasts and her pearly smile. There were no red marks on her perfect tits, that was for sure.

"Do you like her?" Ken asked.

"Yes, ma'am," Michael whispered.

"*Bon.* You shall put on a show for us now, a sex show. Then I shall decide what else to do."

For a brief moment, Michael hoped that things were looking up, but as soon as Cindy giggled, retreated to the side of the room where all the sex toys were and picked up a harness for Ken to approve of, he knew he was wrong.

"So — what are you going to do with Andy, if not put him in the show?" asked Marcy.

"I loan him to you," Ken said magnanimously.

Marcy looked at Chris, who waved a hand in easy denial of Andy's use, and Marcy sighed. "Good. I haven't seen you in a dog's age, Andy, come here and let's make watching this show a little more interesting for me. Parker, feel free to entertain yourself with Stu."

Michael caught a glimpse of the embarrassment and fear that flooded Stuart's face and felt a brief moment of pleasure at the thought of whatever Chris would do to the boy, but stopped thinking right about the moment Cindy reappeared in his line of sight with a large, green dildo shaped somewhat like a corkscrew now strapped between her legs.

"Hello, pretty boy," she whispered, licking her lips and caressing its length with her fingers. "Help me get this nice and hard for you."

"How is his mouth?" enquired Ken, nibbling on a slice of mango.

"I don't have personal experience with it," Chris said. "But Mr. Elliot pronounced him adequate and trainable."

"I hope that he is more than adequate for my Cindy," Ken laughed as he waved at Cindy to command her to begin and then took the seat next to Chris. He glanced down. Stuart assumed the kneeling-to-offer position before him. Chris then deliberately turned away, to face Ken, just as she finished the mango and was admiring the tattoos on his forearms. She traced a line of flames that began slightly above his wrist and wound halfway to his elbow.

"I like the fire," she said. "It is very unlike you, though. Unlike what you appear to be, I suppose."

"Don't confuse restraint with a lack of passion," Chris said.

Cindy was rocking her hips back and forth very gently, letting Michael get used to the width and length of her toy cock. His face was already red, his eyes closed in humiliation or concentration — but not exactly distaste. His cock was tumescent again. Andy's was, too, his body backed against Marcy's, her fingers tormenting his nipples as they watched Cindy work her way deeper and deeper into Michael's mouth.

"So Ken," Chris said, feeling Stuart sway slightly in his posture, feeling the warm energy that came from a person who was so tightly controlled and so excited. He continued to ignore the young man. "For years now, I've supported your contention that they're actually twins. I never even asked them directly, and you know I could have if I wanted to, and compelledthem to obedience, as well. Do me a kindness and end the mystery for me. Tell me the truth."

Ken smiled and they both glanced at the show that was going on for their pleasure when they heard Michael gag. Without moving her eyes away from the scene, Ken said, "No, they are not. They are husband and wife."

"Ah." Chris admired the way Cindy moved her hips — it was just as he taught her, with a little rocking motion to spread the mouth wide. "Stuart, hands and knees, please, and turn to the side. Now shift back. Back. Stop and stay."

Ken obligingly used her new ottoman and leaned back into the chair. "They were almost divorced once, can you believe it? Each wishing that the other would play the master for them."

"Matson found them, didn't he?"

"*Oui.* And then Janna trained them, and then they became mine and then I sent them to you." She sighed and wiggled her toes. "It pleased me that they looked so much alike, twins from the gods, I think. Twin in nature if not in blood. There is — a — what is it, an energy, a synergy? — that comes from the nearness of a brother and sister, yes?"

"Yes, sometimes," Chris said. He watched Stuart's face, saw the color in his cheeks, the slight tremble in his narrow shoulders. Time enough to catch him if he stiffened, and he should have learned by now how to stay in one place for so short a time. "I've seen this sibling energy many times," he said, leaning back, his head next to Ken's.

Cindy looked at her owner and said, "Master — may I?" Ken looked over at the pair and then at Chris, and when he nodded, said "Yes, but *vasi doucement,* eh? Be gentle." Cindy grinned and nodded and patted Michael on the head as he gasped and coughed, and then elegantly walked behind him to kneel comfortably and spread his asscheeks.

Ken watched thoughtfully for another moment and then touched Chris' hand lightly. "I am glad to be friends again," she said. "But I am sad to say that I cannot think of a way to approve of your proposal. I must vote against it." She traced the outline tattoos on his forearm again, this time almost sheepishly. She had liked all of his tattoos when she first saw them two months ago. That was when he first told her about his proposal. And as he glanced at her lowered eyes tonight, he saw that she was annoyed with what she had to say to him.

He sighed, but nodded. "Our friendship was never in jeopardy," he said simply. He took up her hand and gave it a firm squeeze of reassurance. Briefly, he wished he could come up with something that would sway her, even as they sat back to watch her slaves at work, one of them now turned to pleasuring, one tormenting. What a decadent life, to discuss business while people cavorted and posed and fucked for your amusement. How annoying it was that his mind could so easily be turned from this sort of spectacle toward the more mundane aspects of his position. Politics and sex; no matter how you tried to keep them apart, they crowded together. Sometimes, it was exhilarating. Other times, it was just abrasive. And thinking of abrasive things; "Cindy — please be more liberal with the lubricant, girl. I taught you better than that."

219

Ken laughed and Cindy blushed prettily and squeezed out an extra dollop. "She just wishes to make it more interesting, she is a wicked girl that way. So, enough business. You will tell me about this sibling thing, yes? Have you met others like my pair?"

"Yes."

"Slaves you trained as well?"

"Not as much. I'm actually thinking of my sister." He chuckled at her look of surprise. "Not a sister of blood. My sister in spirit."

21 Alex's Choice   by Karen Taylor

Rachel was leaning over her table, rolling a joint, when she heard someone knock on her door. "Go the fuck away, I'm busy," she yelled, since it was at least three hours before her next client was supposed to arrive and she wasn't dressed.

"Too busy for an old friend?" a familiar voice called back, startling her. Rachel dropped the joint back on the table and headed to the hallway. She looked through the peephole. Standing outside her door was a short, stocky man with dark curly hair, wearing a motorcycle jacket. With a shriek, she pulled the door open.

"Parker? Ohmygod, it's fucking Parker!" she cried, throwing her arms around the man at the door. "You surprised the fuck out of me! Why didn't you call or something?"

"I was in the neighborhood, thought I'd stop by," Chris said lightly, embracing her briefly, then releasing.

"Jesus, Parker, the apartment's a fucking mess, I'm not dressed —"

So what's new?" he responded, and she punched him playfully. "Come on, Rachel, I've seen you and your living quarters in conditions much worse than this." He looked around. The studio was in the Meat Packing District, but high enough up that the noise wasn't too bad. Or the smell, although it hovered in the air even late at night. Some of the furniture was still familiar — the kitchen table, the old lamp with the broken chain, the small desk piled high with mail and papers. But there was a new mock-Persian rug, and a futon couch with a stained oak frame with a matching side table. A chiffarobe in the corner had one door open, showing the floggers hanging on the inside.

His eyes trailed up. There, he spotted the eye bolts sunk deeply into the ceiling.

"How's business?" he asked, watching her as she walked toward the refrigerator and pulled out two diet colas.

"Same old shit," she replied, returning and handing him one of the cans. "But I pay my rent and have enough left over for some luxuries." She set her can on the table next to the couch, picked up the newly rolled joint, and lit it. Chris shook his head when she offered it to him, and she rolled her eyes wickedly.

"I know, I know, you don't do it any more. Fuck, Parker, I never thought I'd see you turn down a toke," she teased him. "Time was, you'd match me toke for toke, line for line."

"Match you? I'd beat you," Chris replied, and they laughed together, warmed by each other's company. "Do you remember —" they said simultaneously, then stopped, laughing again. Then Rachel put the joint back down, stepped closer, touched Chris' face tenderly, and kissed him. "Fuck, I miss you, Parker," she sighed.

Chris smiled back, his face more relaxed and open with Rachel than with anyone else in his life. Ever. "I missed you, too," he said.

And suddenly, it was just like old times. They wrapped themselves around each other, kissing deeply. Rachel unbuttoned Chris' shirt, pulled it out of his jeans, and rubbed her hands against the warm flesh of his chest and shoulders, kissing his neck hungrily. Chris was less urgent, but just as ready, using one hand to untie the front of her kimono, using the other to run his fingers through Rachel's thick, curly hair, pulling on it just slightly to pull her head back and kiss her harder. They stumbled, still tangled in each other, to the couch, clothes falling around them. Wrestling for position, like they used to do.

Later, Chris watched her languidly smoke her joint, his fingers tracing a series of scars on her arm.

"You haven't changed a bit," he told her.

"You have," Rachel replied honestly, "but you're still one hell of a good fuck."

* * *

"I'm here to offer you a job," Chris said. They were sitting up, more or less, and Rachel was smoking her joint.

"What kind of job?" she asked.

"Working with me. In the Marketplace," he answered. Rachel took another toke, letting the smoke sink into her lungs as she thought about that.

222

Parker had told her about the Marketplace, told her years ago when he went in search of it. Told her more after he was in it, even though he often seemed to vanish for months at a time without as much as a post card. It was clear Parker loved the Marketplace. She remembered the last time he had come to visit, around Christmas a year ago, after he got his job out on Long Island. He told her about the for real slaves and owners who did this full time. And Parker told her he was going to train the slaves.

Train them? she had asked. And Parker told her about the training program he was developing, the four week, six week, and eight week regimens, and she had laughed at him. Especially when Parker explained to her that he wasn't training them for himself, but for other people. She thought he was nuts.

Rachel couldn't imagine what job would be of interest to her in Parker's world. She sure as hell wasn't slave material. She definitely didn't have the money to be an owner. And after Parker had told her how much money he made training, she had laughed in his face. In Rachel's world, the money didn't balance out the time spent, especially with Parker's extra expenses.

On the other hand, business was . . . boring. Not that she ever got tired of tying clients up and hurting them, sometimes even fucking them. But to do it on a clock annoyed her. Her favorite clients were the ones who took her to clubs or gatherings of other kinky people. There, she'd have a whole weekend to dominate and hurt her client or anyone else she had an interest in. Plus, she got off a lot. In the Marketplace, she knew, the clock would never stop.

"Tell me about it," Rachel said. Chris relaxed. She was interested. He started to explain, and watched her eyes, half—closed from pot and sex, began to twinkle as he described the position he had in mind.

* * *

"Rachel, I'd like to introduce you to Grendel Elliot, one of my employers," Chris Parker said formally. Rachel stuck her hand out automatically, but her eyes were still taking in the room. She had been surprised when the car had pulled in front of big Colonial type house, in a part of Long Island known for its wealthy inhabitants. Now, inside, she was standing in what Chris told her was the library. The windows looked out over a garden, and she spotted a stable. Jesus, the place even smelled like money. She thought the bearded guy who just shook her hand smelled like money, too. "It is a pleasure to meet you, Rachel," he said in a pleasant voice. "My associate will be down as soon as she's finished with her trainee."

Internally, however, Grendel was taken aback. This was the woman

Chris had suggested would be suitable in their house? He could tell Rachel was wearing what was probably her best outfit, but it was definitely in need of pressing, and the skirt was shorter than current fashion. Her shoes were a cheap, shiny leather, the heels a little too spiky and tall for comfort. When Chris took her jacket, Grendel could clearly see the outline of a garish tattoo on her right arm through the sheer blouse. The sheerness also didn't hide the fact that her nipples were pierced. She looks like a biker in drag, Grendel thought in despair. What the hell does Chris think he's up to?

He offered Rachel a seat, and she flopped on the couch, kicking off her pumps. Chris brought her a diet soda, and she refused his offer of a glass, drinking directly from the can. With a sigh, Grendel opened the file Chris handed to him, Rachel's name on the flap. Again, he groaned inwardly. No college degree, not even a high school diploma. Her resume was sparse, waitressing in strip clubs, some phone sex work, and stints in three different Manhattan brothels. No job had lasted more than a year. No references, other than Chris'. He had no idea how to begin. Where was Alex? She should have been downstairs five minutes ago. The silence was growing awkward, and Grendel knew he should start without his partner. But how to begin?

"Tell me, Rachel," Grendel began tentatively, "Do you have any housekeeping experience?"

Rachel stared at him for a moment, then burst into loud guffaws.

"I'm pleased to hear you're getting along so well with our guest," said a voice from the doorway. Immediately, Chris reappeared, and motioned slightly to Rachel that she should stand up again. She did so, with only a slight air of impatience. Grendel was already on his feet, and made the introductions. "Rachel, this is my partner, Alexandra Selador."

Alexandra was small-boned, and elegant, with blond hair streaked with white and piercing blue eyes. Rachel extended her hand again, wondering why the woman looked so familiar. She sat across from Rachel, and made some pleasant comments about meeting a friend of Chris Parker's, making Rachel feel more comfortable. Her presence was also a relief to Grendel, who quickly excused himself from the room, claiming an important phone call.

"Tell me, Rachel, what has Chris told you about us?" Alexandra asked, when the time seemed right. She, like Grendel, was surprised by Rachel, but she was willing to believe there was something about the woman she hadn't yet discovered. If Chris was so willing to vouch for her, willing enough to ask for leave to bring her personally to the house, Alexandra was ready to find out why.

"Well, uh, Parker told me a lot about the Marketplace, and a bit about you two," Rachel began, still wondering where she had met this woman before, "and that you were looking for, well, an extra set of hands around here."

"We're looking to hire someone who is willing to work with the slaves we train," Alexandra explained. "Someone who is willing to be part of the training process, particularly in basic household tasks."

"Yeah, Parker told me. I gotta be honest with you, I'm not really interested in becoming a trainer. At least, not the way Parker explained it," Rachel said. "It sounds like too much work, what with that scheduling and paperwork and stuff. Too much like a real job, you know what I mean?" Alex smiled inwardly. "But Parker said, well, that you sort of need a back-up. Someone who knows how to make a slave be submissive. Keep them feeling that way for their stay, get them used to knowing their place. And I'm *real* good at that."

Indeed, Alexandra thought, looking at the woman sitting before her. If Chris says you are, I'm inclined to believe him. But what about the more mundane aspects of the job? She decided to be more explicit.

"The slaves must also learn practical skills, Rachel. They must be prepared to serve, not just respond."

"Yeah, I know, it's not just tormenting the slaves, they gotta learn something in the process," Rachel said. "Well, Ms. Selador, let me be honest with you. I hate cleaning toilets. I hate ironing shirts. But I like a clean bathroom and clean clothes. You can bet that I'll make sure these novices learn the basics." She grinned. "If I have a little fun enforcing the lessons, I'm sure you won't mind."

Alexandra smiled back. Despite her initial response, she found herself attracted to the woman, her openness and her dominance, and her obvious sadism. She reminded Alex of someone she had seen, many years ago, while attending a party at a professional's dungeon in the City, a young girl with wildly colored hair and brilliant tattoo on her arm. The girl was straddling a young punk who was writhing beneath her, until the girl put a knife to his throat, and told him to stay still while she fucked him. Later, Alex spotted the same girl sitting on one of the benches, this time playing with female, whose face was buried between the young woman's thighs, clearly struggling to breathe. She had looked up and spotted Alexandra watching her, and grinned. Yanking on her captive's hair, she let the woman up to gasp for breath only to push her back down in position, and lewdly moved her prisoner's head up and down by the hair. Alexandra smiled back at her. If only all Manhattan dungeon parties had scenes like that, I'd go out more, Alexandra thought with a sigh.

"Is there a problem?" Rachel asked, noticing that Alexandra's mind had wandered. "No, no," Alex assured her. "I was just thinking about an old friend, a pro in Midtown who used to throw great parties." Rachel snapped her head up. "That's it!" she said triumphantly. "That's where I know you from. You were at that party that Spike and me crashed."

"Then it was you!" Alex said, astonished. Of course, that was the tattoo showing beneath Rachel's blouse. "I remember you clearly."

"Yeah, I remember you, too," Rachel said bluntly. "You were the hottest thing there. But I was too busy dumping Spike getting to know Tikka to find you. Afterward, I mean."

"You were the one person worth watching at that party," Alexandra laughed. "You certainly had the room going." And me, she remembered.

"Yeah?" Rachel grinned. "How about you? Did you like it, too?" She looked Alexandra directly in the eye, and found the invitation.

Amused, but also interested, Alexandra smiled slowly, and waited for Rachel to move closer to her before she leaned toward the dark-haired woman to kiss her deeply. Rachel's mouth had the sweet-turned-bitter taste of marijuana, her lips full and soft. Surprisingly, she didn't immediately thrust herself into Alexandra's mouth, but instead teased her with the tip of her tongue flicking once, then twice, across the older woman's teeth.

There's even more talent here than I suspected, Alexandra thought, responding with her own quick thrusts before finishing the kiss and rising from her seat. Rachel stood immediately, and followed Alexandra out of the room, and up the stairs. After they disappeared into Alexandra's wing, Chris quietly reentered the library, picked up the glasses and the empty can and Rachel's shoes, and departed as noiselessly as he arrived.

Rachel did her best not to stare at the room. Unlike her own experience in the dark, industrial-district loft dungeons of her professional colleagues in Manhattan, Alexandra's room was light, with sunlight flowing through the windows, and beautiful, welcoming furniture that didn't crowd the room, but invited you to sit or recline in comfort.

Alexandra turned back toward Rachel, and shrugged out of her dress with a simple movement, letting the fabric drop and flow over her feet. Damn, Rachel thought, the woman is incredibly hot! She watched as Alexandra unhooked her bra with that curiously experienced double-jointed movement that women so take for granted until they see another woman execute the move. Alexandra stood like a Greek statue, her skin smooth and pale, her blue eyes like sapphires as she reached toward Rachel, and brought her close. Alexandra quickly unbuttoned Rachel's blouse, even as Rachel was unhooking her skirt and shrugging her hips out of it. She stopped, then, and traced her fingers over the tattoo on Rachel's arm and shoulder. It was a fierce-looking cat, snarling, with almost batlike wings and long, vicious claws.

Alexandra felt a set of tiny scars just where the cat's teeth appeared to be sinking its teeth into the muscle of Rachel's upper arm.

"My familiar," Rachel grinned, as she kissed Alexandra and pulled her down on the bed. "She bites, sometimes."

She ran her fingers through Alex's blond hair, then tugged gently, keeping Alexandra's mouth upon hers. She kissed her more urgently, pulling Alexandra's hand down to her dark, thick bush of pubic hair, wanting the woman to feel her arousal. Alexandra felt her own wetness grow when her fingers slipped through the hair and dipped into Rachel's ready cunt. After the years of shaven cunts and cocks that seemed perpetually fashionable in the Marketplace, Rachel's bush held a deep, erotic fascination for her. Its dark, tangled hair implied a sense of wild, sexual pleasure without compromise to any lover.

The older woman's nipples tightened as she pressed deeper, and Rachel responded, thrusting toward the fingers hungrily, demanding more. When Alexandra pushed three fingers, then four through the tangle of hair surrounding Rachel's ready opening, she sighed with delight. Pulling out slightly, she pressing her thumb tightly against the palm of her hand, and rocked it against Rachel's wet cunt. Rachel groaned as Alexandra rocked her hand across the wetness, and thrust harder and more urgently against the fist. With perfect rhythm, her cunt swallowed Alexandra's hand. Both women stopped briefly, enjoying the tightness, the fullness that no cock could ever match. Then the fucking began in earnest.

Rachel was a demanding, hungry lover, who wrapped her legs around Alexandra's thighs, keeping the woman against her and the fist securely in her cunt. Alexandra shifted her hand against the hot, fleshy walls of Rachel's cunt in minute movements which drove Rachel into wild humping thrusts that buried Alexandra's wrist even deeper into the tangled bush of hair. She used her free hand to pull Rachel's head and felt the woman's entire body arch against her.

Rachel growled and wrapped her arms around Alexandra, binding them even more tightly together, then took one of Alexandra's nipples into her mouth and began to suck and tongue it. The intensity of Rachel's hot mouth on her nipple was an erotic counterpoint to the warmth engulfing her fist, and Alexandra began to moan, as well, a sheen of sweat appearing on her neck and forehead. She pressed her knuckles against Rachel's cervix carefully, knowing that some women found that painful and others enjoyed it. Rachel was apparently in the latter category, and bucked hard. Alexandra let out a hiss of pleasure, and began to pull her hand out of Rachel's cunt, then thrusting it back in with a gentle twist of her wrist.

Rachel cried with pleasure, her mouth releasing Alexandra's nipple, only to catch the other in her mouth, this time using her teeth. Rachel bit down harder as Alexandra pumped her hand in and out of her cunt, pressing down, watching with astonishment as her hand appeared, then disappeared into the thick bush of hair. She fucked Rachel harder, until the woman cried out again, releasing her nipples. Then Alexandra bent her own head quickly, grasped one of Rachel's heavy nipple rings in her mouth, and tugged.

It was like riding a tiger. Rachel's cunt tightened almost painfully around Alexandra's fist as she came, thrusting upwards, as if to pull the hand even deeper into her. Alexandra slowed the movement of her hand, wanting to feel the power of the come as it squeezed, then released her fingers. Rachel was yowling, screaming to be fucked harder, demanding it as her right, and Alexandra shifted her hand slightly, amazed as the woman bucked again against her, grabbing the back of her head and pressing her mouth even more tightly against the dark, pierced nipple. Alexandra flicked her tongue against the rock-hard nub of flesh, sending Rachel into another orgasm, feeling Rachel's nails digging into her back as her body jerked again, her cunt tightening once more.

Finally, exhausted, Rachel released her, falling back against the bed, her brown curls spread across the pillow, a satisfied smile on her face. Alexandra smiled back at her, and carefully pulled her almost numb hand slowly out of Rachel's body. When her knuckles were free, another wave of orgasms pulled Rachel off the bed, almost as if she had been given an electric shock, leaving her to flop back like a cotton doll. Then Alexandra realized she, too, was exhausted, panting, and she fell against the pillow next to Rachel, flexing and re-flexing her hand until the blood flowed through it again.

When both women caught their breath, Alexandra rang a small bell on the bedstand, which immediately brought forth a slave carrying a tray with a carafe of light-colored liquid and two glasses. Alexandra poured a glass for her most-recent playmate, then filled one for herself. The slave vanished into the bathroom for a few moments and came back with warm, damp hand-towels, but Alex merely indicated the bedstand and waved a dismissive hand. As the slave quietly left the room, Rachel laughed and used one of the towels to wipe the sweat off her upper lift and around the back of her neck. "Shit, I can get used to that kind of help! Are they all like that?"

"They can be," Alex said after a drink. "Chris is a good overseer for them, but we could use another. How long have you known him?" Alexandra asked.

"Oh, Parker and me, we go way back. Back before he found this Marketplace thing. The 70's," Rachel said. "We met each other on the street. We hung together for a while, and kept in touch after he, you know, went into all this training shit. No offense."

"None taken." Alexandra thought about that. Rachel and Chris must have been in their *teens* when they met. Street kids, in New York, it was amazing they were both still alive.

"How did you live?" she asked.

"The usual," Rachel shrugged. "Parker would stay sometimes with his brother, sometimes with some freakin' mistress this or that. Probably locked up from time to time, if you know what I mean! Sometimes I would find a girlfriend with an apartment. If not, we'd trick for food and dope and blow and find some crib to crash in until something better came along. The piers on warm nights, it wasn't that bad." She smiled. "You know, Parker and I always promised each other that some day, we'd get ourselves our own place, with a dungeon, where we could spank rich stockbrokers for hundreds of dollars." She laughed at Alex's expression of amazement.

"Oh yeah, Parker and me were kinky right from the start," she laughed. "Parker was really into the whole leather-SM scene, sneaking into the bars and picking up the tough guys, sucking them off in the empty trucks on the piers. They liked that innocent face, I think, liked pounding it to shit. Dangerous stuff, sometimes, but when he wasn't doing that, he was getting fucked over by some bitch in high heels. I was pretty much doing the same things with different people. Never had a pimp, either of us, never mainlined, never got into strange cars, we did all right."

"Partners in more than one way?" Alex probed.

Rachel laughed and shrugged, not offended by the question. "We'd try to do this shit with each other, but you know — it just wouldn't ever work for too long. Always hot, don't get me wrong — just not — right. We were too much alike, I think. Then I got into a house and spanked stockbrokers for a living." Her smile faded. "But the leather scene wasn't enough for Parker. When he found out about the Marketplace, he couldn't stop until he got in. And now that he has, well . . ."

"You miss him?" Alexandra asked gently.

Rachel nodded. "Sometimes, its like we dropped out of each others lives," she said. "And he's just, well, different now. Not that he isn't still a real hot fuck," she assured Alex, "but we live very different lives now."

Alexandra nodded encouragingly, hoping that she was covering her shock. The vision of cool, distant Chris Parker having sex with the wildcat in bed next to her was hard to believe. Let alone the woman's assertion that they were *too much alike.* She couldn't imagine two more different people!

"Chris and me were the best fuck buddies," Rachel continued thoughtfully. "Didn't matter who we were doing or how good it was, it was always great to get back together. Even if it was months between fucks, we'd be in the same bed and boom, it was like we never parted. You people — the Marketplace — it's been the hardest separation for us. 'Cause before, one of us would run away or get thrown out, or sneak out or just fuckin' go out and we'd find each other. But for years now, he's had all these rules he has to follow, and I see him only once in a while. It's much worse than all the times he fell in love with someone." Her eyebrows lifted in an unasked question.

"Rachel, Chris is one of the most remarkable trainers to come along in decades," Alex said. "Part of that, I think, is because of his love for the Marketplace itself, rather than for any *individual* within it. There are very few who have that kind of focus. Frankly, I don't know if I could do it without Grendel, or someone like him." Rachel nodded, understanding that her question had been answered. But Alex had a question, too.

"So, Rachel, what about you? Do you think the Marketplace can be the right place for you?" Rachel thought about that.

"I don't know," she finally replied. "I'm not like you, or Parker. The whole thing about training sounds too much like work. And I don't get off on the idea that there might be a bunch of rules that I have to follow. That's why I'm working on my own now — house rules didn't sit well with me." She paused. "But that doesn't mean I'm unreasonable. Someone's got to sweep the floors, clean the toilets, and stuff. I just hate getting attitude from people who think they're better than me. I've done shit most of your owners and slaves wouldn't dare try." She looked at Alex seriously. "I'm not stupid. I'm willing to learn if you're willing to try me. Just don't confuse me with one of the slaves you're training, okay? Give me some room to go out and play in the streets and let me see if I like being a housecat for a change."

"There's no way you would ever be mistaken for one of our slaves, Rachel, I assure you," Alex smiled, her blue eyes piercing into Rachel's.

* * *

"What do you mean, we're hiring her?" Grendel exploded. "She's got no housekeeping experience, no interest in the Marketplace, no resume worth speaking of, not even a goddamned GED, for goodness sakes! I don't care if she gave you a good romp in bed, that's not enough of a reason to put her on payroll!" Alex was waiting for Grendel to finish his rant, but at his last statement, her eyes flashed angrily.

"Are you implying that I, I could be swayed to hire someone based solely on their ability to please me in bed?" she snapped. The menace in her voice sliced through Grendel's anger.

"No, I just meant — no, Alex," he answered. "That was an inappropriate comment to make. I apologize." There was a silence between them, growing heavier with each passing moment, while Alex willed herself to calm down.

"I accept your apology," she said formally, and Grendel sighed in relief.

"Alex," he said more quietly, "you know I trust your judgment. I just don't understand this decision. She made only a bad impression on me."

"She made a remarkably good one on me, Grendel," Alex replied evenly. "And while she comes without any resume, Marketplace or otherwise, she has Chris Parker's recommendation. I'm sure you agree that Chris has an excellent eye for quality. I believe it's reasonable for me to suggest that between my judgment and Chris' recommendation, there is good reason to believe that we are making a good decision by hiring Rachel. Put this down as my choice, and give me a trial period of three months."

"I just wish I had the same faith in her that you do," Grendel said.

"Just wait and see, Grendel, wait and see."

Chris had given Rachel a plain gray maid's uniform to wear, one that covered her tattoos. Grendel had to admit that, in cleaner clothes and with her hair tied back, Rachel was very presentable. Passing by the guest bathroom one morning, he saw her standing over a shivering slave, the heel of her shoe digging into a naked butt while the novice scrubbed the corner. She looked perfectly comfortable, both in this role and the difficult position she was standing in, and her eyes gleamed with pleasure. Not his personal style, but one that certainly got results, Grendel decided. Indeed, the bathroom did shine.

22 Transitions

"I think we need a change in scenery," Marcy suggested after Cindy finished, her body glistening with sweat and her eyes bright with pleasure.

"Good idea," Ken said, casting a glance around the room. "If you are finished with Andy, perhaps he shall have his turn?"

"I have a better idea, if you agree, Marcy," said Chris. He nudged the now visibly shaking Stuart with his foot. "Let me take you up on your offer of putting Stuart to use."

"By all means, Parker, you didn't have to ask. Believe me, he's of more use than a piece of furniture." She stretched luxuriously; but she and Andy had satisfied grins on their faces, and when she nudged him, he crawled, cat fashion, past Stuart to rub against Ken's legs. She laughed and patted him as Chris pulled Stuart up.

"You told me you aren't shy," Chris said, as Stuart stumbled to his feet. "Well then, off with the trousers."

"Yes, sir," Stuart said, and started to unfasten them. He revealed a jockstrap, and Chris smiled over his shoulder at Marcy. Stuart had a fine dusting of almost white-blond hairs on his curved little butt, and down his legs. Chris lightly cupped Stuart's ass in one hand, and Stuart sighed and immediately broke out in goosebumps. Chris laughed and got up, taking Stuart by the scruff of the neck and propelling him toward the center of the room where he said, "Up, Michael. On your knees."

Michael pushed his body up onto his arms and then onto his knees. His eyes were slightly glazed, and he felt Cindy's cool hands steadying him from behind, her cock bumping against his thighs and sore asscheeks. Damn, he thought, he's gonna make me suck the punk anyway. Fucking pretty boy, at least he won't be so big, and he won't know how to really slam a throat. . .

But as Chris pulled at the straps of the jock and Stuart's groin was revealed, the slight bulge in the pouch fell away with the material. Michael blinked several times, because Stuart had no jutting cock between his legs, he had a broad swath of pubic hair just slightly darker than the hair on his head, and then —

Wait a minute, there was a cock. Or rather, Stuart had a positively gigantic clitoris. It was easily as thick as his thumb, and it extended past the hood like a small cock pulled out of a foreskin. Michael gasped and struggled with the urge to look up and see what the faces looking down on him looked like, what they expected of him. But Cindy gently pushed him from behind, and his head dipped forward.

He opened his mouth and gently took this clit/cock against his tongue. The texture was smooth and soft, the skin slightly salty but with that subtle taste of — damn.

It was hot, plain hot. As he breathed in softly around the cock, he could feel his body warming up again, his mind flooding with soothing waves of pleasure that banished the aching in and on his ass into a pleasant afterthought. There was a cunt underneath, he could feel it with his lips, but this cock was what demanded his attention, and it felt so sweet and so exciting to make love to it. He started to lick the length of it, slowly.

"Is he doing it right for you?" Chris asked, holding Stuart's arms behind him and arching his back. His mouth was right next to the young man's ear, and every time he spoke, Stuart groaned. "Tell him what you need."

"Suck it, suck it, please," Stuart gasped.

Michael heard, and did. It was like sucking a finger, like sucking a clit, like sucking a nice, hard cock. But it was a cock that could never choke him — a cock that tempted him with potential pleasure and pleasuring, made him both hungry and patient. Stuart didn't taste like a man and didn't taste like a woman, but damn, he tasted good. And the sighs and gasps that came from him were beautiful. Michael ran his tongue deep alongside the cock and then around it, the way he would play with a cockhead. Then he tried back and forth, the way he would play with a clit, tugging on it with a rhythmic suction.

Both ways seemed to work. He started to bring his hands up to clasp Stuart around the ass, but then stopped himself and put them behind his back. He could feel Cindy's belly against him, her breasts pressing into his back, her breath against his throat as she kissed and nibbled on his ear.

Stuart started to rock against Michael's face, fucking into him with slight hip motions, and Michael felt that there was a strength behind the movements. A quick glance through his eyelashes, and he could see Chris' leg planted firmly alongside Stuart's skinny one. Yes, yes — Chris was right behind the boy, holding him and forcing his body back and forth, so damn sexy to think about, if only he could see it!

If only it was *Chris* directly in front of him right now.

Dimly, he heard Ken Mandarin laughing and saying something, and he was pulled back from Stuart. He blinked again, but before he could even take a deep breath, Cindy was coaxing him down onto his back, and Chris was pushing Stuart over his face again. Good. Better position to make the boy squirm. He felt someone next to his head and heard Chris say, "Take him in your hands, Michael. Work him until he screams."

Oh, yes, thank you, Michael thought. Stuart's asscheeks were soft and curvy under his hands, his flapping shirt-tails like feathery touches on Mike's fingers. As he clenched his hands down on that smooth flesh, he pulled Stuart into the best position for that cock to slide right down over his lips. He began to suck at it, gently and then more firmly, as he felt the way Stuart responded. Apparently, that felt good, too. Michael almost felt like laughing.

Stuart was easy!

When he felt something happening around his own cock, at first he thought it was Cindy — but then he wondered if it was Andy — and he abandoned himself to not knowing and to doing what he was told, and working little Stuart, cute little, how—dare-you-know-my-teacher jail bait space cadet Stuie - until he screamed.

It took a little while — but in the end, it was worth it to hear the punk crying, "Oh, yes, yes, please, please, yes, please, let me come, please," and hearing Marcy, Chris and Ken all say "No!" and laugh together.

And that Michael *himself* was allowed to come, his cock tightly sheathed in Andy's asshole, made it even better. He even had the strength to laugh after Andy eased his body up and off of Michael's shrinking cock and stripped the condom off, when Ken leaned over his face and asked, seriously, "*C'etait bon?*"

In fact, he didn't break down into tears until he came back to his room after bathing and eased his body down onto his futon.

It was a sudden feeling, like a chill that spread through his body. He felt the dull throbbing of the whip marks and the odd feeling of sore emptiness that came after being fucked, and he was content for a few seconds. But as he started settling down onto his elbow, it swept over him. He started trembling uncontrollably, and then he felt the first catch of breath and a tightness in his chest. He desperately wanted to control it, to stop it, but the harder he struggled, the worse the pressure got, until tears squeezed out of his eyes. He tried to hurriedly wipe them away, not wanting Chris to see or hear, but it was too late.

"Michael — what's wrong?"

He wanted to, he really wanted to just say "Nothing, sir!" and be good and make like nothing was wrong, but just the sound of Chris' calm voice shook him even harder. A rough sob broke through, and he curled up on his futon helplessly, still struggling to hold it all back. When he felt Chris kneeling next to him, he couldn't do anything at all. He just let them come, feeling a humiliation that was, if anything, just as keen as what he had felt earlier at his debut as a public sex object.

Chris let him cry for a while, and then handed him a handkerchief. He neither touched him nor spoke, just watched as Michael wrestled himself past the hysteria.

"What's this about?" he finally asked, his voice surprisingly gentle.

"I'm sorry — I'm — sorry," Michael said, taking deep breaths. "It's just — it's just that it all just hit me! I was OK, it was all right, but now — I just feel — so fucking *used*. I feel — I feel like I can't get up and be myself again, like I don't even exist!" The sobs threatened to take over again, and he concentrated on breathing to keep them back.

"Do you feel abused?"

"Yes!" Michael snapped, and then he shook, gritting his teeth. "No. I don't know. I just don't understand how — how they *do* that!"

Chris stroked his chin. "How they do what?"

"How the slaves *stand* it! I did it — I did it because I'm training, because Anderson — because of you, goddammit, I did it for you, and it was hell! I came, it was hot, but I can't believe how — how humiliating it was." The words started to spill, and he pushed himself up, gesturing wildly, trying to calm himself. "How can I face any of them again? How can I just get up and be Mike LaGuardia again, when you — when you all just made me into someone you didn't even have to talk to! How am I supposed to live with this? How can *anyone*?"

"And yet, this is what you used to train people to accept, isn't it, Michael?' Chris asked, still gentle, still quiet and calm. "When you were with Geoff, you told them that this might happen — that it most certainly would happen, since you once assumed that all slaves were to be considered sexually available. So how did you help prepare them for this? What do you remember saying to them that would help you now?"

Michael's stomach twisted, and he bit his lip, desperate not to lash out and scream. Instead, he shook his head, sniffing. "Nothing. I just thought — I thought that they would just — I don't know — enjoy it. That even if they didn't, really, that at least they might be able to — ignore it. Pretend that it was better, different. I don't know."

"Michael, listen to me. What happened to you tonight was very difficult, but it could have been much worse. Ken and Marcy are skilled at distancing themselves, at isolating. So am I. But we did not and would not allow you to come to harm. You were never without observation, or in the hands of an amateur. You were called upon to behave sexually with people who you might or might not have been sexually interested in — but I don't think any of them were decidedly unattractive to you. In fact," Chris let a small smile play on his lips, "you surprised us all with your reaction to poor Stuart, who is no doubt feeling very similar to you right now."

"He wasn't beaten and then raped by that — that horsecock that Cindy had!" Michael was surprised at how cleanly that came out, and felt a moment of gratitude that the hysteria was finally passing.

"Not tonight," Chris said. "At least as far as we know. I have no idea what Marcy does with Stuart. But I would wager that Stuart feels that he has as much to hide about his sexuality as you do — if not more. Imagine how he will feel facing *you* tomorrow."

Michael took another deep breath and wiped the back of his hand over his eyes. "Sir, do you ever get tired thinking of what other people might be thinking and feeling?"

"My God, Michael, yes, I do. Empathy can be exhausting. But it's part of what you learn to do when you are in service. Give it a try right now. What am I thinking? How do *I* feel about what happened tonight in Ken's room?" Chris leaned back comfortably onto his calves.

Michael shrugged awkwardly. "I don't know. Maybe — embarrassed, because you had to punish me in front of your friends, so they knew you had a trainee who was a fuck up."

"Good guess, but remember that I chose to do that; so however embarrassing it was for me, I must have decided it was acceptable. What else comes to mind?"

"There were times when it looked like — when I felt like — you were enjoying it. You liked watching us."

"Oh yes, there certainly were. I enjoyed myself thoroughly, as a matter of fact. Anything else?"

Michael sat up, trying to think. What if he had been in Chris' position — delivering this trainee to be used and abused by my friends — feeling like I had the right to, that he had no choice, but that he was doing it to show how good he could be for me. . .and I enjoyed it. So. . .

Chris began to nod. "Come on, Michael, I can see you're close."

"Were — did you feel — proud of me?" He said it haltingly, and ducked his head, half expecting to be smacked, if only by one of Chris' half-hearted thumps for idiocy. But Chris was still nodding.

"Yes, I did, and I am. You showed up groomed and obedient, you followed orders without hesitation, and if you didn't actually smile through the whole thing, Andy and Cindy provided enough of that to keep us cheerful. You didn't sulk, or protest, and you even managed to keep this little emotional moment until you were safely here. Six months ago, you couldn't have done any of this, Michael, not if Anderson told you that this was the only thing you had to do to become the best trainer in the world."

"But — I'm wasted! I'm a wreck!" Michael hugged his knees up to him and shivered. "Look at me; I can't even stay still."

"It will pass," Chris said. "Lay down, Michael, and go through the relaxing exercises I taught you. Yes, you were used, and used fairly hard for someone of your experience. But you stayed with it, you stayed with *me*. You didn't turn your body off, or shut out what was happening to you. I look forward to seeing how you integrate this new understanding into your studies. But it's time to sleep now."

"Yes, sir," Michael whispered. He made his limbs straighten up, and pulled the soft sheets around him, the comforter on top. Chris patted his shoulder once before getting up and crossing over to his futon. Michael watched him pull the t-shirt off, saw the garish tattoo that covered his lower torso, reaching up to his pecs, the flames and the phoenix.

I wish I could be reborn, was Michael's last thought before drifting off to sleep.

Chris sat up for some time afterward, watching the rise and fall of Michael's chest. What a strange young man he was. Why on earth he had chosen to take this route to mastery was still a major question; and why Anderson had chosen him was an even bigger one. Nevertheless, it was a nice breaking; relatively fast and effortless, and very satisfying. It would be interesting to see how it held.

This was a man who had everything going for him. Charm, a native intelligence that was a bit slow, but that was hardly rare in these days of instant gratification. Handsome to a fault, with those dark ringed sapphire blue eyes and splendid body, men and women appreciated him, and he was capable of responding to both. There was very little that beaten and fucked man sleeping on the futon could not have if he wanted it, and no reason in his upbringing or his sexual orientation or even his dreams and fantasies that he should embrace this — how had Geoff Negel put it? — inhuman regimen of training.

And yet he had. Not to impress Anderson, not because he needed a job, and certainly not because of this pointless crush he has on me, Chris mused. What is he trying to prove to himself?

A dozen respected leaders and trainers here thought it was out-moded, no longer meaningful, perhaps never truly necessary, but this boy chose it. And Anderson was permitting it. Two mysteries.

What a difficult day this had turned out to be. The disappointment of his early meeting with Dalton, the steady confrontations at the debates, the anti-climax of introducing his paper, and then the shock of Tetsuo's gift. Sitting at dinner, trying to be politely urbane and shake the feeling of being manipulated, despite the clear proof that he was. And then, when the entertainment began, to feel so suddenly lonely. Torn between feeling teased and courted.

Michael would ask me why I don't just try to *get along* with people better, Chris thought ruefully. After all, I have the right teachers, I have the right track record, I didn't have to do this. I could easily have taken my seat at breakfast and joked and bitched with the rest of them and gotten involved in whatever non-political events were happening this year and gone home a great success. I could have just waited until someone else took up the cause. I could have let it go another year or two or five, and let Anderson do it before she retired.

Or, I could do the right thing and do it for her before she has to.

Damn the right thing, anyway.

I can get this measure passed tomorrow, even without Negel and his supporters, without the spotters, even without England. Kurgan had great success with the Argentines, even made headway with the Brazilians, and there was some movement from the Australians that they might come on board.

But Ken's refusal stung, as did Dalton's. Neither of them were fools, and they certainly weren't part of the problem. They had to be part of the support network for this, because each of them represented a different kind of Marketplace professional. Each of them had their followers. And dammit, each of them has my respect, Chris thought. But Anderson wants this done. How to satisfy honor *and* instinct? How best to bring in the doubters *and* placate the eventual losers? And how to do this all while maintaining the integrity of the original plan?

He turned to the wall and assumed a meditation position again, this time with his legs crossed, hands cupped upward. Be like a willow, he thought, smiling slightly to keep back the nerves that were threatening to erupt. Bend, damn you, he thought, closing his eyes. It's time to bend.

By the time he went to sleep, he knew what he had to do the next day.

23 A Change in Plans

"Michael."

He heard his name and his eyes shot open. He shifted and turned, and felt the aches all along his hip as he rolled over and onto his knees, the light sheets falling over him. "Yes, sir?" he croaked.

Chris was in his yukata, seated at the table, a pile of papers in front of him, some folded into messages. "Get dressed. I need you to take these around before breakfast."

Michael groped his way out of the bedding and opened the cabinet with his clothing and silently began to dress. When he slipped his watch on, he suppressed a groan — it was six in the morning, dammit. He'd had — what — four hours sleep? But he drew on his trousers and a clean shirt and was knotting his tie as he knelt next to the table to await instructions.

The folded stack was topped with one that said "Ninon" in Chris' neat, spare handwriting. "Take these, and don't wait for an answer," Chris said, waving at them. "Then, arrange a private meeting room for me, anywhere will be fine, get a coffee and tea set-up and at least two slaves to serve. I want it for about an hour before the opening sessions. After that, bring me some coffee."

"How about it if I just have some sent to you right away?" Michael asked, scooping up the messages.

Chris looked up and nodded. "Yes, that will be fine, as long as you make the messages your priority."

"You got it, sir." Michael padded out the door into his light sandals, knowing exactly where to find the small group of slaves who serviced this building. He went straight to the central organizing suite to arrange for the meeting room and check over the registration list. He jogged through the rest of his errand, feeling more alert with every passing minute. Of the people who he visited, only Walther Kurgan was also awake — everyone else had a quiet, sleepy looking slave politely take the message and promised to deliver as soon as it was appropriate. Walther had a naked woman answer his door, and looked up from a tangle of limbs on his bed with a look of half annoyance and half pleasure at being discovered. Michael fought the urge to grin and wink, only nodded a slight bow and delivered the written message and heard giggling before the door was closed behind him. Well, he thought, at least someone is having good old fashioned orgies.

Chris looked pleased when he returned. "Thank you, Michael," he said with a nod. There was a pot of coffee on the table and remarkably, two cups. Chris indicated the empty one, and this time Michael allowed himself to grin as he sat down — somewhat gingerly — to pour himself some.

"Thank you, sir," he said, adding cream.

"I need you on your toes today," Chris said directly, stacking his notes together. "If anyone sends me a message through you, I trust you to find some way to get it to me as soon as possible, no matter what I'm doing."

"I will," Michael promised. He wondered what this was all about, but he kept his face neutrally eager, and wrestled down his curiosity.

"Good," Chris said. "Lay out a suit for me, please, I'll be back soon." He left the room and Michael got up, stretching. But as he brought out Chris' clothing, he paused and thought about the morning. Chris had done nothing but give him instructions — he had done very little but take them. In fact, he had barely said a dozen words to his trainer.

So why did he feel so good? Why did he feel like whistling, even dancing a little? His ass felt like a motorcycle drove over it, but it also felt a little sexy brushing against his clothing. His morning hard-on had subsided comfortably, no aching from desire or frustration, and that was nice. It was earlier than he liked, but he felt awake enough to function, and the coffee tasted great in his mouth, felt soothing to his throat. . .

Is this what it feels like to just be happy — being useful?

He said nothing about his thoughts when Chris returned from his shower, only played valet and then ran down to the bathrooms to take a quick shower and change and then followed his trainer down to breakfast in the eastern wing. He wanted desperately to talk about it, to ask questions and try to get a handle on these new feelings, but Chris had asked him to be attentive today, and that had to come first.

Perhaps not surprisingly, messages did come to Chris as he had his second cup of coffee and sat in the morning sunlight, slightly apart from the tables where most of the early risers were dining and socializing. There were slaves who knelt to deliver notes and whisper messages, and then Walther came striding in, wearing a white shirt open to his waist, his broad chest dotted with iron gray hair.

"I think I understand what you are doing," he said without preamble, beckoning to a slave carrying a tray of pastries. He mused over the selection and chose one and brushed her away, taking a bite. "And I also think it is not a good decision. But I will wait and hear what the others say."

"Thank you, Herr Kurgen," Chris said with a nod. "In about half an hour then?"

"Yes, I shall be there." With a slight nod, he turned on his heel and made his way back through the room. He passed a middle aged Japanese man in a household yukata, insignia over each collarbone, and when Chris saw the man, he shifted from leaning back against the window frame into a more formal seated posture. Michael saw this and frowned; to come to an attentive mode at the approach of a slave? Because the man was clearly wearing a collar, one with two glittering cylindrical beads set into it, but no visible lock or identity tag.

The man walked up to Chris and knelt formally, and Michael could see several other eyes in the room watching. He glanced at the slave again for any clue as to what was so different about the man, but as he rose up and presented a folded piece of paper to Chris with both hands, Michael still couldn't see anything special. Well, no — as he looked into what he thought was a typical stoic Japanese face, he caught a glimpse of something else — a range of things, actually. A sense of self-confidence and pleasure — this was a slave who was proud of himself, or proud of where he came from. And expectation — he definitely expected Chris to be impressed, and he was glad that Chris took the paper with both hands and nodded gravely before unfolding it. It took a lot to display all those things while still looking properly humble. It was like something — an Anderson slave might know how to do.

Michael took a deep breath as Chris opened the message, read the brief contents and refolded it. Then, amazingly, Chris said a few words in Japanese to the slave, who bowed again, deeper this time, and swiftly rose and took two steps backward before gradually turning to leave.

"I didn't know you spoke Japanese!" Michael said.

"I don't, not well," Chris responded. "I have the vocabulary of a child, I think, and probably a . . . dull child at that. And my grammar is rudimentary at best, I have very little understanding of the multiple levels of respect you can convey in different forms of speech. But that's all right; Noguchi-sama speaks perfect English. Michael, please stay here and receive any further communication; I've been summoned. I will be at the meeting room you arranged as soon as possible."

And Michael knew enough not to say anything but, "Yes, sir." But as Chris left the room, he suddenly realized that he had not delivered any message to Noguchi — so why did the old man need to see Chris so early?

He ended up collecting two more written messages and then Ninon came in person. She was not surprised to find out that Chris was engaged somewhere else, and he directed her to the meeting room. And wished desperately that he knew what on earth they were meeting about. They had practically won the debates, that was for sure. It probably wouldn't even be close. So what was there to say?

Chris executed a formal, low bow, his head brushing the stones, and straightened his back slowly.

"Good morning, Mr. Parker," Noguchi Shigeo said. He was seated on a bench, the warm sun at his back, his arm resting on a cushion. A slave waited behind him, in the gray yukata that was a summer house livery, and the messenger slave was kneeling nearby, impassive and at rest. Also in attendance was Tetsuo, who was standing politely to Noguchi's right, closer to him than Chris, his hands behind his back. Only the slaves were in Japanese dress; Tetsuo wore another stylish Tokyo businessman's suit and Noguchi looked like he had just stepped off of Saville Row. The garden enclosure, with the tiny tea-house at the rear, made it all seem like a surreal meeting of East and West.

It seemed only natural to pay honor to the setting, and since there was no seat for him, Chris had gone to his knees, placed his hands about 5 inches apart in front of him and bowed once, and then two more times, fully rising into a comfortable kneeling position only when greeted verbally.

"Good morning and thank you for allowing me to pay my respects to you, Noguchi-sama. I do not deserve this singular honor."

"Much has been said about you, Mr. Parker, but no one has ever faulted you for your manners," the elderly man said. Properly, Chris could have bowed from the waist, since his host was seated, but Tetsuo was standing — it would have been improper for Chris to remain at the same level as his teacher. A test, to be sure. Noguchi showed no surprise at Chris' over-formality. His dark eyes were as sharp as a hawks, and he made no move to signal Chris up from his knees, either to sit cross-legged or to take another bench. Instead, he stroked the silk covering of his cushion slowly and breathed in deeply. Tetsuo and then Chris followed his example, taking in the light breezes of the morning air, feeling the mists rise.

"A most remarkable morning," he finally said.

"Yes," Chris said easily, not stirring. Tetsuo only nodded, and they all stayed relatively still, listening to the bird calls.

Noguchi slowly turned his attention away from the breezes. "Mr. Parker. Are you familiar with the nine qualities of a gentleman?" he asked, his eyes somewhere above Chris' head.

Chris considered his answer carefully. "I have had the honor of studying Koshi-sama, sir. But my scholarship is poor; I have no real understanding of his principles." In fact, he recalled that there were several lists that could be called the qualities of a gentleman — but he had only been taught one which had nine elements, and it was no guess to know that Noguchi was referring to the writings of Confucius. Sakai-san had been somewhat of a devotee.

"Do any of us understand Koshi-sama as we should? Tell me what you recall of his wisdom, if you please. In the matter of the nine principles."

Chris drew in a breath, felt Tetsuo's eyes on him. But he faced Noguchi-sama and recited, "When observing, to see clearly. When listening, to hear distinctly. In his expression, to be — open to knowledge and understanding. In his attitude, to be deferential. In his speech to be loyal. In his duty, to be respectful. When in doubt, to be questioning. When angered, to deliberate on the consequences of anger — and —" He looked up into Noguchi's face, into his eyes. Now the old man was looking back at him, still stern, still distant, but at last engaged. He drew another breath, and said carefully, "And when having gained an advantage, to consider whether it is appropriate and fair."

Noguchi-sama nodded, turning away to admire the hanging branches of a nearby flowering tree. "You seem to have an adequate grasp," he said idly. "I am pleased to see that you have remembered them all, particularly that one. Thank you for coming, Parker-san."

Chris bowed again, deeply to Noguchi, slightly less deeply to Tetsuo, and left with only slightly less deference than a slave would, and when he got back into the coolness of the building, he bent over and leaned against his knees with a heavy sigh. The back of his shirt was damp, and under the collar, and his legs were stiff from not moving, but he had to struggle not to laugh out loud. Yes, he thought. He agrees. They will agree, they will *all* agree. He waited until his heart beat at a normal rate again and then calmly headed to his meeting. With the Japanese trainers behind him, he had no doubt that Walther, Ninon and the rest would be satisfied. Even Dalton wouldn't be able to find a way to not support this.

I did it, he thought. She didn't bother to come, but I did it.

"We recognize the author of the proposal," sighed William Longet, who looked ready to take a riding crop to anyone who spoke out of turn today.

"Honored trainers and spotters, I have asked to speak first this morning in order to offer my deep apologies for the difficulties my proposal has caused this week. It is an honor to be counted at the Academy, and although it was not my intention to create such discord, I must take responsibility for it and humbly beg your pardon." Chris spoke strongly, despite the humbling words, and frowns followed him as he swept his gaze around the room. At the same time, though, the words and his attitude hit many of them like a genetically programmed signal, and they blinked in open confusion.

"However, we all know that an apology is meaningless without an attempt to rectify the condition which caused it to be necessary." Chris nodded to the back of the room and slaves began to distribute sheets of paper to everyone seated. "I hereby ask to re-word my proposal in a such a way as to hopefully provide an honorable compromise that will satisfy everyone on all sides of this conflict."

People took the sheets eagerly and scanned them — it was a simple wording change, with appropriate notes for the subsequent changes that would have to be made in his projected plan of action neatly numbered underneath. It was in English, French and Spanish. There had not been enough time to find someone to set the text in Japanese, which was a regrettable display of discourtesy, but he was willing to be called on that one.

"To make matters simple," he continued, as more of the room read his changes, "I wish to make this committee I proposed a strictly *voluntary* body, made up of mutually selected members at first, to be followed by individuals who choose to affiliate with them by following the guidelines that the original committee agrees upon for training."

There was a low murmur of discussion and translation, and Chris saw Dalton and Mr. Ward pursing their lips gently to keep from smiling broadly. Across from them, Ken Mandarin was also engaged with the text — Paul Sheridan and the trainer from Amsterdam were both whispering to her.

"Point of information here, Mr. Parker," Geoff Negel said, raising one hand. "If this is voluntary, why would it be necessary for us to discuss it at all? Any of us can make any sort of special interest group and do what we like in it. Why involve the formal body?"

"My aims remain the same, even though I admit that my first attempt to deal with them was unacceptable," Chris responded. "I wish to preserve and continue the older, more traditional forms of training. I envision a way to allow trainers to rise through the ranks in an organized and recognized fashion. And, I would like customers and clients to know which among us have chosen that path of teaching. I would like the Marketplace to recognize this voluntary organization in all catalogs of slaves and lists of trainers and spotters. Eventually, I expect that customers will come to know which slaves have been trained by more traditional methods. That level of cooperation from our bureaucracy must be addressed by our Coalition in a formal manner."

"And you think that this will be enough to run the less traditional ones out of business?" Geoff asked pointedly.

"You have admonished me yourself, Mr. Negel," Chris said, "that I need to be more sensitive to the power of the market. I admit that you were correct. Buyers will make their own choices, depending on which methods they prefer, and which results are more — promising. It will be — a free market. Free for us — and our clients — to compete in."

Geoff frowned and was going to ask something else, but sat down to confer with the Brazilian man seated next to him.

"But what if I want to have my own group?" asked Sam Keesey. "I can start one of — I don't know — call it New Wave training. Do I get my own listing in the catalogs too?"

Chris shrugged. "Every trainer here is free to propose any motion they wish."

"Will the Marketplace do this?" asked Tucker thoughtfully. "It ain't the original proposal, that was all our business. This gets the paper-pushers involved."

Eyes turned back to William Longet, who was their liaison to the Marketplace bureaucracy. He examined the wording carefully and nodded. "This is not an unreasonable request for us to make," he concluded. "As trainers and houses are already listed and credited, it would be of no great effort to add any voluntary association."

Walther Kurgan signaled and rose to speak. "I do not think this new proposal will solve the problem of shoddy training that we already suffer," he said with a snort. "But in the interests of detante, I support it." He sat down and folded his arms. It was the shortest statement anyone had made during the meetings, and there was a rush of laughter, which he scowled at.

"I too, support this measure, and announce my intention to be part of the organizing committee for this new association," said Ninon. "And I applaud this young man for his loyal efforts to improve our membership and maintain peace among us." She glanced at Chris and smiled gently.

A few of those on the former opposing side rose to question the motivation behind the newly worded proposal, but it was hard for them to come up with concrete arguments against it.

"This could potentially lead to a . . .a Balkanization of our united resources," Geoff Negel said at one point. "Just as the countries of the former Soviet Union are dividing into territories bounded by ethnic hatred and conflict, this can lead to separation. Will there be two Academies after this, one for the traditional trainers and one for everyone else? We are strong together, my friends, not divided by differences in style. Additionally, this can lead to a feeling of devaluing among those who choose not to be affiliated."

"But if the old ways are so debased and *inhuman*, why would you feel devalued?" teased Walther, now thoroughly enjoying himself.

Several of the trainers and spotters who were opposed to the original and unhappy about it immediately announced that since the new proposal was completely voluntary, it could potentially have nothing to do with them, and so they welcomed the chance to be reconciled with their former opponents. Ken Mandarin was the first spotter to say so, and she did it with an understatement that left several of her friends bemused. And when Howard Ward rose to speak, Chris took a deep breath.

The British man gave a slight nod to him, and his aristocratic face looked thoughtful. "Upon careful consideration, I support this proposal as an appropriate method of creating mutual bonds of fellowship among like-minded trainers. . ."

And it was over. By the time Tetsuo Sakai declared his support for it, the opposition crumbled, leaving only Geoff Negel and a few of his staunchest supporters. William Longet was not the only one in the room who looked relieved when he brought his gavel down, marking the end of debates.

"Thank you, ladies and gentlemen for your wisdom, forbearance and obedience to order," Longet said with a smile. "We shall set up the balloting boxes in this room after today's luncheon. Please bring all properly registered proxies between three and four o'clock, so that they maybe checked against the master lists. Since the proposal has changed, it is advised that you attempt to contact those whom you will be representing. But if that is not possible, please vote according to your understanding of their will, in good faith. This formal business discussion is now ended."

Cheers filled the room, and people thumped each other on the back and hugged. Tucker and Keesey shook hands, and Ken Mandarin kissed the back of Ninon's hand with a flourish, and Walther Kurgan lifted Corinne off her feet.

Many of them came over to Chris, who stood and shook hands with everyone, his voice low and warm. He did not protest when Kurgen grabbed him in a big bear hug either, and took it in good grace when the older man thumped him heavily on the back and said that he wasn't so bad for such a gloomy youngster.

Ken came over to hug him briefly. "I knew you could do it," she said lightly. "Come and sit with us for lunch, hm?"

"Thank you," Chris said, but before he could accept or decline, he saw Dalton coming over, with Bronwyn in close pursuit. Ken patted Chris on the shoulder and waved Paul and Joost and Shoshana over to her to make room. "Well then, Mr. Parker," Dalton said, looking unconcerned and slightly bemused. "Good show. A gentleman knows the value of compromise."

"So I have been instructed, Mr. Dalton," Chris said. "I have had the benefit of wonderful teachers."

"Hmph. I must say, puppy," Dalton leaned forward, his voice pitched slightly lower. "You were an *interesting* boy. But I hazard that you have become a quite adequate man."

"Thank you. . ." Chris started to say, weakly, but Dalton had already pulled back and smiled that tight, thin social smile and the private moment was gone. He wanted to laugh — adequate, used twice this morning as an expression of praise. How wonderful! How Japanese, how British, how perfect. Someone else took his hand and he shook it and mouthed more words of thanks as he saw Dalton join the stream of trainers exiting the room. He nodded and looked into their eyes, into the faces of people whose names he memorized, whose writings and track records he was familiar with, and took their congratulations, whether offered in honest glee or a shrugging acceptance. And when Tetsuo Sakai, Sato-san and Noguchi-sama all nodded to him together, he felt about ready to fall backward into the chair and let one of the exquisite slaves hovering that week fan him and bring him a drink. But instead, he bowed to them in gratitude and waited until they had left the room to finally sit down. His knees were weak, and he folded his hands to keep them from visibly trembling. When Michael came over with a glass of water, Chris kept him waiting for a few seconds, until he took a few deep breaths.

"Is it over now?" Michael asked, still somewhat dazed at how easily two days of arguments had been put aside.

"All but the voting," Chris said. "But for all intents and purposes, yes, Michael. It's over. And — I need — something stronger than this, I think."

Michael laughed. "I'll get you something, what's your pleasure? It's kind of early for Scotch."

Chris sighed and shook his head. "Yes, you're entirely right. But if you would like to make yourself useful, then have some green tea sent to a free bathroom and make my apologies to anyone who wants to see me before lunch is over. I am going to take a very long and very hot bath."

"I'll take care of it," Michael said confidently. "Um — do you want — company, sir?" It was a daring offer. Michael felt the nervousness in the pit of his stomach, but knew, just *knew*, that this was something that a — a person in service would offer. His teacher looked stressed. A massage, or simply a body to play with, abuse or enjoy, was what an owner had a — had someone in service for. He had been resisting offering things, and had been so glaringly *wrong.* How had he not realized that this was something he could — or should be doing? But now, the very thought of providing some sort of release for Chris was like a glowing light spreading around his mind.

"Why thank you, Michael, I appreciate your gesture," Chris said with his wry smile. "How remarkable. But I will have to decline, I am not in the mood for company right now. Just the tea, please, and you need not bring it yourself." He stood and nodded a brief dismissal to Michael. And as Chris walked carefully out of the room and made his way to the ryokan building, Michael finally did whistle as he hurried to take care of that small chore.

That wasn't bad at all, he thought happily. Wow, what a week! When we got here, it looked like it was going to be nothing but my fuck-ups and his fight with Geoff. And now, I'm the good student taking care of business the right way and he's a freaking hero. What a way to end the Academy!

He couldn't wait to record this all in his journal, including the way he noticed how people spoke and bowed and shook hands when it was all over. Man, he would have never understood all the nuances a simple nod could have if he hadn't seen it here.

Everything was going to be just fine from now on.

24 Making Choices

Ken was disappointed that Chris was ducking out of lunch, but that didn't stop her from inviting Mike to join her and her fellow spotters, almost exactly the same crew that Michael had been subjected to on his first day. But their hostility was completely gone now, and so was any agenda but making sure they had all the contact information possible about each other. Business cards and small note pads and flashing pens were much in evidence.

There was also a new energy in the rooms, and Michael was both flattered and amused by several invitations to come to private evening meetings — "with Mr. Parker's approval, of course!". It took him a few minutes to realize that these were — at last — not business meetings or special interest meetings or anything connected to politics or even training techniques, but pure and simple play events. Sex parties. Orgies, maybe.

"Why on earth do you wait until the last night of the Academy to play?" he asked out loud, shaking his head in disbelief.

"Some of us don't," Ken teased, raising a delicate eyebrow toward him. Too pleased to feel embarrassed, he grinned back at her, and Paul laughed.

"You know, I spend so much time going to parties and whatnot, it felt great to come here and lay out in the sun all by myself," the older spotter said, comfortable in khaki shorts and a white shirt that looked like it came from a safari guide. His sunglasses were tucked into the front pocket, and he looked as relaxed as though this whole Academy was nothing but a vacation for him. "Believe me, I don't miss a minute of play. It's almost a relief to come here and not be expected to put on a show or impress a novice or take down some crafty old client who's itching to add notches to their collar."

"I like to see the old friends," Joost said. "If I am in bed with one slave after another, I never have to time to lose at poker and hear all the gossip."

"You have to learn to gossip in bed," Ken suggested. "Or, perhaps you should fuck a slave over the dinner table, while gossiping! Who needs a bed, anyway?"

"You know, I never heard so many people complain that they had too much sex," Michael said.

"Oh, I am not complaining!" Joost insisted, and Paul nodded in agreement.

"You poor men, of course you are complaining," Ken chided. "After all, you cannot fight nature — you can only spend so many times a day, true? While we women have all the advantages. We can enjoy ourselves fully every hour if we wish — every five minutes, if it is our pleasure!"

"Ken, in my next life, I wanna be you," Paul wisecracked.

"Too late, my friend. I have lived such a virtuous life, the gods will return me over and over again, for their pleasure." They laughed and Michael leaned back in his chair, mulling over his subtle invitations and wondering what Chris would do or say when he found out about them. He had to be in a good mood — would he relax enough to let me go to one of these? Would he want to go, or feel that he had to? I wonder if the Japanese trainers will have their own get-together, maybe he would want to go to that one. He idly wondered what that might look like; judging from Japanese porn, things could get mighty kinky.

Michael saw Marcy enter the room with Stuart in tow, and briefly felt a flash of embarrassment. But then, he stopped and tried to think of how he *should* be reacting. After all, nothing especially earthshaking had happened. He had been one of the stars in a vaguely uncomfortable sex show. But when it came down to brass tacks, it had been his choice to do it. *All* of this is my choice, Michael thought. And I have the power to choose how to deal with it, too. I was just laughing at these people for not playing and having sex — but I did play, and I did have sex, last night. Not the type I might have chosen . . . but I got off.

Come to think of it, it really wasn't that bad after all. As far as the beating went, hell, he'd taken worse from Chris. And although Cindy's dick was on the large side, its shape and the humiliation of being fucked for an audience was more of what made it uncomfortable. He certainly didn't feel torn or abused in any way this morning. And he did get to fuck Andy, or at least have Andy bouncing up and down on his cock, which was just as much fun with much less work. And as for Stuart — well, Michael had no intention of blabbing about Stuart's cock any more then he had concerning Cindy's. The very thought was amusing, but in mid smile, he stopped his memories and frowned in confusion. What was I so upset about last night, he wondered. Chris was right — I wanted to play and screw around — and I did. It wasn't on my terms, but it wasn't anything more than I'd been warned might happen, and damit, some of it was downright fun.

So how would Chris deal with it? He'd probably just nod hello to Stu and act like it never happened. After all, it was after-hours and not for public consumption. That was how a good slave might treat it.

But I'm not a slave yet, Michael mused. I'm still free, as free as any apprentice in this field is. And if I had good sex with someone and wanted to say hi the next day, what would I do?

He caught Stuart's eye, and much to the young man's shock, Michael gave him a broad wink and mimed a kiss.

Oh, it was so *good* to see Stuart blush and hurry after Marcy! Kinda mean, yeah, but good, too.

Ken laughed out loud, not missing the exchange and slapped Michael playfully on the arm. "Bad dog," she said. "Naughty dingo!"

"Actually, I'm wondering if I hurt his feelings," Michael said with a regretful sigh. "Maybe I better go talk to him."

"No, no," Ken assured him. "Better he should get used to being . . being made the object of admiration, yes? He is filling Marcy with his new desires to be like you, *mon chien*, to be trained as the great Parker trains, the poor fool."

Michael laughed. "There are worse things," he said.

"Yes, indeed there are. But a man that shy should not even consider delivering himself into Parker's gentle hands, do you not agree?"

Michael nodded after a moments thought. Yes, she was right; part of Chris' technique in distancing was to use surrogates in dominance — to loan out slaves and, well, trainees, to his various experienced friends. Or to give the impression of being loaned. Damn, there was so much to think about now, new ideas were crowding Michael's head like lines of a new song. He wanted very much to sit back and chat with all these hot, important people, but he also wanted to run back to his room and write out reams of notes on all these things. He hoped he would remember all of them when he finally got a break.

"Yeah, Chris isn't exactly the most kind and gentle trainer," laughed Paul, "But he's got a hell of an eye."

Shoshana and Joost both nodded; having a good eye was high praise indeed from people who made it their business to see slaves where everyone else saw mere humans. Dan, the Californian spotter shrugged. "All I ask is that trainers trust *my* eye. Sometimes an old timer like Parker doesn't give a client enough of a chance. That's why I like to send 'em to Negel; he'll hang onto someone for three months at least before giving up. It's the least to ask, when I might have spent half a year scouting them out, waiting for them to get out of bad relationships, testing, researching — it's a pain sometimes! I think we deserve to be taken seriously when we put that much time in."

"We also deserve to be kicked in the *derriere* when we waste our time and the time of others," Ken said with a snort. "Just because you have fun with someone for six months does not mean that a trainer will wish to do the same!"

They laughed and Dan seemed not to take it personally, much to Michael's relief. "I used to think being a spotter would be a great job," he said with a smile. "Hell, it was what I thought I'd do at first. But I had no idea how much time you guys put in on the clients. God, I was an idiot."

"You don't want to be a spotter anyway," Dan said with a shrug. "Long hours and slow turn around. The best thing about is is that it's your choice; the worst thing about it is the rejection rate!"

"No, no, the worst thing is the disappointment when a good prospect doesn't pan out," insisted Paul. "Man, you put weeks into figuring how some-one ticks, you put all your hopes in them, you get 'em ready to go, you're just about to suggest there might be something better for them — and then wham! — they 'fall in looove' — with someone else. Or worse — with you!" He laughed bitterly.

"It is only natural when they fall in love with you," Ken said with one of her slight shrugs. "One can turn that if the client is still suitable, make it into an asset."

Joost nodded thoughtfully, playing with the chunks of pineapple and sections of tangerine left on his lunch plate. "Yes, that is true," he said. "A good trainer can make a difference, I think. It is hard for an independent spotter to do this alone, it works best when you have a training partner. Some-one who can help manage the — the disappointment when it comes." He smiled quickly, revealing beautiful teeth that lit up his dark face. "I am fortu-nate in my alliances; I always have a — what is it you Americans say? A reality check. I know when I have spent too much time on a client who can only go so far."

"God help us when we don't," Shoshana said with a toss of her hair. "Working alone can make you crazy! There are only three spotters in Israel right now, and one trainer. If we didn't keep in touch, we would all be off in the hills, talking to rocks and goats."

Michael laughed. "But why?"

The spotters looked at him in wonder, then among themselves. Paul shrugged, volunteered to answer.

"Because we've got our feet in two worlds," he said. "You've been around a little — how many trainers do you know work by themselves? Not many, right? And even the solos who are out there, what do they do? They assemble a staff, they train juniors, like Anderson does. They live and breathe the Marketplace, and they always have contact with other people in it.

"But we spend more of our time in the soft world — or in situations even less friendly! Like we were saying about sex and play parties — we're at every goddamn leather contest and conference and panel, every stupid fashion show, all year long, it's leather and fetish and sex and SM — but with weekenders and pretenders and well-intentioned novices with grandiose fantasies. With people like us, it's always weird — you have to blend into the weekend world well, but then come back to a place where we do this shit for keeps. It's like building two different lives, two different personalities. Then, look at Kurgan's spotter team — six people who spend their year going from one military environment to another, scoping out the jarheads and zoomies and squids for potential slaves. When they finish one tour, they start another. And the only contact they really have is Kurgan himself, no parties to go to, no Marketplace hang-outs. They have a different problem — they have to walk into the mundane world most of the time and then take a quick retreat into what feels like a fantasy. Hell, most spotters don't even go to the auctions where their clients end up, they came up with some stats to show that it unnerved the clients."

"When you are alone like that, it can lead to some — bad behavior," Joost said.

"Like Matson?" Michael asked, glancing at Ken.

"Matson was never alone," Ken said sharply. "He had friends, he had a local network. But yes, like Matson. He began to believe that he could and should do everything by himself."

"Bullseye also thought the world revolved around him," said Dan. "Shit, I remember him, he was one arrogant bastard."

"We are all arrogant," Shoshana said. "Or, correctly, we are all confident."

"Fine line," said Paul.

"Matson fell in looove," Ken said, echoing Paul's earlier comment. "People grow mad when they are in looove."

"There are much worse reasons for madness," Joost said thoughtfully.

"What do you mean?" Michael asked.

"Envy," Joost said quickly. "A spotter may intentionally spoil another's hunt. Spite, jealousy. Hatred. If I recall Matson, he fell in love with a client and did not wish to relinquish her, am I correct? But at least she had a place to turn, there were those who would be guardians for her. But when a spotter becomes obsessed with someone not in our world, with no one to protect them, then what happens? I know of a certain — person — who — well, it is a difficult tale. I do not think I could do it justice."

"Well, now I must hear it," Ken declared, summoning a slave who bent elegantly to her side. "Do I know this — person?"

Joost sighed, shifted uncomfortably. "Perhaps, Mandarin. Unlike Paul's 'Mr. Benjamin', it would be difficult to masquerade this individual."

"Excellent!" Ken's eyes gleamed with anticipation of something particularly juicy. "Now please tell me that this — individual is not here, so I can listen with innocence, hm?" She ordered iced teas for the table, and no one objected.

Joost laughed. "Well, since you have been kind enough to tell me what happened in Italy last year, I think I owe you something in exchange. Besides that, they are no longer counted among us, so I suppose I may be more free in disclosure." He leaned forward, thinking, and then looked up. Michael drew in his chair as two slaves distributed a milky looking sweet spiced tea in tall glasses. Joost nodded to himself. "I caution you, though," he said thoughtfully after a sip, "I have this story from someone who was already once removed from the situation. I do know that at least some of it is true, but some of the details are — not flattering to us."

Paul shrugged. "As long as it's not about me, I don't care."

"We are all part of one family," Joost said firmly. "When one of us does well, we learn from them. When one of us does not — we must examine ourselves, I think. And learn from them as well."

"Yes, yes," Shoshana said impatiently. "We're prepared, tell us this terrible story already!"

"Well — it took place in Amsterdam," Joost said. "Not too long ago."

25 Redemption   by Michael Hernandez

She parted the heavy leather curtains and entered the bar, one of the oldest on Warmoesstraat, suffering that temporary blindness that accompanies travel from light into darkness. At the moment it was impossible to see without infra-red vision. It was easy to believe that it was the bartenders' fault. The fumbling around in the darkness ensured that the power balance remained with those who were serving. Then again, more than likely the reason for keeping the bar so dark was that darkness invited raw sexuality. Light tended to drive out the beast within. The darkness served another purpose than employee entertainment. It allowed those sitting along the bar to feast their eyes upon their future conquests without the potential "victim" receiving the reciprocal benefit.

Ian knew that if she could just stroll up to the bar without tripping over anyone or her own two feet, her eyes would adjust in the amount of time that it would take the bartender to bring her a drink, and that itself would increase her opportunity to score tonight. In this bar, the balance of power was paramount. Appearances were everything. Anyone who forgot that would soon have the tables turned.

She was the smoothest of operators, clad immaculately in black leather from the Daddy cap on her head, down to her steel toed motorcycle boots, blending easily with the raw masculinity of the majority of the bar's patrons. She wore faded blue button-down 501's under her chaps revealing a rather large basket. As she approached the bar, she absentmindedly reached down and stroked her cock. Her leathers, while clean, did not radiate that polished gleam that came from the pristine butches or leathermen. While she respected the traditional values of the older generation, such fastidiousness was not her style. She was dependent on her ability to blend into the background. All the good hunters in the animal kingdom depended on good camouflage.

255

The respectable fade of her leathers increased her chances of remaining hidden in the alley, of watching from afar without being spotted, and of disappearing without a second glance. She could move through the Warmoesstraat and be noticed at the time of her choosing.

Tonight she wasn't looking for anything in particular. Butch, femme, either/or, punk, something else. Thrillseeker tourists from Germany or the United States were always good and hungry. Anyone would do so long as they were a good time. Gender was irrelevant. It was all about a quick thrill, sex in a public place, and her getting her rocks off. She didn't have to go far nor did she have to take her clothes off to bury her cock in some young mouth. The alley behind the bar would do quite nicely for starters. Her dick twitched. She could smell a potential partner within a two mile radius. A little verbal sparring and the next step was the alley. If "it" sucked well enough they'd go back to her fuck pad in the Jordaan. Blindfolds were used as a matter of course. The combination of blindfold and her neighborhood, which was less than welcoming at night, also prevented visitors from appearing at her play space uninvited. She'd interrogate a scene out of "it" then play to her heart's content, although her heart was not usually the organ that got the action. Actually the word "play" was too mundane of a description of what she did. It was more like . . . feeding.

That was it. She consumed her prey. It was the emotional juices that she craved as well as the physical ones. Emotions such as fear, desire, passion, that is what she sought to elicit. That and the skeletons that everyone hides carefully in the closet.

Barst safe, sane and consensual! It was the edge of nonconsensuality that lured her and in turn lured her victim. No, victim was too harsh a word. Quarry was more like it. She did not feed often. Prey which proved satisfactory were few and far between, but when found, a veritable pleasure. She, like her cats, played with the mousies before the spilling guts upon the floor, metaphorically speaking of course. Through her skill, Ian was able to carefully excise and bring the souls of her partners into the light of day where she played until she tired and moved on to the next one.

If her quarry showed enough initiative to stop the scene, she did so promptly, reapplied the blind fold, and drove back to the bar. No looking back, no regrets, no second chances. She played for keeps. Catch and release kept her skill honed. Only once had the prey *really* meant it. The others complained all the way back to the bar about the scene having terminated. Some begged for a second chance, but Ian was resolute. Rules, while bent from time to time, were never broken. In that she was absolutely intolerant. She had no intention of changing a damned thing. That was the way she did things now. No long term commitments. No mess. No smell. No headaches. No transatlantic phone calls in the middle of the night. No scathing notes pinned to her door with knives. No clothing chopped into tiny bits or personal effects hoarded or destroyed. Oh, her life had drama enough, but it was limited to the drama that she carefully created for herself. She ran the fuck and if the fuck did not want to be run it could go elsewhere. There were plenty of other fucks for the having.

Somehow, she had failed with the last one. Geneviéve. The fact that she remembered a name showed how much that one had gotten to her. It fueled her hunger. A real virgin was a rare find these days. Oh, not that type of virgin. It was innocence that drew her. A clean slate. Fresh, undiscovered, unexplored, untainted by the views of the so-called community. That one filled her thoughts and dreams until she screamed at the walls. She had taken her sweet time and then tossed her out when she had been sated. It had been sweet, but the woman wanted to cling to her for some reason. Unacceptable. It was now a matter of principal. Verdomme! "Never go back," she whispered under her breath, and that statement was enough to create the reality for her. She tore herself away slightly angered at her daydream through the past.

Ian was hungry tonight, very hungry, but she refused to let it show. That would certainly deter her potential candidates for the evening. She slowly unwrapped a cigar and worked it in and out of her mouth, coating the end with saliva. She removed a small silver cigar cutter from the breast pocket of her motorcycle jacket and precisely placed a "V" cut in the cigar. She surveyed the room as she placed the cigar between her lips, rotating it counter-clockwise.

Two young punk dykes practically tripped over each other in an effort to light it for her. The cute punk with the jet black mohawk glared at the shorter skinhead whose scalp was adorned by an elaborate and colorful Celtic knot tattoo. In a split second the room erupted into violence as the mohawk took a swing. Her target deftly removed her face from the fist's trajectory, miraculously causing mohawk to miss. They somehow managed to get into a bear hug and proceeded to knock over several chairs then fly over a table before crashing to the ground. It was a scene right out of an old western.

While Ian was enjoying this entertainment, a set of long, perfectly painted red nails came suddenly into view. The thumbnail expertly flicked the head of a safety match providing the fire for her stogie. "Impressive," she thought, "very promising, indeed. This one knows that lighters are not for cigars." Even more impressive was that fact that the femme was not afraid to split a nail or ruin the polish. *Hmm wonder what she's lookin' for?* Ian flashed a wolfish grin. The *dame* flushed. *Good, good.* This looked promising. Promising indeed.

Ian leaned into the flame and puffed until she was certain that the cigar was lit then turned her attention to the *dame* attached to the nails. She was struck by the intensity of the eyes. Ian was captivated as surely as a black widow spider's mate. The magical moment was broken by Artie's bellow and baseball bat hitting the counter. Patrons went scrambling for the corners. "*Wel verdomme!* Cut that crap out you *rotkoppen* before I collar your *kutten* and chain you to the goddamned bar. Your gonna get fucked nine ways to Sunday and I guarantee that ya ain't gonna like hot pepper oil being used as a lubricant." The fight stopped mid-punch.

Artie, the bartender, was a force to be reckoned with. Her no-nonsense approach to trouble was well known in Amsterdam and gaining speed throughout the leather bars of Europe. Like any story in the community, it was embellished and passed along from flapping lip to eager ear. The latest rumor flying around was that leatherboys and baby dykes disappeared never to be seen again. Secretly, Ian believed that Artie enjoyed the artificially created reputation and did everything to continue its embellishment. Artie continued to glare and the baby butches sheepishly looked down at their Doc Martins.

Ian, threw her head back and started laughing so hard that her eyes watered. The new lady, startled at first, was quickly caught up in Ian's contagious laughter. She had a delicate full-throated laugh which was musical. Artie glowered at them as well. No one was above reproach. They moved away from the bar still chuckling to themselves. No sense tempting fate.

In a better lit corner, Ian sized up the *dame*, taking a puff on her lit cigar in appreciation. The stranger was a tall drink of water or so Ian thought until she looked down to gaze upon the 5" spiked stiletto heels. In the heels were a pair of picture perfect legs enmeshed in black fishnet stockings. Ian's gaze wandered up the legs and just managed to spy the garters underneath the brilliant green velvet dress that the *dame* was l-i-t-e-r-a-l-l-y poured into. Ian's heartbeat doubled. Ample cleavage peeked out from between the sweetheart neckline of the dress. Ian's gaze continued upwards across that white porcelain expanse of cleavage to return to the most probing gray green eyes that she had ever seen. Liquid gold floating in a sea of green. Blazing red hair and not from a bottle either. Cocksucker red lipstick adorned the full luscious lips. Where had this woman come from? A tourist, perhaps, visiting the bars in the Red Light District? In for a little action? Ian hoped it was the case.

The *dame* took in Ian's perusal with a smile. There was an impish glee in her eyes. Something said but not quite spoken. Almost as if she had the inside scoop on a private joke. Ian smiled back. This was more than she could hope for. "Bier?" she asked, checking to see that Artie had calmed down. The lady smiled and, to Ian's surprise and delight, went to the bar herself, leaning toward Artie to murmur the order. The drinks were produced in record speed. When she returned, the *dame* offered one of the beers to Ian. They clinked their glasses, and Ian downed hers quickly, needing the refreshment badly.

Almost before the glass was set down, the woman wove her fingers into the hair at the back of Ian's neck. Situating her lips upon Ian's, she maneuvered her tongue gracefully and insistently into her mouth, running it slowly and deliberately across her teeth and tongue. The kiss increased in its passion. She gracefully insinuated her leg in between Ian's thighs, finding the dildo resting there. She pressed the base skillfully into and around Ian's clit while continuing to explore Ian's mouth with her own. Ian's responded. A moan was torn from her lips as she encircled the woman in her arms. Passion won out over patience. They both parted breathless and full of desire. A fine sheen of sweat had broken over Ian's brow. She had to have this woman. NOW.

"Let's get out of this pool hall," whispered Ian.

The woman smiled and lifted her glass to Ian, "May you never grow bored and live in interesting times."

"*Dank u*," responded Ian, and gallantly held her arm out to the woman. The *dame* flashed a perfectly dazzling smile and took the proffered arm. Heads turned as they walked through the bar. There was a fair amount of whispering and with each step, Ian's ego grew. She was on top of the world and certainly felt it. Pushing the leather curtain aside, she felt as if she were floating on clouds. As they stepped around the corner, Ian noticed that the light emitted by the street lamp had a sharp edge to it, and the canal at the end of the Heintje Hoekssteeg seemed to draw closer, then withdraw. Just then she noticed that she was moving in slow motion.

She tried to mention it to confirm her observations, but her tongue felt thick and dry. The words just would not come. Panic caused adrenaline to flood through her system, but it was not enough to speed the passage of time. Just then she noticed that her legs were jelly. She staggered as the night rushed in to greet her. The last image that she saw was the face of the *dame* above her bearing the most incredible smile. It looked . . . perfectly wicked. "*Wel verdomme?....*" was the last thing that she managed to say before she lost consciousness.

* * *

Morgan had been *furious* when Geneviéve suddenly dropped out of the program. Geneviéve represented several months worth of cultivation as potential material for the Marketplace. Morgan, unlike other spotters, employed the services of various under-scouts to do most of the legwork. This ensured that Morgan did not waste all of her time culling through individuals who would never even be considered for training. The job of the scouts was to bring potential property to her attention. If worthy of consideration, the scout received a fee. A scout was given three opportunities to present talent. Three strikes and you were on your way out. Three outs and you were *kapot*. Morgan had developed a nice network which allowed her to present 10 — 12 candidates for consideration per year. It was expensive for her, but worth it, if she could keep up that pace.

Geneviéve presented rather unique properties. A novice who had very deep-seated desires plus intelligence, wit, imagination and a sense of adventure while exuding a naiveté that was unparalleled. A battery of tests had been performed to determine the extent of Geneviéve's potential.

Then, this, *dumkopf*, no, this *kuttenkopf*, had just waltzed in and done as she pleased, ruining months worth of work, not to mention the lost fees. It was not the first time that Ian had interfered with Morgan's plans, but it would be the last. "Justice, Justice shalt thou pursue," ran through her mind, although deep in her heart Morgan knew it was revenge, not justice. She should not take it so personally, but Morgan took everything personally.

She had carved out a reputation for herself for being a fair, but wicked top. She abhorred femmes who pretended to be stupid or who used their body to manipulate others into doing what they wanted. Morgan's style was more direct. She was the preeminent flirt who was quite able to clearly communicate her needs during the seduction. If the other person was willing to participate then everyone was happy.

In the past few weeks, she compiled information about Ian, her tactics, her prowling ground, what she smoked and drank. That was another thing that the scouting system did well, compile information. Well, someone had to teach this *kuttenkop* a lesson. Ian's interference, coincidental or otherwise, just wouldn't do. Morgan should have moved in a little more quickly on Geneviéve, but wanted to make sure that the proper level of desire had been attained. Geneviéve was more than a bottom, she had service in her blood. Clearly, that little delay gave Ian the edge. Geneviéve was ready and was losing patience for the delays and hoops that Morgan was making her jump through to get what she wanted. Well, little Geneviéve got more than she bargained for. It might still be possible to salvage the situation, but only at great effort.

Morgan owed the two punks, but paying off those debts would be more of a pleasure than a chore. The diversion caught Ian off guard, gave her an amusing distraction that allowed for a spectacular entrance and seduction. Such a challenge, to distract another hunter, even an amateur. So delightful to succeed so utterly. Well, enough of those delicious thoughts for now. Justice would be hers and it was time to pay the piper.

* * *

Ian opened her eyes and immediately regretted it. What little light illuminated her surroundings had a hazy sort of quality. Her tongue still felt thick and her hip hurt. She tried to wipe the sleep from her eyes, learning then that her wrists were securely fastened by thick leather restraints, the kind that they use in psychiatric wards, to the chair that she was sitting in.

The itchiness around her chest and crotch became more acute as she grew more conscious. Ian saw that a small network of wires crossed her body, disappearing under her shirt, down her jeans, and on her hands and feet. The wires all left her body and ended in a black box that Ian recognized as a machine used by physical therapists to make atrophied muscles jump with small, uncontrollable jerks — making the machine popular with certain fetishists, as well. Ian attempted to pull her wrists out of the restraints, but between their design and the strength of the chair, it was impossible. There was nowhere for her elbows to go. The restraints were tight enough to bind her, yet loose enough to be comfortable if she didn't thrash about. No way out of these at the moment. If only she could get to her belt. She had a long wire taped to the inside of it for emergencies such as these.

She heard the sound of heels on concrete and caught a whiff of perfume before she saw the *dame* appear. "How was your nap, dear?" the redhead queried.

"Whoever you are, I'm sure we can work this out. All you need to do is let me go and . . ."

"What's the matter," Morgan's voice dripped with sarcasm, "don't you like my hospitality?"

"Hospitality??! Is that what you call it. Look Lady, I asked nicely. Don't make me lose my temper. This is non-consensual."

Morgan laughed as she approached Ian. "Well, goodness knows that I wouldn't want to do anything like that." Morgan slapped her across the face so hard that Ian's ears rung. She got less than an inch from Ian's nose and whispered in a breathless sexy voice *ala* early Lauren Bacall, "Don't insult my intelligence by mentioning consensuality. That's never stopped you before — or didn't you recognize the recipe for the mickey that was slipped in your drink? Artie told me you should be familiar with it. So then," she lilted mockingly, "you have no idea what this is all about. Do you?"

"*Barst*," Ian spat through gritted teeth, angry at her situation — and astonished that Artie knew about her little helper. Filing that away to ponder at a later date, she glared into the startlingly green gray eyes of her captor and growled. Ian was not a bottom and was not about to be treated as such by the likes of this bitch —*rotwijf,* she growled to herself — or anyone else for that matter.

"Tsk, tsk, tsk," said Morgan shaking her head. "Manners. Manners."

"*Barst!*" Ian spat again. "I demand to be released this instant."

"Release? As you wish." A knife blade immediately materialized under Ian's chin, pricking her ever so slightly. "Ask and ye shall receive. Luke 11:9," the woman said. She deftly began to slice the jeans off her and in the process "accidentally" cut Ian's left thigh. "Oh, dear," cooed Morgan as a thin line of blood started its descent toward Ian's knee, "how clumsy of me. I should tell you that I can be a *dumkopf.* Oh well, it is of no consequence. These things do happen. I suppose that you should be particularly careful if you see any sharp objects in my hands. One never knows," she said as she waved the knife over Ian's thigh, "what may happen." The end of her sentence was punctuated by another rapid slice. Ian felt the burning sting before she saw the knife move and sound escaped her lips before she could stop it. "This will never do," smiled Morgan as she wiped her knife off on Ian's face. "I think I must find another way to release you."

The smell of blood assaulted Ian's nostrils. She closed her eyes as a wave of desire washed over her piqued by the smell of blood, feeling her body dance between fear and desire. Ian had been a blood whore from day one, but this little foray made it clear that, if she was not careful, her passion would betray her in front of this *rotwijf.*

Well this was certainly going to be fun. Morgan noticed Ian's breath catch during the brief drawing of blood. Morgan continued to cut away the jeans, being particularly careful not to cut her prey anymore. In this case, it just wouldn't do to allow the pleasure to outweigh the fear.

"There is nothing like a virgin bottom," Morgan teased the squirming butch. "I've heard about people who exclusively topped, but I've never believed it, really. It's a simple matter of knowing the territory. Exclusive tops lead a rather one—dimensional life, wouldn't you agree?" She paused, as if for a response, but Ian remain silent and struggled briefly against the bonds.

"I have been waiting patiently for this opportunity," Morgan continued, tapping her knife on Ian's crotch. "'To me belongeth vengeance and recompense'. Deuteronomy 32:35 or as they say in Sicily 'vengeance is a dish savored cold' and vengeance shall be mine."

"*Barst,*" Ian answered, spitting a wad of saliva onto Morgan's left cheek.

Morgan knew she could not tolerate Ian's breach of etiquette for even a moment. Sometimes she gave latitude to a person exploring their submission and masochism, as she had with Geneviéve. But of course, it was this *kuttenkop* who spoiled it all.

Morgan wiped her face, and turned her attention to Ian's jockey shorts, poising her knife over Ian's crotch. Most butches had one major weakness, their dildos. She noted that Ian immediately froze, not even breathing, for a moment. Morgan carefully cut away Ian's shorts allowing her meat to spring free. "And what have we here? A Marty. I thought that they stopped making these years ago." Even in her panic, Ian was impressed that Morgan recognized her cock. Italian design, produced in America, a "Marty" was the top of the line. The creme de la creme of cocks. It was comfortable yet practical, soft enough for that deep throat action yet firm enough to fuck with. None of the usual 6, 7, 9 and 13 inch standard sizes. If you wanted one 4 and 3/8's long and 3 inches in diameter, Martino Bagnelli would design it for you. Of course being the artist that he was, he would try to convince you of what he perceived to be the appropriate size based on your height, weight, body type and hands. Apparently Bagnelli did not quite understand the concept of *packing* versus *fucking* dicks.

Her romp down memory lane was interrupted as Morgan's knife touched the head of her cock. Ian began to sweat. She was really attached to this dick and could not bear the thought of losing it. There was no replacement for it, and would not be, since Bagnelli disappeared or retired, depending on which rumor you believed. Clearly, whatever she had said at the bar could not have offended this woman enough to subject her to a castration! She tried to remember the events leading up to this little scene. The concentration required to think and stay still was beginning to give her a headache.

"It is a beautiful piece of work," Morgan said, tapping her knife on Ian's cockhead. "It's a shame to ignore it, no matter who it belongs to." She reached over and imbedded the knife in the table next to the black box, then took a condom, opened it and slipped it into her mouth. She kneeled placing her hands on Ian's legs. Leaning over she slowly moved her open mouth near the cock. Ian felt the warm moistness as the *dame* blew air onto her lower abdomen, her cock, and legs. Once the mouth came near her cock again, Ian pushed her legs towards Morgan hoping to shove just the head into that waiting mouth. Her efforts were rewarded by a severe burning sensation when Morgan used her thumbs to stretch open the cuts on Ian's thighs. Morgan rose on her knees and nuzzled Ian's cheek. Lowering her voice to a breathless whisper *ala* Marilyn Monroe, "thus far I have only corrected your bad manners. Soon enough you will learn that I will hurt you because it gives me pleasure." She leaned back and gazed into Ian's eyes, "Nothing and no one can save you. Remember, you asked for this."

The words shook Ian to the core, making the trickles of blood on her thighs feel ice cold. How was it that a women who she did not know, whom she had not met before, could echo her words so clearly and concisely? It was not exactly a line. Ian did not believe in lines, but she had performed the exact series of moves, that chin nuzzle, the voice inflection, the heightening of the fear factor could be considered her personal trademarks. Edge players tended not to discuss their techniques. She had declined to teach a number of workshops on edgeplay for the weekend kink crowd, the sexual tourists. Her dialogue tended to change with the reactions of her prey, but these words were too familiar.

And then her cock was deep in the mouth of the *dame*, being worked slowly back and forth. Ian felt the friction of teeth sliding across the shaft, and the throbbing of a tongue against the head which vibrated down the core of the dildo to her clit. All the moves she demanded from her tricks. *Wel verdomme!* That thought cleared Ian's head for a moment, a small part of her brain able to still think as the cocksucking shifted in speed and intensity. This little bar pick-up was not a random encounter, but pre-planned and perfectly executed. Ian thought back on her previous expeditions. She would have noticed this *dame* at a bar irrespective of how she was dressed. Ian had a photographic memory when it came to faces. She had not met this woman before and had never seen her at a contest or other leather event. But clearly, she was no tourist.

Ian closed her eyes and tried to think of something else, but she could not escape the throbbing and sticky wetness of the blood moving down her thigh and the pulsing of her clit against her dick. She moaned as the woman swiftly buried her mouth all the way onto Ian's cock taking it to the back of her throat with no effort at all.

Just before Ian was ready to explode, Morgan pulled away, and with a quick flick of the knife she still held in her hand, she cut the dildo harness off of Ian. Removing the Marty, she placed it on the table next to the knife, a bizarrely erotic still life.

Morgan stayed between Ian's thighs, her thumbs resting on the still-fresh cuts. "This is your last chance to apologize, and make amends."

Ian swallowed, her cunt still throbbing from the incomplete orgasm. This bizarre drugging-cum-bondage-cum-fear-and-terror-with-threat-of-electricity scene seemed to be ending. It was clear this *dame* had a few cups missing from her cupboard. Rather than fighting it, Ian figured it would be best to play along, until the bonds were untied. Then she could pull off the electrodes, grab her Marty, and get the fuck out of wherever she was. Later, she would have more than adequate time after her escape to revel in the joys of planning and executing an exacting retaliation. "I'm sorry," she said quickly.

"For what?"

"For not pleasing you." Ian hoped that the sarcasm didn't show in her voice.

"Oh, is that the only reason why?"

Ian was confused. *Why should I have to apologize to this rotwijf in the first fucking place? She fucking drugged me and brought me here. What the hell is this all about? If I can just figure that out, maybe I can bargain my way out of this.* Ian had to maintain control at all costs. Buy her time until she could escape.

"Well?" Morgan asked as her thumbs pressed again against cuts, watching Ian's eyes roll back slightly.

"Umm. I don't know what you are talking about?"

Morgan slowly leaned over showing Ian an impressive cleavage and whispered "Geneviéve" in her ear. Ian's jugular pulsed a little more strongly and that pungent scent of fear emanated from her armpits. "Yes, even *you* remember Geneviéve, don't you?"

"All right, all right, I'm sorry played with your *kut* Geneviéve, or who-ever the fuck she was," Ian growled. "I even admit it was the hottest scene I've have in a long time. But Geneviéve was just a one-time thing." *And she obviously wasn't getting what she wanted from you, rotwijf,* Ian said to herself, forcing her mind away from the scent of the blood and the pleasurable pain of Morgan's thumbs on her cuts.

"That's the problem with you, Ian," Morgan responded "You are one of those dreadfully shallow people who believes that a hot scene is the highest achievement you can reach. It's a shame, really, there's so much more pos-sible. Geneviéve knew it, and was working to get there — until you placed yourself like the proverbial stumbling block before her."

"What kind of *bullshit* are you talking about?" Ian snarled. "Geneviéve never said she belonged to anybody, and the hungry little *kut* certainly didn't stumble following me home! In fact, she was pretty near begging me to take her and keep her forever!" Ian smirked, sure now that this was a lover's quar-rel, and feeling no need to apologize for being the better top.

Morgan slapped Ian again, following it with a caress across her cheek with her nails, enjoying the involuntary shiver it provoked in her victim. Leaning forward, Morgan purred, "Listen and listen carefully. You don't seem to understand that you have committed a grave error. You played with the wrong girl. Not yours to do or to choose. You had the ill manners to enjoy it. In fact, you enjoyed it without thought, without doubt, without honor, and without a price."

"Listen, Lady, I don't know what your problem is —"

"My problem is you, *kuttenkop.*" Ian's eyes snapped up in shock at the obscenity, but Morgan continued. "Your interference has cost me a great deal of time and potential…" Morgan stopped, realizing her anger made her say too much. She had almost said 'fees'.

"What the hell are you talking about?" Ian asked, seeing that the ques-tion made Morgan uneasy, and remembering part of that long-ago conversation with Geneviéve. "Wait. This is about this — this - *Marktplaats?*"

Morgan paused, stunned that Ian knew. Half a heartbeat later, she realized Ian didn't know, and was just repeating something heard, no doubt, from the traumatized Geneviéve. She needed to turn Ian's mind away from that thought, and quickly.

Moving swiftly, Morgan jerked the knife out of the table. Out of the corner of her eye, Ian saw the *dame* hold her Marty down, and, with horror, saw the knife descend toward it like a guillotine.

Ian's stomach dropped. "What the FUCK are you doing?!" she screamed. There were times when the American curses seemed so much more — intense.

"Language, dear, language," Morgan said, clearing the debris from the table, but Ian continued her multilingual cursing, straining at her bonds until she grew hoarse and bruised, and finally, sobbing. Her Marty, her favorite dick, her best, irreplaceable.

Morgan stood watching her, quietly, with a smile *ala* Mona Lisa until Ian finally slumped over, angry tears streaking her face, coughing herself into silence.

"We're back to your need to apologize to me." Morgan didn't even bother to look at Ian, focusing her attention on the black box, instead, knowing that Ian's attention would be drawn there, too.

"Okay, look, lady," Ian said calmly, but through gritted teach. "So I played with something that belonged to you so what? Geneviéve never said anything about an owner or mistress or lover or anything else." But there *had* been someone, Ian remembered, her mind racing as Morgan fiddled with the box. Geneviéve seemed to be expecting someone that night — that's right — she asked Ian if she had been sent by someone or some place. Of course Ian had said yes, knowing it would give her access to that delicious little slice of bottom. But now she was frantically trying to remember exactly what Geneviéve had said.

Morgan set the controls. It was easy to overstimulate using electricity. The trick here was to cause pain when she wanted to, not for the convenience of the bottom. Timing was everything. She could dole out pain carefully and concisely for hours given the right circumstances. The torment would start slowly then build faster and faster until Ian would regret the day that she laid eyes on Geneviéve.

Morgan watched a drop of sweat work its way down Ian's temple. Maintaining a soft and even tone, she said, "You can't just waltz into someone's life, take something that does not belong to you and then discard it with nary a thought when you are done. People, while they enjoy objectification from time to time, are not objects. It took me a long time to find Geneviéve. I

266

cultivated certain tastes in her. Certain hidden desires were disclosed. Certain tests performed. Then in one fell swoop you snatched her up at the bar, had your way with her and without so much as a second thought discarded her. You undid in four hours what took my valuable time and effort to discover and arouse . . . *and* this was not the first time."

"What the hell were you testing for anyway? Cooking? Screwing? Loyalty?" Ian's mind was racing — didn't Geneviéve say something when they first met, something about a test? "What do you mean, not the first time? Have you been stalking me?"

Morgan ignored Ian's questions and veiled accusations. Threats were easy to make when you were all tied up, but it was a terrible loss of face. It was the beginning of the end for her quarry. Morgan had already wasted several months with the Geneviéve fiasco and hoped that word did not get out into the Marketplace. Trainers were particular in their requirements, tastes and in their ethics. She had already lost out twice on pre-selected clients that Ian had taken and then driven into despair and suspicion. No one liked to work with clients who wondered whether the next master would hurt them as much as the last — and in ways they did not enjoy! And yet, there was nothing she could — or should — do to such a dangerous, cold predator in her world, not according to the guidelines her colleagues agreed upon.

And yet, here she was, her prey attached to her slender, painful leashes, and her hands on the controls. It felt good, like salt in the mouth. She had gone too far not to carry this forth to the end.

"I have been waiting patiently for this opportunity," Morgan informed her adversary. "'The time has come, the day is near, I will pour out my fury on you and exhaust my anger at you; I will judge you as your conduct deserves.' Ezekiel 7: 9."

Ian's eyes flew open as the first dose of current ran through her body. Morgan was somewhere behind her, out of sight, or maybe even out of the room. *Wel verdomme, now what,* Ian thought. Electricity was one of those things that no matter how much you fought the inevitable would happen . . . You'd get zapped. Each zap increased the stress which in turn increased the sweat production. Sweat has this marvelous property, salt, which increases conductivity thereby increasing the severity of the sensation. Just when she thought that it was getting better the electricity varied. It peaked and pulsed and zapped at unexpected times. Her body jerked and twisted. Her lips were dry as was her mouth.

Ian tried performing deep breathing exercises. If she could somehow distract her mind it would all work out. She needed to yield to the sensations, as much as she could. She tried to let go as she had seen others do in the past. Having never experienced submission, it was not something that she could simply do. She tried to concentrate on the way Morgan's face looked when she mentioned The Marketplace. But it wasn't enough. The stress of trying prevented the very relaxation that she was seeking. Ian stopped thinking and started screaming. Once she started she could not stop. She screamed to her heart's content. It no longer mattered how she looked or what the woman thought. Survival and pain were all that she thought about. Ian's body finally did the only thing it could to escape, and a smile crossed her lips as the room became black.

* * *

A stream of water struck her face, and Ian found herself still seated, but freed from the electrodes. Morgan was standing before her, with a pair of nipple clamps which did not look like anything that she had ever seen before. They had broad tips and large knobs shaped like a propane valve. Ian's nipples were quickly trapped in the coated teeth. Morgan started tightening the knobs until she had the nipple trapped between them, but not hard enough to have caused any pain.

"No, no, please enough, enough, I have learned my lesson, I swear it," Ian tried to say, as Morgan pulled out a cane and tested it in the air before Ian's eyes.

"But I want you to feel what it is that you have subjected others to." Morgan said, stroking the smooth, flexible rod. "You believe yourself to be devoid of feeling. But is that you really want to be? I will show you a glimpse of your soul. A chance for your redemption. 'The great day of anger has come, and we will see who survives.' Revelations 6:17. Shall we begin?"

In a split second the cane whooshed through the air imbedding itself in Ian's flesh before bouncing back. An intense and fearful shriek was torn from her lips followed by a string of expletives that would make a Swede blush. A reddish welt was already visible across the front of her exposed thighs. Ian had always avoided those damned pieces of rattan. Try as she might, she had never been able to quite master them. But she had to admit they were effective; one strike drove all the breath from her and made her see stars.

These momentary thoughts were interrupted by another cane stroke. There was just no way out of this one. It was bizarre to be caned while seated, her body believing that she could just stand up and leave, only to be defeated by the restraints. The caning continued and Ian thrashed about like a fish on a line, able to see each stroke's mark across her thighs, breasts, and stomach. Her flinching and thrashing finally knocked the chair over.

Morgan's strokes did not slow or alter. No attempt was made to place Ian upright, or even in a more comfortable position. New marks appeared on parts of Ian's body that had not been exposed before. Morgan admitted silently that she was enjoying herself. This was about punishment pure and simple. The cane was an instrument that led straight to the soul. Most people could dish out a hell of a lot more than they could take, but that was not the case with Morgan. She had taken a caning just like this before. It was the one thing that separated her spirit from her body and allowed her to soar.

The caning continued until Ian was reduced to a pile of red, bruised, blubbering flesh. She apologized, she confessed, she told the woman that she would never do it again, she begged and promised and cajoled and even made a threat or two in the beginning. Then there was nothing that she could do. She just wanted the caning to stop. She needed to regain her sanity and that was not possible with the flurry of blows she was experiencing.

Then, quite suddenly, Ian no longer cared about appearances. It was no longer possible to think about appearances. All of her defenses, one after another, came crashing down. She had never felt this vulnerable before and yet at the same time she became aware of a humiliating dampness between her legs. There was a fire of a different sort starting. Even as she begged forgiveness for all manners of sin, she stopped feeling any pain at all. Her eyes were rolling around in her head and howls slowly turned to moans and whimpers.

Morgan, aware of these types of changes in herself was fascinated that the mighty Ian was not above succumbing to her bodily needs. She slowed and toyed with Ian, giving her a taste, just a small taste, of the peace of mind that comes only when one is stripped of pride and arrogance.

When Morgan stopped, she was covered in sweat and her breathing was labored. Not type of breathing that comes from a good work out, but the type of breathing that comes from being aroused. She stood over Ian and relished the sensation. Morgan bent down and with a bunching of her shoulders and arms, righted the chair. With absolute precision, she stepped back, aimed her cane, and she struck the nipple clamps simultaneously, causing them to pop off. Ian was instantly snapped back into her body and the most unearthly sound emitted from between her lips accompanied by an earth-shattering, body shaking orgasm. Morgan turned on heel and left the room.

* * *

Ian was kneeling, her body trembling, focusing her attention on Morgan's feet. She wondered if it would be too desperate to lie prostrate, kissing the tips of the black leather boots. She was terrified that she would be sent away now, just as she had found this yawning need in her. She was terrified, because she knew that was exactly what was going to happen.

"You and I differ in an important way, Ian," Morgan was explaining. "You hunt, capture, then discard. I want you to understand — really understand — what it would mean if I sent you away now, with no way to contact me, knowing that you would never see me again." She watched without moving as a tear dropped onto the toe of her polished boot. "This is, after all, what you do, is it not?" She noted that Ian's tear-streaked face nodded.

"That is because you are a *player*," Morgan continued, spitting the word out. "I do not play. This work I do is my calling. It is, in fact, my profession. Although," she chuckled, "not in the way you might think."

"Unlike you, I recognize my prey has value beyond the beating and the fucking. Until you learn the same, I do not wish to see you again." Ian choked awkwardly, drawing in a ragged breath, but did not speak. Morgan watched her approvingly.

"I am letting you walk out my front door, so you know where I live, and know how to find me again. I am not, like you, afraid to be found. Indeed, I welcome being found.

"Show me you have been redeemed, demonstrate that you recognize the value of the people around you, bring me proof of your repentance, and I may consider working with you further."

Ian stumbled out the front door, the street noises and scents from the Bloemenmarkt easing through the haze in her mind enough to orient herself, and to ensure she memorized the address and street of Morgan's house. She wanted to return as soon as she left, but knew she could not. Not without giving her Lady what she required.

She shoved her hands in her pockets, shivering, and felt her fingers brush against a scrap of paper. Pulling it out, she found a torn piece of paper with a phone number scrawled across it, with the note "G — please call." The "please" was underlined twice. Her loins twitched even before her mind recognized who the note was from. Ian sighed. This could be the way back into Morgan's house. A gift. To lay at the feet of her Lady.

* * *

Morgan was a jumble of emotions. Her anger was spent and now she was simply excited beyond belief. She entered her bathroom and started the steam shower. Leaning over the sink and popping out the green contacts to show clear blue eyes she thought about how Ian not only had talent as a potential scout, but also had the makings of a half-way decent piece of property. A bit rough around the edges with a lot to learn, but definitely trainable. She was concerned about her standing as a spotter for the Marketplace, but then again this little adventure had not involved anyone but outsiders. If Ian remained quiet, whether from humiliation or hopeful obedience, no one would be the wiser. She did not think Ian would go to the police with a fantastic tale of drugged beer and electrical torture in a hidden dungeon. Shame on Geneviéve for mentioning the Marketplace to an outsider to begin with — if she ever regained her confidence and belief in what Morgan had to offer, Morgan would address that issue with her. Perhaps it would all work out in the end.

Morgan removed the red wig, shaking out her raven black wavy hair before entering the near scalding hot shower. As her muscles relaxed she thought of the payoff for the punks then turned her musings to Ian. Mentally, she bet against herself as to how long it would be before Ian returned to her door — to earn back the undamaged Marty that lay on the table in her dungeon. No, Morgan was never one to throw away anything that showed quality. Or lost something of value without *someone* paying for it.

26 In Hot Water

Chris let his head loll back at the ridge of the tub and breathed slowly. The water was near scalding, as most Japanese baths were. It seemed to awaken every scar on his body, old and new, made it a pleasant agony to move. Mostly, he kept still, feeling the sweat trickle through his hair.

The green tea helped settle the knot in his stomach; the hot water was working on all the others. He didn't feel like eating; sleep was the most seductive of early afternoon choices. It might be a good idea — certainly the invitations to private little farewell orgies would be coming in soon.

Not that he was eager to attend them anyway. He closed his eyes and sighed. Now that the vote was all but taken care of, he had the leisure to ponder Tetsuo's plan. There had been no messages from Anderson, no stern transatlantic phone calls, no cryptic indications of approval or annoyance. It wasn't like her to remain silent. Unless she was very, very angry.

Chris struggled with it, but then let the laugh out. His voice echoed against the walls, and his rising chest made the water ripple and splash up against his throat and ears, sizzling and teasing, which made him laugh even louder. It would be the ultimate irony, of course, if she were to be angry with him at this moment of victory.

"I see you are in a good mood, Mr. Parker," came a voice from the door.

"Shouldn't I be, Ninon?" he asked, opening his eyes.

She was wearing the ubiquitous cotton yukata and light slippers, and a female slave scurried in to attend her with an apologetic bow in Chris' direction.

"I apologize for taking this liberty," Ninon said, letting the robe slip away. "I realize that you had specified a private room. I took advantage of my

272

rank." Her generous body was as beautiful as Chris had heard described, a golden olive sheen to her perfect skin, round, feminine expanses of flesh that were lovingly massaged and pampered.

"When you offer me a glimpse of paradise, how can I even suggest that I am wronged?" Chris asked, closing his eyes again. Of all the people who could have over-awed the attendants outside the bathrooms, she was one of the few who he could bear right now. Definitely one of the few he could be comfortably naked in front of. He controlled the urge to laugh out loud again.

"Very good, very good," Ninon said, sitting on the bathing stool and allowing her hair to be pinned up. "As if I did not have the proof of your skill at flattery this morning, hm?"

"It's still awkward," Chris admitted. "I always feel like I'm saying some-one else's lines in a bad play."

"Yes, it is not in your nature to flatter," Ninon agreed. "Still, you apply yourself, and that is to be admired." The slave played a stream of warm water over her body and then gently applied sudsy lather, and Ninon sighed in pleasure.

"Whenever I come to these things, I feel like some sort of underachiev-ing student running into all my old professors," Chris said, closing his eyes again.

"And perhaps you are, although I must quarrel with that word, under-achieving. Is that how you feel now?"

Chris wiped his forehead clear of sweat and let the hot water splash him again. He smiled, slightly.

"Ah—hah," Ninon laughed. "A student no more."

"A student always," Chris demurred. "Just a slightly more cocky than usual one today."

"Deserved, I think, your cockiness, and not merely for your splendid compromise," Ninon said cheerfully. "May I join you in the water now?"

"Please do," Chris said, shifting slightly over to one side. Leaning on the slave's arm, Ninon slowly lowered her body into the hot water, with the slightest of hisses. She smiled briefly before settling down, and accepted a rolled towel for the back of her neck with a moan of contentment.

"I also appreciate that you no longer seek compliments yourself," she said after a few silent moments. "Years ago, you would have asked me what I meant with the phrase 'not merely'."

"I cultivate patience in many things," Chris said. "It's grown easier not to look for compliments or praise. This way, it's always a surprise when I get them." He opened his eyes slowly and Ninon laughed.

"Yes, you and patience," she said. "Your first important writing was on that topic, I believe."

"All right, I surrender," Chris said. "I will show my terrible manners by asking what you thought of my paper. You're probably the only one here this weekend who's read it."

"Oh, I do not think so," Ninon said seriously. "Oh, no, not at all. Certainly there will be those who put it away with all the others. I do not have the time to read everything I get over the year anyway! But you, I look forward to." She closed her own eyes and leaned back comfortably. "It is very sad, this one."

"Sad? I suppose it could be read that way," Chris said. "Denial and frustration are not very happy subjects to begin with. But I hope that I came up with some useful observations and suggestions."

"Yes, I think you did. Many of them will apply to my practice; it is a shame so many owners practice erotic control in haphazard ways. I appreciate your observations a great deal, especially upon the 'eroticism of rejection' as you put it. I have often cautioned clients to use their periods of denial as sources of strength and serenity. I also liked very much what you said, that depression can lead to transformation. Yes, a very odd thing to hear in this age where there are pills for everything. I look forward to the responses you asked for, and will certainly advise my friends to examine your paper thoroughly."

"Thank you," Chris murmured. "That's what I needed to make this morning perfect. Now, I can take a nap."

She laughed lightly, and the water around them rippled. "Is that the way of it? You win your battle and earn your praise and go off to a well deserved rest?"

"Barring a king's daughter to marry, I think that's the best any knight errant can hope for," Chris said.

Ninon puffed her lips out in a dismissive fashion. "I do not think that marriage or anyone's *daughter* would be of interest to you, Mr. Parker. A handsome prince, now. . .?"

"I *have* a handsome prince."

Ninon laughed. "This Michael? Oh, yes, he is handsome. And there is a sense of — what shall it be — a frustrated royalty about him? It is a pity the methods in your paper would not work upon him."

Chris edged his body up a little and cocked his head to one side. "You can tell that?"

"Yes. He does not feed upon his frustration, it feeds upon him. I suppose he must be a miraculous handler."

"You suppose incorrectly," Chris sighed. When she looked surprised, he nodded. "Oh, he is adequate. Slaves will obey him, and he is strict enough.

But he is . . . haphazard in observation, and frankly unimaginative in testing and interviewing."

Ninon's eyes narrowed suspiciously. "And yet, you chose him?"

"Anderson chose him."

"Anderson. . ." Ninon echoed. She pursed her lips thoughtfully, and Chris watched her. There was nothing false about her confusion. She shook her head after a minute. "It is a mystery, then," she said. "How curious. And for this battle, she did not deign to show herself, either. Most curious, indeed. Well, I shall call her when I get home and share gossip, and perhaps she will tell me why this handsome prince of yours is to be a trainer. In the meantime, if you seek a prize of a king, I suggest you look no further than Sakai-san, who seems most impressed with you this week. His third year trainee, Jiro, is very handsome indeed."

"Indeed," Chris said. He left it at that, and Ninon gave herself over to the water, the two of them in silence.

Abe Jiro was in fact a good looking man, tall and slender and slightly feminine, and clearly was surprised by Chris' appearance at their table the night before. But he recovered quickly and spoke a very accented and halting but obviously American tutored English, never ignoring Chris or condescending in any way. In fact, he seemed eager for a chance to practice his language skills. And Tetsuo had seemed pleased with the attention his trainee showed to Chris, which had eased the entire table into a more comfortable mood.

What a marked difference it had been, really. To sit among them as an equal — as a peer — to be acknowledged and spoken to, answered, laughed with. As opposed to being a threat or a curiosity or a thing of revulsion.

"None of the slaves wish to train under you, otachi," jeered Saburo-san, Sakai-sama's chief under-trainer. He used one of the many words that no one had actually defined for me yet but which I had surmised meant things like pervert and freak. "They have said that they would rather be kept back in training until you have gone. Do you understand me?"

Saburo often slowed down his speech to an almost ludicrous level, articulating every word sharply, exaggerating the sounds to make it "easier" for me to comprehend. I knew better than to ever suggest that I didn't need this sort of help. If I did, then everything directed to me would be in the most obscure of phrases — idioms and slang terms would abound even more and conversation would be rapid-fire and I would be lost. So I took the disgrace of his pediatric phrasing.

"Yes, Saburo-san, thank you for speaking so clearly, forgive me for my poor Japanese."

"Better you should leave now and save these poor slaves from having to endure any more time waiting for you, don't you think?" He leaned closer to me,

pushing into my space easily, with all the confidence of someone who knew he had the right, his teeth bared in a hostile grin.

"Thank you, Saburo-san, you are very wise, but I have not been told to go, so sorry."

"I'll show you sorry," he said, the usual phrase of his before something unpleasant, and I prepared myself for a slap or a command. But he did nothing, only stood slightly back and inclined his shoulders. It was not low enough to Sakai-sama. It was too low for another trainer of his level. I turned and immediately knelt for Noriko-sama, Sakai-sama's prodigy daughter and presumptive heir.

"Parker has not been added to the roster," she said to Saburo, also speaking slowly, but not with that edge of ridicule that Saburo cultivated. She, like most of the people there, pronounced my name Pah-kah. She was one of the few who used it as a name instead of making it sound like a vaguely annoying piece of furniture that no one had bothered to move out of the way. I had also noticed that the various nicknames vanished when she was around.

"There are no slaves who wish to have this as their trainer," Saburo said with a shrug. "Your honored father has said that no one shall be forced to train with it."

"Then I will find the right slaves for Parker," Noriko said. "Please tell my father that he will be added to the roster next week."

Saburo almost choked — I could hear him cough back a breath, and I wished that I could grin. But I remained impassive, not showing any sign of listening to a conversation to which I had not been invited.

"Thank you, Noriko-san, I shall," Saburo said. "I'm sure your help in this matter will be most appreciated." Angrily, he turned and left, and Noriko gave me the command to look up. She looked concerned, perhaps a little annoyed. But not, I knew, annoyed at me. She was serious and thoughtful and very precise and the only free person at the school who was younger than I was.

In English, she said, carefully, "Do not disappoint me, Parker." And she too, left. I struggled for almost a full minute, but I couldn't stop the tears that formed in my eyes. I wiped them away with the sleeve of my (American) shirt and tried to compose myself before I had to face anyone else.

It had taken two months — but someone had finally suggested that I might do what I was sent here to do. And what's more — she expected me to do it well. My heart almost broke with the first sign of kindness, and I finally understood how powerful it could be.

"Chris?"

His eyes flew open and he started, disturbing the surface of the water. He blinked and looked at a very concerned Ninon.

"I'm so sorry, Ninon," he said, shaking his head. "Not enough sleep, I'm so terribly sorry. My God, how embarrassing. In the bath with the single most desirable woman here and I fall asleep."

She waved one hand at him. "Never mind more flattery, what was wrong? Your entire body became tense! I thought I would have to summon one of those marvelous massage people to pry you out!"

Chris shook his head and sighed. "A memory. You mentioned Tetsuo and a kings daughter — and I remembered Noriko-san."

"Oh my goodness, how thoughtless of me!" Ninon was aghast at her faux pas. "Yes, you knew her, oh, I am the one who should be sorry, Chris. Her loss was such a tragedy for Tetsuo."

"It's been years," Chris said, stretching and wincing at the lapping water. "I'm just so tired I can barely think. Please forgive me, Ninon, I'm going to shower off with some cool water and take a nap. I'll see you at dinner?"

"Yes, I will be there," Ninon promised. "After all, I must take the first glass of champagne as we celebrate a new era for the Marketplace."

"And I'll take the second," Chris promised. He pushed himself up and out of the tub, and Ninon's slave eagerly waited on him until he gently shooed her away. Wrapped in a robe and his thoughts, he walked back to his room and didn't bother to call for a slave to set out a futon for him. With one arm behind his head, he instantly fell into a deep sleep on the floor, not caring about comfort or, for once, proper behavior.

Two hours later, the main meeting room had been transformed. Chairs were now grouped around tables, small couches brought in to create comfortable seating areas, and all the panels leading to the outer gardens were opened, allowing the slight afternoon breezes to waft through. William Longet's raised table had been reduced to a simple podium for announcements, and a new table was set up for his staff to check the member rolls and register proxy votes. Trainers wandered in after lunch and naps, after swimming or light bouts of sex with slaves or each other. Alcoholic drinks were much in evidence. The mood was light and energetic, and at the chiming of the hour, Longet opened the membership book and locked the ballot box.

"Well, this is a foregone conclusion," declared Tucker, walking in with Michael. They had found each other after lunch, watching an impromptu demonstration of various forms of hand signals from several trainers who advocated different methods. It had been lighthearted and competitive, and the slaves drafted for this use had an eager-to-please amusement that made them cheerfully attractive even when the signals invariably got crossed.

These are people who don't like to fight about important things, Michael thought idly. They may love to argue or show off their skills or compete in all these silly ways — but they don't like to disagree on fundamental beliefs. Of course not. They feel like they're alone in the world, they have no other place to be this way, to do these things. To lose it would mean — tragedy. For anyone, on any side. No wonder Chris' backing down was such a big deal.

"I'm glad it is," Michael answered. "It wasn't pleasant to be here when you guys were all fighting. Now, it's one big happy family again."

"Well, I dunno about that!' Tucker laughed heartily. "But then, I guess we are kind of family, in that sick and twisted sort of way. Thrown together by God, you could say, and makin' the best of it." He leaned over the table and cheerfully accepted a ballot after initialing his name in the member roles. He excused himself to fill it out over by a shaded desk, folded it and dropped it into the box with a flourish. "There — I done my duty for the year."

"Do you train trainers?," Michael asked as they walked over to one side, making room for two others.

"Oh, hell, no," Tucker said with a shudder. "Every once in a while, I take on someone' else's student for a few weeks or months, let 'em help me out a bit, it keeps me on my toes. But it's too iffy, taking on an apprentice. No offense, son, you're a nice fella, very smart. But I've seen it a dozen times — you take on a sharp apprentice and at the end of three years, they're either gone to the block, left the world, or, worse, they want to set up shop across the street from you and take away your business. It ain't like slaves, see, where you lose maybe 3, 4 months. Trainers take years, no matter what that California nutcase says. I'd say it's only one in ten trainers that wants to take on apprentices. Me, I'd rather raise water moccasins. They're as pretty and seductive as a good apprentice, but if they leave you, you don't cry as much."

"And there's always anti-venom in the refrigerator, right?" Chris Parker came into Michael's peripheral vision, and Michael thought that the bath had done him a world of good. He had changed into fresh clothes, and his tie was the one that Michael had given him when Rachel had whispered that his birthday was coming up. It was a rather bold design for Chris — but he had taken a liking to the colorful dancing figures on it, radiating beams of energy shooting from them.

"Yessiree, Chris, that is the truth," Tucker laughed. "Dammit if they haven't come up with ani-venom for human relationships though. You just can't put years in with someone else and not be changed by them, and that's the God's honest truth."

"You won't find an argument with me in that statement, Tucker," Chris replied. And then, remarkably, he winked at Michael, before reaching down into his inside pocket to take out a sheaf of envelopes all marked with the green stamp of the Marketplace's official proxy ballot.

I've had an effect on Chris, Michael marveled. It's more than the haircut, the tie. Jesus, he as much said that to me right now! Could he — is he still proud of me? Is he glad I came?

He shivered slightly, even though the air was heavy and warm, with the weight of afternoon thunder in the distance. Tucker and Chris continued to chat lightly, and their voices seemed to fade as Michael's heart pounded to an ever louder intensity.

I feel like kneeling, he thought, dizzily. I feel like I want to start crying again and just get down on my knees and wrap myself around his legs and thank him. Oh my God, I feel like I'm going to burst! What's happening to me? He blinked rapidly and tried to figure out how to breathe without panting, without gasping for air. Suddenly, the room seemed monstrously calm, as though the breezes from outside and from the overhead fans had stopped. People's voices were only a slight buzz, their faces a blur. Take me out of here and do what you want to me, Michael thought. I don't care what it is, make me a trainer, make me a slave, I'll do it, I can do it now, it's real now.

And then, suddenly, he realized that Chris was turning sharply to one side, and Michael thought he had spoken out loud. But Chris continued to turn, a look on his face of pure astonishment, and Michael's ears seemed to pop as one voice cut through the light buzz of the room.

"Avidan, a-v-i-d-a-n. . .under spotters, there ya go!"

"Ron?" Chris said. "Ron?"

Ron Avidan, quintessential leatherman, gay sexual explorer and, coincidentally, Chris Parker's older brother, turned away from the table with a ballot in his hand and a big grin on his face. His mustache had a little more gray in it than when Michael had last seen him a few months before. He was wearing a black tee shirt and jeans that showed off his handsome, long body, and the powerful muscles on his upper arms, and he had a thick earring in one ear.

"Hey, baby bro, what's up?" he asked, his dark eyes dancing.

"Ron?" Chris repeated. He closed his mouth and then moved forward to catch his brother in a strong forearm embrace, and then in a hug. "What the hell are you doing here?" he asked, laughing.

"Hey, can't a man come and vote for his kid brother's big ideas?" Ron asked, waving the ballot. "Shit, I'm still a spotter, I still got the right to be here, if I want to. I usually just don't want to." He laughed.

Chris took a half step back, and turned his head to one side suspiciously. "You did not come all the way to Okinawa on the last day of the Academy to vote on something, no matter who put it up."

"You're right," Ron nodded. "You know, you always were smarter than me. Truth is, I'm here 'cause someone's a white knuckle flyer. And kid, when she calls and says pack up a tux and a passport, you're coming with me, I still jump."

Chris paled suddenly, and Michael paled with him. "What?"

Ron only nodded, and Chris turned too sharply for such a practiced and disciplined man, to face a tired and rumpled looking Imala Anderson. Both shocked silence and whispered news spread in the wake behind Chris, and he bowed carefully to her as Tucker made a little gesture of welcome as well. One second too late, Michael followed suit, hating himself for not noticing her arrival and warning Chris.

Anderson nodded back to Chris and smiled briefly at Tucker. Her long, navy blue cotton skirt was light and crinkled, her white blouse limp across her upper body. She looked slightly pale herself, and tired, her hair drawn back sharply into a long black and gray ponytail, her wrists, as usual, decked in bracelets that jangled. Without a word, she walked over to Chris and held a hand out.

"Welcome to Okinawa, Trainer," he said softly. He placed the sheaf of envelopes into her hand and stepped back as she sorted through them and walked over to the ballot table.

"What a surprise, huh?" Ron laughed, as other trainers came forward to formally welcome Anderson as she registered her name and had the monitors check off her various proxies.

"Why didn't you warn us?" Michael asked, pitching his voice in a whisper.

Ron shrugged. "I figured if she wanted you to know, she would have told you. Besides, what's the big deal? We heard you got it wrapped up neatly before we even got here!' He punched Chris lightly on the arm, and Chris let him.

"How did you hear that?" he asked, consciously straightening his tie and shooting his cuffs. "How long have you been here?"

"I dunno, maybe 10 minutes. Man, am I beat!" Ron shook his head and stretched a little. "You're lookin' good, squirt, and so's our student here. Mind if I borrow him for some R&R?" He laughed comfortably and leered at Michael, who by now was used to this from Chris' brother. The first time he had met Ron, Ron had knocked a hat off his head and given him a lesson in old-guard leather etiquette, but in subsequent meetings, he had loosened up a little and begun a campaign of teasing that had changed from threatening to flattering. Especially when Chris told him that he had no intention of letting Ron 'handle' Michael, because, as he put it, 'Ron is out of touch with Marketplace mores'.

But if he was so out of touch. . .

"You're a spotter?" Michael asked.

Ron shrugged. "Yeah. Sometimes. I found a few winners, didn't I, Chris?"

"One or two," Chris said slightly distracted. Anderson had finished turning over the proxies from her former students who had given them to her and which she in turn had entrusted to Chris. She then took her own proxy ballot, ripped it up, took a fresh one, initialed her name in the register and voted, all the while returning the greetings of trainers who wandered over to her to pay their respects. As she dropped her own ballot in the box, she seemed to be totally unconcerned with the procedure, and when she disengaged from Walther Kurgan's enthusiastic welcome, he did not pursue her, only backed away and re-joined his own conversation group.

She walked back to Chris and Michael and Ron, and Michael was aware of Tucker also backing away slightly.

"Well." She said the word with a slightly ironic inflection, but her mouth was a grim, straight line. "I think you have some explaining to do, Mr. Parker. Please come with me." And without another word, she turned toward the door leading back to the Western wing. Chris's cheek twitched, right along the jawline, and Michael felt a sinking feeling of shame and fear race through him as Chris merely gave a polite nod to Tucker and his brother and then turned as well, to obey her.

Michael started to follow as well — hesitantly, nothing had been addressed to him, but he was now fully disturbed. Anderson did not appear to be pleased — but she had every reason to be overjoyed! The proposal had been doomed from the start — even if it passed, it would have left antagonisims across the ethical and political lines that had made the past few days so awkward. In compromising, Chris had saved everyone's face and gotten the people who believed in his proposal the ability to at least continue their methods in a more organized and mutually supported fashion. It was perfect. She had to see that! And how could she just pull him out of the room like that, not even allowing him the chance to *vote*, for God's sake?

But even as he started to move, Ron caught one arm, and another hand caught the other. He looked to his left to see Ken Mandarin, a slender cigar in the corner of her mouth, looking slightly amused.

"That is not for you to see or hear," she said, drawing the cigar out and blowing smoke in the general direction of the door. "This time, it is best for dingos to stay out of the house, hm?"

"Yeah, you know better than to get involved in whatever's going on there," Ron said with a slight note of chagrin. "Just let them take care of things."

"But — but — it's not fair! Why is she angry?" Michael almost whispered, not waiting to draw any more attention to what was going on. He struggled and fought down the hint of desperation in his voice. "I don't understand! What is she even doing here? It's the last day, for crying out loud!"

"Not your business," Ron said firmly. "When she wants your input she'll ask you."

"Or give it to you, hm?" Ken let Michael go and winked at Ron. "Hello, there, Ron. You are looking well! Why do you not come out to play more often?"

"Because I don't need the heartache," Ron said, sighing. He let go of Michael as well, and brushed his hand down Michael's jacket sleeve, smoothing it down. "Sorry, kid, didn't mean to grab you like that. Honestly, I don't know why Imala's got a bee in her bonnet, I don't. She called me up three days ago and told me to come with her, and I did. Believe me, there aren't many people I'd do that for, even if they are holding first class tickets to a tropical paradise. But if she's got some bone to pick with Chris, that's their business. I learned my lesson about interfering there a long time ago. Take it from me, just keep your nose out of it and be a good boy, and things will be just fine. In the meantime, why don't you and Ken take me on a tour of this place? I don't even have a room yet. And I need something big and tall and frozen, with some tropical fruit in it and a fucking parasol off the side, so let me at one of these perfect slaves and you can tell me all about what went on here, OK?"

"Yes, sir," Michael said automatically. There was no sense on dwelling on Chris and the Trainer, especially if he had Ron on his hands now. Best to pay attention to what he could do, and hope to get a chance to speak in Chris' defense later on. Surely Anderson would listen to him, if he approached her politely and spoke respectfully and explained things in a way he knew Chris wouldn't. Yes, he thought, idly eyeing a serving slave and getting them to bring something that would aproximate Ron's requested drink. Yes, it'll be OK, maybe I can get one of these other big shots to chip in on this. Ninon, maybe. Or Walther. I'll help. And I won't embarrass him.

"So you took it upon yourself to change the proposal," Anderson said, as she sat down on the couch in her room, spreading her arms along the back.

"Yes, Trainer." Chris stood facing her, his hands behind his back, his posture formal and his words calm. He had taken the walk there as time to compose himself properly, the presence of the two accompanying slaves keeping them both silent until Anderson's luggage had been neatly deposited and the slaves gone with twin bows. Anderson had a room much like Ken's. She had taken a cursory glance out the window before seating herself, but seemed either unimpressed or uninterested in her surroundings. When she lifted her eyes to Chris, they were as cold as they had been in the meeting room.

"Get me a drink," she said, after a moment of silence. "And explain yourself."

Chris took one of the heavy glass tumblers and filled it with ice, sparkling mineral water and a twist of lime. He brought it to her in silence, and then took his place in front of her again, neatly and with grace.

"The disagreements over the proposal were destructive," he said carefully. "Although by sheer votes it would have passed, it was clear that a coalition of spotters were determined to see it as a way to restrict their freedom of choice in trainers. A smaller number of trainers were also convinced that it would restrict their access to clients and customers, if not put them out of business all together. There was a persistent belief that it would lead to disqualification of various types of training, despite the best efforts to demonstrate that it would not. I decided that in the interests of maintaining a unified community, I would sacrifice the compulsory part of the proposal in favor of a voluntary association. This was met with an astoundingly positive response, and I have every expectation that it will pass resoundingly."

"All very well and good, except that it was supposed to be a requirement!" Anderson tapped her fingers alongside the glass.

"Yes, Trainer. I take full responsibility for this turn of affairs. If the Trainer would permit, however, I can explain how this will suit her purposes as well as the first proposal."

"Oh, please do!" Her voice rich with sarcasm, she leaned back, cradling the glass in both hands.

"This new voluntary association will be rich with well known names of experienced trainers," Chris began, seeing the plan evolving in front of him as it did when he was meditating. "Even the British trainers will join. At the end of the first year, slaves trained by members of this group will be so identified in all catalogs and sale meetings, in their personal files and all member records. Owners will begin to know the difference, even if they never have the direct experience of such slaves — what will be remembered is that most of the highest valued property comes with this seal of approval. In time, owners will want slaves with this type of training because they will perceive a kind of ranking that simply sounds better. It's sheer marketing, I admit. But it will work."

"Why?" Anderson put her glass down and leaned forward.

"Because our owners are mostly snobs," Chris answered smoothly. "They want value for their money, true, but mostly they want prestige. If they perceive this new association as representing the very best trainers who use the very best methods, they will want to buy their slaves because they believe it will enhance their standing among other slave owners. In time, it will be considered either gauche or stupid or merely eccentric to buy a slave whose training hasn't been certified. And younger trainers will fight to get received by this association so that they have a support network to become able to make these desirable clients."

"I see," Anderson said. She sat back without further comment, and Chris suddenly felt warmth flooding up the back of his neck. He took a deep breath as her eyes seemed to sharpen in amusement.

"As you intended," he said softly.

"Did I?"

He lowered his eyes for a moment, not trusting himself to speak properly. "Forgive my presumption for asking, Trainer — but why? Why not merely propose the association by itself, and not have to struggle through three days of debates and — and. . ." He took another breath, ashamed of his loss of words, and looked into her eyes again. "Was this another test?" he finally asked.

"No," she said bluntly. "I knew you'd do the right thing. I didn't know that the Academy would, though. And I needed to know who would be in on this because they believed in it, not because they thought they could hike their sales records. Now, I'll know. So will you, by the way."

Chris unclenched his jaw and let his eyes rest at a spot on the wall just over her head. "Thank you, Trainer, for your confidence in me. Although I was too stupid to figure out your intentions, I am glad to have been of service to you."

"Are you really? If you are in my service, why did you accept Tetsuo Sakai's kimono and wear it in public? Why did you actually discuss your *sale* with him?" Her voice scaled up slightly, although she did not actually raise it. It made Chris shiver, it was a rare kind of sound from her, true anger. She put her glass down and stripped her bracelets off, laying them on the table and massaging her wrists. There were red marks on her wrists, Chris noted, and he knew that she really was a bad flyer and had probably spent the last 12 hours in one plane or another, gripping the arms of the seat or her own wrists, while Ron plied her with bourbon and amusing, profane stories. He kept his eyes steady.

"The Trainer is well informed," he said quietly. "This student accepts full responsibility for these actions and further disgraceful behavior in not informing the Trainer of these decisions and actions, and this student sincerely begs pardon. . ."

She slammed her palm down on the table top, and the bracelets rattled. "I'm not interested in your begging," she snapped. "I'm interested in how you broke confidence with me after all these years."

"Sakai-san *knew*," Chris said, his hands clenching tightly behind him.

"He guessed," she corrected.

"I cannot lie to him any more than I can to you, Trainer," Chris said, and he lowered his eyes again. "Again, it is my failing."

"It sure is," Anderson said. "It sure is. Well, you are not for sale."

Chris found his jaw tightening again, and all the benefits of his long soak seemed to vanish, leaving his body tense and almost shaking. He knew what he should do — incline his head correctly, take a step back, accept the final word with grace and silence and wait for further discipline or instruction. But his body was too stiff, his back too straight, his legs almost sunk into the carpeted floor.

"With all due respect, Trainer, why not?" he asked, his voice inappropriately sharp.

Anderson, who had been engaged in taking off a silver ring, laid it down on the table in astonishment. "Excuse me?" she asked.

"Why not sell me?" he asked. "You don't own slaves, Trainer. Everyone knows that. Everyone but me, and now Sakai-san. Let him take me off your hands."

"You owe me, Mr. Parker," Anderson said evenly, her slight drawl creeping into her voice. "Let's not forget that, shall we?"

"I will never forget that, Trainer," Chris answered hotly. " I owe you much more than the money and time you've invested in me, I owe you my life. I have served you without the name to which I am entitled, and yet I will forever be grateful to you. I swore that I would do as you said and give myself over to your plans in five years despite what you know are my own personal desires. And — and I am shamed to admit that I dread that day. I am ashamed to admit that I've hoped that you would reconsider. But I have, Trainer. I have done as you requested, but every day I have hoped that in some way, you would find it in you to release me or bind me to someone else and allow me to live the way I have always dreamed." His face was taut with the effort to say these private and terrible things out loud, and when he was finished, he couldn't even look at her. With a slight cough that didn't quite hide a choke, he gently dropped to his knees and lowered his head, this time the carpet soft under him, this time, a genuflection of humility and sorrow and not mere respect.

"And all I've invested in you — I should pass onto Tetsuo, just like that? Get rid of the trainee I expect to take over for me because he wants the pride of a collar?" She stressed the word 'wants', and the accusation stung.

"Then please, Trainer, keep me. I would be honored beyond belief to serve you forever. But keep me as what I am, not as who you wish I were," Chris snapped back, his eyes flashing. "If I have pride in a collar, it is because you have driven it into me as surely as how to stand and speak and serve a — a glass of water. Allow me my pride or strip it from me if it pleases you, but dammit, acknowledge me for what I am to you."

Anderson stood up, her eyes sharply drawn. "Your voice is raised to me, Chris, and your formal manners are uneven and disgracefully sloppy. It's hard to believe you actually were my student." She walked around the edge of the table to stand next to him, looking down. Chris blushed; it was true, he had slipped in and out of formal phrasing, each time guided impulsively by anger.

"The Trainer is correct," he said bitterly, his voice deliberately even again. "Again, this student begs for pardon. . ."

"I never asked for this from you!"

"Yet the Trainer accepts it when it suits the Trainer's needs," he said tightly.

"Get up," she snapped, and he rose and turned to face her. With cool deliberation, she raised her hand and slapped him, sharply, against his left cheek. Her aim was deliberate and perfect, and the backs of her fingers hit underneath his cheekbone. He gasped, but allowed his head to turn with the blow, feeling the tingle of the flesh with a renewed sense of shock. Quickly, he reached up and took his glasses off, and returned his hands behind his back.

"Bastard," Anderson whispered. "Is that what you want?"

She slapped him again, this time on the other cheek, this time harder. Again, left cheek, and then back, on the right. Each time, her blows got stronger, a measured build up that echoed both in the room and in his ears, and he tasted blood in his mouth, but he did nothing but allow her to repeatedly force his head from one side to another. The walls blurred as his head snapped from side to side and he closed his eyes to keep himself as steady as possible. Eventually, two blows rocked him back on his heels, but each time he righted himself quickly and he never brought his hands forward.

Finally, she stopped, her breath shallow and quiet, and stared at him. His cheeks were red. There was a cut in his lip, from one of her nails. Light red welts streaked across the bottom of his jawline already. His own breath was quickened, and when he opened his eyes gently, without a scared jerk of panic, his pupils were wide, and there was no anger in his brown eyes.

"Is that what you want?" she repeated.

"Yes, Trainer," he said softly, a droplet of blood at the corner of his mouth. "Oh, God, yes." As he spoke, it grew into a thin stream, down his chin, skirting and then mingling with his close trimmed goatee. But he made no attempt to stop it.

Anderson took a step back and sighed. Suddenly, there was no anger in her, either. "Put your glasses back on," she said, unbuttoning the top button of her blouse. "Freshen my drink, send for tea for two, and something sweet. Wash your face, you're bleeding. And then wait right here, in a suitable position for someone in your station, until you're needed."

"Yes, Trainer, thank you for correcting me."

"That wasn't to correct you, Chris," she said, as she headed for the bathroom. "You should know better than that by now. That was for my pleasure."

Chris flushed again, in amazement and an overwhelming need to beg for forgiveness again, or to thank her for that casual off-hand comment that made him so warm in this air-conditioned room. But instead he did as he was told, a little numb inside, his cheeks warm and sore and blood in his mouth, flooding around his teeth and tongue. There would be bruises, he could see where they would form as he patted his face with a folded wet towel. The skin was abraded in several places, but she was precise and careful in her sadism and he wouldn't even have a black eye. He tried to focus his thoughts, wondered how Michael would react when he saw the marks. It would be a good test, especially if Michael felt compelled to display some sort of anger toward the Trainer. An excellent object lesson, as a matter of fact. He called the kitchen and ordered the things she requested. He unpacked for her as well, and when the tea and cakes arrived, he laid them out.

When she came out of the bathroom, she was wearing the light summer dress he had hung in there for her. She ignored him, kneeling by the table, and shook her head at his offer to pour tea. Instead, she put her bracelets and rings back on and leafed through the Academy schedule. When a knock came at the door, she put it down and sighed. Chris got up and went to the door, and opened it for Tetsuo Sakai.

Tetsuo smiled and bowed to Anderson, who rose for him with an equal smile. He thrust something at Chris, and walked into the room, saying, "Imala, thank you so much for coming. You do me way too much honor, especially when I have been so rude to you."

"The day you're rude to me someone will have to let me know," Anderson said, shaking his hand and then hugging him. "Come on, sit down, have some tea. I heard you went to Bali for a few weeks, tell me all about it."

Chris closed the door and walked quickly back to the table, as Tetsuo seated himself comfortably in one of the arm chairs. Chris knelt next to the table and laid the folder that Tetsuo had handed him down, and carefully poured tea, and then inched back out of the way. It was impossible not to notice what Tetsuo had been holding. It was a green folder, not too thick, with a white and gold label on it. It was an official Marketplace slave record, and it had never before been outside of a comfortable, tree-shaded brownstone in Brooklyn.

It took all of his concentration to focus on service. It was his folder. She had sent his records to Tetsuo.

27 Mysterious Ways

Since Anderson had taken a room by herself and not left any instructions for what should be done about her traveling companion, Michael decided to move Ron into Chris' room. After all, there was plenty of room, and he was pretty sure that Chris would like to spend time with his brother anyway. Theirs was a strong and loving relationship — they were obviously very close. It was so strange, though, that they arrived at the end of the trip. He asked Ron how long they were going to stay, and Ron had shrugged.

"I hope she doesn't want to turn right around and go back," he said with a grin. "God knows, I'd do it for her, but two days in the air and in airports is a bit much. Hell, this is a nice place, maybe we'll stay a while. Now tell me all about my little brother and all the trouble he's causing."

After unpacking — and Ron had indeed brought a tuxedo, along with innumerable black t-shirts and one pair of swim trunks — they had gone back to the balloting area, where the last of the trainers was finishing up. Michael told an abbreviated version of the past few days' events, and Ron whistled through his teeth when he heard about the formal kimono, but seemed pretty pleased with the political side of the story, especially with the compromise.

"He's quite a stickler, my brother," he said offhandedly. "Thinks there's something wrong with the world for not seeing everything through his eyes, sometimes. It's good for him to bend a little, it'll make him more friends."

"But if what he did was such a good thing, why is Anderson pissed off at him?"

"Don't know. She sure as hell didn't tell me, that's for sure. Just said, hey, Chris is pulling off a big change in the way we do business, I need to be there, you're coming with me. She's always trying to get me involved in more Marketplace stuff." He laughed and didn't say anything more than that.

William Longet watched the clock until voting time was over, and got ragged cheers when he closed the books and passed the box and key over to the accounting team, who walked off with much dignity. Although his job wasn't over until he announced the results, he loosened his tie and grinned and swept a passing pleasure slave into a kiss as she giggled.

Paul Sheridan met up with Ron in the Eastern garden pavilion and the two men pounded each other on the back and called each other various profanities. Bronwyn was there as well, with Kim and a few of the other junior trainers. Ninon was comfortable on a lounge chair, her hair free and a gloriously handsome woman at her feet, massaging them and preparing to paint her toes, judging from the tiny bottle on the grass next to her and the pedicure tools arrayed on a towel. The thunderstorm in the distance was getting closer, but golden late afternoon sun was filtering its way through layers of clouds, and the breezes also cut through the humidity in a pleasant way. It was nice to sit outside and not broil. Before long, Ken and Marcy joined the small group, and Stuart trailed along behind, turning a little self conscious when he saw Michael. Michael did not repeat his mimed kiss of the morning, but smiled instead and introduced him to Ron. Stuart seemed both shocked and impressed that his hero actually had an older brother.

"So it's true then? Anderson arrived this afternoon?" asked Bronwyn.

"Yep, in the flesh," Ron said, stretching out onto the grass. He had picked up a male pleasure slave in his wanderings and was using the man's buttocks as a pillow for the back of his head. The slave didn't seem to mind in the slightest, and Paul seemed to enjoy just gazing at the tableau they made.

"But why wait until the last day?" asked Kim.

"Far be it from me to ask the motives of my betters," laughed Ron. "The Trainer works in mysterious ways, that's all."

Ken waved a hand. "Oh, it is nothing mysterious. She wishes to impress us all with her power, and voila, we are all impressed. Now, we shall fight with each other on who gets to send a client to her this year, because she actually deigned to join us in public." She laughed lightly. "My, yes, I am already thinking of who I shall nominate to her."

"It is strange how rarely she comes out," mused Bronwyn. "Especially since she is such a valuable role model."

"Role model?"

"Yes! The most sought after female trainer, I'd say. Wouldn't you agree?"

"I suppose so," Ken admitted. "At least, with Ninon here, I should say, one of the most sought after women, yes?"

Ninon laughed. "Oh, I freely relinquish that singular space to Anderson. I know my worth in the world. And while I may make a better lover, she makes a better slave, and we all know which is more important."

"Well, it's very rare that a woman gets the respect she does, or the sheer power," Bronwyn insisted. "I mean, look at what happened — she arrived at the very last day of the Academy, and everyone started talking about her, what did she think, and what did she want, and how did she vote — as if there was any question about that. I'd wager that if she had been here, Parker wouldn't have had to compromise on that proposal; no one would dare oppose her publicly."

"Oh — I cannot say that," Ken said gently.

"I can," Ninon said with a sigh, propping one foot into her slave's lap comfortably. "But then, perhaps that was why she stayed away."

Michael wondered about that. Why did Anderson avoid these meetings, and why did she tend to stay out of the greater affairs of the Marketplace when it was obvious she had a lot of pull with the organization on all sorts of levels? Why stay in her little house in Brooklyn with no real staff to speak of, no luxuries, and no honor when she could easily be the mistress of a vast training house, a private estate with willing clients who would practically pay for the privilege of dusting her credenza? Even Grendel and Alexandra had a major domo, a cook, a gardener and a stableman, and they only trained novices.

"...and frankly, it's good to see a woman in a position of power," Bronwyn was saying.

"Oh, feh," Ken said, leaning forward. "Here we are, you are surrounded by women! I, myself, am one of the world's greatest spotters, no? And here is Ninon, and there is Marcy, here are all the women you need! I think you and Kim here are, what is it — the wave of the future."

"I must respectfully disagree," Kim said with a sigh. "It is true — there do seem to be more women juniors this year — but I have seen the records. We do not stay, we do not rise to the top ranks. There are many, many more men, and truly, many more white men than Asians, even though our own market is quite large."

"Oh, and let's not forget how few trainers are any color than caucasian," Bronwyn declared, her own pale skin flushing. "We look very multi-racial this year, but that's because of location, I think. Last year, in Switzerland, it was a sea of white!"

"Why, did it snow?" Juan Matalino stepped into the garden, a towel around his shoulders, obviously fresh from swimming. He flopped down onto the grass next to Ron and grinned, and Ron grinned back welcoming him.

"No, no, Bronwyn is explaining to us all how white, Western men rule the world," laughed Ninon. "Somehow, this fact has escaped us until now!"

"Well, some white men are acceptable," Juan said, patting the slave that Ron was leaning on. "Have you tried this one yet, sir, he is very nice!"

"No, maybe you could show me how nice he is, sir," Ron flirted. "I'm Ron. And your name would be. . .?"

"Well, forgive me for stating the obvious," Bronwyn groused.

"Oh, don't be cross," Ken said with an exasperated sigh. "Yes, it is sometimes hard to be a woman, but mostly, it is wonderful! And if every other trainer and spotter is a woman, then perhaps no one will notice us, hm? Better to be rare and treasured than to be common, that is what I say."

"Better to have a proper share in the power," insisted Bronwyn.

"Women can have power, even when you think they do not," Ken responded quickly. "I think it is better to know your limitations and work beyond them, yes? Or within them, to the best of your choices. True, not everyone is as fortunate as I — but you might be amazed at what a woman can do when she is clever."

"I love clever women," declared Juan, looking up from Ron's ear, where he had been whispering. "I love clever women and handsome men."

"Then you would have loved this sale I just arranged," Ken said with a laugh. "It is all about a clever woman and a handsome man."

"Excellent, tell me all about it. Leave nothing out." Juan laughed and Ron moved over slightly to make room for him on the slave's backside.

"It is a fairy tale," Ken began.

"Great — I love stories about fairies!" Ron laughed.

"Not that kind of fairy, you despoiler of boys' bottoms," Ken said. "I mean a fairy story as in princesses and princes."

28 Insha'allah   by Karen Taylor

Khadija took the veil off after entering her uncle's house. Normally, she
would only keep her head covered, but out of deference to her uncle and still
in mourning for her father, she had wound the long cloth of the *milayyeh*
around her head, neck and shoulders, and tucked the veil carefully across her
face to hide everything except her eyes before heading through the crowded
streets of Cairo. Anonymous in her dark, shapeless caftan, so different from
the suits and dresses she was used to wearing, she felt enveloped, literally, by
Cairo. Wrapped as our Prophet Mohammed was wrapped in the angel
Gabriel's embrace on Mount Hira, she thought to herself, as she pushed her
way through the swarms of people. Fatma, a servant who had been with her
family before she was born, was keeping pace with her.

Khadija had been invited to the reading of her father's will. Not that she
would be physically present for the formality. While the will was read in her
uncle's private office to the men in the family, Khadija visited with her aunt
and female cousins in the parlour, sipping tea and nibbling at the French
pastries her aunt always served on formal occasions. Khadija hated her uncle's
apartment, with its dusty velvet curtains blocking any natural light, and re-
taining every scent of perfume her female relatives were wearing. The tables
and mantelpieces were covered with three generations of family photographs,
interspersed with trinkets from her uncle's travels, objects Khadija knew were
available in every airport souvenir shop. Gritting her teeth, Khadija sat gingerly on the edge of the overstuffed love seat next to her cousin-in-law, and
endured the chatter about children and answering questions about the latest
European fashions. When her uncle's office door opened and the men poured
out, the parlour bulged to capacity. The din was incredible with everyone
talking at once, calling for more tea, or gathering up various wives and chil-

dren to leave before afternoon prayers.

"*Allahu Akhhah*," wailed the muezzin from a minaret the nearest mosque, calling the Faithful to worship. Was it that late already? Khadija sighed, waiting respectfully in the parlour with her aunt and Fatma until her Uncle had finished his prayers. It was a relief to have her Uncle finally call her into his office. While it was as cluttered as the rest of the house, at least there were only two people in the room. Three, counting the elderly Fatma, who had been enlisted by her aunt to bring tea and still more pastries.

"Khadija, my most beloved niece, here is your copy of the papers." Ahmed handed a closed file to his niece, then gestured her to a chair.

"*Alfi shukir*, Uncle," Khadija thanked him. She placed the file in her lap without opening it. Patiently, she waited until Fatma set the tea down, and waited still further until the proper rituals had been observed in pouring and serving the beverage. She would not shame him by reading the papers before he could tell her his synopsis.

"It is an interesting will, my beloved niece," Ahmed began. "My brother, may he live in our memory, has left a most interesting will." Khadija sighed inwardly. Her Uncle Ahmed had a reputation as a proper, courteous businessman of the old style. Old style meaning hours before business was actually brought up, and hours longer until it was settled. She herself preferred the more direct, approach, but she was a guest in her Uncle's house. She shifted imperceptibly in her chair, in the hopes of finding a position she could maintain while appearing to be alert to every word her Uncle would speak — no matter how often she had heard them before.

"As you know, your dear father did not expect your brother to die on such a peaceful military operation," Ahmed was continuing. "It hurt your father badly, my beloved niece. His sickness worsened at the news, and he never recovered."

"I remember, Uncle," Khadija replied softly, silently willing her uncle to get to the point.

"Your beloved father, my brother, rewrote his will after the death of your brother, may he be with Allah," Ahmed continued. "Your father had your best interests at heart, my darling niece. The will is, as I have mentioned, interesting, perhaps even unusual, but according to the attorneys, it is quite legal. Ah, Khadija, my sweet, your father's wishes are most clear." He paused, and sighed heavily.

"Beloved Uncle, will you enlighten me as to my father's wishes?" Khadija asked politely, hoping her eagerness was unnoticeable. Ahmed sighed heavily again, as if unable to form words.

"*Ya-beyh?* Beloved Uncle?" she prompted him.

"Yes, yes, you were always the impatient one, Khadija. Give this old man time to tell his story."

"*La samaat*, Uncle," Khadija apologized, lowering her brown eyes demurely, silently counting to ten in as many languages as she could. Ahmed smiled at her deference.

"You are forgiven, my sweet niece. Now, where were we? Ah, yes. Your father's last wishes. He has given me ownership in the parts of the business that I am already running in his name. The balance of the business will be given to you. That is, to you and your husband."

Khadija leaned forward in shock. "Husband? But uncle, I have no immediate plans to marry."

Ahmed looked grim. "Alas, my precious one, you do now. For, you see, unless you are married by this time next year, all of the business will be sold, divided to the shareholders, and all your father's dreams will vanish like smoke."

Ahmed leaned forward as well, looking his niece directly in the eye. "Khadija, my beloved niece, you and I shall be honest right now. We both know which of us is better qualified to run the family business. I have done my best with this little office here in Cairo, but you are the one with the business degrees from that American school. You have increased the family's business substantially while running the Zurich office. Your mind is better than that of ten men, but Khadija, my beloved, you are an unmarried woman! You are — what? 27? 28? Almost too old! Your status is in question. No one will take you seriously. Your father, may his memory be a blessing, knew this. We must find you a husband in order to keep the family strong." He straightened in his chair, clasping his hands before him. "Women should be married, Khadija. It is written that it is women's nature to be wives and mothers. You are brilliant in business, my darling niece, but you need a husband or you will not be respected. A husband, Khadija, and *insha'allah*, I shall find one for you."

Khadija was silent. As much as she wanted to shout at her uncle at the unfairness of the will's contents, she knew he was right. Her father had been very permissive with her, encouraging her to continue her education. When she was accepted at Wharton, her father rewarded her with apartments in both Philadelphia and New York, as well as a car and driver. After her graduation with highest honors, her father assigned her to the Zurich office, and soon she was running the entire European branch of the business, where women in business were welcomed or, at least, tolerated. In those years, she visited Cairo rarely, the last time returning for her brother's funeral three years ago. Until her father's death. Ah, *abuyya*, your death brings so many changes, Khadija thought, tears filling her eyes. She politely thanked her uncle for his concern, and as quickly as possible, she and Fatma left.

It was a relief to be out of the disorderly, noisy rooms of her uncle's home. Her father's apartment filtered the light and heat of Cairo through colored glass windows and latticework, instead of the oppressive curtains that covered every window in her uncle's house. Khadija's father had been a collector of rare and unusual objects, but hated clutter. Silk wall hangings with intricate geometric patterns covered the walls, with silver and gold thread winking at her in the dusk. The bookshelves were filled with rare books, elaborate calligraphy on their leather bookbindings. When the muezzin's evening call to the Faithful came through the open windows, Khadija knelt on the rich Persian carpet in the center of the floor, and focused herself on the first pillar of Islam: *"La ilaha illa allah, sayyiduna muhammed ras ulu allah,"* she murmured. "I bear witness that there is no god but Allah and that Muhammad is his Messenger." She let the song of the muezzin, and her own prayers, wrap her in peace and serenity.

Cairo was indeed recapturing her, Khadija thought with a sigh, rising from her kneeling position on the carpet. She seated herself at her father's desk, lit the green banker's lamp, and opened the file her uncle had given her. Indeed, the contents were as her uncle had told her. But there were also personal assets that were to be settled, as well. Her father's apartments in Cairo, Alexandria, Zurich, New York, and London were hers free and clear. The will emphasized that the directive included the apartments' contents. Khadija smiled. She knew, although perhaps the attorney did not, that this included her father's other collection — his people.

Khadija had been told of the Marketplace when her father had purchased a pleasure slave after her mother's death. "It is the quality of their merchandise, my princess," he explained to her. "Women are always available to serve a man with needs. But I collect quality. I wish for my merchandise to please me, even after I have spent myself in her." And the woman he purchased was indeed, beautiful in the Western manner, tall and blonde, with a small nose and blue eyes, and so thin that Khadija wondered how any man could lie with her without bruising themselves painfully on her bones. The slave was friendly, however, and Khadija enjoyed the times they had spent together, chatting in French, playing bridge in the Alexandria apartment, or watching the American movies when her father was out of town. When her father grew tired of the slave, Khadija suggested he give the blonde to Ahmed as a present, but the suggestion was really to keep the woman near to her for company until she went away to college. I wonder where she is now? Khadija wondered. The current pleasure slave living in the Alexandria apartment was unknown to her. According to the papers, her father's other slaves included the correspondence secretary who lived in the London apartment, the *bahweb* who was guarding the apartment and ran errands for the family, the chauffeur . . . and Fatma.

Fatma? Khadija was astonished. Fatma had been a fixture in her life since she was a baby. She even remembered her father telling stories of Fatma when he was a child. It had never occurred to her that Fatma was Marketplace material. She couldn't imagine the ancient crone as a sexual being, much less being placed on an auction block. What had drawn her nurse to such a life? Unconsciously, her hand dropped to the bell, and she rang.

"Oh, yes, *ya madehm*, I was sold in the Marketplace oh, 50 or 60 years ago," Fatma told Khadija.

"That long?" Khadija gasped. "But you have been working in our family all of my life."

"And most of your father's too, may his memory be a blessing," Fatma agreed. "It should be no surprise to you that Muslim families prefer to buy Muslim slaves to care for the children. Your grandfather purchased me to assist your grandmother with her two sons, when your aunt was still to be born. I have remained with your family since."

"But how did you find the Marketplace?" Khadija asked, fascinated with this new knowledge.

"How, how? I don't know how to explain it," Fatma sighed. "I had friends from different places, women friends, with desires similar to my own," she began. "I fell in love, *ya madehm*. I devoted myself to a woman in a way that I cannot explain. She was a mistress to a diplomat who had a house in my town, and she lived there to serve him. No, she was not a woman who had been purchased merely for the purpose of sex, but to provide much more to this diplomat. In fact, she had received special training for her skills, not just in the sexual area, in language, arts, politics, oh, she was so smart!"

"A cultured whore, but still a whore," Khadija sniffed, but Fatma determinedly shook her head.

"No, *ya madehm*, not a whore. The Marketplace is not a dealer of innocent flesh. They do not seek out the unknowing and force them into such lives. They do not even take those who simply exchange money for sexual intercourse. No, the Marketplace exists for people like me, who wish to serve honorably. I knew this when I first met this woman. She was not desperate or unhappy. She had a place inside her soul that needed to be useful to others. And she cultivated this place so that it brought her pride and grace in such a way that I knew that is what I wanted too."

"What did you do?" Khadija asked, drawn into the story despite herself.

"Do? I asked to serve her in her house, to be closer to her. No," Fatma laughed at the question forming on Khadija's lips, "I was not used sexually. With this face? Even 60 years ago, I was no prize. It was not necessary, you see. There are women — and men, *ya madehm* — who are specially trained for such things. Why would their Owners waste their thrustings and groanings with a common house slave? No, but I learned much from my dear friend. I learned how to take such pride in the feelings I had for service, and to perfect the ability to anticipate the needs of my Owners. I discovered that my love for this woman was strong, but my need to serve was stronger. She was kind, bless her, and arranged for me to be taken into the Marketplace. I have remained ever since."

"Have you ever wanted to leave?" Khadija asked curiously.

"Oh no, *ya madehm*, I am very happy in my place," Fatma assured her. "Before the Marketplace, what did I have to look forward to? A life of drudgery, of poverty, of a husband who would make me carry his children! No, I have no use for men. I wanted more for my life. The Marketplace has given me everything I need."

Khadija went to bed that night, her head spinning at the thought of a woman choosing voluntary slavery. What would those radical feminists I went to school with think about the Marketplace? she wondered. Would they believe that some women actually preferred to serve, or would they insist it was brainwashing by the patriarchy? Khadija herself believed that some people, men and women, were naturally inclined toward such service. Even the Prophet Mohammed himself had written of the duties and responsibilities that were naturally masculine or naturally feminine. Lucky women, like Fatma, found a place where they would be permitted to serve honorably. I wonder about the men with those tendencies, Khadija thought as her mind drifted closer to sleep.

Imagine a man of Islam, with a true desire to Submit in more than his religion. A man who would be devoted to his owner, loyal and faithful. A Muslim man, born to service, wanting to serve honorably would probably make a good . . . she bolted upright in bed, wide awake suddenly. He could make a good *husband*. A perfect husband. Her hand reached for the bell, and she rang it furiously. "Fatma!" she shouted. "Fatma, come here! Dilwahti! Dilwahti!"

The next day, Khadija sent an e-mail message to a private address her father had given her when she was first assigned to the Zurich office, requesting an appointment as soon as possible. A reply came within 24 hours: she would receive a visit from within the next 10 days.

Khadija was cutting flowers in the private garden when Fatma notified her of the expected visitor. She told Fatma bring the guest out to the garden, and to prepare refreshments. As she lay her shears aside, her guest appeared in the doorway. "Salaam, salaam," greeted the Asian man, who then lightly touched his heart, mouth and forehead in the proper ritual. No, not a man, Khadija realized as she returned the salaam, a woman dressed as a man. A woman wearing a beautifully tailored suit, designed to flatter her figure. Jet black hair that was cut long in the back.

"Ken!" she exclaimed. "Can it be Ken?"

The woman ducked under a set of hanging baskets, to step closer. Her almond-shaped eyes narrowing, then widening in surprise. "Khadija, is that you? Good heavens, *ma cherie*, I barely recognized you in that costume," she laughed. "Weren't you in jeans and a midriff the last time I saw you — graduate student at Columbia, wasn't it?"

"University of Pennsylvania," Khadija corrected, then continued in French, remembering Ken's fondness for the language. "Papa asked that I entertain his dear friend and business associate's daughter when she came to New York for the Marketplace's winter auction. I fear I was going through my American phase then, bare stomach and all. Not that you were much better, as I recall!"

Ken laughed again, explosively. "You know, I think I still own those elevator shoes. Remember pretending we did not know English, how those college boys struggled with seducing us with their Berlitz phrases. 'I have need to polish your cup with my tongue.' Atrocious accents, and so hard keeping a straight face!" Khadija laughed at the memory.

"Remember how they were talking about us in English? 'I'll take the Asian girl, they're always so submissive.' What a surprise you must have given him that evening!"

"I tell no tales," Ken answered virtuously. "Certainly not mine, nor would I even mention the rather rhythmic thumping and moaning from the room into which you led your young conquest. But I see you've gone native," Ken observed. "No doubt you're a virgin again, too?" she asked wickedly.

Khadija looked down at herself. After just a few weeks home, the dark, shapeless caftan and headscarf were already feeling natural. "My father has recently passed away after a long illness," Khadija explained, and Ken's eyes darkened in sympathy. "I wear the *djellaba* in his memory. What is the phrase? When in Rome?"

"Wear a toga," Ken chortled, and Khadija laughed at her friend's irrepressible humor, as she led Ken to a set of garden chairs and a tea table carefully placed in an alcove sweetened by the fragrance of blooming jasmine. Fatma reappeared with a tray of tea and fresh fruit. "It was time for me to come home anyway," Khadija continued as they settled into the comfortable chairs. "I missed Cairo. My soul is here, somewhere between the souk stalls and the Nile." Her eyes turned toward the garden's trellised fence, as if she could see through it to the streets of the Old Quarter, filled with people and carts and the noise of her home.

Ken opened a cigarette case, arching an eyebrow at Khadija, who nodded permission. The Eurasian lit an Egyptian cheroot and inhaled it with an evil grin. "I never smoke, except in Egypt and Cuba," she explained. "There's something about the tobacco here that makes me feel positively villainous. Ah, but we are not here to talk of my many vices. Let us get to the purpose of this visit, shall we? The message from the central office was vague. I was eager to see you though, and when your name came up, I grabbed at it! I said to them, this lady, I can help!"

"First, I have a simple request," Khadija began. "As I said, my father has recently died, and I am the current legal owner of slaves he had purchased through the Marketplace. I have need to sell one, and I need to purchase another."

"And you need an agent," Ken nodded. "I am happy to offer my services — for a fee of course," she added, and Khadija smiled. Ken hadn't changed a bit. "Tell me more."

"The one I wish to sell is a pleasure slave, and should be easy to move in any manner you feel is best," Khadija agreed, "but the other matter is more difficult." Ken took another suck at the evil-smelling cigarette, and waited expectantly. Briefly, Khadija explained to Ken the pertinent contents of the will. The Eurasian woman listened carefully, and when Khadija finished there was a long silence between them.

"I think see the dilemma. A husband to meet the requirements of the will, but not necessarily the expectations of your family. It's a brilliant plan, Khadija, brilliant."

"I like to think that my *abuyya*, may his memory be a blessing, would have appreciated my creativity," Khadija said, lowering her eyes.

"It is a challenge you place before me. My fee will be high for this service. I assume the man must be of appropriate age, and a Muslim?"

"Naturally. And for your fee, I shall give you 30% on the sale of the pleasure slave, and another fee as you wish should you be successful in the completion of this special search."

"You are as generous as you are beautiful, Khadija. I shall begin immediately!" Ken crushed her cigarette out on her almost-empty teacup, creating a noxious odor that wafted over the table. "But first, let us go to Alexandria to see this pleasure slave of your late father's, so I have a better idea of how much my efforts are worth."

Ken was as good as her word. Khadija received regular reports, beginning with the news that she had several prospective buyers for the pleasure slave. Within the month, Khadija was rid of the extra responsibility, and looking forward to reading about prospective slave-husbands. If only she weren't so distracted!

For Ken was not the only one searching for her husband-to-be. Dear Uncle Ahmed had indeed decided it was his personal responsibility to see his niece wed. It was, after all, right and proper for him to do so, but it drove her to distraction.

Nearly every week, Ahmed would call her, or appear at her door, to present a new prospect. Most of them were business acquaintances of her uncle or her late father, and clearly interested in getting their hands on part of the family fortune. Many of them were old, ancient, with wrinkled skin and beady eyes and wet hands. Ahmed would introduce each of them, then whisper to Khadija, "I think this, this may be the one, *insha'allah.*"

Khadija found faults with each of them, which distressed her Uncle. "But my dearest niece, what is wrong with Ali?" he would ask, and she would reply, "He is rude to me, Uncle, and is only interested in money, not in a marriage. Besides," she added mischievously once, "this one smells of alcohol." Her Uncle would moan and wring his hands, crying at her words, swearing by Allah that he would find her a true husband before the following year. And just a few days later, he would appear at her door again, to introduce yet another man, and whisper to her, "I think this may be the one, *insha'allah.*"

The constant interruptions of her uncle were doubly wearing as six weeks went by and Ken still had nothing valuable to report. Oh, she e-mailed Khadija regularly, sending summaries of several prospects. But none of Ken's prospects were acceptable: too young, not Arab, not of the Faith. But she read the profiles anyway, finding that she enjoyed the descriptions of the men's sexual capabilities, particularly when discussed in such objective ways. Sometimes Ken e-mailed pictures of the men, so explicit that they would make Khadija blush. She wondered if she would treat her husband the way that some of those men had been treated; sending him to sleep at the foot of the bed, beating him if she was displeased with his behavior, forcing him to pleasure her without allowing him any release of his own.

One week, Ken had sent a photograph of a man with rings piercing his nipples and his penis. Light chains joined the man's nipple rings and a single chain ran from its center to the ring in the man's cock, forming a "T" across the man's body. In addition to the chain, metal balls were hanging from each of the rings. Khadija wanted to think it must be dreadfully painful, but she couldn't ignore the fact that the man in the photograph had a full erection. She printed that photo out, and for many nights, she looked at it, then closed her eyes and imagined decorating her own slave that way. Would he, too, keep a full erection under such punishment? If not, she would beat him, yes, beat him as he knelt on his hands and knees on the wool Turkish carpet at the foot of her bed. And he would then sleep on that very rug, until she decided to allow him back into her bed. Her hand crept between her legs as she imagined how he would tremble at her touch, fearing punishment, yet eager to please her again.

Perhaps owning a husband would have more than the *obvious* uses.

It was near the end of the fast month, Ramadan, when Khadija received a promising message from Ken. "Now I shall collect the rest of my fee," the message read at the top, with a file attached to download.

Khadija looked over the file carefully. There was enormous potential here. Farouk al-Wadir was originally from Algiers, but his family was forced to leave during the dreadful revolutions of the 1950's. They settled in Great Britain, where his father and mother entered paid service with a retired British officer who had served in the Middle East. Farouk, as a young man, took a position as a personal servant to the officer's younger son, and followed the young man to Cambridge to serve him there as well. It was through the son's college friends and their servants that he learned of the Marketplace. Farouk was released from his employment when the son eventually married. He immediately sought out training, first appearing on the block in his mid-20's as a common house slave, eventually working his way up the hierarchy to butler. His first Owner encouraged his potential for management, and sent him to finish his education at Cambridge. At the death of his Owner, he was sent to the block again, and was purchased by a British—based international corporation that often did business with her own family's business. Farouk remained there as a valued administrator for the last 20 years. His latest five-year contract would be expiring within the year.

Ken also uploaded a series of graphic files. After waiting an interminable amount of time for them to free themselves from the e-mail, Khadija looked them over carefully. Farouk was in his mid-50's, a short, dark-complexioned man with a tendency toward plumpness. In the first set of photos he was dressed in an expensively cut business suit, and looked all the world for what he was — an administrator of a multinational company. In the second set of photos, however, he was nude, and in the positions Khadija now knew to be standard Marketplace poses. Nude, his weight was more obvious, especially in his belly and buttocks, but he was able to hold even the more awkward positions with a sense of grace and dignity. She noted that his right nipple had been pierced, a small ring of gold drawing further attention to his skin color in a pleasing manner. Then she clicked to the next set of photos. And it took her breath away.

For there was Farouk dressed in the white *galabiyya*, the traditional caftan for the *hajj*, surrounded by hundreds of other similarly dressed pilgrims on the steps leading into the Great Mosque in Mecca. He was staring slightly away from the camera, his dark eyes moist, and a look of intense joy radiating from his face. The photographer captured his desire, his love, his true link to Submission that Marketplace pictures could not, would not have been able to. She sighed in satisfaction, and printed out the entire document, but not before sending her message to Ken: "Please negotiate on my behalf, and contact me as soon as possible."

Ken burst past Fatma into the garden. "May I be the first to congratulate you on your upcoming marriage," she crowed in delight. "What is it you say around here? *Mabruk! Mabruk!*" she added in Arabic, sounding the like the souk peddler who had congratulated Khadija that morning on her clothing purchases, after they had enjoyed a fierce bargaining session. Khadija gave a cry of delight and embraced her friend. "Fatma, some refreshment, please!" she cried, and the ancient slave bustled away, a large smile on her face.

"I see you dressed so that I could pick you out from the crowd in the souk," Ken commented, as she released herself from Khadija's embrace. "Short sleeves? It must be the evil influence of the West, no?" Khadija laughed, her hand reaching up to touch the bright scarf she had wrapped in her hair. "I purchased it this morning, in honor of your visit. Do you like it?" She stood, and swayed her hips so that the material swung from her hips, and the dress' neckline promised the viewer a well-endowed bust.

"Cherie, you look like a luscious mouthful. I could, how you say, polish your cup with my tongue. Hah!" With a leer, Ken flung herself onto the garden's bench and lit a cigarette. Fatma returned with a tray of fresh fruit and tea, and automatically the women switched to French so as to keep the details of the purchase private.

"Ah, cherie, I cannot help but provide solutions to all concerned, particularly where my cooperation will only increase my own family's business," Ken chuckled. "I told his owners that your new position for him might not keep him from seeking employment outside the home. They are prepared to sell him to you on the condition that they have the option to hire him back into his current position for six months to a year to train his replacement. They would also be willing to consider transferring him to Cairo office!" Ken clapped her hands in glee, and Khadija laughed with her. "Naturally, these matters must be left in your hands, but I assured them that you would be most amenable to such a plan. After all, his paycheck would belong to you."

"And then I could put him in charge of my father's business — oh, Ken, it's a wonderful offer. I must meet him at once!"

Ken squeezed her hand. "I knew you would. So I brought the papers with me, and the slave. He is waiting in the library for final approval."

"He's here? Now?" Khadija could hardly contain her eagerness to meet the slave, but forced herself to pay attention to the papers before her. They said exactly what Ken had outlined, and she noted his signature already affixed, as Ken had told her it would be. He was ready to be transferred to her, to become her property. "Do you wish to buy him first, or meet him and then purchase? You can still back out, if he is not suitable."

Khadija looked down at her clothing. Years of cultural and religious training made her hesitate at meeting another Muslim with so much of her skin showing. But then, this man would belong to her. If she purchased him — just by signing these papers and making a transfer of money through her Swiss accounts — then he would see her in a variety of outfits, and even in nothing at all. She took a deep breath. "I shall inspect this man before I sign," she said imperiously, a smile on her face.

Ken rose and elegantly gestured toward the door. "Then let's go."

Farouk was kneeling on the dark, Persian carpet in the center of the room, naked except for a collar and the nipple ring. "Better than the pictures, don't you think?" Ken asked Khadija, as they entered the room. "Present, slave, for this fine lady." The slave moved in a smooth motion until he was standing, his fingers locked behind his neck. At Ken's command, he executed a turn, then bent over, resting his hands slightly above his knees. "Quite a tasty bit of meat, my friend," Ken said wickedly, her hand cupping the slave's ass. "Shall I leave you to inspect him more privately? Take your time. Feel free to — be thorough." Without waiting for an answer, she sauntered out of the room. "I'll be in your garden, enjoying my last cigarettes," she called over her shoulder.

In the light filtered through the latticework of the library windows, Khadija circled the slave, stretching out a hand to caress the slave's back, and saw a shiver run across his shoulder blades. Her touch had done that? How exciting. She trailed her fingers across his back again, then to his chest. She found his pierced nipple, and pulled lightly on the ring. He sighed, and she felt a warmth between her legs. She pulled on it harder, then twisted it. He gasped, but remained in position. She felt the warmth rise through her body, filling her with wetness. This man would belong to her, Khadija thought. Soon he would be compelled to do anything she desired.

The rush of power was as strong as the sexual rush she had felt moments earlier. She stepped forward abruptly, grabbed the slave's greying, short hair and pushed him back into a kneeling position. With her other hand, she pulled her skirt up, and thrust her hips forward toward his face.

The slave needed no further encouragement. He pressed his mouth against her moist undergarment, and exhaled softly. She could feel the warmth of his breath heating the cotton, and her nether regions as well. He pushed his face nearer, and Khadija moaned as she felt his tongue probing her, through the barrier her panties created. She thought briefly of ripping the garment off, but found she took a deep pleasure in keeping herself hidden from her husband-to-be in this manner. Instead, she tightened her grip in his hair, and pushed his face deeper between her thighs, rubbing herself against his nose.

The slave made a low, inarticulate sound, and she felt his teeth lightly tug at the edges of the cotton. His tongue slid under the fabric and she felt its velvet brush against her tiny bud. The intense pleasure of this contact dizzied her; he must have felt her sway, for his hands reached up to cup her buttocks, which steadied her and drove her mad. Her skirt had fallen over him, covering his face, but she could feel him increasing his efforts to stroke her button of pleasure. Khadija rocked herself against him, directing his tongue to the rhythm that would release her mounting need, so tightly focused there between her legs. He obeyed her, flicking his tongue rapidly, using his teeth to increase the sensation across the restricting undergarment. She felt herself reach the apex, and with a cry of release and relief her body thrust against his face uncontrollably. She could feel the slave's fingers digging into the flesh of her buttocks, holding her in place until her thrusts had subsided, and gently releasing her when she could once again stand upright.

Khadija straightened her dress, and sank into one of the library's wingback chairs. She looked under heavy eyelids at the slave, who had returned to his kneeling position, albeit with an erect cock that stirred her anew. That would be hers, as well. In good time.

"Farouk, please kneel here," Khadija said in Arabic, pointing to a spot in front of her. The man complied, and settled again into a kneeling position, looking both alert and patient.

"Farouk, I am Khadija, and I believe I shall be your new Owner," she began. "And if you are capable, you shall have an unusual assignment which is bound to be challenging and, I hope, rewarding." Farouk's eyes grew wider and wider as Khadija explained to him what would be expected of him.

"I know from your records that you are capable of handling such a position," Khadija concluded. "But tell me, honestly, Farouk, because I need to know: are you willing to be my husband yet still my slave? My family must not suspect, nor my father's business associates, that you are not a free man.

You will have a great deal of autonomy. But not in everything. Certainly not when we are alone together. Can you do this?"

Farouk lowered his eyes in thought, and that pleased Khadija. Despite all she had learned in the last months about the Marketplace, despite the scene which had just taken place between them, she still feared she would have a slave who would blindly agree to anything she said, and ultimately ruin the whole plan. But Farouk was taking his time, clearly weighing the challenges and the opportunities. Finally, he lifted his eyes.

"May I speak freely, *ya mahdem?*"

"Yes, indeed."

"To answer your question first, yes, I am willing to be your husband and your slave. But I cannot simply answer you without providing you with my own reasons. To begin, *ya mahdem*, I am intrigued by this position. It challenges me in a way that, to be truthful, I haven't felt challenged in a long time. Business management is interesting, and I have pleased my previous masters with my skill, but in my last few years I began to wonder if there were other ways I could serve that would feel more — fulfilling." His soft, slurring North African accent warmed the room, and sent a delicious shiver through her spine. Oh, she would enjoy listening to this voice in her bed. She wanted to have his voice wash over her again.

"Fulfilling? I wish to know exactly what you mean," she requested, unable to keep a seductive lilt from her voice. Farouk's cock jumped slightly, in response to her tone, but his voice revealed no distraction.

"Yes, *ya mahdem*. I was remembering my days as a butler, and even before that, when I was serving young William while he was in school. The drive to anticipate his whims, to please him before his friends, even the . . . punishments when I was not successful. I became aware that my nature is to be pleased by simple service, to be excited in the pleasure of my employers, my masters and now, my owners. Those elements of service are not as . . . prevalent in business settings. I believe I was beginning to miss them. I began to think about returning to a more personal form of service."

"I see," Khadija breathed, delighted to discover this about her new purchase. "Well, as you may have already guessed, I will expect a great deal of personal service from you, Farouk. But I shall not make use of your lovely and attentive adornment until we are married," she said, gesturing at the slave's erect cock. "That would not be proper. However, I cannot just bring you home and announce to my family that I am to marry a perfect stranger none of them have met. Especially after my uncle has been working so hard to find me a husband. We must be properly introduced. And I am calling upon your talents to suggest a way for that to happen."

"Yes, *ya mahdem*. As you explained the problem, I considered a possible solution." And when Farouk explained to her his idea, Khadija smiled broadly. This indeed, was a resourceful slave to own. And a man to marry. She called for Ken and the papers and signed them joyfully.

"Oh, praise Allah you are home, Khadija," her uncle said over the phone. "I have the most wonderful news. I met a man today — no, don't protest, my niece, this is not like Ali, or Samir, or Nabil, or Mohammed, or the others. This is a man who says you may remember him from business in Zurich. His name is Farouk al-Wadir. He works for Danberry & Ellis, your father's dear colleagues in Great Britain. Do you perhaps remember now? Yes, good. Because he remembers you, my darling."

Khadija could barely control her laughter as her uncle rapturously described meeting Farouk at his favorite tea house (imagine! such a coincidence, a happy one, praise Allah), and lavishly praising his manners and demeanor, his dignity and all the respect he heaped upon her modest Uncle and the obvious esteem he held Khadija in.

"He remembers you fondly, Khadija, and he has asked me to provide him a formal introduction. So wonderful to be talking with a gentleman with such manners, true? And so I would like to bring him by this afternoon."

"Yes, this afternoon would be fine, Uncle," Khadija responded, with a smile on her face. "Thank you, Uncle, for your persistence and your concern for my future."

"Ah, it is my pleasure, little one. And you know, something," her Uncle's voice took on a conspiratorial tone, "I think this may be the one, *insha'allah*."

29 Fencing

Chris poured out the last of the tea from the small pot and removed it from the table, placing it outside the door. Tetsuo and Anderson had covered a variety of topics, including his new investments in Kobe, and her recent visit to California, taking the train across the country and being utterly anonymous for almost three weeks. They did not discuss the proposal, or even the Academy. But finally, Anderson leaned forward and pulled the folder over between them and said, "Now, as to the matter at hand."

Chris stood away from them and coughed politely.

"You may go," Anderson said.

"Please — if I may make a request," Tetsuo said quickly. "If you do not think it inappropriate, I wish he might stay."

No, thought Chris. No, not that.

"During negotiation?" Anderson laughed. "Well, it's certainly unusual, Tetsuo, but so is everything else surrounding this."

"He will not be so rude as to hear things which do not concern him," Tetsuo said with a slight smile.

And so Chris knelt again, across the low table from Anderson, slightly at an angle so that they could both see his face. It was the first indication that Tetsuo had made acknowledging his presence. He composed his limbs comfortably and lowered his eyes to table height so that he could catch any hand signals.

"First of all, I wish to apologize for my presumptions," Tetsuo said, folding his hands politely. "I am aware that this is not what you intended, and of my great — what is the word we used at school — *chutzpah* — in assuming the nature of your property and your willingness to sell."

"As it turns out, your presumptions were more or less correct, Tetsuo, and although you're right, I didn't plan on this, I'm open minded enough to take advantage of a situation that might turn out in my favor. So let's assume I'm willing to bargain." She opened the file and withdrew the stack of contract forms and laid them to one side. "First of all, the photos in this file are not recent, and there have been changes to his body since they were taken. Did you wish an inspection?"

"I've already had one," Tetsuo said with a slight touch of glee in his voice. "And I am content."

"Did you." Anderson shook her head with a laugh. "My God, Tetsuo, you are way ahead of me on this. OK, then, let's cover the modifications — did you see the contract paragraphs on the marks? You've got the right to make additions, but not changes. . ."

Chris struggled not to listen, not to hear. Early in his lessons in Japan, he was told about techniques to screen out other voices, background noises, how to build a fence around himself that allowed peace and yet still permitted him to be alert enough to respond to commands. Noriko had encouraged him to concentrate on the sound of ocean waves, crashing on the shore. Steady roars, pounding, long and multi-layered. Hear the seagulls, if you can. Feel the cool water on the rocks, hear the hissing of the sand. He tried. But it conflicted with his other training, to notice everything, to see everything, to hear everything, from the loudest of cries to the stillness of a thought. . .

A slight pause in conversation. Chris looked up and Anderson was saying, "Your shirt, please."

He unknotted the tie and stripped it off, following with his jacket, and then the shirt. His face seemed hot — he remembered the slaps as he moved so that they could discuss the marks on his back, the ones on his arm. "I will certainly leave this alone," said Tetsuo, waving a hand over Chris's right shoulder blade, "but I may wish to elaborate upon these, here, in the same fashion as they were made."

"More brands? You'll enjoy branding him. I'll give you the original, if you want it."

"Excellent, that would be quite satisfactory."

When they were finished, he dressed again, as gracefully as he could. He tried to summon up the sea again, as they turned pages.

"You will bear the cost of private medical insurance, as outlined here — we will have to discuss local care, but that can be handled after a sale if necessary, unless you foresee difficulties — no? Then let's skip down here, this is all boiler plate for a while. . ."

Waves. Rhythmic waves, I do not need to hear this, Chris thought. He heard a gull, a harsh shriek in the air, cutting through the waves, and embraced the sound eagerly. It was finally loud enough to drown out the words.

But then there was a knock at the door, as more tea was brought, and he had to serve again and resume his place even as they were discussing length of contract.

"Five years."

"I never — never — sell a first time client for more than three."

"Ah, but this is not a first time client. How many years has he been in service to you, shall I do the sums?"

Anderson paused. "I'll permit four, considering his vast experience as a trainer, which should of course count for something. Four?"

"It is an unlucky number in Japan. I prefer not to handle contracts of four years."

"Three then, with an automatic renewal for a year, pending mutual agreement with no contract modifications."

"Automatic renewal for two years, with those stipulations."

Chris could barely trust himself to breathe. He felt sweat at the back of his neck, and struggled to focus his eyes and build the fence again.

Anderson leaned back. "OK, Tetsuo, let's talk turkey. I'll give you the three plus two, if, in exchange, I get one of your three year students and one four year student, in two separate years, for one year each."

"A four year student? You wish to finish their training?" Tetsuo frowned, thinking, and rubbed the back of his neck. "That is — difficult."

"Difficult, but you're thinking of taking away my best pupil. I want full exposure to your best students, and I want your training books with them."

"Ah," Tetsuo sighed. He leaned back, nodding his head in respect. "You want us to be siblings."

Anderson raised her eyebrows. "Isn't it about time? Face it, Tetsuo, you will be the first Noguchi trainer to bring a gai-jin into your House. Don't do things by half. If you're gonna change the world, you can't do it shyly. Let this contract be our bridge, brother and sister."

"And your training books?" Tetsuo asked with a wry smile.

Anderson laughed and jerked a thumb in Chris' direction. "I would say you're negotiating to buy my training books, wouldn't you?"

Tetsuo Sakai gave her a measured look. Neither of then looked at Chris, only into each others eyes, taking measure. Carefully, Tetsuo nodded, and Anderson smiled thinnly and picked up her negotiation again. "You can pick the students, and the time, as long as they are one year apart and they know English, written and spoken. Or, skip the students and send me one trainer of your line for two years, so that I have time to search for a replacement. . ."

Finally, the image of crashing waves caught on again — he could see the droplets of water cascading through the air and falling down against rocks and sand. There was a steady undertone of hissing, the whistling, grinding of underwater sand, and above it all, the screech of a gull, over and over again. The sounds became louder, echoing at last, drowning out the plans to replace him, trade him, send him away, give him away, and at last he realized that the waves were not water at all, but the sound had a more steady and predictable rhythm to it. He could feel the churning of wheels, and the screeching of the gull became the scream of brakes, as the Number Seven train rushed through Jackson Heights and into Corona and Flushing, stops at numbered intersections on the steel elevated tracks above Roosevelt Avenue late at night, on a school night. Each stop shook him awake again, just as the train engines lulled him to sleep, his head resting against the sidewall, his knapsack drawn up between his legs.

It had been a profitable night, almost thirty dollars shoved into his sneakers, where the johns didn't search when they tried to rip you off, which had happened two weeks ago. He had explained the rip in his jeans pocket with a clumsy tale about getting caught in a turnstile. The bump on his head was hidden by his hair, and the worn out army cap with the frayed lining that his brother had given him before going away. It had a peace symbol drawn on it in colored magic marker, all but faded away now.

His throat was sore. But he had the money to add to the folded collection in the ear of the old teddy bear, almost enough to leave, almost enough to get a place for one month maybe two.

The lights of the Shea Stadium stop were bright and hurt his eyes. He blinked as the car filled up with angry, sweaty people, cursing the heat, cursing the team.

"Fucking *twats* can't even win a fucking game," cried a boy who looked like a senior. "Man, I want my fucking money back!"

"*Twats!*" snorted one of his friends, smelling strongly of beer. "*Fucking pussies!*"

He pulled himself closer to the wall, avoiding their gazes. Boys like that beat up boys like him. Or worse. Besides, he was angry. The Mets were a great team. They won the World Series, and he had been there when he was nine. They could do it again. You had to have faith. He kept his eyes closed as the train pulled into the last station on the line, Main Street, and people jostled to exit or just claim seats for the ride back down Roosevelt into Manhattan. As he got up, he saw a flash of bright blue and orange on the train floor, and without thinking, bent down to pick it up.

It was a baseball cap. It was *their* baseball cap, in beautiful shape, barely worn, it seemed. Had one of those older boys actually thrown it away?

Finders, keepers. It was his now.

It was the first thing that his father grabbed when he finally got home.

What the hell is this thing? You went to a baseball game? On a school night? With what money? What do you mean you found it? Lying again? Where were you? Who were you with?

And his mother. Why don't you come home when you're told? Why don't you dress like a normal child! Why can't you just behave? Why do you have to look like a slob?

And his father. You're a curse from God! Your pervert freak brother wears a dress and you go out like — like — I don't know what and you lie and steal and why are you always hiding and what are you hiding, and I don't believe you found this, and until you tell me the truth, you can't have it! Why has God cursed us with two freaks as children?

Sitting on his bed in the dark, his thoughts all dark too. His brother did not wear a dress, his brother was one of the most macho guys ever, he even went to Israel and was in the army there, at least he had a gun, there was a picture of him in a tank top and heavy green pants and boots, a gun in his arms, a cocky smile on his lips. And he didn't steal the hat, he found it, it was his.

He *was* a freak, though. He couldn't do anything about that.

There was one hundred and fifty dollars in the ear of the stuffed bear.

The last thing he did before he left was take the hat from the top of the kitchen shelf where his not very tall father had put it.

He got back on the Seven train sometime after two in the morning and rode it all the way into Forty-Second street and then transferred south. It was still warm enough to sleep under the piers. He couldn't go looking for his brother until he was sure his parents wouldn't ambush him there. Besides — he could still earn some good money under the piers. And the new cap made him look much older, he was sure, and if he bummed a cigarette from someone, they always thought he was older . . . the brakes of the train screeched like a gull, echoing in the tunnel as he got up, feeling tired and frightened but out of there at last, back among people who looked at him and saw what he saw, and not what they all saw at home. . .

"Well, then I think we've ironed out the details, now it's time to give you the final tally," Anderson said, picking up the pen they had used to make notes all over the main sample contract. "This is my asking price."

Tetsuo picked up the paper with both hands and sucked in a breath involuntarily. "This is — most respectable," he said carefully.

"Yes," Anderson admitted. "We're talking years of my time. Not to mention the loss of his services at a point where I have no senior student to replace him with. But you know, I'm warming up to the idea of selling him. If you don't want him, I could just go out to dinner tonight and announce a surprise

311

auction, see if I can get a sweeter deal than this." She was smiling, casually, and there was a slightly playful touch to her threat. But it made Chris snap out of his reverie and clench himself tightly to avoid reacting at all.

"That would be unnecessary," Tetsuo said, laying the paper down. "I am honored to accept your asking price, with all the previous conditions we discussed. However, I must ask for an hour or two to communicate with my bankers to make arrangements, as I have stupidly not brought my man of business with me on this trip."

"Take as long as you need, Tetsuo. We have to have the new contract drawn up anyway, I'm going to rely on you to find someone here who can do that. If I have your handshake, it's as good as done."

He extended a hand and they shook firmly, American style. "I will contact you when all the arrangements have been made and the new contracts drawn up."

"Thanks muchly, Tetsuo, it's always a pleasure to do business with you."

Chris rose to open the door and let Tetsuo out, and quietly cleared the table of cups and trays, and put his file back together neatly. Anderson watched him silently, and when he finally turned to her, she indicated with her eyes where she wanted him. He hesitated — after spending so much time on his knees — but he went to the chair that Tetsuo had most recently occupied and sat down, gingerly.

"You belong on your knees," Anderson said flatly.

"As the Trainer says."

"No. Speak informally. I don't think I will accept formal manners from you any more, unless that's what Tetsuo wants."

Chris winced slightly. "Please forgive me. There is no excuse for my rudeness to you, there never is."

"Yes there is," she said. "You are rude to me because you've found out that it amuses me when you say profane things, or challenge me in such a childish way. You found out it makes me laugh when you tell me to suck your cock, and you say it with a smile. And not as often, you are rude to me when you want to get a negative reaction. I usually don't rise to such behavior in a slave, and so I let you get away with it. You then feel bad for so obviously trying to provoke me, and immediately provide your own punishment. I rarely see the need in hurting someone who is so good at hurting himself. Now Tetsuo — he'll hurt you. He'll never, ever, go as far as he did before, no matter how you provoke him, but he *will* hurt you. And you'll have that collar you crave so much. And at last be free from my inconsistent behavior."

Chris folded his hands between his knees and lowered his head. "May I ask a question?"

"Sure."

"What will you do with Michael?"

"Michael? Since when do you care about Michael?" She raised her eyebrows in mock surprise.

"You — you placed his training in my hands."

"Oh, well, I wouldn't worry about Michael," Anderson said with a sideways wave of her hand. "He'll be gone in six months, a year at most."

Chris' head shot up. "What? I beg your pardon. . .what do you mean?"

"Michael isn't trainer material," Anderson said. "My God, Chris, you've been telling me so for months. After all these years, you still don't trust your own instincts?"

Chris felt the blood draining from his face, the itchiness of bruising beginning. "I — I don't understand, I'm sorry. . ."

"Michael was a test," Anderson said, leaning back. "I wanted to see what you would do with an unsuitable candidate. You lost confidence after that whole Sharon thing. I needed to make sure you still had it in you, that you could still see what was and wasn't there. I needed to kick you again, Chris. And he was a great kicker, you have to admit that. Got your back up the minute you met him. Twisted you eight ways till Sunday. But you kept training and you kept telling me in your evaluations that you didn't see the potential, even though I made you think that I did." She sighed and shook her head.

"You — you brought Michael out of California to — test me?" Chris' hands fell apart helplessly. "I *am* an idiot."

"No," Anderson said carefully. "You are an obedient trainer who knows that the world doesn't revolve around him, and therefore no one would go through all that trouble to bring in someone to specifically to annoy you. Nothing wrong with that."

"I see." There was nothing else he could bring himself to say. He laughed, suddenly. "But — he's improved. Dramatically. I — I was going to write you a report."

Anderson also laughed, only sadly. "Of course he's improved, Chris, *you're training him!* Chris — you could improve anyone, if they gave you half a chance!"

"So — you'll dismiss him?"

"No, I won't need to. Without you there, he won't last six months with Grendel and Alex. And even if he did, he'd figure out right about then that he can't go through with the sale, and he'll come to me and cry and tell me that he'll never forget what he's been through, but he's not strong enough to be in service, or something like that. Then he'll run back to California and find some nice girl to marry and he'll entertain romantic visions of the life he almost had."

"I — I'm glad it's all settled," Chris said, his jaw set. "And I'm sure Michael will be grateful when he realizes that a year of his life was used to teach someone else a lesson."

"Oh my God. You fell in love with the little peckerwood, didn't you?"

"Certainly not!" Chris shot back, immediately.

Anderson nodded. "Oh, but you did, kiddo, you did. Just like you always do. Oh, poor, poor Chris. That was one piece of advice you just can't help but disobey. You love 'em all, the silly things, good and bad ones. And it would all be tragic, if they didn't turn around and fall right in love with you too. That's the difference between us, Chris Parker. They love you and you let them; you love them and they let you. Me? I don't let any of them in. Can't afford to."

She looked at him, his head down again, his hands clenched on his knees, and sighed. "Now get out. You got what you wanted. Don't worry about Michael, he'll get what he wants too, in the end. Someone will find you when it's time to sign the contracts."

"Yes, Trainer," he said, and rose. He bowed to her before leaving, but ever mindful of her instruction, he did not make it a formal bow.

30 Giddy as a Schoolboy

The last dinner together for the Academy was not officially formal, but Ron wanted to wear his tuxedo anyway. "I gotta get some use out of it," he said. Michael went back to the room with him to act as his valet and enjoyed the duty immensely, especially when Ron complimented him on his skills.

"So you're really coming around in all this," Ron said, allowing Michael to straighten his bow tie. Unlike Chris, Ron seemed content to have one that fastened with strap and hook, rather than the old fashioned type that actually needed a knot. "That's great, I'm happy for you."

"Thank you, sir," Michael replied, stepping back to run through the mental list of things to look for. Ron's collar and tie were correct, his shoes polished, his pleats hung and broke just right, his cuffs neat . . . perfect. Michael had chosen Chris' light gray suit for the evening and had it hung up with a shirt and tie, but Chris was still in his meeting with Anderson — which had the entire resort buzzing in concern and speculation.

Michael was about to wonder out loud whether Ron might consider giving Anderson's room a call, when he caught the sound of whistling outside the room, and the door slid open. Chris kicked off the light slippers and walked in, his eyes lighting up when he saw them.

"Well, hello! Ron, it's so good to see you — nice suit! Get that for Aaron's Bar Mitzvah? I was so sorry to miss that, but you know how Mom and Dad are, I didn't think they'd want to see me." He nodded to Michael and looked at the suit hanging up. "Oh, good choice. But since my brother's formal, I'll be, too. The one with the pointed lapels, please, the silver and black studs — and — oh — the European tie this time. That'll be different enough." He sat down cross-legged by the table and laughed, looking at their surprised faces. "Well, Michael?" he asked.

"Yes, of course, sir, right away!" Michael tried to hide his shock at Chris' rapid fire cheerfulness as he grabbed the hanger holding the suit and opened one of the closets to exchange it for the tuxedo with the pointed lapels.

"OK — so I'm guessing she didn't ream you a new asshole," grinned Ron, as he sat down opposite Chris.

"Oh, but she did." Chris said. He tilted his face a little and Ron reached across and ran a finger along Chris' jawline. Ron whistled.

"Uh — that would be pretty rare for her, wouldn't it?" he asked.

Chris laughed again and nodded. "Why yes — I'd say it happens once every few years. When I need it, apparently."

Michael blushed furiously, half in shame for Chris' easy acceptance of what must have been a humiliating scene, and half for being present to hear about it. He could see quite clearly now that Chris' cheeks and jawline were marked up. Damn her for doing this! How could she even think of slapping around a great trainer like Chris? Dammit, she might have trained him, but he didn't deserve to be treated like that just because she didn't get her way. Especially when she didn't even bother to lift a finger to help him! He fumbled with the tray holding the boxes of jewelry and dropped one, and blushing even harder, dropped to his knees to retrieve it.

"Yeah, well, if it makes you happy," Ron laughed. "Which, apparently, it does! So — is everything cool now?"

"Ron — everything is — very cool. No — no — *way* cool."

Michael turned his head sharply to one side, staring openly at Chris, who thought that the sight of him was very funny, and started to laugh again. Ron and Michael traded looks of confusion, and Ron turned back to Chris and said, "Did I just hear you say — way cool?"

Chris caught his breath and nodded, barely suppressing a grin. "Yes. In fact — I feel — awesome. My God, what a stupid way to describe things, but entirely correct. I am full of awe."

"OK, he's gone off the deep end," Ron said, sitting back. "I think one of those smacks must have jarred the brain loose. Listen, Chris, I know you enjoy a good taking down now and again, but you're not making sense. What happened?"

"Did the proposal pass?" Michael asked.

"The proposal? I don't know. I've been in the Trainer's room all afternoon." Chris stood up and pulled his tie off. "No one said anything to me about the proposal." He tossed the tie at Michael, who caught it and rushed over to catch the jacket as well. "I've been busy not listening!" He laughed as he began to unbutton his shirt.

Ron grunted as he heaved himself back up. He walked over to Chris and laid both hands on his younger brother's shoulders. "Great, he's fucking *giddy*. Chris — I can't believe I'm saying this, but calm the fuck down! What is going on here? Someone slip you a happy pill or something?"

316

"No — no — oh, God, Ron, yes, I know — this isn't like me at all, is it?' Chris took a deep breath, gripped his brothers arms for a moment and then looked up into his eyes. "I'm sold."

"What?"

Michael looked up from his place on the floor, pulling Chris' black shoes out, and froze.

"I'm sold, Ron. Purchased. I'm property."

Ron's mouth opened in shock. "No way!"

Chris stood on his toes and brought his brother down to his level. "Way." He bounced back down and laughed again.

Ron closed his mouth and shook his head in amazement. "Well, what do you know? Congratulations, kid, you made it. Jeeze, I can't believe — she came out for that? It wasn't the proposal at all, was it?"

"No, no, I don't think it was," Chris said, finally pulling his shirt off. His tattoo rippled as he crossed the room to Michael and help his arms out. Michael quickly stood and brought a crisp, clean shirt up and helped Chris into it, mutely.

"So who's the lucky guy? I'm assuming it's a guy."

"It's Sakai-sama," Chris said, unbuttoning his trousers and letting them drop. The tattoo of the phoenix that started just under his large nipples extended down his torso and vanished into the waistband of dark colored boxer shorts, bright and malevolent and teasing. As he bent to pull on the tuxedo pants he chuckled to himself. Michael made a choking sound at the name of Chris' purchaser, but got the studs into his hands and didn't even raise his eyes.

"Japanese guy? Hm — is he queer?"

Chris straightened up and let Michael fasten his front studs as he pulled the braces up over his shoulders. "Oh, for goodness sakes, Ron, really. As though 'queer' has any meaning here. He's been married. But he certainly has uses for men, if that's what you're really asking."

"Oh, so you've met him — hey, wait a minute. Sakai-sama — *Tetsuo Sakai*? The guy you went to train with back, what — five years ago?"

"I think eight," Chris said, closing his eyes to think. He fastened his left cufflink and let Michael do the right. "Yes, eight."

"Chris — let me just make sure I have the right guy here. The one who put you in the hospital?"

Chris opened his eyes and grinned a fierce, feral grin. "Yes. That would be him."

Ron nodded, and then walked up to Chris and high fived him. "Way to go, baby bro'." He laughed heartily and shook his head. "So you finally found someone who can take you down hard and let you live to see the next day.

And a man, too. Thank God, now I can stop worrying about you. But Japan? Now you'll never make a family Bar Mitzvah. Shit — I was gonna introduce you to my new lover next week!"

"Write me a letter," Chris said, turning so Michael could fasten the tie around his throat. Michael's fingers fumbled — he couldn't get it right, and then Chris' hands came down over him and gently disengaged them.

"Why don't you let me do that, Michael?" he said, suddenly even voiced and soft spoken.

"I'm sorry, sir, I — I just — please forgive me. . ."

Chris sighed and brought Michael's hands together in his. "Thank you for your help, Michael. You've been very proper and I realize that I haven't even given time for you to digest this sudden news. Sit down for a minute and compose yourself, please."

Michael took that advice. (When you are given an opportunity to do something, take it, Chris said to him, over and over again. You will never know when you have that opportunity again. Enjoy every freedom offered and you will enjoy your return from it as well.) He sat down and leaned one arm on the table as Chris nimbly did up the tie and snapped the collar straight under it.

"So I don't see a lock around your neck there," Ron said.

"No — there were contract negotiations. They have to make up new copies. But they shook hands."

"How long is the contract for?"

Chris looked at his brother in shock, his jacket in one hand. "Er — I don't know. I wasn't listening."

Ron burst out into laughter again, this time until tears formed in the corners of his eyes. "That's my baby brother, all right — they told you not to listen and you actually didn't listen! Chris, I said it before and I'll say it again — you are obedient to the point of impertinence. I don't know how anyone can *stand* you, let alone pay out good money for you." He shook his head, sighing. "Well, since it's not all signed away yet, I'll keep quiet about it. Or at least I'll try to! But I want to go have a drink. Shall we raise a private toast in your honor?"

"I'd love to. Hell, Ron, I think I need to. Why don't we meet you in the bar area by the entrance to the western building?"

"You got a deal. See you there in a few."

Ron left, chortling to himself, and Chris looked down at Michael. With a sigh, he lowered himself to the floor and sat opposite him. "Michael, I'm very sorry I didn't find a more appropriate way to give you this news."

Michael looked into Chris' eyes. "This is something you wanted?"

"Yes, very much so."

318

"Then — then I'm very happy for you. You deserve to get what you want." He lowered his eyes quickly. "Did you know that this was happening?"

Chris pursed his lips and then decided to tell the truth, or at least as much of the truth as he could. "Sakai-sama told me that he was interested in arranging a contract with me the first evening we were here. But I have not been — a free agent, I suppose you could say. I couldn't enter into such an agreement with him unless Anderson — was amenable."

"You're loyal to her," Michael said. "You really live like you write — all that stuff about honor and loyalty and sacrifice."

"Well," Chris colored slightly and coughed to hide his discomfort, "I don't think you can make that judgment at this point. I try to, as you are trying."

"She — she really hit you," Michael observed. He could imagine her slender hands, hard knuckles, crashing into that face, and could actually see dried blood on Chris' lip. In all the time he had been in her house, Anderson had touched him maybe four or five times, and never in anger or discipline.

"Yes."

"And — after that, she negotiated your own contract in front of you?"

"Yes."

Michael leaned forward, his face searching. "And you're not — angry with her?"

"No." Chris said that firmly, with such complete conviction that Michael sat up straight again. "And you shouldn't be angry on my behalf. For one, I deserved every blow, and much worse — and two, it's none of your business."

"But it is my business," Michael said mournfully. "You're my trainer! What's going to happen to me now?"

"That will be up to Anderson," Chris said. "You came to be under her training, not mine. She may leave you at the house on Long Island, or pick another trainer to take over your first year. In any event, we would have parted in six months or so, when I arranged for your sale. You may in fact benefit by being exposed to a different style of training, so look at this as an opportunity."

Michael nodded glumly, and Chris struggled with what to say to him. What would be useful to say to him, now that Anderson's predictions were ringing in his head.

"You've made some great improvements," he said cautiously. "Even in these past few days. I'm very pleased with your progress, and I can send you back home with full confidence that you will apply yourself to your studies. You chose a difficult and rare path to service, Michael LaGuardia. Most don't even consider taking it. And — I am not unaware that part of your inspiration was, I believe, my own journey. I am honored by such thoughts, and I want you to know that before we part."

"Thank you, sir," Michael said, a little bit of pride creeping into his sapphire eyes. "Can I still call you 'sir'?"

"As long as you feel it is appropriate or you are told otherwise," Chris said. "Come on, let's go have that drink."

Tetsuo had sent over a fancy bottle of Jack Daniel's, and knowing the import taxes on American liquor, Anderson laughed out loud, thinking of his confidence, or no, his *chutzpah*. She stripped open the seal and pulled out the cork and poured herself two fingers in a glass and toasted her new brother in the general direction of the East before sitting down with the first draft of their contract changes. She made a few marks, initialed it, and then sent it back with the waiting slave. They could do the signing after dinner, or wait until morning. It would be best tonight, she thought. Give Chris his first night with his new lord here, it's such a honeymoon place as it is. Maybe Tetsuo would want to make a splash, take Chris in his new collar to a party somewhere.

Or, make him wait until morning, just for my sadistic pleasure. Tell him to accompany me to some private gathering — maybe Geoff Negel's. Hell, loan him to Negel. She laughed and shook her head — no, her sadism did have some limits, and so did her masochism. No matter how unbearable such a thing might be for Chris, merely setting it up would be pushing it for her. Watching whatever transpired would be positively painful.

No, better to just keep him isolated, where he couldn't retreat into high formal manners and suffering for her pleasure. Call him to this room, get him out of his pretentious Japanese room, away from the adoring eyes of poor Michael and on the carpeted floor at the foot of my bed, the way he wished to be for so many years. Let him squirm as he contemplates leaving me. The only question would be if that would be a reward, or just another torture. Both, most likely. Emotional masochists were the most infuriating toys to play with. Pay attention to them, leave them alone — either way, they love it and hate it and come back for more.

She paced around the room, gazing out at the garden view with the glass in her hand. She didn't like it. It was too hot, too colorful, too unpredictable. And there were far too many people here, too, dinner would be an ordeal. Oh, she liked most of them, loved to spend time with them. But not so many at once. "Just leave me alone and let me do what I do," she had said once, years ago. And because of how she did it, they generally let her — as long as she always had a trainer in training, someone who could communicate for her with them. Someone who could carry on her traditions, or at least teach parts of them.

It was fun to improve slaves. But it was a challenge to make trainers.

I've just sold my most fun challenge, she thought. She finished the drink and picked a new outfit for herself and changed for dinner. As she slipped on her shoes, the skies outside opened up, and the long threatened thunderstorm began.

31 Clocking   by Laura Antoniou

8AM

Thunder crashed outside as she stepped off the bottom stair into her hallway to face the caller Vicente had announced. Imala Anderson's first thought upon seeing her visitor was "who drowned this feral kitten?" The youth was in fact soaking wet, a sodden Mets baseball cap barely having kept the downpour from showering the aviator style glasses that were already slightly fogged from the heat inside the house. Her visitor was wearing a worn leather jacket with a large, jagged but mended tear across one side panel. Instantly, Anderson knew it had been rescued from the trash, and as her eyes scanned the visitor from head to toes, she knew that this was a person in need of help.

"Come inside," she said, showing the way into the front parlour. It was safe, Vicente had taken her latest client upstairs. In fact, she could hear his steps coming down now, and when she twisted slightly, a towel was pressed into her hand. She passed it to her young visitor and folded her arms, many copper bracelets jangling on her left wrist. Vicente went back to his reserve, the kitchen, leaving them alone.

"You wanted to speak to me?"

"Yes, ma'am." The visitor's voice was low pitched, a little hoarse, like the voice of someone recovering from a long chest cold. Or someone who had done a lot of screaming lately. Little attempt had been made to actually use the towel, other than to wipe the glasses off, and they were quickly returned to their place on the small nose. Droplets from the long, dark curly hair continued to run in rivulets down the jacket sleeves and Imala finally figured out why she had even invited this youth in.

So many boys were wearing their hair long like this now — hell, they

322

were blow-drying lengthy locks just like the girls of a similar age were doing. But even when the visitor looked back up and straightened, it was difficult to really tell exactly what this young person's gender was. How delightful this new age is for old perverts like me, she thought with a slight twinge of pleasure. But that didn't excuse the danger she was in.

"What do you want?" she asked firmly.

"I want to be your slave."

Imala dropped her arms in shock. Well, I've heard that one before, she thought, her mind still delighted at this remarkable turn of affairs. But never from a — a — child. Because whether this one was a boy or a girl, there was unmistakable softness in the facial features, a certain awkwardness in the halting body movements, that gentle lilt of innocence in the voice.

"What is your name? Who sent you? And how old are you?"

The stranger hesitated, as if trying to draw courage, and Imala snapped, "Don't even think of lying to me!"

There was a barely discernible relaxation of the shoulders and a slight sigh of resignation, and then the figure in the soaked jacket and polished boots reached into an inner pocket and removed a wallet. Imala took hold of the proffered learner's permit and High School identity card, and shook her head. "Well. . .Chris. That leaves one more question — who sent you?"

The visitor shook that wet head slowly and said, "I can't tell you that — I swore I wouldn't."

"Hmph. Some slave you'd be, if you can't even answer a question truthfully."

The glasses tilted up, and Imala noted the flash of anger that was struggled with and controlled. Her heart quickened despite the now nearly overwhelming awareness of danger, and she handed the forms of ID back.

"Are you — compelling me to obedience?" the voice was charmingly hopeful.

What a formal way to ask the question. Anderson frowned — it was a training phrase that no teenager should have been able to come up with on their own. "Why do you ask?" she replied, trying to think of who could have possibly spoken those words to a child.

"If you will take me on — I'll be a novice, I know. But I'll prove myself, I promise — then I will answer all your questions honestly and instantly." There was a desperate earnest tone now, one that Anderson was far more familiar with. She left the mystery to itself and shook her head.

"You come back to me in seven months and eight days, and maybe I'll ask again. If you don't answer then, we'll have nothing to say to each other. Because right now, there is nothing I can do for you, and you have to leave."

The towel was tortured, wrung between those small hands until it became a twisted strand of cotton rope. "Please," came a strangled sound from between those soft lips. "I swear — I've had experience. I've been tested —"

"I don't even want to hear about that," Imala said quickly. "You're a minor, do you understand that? Anyone who does anything with you outside of backseat gymnastics is endangering you and themselves. If you tell me anything about where you've been or what you've been doing, I will contact child welfare services."

"Don't you think I've been there already?" came the sharp reply. Imala sighed — this was just an arrogant teenager after all, she could just push this one out the door. She lifted one hand to do just that, and then heard her visitor continue, saying "They wanted to put me in an institution and 'cure' me."

Anderson didn't push. She ran a finger along one of her heavier bracelets and spun it on her wrist. Damn.

"Nevertheless," she said gently. "I won't call anyone. I can try to find you someplace to stay, if you need it. But you can't stay here. I'm endangering my position just by speaking to you. Seven months."

"And eight days," the visitor added, sarcasm, bitterness and grief commingled in every syllable.

"Compose yourself with patience," Imala said automatically. "I don't keep slaves, I train them. I know best when to examine and when to accept new trainees, and I accept them only rarely. You are too young, you don't have the necessary life experience to get one step beyond where you are right now. You will be ready only when I say you are." Oddly, this seemed to produce a new and more promising reaction, as the stranger let loose that terrible grip on the towel and nodded.

"I'll be back," the young visitor said, handing the towel back.

"And we'll speak about all sorts of things — if you're ready," Anderson said. She opened the door and picked an umbrella out of the ceramic vase in the hall. "Please return this when you come back."

The stranger took it hesitantly and for a moment, Imala was sure that she was going to have to deal with a hysterical teenager sobbing on her shoulder. But instead, the stranger's face seemed to tighten in reserve. "Thank you," Chris said, turning to walk down the steps. Imala watched through the open door until the figure had turned up the block to head for the subway station.

Vicente came up behind her again and took the towel back.

"That one was trouble," Imala sighed, closing the door against the rain.

"Oh yes, he is," Vicente agreed.

"She," Imala said absently. "It's those clothes, the hair, it's so hard to tell

324

boys and girls apart these days."

Vicente chuckled and switched to Portuguese, as he did whenever the topic changed to subjects his English just wasn't capable of handling with grace. "You of all people know that clothing has nothing to do with what a person is inside."

She looked at him and shook her head, pleased that he was so completely wrong. "I tell you, that was a girl," she said.

He waved one hand dismissively. "You're de boss," he said in English, grinning. "But you are correct about one thing — that one, he is trouble."

"Just a kid," she murmured, walking into the warmth of her front office.

"But hungry, Imala. Very, very hungry."

Anderson didn't answer. Instead, she sat down in her favorite chair and pulled her calendar to her. She noted the date, and then flipped through the pages until she found the date seven months and eight days away. She circled the day and wrote in her neat, small hand, "Chris Parker".

9AM

On that day, Anderson had made sure she had no time consuming appointments. She was genuinely intrigued with the possibilities that her visitor offered, and aching to hear the answer to the question which had not been answered. Who would dare send a minor to her — a novice is one thing, but a child? Never mind that Imala herself had known as a child, that she had known literally hundreds of people who would have signed over their bodies and souls at an age when their contemporaries were collecting tokens from cereal boxes. Never mind that she knew she had consigned that bedraggled little sodden creature to a world that was not short on people who would delight in such a hungry and willing partner/victim. She had wondered about her visitor several times, both impressed and worried that she had indeed not heard another word from that quarter.

But the day had come, and she and Vicente were sharing a bagel over some fairly inconsequential paperwork when the familiar sound of the mail falling into the hallway came. Neither of them moved. In less than a minute, Emily came in with it on a tray, silent and elegant. She placed the various pieces where they belonged, her presence as unassuming as it could be, considering she was absolutely nude. Anderson noticed the change as Emily examined one envelope just a fraction of a second longer than it usually took for her to diagnose. When Emily slipped it back onto the tray, Anderson instantly knew what it was.

She picked it up by the edges, and examined the handwriting critically.

It slanted a little too much — the product of contemporary grade school. But it wasn't scrawled — it was clean and each line was fairly straight. There was no postage on it — it had somehow been hand delivered along with the mail. Clever.

She slit it open with the long silver knife and pulled out the folded card inside. It was good paper — not exactly what she would have imagined that ragamuffin had access to. Not a commercial card, but something from a quality stationery set, embossed with a silver gray rose, pale enough so that you had to angle it toward the light to see the whole thing. Had the rose been pink, it would have been too frivolous. As it was, it seemed vaguely romantic but not pushy. She opened it, pleased that she had no idea what it would say.

"Thank you for your courtesy and your advice. You were correct; I wasn't ready yet. And I'm not ready now. Therefore, I'm further taking your advice and getting a little more life experience. I hope that this late cancellation doesn't make you angry, please forgive me for it. I promise that I will not fail you this way again. Thank you for your kindness."

"I've been stood up," she said to Vicente, showing him the note. "Well — I hope she's happy."

"He will not be happy until he is here," Vicente sniffed.

"It's better for her if she stays out there as long as possible," Anderson said firmly, her eyes twinkling.

"He'll be back soon," her companion assured her.

Anderson noted with pleasure that Emily displayed not the slightest sign of hearing this confusing exchange, and then snapped her fingers. Emily hurried over to kneel and Anderson's mind counted the seconds, noted the imperfections, even as her hands worked to correct. "Let's get to work, then. No sense thinking about the girl that got away."

"You give that boy a chance," Vicente laughed. "Oh yes, he'll be back soon enough." He went to the front door, opened it and retrieved the umbrella that had been left hanging from the doorknob. A single rose, the kind sold by vendors along the parkways, was tied to the handle with a silver ribbon. He chuckled as he removed the bud to take it into the kitchen, and slipped the umbrella back in the stand. "You will see!" he said cheerfully as he passed the study door. He returned with the rose in a small vase, placing it on Anderson's desk with a wide grin.

It was actually another full year until the visitor returned.

9:15AM

Well, what the hell was I supposed to do? Play with kids and you're playing with trouble, and that's the truth.

326

But here's another truth; Chris knew, and I knew, and a thousand people wake up every day and ache with the knowing of it. We acknowledge it in our hearts and our writings — there are few among us who come late to this self-knowledge. Oh no, we know when we are barely old enough to put words to what it is we feel. And we suffer for this knowledge, through years when our friends are all experimenting with first kisses and lingering glances and tortured love notes left in school lockers.

So what do you do when you have two great truths? You turn to society and the law and you surrender to them because we must at all costs preserve our world.

Back in the 1800's, the Marketplace struggled with a world where parents still practically sold their children to a hellish life of factory or farm work. Already over a hundred years old, the powers who controlled it sustained the essential element of the founding creed; that all who come to us come of their free will and with the full understanding of what they were doing. This by definition meant an adult, and yet they lived in a society where a 14 year-old could join the navy.

Being men, and at that time, mostly British and American men, they based their decision on that central element in their lives. Someone in my trainer line wrote, "if a man might choose to serve his Nation or King in battle, surely he has that choice in personal Service as well."

Oddly, women were assumed to be equally responsible at the same ages, despite the fact that no woman anywhere in the world had a say in their own governing otherwise.

Of course, we raised the minimum age for warriors as time went on. But the 17 year-olds we sent to Vietnam were kids the same, and the country seemed ill-prepared to deal with the adults they became so quickly. We lowered the voting age, raised the drinking age. Who the hell could figure out what an adult was any more?

The Marketplace could. The minimum age of acceptance for any client shall be the age at which they can legally sign a contract without parental or guardian permission, was how we put it in the US. In cases of emancipated minors, we set the minimum age to 18.

These days, there are those who think we should set it at 21.

I know in my heart that had I told Chris Parker to wait until the age of 21, I would have been responsible for a suicide. And I regret with all my heart that I had to send him away and let him show me that he was the trainer of my dreams, the perfect learner and teacher rolled in one. It's not the only thing I regret about Chris, but it was certainly the push which started the avalanche.

This time, the day was sunny and cool, and the Chris was not in that ragged leather jacket, but in a bulky sweater with a blazer over it, slightly preppy looking. This clothing did nothing to reveal a body shape — in fact, it was just as concealing as the jacket had been. Neat, pressed slacks and polished shoes finished the look. The dark curly hair was still longish in the back, but it was cut very short on the top, a strange, asymmetrical shape that suited the soft face very well. A poetic face, Anderson thought, thinking of boys in the summer, laying on the grass, full or import and youthful passion. At least Chris looked like someone who was sleeping in a bed on a regular basis, and clearly the clothing was no longer rescued second hand. Anderson was both relieved and curious; had the youth found a patron? Someone who was concerned with honor instead of utility?

"Thank you for seeing me, Ms. Anderson," Chris said, standing in front of her desk. There was a black book bag next to the visitor's chair, but Chris remained standing until Anderson nodded. Better manners than some might expect, but Anderson expected more than most. She didn't know whether she wanted to find fault, though. Not yet. She wanted to see how long this child — for the stranger before was her was just as much a child as she had been almost two years ago — could maintain this air of competence and self-assurance. Struggling to remain calm and aloof.

How she would enjoy stripping all of that away.

But of course her face betrayed nothing but polite and slightly distant courtesy. "Why the additional year?" she asked, leaning back into her chair.

"Because you deserved better," Chris said, with a bashful lowering of eyes that was simply delicious. Chris' eyelashes were unexpectedly full and lush, positively girlish. The answer was unexpected, too. What fun!

"And how are you better, other than being that much older?"

Anderson expected the usual recitation of deeds, mistresses served, floors cleaned, that sort of thing. But instead, Chris reached down into the book bag and pulled out a green file folder with a white and gold label on it. Anderson's heart quickened — had some other trainer taken this one on already? Was that the reason for the one year delay? She picked it up delicately from the desk and flipped it open.

It was in fact a Marketplace slave record; but it was not for Chris. The woman whose photo was clipped to the cover sheet was unknown to her — an attractive light-skinned girl in her early twenties, with long, sun streaked blonde hair and a bright smile. Anderson's hand shook as she turned onto the second page to see her nude — very pretty, a clean lined body that was made for giggling and cuddling. Next page, to the sales record, a page with only one notation, and a date of barely thirty days ago.

I'm not really going to see what's on the next page, she thought, her hand actually frozen above the file. But she turned to the final page and sighed. The trainer of record was one Chris Parker, with supplementary training by a spotter and trainer who was currently quite active in the NY soft world arena.

"How?" she asked, closing the file.

Chris was actually shaking — so tense, Anderson thought she would have to re-glue the legs of the chair later. "I — I went back to the person I was living with," Chris said, "after you sent me away. I had no where else to go. And — I stayed with her for the next six months. But whenever I was away from the house, I hunted for your people. Marketplace people. And I found them. I — studied whatever I could get. When I was. . ." Chris took a deep breath. Anderson waited for the moment of self composure to pass, and was pleased that just when she was about to snap something demanding, Chris continued. "When I was freed, I decided to do something to impress you. I found Alice on my own, and trained her according to what I'd learned, and presented her to Kyle Van Dien for testing. He decided that she was acceptable for a novice and told me that when I wanted to hook up, he would take me on as his apprentice."

Well, that was impressive. "Why didn't you?"

Chris actually looked astonished — those soft brown eyes widened as if the answer was obvious. "I wanted to be a slave, not a trainer, ma'am. And I wanted to be here. With you."

"Why?"

"Because you're the best."

Anderson smiled to herself. "And now you think you deserve the best?"

"I want to be the best," Chris said softly, eyes dropped again.

"Can you afford me?"

Those eyes remained glued to the floor. "No, ma'am, I can't. I can give you all of my share of Alice's sale, but it isn't much, because Kyle took half. . .and I. . .I had some debts. I have almost no other savings, and my — my former owner isn't interested in having me further trained, and wouldn't pay for it if she was. She — is not Marketplace." That was said completely without bitterness or anger, just a clean statement of fact. But it was clear that Chris was tremendously embarrassed by this financial state of affairs. "I — I can give you all I have to give. I know that with your training, I can be worth quite a bit — it's all yours, if that's what it takes."

"You'd give up your entire purchase price?"

Chris' head shot up instantly. "Yes."

"But what if I decide you wouldn't make a good slave? What if I decided that because of your precocious talent, I wanted to make you — a trainer?"

That caused another brief moment of thought. "I think I'd be a much better slave than trainer," Chris finally said.

"What you think right now is of so little consequence that it's not worth discussing," Anderson replied, letting a little bit of steel into her voice. "If you give yourself to me, then I decide where you go and what you do, isn't that true?"

"Yes, ma'am," Chris said, that light voice almost a whisper.

"Speak up!" Anderson snapped, standing. When Chris froze and looked up, she continued, "Don't just sit when I'm standing. On your feet, and answer me directly!"

"Yes, ma'am!" Chris said firmly, leaping up.

"I think you're nothing but trouble," Anderson said, walking from around the desk. "I think you're a snot-nosed, arrogant little brat. So, you found someone who you could successfully lie to, and you got basic training in Marketplace techniques and you got lucky spotting. I can read that story a dozen times a year if I want to, and none of those folks will even get past my front door. I think you've spent a lot of time in your own head, which is now full of the worst kind of nonsense imaginable, and that you're so hungry that I could touch you and you'd scream. You're the worst kind of novice candidate, requiring the greatest amount of sheer work from any trainer. Give me one damn reason why I should even examine you."

"You should examine me just because you've been wanting to for a year," Chris said back, as they stood toe to toe. Chris had to look up into Anderson's face, it allowed her to get another glimpse of the thick eyelashes that were so artfully hidden by the rim of those aviator frames. "Ma'am," Chris added, just a second late.

What a little wise ass, Anderson thought, even as she stepped slightly back and effortlessly cuffed Chris across the cheek. "Apologize," she said calmly. "That was a calculated act of rudeness."

Chris was startled by the blow, and as a slightly pink area rose on that smooth, soft cheek, there was a look of shock that seemed to start at the eyes and then spread with molten fluidity throughout the rest of the body. Chris took a deep breath and said, in a more controlled voice, "I'm sorry for offending you, ma'am."

"I think the first thing that will have to be done is to teach you how to apologize," Imala said as she turned to the door. "You're going to be doing it often. You think you proved yourself to me with this little stunt? You just proved that you can't be trusted. Wait for me."

She left the room with a swirl of skirt and hair, and suppressed the smile

330

that threatened to break through her stern demeanor. She waited until she was upstairs, and then shook her head even as she began to dial a phone number.

When she returned, Chris was waiting in exactly the same spot, and gave no impression of having moved at all. She placed an index card down on the desk and sat down again. "You are expected at the address on that card tomorrow," she said, taking in the array of emotions playing across the youth's face. "Ten o'clock in the morning, bring your clothes and personal items and don't disappoint me by disappointing her."

"Ma'am?" Chris picked the card up, and Anderson felt like she had just kicked a puppy. She turned away from her would-be client and waved a hand dismissively.

And didn't hear anything else but the clinks of the bookbag being gathered up and the click as her door closed.

My God, my God, she thought, her heart pounding. This one is real.

11:15 AM

As much as I wanted otherwise, I sent Chris to Janna Corliss, one of my former trainees. She had a nice little operation going, doing entry level training from her house in southern New Jersey. She had sounded delighted on the phone — a novice who faked Kyle Van Dien out? A shining example of raw talent who I needed shown a lesson in patience? She was only too pleased to take him on, and we agreed on three months for her to make something out of this mysterious kid.

Two days later, I got a call from her. What did you send me? she asked, her voice oddly strained. Is this — a test?

I was right, Chris was the real thing. Break her, I said.

OK, Janna said, carefully. I'll call you when I'm done.

Janna showed up at my house at the end of those three months. I had never gotten that call.

NOON

"OK, where do you want to sell him?" was the first question out of Janna's mouth after they settled over coffee and cookies in the front parlor.

"Who?" Anderson asked, settling back.

"Chris, of course. He's ready. Hell, if he stays with me much longer, I'm going to buy him." Janna pulled her charts out of her briefcase and passed them over to Anderson with a barely contained look of glee on her face. "Trainer, I don't know why you sent him to me, but he's a treasure.

Picks things up almost by osmosis, I swear. Remembers everything he's taught, and can pass it on using better language and better technique than most of the trainers I know, including me! I've already changed some of the language in my workbook."

Anderson's coffee cup clinked sharply as she set it down on the saucer. She took the folder and opened it in her lap, her mouth pursed in consternation. Damn it if Janna didn't fall in love with the little wiseass, she thought furiously.

"What do you mean 'he'," she asked crossly, scanning Janna's neatly printed notes.

"Well — frankly — I'm not quite sure what to call Chris. He is bisexual, at least from a functional definition; shows no real preference for men or women, responds mostly to dominance and submission, period. But when it comes down to his own sex — it just seems right to call him — him. And he prefers it."

"Slaves don't have preferences," Anderson muttered.

"Of course not," Janna said with the right air of submission. Anderson sighed and kept reading. Truth was, she disliked being a bully — but it came in handy now and again.

"What did the doctor say?" she asked, her voice gentler.

"There's a full report in the back, but basically, he was as puzzled as I was," Jenna said, recovering neatly. "He said he could call Chris a crossdresser, but we decided that Chris doesn't get an erotic charge from being mistaken for a man — Chris just feels right when looking masculine. I'd say he was a candidate for a sex change, but the Doc said he never heard of such a thing. He was supposed to get back to me on that, but I haven't heard from him."

Anderson snorted. "Follow up, I'd love to hear what other theories he comes up with. Drugs? Home abuse?"

"Some drug use, but not for a year now," Janna said immediately. "Said he went cold turkey to help clean up his act for you. He's a run-away, as I'm sure you realized, but he was pretty clear that his parents didn't smack him around much or anything. Just the usual tomboy stuff, you know — always on him for not fitting into the pink box."

Since Janna was herself on the butch side of things, Anderson only nodded and turned her attention back to the report.

The file format was easy to read, comfortably familiar. It was, after all, her style. So it was easy to find how much time it took to teach Chris the basic positions and responses — no surprise, anyone who had trained someone else could be assumed to know them already. OK, then, the more advanced work, the logic problems, the distraction exercises. Hm. Here, you could see a talent beginning to show through. The service training took a more normal length of time, but that was mostly because Chris had apparently been taught less-than-correct styles of table service, and had no idea what it took to manage things like financial records.

But after that, Janna had entered her program of breaking. This was the reason why Anderson had sent Chris to her, because when Janna got it in her head to break someone, she went at it with the single minded devotion of a pit bull. She was truly merciless, and had a delightfully perverse sense of humor that lent itself to pretty extravagant humiliations. It was one thing to chain someone up and beat them every day until they cried and begged you to stop. It was another thing entirely to reduce someone to tears with a word, a touch, even a caress. Plus, this sort of program often revealed the true nature of a client — are they a stubborn fighter with no sense of scale, holding on to dignity way past when it would have been appropriate to surrender? Are they afraid of things that might be central to service to a particular owner down the line? Do certain behaviors, names, articles of clothing, roles — make them angry? Unavailable in any way?

In other words, what would make Chris flee from this life?

Nothing, apparently. Or rather, there was something; but Janna had not completed her own program. Curious.

"Tell me a story," Anderson said, putting the file down. "What is he like to play with?" Instantly, she realized which pronoun she had used and cursed to herself.

Janna nodded and thought for a moment. "Takes a beating like a cross between Gary Cooper and a porn star. Stands up to it bravely and willingly — but then surrenders to it. I had to do a little work around permitting him to express the pain, but once he understood, he let it all go for me. Apparently, he's done some heavy, heavy shit — excuse my language, Trainer — but look at the photos if you doubt me."

Anderson fingered the envelope of photos, pulled one out and whistled, low. "Hm. Whips. Cutting ones. Is that — a brand? On his arm?"

"Yep."

"Who the hell would brand such a child?"

"Would you believe the child? Wait 'til you see the transcripts of my tapes; apparently, he had a friend of his do that sometime last year. Made the brand himself out of a cut up coffee can, and they heated it up — get this — with a shop—lifted butane torch. Made a clamp out of Chinese take-out chopsticks and a rubber band."

"My God," Anderson muttered. "Real masochist, then."

"Oh yes — definitely a turn on. But more than that, this kid comes *alive* when you're cruel. Beautiful responses, really, deep breaths and hissed intakes, little cries, building up to full throated screams. For someone who used to work with one of those 'just stand there and don't make a sound' types, it's positively miraculous. Add a touch of humiliation to anything, and his entire body reacts. He stiffens just enough to make it interesting to really push. On the negative side, he's definitely not a bondage fetishist. I think he's *offended* by bondage, somehow."

"What is — Chris — good for?"

"Practically anything, for the right owner. And that's the tricky thing. I'm not quite sure why, but he's got to belong to someone who — will understand him? I don't know if that's right. Basically, I've been treating him like a transvestite, and that seems to be the best way to handle him." Janna spread her hands in a shrug. "But with that aside, he can be a great house-servant, absolutely a demon when it comes to details. A personal assistant is also another way to go. He has no real education to speak of, but with a college degree in something useful he'd shoot up in value so fast your head would spin. About the only limitation he has is as a sex slave."

"Not interesting in that area?" Anderson asked, one eyebrow raised.

"Oh, no, he's very interesting, sorry to be so imprecise. But, well — he's — not attractive in a conventional sense. Not masculine enough to be right for the gay men or the straight women, and if we tried to make Chris into a pretty girl, well, I think we'd lose all his value in a minute. As a butch lesbian type, I think we could make a really good case — but that market is nearly non-existent as far as I know — only six sales I could find last year, and that was world wide. But he's willing, and talented, in a charmingly eager way. The right owner could make him into a great pleasure slave — but there's that right owner to come up with again!"

"Now tell me why you didn't obey me."

Janna's dignity didn't allow her to blush easily. Instead, she hardened, one of her few faults. "In my judgment, breaking Chris would have been a vast mistake. He's strong, but he's as bendable as a reed with the right motivation. As you have frequently noted, playing with clay is a lot more fun than playing with dust. You want to know how to break him, it's in the final notes. Pretty easy, too. But if you do that, Trainer, with all due respect, you will ruin him. I swear to you, on my honor, that every piece of training I have tells me that."

"But you still think I could sell him right now?"

"Like I said, I'd buy him."

"And what would you do with him?"

Janna bit her lip and then gave her trainer a crooked grin. "I'd make him a junior trainer under me," she admitted. "And that's what you want, isn't it?"

334

"I have ten applications sitting on my desk right now, from people who went through the accepted route to find me," Anderson said. "I don't need an arrogant, confused child to get underfoot. Tell you what — Chris is useful as an under-trainer? Take another three months, and then I'll let you know what we're going to do. I'll cover any additional costs of the training myself."

"That's very generous of you, Trainer."

Anderson waved her hand and then reached for her cooling coffee. "I know. Just don't ask me why, I'm never going to see a cent back on this troublemaker, I know it."

It was later on that evening, after Janna had left, when Anderson re-called the mystery of exactly how Chris had found her. She re-examined the events in her mind, and realized that she had been assuming that it was Kyle who had been Chris' first contact. And what was that phrase that Chris had used, that first day? "Are you compelling me to obedience?" Damn if it wasn't one of her own phrases, but none of her trainees would have been so sloppy as to let it slip to a street kid. Someone who had to give you a learner's permit for identification, she could see the blurry print even now, in her minds eye, Chris Parker —

That was when she realized who had sent her this talented little mystery.

She had last been there almost three years before, shortly after he had told her that he had moved. It was his dream apartment, a few blocks north of Christopher Street, in that area that was half filled with charming tree-lined streets and meat packing plants. Not to mention the gay sex clubs that dotted the area, and the easy access to the piers, where all manner of sexual behavior took place. He had told her about the men who had their little adventures in the backs of the parked 18-wheeled trucks and then took trains home to the suburbs. And of course, the back rooms where men could take on all comers in hours of carnality that boggled even the mind of a professional slave trainer.

She walked up to the second floor and knocked on his door, and heard him shout, "It's about time, you cocksucker, get in here!" Sighing, she opened the door.

"Is that any way to speak to your trainer, Ronald?"

He was lounging on a dilapidated couch, dressed in nothing but a pair of green khaki-colored boxer shorts and a stringy tank top, neither of which left much to the imagination about his sexy body. His jaw, dotted with a few days worth of dark beard, dropped in suitable shock even as his body un-folded to rise gracefully and eagerly to greet her. "Anderson! I can't believe it!" He ran to her and threw his arms around her in a crushing embrace, which she accepted for a few seconds before poking him strongly in the chest and pushing him back.

"Parker?" was all she said.

"Oh, sh—ooot," he said, catching the profanity as it started to come out. He had the decency to look somewhat abashed, lowering his head shyly as he scratched his chest where she poked him. "So, you figured it out, huh? Or did the little faggot finally tell you, so I have to kick his ass next time I see him?"

Anderson shook her head in disbelief. "I don't believe you, Ron," she said, moving through the apartment and kicking various garments out of the way. He scooped some more off the best chair for her and she sat down. "I don't believe that you would send a minor to me. And I just don't understand why you — why *everyone* is so eager to deny your sister's real sex!"

"Huh. Well, I figured that would be the easiest thing about Chris to understand, Trainer," he said, pulling a pair of jeans on over the shorts. "You Marketplace folks never run short on guys liking to be girls, you know. Chris is just the *opposite*, that's all. The little punk's always been like this; hell, he was on the street sooner than I was! Well, I guess I wasn't the best role model." He found a long sleeve shirt and pulled it on, and as he tucked it in, headed into the postage stamp sized kitchen.

No, Ron wouldn't have been the best role model for anyone, Anderson reflected. A brilliant scholar who left home to go to Israel, left the kibbutz to go to school, left college to become a slave, and then left slavery because it was too "boring" and became a leather clad master, a pool shark and occasionally a very expensive hustler.

So much potential there, so much grand potential. But he was restless, and needed change. No amount of training could stop the urge for novelty in one's life. She had told him so herself, when she let him go from the advanced training he had requested. He had seemed disappointed, for a little while. But then his eyes lit up, and he had asked, "So, can I call you Imala now? Can I take you out for a drink sometime?"

Surprised, she had said yes to both. And now, years later, he had sent her this . . . this strange problem.

He elbowed himself back into the room and gave her a glass of soda and sat on the couch again. "Look, Anderson, I didn't know what else to do with him. The idiot was getting into trouble like you wouldn't believe. Every couple of weeks, he'd show up with the snot beat out of him, and short of calling the cops, I didn't know what to do. I swear, he has a talent for finding the most psychotic freaks you can imagine, the crazier, the better. And only two people in the whole world cared about his ass, and neither of us could do much to help him, not really."

"How about your parents?"

"What about them? They fu— they tried to have him committed, OK? The kid's not insane, he just needs, you know. Direction. Training. Someone in charge."

"So I'm a baby sitter?"

"No! Jeeze, you think I'm stupid or something? I was in the world, Anderson; I can see that he's got what it takes. In fact, if it took you this long to figure out who he was, I'm betting you're not even training him yourself, are you? You passed him onto someone." He grinned, his heavy black mustache turning up charmingly, and she sighed. No, Ron was never stupid. In fact, she thought, why isn't he spotting for us? She would ask him later, when she wasn't so mad at him.

A knock sounded on the door and Ron yelled, "Beat it, you're late! Come back tomorrow, asshole!"

Footsteps on the stairs, no hesitation. Anderson raised one eyebrow. Apparently Ron had turned out to be a much better top than bottom. "And you couldn't provide Chris with a little direction and training?"

Ron shrugged. "Incest is not my bag."

"You pervert, that wasn't what I meant and you know it."

"Yeah, I know, I could have kept it all clean and everything. But that wouldn't have been enough for Chris. It wouldn't have been right. The two of us playing with that kind of power is just too nasty to think about." He looked around the apartment and kicked at the underwear on the floor next to him. "Though I have to admit that whenever he was here I never worried about the laundry! So — what are you gonna do with him?"

"Chris looks like a trainer to me," Anderson said.

"Damn! That would suck."

'Why?"

"Because it's not what he wants, man," Ron said. "Hell, anyone could see the kid was born to be a slave. Forget the trainer thing. You know he's good, and you got more trainer applicants than you can shake your riding crop at."

"You're assuming that I'm keeping him. Are you paying his training fees?"

Ron blushed — why hadn't she seen the resemblance between them before? "Aw, you know I don't have that kind of money, Imala. I spent half my slave fees getting set up here — the rest is the only retirement money I'll ever have, if I keep myself in the lifestyle to which I have become accustomed." He sighed, cursed under his breath and then shrugged. "OK. You want me to get it out of the bank and turn it over to you? You can have it, every dime. If you need more, tell me and I'll get it. But you can't tell the kid

I did it, or he'll have a fit."

Anderson put down her cup and shook her head. "You're a good brother, Ron. Actually, you're a sorry excuse for a brother. If you had any sense, Chris would be in school, well dressed and dating and going to the movies, and not — confused."

"Oh, take my word for it, Anderson, that kid is not confused. Give him a few weeks at your place, and you will make him confused, sure. But I bet you that right now, he knows exactly what he is and what he wants." He stretched, drawing the shirt tightly around his body. "It'll take me a day to go down to the bank and see about making out a check."

"Forget it," Anderson said, rising. "It's taken care of."

"Really?" He gave her a slow, sleepy look, and then his lips twitched again in amusement.

"Just tell me something — why did you call Chris a . . . faggot?" She worked her mouth around the harsh word distastefully.

"Because he is," Ron insisted. "Queer as a three-dollar bill. I don't care what that hellion he hangs with says or, sh—oot, what she does with him. In fact, I don't even want to *think* of what they do together." He winced theatrically. "No, Chris is my baby bro' in every way you can imagine but one. Oh, and the name, I guess. What can I tell you? I always hated 'Parker', made me sound like a damn goy or something." He laughed.

"I had actually forgotten that you changed your name," Imala admitted, looking down at him. "But then, I'm getting old. I must be slipping."

"You? Like hell! I'll tell you what the problem is, oh Lady Trainer." He stretched again and grinned his feral grin. "Imala's in luuuv," he purred.

"Now you're being rude," she said, picking her way to the door. "Ron, do me a favor and never send me a minor again. But call me, sweetheart. You could be a fabulous spotter."

"Ah-hah!" His cries of satisfaction continued even as she let herself out. "I told you so!" he was crowing. Smart-ass, she thought as she left the building. Just like his brother.

Sister, dammit! Sister!

12:15PM

Janna had Chris appraised at the end of the next three months. We were both impressed with the values that several pricing specialists posted. But every one of them said roughly the same thing; this was a specialty slave without a specialty. Chris had never stopped asking to train with me, although he always waited suitable intervals. He occasionally asked when his projected sale might be. Janna and I gave the matter some thought, and then

338

I pulled rank. If Chris needed a special skill, I would provide what would become a perfect role for him to take on. I sent him to my brother trainer in England, Dalton.

Dalton, the perfectionist. Dalton, the disciplinarian.

Dalton, the butler.

So why keep Chris at arms reach? I was only doing what we have always done; I kept a goal slightly beyond a client's reach. Oh, yes, it was an object lesson in and of itself. But it was also showing me what Chris was really made of. Every time I passed him on to someone else, I learned new things. Every report that got back to me taught me things that I might have missed in personal contact. And yes, I was very afraid that if Chris was in my hands, I would let my own plans get in the way of my client's real potential. I had to know, for sure, whether what my instincts told me was right. In this case, I chose correctly.

Janna's reports had been positive and wonderful. But what Dalton told me was just short of miraculous. Every month or so, I'd get his fascinating reports on what Chris had learned, and how Chris was bearing up, and as the time passed and I personally trained three clients and finished a new trainer myself, Chris was on his way back to me, certified as a butler or a major domo. He could manage a house staff, train footmen and valets and maids, organize work details, or he could do all of the tasks related to that kind of service himself. He took to the discipline of management with the same zeal he attacked almost every other assigned task, and Dalton reported that this puppy had a firm bite and a taste for control that was a delight to watch.

Now, he was genuinely valuable. Now, I would test him myself. And thanks to Dalton's detailed reports and Janna's very clear instructions on what she might have done to break him, I knew exactly what it would take to test this client's mettle.

Vicente disapproved. But he did as I said and collected Chris' suitcases and locked them away. And showed Chris the new wardrobe that would be his — hers, dammit.

This client, Dalton had written, *positively thrives when put to use at the table. His marks at Kaleigh were top-notch in all areas, displaying a firm sense of responsibility mingled with a level of confidence rarely found in a young client. When appropriately dressed and addressed, Chris displays excellent behavior and instincts. I would recommend finding an owner who appreciates this particular fetish, for although Chris' behavior does not suffer when dressed in maid's garb, it is clear that "he" suffers from loss of sleep and depression. The apparent difficulty this client has with being attired in feminine wear should be considered a reason-*

able limitation requiring owner notification before sale. This is no mere paraphilia, such as recreational cross-dress, but an honest example of gender identity. It is almost certain that owners may be found who will be entertained by such an individual. I believe that there is great value to be had in permitting Chris to present as male, and none whatsoever in the reverse.

Oh yeah, I thought?
Too bad.

If you find yourself in a battle of wills with a slave, there are only two explanations. Either you have a bad slave, who refuses to bend to your will or break when it is sensible, or you have a bad trainer, who doesn't realize where her place is.

After all, we have all the power. Never mind the philosophical arguments that the slaves are the power holders here. The slaves have one power only — to quit. We have everything else, including the threat of dismissal. We can make their lives rewarding and challenging or hellish and degrading. However, in order to create from a position of power, you can never find yourself in combat; it elevates the slave and lowers you. A minor scuffle, a small rebellion, these are the things which can make the whole master/slave relationship interesting. But a battle of wills should only be between equals.

Breaking starts off unfair and gets worse. But the rewards are nothing short of magnificent. A broken client touches the core of their existence and recovers with a strengthened sense of purpose. Sometimes, it turns out that the breaking shows them the way out the door. That's a risk I take every time. But in the long run, I'd rather break them than wait for some very smart or very stupid owner to do it. It's easier for us all if the trainer takes the heat.

I was prepared for Chris to do battle with me. I wanted Chris to come out stiff lipped and somber, showing every inch of that lovely adolescent arrogance now further molded by Dalton's British reserve, daring me to push further. I brought in another student, Ray, and two clients, a full house, and cast Chris into Silence, the first step in ego breaking. And I gave Chris nothing but girls clothing — not especially humiliating or sexual — but girls clothing just the same.

And then I ignored this new girl in my house. Ray was given full authority to supervise her, and was instructed to deny all attempts to speak to me directly. This he was only too pleased to do; most of my students are jealous of my attention, for better or worse. I count on that. It is part of the breaking and molding. Part of the test.

I expected sullen obedience. Stiff, monosyllabic responses. I expected breakdowns, little moments of despair that were quickly hidden under smol-

340

dering, thin-stretched patience. I expected to be begged for a chance to dress and act differently, to hear from Ray that the new girl was constantly asking for a private meeting with me.

But I had left Chris with Janna for six months, and with Dalton for longer. Even considering the effect that their training had, I was unprepared for what I got.

Chris' eyes widened, according to Vicente, but there was no sign of rebellion when the new wardrobe was revealed. Only a careful nod and an immediate change into the new costume. Chris did not ask to speak to me, did not beg for anything, only took instructions and asked the most direct and simple questions necessary.

In fact, it was over a week before I even saw more than a glimpse of my newest junior client. I was a little surprised — I had almost forgotten what Chris looked like. Frankly, I was disappointed. The features that made a handsome boy made a plain girl. And the short haircut that Dalton had apparently approved of looked just *wrong*.

But the way Chris slid silently to one side and waited with a lowered head for me to pass — oh, that was perfection.

I was so surprised, I didn't even linger to find fault.

I instructed Ray to watch for signs of dissatisfaction and discomfort, and much to his annoyance, they were few. Chris was obedient to a fault, a hard worker, respectful and unobtrusive, attentive and thorough. Up early and asleep late, there were never assigned tasks that went undone, except for those designed so. And when Chris was punished for these "failures", there was never an unattractive display of either rebellion or terror.

It would have all been very annoying had I not started to look into Chris' state myself. Despite Ray's claim that Chris was sleeping well every night, I knew better. Vicente passed on a comment one day, something about dark circles under Chris' eyes, and the next time I saw the figure in the gray dress, I picked up that soft chin and took a look myself.

That was when I knew the breaking would start. You can always see it in their eyes — a certain tired hollowness, that hint of panic around the edges. Chris looked tired, yes, but also just plain *worn*. And although there was a spark of interest and even excitement in those eyes, deeper back there was a touch of despair. Chris was so eager, so ready for my touch, and yet fully aware that I wasn't going to engage in any personal contact. Looking into those eyes, I saw all of that.

I walked on without saying a word, and heard my own heart beating with excitement. Surely, now we would see the cracks in the facade.

I ended up waiting another two weeks.

It doesn't sound like much, does it? After all, I rarely take clients for less than two months, even the well-trained ones coming back for follow ups. But living under Silence is one of the hardest things for human beings to do. We are such social creatures; we need to hear other voices, and we especially need our own. Even loners will talk to pets, to plants, back to television sets. To be in a crowded house with chatty slaves and lecturing trainers — not to mention the gossiping Brazilian in the kitchen — and be forbidden to speak in anything other than the briefest of respectful answers to direct questions is just damn hard. Add that to being dressed and addressed as something you hate, being assigned to the lowest level of service when you've been told you can be among the highest and being denied access to the one person you've been enduring all this for. Then try to imagine what you would feel like. What you would do. Scream? Cry? Pick fights with someone? Quit?

Chris picked up a bad habit.

Ray told me with glee that he had taken a cane to Chris for the crime of fingernail biting. The next time I found Chris industriously at work on the laundry, I asked to see her hands. My first words to Chris Parker since she was returned to my house were, as faithfully recorded in that night's journal entry:

"You are a disgrace, missy. If you can't be trusted to keep your hands looking presentable, you should consider another line of work."

Not the worst thing I've ever said to a client, but I might as well have told Chris that she had destroyed my great grandma's heirloom china or accidentally killed my favorite pet goldfish. I got a perfect apology which I ignored, despite being very pleased at its content and delivery.

Instead, I simply told Ray what to do, and when Chris went back upstairs that night to sleep, there was a bucket and a toothbrush waiting. There's nothing like a good old fashioned punishment to stir the pot. And frankly, the copper plumbing and walnut baseboards really appreciate a careful, patient cleansing. It wasn't until the third night when Chris actually got into the kitchen and I finally heard a more audible crack.

My house is an old one; it has been renovated twice. During the first renovation, the owners saw fit to close off the old dumbwaiter in the kitchen and wallpaper over it The paper neatly covered the edges of the door, but did nothing to disrupt the sound-carrying properties of the shaft.

Parabolic hearing my ass; I just know where the best places in my house are to eavesdrop.

I found myself leaning against the wall at about three in the morning, everyone else asleep. By all rights, Chris should have been finished and in bed as well, but instead, my special client was sobbing.

I'm used to hearing crying — little squeaky tears of fear, loud, shaking sobs of pain, twisted groans of humiliation — I've cataloged them all. Even secret tears were no secret to me; after all, we tend to show when we've been crying, with red eyes and sniffling noses and pounding headaches.

But Chris' little private sobs were different for me. As I listened to them sputter out, almost strangled into silence, and then the sounds of renewed labor and the harsh words that were aimed at my august person, I didn't feel the breaking, the sense of futility. Oh, there was frustration and anger, definitely. And that particular sound of a person's pain when they blame themselves for it. But these were not the despairing cries of someone who doubted their courage, but instead someone who was frustrated by their own weakness.

Yes, I could tell the difference.

There had never been a client broken under me who did not give off that particular wave of hostility, fear and defeat that a trainer can almost taste in the air around them. Chris was hurting, yes, but not breaking. Angry at me enough to curse me, but controlled enough to not let anger get in the way of training. Or, for that matter, in getting the tile grout as white as possible.

For the first time in years, I doubted my program. This was getting me — and my client — nowhere. Chris wasn't going to break publicly, and was going to continue to work until exhaustion caused foul-ups. And for what? The humiliation of failure? That would have to be nothing compared to the humiliation of being told to paint those gently chewed fingernails pink and keep those hands looking like a lady's.

The more I thought about it — and I stayed awake until far past the time I heard Chris's slow footsteps on the stairs — the less satisfied I was. I wasn't going to get a trainer out of this one, not the way I was going. All I was going to end up with was an exceptional slave who was designed for an owner with a particular fetish; not a bad thing, but not what I expected.

And the whole thing was compounded by the just plain feeling of "wrong, wrong, wrong" that I got whenever I looked at Chris. I've had plain looking clients, even just damn ugly ones from time to time, and I've had clients who were not comfortable in their bodies, not satisfied with how they looked or sounded or felt. But there was just something *wrong* with Chris in a dress.

As wrong, I reminded myself, as a transsexual.

Except that there were no female transsexuals. Or whatever you would call them.

I stayed up until dawn, looking through my notes and Chris' original file, with the doctors report. And then I took out older files from previous clients, people who had once been men, but had taken the hormones and had surgeons alter their bodies. And finally, when the older slave whose job it was that week found me and brought me coffee, I swallowed my pride and called in a second opinion.

Al Cruz — now Alison, Anderson reminded herself — was looking better these days. Or at least she was looking happier. Once there had been a slim man with haunted eyes and a nagging sense of not belonging which drove him to seek ownership as an answer to his problems. Now, there was a vivacious *cafe au lait* skinned woman who probably made more than a few men look up in order to be fascinated by her flashing eyes and long, wavy hair. Her facial bones looked a little prominent, and she favored sweeping, colorful and conservative clothing with long scarves and vests, but that fashion was only slightly out of date.

"Anderson!," Ali cried as she swept through the doorway into the sitting room. "Ohmigod, you look stunning! I love the beads, are they Indian?"

Al used to be shy, too.

Anderson glanced down at her braided necklaces and shrugged. "I'm fairly sure they're Bloomingdales, Alison."

"Ali, Ali. I decided I need a nickname." Ali took the pretty chair by the window and sighed. "I haven't seen you since the nip and tuck, Trainer, how's business?"

Anderson laughed. "As good as it always is; and how is life now that you're all settled into the new skin?"

"Oh, you know, it's just fine. *Mira*, no more facial hair, all gone! For good, too." Ali smiled with satisfaction, stroking her own cheek. "It's like a dream come true. And mama, you should see the handsome macho man I have calling on me now, also like a dream come true!"

"I'm happy for you, Ali," Anderson said honestly.

"I know, I know. I used to hate you, but now, I know you were sent by God to make sure I did the right thing. Now that I've honored you, tell me what I can do to help you." She sat forward, all attention.

"There's someone I want you to meet," Anderson said gently.

"Another transsexual, you mean? Bring her on, I'll gladly do a little social work for you, any time! I don't believe you're making such a fuss over it, you know I owe you a thousand thousand times." Ali waved her hand and laughed again. "Take me to the poor thing, or tell me where she is."

"Funny you should say 'she'," Anderson said. She rose and headed for her office across the hall, and Alison followed her, curious.

"What do you mean?"

Anderson opened the office door, and Ali peeked in around her shoulder, to see a very composed if not happy looking young man in the servant's drag of a kitchen maid, hands folded demurely in his lap. As the door was fully opened, he rose gracefully and curtsied, and although the move was very nicely done, there was something lacking to it — something she couldn't put her finger on. His head was lowered in a charming way, and she could see that his hair was much too short for the role, and she wondered why on earth Imala hadn't allowed it to grow out. . .

Or — Ali blinked and shook her head.

"*Ay, dios mi,*" she said softly. She turned to Anderson, a sharp look of curiosity in her eyes. "Is this a boy or a girl?" she asked.

You tell me, Anderson thought. She said, "This is Chris. Chris, this is Ms. Alison Cruz. Please answer any questions she puts to you honestly and directly."

"Yes, ma'am."

Alison glanced from the figure in maid's clothing and then back to Anderson. "I'll need some privacy," she said. "You go hit someone or something."

"Thank you, Ali," Anderson said, and with a light touch on the woman's shoulder, she left the doorway.

Alison walked into the room and closed the door gently behind her. She made her way to Anderson's desk, and sat down, indicating that Chris sit as well. When Chris sat down facing her, she sighed and stroked her smooth chin, thinking.

"Well, Chris," she finally said, pulling a sheet of paper from the box next to the typewriter. "I would like you to draw a picture for me."

"I beg your pardon, ma'am, but I've had no formal training in drawing," Chris said. Chris' voice was a definite tenor, a little high, perhaps, from nervousness. From fear of disappointing, perhaps.

"That's OK, I don't want to hang it on the wall." She passed the paper and a few pens across the desk and waited until Chris drew up to a more comfortable position for drawing. "Make me a picture of a house, and a tree, and a person."

Chris digested that for a moment. "Any special types of these things?"

"No — just whatever you think of. In any order that you wish."

"Yes, ma'am." Chris chose a black pen and immediately drew a long, sweeping line on the sheet of paper. In seconds, there were suggestions of branches.

I don't know who you are, Ali thought as she sat back, trying to remember the questions they had asked her years ago. Trying to envision the thick books that now filled her shelves and what she had read in them, about her and about people like this young man. I don't know *who* you are *muchacho,* but I can tell *what* you are, you obedient slave. You Anderson slave.

Anderson knew it would be a while, but wasn't quite prepared for four and a half hours. And she certainly wasn't prepared for Alison Cruz to come out of the room with a look of anger on her face. It dissipated into annoyance as soon as their eyes met — there were very few who faced her with sustained anger.

"We have to talk," Ali said. "Privately, please."

"All right," Anderson answered cautiously. "Chris, you are excused, report to Ray for the completion of your duties today."

"Yes, ma'am." There was a quick reverence, and Chris slid out of the room almost too fast, absolutely not within acceptable guidelines, and Anderson heard a quavering in Chris' voice that she had never heard before. She looked at Ali with one eyebrow raised as they walked into the room.

"If I were you," Alison began, picking up sheets of paper and stuffing them into her cavernous purse, "I wouldn't send him to clean the toilets, I'd put him in his proper clothes and get him to a doctor, fast."

Anderson sat down, feeling the weight of her fear settle into her stomach. "Him," she said softly.

"Him," Alison repeated. "I don't know anyone else like that, but I've read about it. And I remember what I said and felt and thought and dreamed about. It's like looking into some mirror at a carnival, all twisted wrong, but you know what's in there any way." She perched herself on the edge of the desk and leaned forward. "He's a transsexual, Trainer, like me, and you've been making him crazy. Sorry to be so blunt, but you know, I say what I think."

"Oh, dear," Anderson said. "But — the doctor who examined him said there was no such thing."

"He's out of date, then. Or stupid. Or both, I don't know. And you know what else? I don't even know if my doctor will be able to help, either, all he works with is ladies like me. Maybe there's someone at Johns Hopkins, but that's where that whacko is who thinks if you talk about it, you can grow tits and stop needing to shave." She tossed her hands up in frustration.

"What?"

"Oh, I was just reading this report from this doctor who says that people like me don't need surgery, all we need is a good psychiatrist. Honey, I could talk your ass off from here to when Jesus comes, but it wasn't talking that got me this gorgeous body, it was the knife and lots of drugs."

Anderson shook her head. "I have to think about what to do now," she said.

"Don't think too long. You remember how unhappy I was when you told me I needed to leave and get real help? He's worse. The only reason he's not dead now is that he wants to be a slave more than he wants to be a man, or at least that's what he thinks. You have to convince him he's wrong."

"I do?"

"It's what you would do if he was a young man who you felt was a woman, right? Anderson, tell me something — you can feel so much from a person, I know that. I took one look at him, and I read him like a clock. Don't you just *feel* it from him?"

"Actually," Anderson said, standing with a heavy sigh, "apparently I was the only one who didn't. How about that? Thank you, Alison. Can I ask you for another favor? Can you help me find someone for him?"

"I will," Ali nodded and shifted her purse onto her shoulder. "But get him out of the life, Trainer. You know they won't take him seriously if they know what he's been doing with you."

"Yes," Anderson said, her voice a little hollow. "I know that." She saw Alison to the door and went back onto the office to sit alone for a while. When she was composed, she thought of calling Ray in, but changed her mind and went to see Vicente first. And after her apology to him, she was the one who went upstairs to tell Chris that he was relieved from chores and to give him back his clothing.

And that was precisely when Chris broke.

1:15PM

"Please, please, Trainer, ma'am, I promise to work harder! I'll be happier, I'll smile more, I'll never, never show discomfort again, I swear!" Chris' eyes were red-rimmed now, and wide open in desperation. It had been difficult for him, those moments of trying to be obedient and calm, to collect himself and follow my instructions. But he crumbled gradually, like chipped limestone, cracking around the edges until the huge fissure down the middle left him unable to stand.

Of course the only proper place for him was on his knees anyway, so when he suddenly doubled over and keened, there wasn't much more road for him to travel. He was much too well trained to grab for my legs or even make a move toward me, and so he hugged his arms around his chest instead, as his gut twisted him down, head lowered so he could dash away tears with the back of his hand before raising his face to me to plead again.

"Please, ma'am, don't send me away, I've worked so hard to get here — it is all my fault, yes, I haven't been as good as you deserve, but I will be, I'll accept any punishment you chose, any duties, any clothing, it doesn't matter to me, but please, don't throw me out!"

I did expect something dramatic to happen. It always does, when I have to tell a client why they can't pursue their dream. Some of them break down and cry, others scream at me, a few will coldly shut off all feeling and start calmly packing. Four times, I had to dissuade people from killing themselves.

347

Three times, I succeeded.

It doesn't get easier with time, but at least I learned to figure out what people really mean in those unguarded moments of hysteria. And now, I could feel the panic, the desperation I so wanted from this client a week ago. I had a choice; coddle and soothe him, or see whether this colt could stay the course. The humane thing, of course, would be to get on my knees right next to him, take him in my arms until he calmed, and then explain what was coming in as gentle and supportive tones as I could manage. Most people don't know, but I can become mamma when necessary. When I mounted the stairs, I fully intended to be humane.

But humane or not, dammit, this was my fascinating client here; driven into desperation by the slightest glimpse that Ali Cruz had allowed him of himself, and now, just at that state I had wanted the day before.

"Compose yourself," I snapped. "This behavior is unseemly in someone with your training."

The reminder of his training seemed to spark something; his breath caught sharply and he coughed, choking on it, but as he rubbed his eyes even more and straightened his clothing, he was clearly winning the battle with his emotions. Shaking violently, he brought his arms behind his body tightly, and I felt my heart break with pride. The display itself was loud and ugly, but it had the virtue of being honestly shown and strongly controlled. It was the recovery that was impressive.

"You will do as I said, and change into the clothing you came here in," I said, deliberately looking into Chris' eyes. "In fact, I want you fully groomed. Take a shower, and fix your hair the way it used to look. When you dress, find something appropriate for this house. And when you are fully composed, I will see you in my study. Take as much time as you need."

Oh, how badly he wanted to plead with me again — I saw the sudden intake of breath, and the renewed desperation in his eyes — but instead, he lowered his head and said, "Yes, Trainer," in a shaky but quiet voice.

I turned on my heel and left the room, and wondered what the hell I was going to do now. Ray met me in the hallway, questions on his mind, but when he saw the way I looked, he sidestepped neatly and let me pass without a word.

What Ali said was true; few reputable doctors wanted to hear that their transsexual clients wanted to be anything but someone of the opposite sex. A heterosexual person of the opposite sex at that, with nice, middle class aspirations of a pale faced family living in suburbia with two cars in the garage. We'll change you, they are saying, if you will only be the fantasy we want you to be.

Voluntary slavery did not fit into this picture. Chris had to leave my house and leave training if he was to become at home with himself. And yet the Marketplace was now his home, at least as much as his skin was.

When men who became women left the Marketplace, many of them were assured that there would be a place for them should they wish to return, regardless of how far they went with their change. Heck, there were so many requests for folks with breasts and penises you would think God might have forgotten one of the sexes during those hectic six days, and some of us miss it real bad.

But how could I promise there would be a place for Chris?

I couldn't. Not reliably. Except that he had broken — and had begun to show me what he was really made of, the strength of will and determination that made him so damn attractive. Attractive to me.

I had to salvage him, if not for the auction block, then for my own purposes. I'd be an idiot to let him wander away to continue thrill seeking among the amateurs. Or, more likely, lose him to Dalton, who had been so sure that there was a place for him somewhere.

He already belongs to you, I thought wryly. He told you so; why not call him on it?

Because I don't own slaves, that's why. I don't think that trainers should own slaves, especially trainers who work alone. I don't keep my own trainees when they do their service terms, I send them to friends and associates. To me, the relationship of owner and slave is too intimate, too unique to ruin with a spill-over into the realm of trainer and student. Plus, the minute I own a slave, I immediately set up the possibility I can own two. It's hard enough to be a perfectionist trainer; I can't also be a dream master too.

I pulled Chris' file again and read through it, turning the pages idly. All this time I had invested — and not only my own time but Janna's and Dalton's as well. Dalton seemed sure that he could find someone who could agent Chris into the right home; but to toss this gifted youth into an English household just might lose him to me forever. Lose his potential as something better than a single purpose slave, a curiosity.

It might make him happy though, my conscience nagged me.

I closed the file and opened one of my old cabinets and leafed through a folder of old contracts. And when I found the one I wanted, I put it on the desk and waited for my client to present himself.

2:00PM

Chris Parker finally looked right again, in a white shirt and tie, a slightly oversized pull over wool vest and trousers that looked like he had just ran an iron over them. Even his shoes were shined; well, Anderson had told him to be groomed and appropriate. His eyes were red-rimmed and his body just a little stiff — but nothing near the stiffness that he had when in a dress.

He was also quiet and attentive, sitting in a composed posture that signaled nothing but patience and obedience. His jaw occasionally moved as she began to explain, but he never interrupted. She was blunt, as occasions like this often required. And when she finished, he nodded.

"Thank you, Trainer," he said softly. A low voice for a girl, Anderson thought, but a sweet voice for a boy. "Thank you for everything, you've been more than generous and kind to me. May I ask some questions?"

"Please do."

"Do I have a choice in this? Do I have to see a doctor? What if I just kept on training and you had me appraised again — couldn't I just be sold without all this — psychiatric — care? Mr. Dalton said that I could be sold in England — and I was offered a place at Kaleigh, I could go there, couldn't I?" He was trying to look calm, but there was a beautiful edge of panic in his voice, just a touch of pleading.

"We all have some choices in our lives," Anderson said, leaning back. "But I wouldn't continue your training, and I would advise Dalton about your situation as well."

He swallowed hard and closed his eyes for a moment.

"Understand me, Chris, it isn't because I think there's something wrong with you. But keeping you on as a client when you haven't finished the business of what gender you are — that would be a mistake."

"But — excuse me, Trainer, please forgive me for arguing with you — but I don't have any money for this. I don't have anything! And — and — it could take years! Ms. Cruz said it took three years for her — for her to — change." His hands clenched each other as he forced them down into his lap.

"As luck and fate would have it, I have a solution to both problems," Anderson said, fingering a multi-page document in front of her. "But I have to ask you a serious question first. Do you remember what you offered me for your training?"

"Yes ma'am. I told you that you could have my entire sale price." There was a flicker of interest working its way past the wide-eyed panic.

"And what did Janna tell you when you were with her?"

"That in fact you would take a straight fee out of my first sale price and up to three sales past that, with a portion going to her, and that the rest would be held in trust for me when I left service." Interest grew into hope, and his face seemed to open to her.

"Well, Chris Parker, I'm going to revisit your first offer," Anderson said. "To be frank, I have every confidence that you are born to service and will make an excellent slave — or trainer."

The unexpected praise pushed him back in his seat — he blinked in shock, but she didn't let him wallow in it.

"But, as Dalton put it, you are abysmally ignorant in matters of literature, music and art. You are lacking in the classical education that he felt was necessary to be a fully qualified gentleman's gentleman. And now, we have this — issue — with how much time you might need to make changes in your life that will at least allow you to present as the kind of person you see yourself as when you close your eyes." She raised an eyebrow at him, and he nodded sadly.

"I estimate that you should need between two and four years to do whatever the doctors we find for you tell you to do, or what you decide needs to be done. We don't know right now exactly everything that might happen, but judging from my experience with men who become women, that seems reasonable. You also need an education. And finally, you need to be out of full time training so that you can dedicate yourself to both of these things." Anderson ticked them off on her fingers and then gave her client a long, measuring look. Yes, he was starting to understand.

"Depending on what happens when Alison finds you a doctor and what he says, I intend to send you to school," she said, watching his eyes flicker and his hands start to shake again. "I will support you while you study, and while you are under a doctor's care. And in return—" She pushed the contract across the desk and with a flicker of her eyes, told him to pick it up. He examined it for a moment and then looked up at her in confusion.

"A — bondsman?"

"Debt bondage," Anderson said with a nod. "Pretty rare these days, with so many eager volunteers who would pay for the right to be someone's doormat. But acceptable within our guidelines."

"But — ma'am — it's too much," Chris whispered, putting the contract back on the desk. "I owe you so much already — I can't ask you for all that as well — it's too much!"

"You didn't ask me, I made an offer," Anderson countered. "I think the time and money invested in you will pay off handsomely, if you apply yourself the way you have since you started training. It won't at first — you will still need experience and some more training to be the kind of client I see you have the potential to be. But if you don't take my offer, I run the risk of losing what I've already invested."

Chris looked at the contract for a moment, and Anderson almost grinned. Yes, Dalton had complained that Chris lacked an acquaintance with the higher arts, but he also noted that Chris wasn't at all stupid. Find the trouble with this offer, Anderson encouraged silently. Find my trap.

"I mean no disrespect, Trainer," he said carefully, nervously. "But — I have learned that you do not keep slaves. If I am in debt to you and there isn't a buyer who can afford to pay you for what you — invested in me — what will happen to me?"

"Oh, I can guarantee that no one will afford you when you get out of school," Anderson said easily. "At least, those who could afford you could also get better for the same amount of money. No, Chris, I am counting on a period of time in which you belong to me — or at least, when your *labor* belongs to me." Think about it, she thought, watching as indecision swept over his face.

"I agree," he said softly.

"You should take some time to think about it," Anderson said.

"I have no choice," he said, taking a deep breath. "Trainer, I have nothing but what you see in me. If you think I need to do these things, I have to trust you, because — I don't know, myself. I once told you I wanted to be the best, Trainer. I — I've learned that I was arrogant and rude, and that I didn't know anything about what it might take to be anything better than — well, like you said, someone's doormat."

This was a long speech for someone who was not used to talking. Anderson crossed her legs comfortably and cocked her head, encouraging him to continue.

"If what it takes to complete my training is to serve you as a trainer, then I will," he said simply. "For as long as you think is fair."

Anderson sighed. "You still believe things should be fair?' she asked. "After all you've been taught?"

"I have to," Chris said.

2:15PM

The temper tantrum I threw when I found out how many people like Chris there were and realized that we had been relying on outdated and/or edited information from our so-called mental health professionals turned out to have a great effect on the way we did things. Janna was also a bit put out; she had accepted her doctor's opinion without question and hadn't done her own research and she felt that it should have been her responsibility since I put Chris' initial interviews in her hands. But how could I criticize? Even my damn cook knew more than I did. Which he didn't fail to remind me of for years.

It took several weeks to settle on a local professional who had experience that Alison respected, and actually get Chris into his care. Torn between wanting to get him out of my reach and not wanting to leave him alone, I finally

352

moved Chris into the attic room that I used for overflow. Poor Ray took a little time to understand what had happened, but he had his hands full of the clients I neglected while I talked to Alison on the phone and called in favors and engaged myself in figuring out how to do what I had proposed to Chris. The flurry of preparations distracted me long enough to get used to the idea of sending him away again.

And when the paperwork was finished and the details ironed out, I could send for my soon-to-be debt slave and present him with his new address and his new bank account, and his contract.

"You will keep a running ledger," I instructed him, giving him the bound book. "I am not interested in proofing it, so I rely on you to be accurate. You will also continue to keep a journal, and in addition to that, I will expect a monthly report on your progress. No less than three thousand words, please. If you anticipate new expenses or have a problem, you may call Vicente; but keep your communication with me limited to writing. While you're at it, improve your handwriting and learn to type."

Chris nodded. "Yes, Trainer," he said. He had stopped crying, settled himself into cooperation, which was nice. But also a little disconcerting.

"Alison will prove to be one of the best friends you will ever have," I continued. "Treat her with respect. Since she has offered to remain your mentor, I suggest you take her up on that and remain in communication with her as well. You may not indulge in any illegal drugs, and if you value my advice, you will also abstain from alcohol. Don't take this opportunity to be a typical college student; be an exemplary one. I want you to concentrate on your therapy and your studies and anything I turn your mind to, and not to waste a single minute doing things that are self-destructive. You will not be in my house, but you are damn sure part of my household, do you understand?"

"Yes, Trainer," he immediately answered. And glad of it too, I thought, looking at the way he relaxed when I gave him instruction.

We were standing together in my office, and when he looked up at me, I gave into my own impulse and touched him, running a finger along his jawline. He shivered slightly, but allowed me to turn his head, examining his face.

"As for the rest of your life — I am not sending you out into the world to be a hustler, Mr. Parker. There will be no late night searching for easy sex, no sex for money. I've read your early interviews, and I disapprove of that sort of thing. No SM play with strangers, and if you are desperate enough to feel like you need to be taken in hand, you will contact me and leave that up to my judgement. I do not want you to pursue any kind of romantic or physical relationship without my permission. Do I make myself clear?"

"Absolutely clear, Trainer," he said softly. A touch of shame touched his cheeks. I walked around him, and ran my finger down his spine, feeling him shake and straighten up just a little more.

"If you want to visit your brother," I said, feeling his body react in surprise, "don't do it in a leather bar."

Oh, it was so much fun to surprise him; watch the struggles he went through, trying to figure out whether he could or should say something, ask something. Janna had mentioned this, and so did Dalton, although from his perspective, it was a flaw. No, Dalton would never want to push someone across a desk and press them down while whispering questions into their ear, making them blush and stammer as you found out how excited they were by the process.

"How many other secrets do you think you're hiding from me?" I asked as I pushed him down. He bent under me, alongside me, gasping; I had never been so close to him. At first, he didn't understand what I wanted, and almost braced his arms — but as I pressed, he bent, and when his cheek hit my blotter, I plucked his glasses off his nose and put them aside as I leaned in.

"That was not a rhetorical question, Mr. Parker."

"Yes, Trainer, I beg — I beg your pardon," he gasped out. "But — I don't know how to answer you, since — since it seems that you already know at least one, so I don't know which other secrets you might be interested in."

I almost drew back to laugh. In fact, the urge was so strong, I did smile, glad that from the angle I was holding him, he couldn't see my face. I gave him a rough shake, my hand at the back of his neck, and listened as he let go the slightest of whimpers, his legs bracing.

"Impertinence is something you seem to have difficulty controlling," I said, when I could count on my voice to be steady. "And I'm not interested in playing 20 questions with you today. But you will tell me everything, my. . .boy." There was an appreciative shiver when I said that word, beautiful positive feedback from a slave who got off on precise wordplay. "You have a few years in which you will make me the world's expert on Chris Parker. You'll learn how to talk to me, how to tell me things, how to ask me things. And you will never forget how this feels, will you? To be handled like the piece of property you aspire to be. I wanted you to leave this house today absolutely sure that I will have a place for you when you get back. Do you understand where that place will be?"

"Under — under your hand, Ma'am," he said, and I heard the inflection that would later grow to be one of his specialties and damn if I didn't feel like keeping him exactly where he was and doing something very un-Anderson-like.

"Strip to the waist," I said, barely hearing my own voice. As he obeyed me, his legs still pressed up against the desk, but his body raised only far enough to handle that task, I walked over to the glass case that held the few items in my house that could be qualified as my sex toys.

I chose a small box, and still in an almost trance, pushed Chris back down, firmly. I moved the tray of papers out of the way so I could be close enough to do my work, and I told him, "Keep your shoulders from bunching. Keep the lines of your back supple for me. But don't move unless you warn me that you have to."

His head was turned to the right; frozen, he whispered his understanding of my instructions, and I deliberately put the box down next to his cheek. He would see each knife that I drew out, and what they looked like when I placed them back in the lid.

It took four knives. Human skin dulls blades quickly, and a rose is an intricate design. My hands were perfectly steady, they always were when I used the knives, and I saw clearly the design on the card he sent me, the way he had shyly courted me with the rose on my umbrella. Would the doctors puzzle over this mark? Undoubtedly. But young men were expected to do stupid things, like get themselves adorned to impress young women. More important to me was the way his breathing quickened when he saw the silver edges, the way he groaned when the first cut spread open on his back, the way he sighed with every turn of the small blade as I cut another thorn into the stem. I breathed in his pain and delight until the design was complete, and stood back to watch the red trickles down his side and across the back of his throat. It had spilled onto my blotter, which did its job admirably, spreading the stain all around Chris' face. And it had dripped a little beyond it as well. The blood would stain my desk a little. I liked that idea.

"It's very becoming," I said out loud. The first words in the room since he had acknowledged his instructions.

"Thank you, Trainer," he whispered hoarsely.

He thanked me again after the alcohol. And again after the ink, although by then, they were thanks mingled with tears. I bandaged the mark myself and I stepped back to watch him dress, watching him wince as the cuts crinkled when he flexed his shoulder. His own blood stained his face and his neck, there was even some in his hair.

It had tasted sweet.

I let him go then, knowing that he would never doubt he had a place to come back to. No matter how lonely or frustrated or angry he got, no matter how far he let himself sink into despair — he had something of me that very few in this world did. I had let him feel my passion. He was mine now, for as long as I wished. In time, I too would read him like a clock.

32   I'd Like to Thank the Academy

A good dozen trainers had already left before dinner, a mixed, casual affair with no set hosts and no scheduled entertainment. The last night of the Academy was set aside for parties and final meetings and one last opportunity to make connections. Chris and Ron were not the only ones to dress up, although the formally dressed contingent was definitely in the minority. Some fetishwear made it into the room as well, although it was limited to a corset here and there and a pair of leather shorts or a skirt or two. The slaves were apparently in whatever they tended to wear at home, outfits ranging from nothing at all to full serving uniforms to the stylized brief bands of silk favored at auction houses and other display areas. Their motley appearance suited the dinner nicely, and at last, their owners' — and trainers' — names were appended to their collars, so that they could be honored.

Anderson came late, in a long black dress, with Tetsuo as her companion. They sat at a table with the other Academy gods, Ninon and Kurgan, Corinne, Arturo and the rest. Michael and Ron stayed with Chris, and ended up near Anderson's table, along with Marcy and Stuart.

At the end of dinner, as fruit and ices were being distributed, William Longet, elegant in a tailed coat and cravat, got up to make his announcements. Shushes followed his polite cough into the microphone.

"Ladies and gentlemen of the Academy, I have a few thanks to offer and decisions to report, with your kind permission."

He was met with sustained applause, and he smiled briefly and slipped reading glasses onto his nose, peering down at the sheets in front of him. "All of the members of the Academy extend their profound thanks for the consideration and generosity of the Okinawa Guild of trainers, the greater Japan Guilds, and the Shimada family, for a splendid example of hospitality. . ."

He went down the list, thanking all the trainers who sponsored and arranged for the slave staff, the supervisors, the entertainment, the chefs — everyone who could possibly be thanked. Applause was genuine, and there was much back slapping and hand shaking among the tables.

"I would also like to announce that next year's Academy will be held in the country of Canada, in the province of — British Columbia. Our host, in addition to the Canadian trainers and spotters, is the Rysbeck Corporation, owners of the Lion's Mane Resort."

"Woo-hoo!" crowed Stuart, who immediately blushed as the people around him laughed.

"Finally, an Academy that won't cost an arm and a leg to get to," sighed Marcy. But she was obviously pleased that her northern neighbors got the honor, and Michael could see the Canadian table all grinning and acknowledging more applause.

"And finally, I would like to announce the results of our afternoon vote," William said, after people settled down.

"As if we don't know," cried Tucker, and several people laughed. William Longet didn't. He took this part of his job very seriously, and only raised an eyebrow in Tucker's direction as he broke the seal on the envelope.

"In the question of the Parker proposal, forming a voluntary association of trainers which shall be duly recorded and supported by the Marketplace, membership to be decided within that association, with no penalties nor rewards for membership. Proposed: That the International Coalition of Trainers and Handlers permit to be created a volunteer association of training, including a certification process for accrediting new trainers within it, entering membership in said association as part of the available records maintained by the organization.

"The vote is — in favor of the proposition, by a four fifths majority."

Cheers came up, and more applause, this time accompanied by foot stamping, and both Marcy and Ron leaned over to slap Chris on the back. He smiled thinly, embarrassed by the attention, and stood reluctantly, when he heard his name chanted by a table led by Tucker. He bowed slightly to the group, nodded, and sat down again, blushing.

When the applause ran out, William Longet gathered his papers and said, "I thank you for your kind attention this year, and ask you to welcome Herr Walther Kurgan for this year's specialty awards."

There was laughter as Walther got up and strode to the podium. He was one of the people there ready for play — he was wearing leather jeans and a vest, his bare chest broad and firm. But it wasn't his appearance that was amusing, that was just Walther. It was the awards he was about to bestow.

"Friends and not friends," he said genially, to more laughter. "Once again, we have been gifted with a fine week of pleasure and politics — teaching and fucking. And once again, we have noticed the rare few among us who deserve our attention for service to the Academy above the call of duty! or well below! For example — our role model in timeliness, the great trainer of trainers, Anderson!" The room rocked in laughter as he continued, "She has shown me the valuable lesson this year that when one arrives late to a party, one may arrive very, very late!"

He went on, singling out Ninon as the best dressed trainer and the Canadians as the group most likely to use flea collars on their slaves. He awarded Michael the "most admired by men, women and sled dogs" certificate, and in fact had one of the Canadian slaves deliver it to him in her teeth, which made him freeze in embarrassment before Ron slapped him on the back and he finally exploded in laughter. It had been a while since someone had complimented him so publicly.

Finally, after complimenting or embarrassing about a dozen trainers, he held one last sheet of paper and said, "And what would this week have been, if not for the honorable opposition, eh? For Best Loser, the award goes to Mr. Geoff Negel, from California, America!" He laughed so had he almost doubled over, and Geoff got up to bow to the laughter and applause of his peers, a rueful smile on his face. When Walther got control of himself, he wiped the tears from his eyes, and said, "So remember, all of you — you cannot escape the eyes of the special awards committee — we shall see you in Canada next year!" People threw balled up napkins at him as he made his way back to his table, still laughing. But when Anderson rose and approached the podium, silence swept the room.

She and Walther were of a similar height. The microphone was right where it should be, she gripped the sides of the podium for a second, and then spoke.

"My friends," she said. "My apologies for my lateness and my thanks for this award, which I have already stopped treasuring." She smiled, and they laughed. "I come before you this evening, in our tradition, as a master trainer, and I beg your indulgence. It has been some time since I addressed this body, and I shall be brief.

"It should come to no one's surprise that I supported the proposal placed before this body. I am also pleased to announce that I supported the amended version, and am gratified that my peers see both the value in the new association and the value in keeping peace among ourselves. But what pleases me best is that this was accomplished without my presence, and with the leadership of my favored pupil, the trainer Chris Parker."

Chris froze as Ron and Michael grinned on either side of him. Some scattered applause began, but Anderson raised one hand and stilled it.

"It has been a singular pleasure to train Mr. Parker, and to see him grown as an independant trainer. I am sure many of you have studied his writings, whether they were combined with my own or the few times he has been allowed himself the credit. I certainly, have learned much. But his modesty aside, I can honestly say that there are few trainers with his love — no, his passion — for the Marketplace and the purposes we serve.

"It is a hard thing, to train a trainer, as many of you well know. But every year spent in this task is well rewarded on a day like this, when I can announce to all of you present that I wish to bestow upon Chris Parker the title of Master Trainer, and I ask for your approval."

The applause and chanting and cheers became an astounding roar, and as a body, the room rose, and Chris swallowed hard. The bruise against his lip was obvious now, and so were two dark red ones on his cheekbones, heightened by the blush that crept up from his collar.

"Get up," Ron said in his ear. "Give 'em a wave, who knows when the fuck you'll see 'em again?"

He stood, bowed again, this time first to Anderson, who was applauding with a look of mild amusement in her eyes, and then to the rest of the room. There were no more announcements, no more speeches. People came over to congratulate him on receiving the new title, a few asked him if he was considering starting his own house. Knots of friends began to form as the private parties were to begin soon, and Michael remembered that he had never even asked Chris if he could attend one.

Now, he was pretty sure he didn't want to.

Anderson left as soon as it was polite, with Ninon at her side. Finally, Chris stood up from the table and Michael shot up after him.

"Is there anything I can do for you, sir?" Michael asked eagerly.

Chris smiled a little. "Yes, Michael, there is. Please enjoy yourself tonight, take whatever invitation pleases you. I give you your freedom until morning, when I or Anderson will see that you are given instructions on departure. I suppose it all depends on what her plans are, so please make sure that you are not hung over or otherwise unavailable to either of us."

"But — but," Michael stammered. "Is there anything — I can do for *you?* Personally? Um — a massage? Another drink? Want some company? Wanna beat the snot out of me?"

Chris laughed. "Excellent use of humor, Michael, very good! Appropriate, too. But no thank you, I am — going to be meditating. So go on and have a good time. I'm sure someone admired by all genders and sled dogs will have no problem finding a welcoming group to play in. You may top or bottom, as it pleases you."

Michael knew better than to argue, but he didn't much want to go off and party, either. He grinned to show that he was fine, and wandered off as though he knew where he was going, and then ended up at the bar sitting by himself, wondering how drunk he could get without causing a crippling hangover.

Ron, typically, had already made an assignation with Juan Matilino and the slave they had shared as a pillow earlier, so after patting Chris on the shoulder, he got up and sauntered out as well.

Chris went back to his room, where he could be easily found. And sure enough, by nine in the evening, the call came. Jiro, in house livery for the first time during the Academy, came to bring him the message. Chris himself had not changed clothing; how do you choose clothing for such an event? It seemed appropriate to be dressed in a tuxedo, with a high collar much in the style of his major-domo formal dress at home, crisp black and white. He pocketed the gold pen that had been his sole graduation gift and followed Jiro over to the other building, passing rooms where music — both instrumental and human — escaped half open doors. He slipped into his shoes when they passed between buildings, and Jiro smiled calmly, waiting for him without a note of impatience.

Slaves carrying trays of beer and sake and champagne passed them with respectful smiles and nods. Anderson's floor seemed quieter. Jiro knocked and bowed Chris in, and Chris wondered if that would be the last time he would get a deeper bow from him. He acknowledged it correctly, walked in, and stood where he had been earlier, when he had explained himself to Anderson. Jiro did not enter the room, but closed the door quietly.

They were all dressed as they had been for dinner. Champagne was open on the sideboard, and it seemed that Tetsuo and Anderson had already drunk a toast or two before Chris arrived. The box containing the collar was on the table, along with Tetsuo Sakai's personal chop, next to the newly drawn up contracts.

"As your trainer of record, I have examined the contract and it is acceptable to me, Mr. Parker," Anderson said without preamble. "Do you wish to examine it?"

"With your permission, Trainer."

She handed it up to him. He glanced at the first page and noted that it was in fact a three year contract with an optional two year continuation at the same terms, no renegotiation, no rise in fees. All he could do was say yes or no. It was a style of contract he never advised people to take, the stakes in it were too high.

Excellent. Quickly, with a practiced eye, he swept through standard wording and mentally absorbed the special stipulations. Tetsuo had reserved the right to pierce, tattoo and brand him, although he had promised not to alter any existing body modifications. He had the right to profit from Chris' professional services as a trainer, or to use him in personal or general service, to loan or otherwise arrange for fostering at his will. The usual international riders were there, that Tetsuo would bear the legal costs of getting Chris the proper documentation to work and live in Japan. He promised to provide transportation to the United States and a reasonable amount of time on an annual basis for medical checkups if Chris requested it, to provide any support necessary to keep Chris' medications available to him. And, spelled out in the contract was one line that almost made Chris crack; instead he took a deep, slow breath.

"Client shall present exclusively as male and shall be treated as such."

He wondered who added that line. But he continued through the document until the end, nodded, and laid it down on the table. He would have easily been able to sign it unseen. But that was not what he told his clients to do. He had to follow his own advice.

"Thank you, Trainer."

"If you have nothing else to say, Mr. Parker, then please sign."

Chris pulled the pen out, and if Anderson recognized it, she didn't show it. He knelt carefully, turned the pages on all three copies and signed. His hand, suprisingly, did not shake. He leaned back on his calves as first Anderson and then Tetsuo signed as well. Tetsuo also affixed his chop, as befitted a formal contract.

"Congratulations, Sakai-san. You might not think it right now, but you got a bargain." Anderson gathered two of the three copies and put them to one side as Tetsuo placed the third into a folder.

"Thank you, Sensei Anderson, I am honored to accept my prize." He opened the box, and touched the magnetic key to the smaller of the ceramic disks. It clicked open with a very slight sound, hardly the snap of a key in traditional lock. He turned to Chris and said, in Japanese, "Come."

Chris moved forward on his knees and lowered his head, felt Tetsuo's hands as they clasped the collar around his throat, letting it fall over his shirt collar, over his tie. The identity cylinder fell right over the knot of the tie, and the cool metal slid down the back of his neck. The click of the two joined ends as they locked together again was louder closer to his ear. He felt Tetsuo's hand brush his hair and was startled when it gripped a handful and jerked his head up.

"Before I take my leave of you," Tetsuo said, as Chris' heart pounded, "I wish to inquire about this." He pointed to the bruise on Chris' lip and the slight discoloration and abrasions over the cheekbones. "Previously, of course, this was your matter. But now, it is mine. Is there some fault in this slave which needs correction? Has there been discourtesy which needs addressing?"

Anderson's mouth curled up in a slight smile. "Oh, no, Tetsuo, would I pass on discourteous property? No, that was merely — for my amusement."

"That you still find amusement in this slave is the highest recommendation you could make, Imala," he said, releasing Chris' head. "I thank you for your valuable time, I'm sure there are numerous things you wish to do tonight. I will speak to you in the morning regarding our travel plans."

"Thank you, Sakai-san, I'll see you in the morning."

When his new master rose, Chris did as well, and bowed deeply to Anderson before opening the door. She nodded, and turned away, and he followed Tetsuo — Sakai—sama — out. The chain felt heavy around his throat. He moved naturally into position and followed, struggling to keep the smile from his face.

33 Farewell to Okinawa

Michael woke up in a western bed, and for a moment wondered where he was. Then, he saw the beautiful russet hair touched with gold highlights and remembered that he had come up with enough Italian to make Luciana understand that spending the night with her was definitely a doable thing. Thankfully, Arturo Massimiliano, her boss, had placed no restrictions on *her* sex life.

They had met each other at a party, at Walther's orgy, as a matter of fact. They found each other looking over what was a sea of bodies, and they had smiled ruefully. Soon after that, they left together.

It was strange, making love to a woman — a free woman, he had to wonder about, pay attention to, speak to. He had not really had sex with anyone in a long time without there being a top and a bottom, without there being some understanding that one person was due complete pleasure and the other devoted to providing it, or at least suffering for it.

But it had come back to him, and it had been as magical as it always was, a complete drowning of the senses, a spirit of timelessness falling over him that made him laugh out loud when he came, which made Luciana laugh as well. They rolled over together, his cock still inside her, and she teased him to erection again and rode him pleasantly, murmuring endearments in Italian and playing with his nipples the way that most straight girls never do. Then they showered together, and he couldn't resist getting on his knees under the water and loving her with his mouth, until she gasped and laughed again and they splashed all over the floor, wetting every towel. They fell asleep finally, entwined in each other, and Michael knew a kind of peace he hadn't in a long time.

But when dawn came and light woke him up, he quietly and gently disengaged himself, put on his trousers and his shirt, but didn't bother with buttoning anything up. He just threw his jacket over his shoulder and tiptoed out of the room with his shoes in the other hand.

As he passed into the eastern wing, he saw slaves carrying luggage down to the drive-up area by the western building. Almost all the trainers would be leaving today, a skeleton crew of slaves left to clean and return the ryokan to its former state for the regular staff to find when they returned. Technically, he and Chris had flights out of Okinawa in the late afternoon. He wondered if either of them would be taking one.

He got to his room and slid the door open, and grinned. Ron was laying on his back on the futon, the covers scattered across the floor, totally and impressively naked, and there was the smell of sex in the entire room. Ron lifted his head wearily.

"Well, look who went out tomcatting," he said cheerfully.

Michael raised his hands. "I was given full permission!"

"Yeah, for however long that lasts," Ron said. "He sure didn't show up here last night. I'm assuming he's at the base of one of these overstuffed maxi-pads somewhere right now. Damn, when you already sleep on the floor, where do you put the boy?"

"Wrap him in a blanket and no maxi-pad," Michael snickered.

"Give me a posture-pedic any day," Ron groaned, sitting up. "Well, show me to the bathhouse, junior, I need to freshen up and see what the boss lady has in store for the universe today."

They walked to the communal bathing area, and it was still too early for many people to be up, so they had it to themselves, not counting the attendant slaves. Michael asked, softly, "Ron — sir — did Sakai really put Chris in the hospital once?"

"Yep. Broke two ribs, as I recall, dislocated a shoulder — some other stuff too, I can't remember exactly. Ever see the scar on his cheek? That's from Tetsuo-sama."

"Oh my God! And they let him be a trainer?"

"Two things have to happen to get thrown out for abuse, Mike. One, there has to be a complaint filed — and there wasn't — and two, there has to be an inquiry, and there wasn't. No complaint — no abuse. Besides, Chris is one kinky motherfucker, probably enjoyed it. Didn't tell me about it for a year, if I remember, maybe two, and then I had to drag it out of him."

"But — what's to prevent that from happening again? How can he want to go back to someone who hurt him like that?"

"One, nothing except the man's self control, and two, because I guess there's something to the guy that goes beyond a moments insanity. Keep in mind that he's a big shot in this field. If he was smacking heads and breaking bones left and right, he wouldn't be who he is, he'd be gone. And Chris has filed his share of complaints against abusive trainers and masters, he knows one when he sees one. If he's happy to get sold to this guy, then he must be clear on what he's walking into. I wasn't kidding when I said he was smarter then me."

Michael shook his head sadly. "I don't even know what to think about it all," he said. "Everything's happening so fast."

"You're telling me!" laughed Ron. "I don't even know what day it is!"

When they got back to the room, Chris was there. He was wearing the gray suit that Michael had picked out for him the day before, his shirt still open at the collar and a tie draped around his neck, and there was a Sakai house yukata hanging on the wall. He was busy putting his tuxedo back into a garment bag. His hair was still wet, and he looked wide awake and still rather cheerful.

"Hey, bro'," Ron said, springing into the room and catching him in a hug. Playfully, he sniffed at Chris' hair until Chris laughed and brushed his hands away.

"What on earth are you doing?"

"Sniffing for piss, my kinky brother. Suddenly I remember *everything* you told me about Sakai-sama!" He laughed and released him.

Chris snorted disapprovingly and pulled the sleeves of his jacket down. "And I'm suddenly regretting telling you *anything*, you foul mouthed tell-tale. Kindly do me the courtesy of behaving in a slightly civilized fashion before a novice trainer, if you will."

"Hey, you're in a peppy mood! I guess Sakai-sama rode you hard and put you away wet!" Ron laughed, actually slapping his knee. "Oh, damn, I can't help it. I'm sorry, I'll behave. Don't even listen to me, Mike, I'm a bad influence."

"Yes, sir. Um — sir — I can pack for you, if you like. Can I help with anything?"

Chris nodded. "Yes, thank you. I'll be keeping pretty much everything except for one tux — you can take the round lapeled one back with you. I'll also be sending a list with you, and if you would be so kind as to ask Rachel for her help, I'm sure you will be able to pack a suitable wardrobe for me and ship it."

"Of course! I'll do anything you want!" Michael struggled to keep the desperation out of his voice and didn't exactly manage, but Ron seemed oblivious and Chris did nothing but nod gently in his direction. There came a tapping against the doorframe and Michael turned, saying, "I'll get it."

On the other side, dressed in a yukata himself, was Tetsuo Sakai.

Michael found he didn't need to think. Quickly, he stepped aside and sank gently to his knees, and for once, he beat Chris into formal posture, because Chris had to wait and see who stepped through.

"Sakai-sama," Chris said, as he sank to his knees and bowed.

Michael could barely keep from closing his eyes. I don't want to see him like this, he realized, achingly. Please, someone, send me away! But no one paid any attention to him at all, and frozen in indecision, he could only remain by the door, seeing but trying not to look.

Tetsuo bowed slightly to Ron in greeting, and Ron, suddenly serious, bowed carefully back. Chris raised himself and said, "Please allow me to introduce Mr. Ron Avidan, Master, my elder brother."

"It is a pleasure to meet you, Mr. Avidan," Tetsuo said, offering his hand. "It was kind of you to accompany my friend Sensei Anderson on her journey here."

"Thank you, Mr. Sakai. I've heard quite a lot about you." Ron managed to say this without the slightest hint of humor. "And may I offer my condolences on picking up the most annoyingly perfect slave on the whole planet?"

Tetsuo laughed even as Chris' eyes flashed at his brother. "I have always been confused by the lack of value you Americans place on perfection," he said cheerfully. "Here in Japan, perfection is sought after and admired and cherished."

"Then you will cherish him," Ron said with a crooked smile. "And I'm glad. Nice to meet you, Mr. Sakai, but if you'll excuse me, I have some travel arrangements I need to figure out."

"Of course. It has been my pleasure."

After Michael closed the door after Ron and wished that he could excuse himself too, Tetsuo turned to Chris. "You are packing?"

"Yes, Master."

"I wish to see this strap of yours."

Michael tensed and closed his eyes. Please, please don't beat him in front of me, I don't think I could stand it, he thought.

Chris rose carefully from his knees and found the strap in the drawer and delivered it back to his owner, standing to offer it with both hands and a bow.

Tetsuo turned the worn brown leather over in his hands, caressing it. "This is very fine," he said. "Anderson tells me that it is your property and not hers."

"Yes, Sir."

Tetsuo dropped it deliberately on the floor.

"You may not own this while I own you," he said.

Michael blushed, down the sides of his face and across his throat. Why didn't he send me out? he wondered. Why keep me here for this?

Chris looked down at the strap and up at Tetsuo's face. Their eyes met.

With the slightest of nods, he went back down on his knees and picked it up thoughtfully. He glanced for a brief second at Michael's back, saw the red along his face, and then looked up at his new owner and offered the strap up again.

"Please do me the honor of accepting this as a gift, Master," he said.

"I accept it," Tetsuo said. "I will see you at the main meeting area at ten o'clock."

Chris bowed again, holding position until he heard the door slide shut after Tetsuo. Then immediately got to his feet, went over to Michael and jerked his head up with a hand in his hair. Michael yelped in shock, his face red and his eyes angry and hurt.

"How dare you judge my Master?" Chris asked.

"But — but. . ."

Chris shook him hard. "No buts, Michael. You were sitting here thinking that what was happening was unfair and ugly and shameful and you broadcast it to me and to Sakai-sama and probably to my brother!"

"Yes!" Michael said, squeezing his eyes shut. "Yes, and I'm sorry, but I can't help it, it just seems so harsh. . .why did he have to do it in front of me?"

Chris let Michael go, and squatted down next to him. "Listen to me very carefully, Michael. What he did was his *right*. What I accepted was for me, an intense pleasure that defies explanation. *But no one did anything to you.* You opened the door. You closed the door. But you were not even *here* to Sakai-sama, unless you advertised your presence, which you did.

"You do not have the right to feel offended for me, or angry for me, or humiliated for me, Michael. Only I have the right to those things. But I need you to remember this feeling and watch for it, Michael. You were just in two places at once, you were witnessing what was happening to me and you were identifying with me. *That* is what a good trainer does, Michael. That is how a trainer feels. Otherwise, they may never be able to give a client the advice they need in order to deal with the emotions that are tormenting you right now. I'm sorry I can't be more thorough in this lesson, Michael. But I am compelled to obedience." He leaned forward and kissed Michael on the forehead and said gently, "And I love it, Michael. Believe me. Now get up and help me pack and say no more about it."

Word got out very, very slowly, and several people left before they heard. But the bath slave who overheard Ron and Michael told Ninon's personal slave, who told Ninon, of course, but only after she also told one of Walther Kurgan's favorite bedmates for the week, who after telling the slave who was her husband back at the house they served in in Sweden, teased Walther with the information while she kissed him all along his spine.

Ninon told Corinne while they shared a bath, in French of course, so that the Japanese bath attendant would not understand. But he did understand the names involved, and he asked one of the other slaves traveling with Sakai Tetsuo why everyone was mentioning his name in conjunction with that American trainer who caused all the trouble, and that slave told him that the American had in fact spent the night with Tetsuo and was seen wearing the house livery this very morning. The bath slave argued that Tetsuo-sama could have just lent the gai-jin a robe, after all, they tended to be very shy about their bodies.

But then one of the kitchen slaves interrupted them and said that she had delivered three pots of tea to Sensei-Anderson's room yesterday, and who was her guest? Teusuo-sama. And who served the tea? Pah-kah-san.

The secretarial staff, who would have been the ones to make any contracts were consulted, but true to their profession, they remained noncommittal, saying only that records of all contracts and sales were made available thirty days after filing.

Juan Matilino heard it from Ron, as they drowsily allowed the slave they had shared the night before to thank them for their attentions with massages. He then told his Brazilian friend Conrado, who told his apprentice, Hugo, who had spent an evening in the hot tub with Kim and Michael, and so the minute he saw Kim, he grabbed an interpreter and told her, after which in shock, she told Choi Jin Yong, her trainer, who after slapping her for spreading gossip — the first time that morning this had been the reaction — immediately turned and called his friend Ken Mandarin.

Who, when she got off the phone, stamped her foot angrily and screamed, "You mean I only had to buy him!?" and while Andy and Cindy hid behind the couch, launched into an array of obscenities that they silently rated as one of her best. And then she collapsed onto the couch laughing until they came out and laughed with her, trading confused glances until she explained. At which point the very idea of their former trainer as a slave to such an important and good looking and — well — sadistic man made them both so hot that they begged Ken for an outlet. Ken let them fuck while she called Marcy, who sat Stuart down shortly afterward and told him as well.

The only person Anderson told was Alexandra Selador, in a private meeting. Alex decided to wait until she got home to break the news to Grendel and Rachel. And although of course Shigeo Noguchi already knew — knew before anyone, really, since Tetsuo had announced his intention to do this thing weeks ago, and Noguchi-sama was used to his headstrong pupil getting his own way — Tetsuo had only explicitly told Jiro Abe, when he informed him that at the end of this, his third year in training, he would be going to America, to work with the great trainer Anderson, since Tetsuo had deprived her of Parker's services. He added that the appropriate response to this news would be deep gratitude for this remarkable opportunity and an immediate desire to learn better colloquial English.

Jiro, who had been practicing his more romantic slang with Bronwyn in private, whispered to her over breakfast. She whispered to Dalton, who turned out to be the only one who told no one, only sat back in his chair with a satisfied smile on his face.

So by ten o'clock, when Chris accompanied the slaves who brought his and Michael's luggage out of his room, he was getting a few raised eyebrows, a few knowing smiles, and a few envious ones. Always hating to be the center of attention in a crowd, he ignored them.

Until he found himself face to face with Geoff Negel.

"Good morning, Mr. Parker," Geoff said, looking down at him. Geoff was in traveling clothes, a short sleeve silk shirt and comfortable khakis.

"Good morning, Mr. Negel. I hope you enjoyed this year's Academy."

"I did, thank you very much. Listen, Parker — I was wondering if you might care to confirm or deny a strange rumor I caught this morning."

Around them, conversation stilled and several people moved out of the way, distastefully. Others somehow managed to move closer, among them a rather afronted looking Dalton, who touched Howard Ward lightly on the arm. They two men turned toward the conversation.

"Why Mr. Negel, I didn't realize you listened to rumors," Chris said.

"Oh, of course I do. We all do, it's part of the game, whether we admit it or not. Of course, some of us use rumors as well, don't we?" If that was meant to bait Chris, it failed. Chris merely raised an eyebrow, his face an encouraging blank. Geoff compressed his lips and looked down at him. "But this rumor — I heard that Tetsuo Sakai has purchased you."

"I say, Mr. Negel," said Howard Ward, clearing his throat. "Perhaps this is not an appropriate time . . .''

"The Academy is over," Geoff interrupted firmly. "Besides, if it were true, it's hardly something shameful, is it?"

"But hardly topic of discussion in such a way, Mr. Negel. May I suggest a continuation at some more agreeable time?"

"Yes, Mr. Negel, the rumor is true," interjected Chris. He nodded slightly to Dalton and Mr. Ward. Ward shrugged and nodded grimly in return. "Will that be all?"

"That's a bit snippy for a slave, don't you think, *Chris?*" Geoff smiled slightly, and behind him, Sam Keesey snorted in amusement, just as he was turning away. "You might have to learn to curb that attitude the same way you broke Michael's spirit and made him into an automaton."

Chris smiled, thinly and gently. "As you say, Mr. Negel."

"As I say," Geoff repeated thoughtfully. "You know, I have to wonder whose words you said this week, Chris. At first, along with everyone else, I assumed you were speaking for Anderson. But were you in fact speaking on behalf of our hosts the entire time?"

Michael heard that as he was accompanying Ron to meet up with Anderson. He stopped in his tracks, horrified, barely able to see over the shoulders of the people who were now crowding around the two men.

"Mr. Negel, I can only say that every word I have said this weekend has been my own, including the following; you sir. . .are an arse." Chris straightened his back and shot his cuffs as Geoff frowned. Out of the corner of his eye, Chris could see Dalton shaking in barely-contained laughter. But he looked back up at Geoff, who was taking a breath to respond and cut him off neatly.

"And if you wanted to intimidate a slave not your own by suggesting that you could judge their behavior, I suggest you choose someone who is a little less experienced than I. Now, if you wish to consult with someone about my poor attitude toward you, my Master is Mr. Tetsuo Sakai and he will be here shortly. In the meantime, sir, you are impeding me in my duties and I am forced to ignore you."

Michael found himself laughing with most of the other people there who heard this exchange, and he even heard applause. He saw Geoff's arm move, and wickedly, he thought, oh, yes, yes, Geoff, raise that arm, hit him or grab him or try to, because the next thing you'll know, you'll be counting beams in the ceiling. But Geoff only waved one hand dismissively and turned away, and Chris was granted a wide berth full of grins as he directed the slaves accompanying him where to put their burdens down. He gave only a nod to Dalton, who smiled gently back and inclined his head in that perfect butler bow that was the first thing he had taught Chris when he realized that a curtsey simply *would not do*.

There was no better farewell than that.

People had mostly drifted away by the time Anderson came down with Alexandra and Sakai, and the three of them joined Michael and Ron where Chris had arranged the luggage.

"This is the way it's gonna go, folks," Anderson said. "Mike, you're heading out on tonight's flight as planned, you're going back to Long Island. I'll be in touch with you when I get home, but assume that you will be there until your sale. I am going to Tokyo with Tetsuo for a week — I sure as hell didn't spend a day on planes to turn around and go right home. I might as well see the sights. Ron, I'd like you to stay, just so I can have company on the way back, but if that's not possible, speak up now, and you can ride out to Tokyo tonight."

Ron pursed his lips. "You buying this trip?" he asked bluntly.

"My treat."

"Then I'll call home and get someone to feed the cat," he said cheerfully. "Like I'd turn down a week in Japan! Look out Shinjuko!"

"Excellent," Tetsuo said cheerfully. "There will be students and slaves at your service to make sure you enjoy your stay."

Ron laughed. "Gonna send my own brother to serve me breakfast in bed, Mr. Sakai?"

"Ah, regretfully, if that is your desire, I will be unable to fulfill it. After staying here one additional day to help in the clean up, Chris will be going to Kobe, to join my apprentice Jiro Abe in making my new school ready there."

Chris' head snapped up — apparently this was the first time he had heard this. But he displayed no other sign of surprise or dismay, only interest in hearing his instructions.

"Oh," Ron said, a little deflated. "Well — with your permission, Mr. Sakai, I'd like to say good bye before I head off with you all."

"Of course, Mr. Avidan." Sakai-sama nodded at Chris, who excused himself from that company with a bow and walked outside with his brother.

"Wow, well, this happened kind of fast," Ron said with a grin.

"Yes," Chris said. "I'm sorry there wasn't more time to prepare you."

"Shit, I'm not the one in the new collar, Chris. And you've been preparing for this your whole life." He looked down at Chris and sighed. "Do you want me to tell the parents anything?"

"Tell them I've moved to Japan. With any luck, it'll make their therapy easier if they don't think they might run into me somewhere." Chris smirked.

"Fine with me. You got any stuff I need to look after?"

"Nothing," Chris said. "Thank you. But write to me — and send me a photo of you, will you? And one of that new boy of yours."

Ron slapped his forehead. "Jeeze, that's what I didn't tell you! He's no boy, kiddo. This one's as old as I am. And guess what — he lives in New Jersey!" He laughed, and Chris smiled. "Man, is that a sign of my age, or what? But I like him, I really do. He makes me laugh."

"Good, you're much too serious," Chris said, punching him. They hugged.

"Take care of yourself, baby bro'. And take care of handsome Mr. Sakai, too."

"I will."

"But tell me one thing — did he really piss on you?"

Chris pushed his brother away. "Oh for crying out loud, Ron!"

"Well, did he?" Ron's eyes were wide and innocent and pleading, and he looked about ready to throw himself down on his knees and beg.

"Go to Tokyo, Ron. Get out of my Master's bathroom."

"I bet he'll tell me!"

"Then you'd better ask him!"

Michael didn't have a chance for a private good-bye. He wanted to ask for one, but didn't know whom to ask. Anderson? He was technically hers again. Sakai-san? But could he even talk to him without permission? That sort of hierarchical tangling was too complicated, and by the time he figured out that he should ask Anderson if it was OK to ask Sakai-san, it was time to go, and Chris was not in the group waiting at the gate while the cars lined up for the airport. He was upset — he hated to think that his last scene with Chris had been that angry moment when Chris was trying to explain that trick of empathizing with slaves, angry that Michael had dared to feel badly toward his new Master. Michael wanted to apologize, and most of all, he wanted to thank Chris for everything, especially for what he had learned here in Okinawa. But he didn't get a chance, only got to wave from the car that he got into with a somber Alexandra Selador. And that was when he realized that maybe he wasn't the only one who would miss Chris. He couldn't even imagine what Rachel would say.

But he promised that he would do Chris proud. I'll be the best trainee they've ever seen, he thought. And I'll write to him and thank him in a letter.

Chris made himself useful in Sakai-sama's staff as much as he could, with Jiro's enthusiastic help. No one treated him like a strange outsider, no one stared at him rudely or sneered at him. And when Sakai-sama and Anderson left together, with more than half the staff, Jiro had stood next to him as they bowed the car away, repeatedly saying good-bye until it was out the gates and down the road.

"I will find a room for us," Jiro said, as soon as they were out of sight. His r's slurred a little, but his diction was very clear otherwise. "And I will send a — a — supa-visa? for you, to tell you what to do, is that acceptable?"

"Hai, arigoto," Chris said. They had agreed to speak only each other's language to each other as much as they could, to better practice. At least when Sakai-sama wasn't around. Sakai-sama had already instructed Chris that he was to speak whatever language the Master was speaking to him, and if, by the end of one year he was not suitably fluent in daily speech, he would be subject to discipline. That seemed more than reasonable, especially since it seemed that no one was actively hostile toward him this time around.

Jiro walked away, leaving Chris to stroll slowly toward the main outdoor pavilion, where so many discussions had taken place over the past few days. He could see people watering the pathways and scrubbing the benches, but one bench was free. He sat down and at last drew his treasure out of his breast pocket.

Romeo y Julieta. Mandarin had *damn* good taste. He unfolded his pocket knife and snipped the end neatly, and rolled it gently in his mouth. Putting the knife away, he pulled out his lighter — when was the last time he used this, a year? He had left it with Rachel at the house on Long Island, thinking that he would not smoke when he went to Anderson's. That lasted for about a week.

He lit the cigar carefully, drawing the smoke into his mouth and letting it swirl out again. Dropping the lighter in his pocket, he leaned back and enjoyed the rich taste of the tobacco. Congratulations to me.

When he was about one quarter down its length, an older Japanese woman approached him and bowed. "Excuse me, sir," she said, in lilting, accented English. "Are you Pah-kah-san?"

"Yes, Elder Sister," he replied in Japanese, sitting up. "Are you my supervisor?"

"Elder Sister?" she tittered nervously. "You are a brother to me?"

He reached inside his shirt collar and brought out his new chain. She leaned forward and examined the chop on the cylinder and sucked in her breath and tittered again.

"Ah, so, you are my Younger Brother!" she laughed. "A fortunate Younger Brother, fortunate in your Master!"

"Thank you, I am. Please tell me what I can do, Elder Sister." He stood up, and to his amusement, found that he was actually taller than her.

"Well, Younger Brother, what can you do? Can you clean tatami? Can you polish silver? Clean floors?"

He laughed, understanding every one of her options. Perhaps his Japanese wasn't as forgotten as he thought. "Yes, Elder Sister, I can do all those things. Please — use me — as you think best, and excuse my bad Japanese."

"Oh, but your Japanese is very excellent, Younger Brother! Come with me please, and put out that stinky thing, we must not leave that smell in the building!"

Chris laughed again, and obeyed her and followed her inside. Yes, he thought. I can do anything, now.

Epilog

Six months later

Chris Parker bowed his way politely out of his Master's suite and closed the door gently. Rubbing his wrists one at a time to work down the slight red marks, he walked down the hall to the stairs instead of taking the elevator. When Tetsuo was in town, he rarely had the time to get in a run, so he had gotten used to taking the stairs whenever possible just to keep up a little aerobic activity.

Two floors down, he passed a slave who was industriously polishing the banisters. They, like every other part of the building, got cleaned thoroughly on a schedule that made plenty of work for any number of staff or trainees, and in a nation of people who grew up cleaning the halls of their schools as children, it was done without a second thought. She backed away and formally bowed, and murmured, "Good morning, Teacher."

"Good morning, Mariko," he said. "Have you seen Abe-sensei this morning?"

"Yes, Pah-kah-sensei, he was in the dormitory fifteen minutes ago. May I have the honor of taking a message to him?"

"No, thank you, please continue working."

"Yes, Teacher, thank you," she smiled gently, almost shyly and bent to her task again.

The stairways were unheated, and the early spring chill easily penetrated Chris' yukata. He still missed his boots. Later in the day, he would change into a suit and tie again, after the morning meetings were done. But the first thing he wore every day was his household livery. He had in fact finally learned to tie his sleeves back with an ease that suggested that he had been doing it all his life. The jokes about his being a member of the Yakuza had also gotten under control, especially since Sakai-sama's first tattoo was in place.

His Master did not waste time.

There were seven slaves in training here in Kobe, and three junior trainers, all at different levels of skill. The school was a refurbished office building, with Sakai-sama's suite on the top floor and room for everyone to live and work. While everyone else shared dining, work, training and sleeping areas, Sakai-sama had the entire top floor to himself, an almost obscene amount of space and privacy. What's more, it was thoroughly modern in layout and furnishings, as was most of the rest of the building. There was only one floor with traditional tatami rooms, and that chiefly used for training or entertaining. The school could easily sustain two more trainers, a full staff of twelve employees or household slaves and up to fifteen slaves in training, although it was unlikely that they would ever be that busy. Chris and Jiro shared the management duties, although Chris' duties were heavier when Sakai-sama was in town.

Which was, frankly, wonderful, although occasionally exhausting. He had only gotten a few hours of sleep during the night, but his back was deliciously sore. The tradeoffs were certainly acceptable.

He went directly to the office he shared with Jiro and pulled out the day's training schedule. He wrote a few notes about Mariko to pass onto Jiro — technically, she was under Jiro's supervision. While he was writing, one of his clients came in and delivered his second cup of coffee. Thank goodness Sakai-sama was a coffee drinker. Giving it up would have been more challenging than tobacco.

"Hey, you pale excuse for a human being," Jiro said in English, walking in. He was dressed in black jeans, a neat white shirt and a narrow tie. Only his indoor slippers were not completely American, he was probably intending to do some work on the tatami floor later on. He had been encouraged to dress this way to get him used to it, and he was quite pleased with the effect. "I see your lazy behind is finally out of bed today," he continued, waving the slave away.

"At least I was hard at work, pleasing our most honored Master, when some other people just stuff their faces with sweet bean buns and watch wrestling all night long," Chris answered in Japanese.

"At least it is sweet buns in my face and not my face is toilet, OK?" Jiro cackled.

Chris tried to suppress a grin. "I win. That should be 'at least I have sweet buns in my face and not my face in a toilet', Jiro-san, or, 'and not urine in my face.' If you meant to make a — word-trick —" he couldn't recall how to say "pun", "then you could have said 'at least I had sweet buns in my face rather than the Master's buns.' 'Buns' is American slang for buttocks, do you understand what I mean? Besides, you're just jealous."

"Damn! Shit! Fuck!" Jiro said, annoyed. They had been working diligently on colloquialisms, especially insults. "Jealous? Jealous my ass. You keep the Master's love, and his beatings and his *buns*, and I will be happy not to take the extra work." He laughed again, stressing the English word, "love", which he found hilarious for some reason. In truth, there was neither jealousy nor dislike in him. Tetsuo Sakai was truly a trainer of the old school — he did not miss a chance to use any of his under trainers in any way he desired. Jiro had of course, taken all the attention offered him with appropriate gratitude, but it was not, he privately admitted, to his taste. He was glad to be freed from such use, especially by someone who seemed to enjoy it. He never indicated that it was Chris' slave status which made it more endurable or appropriate — only noted that it was best when persons suited to each other sought pleasure together. The two men had grown to be friends, and each was openly sorry that they would soon be separated.

Jiro had spent the first month or two gently asking questions about American culture and some innocuous training questions, and then one night surprised Chris by asking, right out of the blue, "Will Anderson-sensei want to be sexual with me?"

"Well, no," Chris responded.

"No? Not at all?"

"She is well known for not doing so. You can read it in her papers. You might be asked to sexually evaluate any slaves you might be working with, and she may send you to some other trainer who might make that request, but you will not be expected to perform with her."

Jiro digested that with some measure of disbelief. "Will she beat me then, if I am disrespectful or do not perform in my duties?"

Chris smiled a little. "Only if she likes you very much," he had said, and from then on, he and Jiro understood one another.

"So, here is your shitting mail, shitface," Jiro said, handing the envelopes to Chris politely, with both hands. "Please eat shit and die."

"Thank you, beanstalk. Please go away and spare me from your stench."

"Aieee, that was not nice," Jiro said. "But stench is good, better than smell. Beanstalk is good, too, Shorty, but not very dirty. I will have an excellent insult for you later. I am going to breakfast, are you coming?"

"I've already eaten."

"Yes, I bet you have!" Jiro laughed and mimed cocksucking, and made exaggerated choking sounds and Chris tried very hard not to blush. He had forgotten how explicit and ribald the Japanese trainers — and slaves — could be about the sexual activities around them. It was especially hard to handle such casual, borderline insulting jabs at sex with the Master, something never

— never! — done in either British or American Marketplace culture. But the rule was as long as the Master didn't hear — or, failing that, if he was flattered — then it might be all right.

But it was open season, of course, on those of lower ranking who provided Master with such diversions. It had taken a little time — made worse by the fact that anyone could see that Chris was uncomfortable with any discussion of what went on beyond the eyes of his peers and juniors between himself and his owner. The very fact that he could be sensitive over such a minor thing made it even more fun to tease. His only defense was to surrender to it.

"It is true that the Master is huge and virile," he said, choosing his words carefully. "Unlike the many examples of small and . . . puny men I would have to choose from when he is not here. Do you have wonder that I devour every inch of him when I can?"

"Ha! Now I win — that should be 'is it any wonder,' I think." Jiro giggled happily. Chris dutifully repeated the phrase until he got it right, and Jiro excused himself with a polite bow.

Chris examined the air mail envelope on the top of the stack of mail and slit it open carefully. The return address was unfamiliar, but the handwriting wasn't. He sipped his cooling coffee as he read the slanted script.

Dear Chris;

I'm so sorry to have to write you, I really wish I could talk to you in person, to explain. But I guess this is the only way I can do this without making a fuss, because no one will tell me how to call you and I don't want to bother your master or make trouble for you in your new life.

I'm leaving training.

There, I wrote it. I tried to write this letter five times and I could never get it out. I know you must be angry right now, and I don't blame you. I'd be angry if I were you, hell, a saint would be angry. But I knew I had to tell you myself, and I thought I'd explain what happened.

I fell in love.

Sounds stupid, right? I mean, what do I know about love? But that's what happened to me, really.

I met her at Alex and Grendel's house. You've actually met her yourself, her parents own two slaves that you helped train! Mr. and Mrs. Cameron, from Manhattan. In case you don't remember, he's a television executive, and she's a newscaster. Their daughter — my fiancée! — is Claire. She's beautiful, smart — you'd like her. She remembered you, said she thought you were very impressive. In fact, the fact that I trained with you seemed to impress her parents a lot, when they found out that I was a trainer in training and not a slave.

I guess I'm getting ahead of myself.

Well, I told you that Alex and Grendel were allowing me more time off and stuff as I took over more responsibilities. Claire asked me to go out with her one night after we met, and I did, and it was like magic. We seemed to know each other so well. So I asked her out and she asked me again — and the next thing you know, we were dating.

I called Anderson to ask her what I should do, and she said that if I wanted to, there was nothing stopping me from dating. I knew what she wasn't saying — that the only thing in my way was that I was gonna be sold as a slave for two years in a few months, but I couldn't stop seeing Claire.

I just couldn't.

And finally, I told Claire what I had promised to do, and we talked about a future together and suddenly, I realized that I wanted to be with her more than I wanted to be a classically trained trainer.

I'm so, so sorry. Can I say it a hundred times? I wish I could.

I proposed last week, and she said yes. I can't believe it, I'm nothing compared to her, poor, dumb, and now a promise breaker, but she said yes.

Naturally, Anderson was pretty pissed, as I am sure you are as well. I sent her a letter too, after she hung up on me twice. But we talked again last night, and she said that it was better I figured it out now than wasted some owner's time and money, and boy, is she right. I hope you see it that way too.

So, I made up a resume and I think that Claire's dad will pull a few strings and get me a job down at the studio he runs. I figure my Communications degree will finally come in handy, right? And we set a date for the fall. I'll send you an invitation, although I guess you wouldn't come even if you could. I'm so sorry. I keep writing that, and I wish I could give you one of those perfect apologies you were always on me about, in person.

You made a difference in me, Chris, I hope you know that. I think you made me a better man. No, I know it. And even though I let you and Anderson down, I hope you find it in your heart to forgive me. It seems you were right all the time. I was not made to be a trainer, or even a slave.

But you know what? My new in-laws said that they'd give us a slave or down payment on a house or a co-op for a wedding present. So I just might become a slave owner! Now, that's funny.

Your friend,
Michael "Dingo" LaGuardia

Chris sighed and folded the letter up and put it back in the envelope. He flipped open his calendar and wrote in a small note to remind himself to send a gift. Then he got up and stretched, and went to find Jiro and start the training day. When Tetsuo came down, all the slaves would be prepared and arrayed for his inspection and the trainers would be tightly in control and everything would be perfection.

About the Authors

Laura Antoniou

Laura Antoniou's work has become well-known in the erotically alternative community as the creator of the Marketplace series (The Marketplace, The Slave, The Trainer, and The Academy), originally written under the name Sara Adamson. One Marketplace character also appears in her first book, The Catalyst, but she leaves the reader to figure that out. The only independently written Marketplace short story, "Brian on the Farm," appears in Lawrence Schimel and Carol Queen's ground-breaking anthology, Switch Hitters: Lesbians Write Gay Male Erotica, and Gay Men Write Lesbian Erotica (Cleis), which has been published in English and in German.

Antoniou has also had great success as an editor, creating the Leatherwomen anthologies which highlight new erotic work; By Her Subdued, a collection of stories about dominant women; and No Other Tribute, which features submissive women. Her nonfiction anthologies include Some Women, and an homage to author John Preston entitled Looking for Mr. Preston. Antoniou's books have been published in the United States, Germany, Japan, and Korea, to international acclaim.

Antoniou's short stories also appear in other anthologies, most recently in SM Classics, edited by Susan Wright; Things Invisible To See: Gay and Lesbian Tales of Magic Realism, edited by Lawrence Schimel; The Second Coming, edited by Pat Califia and Robin Sweeney; Once Upon a Time: Erotic Fairy Tales for Women, edited by Mike Ford; Ritual Sex, edited by Tristan Taormino and David Aaron Clark; and Best Lesbian Erotica 1997, edited by Tristan Taormino. Antoniou was also a columnist for Girlfriends magazine from 1995-1997, the submissions editor for Badboy and Bi-Curious magazines from 1995-96, and is a regular contributor to The SandMUtopia Guardian.

Antoniou is currently finishing the fifth book in the Marketplace series, entitled The Reunion, which is expected out sometime in 2000, and beginning the sixth book, entitled The Inheritor. She is also currently working on a collection of her short stories, and a new book titled Serious Player.

M. Christian

M. Christian's work can be seen in Best American Erotica, The Mammoth Books of Erotica series, Best Gay Erotica, Friction, Quickies 2, and over one hundred other books and magazines. He is the editor of the anthologies Eros Ex Machina, Midsummer Night's Dreams, Guilty Pleasures, and (With Simon Sheppard) Rough Stuff: Tales of Gay Men, Sex and Power (from Alyson books). A collection of his short stories, Dirty Words, will be out sometime next year also from Alyson Books. He also writes columns for www.scarletletters.com, www.bonetree.com, and www.playtime.com. He thinks WAY too much about sex.

Michael Hernandez

Michael Hernandez is a rather twisted, gender variant imp who speaks nary a word of Dutch. Writing credits include a sex column in the FTM Newsletter and contributions in Transliberation: Beyond Pink and Blue, edited by Leslie Feinberg (Beacon Press), Looking Queer, edited by Dawn Atkins (Hayworth Press), Dagger: On Butch Women, edited by Lily Burana and Roxxie Linnea Due (Cleis Press), and The Second Coming, edited by Pat Califia and Robin Sweeney (Cleis Press). He also appears in Transmen & FTMS: Identities, Bodies, Genders & Sexualities by Jason Cromwell (University of Illinois Press). Mike has a penchant for polar bears and fishnet stockings, but prefers to keep these separate. An avid addiction to the internet ensures that the inner-voices are kept at bay, so write — Lbear@koan.com

david stein

david stein has spent decades looking for a Master with a will of iron, a heart of gold, a mind like a steel trap, and the patience of a saint. In the meantime, he overworks for a living in New York City and puts his heart into his educational and erotic writing about BDSM and D/s. Credits include guest-editing issue 14 of International Leatherman magazine (the special issue about real-life gay Master/slave relationships), six years of "Bond+Aid" safety columns in Bound & Gagged magazine, an essay on "what slaves need" in SM Classics edited by Susan Wright (Masquerade); two pieces in the anthology The Horsemen: Leathersex Short Fiction edited by Joseph Bean (Leyland), and additional fiction and nonfiction in Checkmate/Dungeon Master, Mach, Powerplay, and Drummer. Some of the work he is proudest of can be found on his Web pages at http://lthredge.com/ds, including several chapters from his still-unfinished novel about a gay Master/slave relationship, "Carried Away." In 1980 david co-founded Gay Male S/M Activists

(GMSMA), now the world's largest gay male s/m organization, and he served GMSMA in a variety of offices through 1992. Among other achievements during that time, he coined the terms "pervertable" and "leatherfest," and it seems likely that he originated the phrase "safe, sane, and consensual" as applied to s/m. Online he founded and manages the gl-subs mailing list for queer slaves and other submissives, and he contributes to other lists including gl-asb and theslaveboynetwork.

Cecilia Tan

Cecilia Tan started writing about the same age she started masturbating (about age 5). But she didn't start finishing stories until she came out into S/M at age 23. Now in her 30s, Tan has published dozens of short stories and articles, and is the author of the book Black Feathers: Erotic Dreams. She has contributed to Best American Erotica, Best Lesbian Erotica, Ms. Magazine, Penthouse, and Isaac Asimov's Science Fiction Magazine. She is hard at work on her next erotic book, tentatively titled The Book of Want.

Karen Taylor

Karen Taylor first offered to write stories in the Marketplace universe as a courting gift, which demonstrated its success as a ploy when she and Laura were married in 1998. Other stories have appeared in No Other Tribute and Leatherwomen III both edited by Laura Antoniou (Masquerade), Friday the Rabbi Wore Lace, edited by Karen Tulchinsky (Cleis), and the 1997 Small Press award winner, First Person Sexual, edited by Joani Blank (Down There Press). The first Marketplace story she created, "The Nurse," was written in 1996 and is dedicated to the memory of Michael Max Young. Her current labor of love is the compilation of the Marketplace Codex, excerpts of which will appear on the Marketplace website, http://www.iron-rose.com/marketplace.

Preview: The Reunion

Robin stared at the colorful map glued to the back of driver's seat. There wasn't much to see out the windows, just flashes of highway lights and other cars crawling along with them. She raised her voice above the drone of the wheels and said, "This map is wrong."

"Yes, it is," agreed the driver, nodding vigorously, his turban neat and tight. "It is wrong, no one cared to make it right before it was put in the cars!" He tsked, heavily. "And we had no choice, you know? Just went to the garage that morning and they were there. No one asked us, and we know where all these things are, right? But all we are is drivers, not people. We could be slaves for all they care!"

Robin chuckled and leaned back into her seat. "I know what you mean," she said wryly.

He continued to speak - something about shifts and other drivers being messy - but the engine was lulling, and her false cheer heavy. She had packed some jewelry, but couldn't bear the thought of putting anything on, and her throat felt achingly bare and chilled. She pulled her coat closer around her and was grateful to see the welcome signs for Kennedy Airport at last. She made affirmative noises as the driver spoke, and he seemed pleased by the attention all the way to the curb. She tipped him heavily and stood awkwardly while he unloaded her bags and beckoned to an agent to check them in. Just like at Dulles a month ago, she fumbled, forgetting that they needed photo ID now. Yes, she had packed her own bags. No, no one had given her any strange packages. Yes, they had been with her since she packed them.

Which was not entirely true. One of the bags had been in storage for years. She had not needed her formal dresses since she had a life outside of the Marketplace. When she pulled the wardrobe box she had stored them in out, she was surprised to find that most of them still seemed fashionable.

I'm the best dressed slave in the joint, she thought, watching the burly man toss her garment bag onto the conveyor, the special green tag vanishing under the skirting as it went through the little door.

Not any more, she reminded herself. She took the packet containing her ticket and all the luggage receipts back from the man who helpfully repeated the gate information for her. She had to check what he had written down anyway.

It was surprisingly busy in the terminal; of course, all sorts of flights to Europe took off at night. A young man carrying a duffel bag bumped into her, and she almost found herself backing away with a bow of shame, but he was gone before she was finished struggling with the impulse.

"It's going to take some time to get used to the soft world," the nice man told her during her exit interviews in DC. "Don't push yourself too hard to fit in too fast. If you haven't been allowed to drink, don't go out to a bar and get drunk. Give yourself time to feel comfortable again. We don't recommend one night stands for a while, either. And don't worry about little moments of fear or confusion, they are normal. Call me, or the emergency number at any time if you need help - we'll be here for you."

It had seemed so strange, so softly therapeutic. Some of it was obvious, at first. But the second night in her hotel room in New York, she felt a strong urge to go down to the bar and find the most attractive person attracted to her - no matter which gender - and take them back to that large cold room and just fuck until she lost her senses.

That was when the phone rang, and a voice asked her, very politely, to please hold for Anderson.

She looked up at the tote board and glanced back to the ticket in her hand. It was a long walk to her gate; wasn't it always? And what was with checking in two hours before a flight anyway? There was a paperback in her purse, something light, a mystery. It had looked good when she picked it up, but suddenly she had no interest in reading it. And as she passed them, the newsstands beckoned her with magazines she hadn't glanced at in years. She now planned to spend an uncomfortable hour in one of these plastic seats and then six hours crammed in with other tourists - what was she going to do with all that time? What on earth was she doing, period?

Running away, whispered a little voice in her head.

Bullshit, she thought right back at it. I'm taking some time to think. I'm entitled. I'm expected to. It's the right thing to do.

People were already lining up to get their boarding passes. She joined them with a sigh and handed over her envelope to the cheerful woman behind the counter. Her hair was red and curly, like a grown up Little Orphan Annie, but her eyes were sharp and dark, dark gray. "Good evening, Ms. -" pause to read the ticket, even as her fingers flew across her hidden keyboard,

"Cassidy! Going to the homeland, are you?"

"Never been there before," Robin admitted.

"Oh, you'll love it, it's beautiful!" She smiled again, and this time, Robin could feel something a little more genuine in her warmth. As usual, this startled her. She couldn't help but try to smile back.

"Well then! It looks like your upgrade came through," the woman was saying, as a printer started to churn.

"My what?"

"You've been upgraded to Business Class, Ms. Cassidy. Your seat is on the boarding pass. Thank you for choosing to fly with us!"

Robin blinked and looked down at the papers, at the boarding pass sticking out of the top.

"But - I didn't ask for an -"

"You may use our executive lounge until boarding time, Ms. Cassidy," the agent said, waving an elegant hand toward a nearby corridor. "Enjoy a taste of Irish hospitality before you even get there."

Robin took the ticket and walked away, suddenly realizing that she shouldn't argue with someone telling her she might escape the prison of coach class. It's all a mistake anyway, she thought, pushing the door to the lounge open. I'll sit on the plane and someone will figure it out and I'll be packed in the back before you know it. But I might as well have a real Irish coffee while they're confused.

She ended up having two, and felt a little more relaxed as a result. Unfortunately, the whiskey also had its other well-known effect. She had picked an American published Irish newspaper out of a rack by the door, and had turned every page from front to back without registering a single thing before she realized that she wanted to cry again.

No more crying! she told herself sternly. There is nothing to cry about. You are fabulously lucky. You got to live a life people only dream of. You had happy years, many happy years. You've got enough money to keep the wolves away for a while, and infinite options for the future. And memories are a kind of wealth, too.

And there were some great memories. Tons of great memories, from the thrill of being trained and sold to the fascinating reality of negotiating the life of a slave in a household that had more slaves than free people, to the incredibly difficult but endlessly rewarding life of being a single person's single slave.

If only she could take comfort in these cut and dry descriptions of her life! How nice it all looked on paper, three contracts well served, high recommendations from her owners, seven years in a collar, how wonderful for her.

Yippee for me, she thought, turning the paper over again. The cocktail waiter hovered, asking silently if she wanted another mind-numbingly good, whiskey rich coffee, but she asked him instead for some seltzer, a twist of lime, please.

She did have a treasure trove of wonderful memories, she thought. Think of how many people don't even have that!

Think of waking up every morning and getting coffee and breakfast ready for a woman who hadn't had that kind of pampering treatment in years, seeing her smile as she rolled over in bed, hearing her scratchy thanks as she allowed pillows to be rearranged and papers to be arrayed.

Think of the satisfaction of getting all the "little things" done, being home to get and send packages, meet repair people and then learning to do the repairs herself. Running errands, cleaning, cooking, shopping, keeping the home in order so that when its owner walked in the door, there were no worries, nothing that needed immediate attention.

Her trainer, Chris Parker, had laughed once, well, he had grinned that wry, crooked smile of his, as he told her that many slaves ended up doing all the very things once routinely expected of housewives. She had shuddered; it didn't seem very erotic at the time.

Odd how that had changed.

Not that dusting the ceiling fans and folding sheets and pricing cilantro ever made her wet; she was never that much into housekeeping. But the satisfaction she got when the last detail had been wrestled into place, the last piece of china set, the bed always clean and welcoming and sensual - was nothing short of intoxicating.

And Monica's appreciation was even better. Every time she went hunting for something and found it where it should be, or came home after a long trip to find a car waiting for her at the airport and hot food and warm sheets waiting at home, she purred with delight. Robin often surprised her owner with that Holy Grail of slavery, anticipatory service, bringing a drink just as Monica had decided she wanted one, or making a favorite dessert just at the right time, producing some odd object or file right as Monica had decided she needed it. And every time that happened, Monica's eyes would light up, and a big smile would crease her face and she'd say, "Robin, I don't know what I'd do without you!"

Don't even think of that snappy, smart mouthed question lingering at the back of your mind, Robin warned herself. It's not nice. It's not proper. It is not what an experienced, valuable slave should be thinking.

Think instead of one of the really good days. Like the day Monica closed on the new house.

Robin had gone with her to the closing, holding the briefcase of paperwork, the various checks and forms. Monica, flush with overwhelming success, had both a lawyer and her 'personal assistant' on hand to make sure that nothing was a surprise, that everything went smoothly. And everything had been going so perfectly, it was hard to imagine that anything could turn against her.

In two years, she had gone from an underpaid, overworked left-wing political lobbyist to an overworked and finally, in her opinion, properly compensated left-wing political lobbyist. Finally, someone had made the right offer, the one that would make it easier to leave behind cramped, shared office space and a sense of righteousness. Righteousness, she had often said, had a price of its own. It was high time she stopped paying it.

With the security of a steady, high paying job, she could finally look to her well-managed investments and make the big plunge. Get out of her dark, narrow row house and into a sprawling, light filled home with a yard and a garage, a place large enough to hold fundraising dinner parties and just-for-fun pool parties. A place, she had joked, big enough to keep a slave nice and busy.

And since Robin had just joyfully signed a three year contract with her, there was no doubt who that busy slave was going to be.

And so she closed on the new house with a minimum of trouble and drove right out there with Robin at her side. They pulled the car into the garage and walked deliberately to the front door so Monica could feel like it was a formal occasion. The empty house, echoing, had a familiar feel already. Robin in particular had been all over it with a flashlight and a notepad and a book on house inspection under her arm. But it was thrilling to walk with Monica as they circled through the building, each room nothing but color and space. They got to the master bedroom suite, with a dressing room and a private bathroom with a Jacuzzi tub and separate shower stall, and that was where Monica said, "Strip."

Robin's fingers shook in the way they rarely did - after all, she was a very experienced slave now, and beyond such nervousness. But the sheer emptiness of the house, and the way everything seemed stark and open, was almost scary. And Monica's command had been unexpected.

But she took all her clothing off, carefully and gracefully, and laid the pieces on the floor in neat precision. Monica watched her without moving, and Robin was used to being watched, too. But it was exciting nonetheless.

"Do you know what this house is?" Monica asked, with a slight smile.

"No, Monica, what do you mean?" Robin's breath was quickened. She always used Monica's proper first name, never called her ma'am or mistress, or the more familiar Mo, as her friends did.

"How many rooms does this palace have?"

"Ten, Monica, not counting the basement or the bathrooms." Robin could list the exact dimensions of each one, too.

"So. . ." Monica stepped closer to Robin and gently touched one erect nipple, making Robin shiver. "So - including the basement and the garage and all the bathrooms, that's - fifteen new places you'll have to be fucked in, isn't it?"

Robin could barely keep herself from giggling with delight. She smiled and blushed instead and nodded. "Yes, Monica!"

"And fifteen new places for you to get me off, isn't that right, too?" Monica's hand trailed down Robin's body, to her shaved pubic mound, touching the rings there. Robin immediately slid her legs apart more and moaned.

"Oh, yes, Monica, yes, please let me serve you in every room! Tonight!" Together, they finally laughed, but Monica was so close now, and Robin was already wet, and when Monica hugged her close and kissed her, Robin's body shook with need.

They fell to the floor naturally, Monica cupping Robin's breasts in her hands and pinching the nipples sharply, until Robin whimpered. The carpet was rough against her back as Monica pushed her all the way down and took hold of Robin's labia rings, hooking one finger through them and tugging. Heavy gauge and set well into Robin's outer labia, the pressure was like being led along by her clit. Her cunt throbbed with every jerk and twist of Monica's fingers.

"Maybe I would have gotten a better deal if you blew the agent, hmm?" Monica teased. It was an old joke between them now, Robin's bisexuality. Monica had few male friends, period, and was not interested in using Robin as either bait or reward or bribe for any of her various professional colleagues. (Not that this would have been a new experience for Robin, whose last owners had used her for that exact purpose more than once.) But it didn't stop her from suggesting that she should, teasing Robin with improbable scenarios such as sleeping with hotel managers to get the Presidential suite, or sucking off the fast-talking, cheap suit wearing real estate agent who had taken so long to figure out that no, Monica would not have to check with a man somewhere to do anything about buying her own house.

"I bet if you just took him into the back office and sucked his cock, he'd forget about where my husband or boyfriend or sugar daddy was," Monica had whispered to Robin one frustrating day. Robin had blushed as Monica continued to speculate how big that cock was, and whether Robin could find it, and if so, whether it would take three or four minutes, and whether he would whine or whimper when he came. Whimper, was her decision, just as he came back with a smile and another inane question.

If he didn't have the house as an exclusive, they might have gone elsewhere. But they dealt with him, and eventually he stopped wondering and started leering, but by that point, there was a mortgage ready and a price agreed upon and there just wasn't anything else he could do to delay things.

And Robin didn't have to suck his cock. But she could imagine the humiliation of it, the strange moment of disorientation when an owner tells you to do something unpleasant or unexpected, when even the best instinct to serve doubts the command heard.

As Monica whispered to her, Robin struggled to keep her thighs apart and not just buck up against her fist, her fingers entwined in the rings, her knuckles pressing against warm, slick cunt lips. The carpet scraped her back nicely, and the stark light of the simple lighting fixture that had replaced the ornate one they had seen earlier was so unnaturally bright in her eyes. So exposing against her naked body, especially when Monica was still fully dressed.

"So many boys you could have serviced to ease my way, cutie," Monica was saying. "The house inspector. That banker we spoke to before I went to Patty. The architect. The seller himself - and his high powered lawyer. Hell, I could have just invited the whole pack of 'em to a hotel room and let them gang bang you and sign the next morning. You might have liked that, don't you think? Five guys and their hard cocks, all for you? One in your mouth, one in your pussy, one up your tight little ass. . .what do you think the others would have done, just watch? Or would they have you jerk them off, one in each hand? Can you see it?"

Yes, Robin could, and it was terrible, cheap and tawdry, the men all perfectly unhandsome and crude. She could smell their beer and whisky breath, taste their excitement and sweat, feel their hands on her body as Monica rocked her closed fist against her cunt.

"Oh, noooo," she had whispered back, afraid to make more noise in this empty, echoing room. An orgasm was imminent - already! But Monica could do that to her, with her hand or her voice alone, sometime with as little as a look.

"You're right," Monica said suddenly, and she let go of the rings and laughed as Robin gasped, surprised every time, dismayed every time, but also accepting and never sullen.

"You're right, I just couldn't do that to you," Monica laughed. "But you never know, one day I might - unless you keep me happy in every one of these rooms. . ." She stood up, and Robin moved to follow her, but Monica pressed her slave back down with the heel of her shoe, and then hiked up her own skirt and pulled her panties down. Robin smiled and lay back as Monica knelt down, straddling her shoulders, her own pussy covered with dark, close cropped hair.

"I'll do my best, Monica," Robin said mischievously, as she licked her lips.

"You always do, my love," Monica had said with a laugh. "Yes, you always do!"

So, how are you doing without me now, Robin thought suddenly, that terrible, bitter thought she had successfully kept back before. It escaped her now with all of its disappointment and anger and self-pity, and she almost swayed in her chair from the intensity of it. She hadn't realized that her eyes were closed. There was a glass in front of her, beads of moisture dotting the sides and soaking the paper napkin underneath it. A limp wedge of lime was crushed against one side. She stared at it and forced herself to drink some, the bubbles harsh in her tight throat. I am not going to cry, she told herself again, as she fished a couple of bills from her purse and tossed them onto the table. It was time to board and find out who was really in her upgraded seat anyway.

For the first time since she flew on business for the auction house she had once worked for, she boarded first. The smiling steward at the Business Class compartment directed her to the left side of the plane, and when she got to the wide leather seat, she found that she was holding the boarding pass for the window seat.

For a moment, she was actually disappointed, which made her laugh. She hated the window seat, didn't like being trapped against the side of the aircraft, clouds and water and land her constant companions. She always requested an aisle seat when she flew.

But a window seat in Business Class is better than an aisle seat in coach, she thought, as she slid in. A stewardess came by, and asked if she would like a pillow or a blanket and passed her a little courtesy kit.

"Do you know if there's an available aisle seat in Business Class?" Robin asked, almost laughing at her own boldness.

"We're quite booked up, Miss," the young woman said cheerfully. "But I can inquire for you after we are aloft, if you like. Perhaps your seat mate might trade. Why don't you take it now, and see if that will work?"

"Thank you," Robin said. She declined the pillow and blanket and gingerly sat in the aisle seat, marveling at the room and comfort. This really is the only way to fly, she thought. She declined the champagne, feeling a little woozy from the two Irish coffees already.

Other people made their way into the plane, and she could hear the crowds obediently shuffling down the narrow aisles toward the coach section. As the other Business Class passengers arranged themselves comfortably, she gave her first thought to who might be her seat mate.

Please, she thought, please, not some chatty old lady who wants to know what a nice girl like me is doing all alone. Or a little-bit-too-friendly businessman who wants to know if I can meet him for dinner in Limerick one night. Or even someone my age who will ask some innocent question like "so, simple, and you won't panic. Remember that you don't have to answer every question quickly and honestly any more, but don't go overboard making up lies, either, you'll only end up digging a pit for yourself to fall in."

"I'm an art appraiser, and a buyer," she whispered to herself. "Between jobs right now. I was a housekeeper. I was a professional companion. I used to be a slave. Yeah, funny thing, isn't it? Free now, isn't it a bitch?"

She started to shake, and to combat the feeling, turned toward the window and wrapped her arms around herself. Suddenly, she didn't want to be here at all, not on this plane of happy vacationers, not even sharing this wide, soft seat for a few hours, not with a bunch of strangers in some country she didn't know, castle or no castle. She wanted, like Dorothy, to just go home.

But there wasn't a home. There wasn't a family to welcome her back, to praise her for her success, to love her unconditionally and listen to all her stories. She had visited her parents' home several times during her enslavement period, gone there for Christmas once, but her world was now entirely alien to them. Her mother never got over the disappointment when Robin told her she had given up her "job" in California to move in with a woman in Washington DC. It was hard enough for her family to understand that she was bisexual - she never even tried to tell them that she was a slave. No, there was nothing there but that confused parent love any more, no real connection but one of blood. She had no family connected to her by soul. It hurt. It hurt more than being freed, being abandoned.

But that's why you're going to this Reunion thing, isn't it? she asked herself. To meet other slaves, other people like you, who will understand, people who will help. . .

Help me what?

Go back to the block? Take another chance on a complete stranger and then get cut loose after two years, or get stuck in some weird place I might not like for even longer?

Help me get sold to someone I'll helplessly fall in love with and then wait until they want someone new and have to smile as I pack up my life to move on?

Help me leave the Marketplace all together? To do what? Get another job at a museum or an auction house, so I can get another small apartment and eat more take-out Chinese dinners while I dream about the great experiences I had once?

I'm nuts to think anyone can help me with this, she decided. I'm nuts, period. I need to hide. I'm gonna go back to the hotel and hide.

She almost bolted out of the seat to leave, but was instead frozen in place by a familiar voice.

"Might there be someplace to hang these?"

"Of course, sir, if I could just have them, I'll put them in the closet. Shall I stow the bag as well?"

"No, thank you, I will keep it. You're very kind."

Robin couldn't move her limbs. She couldn't even turn her head. It couldn't be true, she was not hearing that voice!

"Hello, Robin," he said lightly, standing next to the seat. "I'm afraid you must take the window seat, I don't like them much."

"Chris," Robin whispered. She half turned and saw him unbuttoning his suit jacket, and then lifting a black leather case into the overhead compartment. When he lowered his arms and smiled down at her, it was true. Somehow, he was really there. Her mouth opened in shock, taking him in as he smiled at her, and then he proved once and for all that it was truly her former trainer in the flesh.

"If you don't move over now," he said softly, in that polite tone that always heralded an uncomfortable command, "I won't spank you when we get there."

Robin gasped nervously and hopped over to the window with a slight blush. As Chris took his seat, he kept himself turned toward her and then said, patiently, "You know, a greeting would be appropriate at this time."

"Hello, Chris."

"Nice to see you, Robin. Now buckle your safety belt and tell me all about your adventures, we have six or seven hours to catch each other up."

That was when the tears started. Now half from relief, but still half bitter, they welled up in her amber colored eyes, and Chris made a tsking sound as he pulled a white handkerchief from his breast pocket. "Now, now," he said, passing it to her. "It'll be all right."

Robin buried her head into his shoulder and missed the entire safety video, but she was sure at last that going to Ireland was a good idea after all.

"Ireland this time of year, what idiot came up with that?" Richard Nelson groused as he looked through his pockets again. "Dammit, Lisa, are you sure they aren't in your purse?"

Lisa raised dark eyes with one elegant eyebrow arching at the tone of his voice. Richard sighed and threw up his hands in despair. "Great! I left them home, it's all my fault. Our luggage will end up in Yugoslavia for all I know."

"There is no more Yugoslavia," Lisa said wryly. "Are you sure they're not in the outside pocket of the garment bag?"

"Mom, Todd's bothering me!"

"Am not! Am not! Are we going to 'slavia, Mom? I thought we were going to Ireland!"

Lisa grabbed both kids firmly and pulled them into positions on either side of her, parking them down on the plastic chairs. Amy, filled with the great dignity of an eleven year old, folded her arms and stared ahead of her. Lisa pointedly ignored Todd, who was trying to edge around her to stick a tongue out at Amy and watched her husband check the luggage pockets again. He was getting harried, typical. He always wanted things to be perfect, wanted his mere presence to assure that complicated things like traveling with a family happened as easily as - well - as he had probably handled things years before. When life was so much simpler.

"It'll be OK, honey," she said calmly. "I'm sure we can help find our own luggage when we get there."

"Well, that'll be a great start to the vacation," he mumbled.

Lisa was about to reassure him and suggest that they write all new tags with the name of the castle on them, when Amy sprang up and started waving energetically. "Hey, Uncle Al! Over here!"

"There's Princess Amy," cried an older man from about thirty feet away. He dropped his own single piece of luggage and crouched down, as both kids ran over to him and leapt at him. He was a little unsteady as they hit into him, his heels rocking, but he laughed, and let them plant kisses on his pink cheeks.

"It's the terrible twosome!" exclaimed Al's companion, picking Todd up by the arms and groaning. "My God, you're gigantic, Todd-boy!"

Todd giggled and kicked as his Uncle Lloyd let him gently down. Lloyd rubbed the center of his lower back and laughed. "Damn, kiddo, I won't be able to do that for much longer! You've got to stop growing up, right now!"

"Hi, guys," sighed Richard, sinking down next to his wife. "I see you're all checked in."

"Yeah, we did the curbside thing," Al said. "Atlanta traffic, post rush hour, I was glad we got here before the damn plane took off. Rick, buddy, you look like a wreck. How come you still have all your luggage?"

Richard rolled his eyes. "Because brilliant me left the special tags at home. Nice way to take care of the family, huh?"

"Well, we have extras, don't we, sweetie?"

Lloyd, having come in closer, nodded and pulled open his little carry-on bag. "Yeah, I think we have three."

"Thank goodness," Lisa said, stopping Todd from wrapping himself around Lloyd's leg. It was hard - both kids adored this man who looked so much like Santa Claus, and he was often willing to engage in horseplay for much longer than his body could comfortably stand. His postman's legs were strong, but there was no denying that his pot-belly and many years just slowed him down. He hated to admit it, though.

The green luggage tags were produced and filled out with the Nelson family information and duly attached, and then Al and Richard went off to check the bags in. Todd went with them, importantly dragging the smallest bag that had wheels, and Amy pounced on the little paperback book that Uncle Lloyd produced from one pocket and curled up away from her mom, on the floor by a pillar, to examine it.

Lloyd sank gratefully down into the seat next to Lisa and smiled gently. "I'm guessing he needs this vacation," he said softly. His green eyes met hers warmly, and she couldn't help but smile at him.

"We all do," Lisa sighed. "I swear, I was ready to send him by himself if he didn't agree to take the whole family. He's driving himself nuts these days, angling for that promotion, trying to manage our investments by himself. And I'm so busy with the kids, sometimes I think the most adult conversation I get is online."

"Yikes! Don't find too much of it there, either," Lloyd laughed. "Remember, I live with an Internet junkie myself."

"I am so glad you guys are along for this one," Lisa said, laying a hand on top of his. "The kids haven't seen enough of you. And I know Richard is just itching to drag out all the old war stories again. I think when he can't talk about his Marketplace years it just builds up inside him, like, well, I don't know. . ."

"Like plaque?" Lloyd laughed and she pushed his hand away with a smile. "Oh, I know what you mean. At least when I talk about my old golden days, I'm talking ancient history. Poor Richard is just a little baby compared to an old fart like me. It'll be good for him. He'll find some new ears for his stories and remind himself how good life is now and we'll all come home happier."

"Well, I hope so," Lisa said. She looked over to Amy for a moment and then back at Lloyd. Lowering her voice, she said, "Sometimes, I think he wants to run away, Lloyd, I really do. I don't know what I'd do without Al and the support group."

"Don't you worry, sweetheart," Lloyd said soothingly. "He loves you, and he adores the kids. You know he wouldn't leave."

"Yes," Lisa admitted, her eyes a little sad. "But I don't want him to be unhappy, either."

"Everything will work out," Lloyd said. "You know it will. Look, here come our handsome husbands, back from the baggage check in. Hey, Princess, want to help an old man out? Give me a hand here!" Amy giggled as she and her brother each grabbed one arm and 'lifted' Lloyd out of the chair as he groaned and moaned.

Lisa took her husband's hand, and squeezed it gently. "Come on, honey, loosen up. It'll be a great time."

"Sure, babe," he said absently. He leaned over to kiss her hair and sighed. "I hope this wasn't a mistake."

"A week in Ireland in a real castle? People to take care of the kids, time alone, formal dinners by candlelight and an indoor swimming pool? Sweetie, if this is a mistake, it's one of our better ones."

He smiled suddenly, and this time gave her a real kiss. "You're the best, Mrs. Nelson, do you know that?"

"I do indeed, Mr. Nelson, so get that cute butt moving and let's have some fun."

Carol waited on the slowly moving line to board her flight with an increasing tightness in her stomach. She was holding her carry-on bag in one hand and keeping her purse close with the other, the boarding pass in her clenched fingers. Everyone around her at LAX seemed cheerful or excited, and her own quiet confusion was like a wall around her.

At least it wouldn't be hard to sleep on the flights, she was exhausted. She had spent the last two days in a motel near the Marketplace regional office, going back and forth to the welcoming suite belonging to Winifred Pembroke, who made her tea and held her hand and reassured her, over and over again, that she was doing the right thing. And to be truthful, Carol knew it was the right thing. She wanted this with all her heart and soul.

She just didn't know if it was within her reach. Until a few weeks ago, she didn't realize that there was anything the Marketplace could offer her any more.

"Of course there is, my dear," Winifred had said cheerfully. "The Marketplace is always here for our clients, even the former ones. Maybe especially the former ones." She had smiled encouragingly, and that smile almost made Carol cry. Eventually, she would cry, in that airy, comfortable office and Winifred would pat her on the shoulder and listen to the whole story, with Carol's old file on her desk.

Carol didn't look the way she did in that file anymore, and that was maybe one of the things to cry about, but dammit, life went on and gravity and time and maybe a few too many cheeseburgers just did their work. But she sure wasn't that trim, golden skinned girl with the perky tits and the blow-dried hair, flung back like that Charlies Angels lady. For goodness sakes, she was almost forty. And her hair had been bleached even lighter than it used to be by the same sun that made her skin into that darkened desert color. *I can be pretty*, Carol thought, *but I'm sure not that stunner who took Vegas by storm, that's for sure.*

"Tell me about yourself," Winifred had said, closing the file after only a short glance. "This covers your two contracts. What's happened with you since then? How were you referred here, was it through your trainer of record?"

Ha. Carol had sighed, fighting to keep calm. How different Winifred's welcome had been from the one she got from Sam Keesey after she tracked him down and arranged for a meeting.

He hadn't even waited for the casino waitress to return to their table before he told her he wouldn't work with her again. "I can't take you back, Carol," he had told her abruptly. "I barely train myself anymore, and when I do, I train hot babes and boys that can squirm easily on their owners' laps, and look like they can fuck all night. Even if you lost the extra 30, 40 pounds, you're not going to hide those age lines."

She couldn't repeat his exact words to this nice lady, so instead, she said, "Sam isn't interested in training me further. When I asked him, he suggested that I visit a regional office to explore . . . other options."

"I see," said Winifred non-committally, although Carol thought she could read sympathy in the older woman's eyes. "And have you considered your options?"

A short burst of nervous laughter came from Carol. "Well, frankly, I'm not sure what options there might be," she said. "I mean, I only had two contracts, both were over a dozen years ago, and, well, I don't think I could go back to the type of slave I was then." Winifred silently indicated for her to continue.

"I was young and hot and eager, when Sam Keesey found me in Vegas serving drinks," Carol explained. "I was already popular with the gamblers — the big time money men, you know, because I just always knew what they wanted — drinks, cigarettes, or just company. One thing led to another, I guess you know about training and everything, and less than a year later, Sam put me on the block in Los Angeles. I was one of the best slaves he'd trained, or so he told me at the time." Carol remembered hearing his praise and half-smiled. "I read all of his etiquette books, refined my card skills, cleaned the chrome in his bathroom and on his motorcycle — and even learned to take a real beating, although I wasn't a heavy masochist. Wouldn't you know, in the end, I was sold to one of the men who used to come to the casinos?" She laughed, and Winifred smiled encouragingly. "So there I was, traveling with him to Reno, Vegas, sometimes Atlantic City, once even to Monaco," she recalled, her eyes beginning to cloud from the memory. "And believe it or not, I started to get bored. Luckily, I guess, because he did, too. After my contract was up, he didn't renew, and I went back to the block."

"And then?" Winifred prompted.

"Same thing happened," Carol replied, her smile turning a little forlorn.

"I didn't know this guy, but it was the same deal. I mean, I enjoyed the traveling, the glamour, the parties, but I never felt like I was really, I don't know, useful. I would bring them drinks or massage their shoulders, but so would the casino staff or any hooker, if that's all they wanted. I always wanted to be more useful, I mean, I'm smart. I got good grades in school, I was ready to learn anything, secretarial work, bookkeeping, fancy serving stuff, anything, but they just laughed and told me not to worry my pretty little head and just keep the drinks coming and the bed warm. It was almost insulting," she admitted. "So when the second contract ended, I decided I didn't want to go back to the block. I just moved to Palm Springs, got a job, and, well, suddenly it's 10 years later. Tried marriage once, that didn't work. And here I am; single, thirty-nine, fat and going nuts because I can't forget the Marketplace. As disappointing as it was, it was the closest thing to happy I ever had."

"We're pretty unforgettable," Winifred agreed, her playful tone almost cheering Carol, enough for her to raise her head and brush the strands of hair out of her eyes and feel just a touch of hope.

"But what can I do?" she asked, her frustration showing in her tone. "I'm not 23, and I know I'm not exactly the ideal of sexual beauty, but, well, isn't there a place in the Marketplace for someone like me?" Her eyes were pleading, and Winifred looked almost ready to scoop her up against her generous breast and soothe her. But, as she did for every other Marketplace slave or former slave who came through her door asking the same question, she merely leaned forward, reaching gently across the table to hand her client a tissue.

"Carol, there is always a place in the Marketplace for someone like you," Winifred said softly, "we just have to help you find it."

And here I am, Carol thought, showing her boarding pass to the stewardess and walking up the ramp. Turns out the Marketplace has a place for me in Ireland.

Hysteria was close to the surface sometimes, and Carol fought with it successfully. I'm going to get nowhere with that kind of thinking, she thought with a mental shrug.

She wasn't going to Ireland to some new owner, after all. In fact, there wouldn't be any owners there are all. It was some sort of vacation for slaves, for crying out loud. Current and former ones, all at this ultra-posh resort hotel that was a real castle. Winifred had shown her pictures, the place was huge.

"But why go on a vacation of all slaves?" Carol had asked.

"It's not just a vacation", Winifred said firmly. "It's a Reunion. Slaves from all walks of life, from all over the world go to Reunion events. Some will be taking their scheduled breaks, and others, who were retired, will be there for the camaraderie and the shared history. But many attend when they are in transition." Winifred looked at Carol meaningfully, and Carol grasped at the word. "If they're between contracts, thinking of expanding their skills, considering retiring, or, like you, wondering about returning, the Reunions are wonderful opportunities to network and gather information from other slaves. It's a chance to meet pleasure slaves from the Middle East, butlers from Great Britain, executives from the corporate owners — Reunions are the place to find them all together. And, they're a perfect place to be able to safely talk about your experiences and dreams with people who will understand you."

Carol got that point all right. And once she saw the subsidized prices for the gatherings, it wasn't that much after all, and money was the least of her problems anyway.

She reviewed the locations of the upcoming Reunions, regretting that she had just missed one at a Mexican resort, sorry that the Fiji Islands were really beyond her finances, deciding that the Kyoto and Budapest reunions might be a bit too exotic, and finally picking the one in Ireland.

"An excellent choice, my dear," Winifred reassured her. "Primarily English speakers, and it will no doubt include slaves from both the United States and Europe. You'll find a good mix there."   And, Carol hoped, some ideas for future training. Or at least some clue about what she could do now, some idea how to get back into the lifestyle.

Her seat came up at last, and she stowed her carry-on bag in the over-head compartment. She was sitting next to, of all people, a woman she had seen looking at her back at check in.

Her seat mate was busy scanning the emergency card for the plane, so Carol had another opportunity to take a brief glance at her outlandish appearance. She was a young African American woman, tall and sturdily built, wearing an oversized hockey jersey that showed her powerful shoulders. But it was her hair that really stood out - cropped short all over her scalp except for a tangle of dreads hanging over her forehead, it had been dyed a brilliant yellow color. The dreadlocks were still black.

She had four piercings in the ear turned to Carol, and one along the side of her nose, and was wearing a heavy gold chain under the jersey. Great, thought Carol with a half smile. What the hell are we going to talk about? She took her seat gingerly.

"Hey," the woman said, leaning back in her seat.

"Hey," Carol meekly answered.

"You ever been to Ireland before?"

"Well - no. Have you?"

"Nope. Been to London a few times, and Glasgow and Paris and a shitload of other places, but never Ireland. I got a book, though." She reachèd easily under the seat in front of her and Carol remembered when she had been that limber. When she sat up again, she was holding a Frommer's guide, with post-it notes sticking out the sides. "It's a cool place! It's got tons of history and shit. I'm gonna see everything I can."

"That's nice," Carol said.

"Yeah, I am gonna have a goood time, I tell you," the woman said, flipping through several pages. "Gonna stay in a real castle, gonna meet some hot slave babes, get laid every night, gonna see everything there is to see." She glanced up at Carol's surprised face and laughed, showing two front teeth that had what looked like diamond chips imbedded in them.

"Yeah, we're going to the same place," she laughed. "Don't have a coronary, girlfriend, I spotted your luggage tags down at the check in!" She pulled her gold chain out from under the jersey and showed Carol a lock and winked. Then, she extended a hand. "I'm Tequila, Blondie, Tequila Gold! And ain't we gonna have a time?"

"To whom do you belong?"

"To you, Mistress!" Lucretia's favorite victim was stretched across his own desk, wrists bound, blindfolded, his back showing the faint marks of her nails and her whips, all laid on with a fairly light hand today. Today, her torments were of a more - internal nature.

She snapped the glove off sharply and tossed it across his face, so he could feel it slide along his cheek, cool and silky. He shuddered prettily, shook in his bonds, getting ready for what would follow.

"Your little butthole is tight today," she purred. "Do you think you can take me, bum-boy? Do you think it will hurt?"

"Yes, please, hurt me, Mistress, please hurt me!"

"Pitiful slut, you can't help yourself, can you? You have to feel me inside you. Hungry little whore, with your ass turned up for me, look at you stretching on your toes to meet me!"

"Yes, yes, I need it, I want it, please, Mistress, hurt me again!"

Lucretia was already hard. She smoothed a condom over her cock and ran her hand across her flesh, warming the slick rubber. His ass was full of lubricant, she didn't add more to herself, only pressed the head of her cock into his asshole and slid in gently. He whimpered as he felt it, and then sighed, and she could feel his ass muscles clenching her, drawing her in.

"Take it, take your mistress' cock," she commanded, somewhat facetiously. But he responded as though she had told him something new and terribly wonderful, and he started to pant furiously.

"Yes - harder, please, I beg you, harder, Mistress, hurt your slut, please!"

"You filthy thing, you deserve to be hurt, you deserve to be stripped like this, bent over and fucked, used like a little tight backstreet whore, don't you?"

He howled in shameful pleasure and tried to arch back onto her, but the bondage prevented him. So instead, he moaned, lowering his head to the rich leather of the desk top and wiggling as much as he could. "Yes, please, oh, yes, please, Mistress, my Goddess, take me, make me yours, that's right, make me your slut, whore, filthy little sex toy. . .yes, Mistress, thank you, yesss, yesss!"

She laughed in pleasure as he worked himself up to an orgasm - was that his fourth or fifth since they started? Her favorite victim was one of the most insatiable men she had ever met, always ready for another round. She slowed her thrusts as he breathed heavily, and as usual, she felt the tight contractions of his body as he worked every inch of her flesh hungrily. She did not often experience orgasm with him, and today was not one of those days.

Instead, she pulled out, still hard, and stripped the condom off. It, too, slapped across his face, and he almost sobbed in pleasure.

You are pathetic," she snarled, close to his ear.

"Yes, yes, I am," he admitted. "Thank you, Mistress!"

"I am going to shower. You will not be permitted to even see me naked." She untied his wrists and jerked him by the studded leather collar over to the steel cage in the corner of the room. He heard the door opening - it was a little squeaky - and whimpered, but he didn't fight her as she strapped him to the bars at the back of the cage. He did beg, though.

"Oh, please, please, Mistress, let me gaze on your body one more time! Please allow me to bathe it with my tongue! Bathe me in your essence! Let me be your mat when you step out of the shower, stand on me, please!"

"Quiet, you slut! Don't make me gag you!"

She did add nipple clamps, though, and gathered his balls into an elaborate parachute and added appropriate weights. He moaned, but stopped begging, and she could see that he was starting to get aroused again even as she slammed the cage door loudly.

She stripped out of the beautiful leather waist cincher and the stockings and boots, putting them all onto the desk for him to put away later. She returned to the cage to rub her g-string across his cheeks and tie it around the head of his cock. "Now, don't get that all dirty," she said in a teasing sing-song. He moaned again, and his cock stirred even more.

Her shower was hot and short, the way she liked it. She combed through her saffron colored hair, drying it in her fingers while she studied her face in the mirror. Not bad at all, really. She always liked her pert little chin and small nose, and the severe hairstyle gave her sharp eyes a nice touch of menace when she needed it. Cool, and elegant. Distant. As she dressed in a prim, tailored wool business suit and a silk blouse, she watched him struggle in his bondage, keeping as silent as possible to prolong the illusion that he was entirely alone, abandoned. He was humping the air by the time she had carried her luggage to the front door and laid her travel documents on the hall table. It was chilly in the hallway, but the crisp air outside was welcoming and inviting, and she was eager to go. A few final things, though.

"So, slut, do you think I should let you look at me again, before I leave?"

"Yes, yes, please, Mistress, haven't I been pleasing? Give me the treasure of your image before I am left all alone, please, I beg you!

She stepped into the cage and let the straps free, and his arms came down, slightly shaky. Grabbing him by the ring in the collar, she jerked him out and down, onto his knees. "Then make that tiny, insignificant little cock of yours come again for me, you sex hole, you shivering little boy. Shoot for me, or I'll leave you like this, trembling on the floor with no sight of me until I wish to return again."

Looking exactly as she described him except for the fact that his cock was rather standard in size and well shaped, he grabbed onto it with his left hand and began to jerk and pull. He used her g-string, rubbing the damp material against his shaft with a groan of ecstasy, even as his fingers fumbled and his rhythm was off. That was one of her commands - when he was allowed self pleasure, he had to do it with his less-dominant hand. He whimpered when she had told him so, and had loved every reminder of how differently he behaved with her.

"That's right. little boy, show me that you can make that undersized twig shoot like a man, and I'll take the blindfold off. Maybe I'll even allow you to kiss my boots before I leave, wouldn't that be nice?"

"Yes, yes, yes, Mistress, yes," he moaned, working his cock frantically. "Yes, please let me cum on your boots and lick it all clean, I swear I'll get every drop!"

Lucretia looked down at her boots. They were very clean, gleaming, as a matter of fact, as all her shoes were. He was very concerned with her footwear. She moved closer and pulled the blindfold off and he gasped.

"Do it, you filthy slut," she commanded. "Shoot your dirty jism all over these lovely boots so you can lick them clean with your tongue."

He shook and moaned and as his hand fairly flew across his cock, a thin stream of cum shot out and in fact landed right across the top of one boot, dribbling down the side of the other. She was always amazed that he had any left by the end of a session.

"You disgusting thing, look what you've done," she hissed. "Clean them off immediately. Put that useless tongue to work and clean up all your dirty

401

juice, right now!"

He was already at work before she finished speaking, and was still lapping happily away when she heard the horn of the taxi out front.

"Enough," she said as gently as she could. With a sigh, he leaned back onto his heels, panting, and she turned from him to wave out the front window. When he was gone from the room, she opened the door and indicated that she had luggage. The uniformed driver came up to take them, tipping his cap to her politely. She closed the door behind him for privacy, and turned back.

"Here, Lucretia," her favorite victim said, standing behind her. He had slipped into a silk robe, and looked as urbane and cool as he did when he went off to his office in the mornings. He was extending an envelope toward her, heavy, parchment colored paper. With a smile, she took it and peeked inside, and saw nestled there a neat stack of Irish pounds. How sweet, he didn't even give it to her in Swiss francs, and make her exchange it later.

"Thank you, Master," she said with a smile.

"Spend it all on frivolous things," he said, as he always did. "And I'll call you when you get to Brussels. Don't call me unless there is an emergency, all right?"

"Of course, Master," she said. "Thank you. Enjoy the time with your children."

"I will; and you enjoy the Reunion. I'll miss you every day."

She smiled at him and gave him a slight curtsy; he never asked for more than that. When she walked down the path to the car, she could feel him watching from the window, but the little house and he were already gone from her mind.

Ireland! She had never been there before. Full of handsome, laughing red-haired men, or so the travel brochures suggested. And to stay in a real castle, how decadent. She would get a massage every day, she decided, a real, professional massage. Her Master loved to massage her when she told him to, but he didn't have the strength or the skill to really work her muscles. But most of all, she would talk, oh yes, talk with other people and share stories and listen to gossip and maybe even get lucky. To hear different voices, from new people, about places she didn't know, what a pleasure that would be.

It was sometimes a little lonely, being a Master's Mistress.

Nigel woke up early, courtesy of his upstairs neighbor, the bloody bus driver, who never understood that normal people slept past dawn, and persisted in stomping around his flat in what sounded like hobnailed boots before he went to endanger lives out on the streets of London. But on this day, Nigel had to get up early anyway, so he just tossed a beer can up at the ceiling and went to take a lukewarm shower. His beard was as rough as carpet. He scraped it off again, cursing the almost dull razor and his continued forgetfulness about getting a new packet of them. He combed his hair and stubbornly applied some new lotion to keep it from becoming unruly. It, like his beard, would defeat him at about four o'clock, every day. Five o'clock shadow, be damned. By four, his hair would be all curls and he would look like some crazy prophet on a box, crying the end of the bloody world.

He tossed two cases onto his bed. In the larger one he threw some vests and all his clean y-fronts, the clean shirts still in the wrapping from the laundry, a pair of blue jeans and another pair of trousers. All his socks. With a moment's reflection, he tossed in a sweater and a decent looking blazer and his cleanest tie, just in case he needed to get somewhere snazzy. He'd have to remember to get razors at the airport or something. He went back to the bathroom and came back with his comb, aftershave, toothbrush and paste. There, that seemed to be everything he needed in that bag.

The second one was a little more complicated. He took boxes off his shelves and examined their contents. The tape recorder and some blank micro-cassettes. His Nikon, and three lenses, including his best telephoto lens, all packed in its lined case. His discreet camera, the one that fit into the palm of his hand. And the new digital monster, with extra storage disks. Plastic covers for everything, because if he was going to be in bloody Ireland, it was going to fucking rain, that was for sure. He tossed in a box of lens cleaners as an afterthought. His battered laptop computer and extra batteries and the battery charger; he'd learned his lesson when his online connection was lost when he was sending those photos of the rock star with the rolled up paper sticking out of his nose. He paused to laugh, remembering the look of shock on the man's face was he heard Nigel's shout to get him to look up. Damn, but that had been a good shot. Pity the lawyers got to his paper before the pictures did. He sold them on the side, anonymously, to an American tabloid, where they were renounced as fakes.

Another potential big story all shot to hell. Story of my fucking life, he thought. He picked up the brown file folders he had all lined up in one box and started leafing through them. Ah, here were the ones he wanted.

Phillip Harrington, Lord-Bloody Southerby and his wife Angelique, the American computer genius. Those shots he had of them frolicking naked on the beach sure didn't make him any new friends, especially when he enlarged the pictures to their grainiest details and showed that the new Lady Southerby had a ring in one nipple! They had to put that one up on the paper's web site, with a banner over it declaring that it was not meant for minors to see. Naturally, they had a record number of hits that week. Nice bonus for that one.

But the bigger bonus came later, when he realized that Lord Southerby was tied in with some pretty interesting people. Like Howard Ward, no, Sir Howard these days, after the Queen knighted him for his charity fund raising work. The ever mysterious Howard Ward, who maintained a house outside of Cheltenham, in Gloucester, where his staff were as silent as monks about the owner's habits and many people came over the years to stay for a few months - or a few years - and then vanish into - what? Where?

"The bloody Marketplace, that's where," he muttered out loud.

He fished through the folders, pulling out a few. Some had transcripts of interviews, others had photos, some had copies of documents that he was certainly not supposed to have. He looked through the American ones, glancing at the familiar names. Ah, Karen, that young girl from California. She had seemed so promising at first, certainly her story rang true. But in the end, she had only one name for him. Michael LaGuardia, now from New York, whose secretary was obviously trained by former KGB agents. Nothing got through the ring of people he had surrounding him and his actress wife - but there had been that newspaper article about the Christening of their son. That one came up with a real connection.

Chris Parker. Vanished from New York five years ago, but turns up for this little society affair, and that was a picture of him right there, holding the little sprat. Now, that was a familiar name, connected with Ward's old mate, Dalton from Surrey, and that Anderson woman in New York. And now Mr. Gets-about Parker just happened to be in the same house as that Japanese businessman whose name turned up over and over again with Nigel's pal in Hong Kong, Henry Tok. Henry had come up with a lot of Marketplace dirt over the years, not as much as Nigel for sure - but then who the fuck really knew? Nigel certainly didn't share everything he knew with Henry. But Henry had caught a photo of the Parker fellow in Kobe, standing outside of a building that was owned by one Tetsuo Sakai, a businessman who spent quite a lot of time not managing the businesses he owned, but doing 'other things'. Like hosting people who stayed with him for months and years and then vanished outside the workforce again. Just like Ward, just like Anderson.

And I've got another picture of you, my fine American friend, Nigel thought, pulling out that file. And I bet you'd rather folks not see this one. Ah, at last, I've got the keys to the whole bloody thing. It's all coming together.

The last file he needed to take were printouts of his correspondence with LrdDom@sizzlemail.ie. (Never trust the back up files on the hard-drive, never trust the bloody disks that can be erased by a fucking swipe from a magnet.) Lord-bloody-dom, indeed. Well, whatever the fellow wanted to call himself, he finally had the goods. After years of people who told Nigel improbable but seemingly honest accounts of being seduced and edged toward being stolen away, of stories leading to dead ends, interviews ending in puzzled shrugs, slammed phones and doors and simple silence, he finally found one who not only was willing to talk, but was willing to provide proof.

And here was part one; the registration list for Kaleigh Castle. Not a terribly hard thing to lift at most hotels, there was always a clerk who could use a new stereo or something. But Kaleigh was one of those damned properties owned by Danberry and Ellis - and what a file he could build on them, too. Pretty shifty group that one, huge and multi-national, although their home offices were here in London. Real estate and hospitality, shipping and manufacturing, media and travel; there wasn't anything they didn't have a finger in. And, their security was studied the world over. And wouldn't you know, that was where Lord Southerby worked for a while, and his pretty ice-queen wife, with the ring in her nipple.

Yes, it was all coming together. If you had to have a world wide slavery ring, why not manage it with the help of a huge mega-corporation? And if the people who were sold through it were even allowed a few days off from their illegal and immoral activities, of course they should be secluded in some privately owned piece of property where you could hide them and keep them safe.

Well, not from Nigel Pepper, he thought, tossing the stack of folders into the case. I've got you this time, all of you. It had to end sometime - there was no way to keep something this big so secret. Someone will let you down every time, and I will be there to see you fall.

Finally, he packed the money. Gimpy Scott, his editor, of course wouldn't release the entire payoff until the proof was in the offices and the legal buzzards had done their work. But Nigel had pulled a few hundred pounds of cash out of the stingy little turd to flash in front of LrdDom if additional incentives were necessary.

But Nigel knew they wouldn't be. The recent e-mail from the bugger was sounding quite cocky. The images that Nigel could spin for him, of interviews and fame, glory and lots and lots of money for his story, were doing their work nicely. Oh, he'd roll over nicely when the time came. All he had to do was get those last bits of proof that Nigel asked him for and get Nigel onto the property, and everything would be taken care of.

And, if LrdDom didn't come through, maybe Parker, or any one of these other people might play along. Or be convinced to act nice, anyway. Bunch of perverts, all of them, highly susceptible to reason, no doubt.

Nigel closed both cases, picked up his airline tickets and rode the elevator whistling. This is the big one, he thought. A holiday for slaves! Who could have imagined it? And it's all mine. Eat your heart out, Henry Tok, I'll nail these bastards first.

*(excerpt from **The Reunion**, Scheduled for publication Spring 2001)*

The Marketplace Series by Laura Antoniou returns to print!

Mystic Rose Books follows the publication of the fourth book in the series, The Academy, with the reprinting of the first three novels and publication of a new book, The Reunion. The Marketplace, The Slave, and The Trainer return enhanced with the addition of new material. The series chronicles the adventures of those who inhabit an enticing alternative reality built around a slave based hierarchy. Following is the publication schedules for the series.

THE ACADEMY, TALES OF THE MARKETPLACE   March 2000
The long awaited fourth book in the Marketplace series! Taking up where The Trainer left off, as Chris Parker and dozens of other Trainers journey to Okinawa. This book explores both the strict, hidden order behind the men and women who train the exquisite Marketplace slaves and the mysteries behind Mr. Parker himself. The Academy is a full length novel incorporating independent short stories written by Guest Authors. Karen Taylor, Cecilia Tan, Michael Hernandez, david stein and M. Christian delve into the world of the Marketplace and turn up tales of power, sex, and surrender, the kinds of stories Trainers tell each other to inspire, teach. . .or warn.

THE MARKETPLACE   June 2000
"Compelling, charged with electricity . . ."   - Kitty Tsui

The first volume in the landmark Marketplace trilogy, the series that set the standard for contemporary SM erotica. After Sharon, Brian, Claudia, and Robert are accepted for training by Marketplace representatives, they struggle to overcome their shortcomings: pride, selfishness, immaturity and perfectionism. Who among them will survive the training meted out by the rigorous and unrelenting Chris Parker? And who will uncover the truth of his or her own sexual need to submit?

THE SLAVE   September 2000
"There's a new voice in S/M fiction these days, and none too soon . . . Thank goodness Sara Adamson has exploded onto the scene!" - Kate Bornstein

The second volume in the Marketplace Series, The Slave describes the experiences of Robin, an exceptionally sensitive submissive who longs to join the ranks of those who have proven themselves worthy of entry into the sexual training ground of the Marketplace. Follow Robin as she is educated in the arts of submission and service by the meticulously ethical Chris Parker, the person in whom she will confide her deepest sexual secrets.

THE TRAINER

December 2000

"This is domination and submission at its best - a very well-written work that holds from page to page . . ." - Shiny International

In the third book of Sara Adamson's Marketplace Series, would-be trainer and spotter for the Marketplace, Michael LaGuardia, learns there is more to the art of commanding respect than meets the eye. Moreover, iconoclastic master trainer Chris Parker doesn't seem to appreciate Michael's potential. What can he do to get his attention? What does Michael really want from Chris? And when will Chris finally divulge his long-hidden secrets?

THE REUNION

April 2001

More from the characters we have come to love as book five of the Marketplace Series reunites Chris Parker, Anderson, Robin, and others in a castle in Ireland. Once again Antoniou brings us a compelling novel bursting with raw sexuality, set within the hidden world where slavery is absolute and personal honor is valued above all.

Other Titles from Mystic Rose Books

DHAMPIR: CHILD OF THE BLOOD

by V.M. Johnson

Vampyres walk amongst us. Here, for perhaps the first time in this century, a vampyre of the Clan of Lilith invites us into her life through letters to her newly made "cub" and to those she calls her "food." In Dhampir, Child of the Blood, the myths come alive, but they are not as one expects from the myriad fictional accounts. Courageously, Johnson uses her real name, discusses real people and events and passes on to us the history, legends and wisdom of The Clan of Lilith handed down by her sire when he made her. Frank, explicit letters from a mother to a daughter about life and survival as one of the newest members of the vampyre Clan of Lilith.

TO LOVE, TO OBEY, TO SERVE

by V.M Johnson

Within these pages are the real life experiences of an extraordinary woman as recorded in her journal. Vi Johnson is one of the most loved and respected women in the leather community. She entered the Leather s/m scene in the 1970's, as a slave. A slave's duty was to Love, Honor, Please, and OBEY, sometimes blindly, often at great personal cost. To own or live the life of a full time slave is, and has been, the stuff of s/m fantasies and erotic stories. The life recorded here reveals those realities, which are quite different from the fantasies. Most of all this is the journey of a woman following her dream.

SCREW THE ROSES, SEND ME THE THORNS
The Romance and Sexual Sorcery of Sadomasochism
by Philip Miller and Molly Devon

"Screw the Roses, Send Me the Thorns is about enhancement of the human sexual experience through the use of restraints and disciplined applications of tactile sensations. It is a gentle and experienced guide taking the reader from the introduction of the principles of S/M to step-by-step instructions on how to apply and receive 'discipline'... Dominants and Submissives practicing within the guidelines... in this book can find a safe and rewarding way to make reality of their fantasies." Dr. Wm. Granzig, President, The American Board of Sexology

A thorough guide to sadomasochism by two experienced players. This popular book strips away myth, shame, and fear revealing the truth about an intense form of eroticism too long misunderstood and condemned. It is fully indexed and includes over 225 photos and illustrations, a 250-plus word glossary, appendices with contacts for SM resources.

Order by mail at:	Mystic Rose Books P.O. Box 1036/SMS Fairfield, CT 06430	Or online at WWW.mysticrose.com

___Dhampir: Child of the Blood
     by V. M. Johnson $8.95
___To Love, To Obey, To Serve
     by V. M. Johnson $17.95
___Screw the Roses, Send Me the Thorns
     by Philip Miller & Molly Devon $24.95
___The Academy, Tales of the Marketplace
     by Laura Antoniou $13.95
___The Marketplace
     by Laura Antoniou   (anticipated, Spring 2000) $13.95
___The Slave
     by Laura Antoniou   (anticipated, Fall 2000) $13.95
___The Trainer
     by Laura Antoniou   (anticipated Winter 2000) $13.95
___The Reunion
     by Laura Antoniou   (anticipated, Spring 2001) $13.95
___Shipping   (add $3.75 per book shipping)

___Total (check enclosed)